BEWARE OF CHICKEN

— BOOK 2 —

— BOOK 2 —

CASUALFARMER

Podium

Copyright © 2023 by Torsten Hewson

Cover and interior art by Tsuu

ISBN: 978-1-0394-5227-5

Published in 2024 by Podium Publishing
www.podiumaudio.com

Podium

To everybody who believed in this little story about a man and his rooster and helped make this possible—especially my beta readers, who have put up with far, far too many late-night revisions.

BEWARE OF CHICKEN

— BOOK 2 —

CHAPTER 1

FULL STEAM AHEAD

The Crimson Phoenix Empire. A name that resounds across the known world.

It is a land of power and glory. Of industry and of art and culture. A superpower that dominates an entire continent under the watchful eye of the Son of Heaven, His Imperial Majesty. The Divine Mandate of Heaven secures his right to rule, and his legions of officials and functionaries span the length and breadth of the continent.

Its grand cities house millions. Its sheer expanse could not be fully explored in a hundred mortal lifetimes, encompassing floating islands, hidden realms, and untamed wilderness. There are poison bogs, befuddling forests, and mountains that scrape the very edge of the sky, too tall for any to climb.

It is a land of cultivators, those who strive every day to defy the heavens. A hundred thousand battles, great and small, rage across the continent. Martial tournaments. Bandit attacks. Rampaging Spirit Beasts. Pub brawls. Wars in all but name between the Sects. The great battle at the Five Immortal Phoenix Gates rages against the latest round of demonic invaders.

For the people who inhabit this land, it is a never-ending climb to the top. To train and fight and struggle and strive. To win glory, fame, merit, accolades. To rise above your birth and defy the heavens.

A thousand tales are told of the most noble of martyrs, of the most vile of villains, and of the greatest of heroes. There are battles that shake the heavens and upend the status quo.

Even the least of these people dream of it; even the weakest wish to climb.

Upon the northern reaches of the sprawling Crimson Phoenix Continent lies the Azure Hills. It is a mostly landlocked province, with only a tiny stretch of land that touched the ocean along its southwestern edge. The province is full of giant rolling hills and grassy knolls. It is so named for the purity of its clear sky and the prevalence of said hills. As befitting a northern province, the seasons are temperate, and a great amount of snow falls each winter.

Like all provinces of the Empire, the Azure Hills are enormous, nearly a country in their own right. But they are guilty of a nearly unforgivable sin.

The Azure Hills are *weak*.

They are absent from every grand tale and every battle worth mentioning. No name from their pitiful lands has ever been able to reach the heavens. While other provinces can lay claim to wondrous foundries, or high culture, the Azure Hills' only outstanding quality is its weakness. There were no grand battles here. Very little court intrigue. It was a complete and utter backwater.

Yet even these people, in this Qi-less desert, strive. They battle! They defy the heavens!

To be victorious, one only needs to pick up their sword, steel their resolve, and fight—

□

Cai Xiulan, the Young Mistress of the Verdant Blade Sect, stared blankly at the object that had been placed into her hands. It was not a sword. It was not a spear, or even a bow.

Instead, it was something that a farmer would be intimately familiar with.

It was a hoe. A hoe used for tilling the earth.

"Is . . . is this it, Master Jin?" she asked carefully, looking up at the Hidden Master. He grinned at her, his cheeks covered in freckles. His smile lacked any sort of malice or guile, that this was just some strange joke he was playing on her. Well, was that not the way of Hidden Masters? their methods were always strange to those who could not comprehend them.

"Yup! I thought I would start with the basics. I bet you haven't used something like that too much, eh?" Master Jin asked as he stretched out his arms. Still, Xiulan could not help but to glance at the other with the

Hidden Master. Bi De, the resplendent rooster on his shoulder, a regal beast whose plumage was the colour of fire and who wore a fox-fur vest, raised an eyebrow at her.

"I am inexperienced in its use, Master Jin," she replied. Xiulan *certainly* hadn't ever used a hoe before. Her Sect Elders would have probably spat blood for her just holding the farming implement.

"Well, there ain't nothin' to it! Come on, let me show you how to use it properly!" The Hidden Master was full of energy as he got into a stance holding a hoe of his own, and Xiulan rushed to copy him. He smiled as he saw her attentiveness. "Right, now swing it down like this—!"

Both of them swung the hoe, Xiulan's concentration fully on what they were doing.

She had asked to learn the Hidden Master's ways; if a man as powerful as Master Jin said that this was his way, then she could only be blessed to follow him.

Surely, working like this would pay dividends in her cultivation, just like she hoped it would!

They spent a few minutes working together before Master Jin was satisfied with her form.

"Hey, that's pretty good!" Master Jin said, nodding at her. Now, you're going to be in charge of that field over there, okay? Try to make those rows even!"

"Yes, Master Jin!" Xiulan shouted, her mind and spirit focused.

Thus began Cai Xiulan's life on Master Jin's farm.

↔

I woke up content. Well, I hadn't just *woken up* content. Contentedness had been my state of being ever since the wedding. It was hitting week three since the wedding, and I was still on cloud nine.

There was a pleasantly warm body pressed against my chest, and I was curled around it. My arm wrapped around her chest and my palm was held over her heart by her own hands. I could feel the steady slow beats of her heart, pulsing gently against my palm.

She was my wife. I was *married*. Still something I was getting used to. It was . . . a bit weird, I will confess, yet that was mostly lost in a haze of good feelings.

My wife was beautiful. Idiots called her eyes sharp, her freckles blemishes, and her tongue a dagger.

Her eyes were beautiful amethysts, her freckles made her cute, and her tongue . . .

Her tongue was very nice too. Uh, yeah. *That's all I'm going to say about that.*

To my sensibilities, we had moved extremely quickly. Like Las Vegas shotgun wedding fast. But to the people here . . . well, it wasn't so abnormal.

It was good. *Very good.* Especially the sleeping-in-the-same-bed part. It might just be the honeymoon period talking, but we were getting a bit less sleep than we probably should have.

I pressed my nose into green-tinted hair and took a breath. She smelled like herbs. It was a *very* nice smell.

Meiling stirred in my grip, and her hands tightened briefly against my hand on her chest, trying to pull me closer. She let out a little sleepy murmur before sighing in contentment as she let go.

Good morning," I murmured into her hair.

"Morn—morning," she replied midyawn, raising her arms above her head and stretching, wiggling against my body in interesting ways. After a moment of that, she rolled over in my arms. Her wonderful violet eyes were still lidded with tiredness.

She pressed a kiss to my lips, and then we just cuddled for a while. Her body was warm and smooth, and listening to her heartbeat nearly lulled me back to sleep. Our breathing synchronised as we lay together.

Everything felt *right*.

I pondered what I was going to say.

"I like swimming, and the smell of rain, but I *really* hate getting rained on," I eventually said, deciding on my "fact of the morning."

We were married but didn't actually know too much about each other. So we had started this little ritual, telling each other something random about ourselves. It was mostly knowledge that didn't really matter, but . . . well, it was nice to learn more about the person I was hopefully going to spend the rest of my life with.

Meiling hummed, amused. "So *that's* why you were so grumpy yesterday. I thought it was because Gou Ren messed something up."

I shrugged. What can you do? I liked the outdoors, but getting soaking wet when I didn't want to be always put me in a bit of a bad mood. *I chose a great profession in farming for that, didn't I?* I needed to go outside in the rain all the time.

Meimei smiled up at me. "Well, something in common. I really hate getting rained on too."

A second later, there was a loud call from outside as Big D sounded the morning bell.

I sighed, wishing I could just spend the entire day in bed. Instead, I kissed Meiling on the forehead, and we both got up to get dressed. Before we started the day, we had one more morning ritual we'd decided on that let us have a few more moments together.

I ran a comb through my wife's hair. It was simple. But the feeling of silky-smooth locks underneath my fingers calmed me down and let me think a bit better.

We prepared the rest of the morning in silence. When we reached the door, we both took deep breaths, preparing for the long, long day ahead of us.

"This is the hardest part. Once summer hits, we'll have less to do," I muttered to myself.

I reached out for Meimei's hand, entwining our fingers.

"All right. Let's do this," I declared.

We marched downstairs. I started the fire while Meimei went and got the eggs. Eggs and rice, an *imaginative* breakfast. I was craving an egg and cheese sandwich, and while I could probably go running around to find all the ingredients, it was more trouble than it was worth. Instead, I would be patient. My first more western-style breakfast would be made with *my* eggs, *my* bread, and *my* cheese. With *my* hash browns too.

Think of it, Jin. Let the desire fuel your movements!

By the time breakfast was ready, everyone else had already sat down and was ready to start the day. Big D bowed slightly as we came in with the food. His colours were as vibrant as ever, and his fox-fur vest was just as pristine as when I first gave it to him. Beside him sat Rizzo, the little rat still sleepy and seemingly dozing. Washy, the dull brown carp, was in his trough, slapping his fins happily in anticipation for food. Chunky was next, the big boy curled next to Peppa. His scars had faded to white lines, but they still lent him a dangerous air.

Tigger was the last of the animals; the orange and black striped cat immediately trotted up next to me, curling up in my lap and sulking. She had been in a terrible mood ever since me and Mei stopped letting her into our room. She yowled at me, and I sighed.

"Yeah, yeah. I'm sorry, Tigger. But you should go out and explore a little more, yeah?"

That was obviously the wrong thing to say, since she started sulking more. I couldn't really understand her yet, but I probably should see about having a night where I actually slept, and let her sleep with us again. She was basically just a kitten who had been kicked out of her parents' nest.

I held back a sigh at the thought. *Worrying about how animals are taking your marriage. How surreal my life has become.*

The other two guests at the breakfast table were human. The first was our friend from Hong Yaowu and acting farmhand, Gou Ren.

Gou Ren had a bit of an . . . unfortunate face. His nose was a bit too wide, and his sideburns grew in *just* the right way to make him look like a monkey.

He appeared well rested and was scratching Chunky behind his ears.

Our other guest—and other farmhand—was sitting with great dignity at the table. Cai Xiulan, a cultivator, bowed in respect when she was served. Her silky brown hair was immaculate, and her white robe pristine.

Peppa, sitting demurely beside Chunky, bowed in thanks for the food I set in front of her, though I could tell she was distracted by something. With a single, dainty bite, the eggs and rice were gone, the bowl cleaned.

We ate, largely in silence, as I considered my options.

Each and every day was a learning experience. What I was currently coming to grips with was delegation. It's amazing how much you get stuck in your ways over the course of just a year. But now I had people to help me. I had to talk to people. The first day of work this year had been hilariously awkward, as I had just kind of gone off and started to do my own thing, while everybody else had been waiting for direction.

"Gou Ren, you're on the rice paddies today," I decided. "Shore up the walls like I taught you, and then we'll move on to sorting the seed."

Gou Ren let out a groan. "Qi reinforcement is the bane of my existence," he grumbled. "Do I really have to do the whole thing?"

"Yup. Gotta make sure it won't collapse, else we're going to lose the entire harvest." Gou Ren sighed and started to grumble. He liked to complain a lot, but I would be sure he'd finish the job, come hell or high water.

"Xiulan," I continued. The other woman perked up immediately at the mention of her name, leaning forwards eagerly. "The western field, please." She nodded, yet she seemed a bit disappointed.

"Meimei, are you still working on the garden today?" I asked, and she nodded.

"I'm going to be out with Babe. Work with him for a little." Honestly, I felt a bit sorry for the ox. I had named him after Paul Bunyan's companion, but he barely had anything to do. I could pull the plough better than he could—and do it faster than him too. Every job that we would need an ox for was more easily accomplished through the strength granted to us by cultivation. Ironically, the big, strong ox was one of the weakest things on the farm. *Maybe* he was stronger than Rizzo . . . but I wouldn't bet on it.

Still, it wasn't good to just leave him without anything to do but chewing cud all day, so I decided to try to use him for his intended purpose.

We finished our meal, then got started for the day.

↔

It was slowly getting hotter as the sun beat down on the land. The snow had long since melted, but the river was still ice cold from meltwater. The ground had hardened up a bit, firming in the sun from a quagmire to something that was workable.

"Ooh, this is nice," I mused aloud as we used the new plough. The edge of the formerly demonic blade bit deep and sliced through the soil like a hot knife through butter. It took my Qi easily; it was a *lot* better than my last plough. I patted the ox on his rump. He was a good boy. Obedient, calm, and easy to control, but still a regular animal instead of a Spirit Beast.

He needed something to do other than sit around and get fat, and he seemed to enjoy being hitched up well enough.

It was a really nice plough, though. If a bit unadorned.

My mind wandered as we worked.

I was on field two. This one was going to be the root vegetable field. Radishes, turnips, and most importantly, *potatoes. There are hash browns in my future.*

Behind me, a gaggle of chickens followed, pecking eagerly at the bugs unearthed by my efforts. The flock fluttered and squawked, making little clucking noises as they ate.

And, there was a certain someone on my shoulder. Big D was in his usual place, gazing imperiously from his perch. He watched over the rest of the chickens, making sure they didn't go too far; if they did, a single, sharp cluck would bring them back into line.

Occasionally, he too would hop off my shoulder and pluck a particularly fat-looking bug out of the air before returning to his position. I scratched his wattles affectionately when he did.

Back and forth across the field we went, pulling the plough. Each step was perfectly even, and each furrow was at an exact distance. Hells, I could probably use these things as a ruler!

I idly looked at the plough again, and my lips quirked into a smile.

I patted it twice. "I dub thee Sunny," I declared. I could almost imagine Sun Ken, the blade's previous owner, spinning in his grave.

I imagined sun carvings on it, along with a nice coat of yellow paint. *It's going to be a happy, cheerful plough.*

In what felt like no time at all, I was finished. By that point, the sun had risen high in the sky, and I was terribly thirsty. I took a swig from my bamboo drinking container, then wandered over to the river with Babe to splash some cold water on my face and wash away some of the sweat.

It was brisk, but invigorating.

I sighed in contentment and leaned back. I felt good. I had a hell of a lot of work to do to expand my farm for winter—but it was a wonderful start to a wonderful spring.

Big D agreed with me, ripping loose a call from his place on my shoulder, happy to be planting again.

"You tell 'em, Big D," I said with a smile.

CHAPTER 2

EACH DAY A BLESSING

Bi De sat upon the Great Pillars, a piece of paper laid out on the wood before him. He examined it and the rough drawing of the Formation of Fire he had drawn on it: that grand thing he had seen on the winter solstice. It was an intriguing puzzle he had witnessed that night. One that he constantly found his thoughts going back to as the fiery Qi spread across the land.

But for all it consumed his thoughts . . . he could not yet act upon his desire to investigate it. The rooster shook his head and stowed the paper in his fox-fur vest, the trophy he had gained from Basi Bu Shi. He made special care not to disturb Sister Ri Zu, the rat asleep on his back.

He instead turned his gaze to Fa Ram. Another day upon this Blessed Land, and another phase of the moon to observe. Tonight, the moon was once more full, shining brightly in the heavens.

It was the start of the second cycle he had witnessed in this world. The second year since he had awakened. Or, Bi De supposed, as it was a cycle, it had no true defined beginning or end, did it? It simply *was*, turning through the seasons whether he was aware of it or not. A never-ending spiral through time.

He was satisfied with this. To know that this cycle had been here before him and would be here long after. And yet though the cycle continued, it also changed. Though they went through the same motions, they progressed. Each foot in front of the other, following their own path.

Bi De reflected upon his own march forwards.

The rooster followed the way he knew. He announced the sun's arrival in the morning. His voice rose, and his Great Master praised his calls. He patrolled vigorously at night. He exalted in the world around him, in both the base mysteries and the profound.

And, he got to relive his most enjoyable memories. At first, when the Great Works began anew, he'd assumed that he would be assigned some other task. Yet his Lord had held out his arm and welcomed Bi De once more unto his broad shoulders.

He recalled the memories of when he was just a young, jumped-up and foolish bag of bones and feathers, arrogant and stupid.

He had changed, progressed. And in this new cycle, he would endeavour to continue that growth.

He descended upon the base creatures that dared to impede his path, and left those broken by his charge for his gaggle of hens and offspring. The Great Master was training Bei Be, the ox, in the use of a powerful artifact. He would watch the ox closely, for if his Master was bestowing such a gift upon him, then the creature was sure to have some sort of potential.

Even if for now, the ox was just that: an ox.

Bi De shook his head again, clearing the thoughts, and stood so that he could continue his patrol. He reached around with his beak and preened the sleeping form of Sister Ri Zu. Then he set off across the land.

Each day was a gift from the heavens.

↔

I took deep breaths, filling my lungs with sweet spring air.

I had really missed this feeling. There was just *something* about it. The air was almost charged with energy, and it was driving into my soul, stirring me to action.

My plans were ambitious this year. Very ambitious. Last year I had created an entire farm from nothing, but that was small potatoes. I hadn't even used half an acre. This year? I would expand. Now, I had more than just rice and a few veggies. I had so much stuff to plant!

The fields were big enough that in this time period, you'd have to have entire families, or entire villages, to tend to them. It was going to be a lot of work even for cultivators.

The faster I got the prep work done, the faster I could take it easy. Farming was hard work, but you had a surprising amount of time to kick back and relax, outside the crunch periods of spring and fall.

My section of the fields was mostly done being prepped. On the other side of the farm, both Xiulan and Gou Ren were a bit slower.

But it wasn't like I was waiting on them. They would finish when they finished.

I had a little bit of time on my hands, so I took a bit of a walk to see Meiling. I was curious how the garden was going, back at the house, and I needed to prep the potatoes for planting.

"All right, which one is this?" I watched Meiling ask her student, offering her a seed. It was the third one she had given to the rat, and each one before then, Rizzo had guessed right.

I smiled at the scene as I worked, cutting the eye off a potato. Rizzo examined the seed intently, her little nose twitching away.

'Coriander, Master!' the little one finally squeaked authoritatively. *'Grows best in light shade, in a cooler part of the garden.'*

Meimei nodded with pride.

"And this one?" she asked. Rizzo actually looked a bit insulted, and I could tell why. Peppercorns were easy.

'In the pots over here, Master. They require little, though must still be tended for the best results!' Rizzo declared again.

"Good, good. Now, which of these is poisonous, and which is medicinal?" Meiling brought out two identical-looking mushrooms.

I turned my attention to the potatoes but kept an ear open to Rizzo's lessons. This stuff was interesting!

The potatoes, or "earth apples," Xiulan had been given by the merchant weren't any kind that I was familiar with. They were kind of like russets in size but had smooth, bright purple skin once you got the dirt off.

They tasted pretty good too. Nice and fluffy, and they took the butter we had well.

I cut into a potato, carving off a section with a sprouted eye and laying it to the side so that it could dry for a couple of days. Letting them get "calloused" helped prevent rot, which was why you let them dry out a bit instead of burying them immediately. Small potatoes you could just chuck in the ground, no questions, but these bigger ones needed to be taken care of.

After a bit of cutting, I heard Rizzo's answer.

'Master tries to trick-deceive this one!' she cried. *'Both are poison, both are medicine!'*

Meimei's grin was massive. "Good!" she praised, and Rizzo preened. "You're absolutely correct. In small doses, the Two-Colour Gill Mushroom can reduce swelling and inflammation and open constricted blood vessels. But taken in too large a dose, it can render the muscles unable to contract properly, leading to paralysis and, in extreme cases, death."

Huh. You learn something new every day. Xianxia-land mushrooms are kind of nuts . . . And this is the province with the least *amount of Qi fuckery.*

"Now, for today, we shall finish planting this section of the herb garden," Meimei demanded. "Remember to mark each section carefully; some of these are mildly poisonous."

Rizzo nodded eagerly and got her little hoe out, ready to work. It was cute as heck. Meiling walked over to look at the taters, and I knew she planned to work more on the little signs she was making for the herb garden. I wasn't too familiar with some of the stuff Xian, my father-in-law, had given us, so she had started making the signs for me, and in the meantime, I was to study a scroll.

"Rizzo is doing well, then?" I asked.

"Yes. She hasn't studied food as much as medicine, but she did very well today. I'm quite proud of her for figuring out the trick question." She had a familiar look of half pride and half affection on her face.

We worked side by side in companionable silence for a little. I cut up our bag of sprouting potatoes, and she checked her father's written note against little satchels of seeds.

Our silence was broken by Peppa, who appeared out of the forest. She had two baskets tied to her back, filled with mushrooms and fiddleheads. Big D wandered beside her, looking incredibly pleased with himself.

She didn't have just any mushroom—they looked like morels.

I was about to offer to cook dinner when Meimei noticed the bounty and her eyes widened in pleasure.

"I'm cooking tonight!" she demanded, looking the fiddleheads and morels over and sniffing at them eagerly.

I raised an eyebrow. "You like these that much?" I asked as I took a drink of water.

She nodded happily. "My mother used to make this dish. It tastes really good." She paused for a moment and gave me a sly look out of the corner of her eye. "It also supposedly improves stamina and fertility—though I hardly think we need help with *that*. I wouldn't be surprised if I was with child already."

I nearly choked. The thought was both terrifying and exciting and drove home how much I really *hadn't been thinking. Sex makes babies.*

Yeah, tilling fields with a beautiful woman was fun and all, but actions have consequences. And the joke was a splash of cold water on me.

I grabbed her hand when she went to get up, pulling her into my lap instead. She was all tense and tightly wound, her muscles bunched up.

"Meiling . . ." I began, at her curious look. I swallowed thickly. "Are . . . are we ready for that? Are *you* ready for that?" I asked nervously.

She seemed surprised that I was even asking. "It's a . . . little bit late to be thinking about that, no?" she mused, raising an eyebrow. "That's something to think about *before* we engage in nightly activities."

I grimaced, which prompted her to sigh, then bonk me on the head. "Did you hear me complaining?" Meimei asked, and I conceded the point. Meiling was an . . . *enthusiastic* partner.

"We can stop?" I offered, a bit reluctantly. "Just so that we can think about it more?"

She sighed again, and leaned back into my chest. "If I were against the idea, I could have been making a medicine that reduces the chances of conception," she finally said in a quiet voice.

Huh, they have those here? I guess it made sense.

"That I have *not* taken any means that I am as prepared as I can be. Besides, you were right when you said we nearly had children already. It can't be too much different than this." She glanced over at Rizzo and Peppa.

"Our kid is going to be worse than both of us put together, tempting fate like that," I mused.

She laughed, which turned into a hiccup as she stared out over the land.

We sat together for a while, enjoying the sun hanging low in the sky. Finally, a brief moment where we weren't working. Just . . . sitting together. Some of the tension drained out of her shoulders. Dinner might be a little late tonight, but that was fine.

Her grip tightened on my hands. I could feel her fingers shaking a little—and then she suddenly firmed up and sniffed back the snot that had been gathering in her sinuses, and wiped away the beginnings of tears.

Ah, I was wondering if and when this would hit.

"I should . . . really go and make supper, I—I need to . . ." she muttered, tugging at my hands, but I wouldn't let her go.

"Homesick?" I asked her. Hey, I could be a *bit* perceptive. I . . . knew the feeling. I knew that feeling *very* well. It had been a constant companion in the early days. The sheer misery had been hard. You could cry all you wanted, and it wouldn't change anything. Staring at the ceiling and wondering whether the void in your heart could be filled.

Working till you dropped was one solution, if not a very healthy one. People and emotional support were better.

"Hu Li said that it would pass if I kept busy . . ." she mumbled, mentioning the Xong brothers' mother. "Just need to keep busy so I don't think about it. Besides, *this* is my home now, and I . . . *I* . . ."

She took a deep breath, and her eyes firmed up. I smiled at Meimei. She was made out of pretty stern stuff, my girl.

"We'll go visit soon. I want to see Pops and your little brother again," I told her as my hand went in circles around her back. She nodded. "And tell me next time, if you think things are getting too much. We need to talk more as it is, anyway."

"I'm not a delicate flower. You don't need to coddle me," she said with a grunt.

"Never said you were. You have to hold me when I feel like this too, ya know?"

Meimei took her head away from my chest and scrubbed her eyes. "Men are to be stoic in bearing, and never show such unsightly things," she said stiffly. "But be thankful, for your loving wife will forgive any weakness you might have." Her smirk was a bit crooked, but at least there was a spark of amusement dancing in her eyes. "Thank you," she whispered. She pulled away, and this time I let her. After a moment, she cleared her throat and brushed down her robe. "I'll go get started on dinner now. You go and collect the others," she commanded.

I got up to do as she asked. "And Jin . . ." I turned back to my wife, who had a bit of a flush on her face. "No slacking on your duties, husband."

I chuckled.

"Lewd woman."

"I am not lewd, I am a *proper* wife, attentive to her duties!" she shot back, glaring.

"You're the one who got the recording crystal out last week. You're *lewd*."

Her eyes narrowed into slits. "Go get the others." Her voice was a razor blade.

I beat a hasty retreat, heading for the rice paddies. I was probably going to be paying for those words later, but at least Meimei was in a better mood now.

Upon reaching the area, I was treated to quite an amusing sight.

I struggled to hold my laughter in as I watched the scene unfolding before me. Gou Ren was stripped to the waist and absolutely *covered* in mud. Both of his hands were pressed against the terrace wall as he concentrated, sweat pouring down his body while he made sure it was well and truly reinforced.

"All right, *Chunky. Go for it,*" he declared.

My Chunky Boy squealed happily and launched into motion. His trotters tore up the ground and a slight rumbling heralded his charge. He lowered his head and slammed into the wall with earth-shattering force.

Massive, hairline cracks radiated out from the impact point, but amazingly the wall *held*. Gou Ren whooped like a madman and started dancing around, pumping his fist and thumping his chest.

I was impressed. He had gotten *good* at Qi reinforcement.

Chunky hopped and danced with him.

"HAHAHAHA! My castle walls are the greatest in the realms!" he cackled.

"How's this going, boys?" I called out, and Gou Ren turned to me with a smile and a salute.

"No rain is knocking *these* over. The toughest terraced walls, bar none!" he stated triumphantly.

Sure, I had asked him to reinforce the terraced walls, but I had no idea how or why he'd decided that they needed to be able to stand up to a *Spirit Beast*.

I nearly asked him why, but at the eager, victorious gleam in his eye, I just didn't have the heart to. Chunky butted into my leg happily, proud to have helped, though that left muddy head marks all over my pants. I gave him a good scratch.

"Good job on the terraces," I praised, looking him up and down. He was really, *really* muddy. "Go wash up," I suggested. "I may have . . . *poked* Meimei a bit, and unless you want her to drag you to the river by your ear again, I'd go in willingly."

He finally seemed to notice just how dirty he was, then nodded. He eyed Chunky shiftily. "Race you to the water!" he shouted, and immediately started running.

Chunky squealed in protest and shot off after him, incensed at the foul cheating.

I shook my head with amusement while I went to grab my other "farmhand."

On the way, I wandered past Afro, Pompom, and Fuzzy. The sheep were grazing and were supposed to be watched over by Tigger, but my cat was conked out on top of Afro, fast asleep in the warm afternoon sun.

Xiulan, in contrast to Gou Ren, was leaning against a fence post with her arms crossed, deep in thought. Her hair, normally left to flow freely, was tied into a rough bun, and she was wearing one of my spare rough shirts instead of her normal silk getup.

She was wearing one of mine because she couldn't close any of Meiling's properly. It was better to have something too baggy and cinch it closed, rather than something bursting at the seams.

She sighed as she stared up at a cloud.

"Xiulan," I called, and the woman nearly jumped out of her skin.

"Master Jin!" she yelped, looking like a kid that had gotten caught with her hand in the cookie jar. She bowed immediately. "This one apologises—she did not—I was merely—"

"It's all right. Everybody needs a break now and then." I waved her off, and she raised her head, looking a bit confused. I guess she had been expecting me to scold her for slacking, like the Seniors in my old Sect.

"Ah . . . I see?" she asked.

I leaned against the fence post and looked up at the sky. It was a beautiful blue colour, with only a few white, wispy clouds travelling across it.

I patted the post next to me. Xiulan tentatively walked back and resumed her position. However, she got antsier and antsier as we waited, until she caved.

"Master Jin . . . this one does not understand. What purpose does this lesson serve? Your other disciple practises Qi reinforcement, yet I am here. Have I displeased you?"

Ah. I guess it was a bit rude of me to use her as free labour, but she *had* offered. Maybe I'd misunderstood her intentions? Meimei had said she didn't think Xiulan was here to learn farming, though Xiulan had seemed real eager for the first few days.

Maybe she was just having an off day?

"What purpose does the lesson serve?" I said, "Well, what were you trying to learn from it?"

Xiulan paused, then lowered her head again, looking embarrassed. "This one stands chastised, Master Jin," she whispered.

I looked at the field. The rows were neat enough, but . . . I could tell her attention had started to waver. It was just a sense—just by looking at it, I saw she'd screwed up the depth in some parts.

Well, everybody had their own skills.

"I'll teach you how to water the Spiritual Herbs tomorrow," I told her. Hopefully that would be a bit more interesting, but instead, she slumped.

"As you say, Master Jin," she murmured.

"Come on, let's go get dinner," I said.

She was still frowning at the field, but she left with me.

→

Meimei's mom's mushroom and fiddlehead recipe was really, *really* good. The flavours weren't something I was used to, so they were distinctly exotic to my palate. There was also a strange drink she had given me. It tasted a bit weird, almost like a medicine mixed with coffee, but surprisingly it fit with the meal.

I got my dishes together and brought them into the river room. I was one of the last to clean up, and Washy was there, waiting for me eagerly. The carp slapped his fins against the stone, hungry for more leftovers even after he'd gotten a full meal.

Smiling, I handed my plate to him. He lunged forwards like he had been starved for a week, splashing sounds echoing through the house. I smiled as I watched him first lick it clean, then take the washcloth I had set on the stone step and wipe it off properly. I started tapping my finger against my arm to an invisible beat while I watched him work. It was kind of fun to have a live-in dishwasher.

He finished up, then pushed the plate out of the water towards me. Nodding in thanks, I picked the clean plate up and spun it around a few times before putting it away, a bit of a bounce to my step. I was feeling a little bit antsy.

My fingers were tapping rapidly against my leg. I was starting to get a bit jittery. Looking down at my hand, I frowned.

Okay, this is a bit strange. I bounced up and down a few times.

I walked back into the main room and noticed that everybody else was missing.

"Meimei. What was in that drink you gave me?" I asked. I was getting really, *really* bouncy at this point.

She looked like butter wouldn't melt in her mouth as she stirred something into a cup of water. It smelled exactly like the drink she had given me.

"I have *no idea* what you're talking about, dear husband."

Some kind of prank, then? Would my skin turn blue, or was I about to start itching?

"Are you kidding? I've been waiting for you to try to get your revenge ever since I threw you into the mud pit!"

She looked almost offended by that statement.

"Jin, I've been trying to get you with *something* ever since Meihua's wedding. You've ignored the itching powder, the blue-skin dye, *and* the coughing candy. You didn't even notice," she deadpanned, frowning at me.

That . . . was hilarious, actually.

"And what's this?" I asked, bouncing on the balls of my feet.

She shrugged, her face starting to flush and her pupils dilating slightly.

"My father's energy tea. He takes it sometimes, when we have big orders from Verdant Hill, or when lots of people get sick."

I stared at her.

"You spiked me with an *energy drink?*"

"Yes. After all, I'm just a lewd woman. We won't be getting much sleep tonight." She pulled one of the ties on her robe, undoing it.

I felt my cheeks flush as my eyes locked onto the exposed flesh.

"You're . . . sure?" I managed to get out.

"Yes. This is my answer. So . . . let's go and *do our duties*, husband." Her voice was entirely too flirty, and I couldn't take it anymore. I started forwards, and she fled for the stairs to our room, giggling all the way.

But I caught her, throwing my wife over my shoulder like a sack of rice and racing towards the bedroom.

She was right. We didn't get any sleep that night.

CHAPTER 3

CROSSED BLADES

I t was another beautiful night. A cool breeze carried through the trees as Xiulan raised the hoe again, bringing it down to bite into the earth.

What are you trying to learn from this?

What was she missing? What profound secret eluded her? What was the purpose of this?

What was the advantage?

She could not comprehend it.

She knew that those with powerful wood-aligned Qi could grow entire forests in moments, or complete fields like this one faster than she could blink. Yet he didn't.

Why? Why *wait*?

The first few days, when Master Jin had taught her how to use the hoe, had been interesting, and she had been eager to accomplish what he had shown her. To learn his ways, like she had begged him to. She pushed some Qi into the ground like he had said, even though it was rather wasteful. She'd done her tasks with diligence. She supposed this was her own fault, for expecting to learn things so swiftly.

She *should* be content. She was receiving enough cultivation resources that it was as if she were Master Jin's favoured disciple rather than her own Sect's! Especially the "maple syrup" they had often. The Wood Qi within it was added to her own, without concentration. It filled her reserves and strengthened her body. It was less effective in a single sitting than the few pills she had consumed, but she could consume it far more often than the pills. And quantity had a quality all its own.

Yet it was the Fire Qi within the syrup that astounded her. If she consumed a pill of a Fire Nature without extreme care, it would ignite her own Qi. It had the possibility to burn her cultivation, just as a fire would burn across the grasslands. When she consumed it as one did mortal food, it passed from her body without a need for careful monitoring and purging.

There was no worry about that here. It simply dissipated through her digestion, never once threatening her.

She was being largely treated as an honoured guest. She was fed, she was clothed, and she was given places to cultivate. Master Jin even drew a bath for her every day, and Senior Sister washed her back! She returned the favour, of course, as it was only polite.

Yet she was unsatisfied.

There was a burning hunger for knowledge. For ascension. For a life, lived on her own terms.

And for an escape from her ill feelings back at her Sect.

Xiulan shook her head, dispelling the thought. When Master Jin had offered to teach her how to properly grow the Spirit Herbs, it had felt like a failure. That she was being assigned a different task because she was too slow and too unskilled to comprehend his methods. *Animals* understood what he was doing! Spirit Beasts!

And yet *she* did not.

She sighed as she stopped fixing the rows of furrows she had been tasked with creating. She eyed the house of Master Jin, and her face flushed. She would be outside tonight. Senior Sister had asked for privacy.

She had to credit Disciple Gou Ren. He looked like a monkey, with the cunning of one as well, swiftly laying claim to a shack to have a roof over his head.

He had even offered to share it with her, but she refused. He was growing tolerable, as he no longer stared openly at her—but she would *not* be sharing a roof, especially a roof that small, with him. Trading commiserating expressions over how loud Senior Sister's voice got was one thing. This was another.

She raised the hoe to strike the earth, but then paused.

What *was* she trying to learn from this?

She didn't know.

She slumped against the fence and looked up to the moon.

'A little blade of grass, grasping desperately for the heavens she can never reach.'

She froze at the voice, fury filling her veins. Her head snapped up, and she glared at the smug-looking cat, licking her paw.

"Begone," she snarled at the cat. "Do not test me, little one."

How the damnable little beast had somehow chanced upon that insult was infuriating. Her fists clenched at the familiar words that had been levelled against her Sect countless times. Dismissing their actions, and their cultivation. That the Verdant Blade Sect was as worthless as the grass that covered the ground.

It hurt because it had truth to it. They were a middling power at best. And a middling power in the Azure Hills meant that they would not even be a *servant's* servant in other provinces.

The cat scoffed, lying down and watching her.

Xiulan grabbed the hoe and began again.

How many times had she seen sneering faces looking down their noses at the Verdant Blade Sect.

If she was honest with herself, sometimes she thought they were right. She never would reach the heavens in a place like the Azure Hills.

Yet simply striving upon this path was admirable in itself. She knew she was too weak to survive outside this small pond; that was why she had jumped on the opportunity to train under Master Jin.

'*She cannot figure even* this *out, how disappointing,*' the cat mocked, and it took all of Xiulan's self-control not to throw the hoe at her. '*You should leave. You are barely tolerated here, interloper. A worthless parasite, flouncing around and dining off our benevolence,*' Tigu purred.

"I am not the one who was kicked out of Master Jin and Senior Sister's bed," Xiulan shot back. The cat recoiled, her eyes going wide. "I've seen you skulking about and pining up at the windows." Tigu hissed angrily, yet Xiulan continued.

"Shall *I* join them?" she mockingly pondered, purposefully straightening her back and pressing out her chest. "If I asked, I do not think they would deny me your place—"

She jerked her head back. Two strands of brown hair drifted on the breeze, severed by a blade of pure cutting Qi.

Xiulan smiled. She hadn't had a proper spar in a while. The fox boy, Yun Ren, ran away from his punishment at the wedding after goading her. The monkey boy was subdued and had not offered her a reason to work out some of her stress.

She needed this. This . . . this would make her feel much better.

"I will gladly trade pointers with you, *little sister*," Xiulan said, a smile spreading across her face. The Jade Grass Blades leapt into the air and floated obediently behind their Mistress. "Come, let us go to the forest, so we do not disturb Master Jin."

The cat scoffed but followed, glaring daggers when Xiulan purposefully turned her back on the predator.

She was honestly surprised that the Spirit Beast did not pounce upon her. For all Tigu's mocking, the Spirit Beast did seem to have *some* honour.

They met in a clearing in the forest, far enough from the house so as to not disturb the occupants. The cat was clearly seething, while an odd calm settled over Xiulan.

[Claw Arts: Five-Fold Blades]

Five disjointed claws made of Qi formed shards of light and murderous intent.

[Verdant Blade Sword Arts: Six Blades of Grass]

The swords grew and rose like blades of grass, thrusting proudly towards heaven.

The cat's eyes narrowed at the number of swords—she knew it was less than Xiulan was capable of making.

"It is uncouth to bully the weak," Xiulan informed her with a mocking grin.

At that, Tigu exploded into motion, her form blurring as she struck at Xiulan.

Perhaps, before Sun Ken, before she'd broken through to the Fourth Stage, such a strike would have been difficult for Xiulan to counter. Perhaps she might have strained a little. But Cai Xiulan had grown, and now her control over her floating blades did not waver. Five blades met five blades and stopped them dead. The sixth sliced up from beneath, forcing Tigu to throw her body out of the way.

"Who was reaching for a heaven they could never grasp?" Xiulan taunted. "The first blow is still yours, *little sister*."

The bout continued and Xiulan had to admit, the cat was fast. Her leaps were nearing the level of a movement technique! Tigu had great instincts and struck with unrelenting ferocity. She was a small target and leveraged it well, bouncing like a demonic ball from one tree to another.

Xiulan didn't move, rooting herself and simply standing with her arms behind her back. Blades of light struck blades of grass and were rebuffed. It was a stalemate.

Tigu was not a creature that gave up easily. Each moment she was in combat, she adapted and she grew stronger, feeding off battle like it was a bowl of rice. She got faster, her rage driving her forwards—yet not to the point of recklessness. A cold, calculating fury of a born fighter. Xiulan was impressed, even as the cat tried her damnedest to slash her to ribbons.

Finally, Xiulan could no longer just sit and defend. She had to start moving too. They sped through the forest, dodging and weaving between trees, yet their blades left not a trace upon their surroundings.

In one exchange, a leaf fell between them, floating between slashing claws and spinning swords. It touched the ground unmolested, not even the air disturbed along its passing.

The moon rose in the sky as they fought, blades slashing thirty times in a heartbeat, yet their exchange couldn't last.

Tigu was visibly tiring, even if her blows were stronger than when she had started. Her eyes narrowed and her blades shot out like spears, carrying enough force to actually halt Xiulan's own swords and forcing an opening.

Tigu shot through the gap, her eyes gleaming with victory—five more blades formed, all ready to strike at Xiulan.

To Xiulan's surprise, they were partially blunted. They would hurt, yet they were not designed to kill. It was a little insulting for the cat to think she would strike true. But it was appreciated. Xiulan's return strike would be just as measured.

Two more blades of grass formed, meeting five blades of light. Skill trumped talent. The blades, arranged like a flower bud, penetrated the center of Tigu's formation and bloomed, shattering Tigu's guard.

Xiulan's palm impacted Tigu's stomach, throwing the cat backwards and into a tree. A light blow, mere chastisement.

Yet the cat's shock was clear as she lay there, glaring at Xiulan.

Tigu sprung back to her feet, full of fury and humiliation. In response, Xiulan raised an eyebrow and inclined her head.

"A good bout, little sister," she said. The cat would have none of it. Her eyes narrowed.

Tigu hissed angrily. Ten blades of cutting intent formed. Twelve blades of grass rose at their Mistress's command.

They prepared themselves for another round—

And then, there was a *presence*.

'Who dares disturb this land's peace?' Ri Zu's voice echoed.

They both froze.

A mighty cock strode from the trees, his eyes focused fully upon them. He nearly glowed under the light of the moon; his bearing was resplendent. Upon his back was a dark shadow.

'The First Disciple says that you might have interrupted the Great Master and the Healing Sage with your roughhousing. Such things are unacceptable,' Ri Zu's voice squeaked.

"We were trading pointers, First Disciple," Xiulan declared, clasping her hands in respect. Tigu looked once at Xiulan, then nodded. Bi De observed them, his head cocked to one side.

'Oh? So late at night? Very well, then. The First Disciple begs you to allow him to trade pointers with you, then. We are all disciples here.' The rooster's Qi rose above his form as Ri Zu translated for him.

Xiulan swallowed. She was not used to being the inferior in these situations. "Treat us kindly, First Disciple?" she asked.

The rooster raised an eyebrow, studying her for a moment. Bi De inclined his head.

Xiulan shared a quick glance with Tigu. The cat nodded.

[Verdant Blade Sword Arts: Sixteen Blades of Grass!]

[Claw Arts: Ten-Fold Reaping Blades!]

They struck as one.

The rooster stroked his wattles with a wing . . . and then raised the limb into the air. The other stayed tucked against his side.

→

Xiulan staggered back to the field and collapsed against the fence post. Tigu flopped down beside her. Xiulan was exhausted and sweaty, yet she could not even say her pride had been too badly wounded. Bi De was in the Profound Realm—their fate had been sealed the moment he laid eyes upon them.

A clucking laugh echoed out as Bi De alighted in front of them. There was not a feather out of place.

'The First Disciple declares that was most invigorating,' Ri Zu said for him, never having moved from her position on the chicken's back. Not that she had needed to.

"Thank you for your pointers, First Disciple," Xiulan intoned. The cat just snorted.

The rooster nodded, his eyes on Xiulan as she staggered upright.

She was defeated, tired, and sore. That meant it was once more time for training. She locked her eyes upon the hoe. Maybe this time she would be able to learn something. She started her work again, trying to comprehend.

There was a cluck. Bi De was gazing at her. Slowly and with great purpose, he pulled back a leg, fixing a furrow that was inexact. There was *something* there. She watched intently as he did it again, energy swirling about him.

And then he turned and walked away. Xiulan sighed in frustration.

'Disciple Xiulan,' Ri Zu said as Bi De began to leave. *'The First Disciple says, "Some things cannot be forced. Time is the only way. Rest for tonight, and meditate upon this."'*

Xiulan paused and lowered the hoe again, the feeling of defeat growing worse.

"Yes, Senior Brother," she whispered, bowing in respect. The rooster nodded, then left, leaping into the air heading back towards the house. Xiulan sighed, limped over to the post, and sat down beside Tigu.

The cat gave her a halfhearted glare.

'You were defeated most embarrassingly,' the cat told her.

"And you were not?" Xiulan asked back.

The cat hissed.

'I require a sparring partner. You can understand me the best, so I will allow you the honour.'

Xiulan pondered refusing her, but the cat was good. She just needed more technique.

And Tigu was surprisingly polite, as far as sparring partners went. Tigu had pulled her strike, even after their harsh words, which meant she was . . . safer than a good number of Xiulan's previous sparring partners. Most, Xiulan knew, would not hesitate to "accidentally" run a rival through.

"At night, in the forest," she agreed. "Smacking some sense into such a rotten child will do wonders for my health."

Tigu sneered. *'Wait for me, harlot. I will transcend the limitations of this small form!'*

Xiulan nodded, amused. "I'm sure your human form will be as miserably ugly as your personality."

The cat glared at her, and then a look of confusion crossed over her feline face.

'My what *form?'* Tigu asked.

CHAPTER 4

A FINE MORNING

Gou Ren yawned as the first light of dawn filtered into his "home." He had originally planned on staying in Jin's nice, big house. But, well . . . *things* happened. Good things, as far as he was concerned. He had gotten a good friend, gotten to see his sister in all but blood married, and now he had a great, if tiring, job. Plus he got to eat as much as he wanted while helping his village.

His only complaint was that they were extremely inconsiderate of their guests' sleep. At night, Meimei got a bit . . . loud. Loud enough to keep him awake. But he supposed he would be just as inconsiderate if *he'd* just gotten married.

So he had claimed Jin's old shack. It was strange, having a place mostly to himself. He normally slept in the same room as his brother, and he heard his parents occasionally move around during the night. Outside Jin's, it was oddly silent, and he had a bit of trouble falling asleep, with only the sounds of nature as his company.

Most nights, Chun Ke and Pi Pa joined him. They never slept unless they were together, and their breathing and soft shuffling around did wonders for his peace of mind. He had spent his entire youth wishing for more privacy, yet now that he had it, the first thing he'd wanted was more people around.

It was still a bit strange to think of animals as "friends," but Chun Ke was more expressive and a better companion than most he had met save his own brother and Jin. Pi Pa was odd, prancing around like she was some high-class lady, but he didn't really find it strange anymore. Ever since Jin had arrived, Gou Ren had found himself increasingly able to ignore weird things happening.

He patted Chun Ke on the side, and the boar opened his eyes, not looking tired at all. He oinked at Gou Ren in greeting, then nudged Pi Pa, who also awoke.

Gou Ren got up and wandered out into the morning light. He stretched, grumbling under his breath, and both pigs beside him stretched as well.

The rooster crowed, though it was a lot quieter than normal—just enough to let people know that it was morning.

It was peaceful in the early dawn.

Jin was right, Gou Ren decided. There was something special about waking up like this. He wasn't normally introspective, but . . . he was glad he was here, even with the minor inconveniences.

He wandered over to the main house, scratching his belly.

"Mornin', Bi De," he greeted the rooster, who bowed back. "Oh, and mornin' to you too, Ri Zu." He caught sight of the little shadow, and the rat squeaked and waved back at Gou Ren.

Gou Ren got some eggs from the coops along with cold, day-old rice, and some venison from their pots in the river, the water keeping the jars and the meat inside cold enough to stave off spoiling. He glared at the bastard fish as the beast exacted his daily toll. His smug, fishy eyes locked on Gou Ren's as he received some rice—a necessary payment, otherwise Wa Shi would do his damnedest to get him wet for the rest of the day.

He was happy he didn't have to deal with the greedy little bastard on a daily basis. Getting a spray of cold water to the face when the fish thought you were being stingy was not something he needed or wanted first thing in the morning.

It was too nice a day to prepare food indoors, so he decided to eat outside.

He stoked the firepit, got out the wok, and started on fried eggs and some slabs of venison over rice. The fire was roaring, the eggs were cooking, and he was absently scratching Chun Ke behind his ears when he heard a voice.

"Perhaps meditation upon the human form would be most effective? One must first understand what they wish to be, before they strive to realise such a thing," a woman mused, her familiar voice a wonderful melody, before pausing and sounding rueful. "As this one was reminded."

Gou Ren's heart started thundering faster at the mere sight of her, at the vision of beauty that haunted his dreams at night. Xiulan approached, along with Tigu.

Xiulan's borrowed, too-big robe had opened slightly, exposing an expanse of smooth, pale flesh and a deep valley—

Gou Ren tore his eyes away and chastised himself. The cultivator was ethereally beautiful, but it was no excuse to stare. She had finally stopped looking at him like he was a pile of dung, downgrading from absolute disdain to mild distaste over the course of the week. *Progress!*

Tigu meowed and Xiulan frowned.

"Observe the full body? I suppose it *would* be best to do it that way. This is a debt, however, and one you must repay."

The cat glared at Xiulan but eventually bowed her head in what almost looked like respect and acknowledgement.

Okay. Strange. But not important, Gou Ren thought. *Don't mess this up, don't mess this up—*

"Good morning," Gou Ren called, raising his hand in greeting and trying to sound nonchalant. Tigu nodded to him, while Xiulan's eyes narrowed.

"I bid you good morning, Disciple Gou Ren." Her voice was cold to him, but she inclined her head ever so slightly.

Inside, Gou Ren was cheering his heart out. She had actually *talked* to him! She had stopped calling him monkey boy! It was a better reception than last night, when she had just frowned and walked away. He supposed he had been a little forward, offering to share such a small shack, but he had the best of intentions!

That went all right, right? She didn't look particularly irritated at me. Now, step two.

"I'm making breakfast, do you want any?" he asked, his voice a little gruff. The woman's eyes flicked to the wok, then back to him. She nodded.

He concentrated valiantly on the cooking as Xiulan sat down. He held out his hand for Tigu, and the cat allowed herself to be stroked a single time. She meowed at him, her yowling almost sounding like words, but when Gou Ren just stared in incomprehension, she batted his hand away and sat beside Xiulan.

There was silence as he cooked, and then he served everybody but the Master and Mistress of the house. Xiulan nodded in thanks, remembering him cooking pancakes for her before. She didn't make any of the noises he was so fond of, or even squirm around, but she was enjoying the meal he'd made. There was a slight smile on her face.

It was as if the sun had just risen again. Gou Ren smiled dopily back, his entire day brighter from seeing that smile.

They ate in silence for a while, before Xiulan heaved a sigh.

"Rough night, huh, Miss Cai?" he asked, searching for a topic of conversation.

The woman sighed. "Quite" was all she said, returning to silence. Gou Ren shrugged. Not really his problem. If she wanted to talk, she wanted to talk. If she didn't, well, that didn't matter either.

But . . .

"What's it like, going to a tournament, Miss Cai?" he asked. It was one of the burning questions he wanted to know the answer to. He knew about the massive fights between cultivators, which were apparently a great show to watch . . . but none of them happened around here. He had never even *seen* a cultivator before he'd met Jin. The woman seemed confused for a moment, bewildered that he had never been.

Eventually, she answered.

"It is exhilarating. Displaying your skill and winning glory for your Sect in front of a hundred thousand people—meeting people from all over the Azure Hills, and defeating their techniques. The roar of the crowds, the taste of the food—it is like the biggest festival you've ever been to." She was smiling a bit, remembering something fondly. Tigu was staring at her, the cat's eyes wide.

Her smile faded, and she took another bite of food. "The Dueling Peaks Tournament is the most important one of my life. The largest in the Azure Hills. It is held once every eight years, at the end of summer. There will even be those from out of the province, and rewards beyond imagination. The winner's name will surely resound through the entire province. My Sect has . . . great expectations of me. I must perform adequately—no. No. I must *win*." She took another bite, frowning.

"Why? Do you wish to participate, Disciple?" she asked him. Gou Ren pondered before responding. Probably not. He knew how to throw a punch—Elder Hong had shown him how to put his full body into the strike, and it had served him well in the few scraps he had gotten into, but the thought of fighting against people who had trained their entire lives?

Gou Ren shook his head. "I'd like to see it. I don't think I could compete, but maybe I'll be able to come watch? I'll just cheer for you instead of fighting." It would be cool to see that many people. The farthest away from the village he had been was the one time he had visited Gramps up north.

Maybe Jin will let me go?

Xiulan looked, well, he wouldn't say "touched" by his statement, but her eyes softened slightly.

"Thank you, Gou Ren," she said with a soft smile. "And thank you for the meal."

Gou Ren tried to hide his blush as he looked away. He finished his meal and thought about the day ahead. He would go hunting today, he decided. He had finished the terraces yesterday, so he deserved a break!

There was a sharp cracking sound. He jumped and looked up, startled.

He saw Tigu and Xiulan punching rapidly at each other, the cat looking annoyed, and Xiulan amused. Their hands and paws were nearly too fast for him to see, but both of them seemed amused, treating it more like a game than anything.

"What? More information, Tigu? Very well. First, there is the tournament, and then the Hill of Torment, where one can attempt to find resources. The Slash-cloud Nests are the things one has to be the most wary of . . ."

Gou Ren observed the tableau for a moment longer before deciding this wasn't his problem. He could barely see the strikes they were throwing out, and they looked like it was just a game to them.

He patted Chun Ke on the head, then went to get his bow. He was just taking stock of his last supplies when Jin staggered downstairs, looking a little worse for wear, but in a good mood.

"I made breakfast. Xiulan might still be out here," Gou Ren told him. Jin nodded and clapped him on the back.

"Thanks for breakfast, Gou," he said earnestly.

Gou Ren smiled. "Any time, Brother Jin." Jin rolled his eyes at the respect Gou gave him, and Gou Ren smirked.

"You better catch us something big, you slacker," he chided, glancing at the bow slung on Gou Ren's back.

"Me, a slacker? You bastard, you're just a slaver!" he complained.

Then, after a moment, Gou Ren held out his fist to Jin. The cultivator grinned, and they bumped knuckles.

Gou Ren loved his new job.

↔

You know, of all the things I could be doing, I hadn't really thought I'd be holding hands with a woman other than my wife not long after I woke up. Though I *had* woken up pretty late.

In my defence, my wife was holding my other hand and was entirely on board with this. A flower in both hands. Truly, I was a harem Isekai protagonist!

Pffft. Yeah, right. Xiulan is cute, but I'm not going there. Hell lies in that direction.

Originally, this lesson was just supposed to just be me and Xiulan, but Meiling had wanted to learn as well, so she'd pulled herself out of bed and limped over. Now I was teaching Qi infusion to two people.

Qi infusion was difficult to learn, from what I remembered. Many, many exploded plants had followed Jin Rou before he learned how to do it properly. And then make it work *better*, because the scroll he was working from was stupidly vague, and he'd had to research it in the Sect's library. There were so many pitfalls you could fall into. Some of them made the plants wilt a bit, and if you didn't monitor the soil properly, you got substandard results. Infections, diseases, bugs, and even some sort of Qi overload were common mistakes, damaging the final product.

There was nothing I . . . *Jin Rou* had hated more than not doing your best on an assigned task, even if it was shitty, and even if you were forced into it. But once you could do it well, then you could cheat. If you had a quota, and then managed to get fast enough to do more than your quota, you could skim off the top, like Rou had done with the Spirit Herbs. It was devious, and could have ended poorly if anybody found out, but considering Jin Rou's experiences? I approved. The Sect hadn't even noticed. In fact, one person had even complimented the Outer Sect Disciples for producing so many herbs. Jin Rou had been a little upset that all of the disciples had been complimented, seeing as he was doing nearly all the work, but he'd gritted his teeth and dealt with it.

Since I didn't have that scroll on me, I had to take a different approach. Show directly. And that needed physical contact.

Xiulan was a bit sweaty from whatever work she had decided to do this morning, although she seemed a bit less frustrated today than she had been yesterday, which was good. I had even seen her getting along with Tigger, sitting beside the cat and whispering to her. That was a relief. I was afraid that they might come to blows.

I took a small breath and concentrated, moving my Qi slowly so they could get a good feel for it. The flow gently wrapped around and guided both of their Qi.

After Meimei said my Qi was easy to control, I'd assumed hers would at least attempt to follow me, and I was right. It obediently trailed behind me and did everything I was trying to show it.

Xiulan's was surprisingly obedient too, but I guess that was just her control. She *had* to be good if she could make swords float. The energy followed along the pathways I made for her, like the roots of a plant following water. And that was what her Qi reminded me of: a plant. It was a bit similar to Meimei's, but while my wife's Qi felt almost gentle, Xiulan's was closer to razor grass.

It took about an hour for me to carefully show them what to do, guiding them over and over in creating the little formation in the plants, and in the water that we would use. Eventually, I had to direct them less and less, and observed as they had to form their Qi themselves.

Finally, it was time for a practical lesson.

"All right, your turn," I declared, handing them each a pot with a dandelion in it. That way, when they inevitably turned it into goop, we didn't lose anything valuable.

Both women nodded. I'd need to teach this to Gou Ren later too, but he was out getting us some more meat. Hopefully we'd have a deer or some rabbits tonight.

I looked at the two women as they focused on the weeds, their eyes narrowed in concentration. This part didn't really need much supervision, so I went to check on the rest of the herbs—specifically, one of the new Spirit Herbs that Xiulan had given me as a wedding present.

The Ten Poison Resistance Herb had been in the scrolls when Meimei and I had gone looking for the root at the Archives. They hadn't contained any growing instructions, but they had contained where it liked to grow. It preferred rocky soil and needed cold water. Its leaves were mostly green, but they had purple edging, and the underside was covered in soft fuzz.

It was looking much better in its little pot. It had been looking a little droopy when I'd replanted it, but I knew after a little bit more watering it would look big and strong.

I . . . honestly didn't know what I was going to use it for. If I could somehow get some seeds—or figure out however it reproduced—I could start growing more, but I didn't think I needed it for its poison resistance. I mostly just wondered what it tasted like.

The girls worked on their Qi stuff. I heard a muffled curse and looked behind me. Meimei had melted her dandelion and was wiping green sludge off into the soil.

As I'd hoped, Gou Ren came back with a deer for us, and we had a nice dinner. All in all, the slow, relaxing day was something I needed, especially after how much work we were putting into the farm.

→

"Hey, Meimei, have you seen Tigger?" I asked a few hours later as we were getting ready for bed. My wife considered my question while she got into her night robe.

"I think she's with Xiulan," Meimei guessed, sniffing the air.

I nodded. "I'm glad she made a friend. I was going to ask her if she wanted to sleep with us tonight, but if she's off having some fun, I'll leave it."

CHAPTER 5

BUT ONE FLAW

Meiling was in the middle of a field. The sun was high in the sky, and the world was warm and pleasant. There was a little girl who seemed achingly familiar yet a total stranger. A tiny, emaciated, broken slip of a thing, her body marred by gold cracks. She was missing an eye, she had a split lip, and her smile was full of holes, teeth that looked like they had been knocked out. She should have been sobbing in agony. But instead, she smiled.

Meiling felt her heart rend in two at the sight. She had seen devastation before, in the aftermath of one of Sun Ken's rampages. She had witnessed the lost and broken in Pale Moon Lake City when she was but a girl.

Yet nothing compared to this little cracked vessel. Meiling wanted to run to her, scoop her up, and murder the wretched people who had done this to the little one.

And yet, for all the ruination done to her body, the child still seemed to be in good spirits. Enough to hop and skip and hum.

She turned to Meiling. With that heartbreaking smile, she asked if they could go catch frogs.

Meiling couldn't bring herself to deny the little one. They walked hand-in-hand to the stream. Meiling hiked up her skirts and hopped in, taking the little one into the water with her.

Meiling liked catching frogs. She especially liked the way their little cheeks puffed up as they croaked. They were cute, if a bit slimy.

The frogs here were easy to catch. They were big and fat, wallowing in the mud. It was fun. It was so fun, getting covered in mud, and watching that brilliant smile, which was so full of joy even through the girl's missing teeth.

They must have played for hours, yet the sun never moved. They ran around the grassy hills. They played catch with a big seed. Meiling wove flowers into a crown and put it atop the little one's head.

She stood on her tiptoes and kissed Meiling on the forehead. Meiling ruffled the little girl's hair. It felt a bit like soft grass.

"What is your name?" Meiling asked her, even though she had a feeling she already knew it.

"[XXXXXX]," the little one replied. It was a cute name. It suited her well.

They played for a while longer, teasing the tail of a giant black turtle, who never even glanced in their direction.

Finally, the sun started to set. The little one, broken and beaten as she was, smiled happily. The golden veins that went through her body reflected the setting sun. Meiling scooped her up in a hug, then swore that she would do everything in her power to help fix the child.

Meiling woke up crying. Her body was positioned as if she were cradled around her little brother, yet no one was there. Jin's arm was around her, and there was dampness on his cheeks.

She scrubbed at her eyes, confused, and wondered why she felt a bittersweet smile on her face.

□

The best part about everybody you know being superhumans is that you can turn mundane, backbreaking labour into a game. It certainly improved my mood, as I had been feeling a bit down earlier in the day.

Seeds flew through the air and embedded themselves into the soil, perfectly equidistant from each other and with terrifying speed. Tigger's and Xiulan's faces were masks of concentration as they hurled them from the line, trying to see who could get them in faster.

The rest of the seeds were tossed far more slowly, and with more care, but they were still thrown. Both Meimei and Gou Ren were laughing at the sheer absurdity of the exercise, but it was honestly good for control. Probably.

Who am I kidding, I'd just invented martial arts wheat farming. Now I just needed my next disciples to be a panda and a dude with a pigtail.

People who were good at this whole "transported to the past" thing would have already made a seed drill while praising the wonders of science, instead of still planting everything by hand.

I had no damn idea how to make one, and I hadn't been to a black-smith who might be able to understand my ramblings and shitty draw-ings. It's just . . . did I need a seed drill?

Judging by how fast Xiulan and Tigger were tearing into the field in their new "shounen rival" style of friendship, the answer was no, because this was probably just as fast, or faster.

I should probably just ask Brother Che about it, though. No sense not to try to spread a bit of the modern knowledge around Hong Yaowu, and make their lives easier.

It was damn hilarious watching the normally rather prim Xiulan start arguing with a cat. They'd gone from hating each other to thick as thieves in a single night. A strange friendship, but it was good that Tigger had made a friend.

I wasn't taking part, because it was "unfair." They were right, but I kind of wanted to kick somebody's ass at something. Instead, I got the actual work portion: fixing any of the wheat seeds that had missed the target, making sure they were covered, and giving them a nice drink from my magical Qi bucket.

If I was lucky, I could get a double wheat harvest. If I wasn't . . . well, I would be fine with just one.

There was a soft moo, and the sound of cowbells. The two heavily pregnant cows, Lonlon and Malon, were getting taken for a walk by Chunky and Peppa, who were cheerfully watching over them. Babe the ox meandered with them. In their wake Big D and his hens followed, cluck-ing away and snapping at the flies that dared to bother the big animals.

Man. This was *really* starting to feel like a farm. I just needed my big red barn, and then everything would be perfect. The cows and ox lived in a temporary shelter for now, but after the fields were done, they were my next project.

I watched everything with a fond eye. The animals wandering. My wife and friends trying to one-up each other while chucking wheat seeds. The cultivator and the cat glaring at each other like they were mortal enemies.

The melancholy, wistful feeling from the morning had long since faded and the day was slowly getting better.

I relaxed for a while, watching Washy and Chunky share some spring berries at the edge of the river, each one having brought his own snack for the other to try. It was cute.

↔

Xiulan stared at herself. Or rather the statue of herself, carved out of wood, as she put back on her robe.

The first half of the morning had been spent . . . *enjoyably*. She did not know training could be . . . fun, but she had enjoyed herself. She had enjoyed bruising Tigu's pride more. The cat had turned from a haughty princess to a sulking child after Master Jin had declared Xiulan the winner of their bout.

Xiulan would much rather be working on the technique she had been given, but this was an interesting enough distraction: observing a Spirit Beast attempting to ascend.

"You're really quite good at this," she said. Tigu turned to stare at her and huffed.

'Of course I am skilled at this. I am unsurpassed in everything I do,' the cat declared. *'The Master has seen my skill, and approves. I shall allow you to gaze upon the ones made of ice later. He preserved them especially for me.'*

She seemed particularly proud of that, sticking her nose in the air.

"You also did the pillars for the wedding, did you not?"

Tigu nodded, settling in front of Xiulan. *'You are at your best when praising me, little Blade of Grass. Continue,'* the cat demanded.

"The composition was utterly amateur, but I suppose the technical skill was competent," Xiulan mused. Her honourable father had many fine carvings that surpassed what this little beast could do. "You have a long way to go."

The cat stumbled, then glared back at Xiulan—who put on her most innocent expression.

Tigu grumbled under her breath and turned to look at the statue.

'No tail for balance,' she stated, wandering around the statue. *'No proper teeth to bite, nor claws to rend. Eyes useless in the night. No good ears to hear, and a nose that is pathetic. Why would one even consider abandoning their form? This one is superior in every way to this . . .* thing.'

The cat turned up her nose at Xiulan's body.

"Are you claiming your form is superior to your Master's?" Xiulan asked, incredulous.

Tigu shrugged. *'He has but one flaw. I shall overlook it.'*

Xiulan huffed out a laugh at the sheer arrogance. Some would find it enraging, that a mere cat claimed itself superior. Xiulan took it as it was.

The empty boasts of a child. Despite her words, Tigu was looking at the body in longing and if Xiulan wasn't missing the mark . . .

Envy.

'I suppose the hands are useful enough,' the cat conceded. *'But the rest of this needs to change. Fear not, Xiulan, I shall improve your form.'*

Tigu's claws flashed, and Xiulan winced as two large objects hit the floor.

'Useless. Gets in the way,' the cat declared. Well, the cat was right, they *did* sometimes get in the way. Thinking about it made her appreciate that she was a cultivator. Some mortal women complained about their backs, but she had never felt any strain.

'Too tall. Needs better eyes.' The cat went to work, cutting and shaving down her sculpture of Xiulan into a sculpture she was more pleased with. The cuts were quick, with minimal thinking. Tigu already seemed to know what she wanted.

'Hmm. Much better,' the cat decided a few minutes later.

It looked a lot more like Senior Sister than Xiulan, with sharp, predatory eyes . . . though it was oddly stocky. The top half of the body was almost Master Jin in miniature. Far more muscle than a woman should possess.

The muscles in the thighs were Xiulan's, though.

'I shall meditate upon this,' the cat declared. *'Now come, witness the Master in all his glory.'*

Xiulan sighed but followed the cat. She wondered if the little beast would actually be able to take a human form.

Ah well, she had earned a favour from it, and she would be collecting that favour, whether the cat could transform or not.

Cold air billowed out from the pit in the ground, sharp and frosty. Xiulan opened the door and was met with . . . a sight.

Jin, nude. Jin, defeating an enemy, also nude. Jin, doing a flip. Again . . . nude.

She stared blankly at the ice sculpture's waist along with what was there—her face flushed.

'Is he not magnificent?' Tigu asked, rubbing up against the sculpture's leg.

CHAPTER 6

THE BUZZ

B i De stood at the head of the disciples. His countenance was calm, and his Qi was as still as a lake. The others had been called to assembly.

Indeed, they had been commanded. A mission, a charge, a *directive* from the Great Master! It had been given to Bi De that morning. He was overjoyed at the trust, and the order. So he had ordered the disciples to assemble. Brother Chun Ke was humming happily, his Pi Pa beside him, leaning against his bulk. Wa Shi was in his trough, chewing on a selection of river reeds, tilting his head from side to side, considering their flavours.

Sister Ri Zu was at the head of the table, going over the scrolls she had from the Healing Sage. Her little whiskers twitched, and she nodded to herself every few moments.

Brother Chun Ke oinked inquisitively, and Wa Shi perked up at the mention of honey.

They were just waiting for one more arrival.

They did not have to wait long. Tigu entered the building, looking irritated and dishevelled. She huffed at the assembly but went to her place, to the right of Bi De. The head of the table was the position of the First Disciple, but she had demanded a place of honour. None had sought to challenge her for it. Ri Zu took his left, and Pi Pa and Chun Ke didn't care. Wa Shi stayed as far away from the cat as he could.

'*We thank you for your attendance,*' Bi De greeted her and nodded at the cat. The cat grudgingly nodded back, her fur still ruffled from a recent spar. She had likely been training with this . . . *Cai Xiulan.*

Bi De knew not what to think of the female human. She wished to learn the Master's teachings, yet she always seemed so tense when she was meditating. Her muscles were coiled, and though she was pushing her Qi into the ground, the Land categorically disregarded her offerings. He deduced that she was being too forceful and not deliberate enough in her attempts. She was trying to go too fast, and thus the Land was ignoring her.

He had the ability to admit he might be wrong, however. He had counseled her to slow herself and properly reflect. She had taken his teaching to heart and directed her attention away from such forceful and swift infusions.

After that, she had begun trading pointers with Tigu regularly. At first, he had been concerned about her intentions. Yet Xiulan had proved the Great Master's trust in her. Her blows were chastising to the cat, yet not harsh. Tigu refused to call the woman Senior Sister, yet that was what she was. Bi De watched but left them to it. Although he wished to participate, if he traded pointers with them too much, he might stunt their growth! Such a thing was unacceptable.

When Tigu had settled and began to clean her paw, he gestured to Sister Ri Zu to begin.

'*The Lord has given us a request-command,*' she squeaked. Tigu's eyes sharpened immediately at the words, and she sat up straight, ceasing her grooming.

'*We, the disciples of Fa Ram, have been tasked with finding a creature for the Lord, and Master Sage.*"

Ri Zu went to Brother Chun Ke's piece of slate, laid upon its side, and picked up the large slab with a heave. It dwarfed her utterly, and she strained slightly with the weight but revealed its contents for the rest of the disciples to peruse.

Upon it was a stripy insect, and there were multiple views of the creature. It had two sets of wings and a long tongue. In its behind it held a weapon, a dagger, long for its body size.

'*This is a bee,*' Ri Zu declared, propping up the slate and making sure it would not fall over.

It was a creature he was marginally familiar with. At first, he had slain them for daring to sup upon the Great Master's plants, yet he had been chastised for the action. The buzzing things were apparently necessary for Fa Ram to function. Pollination was a fascinating topic, and it revealed the similarities between plants and animals.

'*This insect lives in great-big communes, of one hundred to ten thousand. They are an industrious creature, crafting great hives filled with honey and wax. These have great-much value to both the Master and the Mistress. Yet it is not the honey or the wax we have been tasked to find-seek.'*

Ri Zu paused.

'We shall be finding a queen.' She gestured to one of the other drawings, this one of a larger individual. *'From this one do all the lessers spawn, and thus do they go and create honey and wax. Should we capture this queen, we are to return her to the Master.'*

Brother Chun Ke oinked, sounding inquisitive.

Ri Zu nodded. *'The Lord has built for them many homes. The white boxes. In return for his protection, he will harvest-tax a portion of the honey and wax.'*

Chun Ke considered this for a moment, then nodded, satisfied at the explanation.

'Now, we shall learn of our quarry. You see-observe this long dagger? It secretes a venom, yet the most fascinating effect is that once the bee stings, the dagger rips out!' Sister Ri Zu's eyes were wide and fascinated, as she pointed to another drawing, this one of the insect's distended organs. *'They perish-die after this act, but it is most interesting! They give their life for the hive and the queen, so devoted are they—!'*

'Are they Spirit Beasts?' Tigu interrupted, bored. Ri Zu paused.

'Nay, they are normal-mortal insects—' the little rat began, looking dejected.

'Then we have no reason to hear of their weapons. What shall they do, bounce off our skin?' the cat scoffed. *'Enough of this. We shall begin a search for these "queens." How pretentious, claiming one's self a queen when the Master exists! If he did not desire them alive, I would bring him fifty of their heads for their arrogance!'* She raised her nose in the air and summoned her blades of Qi.

Ri Zu frowned at the cat's arrogance and boasting. Tigu noticed the glare.

'Ah, finally grew some spine, did you? Shall we trade pointers? I shall give you the first blow, little sister.'

Tigu's eyes were wide with predatory glee as she met Ri Zu's frown. The glare held for a moment, before the rat looked down and away. Bi De frowned at the interaction.

'This one thought so,' the cat smirked. *'Fear not, you need not bother your- selves with this task. This Tigu shall gather a hundred of these queens before the rest of you collect but one! The Master will be most pleased with me!'*

With that, Tigu left, sweeping eagerly out of the room with her tail held high. Bi De sighed as he watched her go.

Ri Zu glared at the door where the cat had retreated to.

'Ri Zu will poison her one day,' the rat declared. *'Then we shall trade pointers and see who has fun.'*

The rooster frowned at the rift between the two of them. He didn't exactly know how to address it. Indeed, this disciple took after her instructor—the Mistress. Tigu was likely going to learn a very, *very* nasty lesson in the future.

He paused, wondering what he should say. Ri Zu had saved his life. He would defend his Sister if Tigu came after her, but how to prevent the battle before it began? In that, he had no experience.

Ri Zu looked at the slate and sighed, dejected at the interruption of her lesson. She looked like she was about to place it back down, when Brother Chun Ke oinked again. He was sitting like he did whenever the Great Master offered lessons. Pi Pa and Wa Shi also remained, though the fish was here likely more out of laziness.

'You wish to hear-learn more?' Ri Zu asked hopefully. Brother Chun Ke oinked again, wiggling from side to side.

'A-ah! Well, ahem!' Ri Zu stood tall once again, and some of her excitement came back. *'We shall speak upon the medicinal qualities of honey, and the habitat of the bee!'*

Bi De traded a glance with Pi Pa. In her eyes was nothing but contentment, as she leaned further into Chun Ke's side. Bi De understood her affection. Brother Chun Ke's heart was a treasure that surpassed heaven.

Truly, if Bi De had been a hen, he wished he could have known a Chun Ke. Instead, he would be content with their friendship. Truly he was blessed to have their support, and he treasured their forgiveness for getting Brother Chun Ke hurt.

Bi De settled down to listen to Sister Ri Zu's returned enthusiasm. She hopped about, and her whiskers twitched as she pointed to different parts of the insect, explaining how it flew and where it liked to burrow into the ground or construct upon the trees.

Her lesson lasted perhaps an hour longer, and then they were done.

'This concludes Ri Zu's knowledge on the bee! We shall go and seek-find them now!' Ri Zu shouted in excitement, waving her little hands about. Brother Chun Ke nudged her affectionately with his nose, and Ri Zu

pushed back, nuzzling into him. She looked like she was about to hop onto his back, but Bi De drew their attention, coughing slightly.

He had wanted to spend some time with her, just the two of them.

Ri Zu's eyes widened. Chun Ke gave her a little push.

'Ah, Ri Zu will be joining-travelling with the First Disciple—ah, Brother Bi De?"

Bi De nodded, happy at her use of his name. She took her place upon his back, and the rest of the disciples exited the house together. They paid their respects to the Healing Sage, out in her herb garden. They wandered past the Great Master, who was separating the rice seed with Disciple Gou Ren and Disciple Xiulan. He was pointing at the water and musing on how the salt made the density of the water different, which allowed the rice to float or sink.

Bi De observed the odd, fluffy balls and the puller of the plough as they ate the grass, content with their lot in life.

It was another wondrous day in this Blessed Land. The sun was high in the sky. The wind was beautiful and warm. The land was hale and hearty. Wa Shi split off first, headed to the river. He likely wouldn't be able to help much, confined to the river as he was, but he would most assuredly be on a sharp lookout for any beast that could produce the sweet snack.

He nodded to Sister Pi Pa and Brother Chun Ke as they too began to split off from him and Sister Ri Zu, covering more ground in two groups, rather than one. He was disappointed he would no longer have their company, but the task from the Great Master was paramount.

That was not to say that he could not enjoy himself while completing this task. Sister Ri Zu's Qi, almost absent-mindedly, went to the places where wicked Chow Ji's impurities had once lay, though they were now only scars. They still ached occasionally, or twinged a bit when he moved too fast, but they had healed well. Better than poor Brother Chun Ke's wounds. The boar was . . . slow of mind—permanently crippled by wicked Chow Ji. It was a deep and lasting wound, but it made Chun Ke's cheerful demeanor all the more precious.

The Qi circled in Bi De's body, and he knew peace.

They entered the forest and began their search. His eyes were sharp, and Ri Zu's nose was sharper. No bee would evade them.

They wandered through the forest together, simply enjoying one another's company.

'Willow, reduces inflammation and joint pain,' Ri Zu said, pointing to a plant and listing off another medicinal fact. Bi De committed her hard-won knowledge to memory. He took note of everything she pointed to, her excitement infectious. They harvested little bits here, little bits there, to help build up the Healing Sage's medicine room. They were not searching especially hard, simply travelling together and enjoying the world.

As they walked, they observed the buds, the new shoots, and the spring flowers. The wonder and bounty of spring.

Bi De preened little Ri Zu, and she giggled.

Their walk was leisurely, since the Great Master was in no urgent rush. They wandered all throughout the land, drinking in its sublime atmosphere. Bi De allowed his whims to guide them, occasionally hopping up into the trees for a better view or dropping down to inspect something Sister Ri Zu pointed to.

Their patience was rewarded. Buzzing around a flower was a bee. A large bee. She was ragged-looking, and her flight was lumbering and laboured. If Ri Zu's drawings were right . . . it was a queen bee, yet one without a hive. They observed her for a while. The bee was damaged, and hurt, yet still seemed healthy enough as she attempted to gather more materials and remake her hive. How admirable. A most fortuitous encounter.

With a beak that could rend steel and tear men limb from limb, he plucked the bee from the air. So gentle was his grip, and so sublime was his control, that the insect did not even notice she was caught despite being held fast.

They could go out and search for more . . . but Bi De decided that if his Great Master required more bees, they would venture forth again tomorrow. He would gladly do this duty.

↔

I was humming to myself as I set up the beehives. You couldn't just shove a bee in there and expect it to do what you wanted; like everything else on a farm, a bit of prep work was required first. In this case, I had to put some wax along the frames, so the bees would know where to build. It was a simple task, fast and easy to complete. I put the hives in a few locations. Most were back towards my old shack, and the others were in the forest where Big D had fought with the fox.

I knew they had to be far enough from the house that the bees didn't buzz around the windows too much. Bees were useful, but if you've ever been to an apiary, you would know that they get absolutely *everywhere*.

After I'd finished, all that was left was finding the bees. Or more precisely, the honeybee. I had already seen something that looked a bit like a bumblebee earlier, and maybe some mason bees. For the mason bees, I had actually decided to build them their own little "hotel." The solitary bees could use them since they didn't create hives but rather worked alone, doing their duty.

I still had some little odds and ends of bamboo. Nothing useful, save for maybe use as a straw, but perfect for this project. Punch out the center, then build a container to hold them with a little roof to keep off the rain. Put it facing the morning sun, and you've got yourself a solitary bee hotel!

Not bad, for like five minutes of work. Sure, they wouldn't make me honey, but you should always do something nice for the native bees. They're good for the environment.

I was examining my handiwork when I heard a cluck from behind me.

Turning, I saw Big D and Rizzo, both looking pleased. He had a bee in his beak. A honeybee. It was just sitting there, not even struggling, looking around at the world.

I stared blankly in shock. Just a few hours ago, I had said to keep an eye out for any bees, so that we could get started on the hives. But this? They had immediately dropped everything to go and find one for me?

I laughed.

"Good job, Big D, Rizzo," I said, reaching down to give them both a pat. I always felt a bit odd doing that—they were people . . . but they liked their head pats. Well, Rizzo tolerated them. She never actually said no to them, but she was the only one of them that wasn't that affectionate with me, but I didn't mind.

I crouched down and looked closer at the prize they had brought me. It certainly looked like a queen; however, honeybees travelled in swarms. This was just a single, lone bee, though a bit larger than average and slightly iridescent. Was it some kind of native bee?

In that case, it might be better to put it with the rest of the mason bees . . . but hell, I was in no rush. *Let's give it the big hive, see what happens.*

We sat in silence for a moment as I just looked at the hives, imagining all the buzzing honeybees.

CHAPTER 7

A MEETING

It was always fascinating watching another's cultivation style at work. Xiulan looked on, interested, as Master Jin walked through his fields and beehives, deep in meditation. It was odd to use moving meditation so heavily. She knew not of a single Sect in the Azure Hills that employed it to this extent, as Disciple Gou Ren was deeply cultivating as well. He carefully planted the rice seed in the barrels so that he could continue upon the path he'd been given by Master Jin.

She knew of the technique, of course—she had even managed to perform it once. That had been when she had first received the Jade Grass Blades, the treasures of her Sect.

She had been overjoyed, immediately going off to practise. It hadn't been out of any desire to train, but . . . because she wished to. It was more a dance than a form. She had whirled through *something*, light on her feet, completely ignoring the style of the Verdant Blade Sect.

She knew that was folly. Deviation in one's cultivation was dangerous at the best of times, and giving in to a whim? That was unacceptable.

Even if those footsteps sometimes found their way into her forms in the heat of battle.

Still, she observed closely, then concentrated intently upon his Qi. How deeply he drove it into the earth. While the amount was beyond her, she could feel it. She could feel the beginnings of something taking hold and then fading.

She took a breath and tried to copy it. Deeper and deeper, she drove her Qi, searching. Reinforcing. Trying to find whatever it was the others had found.

She encountered nothing that day, despite all of her efforts.

She was just about to enter deeper meditation for the night, when her sparring partner approached, looking absolutely enraged.

Tigu's fur was matted and looked slightly sticky. Xiulan could smell honey on her, and there was a bulbous welt on her nose.

She was trying to look dignified as she approached for their nightly spar. The cat really didn't appreciate Xiulan's stifled laughter.

Blades of cutting force arced out and Xiulan's feet unconsciously moved in time to a dance only half remembered.

The battle was short and the scuffle vicious, but she ended the battle with a cat in her lap, glaring petulantly at her.

Her fingers wove through soft fur. There was something to be said for being able to play with your sparring partner like this, after you defeated them. It was quite . . . pleasant.

She began her meditation again, searching for whatever eluded her.

Time, she told herself. She just needed time.

☐

"Senior Sister! Senior Sister! Tell us about how you slew Sun Ken!" one of the disciples eagerly asked. They crowded around, as close as they felt they could get. Their eyes were full of stars, each one of them eager to hear her tale.

"He was wounded from the first fight. Jiang Yuan, one of our noble fallen, managed to strike a blow," she lied. She had chosen Jiang Yuan, who had stood faithfully behind her. He'd been old, so old for a disciple, stuck on the First Stage of the Initiate's Realm for decades. He was full of good humour and was kind to the mortals. He had faithfully followed the teachings of righteousness, and had been the first to volunteer when called upon to hunt Sun Ken, offering his blade without hesitation. He was loyal and stalwart, a fixture of the Sect for as long as she could remember.

Sun Ken had split him in two, like a man splits a log, laughing all the while. Poor old Yuan had barely managed to slow him.

"They were easy to follow after their failed ambush." Lie. "They were bandits, after all, and they fled like chickens with their heads cut off." Lie. "I found them, about to set upon the village, and did to them as they managed to do to so many others. They were far too focused on their escape to notice my own ambush." Lie, lie, lie.

She wove a tale of a daring, audacious assault. The other disciples laughed at the irony of bandits being ambushed. They gasped at the account of her "duel" with Sun Ken, her own swords meeting and exceeding Sun Ken's own.

She told them how she left Sun Ken's corpse for the dirt, not even bothering to bury him—how her own strikes had destroyed him so utterly that bringing back even his head was a worthless endeavour.

The disciples laughed and cheered. The women looked on with wonder and admiration. The men with awe and desire. Xiulan's face was locked in an imperious, self-satisfied smirk.

As one expected from the Young Mistress.

She was lucky they couldn't hear her thoughts.

→

The next day, despite her troubled rest, Xiulan had her attention fully on her current task. The Qi structures and infusions were not overly difficult to grasp, but it was as if they had all come from separate techniques. There were too many differences. One was a spiral, one was almost spiky, and yet still others were like solid earth. Five—no, *six* of them had fused into one.

She thought back to the guidance she had received two days ago. The touch of Master Jin's Qi was firm, yet gentle. Her Wood-aligned Qi had responded instantly and obediently, remembering the patterns he'd guided it through, like it was growing into place. She had to stop it from automatically just repeating the same actions, so she could actually understand what she was doing.

There were parts that should have caused the Qi to run out of control. They *did* if she did not exercise her control properly, which then burst the plants that she was working on. But once properly accounted for, it was a truly profound art.

When functioning correctly, the formations supported each other, smoothed out odd ripples in the structure, and targeted everything: the plant, the soil, and the water.

She finished one more iteration of the technique and, satisfied at her progress, she stood. Master Jin was teaching Disciple Gou Ren the technique and the monkey—no, that was rude of her. He had some bad habits and wandering eyes, but he was *tolerable*. At least he tried to hide his glances, and even unprompted would tear his eyes away, obviously chastising himself.

It was . . . nice. If she was being honest, she almost felt fondly towards the boy.

She waited patiently until he was finished instructing the other disciple and had turned to acknowledge her.

"I'm guessing you've got it down?" he asked her. He seemed a little surprised, but also impressed. "Well, I suppose I did get all of the trial and error out of the way. It took me *months* to make sure everything worked together. *So much plant goo,*" he muttered, his eyes unfocused.

As expected of a Hidden Master, it was an original creation! He had passed on to her one of his techniques! Even when she did not comprehend the first lesson he had given, his generosity knew no bounds!

A hand clapped onto her shoulder. She nearly flinched at the sudden contact, though it bore no ill will. It was meant to be encouragement. "Time for a practical application," he declared. "Grab one of the tubs and follow me."

She was quick to obey, following her Master outside to a pile of dirt. It was black as pitch and smelled of life and decomposition, yet it wasn't unpleasant. Master Jin appeared to be pondering something as he leaned down.

He dug his hands deep into the loamy earth and brought up a handful. Examining the earth in his hands, he took a deep breath and sighed happily.

"This is our foundation. Each year we add to it, and each year, hopefully, it will get better. Lots of people forget that the dirt is alive," he mused.

Xiulan listened intently.

He held out the dirt for her to peruse. "You know what bacteria are, right?"

Xiulan nodded as she examined the offering. They were the tiny attackers who invaded the body and slew the host if they were able. She had known vaguely of their existence; Senior Sister had explained them in greater detail.

"Well, they're not all bad. Just like you need some insects, you need some bacteria in the soil. The bacteria break down the plants and the waste you put into the dirt, so that what's left is usable by the next things you grow. It's a balancing act. Too much of a good thing can be harmful." He paused and seemed to be thinking of a metaphor. "Think of it like . . . pill toxicity. A pill may help you grow your cultivation, but what would happen if you took a pill every day, damn the consequences?" Master Jin asked. At first she thought it was a rhetorical question, but she answered anyway.

"The impurities would build up in your body and harm you, eventually," she replied—before she realised the reason why he'd asked. "Is this why you don't command the plants to grow?" she asked.

He seemed taken aback by the question.

"These things work on a different timescale than us. I suppose I *could* command the plants to grow—maybe even twice—without unduly harming the soil." He paused, seeming to think deeply on her question. "But make no mistake, it *would* harm it. There are simply too many things in the soil, too many connections, and you can't target all of them. Or at least *I* can't," he said, seeming rueful, and shrugged. "Like that forest there. All the tree's roots are connected through strands of a tiny fungus. In times of drought, or poorer soil conditions, it helps transport nutrients and water to all the trees in the system. If I forgot about that portion and just made the trees grow more, what would happen? Would they consume the fungus for more food? Would the fungus grow out of control and eat the roots? If it destroyed the fungus, the rest of the forest would suffer. If it depleted the soil, nothing could grow there for years. It would be a cycle of waves. Bursts of plenty, followed by bursts of famine. My goal is a more consistent approach. If you even out the bursts, then you would, in the end, get either the same yields or maybe even more in the long run, because you just keep building it up better."

"There's a whole world in there. It would be a shame to carelessly destroy it."

Xiulan digested this information the best that she could. Of course, it all came back to his first lesson. *Connections.* Especially the connections that did not seem obvious, or were too small to notice at first. Xiulan bowed her head at this wisdom.

"Now, let's learn about *phosphorus, nitrogen, potassium,* soil density, and their relation to good growth!" Master Jin cheered, enthusiasm shining in his eyes.

→

Later that day, Xiulan searched once more, letting her consciousness flow outwards. Now that she knew what to look for, she could feel the little roots connecting to each other and forming into a web. She could also feel the depths of Master Jin's Qi.

She could also sense the other force present: the beating heart of the land. That was what Master Jin had been driving his Qi into. It felt so much like him and yet not. In truth, she still couldn't tell where he ended and this separate entity began.

There was focus. There was intent. She was being watched. She observed the glorious entity, overflowing with Qi, and with shining golden cracks running through it.

It was almost a body. Almost a human form.

It was a spirit. An Earth Spirit. Xiulan had read about their existence—yet she'd believed the Azure Hills were too weak, too Qi-deprived to have anything like this!

Yet here it was. An Earth Spirit, in the Azure Hills. This was what Master Jin's Qi had to be nurturing. He . . . he was building it up. He was building up the Azure Hills.

Was that his goal? To see if he could fix this Qi-deprived province?

Xiulan approached, in a trance, travelling deeper and deeper, towards the entity. It was shining with power and so, *so* beautiful. She could feel its benevolent power—so much like Master Jin's—radiating off it. It was a thing of absolute beauty. It recoiled and yet still she approached, her Qi spurring her onwards. It was like there was something ancient, hidden within the Verdant Blade scriptures, that drove her forwards.

She had to get closer. She had to see this spirit, the fruit of Master Jin's labour. Perhaps this was what was empowering the Spirit Beasts? Perhaps all she needed to do was claim a part for herself!

The Qi stopped recoiling. Instead, it held out its arms.

The hands reached out, as if to cup her face. Xiulan approached the embrace, raising her own arms to receive the spirit.

The spirit's hands firmly gripped the braids on either side of her head.

A spiritual forehead connected with her own, in a rather vicious headbutt.

CHAPTER 8

A NEEDLE

There were some things about life as a farmer that Meiling didn't particularly enjoy. One might think, as the headsman's daughter, she would be exempted from the difficult or disgusting tasks. That she merely tended to herb gardens and made medicine. But that was not how Hong Yaowu did things. Hong Xian was just as ready to lend his aid toiling in the fields as he was in preparing medicine or healing the sick and wounded.

It was an ancient pact. The pact of feudal lords, and her father, carried on the duties of the village patriarch, unbroken for generations. To be the patriarch *meant* something, in Meiling's opinion. Maybe it was her birth, but she considered few of the men with the title of patriarch to be worth the name. They might have power and wealth, but if one neglected their ancient duties of caring for and protecting their charges, they were not lords at all.

But she digressed. She had to do her share of fertilizer shovelling and cleaning up after patients in her father's care. One lost fluids rapidly when affected by the flux—normally out their ass.

And speaking of asses, she was about to stick her hand up a cow's. She put her hand into the water and focused, heating it once again to boiling. It stung a bit, but it was bearable, and it would kill any bacteria on her hand, which was necessary if she was going to shove it into the cow in front of her.

"You were right, everything looks normal," Meiling told her husband. Jin smiled sheepishly.

"Sorry for making you do that again, but I'd rather have a second opinion, and you've done this more than me." Jin went to scratch the back of his head, paused, and switched to his other hand with a grimace.

She smiled. She would have preferred not to stick her hand up there, but . . . he trusted her. He trusted her skills and knowledge and didn't mind asking her questions. It was nice. Even if she had to occasionally get a bit dirty.

Indeed, examining the heavily pregnant cows was a filthy task, considering where one's hands had to go. That was the easiest way to check the calf and examine it. One just had to go elbow deep and feel through the intestines and uterine wall to make sure there were no complications, like a breech birth where one might even be able to feel if the umbilical cord had wrapped around the neck.

A smirk formed on her lips as Jin patted the mildly distressed cow, trying to calm her down from the intrusion.

"Hey, Jin. We're hole siblings," she said cheekily, using the crude idiom referring to men who had shared a prostitute.

Jin's face went from incredulity to disgust before he burst out laughing.

He raised his hand in bewilderment when he finally regained his breath. "What the *hells*, Meimei? That's disgusting!" he managed to get out through wheezing laughs.

They looked at each other, then burst into laughter again.

"How soon do you think?" Jin asked her, still smirking.

"Soon. Maybe even this week," she replied. The cows were extremely close now, and they would be calving in no time. One of the disadvantages of a spring calving was that the spring rains sometimes made the calves sick.

That most likely would not be an issue here, however. She looked up at the tall ceiling. Two of the walls were not yet complete, but the barn was coming along nicely. However, that work had only taken Jin two days, interspersed with him making sure the hives were ready. It was still something wondrous, to see the barn raised so swiftly and surely, and just as humbling. Meiling was very used to life in her village, and these days it felt like time was moving twice as fast.

"Right, let's go take a bath," Jin declared. He wrapped his clean arm around her shoulder and started walking. She allowed herself to be dragged along. Jin was obsessed with cleanliness. She was clean by nature and practice, yet Jin demanded a bath every night, instead of just a wipe with a wet cloth. However, she supposed since the bath was so easy to fill, it was feasible. Dragging the water from the river for a weekly bath was a source of great grumbling around the village.

The heated water was extremely nice, she had to admit, and Meiling was getting used to the feeling of always being clean.

"Indeed. We must clean ourselves of our effluvium, after our strenuous time penetrating the fine ladies of this establishment," Meiling japed, earning another bout of laughter from her husband.

They strolled along the property. Things were finally slowing down after the mad dash to complete the fields. Essentially, all that was left was to plant the rice, finish the barn, and have the calves birthed. Then they would finally have some time to rest.

Jin had promised her, at the first available opportunity, he would take her home—back to her village, to see her father and brother again after the month she'd spent away.

She couldn't wait.

She was in a great mood until she smelled cut grass. Normally, the smell of freshly scythed grass was one she enjoyed immensely. This, however, was just on the wrong side of pleasant and was tinged with Qi. She had noticed it in the morning, and it had gotten worse throughout the day.

She looked around and found Tigu and Xiulan. Both seemed to be in a foul mood. Xiulan appeared downright *exhausted* and was rubbing her forehead. Tigu was . . . sticky? Her fur was matted, and she looked just about to kill something.

Jin's arm tightened on her shoulder. He caught her eye and nodded in the direction of the two irritated-looking girls.

"Are you sure?" she asked. She was rather looking forward to leaning back against his chest and letting her own worries slip away into the heated water.

He nodded. "I'll wash the clothes instead."

Women's work, her mind supplied. Jin didn't seem to care.

She got up on her toes, and they shared a kiss. "Acupuncture kit, please," she whispered. Jin nodded obligingly.

Well, time to see what the matter was.

"Xiulan, Tigu! Come join me!" Meiling called. The woman and the cat looked up, a bit startled, but after a glance at each other, they nodded.

They really looked like they needed a bath.

→

"How did you get this all over you?" Meiling asked, aghast. There was wasp paper, honey, and bits of bug strewn throughout Tigu's fur.

Tigu yowled an answer, her speech a series of chatters and grunts. Meiling sighed and rubbed the cat's head. "Yes, yes, I'm sure," Meiling replied to the cat before turning to Xiulan. Tigu wilted slightly.

"After her failures yesterday, she asked me to accompany her. She mistook wasps for bees, again, and raided a yellow-lance nest head-on," Xiulan muttered. "Then she tried to dig out a bee nest that was underground. She disturbed the earth too fiercely and ended up in the honey. In the confusion, the queen escaped."

Tigu turned, absolutely scandalised, and hissed at Xiulan. She struggled for a moment, like she wanted to get at the woman, but Meiling simply gripped her by the scruff and the cat went limp.

"You are going *nowhere* until I clean you," Meiling stated. Tigu let out a few token grumbles but remained limp. The little beast even started purring when Meiling's fingers went to work, cleaning the silky fur.

Meiling watched Xiulan out of the corner of her eye. The woman was morose, hugging her knees to her chest while sitting on one of the benches.

"And you?" Meiling asked. For a moment, Xiulan looked like she wasn't going to say anything, before she deflated.

"I made a mistake and pushed too hard, too fast. *Again*," Xiulan explained. She winced, then rubbed her forehead again.

"Did whatever happened hurt you?" Meiling asked, concerned.

Xiulan paused and took stock of herself.

"Only my pride, I think," she whispered. "And my forehead. I was hit with a stone."

Meiling shrugged. "Then there is little problem in trying again, but slower this time, no?"

Xiulan sighed, a tired smile coming to her face. "You are right, Senior Sister. This was a light rebuke. I shall try again. Slower this time."

Meiling nodded. She ran her fingers through Tigu's fur one last time, then turned to the other woman.

"Grab a towel and lie on your front, Xiulan. You look like you could use some relaxation."

Xiulan's eyes focused on the acupuncture needles, her body tensing further, before she abruptly relaxed.

"I entrust my body to you, Senior Sister," Xiulan said, her voice soft. Meiling coughed at the phrasing.

Meiling set Tigu aside, the cat mewling softly as her fingers left.

Xiulan's skin was impossibly soft and smooth. Every time Meiling had touched it she'd wanted to just run her hands up and down the other woman's body for the pure tactile sensation. Not in any sexual sense. It just felt so *interesting*.

But it was a veneer. The smooth, soft skin ended abruptly and gave way to unyielding flesh that was like metal cords. Especially when Xiulan was this tense.

Meiling frowned. She knew mortal acupuncture, but not cultivator acupuncture. She was fairly certain she wouldn't hurt the other woman, but she would only focus on the muscles, just in case.

The first needle refused to penetrate flesh, instead just bending.

Meiling took a calming breath and got out another needle. This one, she carefully reinforced with Qi.

She took her time, observing every reaction, as she placed the needles carefully into the muscles. It took a strange amount of effort to complete her work. She stuck each one in precisely, like she did for Elder Che when Father could not do it.

When she placed the last needle, Xiulan's body abruptly relaxed, and the other woman let out a groan of pleasure that turned Meiling's ears pink. Seriously, this woman! Meiling shook her head. She would need to ask Jin, or Xiulan herself, for more scrolls on acupuncture. They were all cultivators, so that meant she needed better arts if she was going to adjust their bodies properly.

Or, at least that was what she assumed. Maybe she didn't need them? It never hurt to learn.

A paw batted at her arm, and when she looked down, she saw Tigu staring at the needles, entranced.

"Okay, fine, yes, you too," Meiling said with a sigh.

She soon had an utterly relaxed cat, and a puddle of a woman, both steaming in the water.

I'll have to see if Jin wants to learn acupuncture. It just isn't the same to do it to yourself.

Yet all good things come to an end. The other girls staggered out of the bath and into the evening air. Well, Xiulan staggered. Tigu just curled up in Meiling's arms. Jin was sitting with his back against the house. He had the bee that Bi De had collected in the palm of his hand and was carefully feeding it some maple syrup. The rooster was looking on, interested in the small, surprisingly docile insect. Meiling knew that while the young queen *could* feed herself and make a new hive by her lonesome, it was best that she didn't work too much, especially after being separated from her swarm.

He raised an eyebrow and gestured towards Xiulan. Meiling shrugged. Even though Xiulan had told her what was bothering her, Meiling didn't think she had spilled everything. Still, she seemed to be in a bit better mood now.

There was a commotion as Chun Ke, Pi Pa, and Gou Ren exited the forest. Chun Ke had a thick branch in his mouth with a hive upon it, yet the bees were nowhere to be found. Gou Ren raised a hand to Jin.

"We've got more!" he shouted, patting a box on his back. "A whole hive, thanks to these two!"

CHAPTER 9

DREAM

Xiulan took another bite of rice and exhaled in pleasure. It was . . . well, it was perfect. Her back felt so good. Senior Sister's Medicinal Qi had worked out knots she didn't know she had, and it was absolutely amazing. Senior Sister had avoided all of Xiulan's meridians, focusing merely upon her more mortal aspects, but it had done *wonders*.

She glanced around the table. Senior Sister was gesticulating at a medicinal scroll excitedly while mentioning technical details of acupuncture. Master Jin nodded, focused entirely on her words and asking the occasional question that, if possible, made her already bright eyes light up even more.

Disciple Gou Ren was lazing against Chun Ke and Pi Pa, having already finished his meal. He tossed a stone up into the air and caught it as it came back down, humming to himself and looking content.

One hand reached down and Xiulan absently patted Tigu, the cat long since having fallen asleep.

She didn't know what she felt. Was she at peace? Or was she simply so drained that she couldn't feel anything?

"Now, we just need a test subject for this," Senior Sister said, her voice considering, before she sighted the boy tossing his rock in the air. A vicious grin spread across her face. "Gou Ren," she called leadingly, her voice sickeningly sweet.

The disciple's eyes widened with abject terror, and he flipped backwards over the boar, landing behind him, then peeking up over his bulk at Senior Sister like the boar was a castle wall.

"Like hell!" he roared, his eyes searching for an escape. "My face was stuck like that for a *week* the last time!"

Senior Sister winced at the accusation.

"His facial nerve is a bit farther to the left than it is in the scrolls," she explained to Xiulan, and turned back to him. "I made you meals for that entire week, didn't I?" she asked, smirking at the boy.

The disciple kept glaring, not moving from his position behind his shield, but tilted his head to the side to concede the point. He glanced at Xiulan, something warring in the back of his eyes.

He pointed. "Take her instead," he demanded, as if sacrificing her to a demon.

Xiulan froze as Senior Sister's teasing attention turned to her.

"Oh?" Senior Sister asked. She stood and walked over, her hips swaying slightly. Her gaze was predatory.

"Will you allow myself and my husband to examine your body . . . *thoroughly?*" she enquired, licking her lips while her eyes roved all over Xiulan's form. Her hands made odd grasping gestures.

"Yes, my body is at your disposal, Master Jin, Senior Sister," Xiulan agreed easily. She doubted whether anything they did would harm her. They'd had plenty of time to do that already. No, an examination of her body would only benefit her. At her response, Master Jin choked, and Senior Sister recoiled, both of their faces flushing.

Senior Sister recovered first, shaking her head and sighing.

"Ah, that's no fun. You're not supposed to agree. Where's the floating swords to ward us off?" Senior Sister complained, sitting down beside her.

She was not about to point actual blades at Senior Sister, but if this was some manner of game . . .

Xiulan focused intently. They were no treasures of her Sect like her Jade Grass Blades that assisted her as loyal servants, but she managed to make her chopsticks float.

It was a good Qi-control exercise. It was *not* childish. It was unbecoming for the Young Mistress to do such a thing, it was true . . . but she wanted to.

"Back, foul demon, you'll never take my body?" she tentatively commanded as she concentrated, bringing her weapons to bear.

Senior Sister laughed in delight as the chopsticks bounced against her forehead ineffectually. She fell over anyway, as if defeated by the worthless attack. She was still giggling, her smile bright.

"And you, how dare you betray your comrade?!" Xiulan demanded, a smile starting to form. Her newest weapons levelled themselves at Gou Ren. He fled before her wrath, dodging around the room.

Her smile got wider. She managed to trap him by adding a third weapon and striking him from behind. He fell over, an obviously false death howl escaping his lips. "Chun Ke, avenge me!" he demanded as he "died."

The boar just snorted with amusement, not moving from his position.

Finally, she turned her "blades" at Master Jin but then hesitated. He looked eager to receive her blows, holding a spoon up like a weapon of his own.

From all sides, the chopsticks struck, and from all sides, she was foiled.

She tried to add a fourth, and the chopsticks began wavering in the air. She tried to hold on to them with Qi, but it was too much. They were too thin and were not attuned to her Qi. Her concentration failed entirely, and the chopsticks dropped out of the air.

She paused, waiting for the rebuke for her failed concentration, but it never came. Instead, there was only laughter. Senior Sister hugged her from the side. She suppressed a flinch at the sudden touch, but it was no chastisement.

It was . . . pleasant. There was no grand politics. Just inane chatter and talks of tomorrow.

She wondered if this was what the mortal soldiers did.

Xiulan's fingers gently wove through Tigu's fur, the cat purring softly in her sleep.

She yawned mightily, then nearly collapsed onto the table.

"Xiulan, go to bed," Master Jin told her kindly but chidingly. Her face flushed with embarrassment.

Yet she did as she was told. She climbed the stairs, one step at a time. Each step she took away from the light and into the darker top floor was made with just a slight bit more trepidation. She entered "her" room, casting about in the darkness, and her eyes alighted on her little-used bed.

She tried to sleep as little as her body would allow.

Grimacing, Xiulan got into the bed, exhaustion and conflicting feelings swirling around her mind . . . and settling into her heart.

□

Xiulan was back in the valley, again.

They had managed to catch three of the bastard's raiding parties, destroying them utterly. The others, the groups that had risen to her call, had completed the encirclement, led by their own experts and practitioners, ready to finally bring Sun Ken to justice.

She was equal to Sun Ken in cultivation—that much was true. She could trade blows with the legendary Whirling Demon Blade, and with their superior forces she could bring him to justice.

Of course, it had been a trap.

It was a desperate ambush. Sun Ken had been running out of places to flee to. The noose was tightening.

So he'd chosen to fight. Chosen to strike at the ones who had levied arms against him first and hunted him for so long, for his pride would allow nothing less. He had spat in the Verdant Blade Sect's face once. He couldn't resist trying again. That "only a daughter" had been sent against him had surely set his blood boiling.

The scream of "ambush!" split the air, and then everything happened so fast.

The rumble as the rocks fell. The howls of the bandits, their eyes mad, and spittle flying from their mouths from whatever combat drugs they had consumed. The hail of arrows. Then the impact.

Blood. Blood, blood, *so much blood*. Many of Sun Ken's bandits, though cultivators they were not, had a little bit of Qi. Fueled by whatever drugs they had taken, the bandits were mad, whirling demons. Their blades spun; they ignored wounds that should have killed them; they struck with absurd strength for mortals, and the soldiers died.

The ambush was effective. Yet in the end, the mortal bandits could not match a true cultivator.

She danced among them. To these bandits she might as well have been the heavens, for all that they could reach her. What she did to those vile men couldn't be called fighting them, because that implied they had a chance of hurting her.

They were rice to be harvested, but every drop of her Qi she spent cleaving through the men and intercepting attacks meant for allies was a victory for them. It was wearing her down. For other provinces, cultivators had nothing to fear from even a hundred thousand mortals. A cultivator in the Initiate's Realm, in the Azure Hills? Quantity had a quality all its own.

And then, Sun Rong had appeared—the lesser of the two bastards. He was so full of pride, boasting about how he would defile her along with his brother.

Sun Rong was no Whirling Demon Sword. She met him head on, even after the slaughter had made her green blades crimson. She was stronger, she was faster, and even the amount she had killed over the course of the battle had not truly tired her. His mad spins were not befuddling. His footwork was poor. His foundation, built out of rape and murder.

He was unused to fighting people who could actually fight back.

The first exchange launched him backwards and had gifted him with three cuts along his arms. He tried again to strike but had to throw himself out of the way again as her blades closed like the jaws of some beast.

The transition from cocky strikes to panicked backpedaling had been swift. He started to get desperate. He started to get reckless. He managed to score a small hit along her chest—Xiulan accepted the blow willingly, since it let her cleave his head from his shoulders.

She turned to help her compatriots but froze when a roar of fury echoed through the battlefield. Sun Ken witnessed his brother's death.

Blood. Desperation. Terror. *Pain.*

The dreamscape changed.

Sun Ken's face twisted as the sky took on a nightmarish hue and started to drip crimson demonic energy. The ground transmuted into the screaming faces of the fallen in that butcher's valley. She screamed, screamed that it was her fault. That if she had been better, she would have seen the ambush coming. They grasped at her legs, trying to pull themselves up as blood and Demonic Qi began to flood the valley.

Skeletal hands, attached to rotting soldiers, grabbed her legs. Sun Ken, ten feet tall and his eyes blazing with malice, raised his sword high.

This time, when Sun Ken's blade struck, it bit deep.

□

Xiulan woke up drenched in sweat. Her breath came in gasps as she raised her hand to cover her forehead.

That dream again. The dream in the valley. It had been a recurring problem back at the Verdant Blade Sect, plaguing her sleep and contributing to her desperation to just leave. It had faded when she'd left on her journey. It had been silent during her first weeks here. But now it was back.

It was back.

The glow of happiness from dinner was a bitter echo.

As it should be. Why should she be happy, when she was such a failure?

She rose to a seated position in the too dark, suddenly oppressive room. She tried to breathe.

Jiang Yuan, Lie Quan, Ming Po, Hi Shin . . .

It was folly, her father had said, to dwell on such things.

Jing Ri, Lu Hin, Xi Xing, Mao Hun . . .

It was a weakness of her heart. She was a cultivator! One who defied the heavens! A few deaths shouldn't bother her!

If it didn't bother you, you wouldn't have made it a point to remember all of their names, would you?

She whispered the names in her head. They had all died valiantly. Honourably, she told herself.

Yet they had died all the same. Died, because she hadn't been good enough.

Sunlight streamed in the window. Bi De crowed.

She began her morning routine, her face a mask of serene grace.

CHAPTER 10

ROUTINE

Routine. Structure.

When I had first arrived, it had been a necessary thing. Self-discipline did not come naturally to me. It had to be focused on and worked at every day. Things needed to get done, and I was the only one who could do them. It had been a desperate sort of drive, at first.

But quickly, that changed. I enjoyed my work. The reason why I was able to get off my ass and start every day was because it was fun. Because it was interesting. Because I could see the tangible effects of my efforts.

It started by myself. Wake up. Eat. Run through the stretches Gramps had taught me—*Jin Rou*. "Each and every day!" the old bastard had commanded. It . . . it wasn't particularly cultivator-y. It was basic, so I did it, since it got the blood pumping in the morning.

It was one of the few vibrantly fond memories Jin Rou had too, so . . . well, it didn't hurt to remember.

After that, I was refreshed and ready to begin the day. Time passed in a blur. Wake up, eat, stretch, work, sleep.

Each and every day. One man against the world.

I . . . honestly wouldn't recommend it. One man against the world sounds all nice and inspiring . . . until you *are* that one man against the world. It was soul-crushing. Humans are by nature social animals, and living a life of complete isolation and drowning yourself in work just wasn't healthy.

Slowly, that routine changed. First, it was a chicken I had ignored, hopping and kicking along my fence. Then, there were two pigs, a cat, and a rat. Then a fish, and now . . .

I ran through my stretches. Big D hopped and kicked. Chunky and Peppa were lying together in the morning sun. Tigger was standing beside Xiulan as she went through some kind of kata. It was nice-looking. Elegant. Gou Ren was stretching beside me. Meiling and Rizzo were seated on the veranda, sorting through dried herbs.

My mind added a third participant: a child, who looked vaguely like a combination of myself and my wife.

It was a good image.

"Hey, Jin?" Gou Ren asked, interrupting my thoughts.

"Yeah?"

"Could you go through that form a little slower next time?" he asked hopefully.

Ah, I did go through it pretty fast. Muscle memory was one hell of a drug, and I'd . . . we'd . . . he'd? Whatever, *I* had been doing it for years.

And if he wanted to learn, that was fine. It was a nice way to wake up.

"Hey, Meimei, you want to join us?" I asked. My wife paused in her teaching and turned to us. She smiled softly, then nodded.

"I'll try," she agreed, looking both interested and excited.

And while she probably had better things than this . . .

"Xiulan?" I offered tentatively. She too paused, her face twisting for a moment, before settling back into a placid look.

"I thank you for the offer, Master Jin, but I must decline," she stated apologetically.

A moment later, she bowed her head and walked off. Tigger followed.

Meiling eyed her back as she left, concern in her eyes.

"The smell is getting worse," my wife whispered to me.

"I heard her muttering last night," I replied, sighing. Xiulan was wrestling with some demons when she slept. It was something . . . well, I recognised the look in her eyes when she'd woken up—before the mask had clamped firmly into place.

"You should talk to her. She's . . . nice. A friend," she recommended, looking up at me.

I frowned, considering her question. "I don't know if I'm the right person to ask her about it. She's more guarded around me than around you, and . . . I've seen the way she looks at me sometimes. Like I'm going to smack her for getting something wrong." Honestly, it hurt a little. I'm fine with roughhousing, but did I come off as violent? I hope I didn't.

"But . . . wouldn't you be better for cultivator problems?" she asked, chewing her bottom lip.

"One of the last times I encountered a cultivator problem I ran eight thousand li in the other direction and became a hermit for six months," I mused. "The other time, you talked me out of it." I smiled at Meiling, and she nodded, still working at her lip. "We'll make ourselves available, but . . ."

She sighed, looking at the ground. "Most would say 'just get over it,'" she whispered.

"That's what she's probably been told. 'You face the heavens alone.'"

You face the heavens alone. It might as well have been the cultivator mantra. It was, for them, a guiding principle. "Only *you* can decide your own fate. Only *you* can fight your own battles."

A cultivator was alone against the world, and to that end . . . other people didn't really matter. Asking for help in a trying time? For a lot of people that was nearly unthinkable, unless it was their direct family.

My wife frowned once more at the quote. Some of Gramps's lines were better than others. "That's no way to live," she whispered.

↔

As always, the Great Pillars were truly the best place to be in the whole of Great Fa Ram—even greater than the Great Master's coop. Bi De stood upon them, going through his daily forms. His legs whirled through the air. His beak thrust and stabbed. His wings swept, redirecting his momentum and making the very air cry out in pain when he struck with all his might. When he commanded, gales exploded outwards to rush along the grass and stir the trees.

It was not a technique—not yet. Currently, it was only brute force. It was an inelegant thing, meant only to chastise and rebuke. But . . . he was getting closer. In time, it would be refined. In time, it would be elegant. Perhaps not as elegant as the moon, but something beautiful. His eyes turned from his training, from the spiralling gales of wind, and observed far and wide the Great Master's domain.

He catalogued each change, comparing it to his earliest, haziest memories. Most were blatant changes. The lack of giant rocks, the thinning of the softwood forests, the Great Master's new coop, and the rising coops for the larger animals. These things were easy to spot and reflect upon.

Yet it was the subtler things that Bi De focused upon. The sweetness of the air. The soft breeze. The soil, which was ever so slightly darker than the previous year. The plants were ever so slightly greener.

Fa Ram was growing in strength. Its might was so clear, the vast majority of interlopers had finally abandoned their assaults. There was the occasional one of Chow Ji's ilk, but Tigu took care of them with brutal efficiency. The rest, those like Basi Bu Shi, had retired, rather than attempt to brave the defenders.

He checked the position of the sun. The time for his contemplations was over. He had a job to do, proof of his Great Master's trust. First, he'd had to find the bees, and now he had a mission of even greater importance.

He hopped down from the Great Pillars and began a sedate walk towards the new, large coop. There was a bit of an urge to simply leap the distance—and he had once, just to see if he could. That had been an enjoyable experience.

This time, he restrained himself. This sedate pace was superior. He plucked the occasional interloper out of the air as he strolled. These were the only interlopers that came in their multitudes. Though he supposed that they were barely interlopers at all. They were merely food, sustenance like the rice and the leafy greens.

The Great Coop, another house for the animals, loomed in his vision. Half the planks were red, and the other half were ready to be painted.

His Great Master seemed to enjoy the lucky colour. His mighty sleigh, his hat, and now his new coop. Perhaps he meant it as protection?

He landed at the entryway, then heard murmuring from inside. He cocked his head to the side at the sound of Pi Pa's voice.

'Oh yes, girls, it was dreadful. The little things tried to sting my dear, even after he was so kind to them! He asked them so gently! Well, such a thing is not permitted, no, such a thing is not! I scooped them up and put them in the box Young Sir Gou Ren had for them. They were quite a bit more docile after that!'

Bi De's eyes widened at what Pi Pa was saying. She was speaking to the newest additions? Had they ascended already?

He quickened his pace and entered the coop, excited. Sister Pi Pa was lying on the floor in the Great Coop. She was surrounded by his own offspring, against her side, while some sat on her back. He paused at the image, a sharp pang in his chest at the lack of sparks among them. He shook his head and turned to the cows—they were sure to have a spark!

Instead, dull eyes stared back at him, each beast placidly chewing cud.

'Ah, Bi De. Here to assume your watch?' she asked him pleasantly, offering him a smile.

He recentered himself. His Great Master spoke to the new ones as well and lavished affection on them. He lavished so much affection on them, and checked on them so often, that the Healing Sage had gotten annoyed. For some reason, the Great Master had been greatly worried about the cows giving birth. The Healing Sage had decreed if he was that worried, he should set up a watch.

Bi De had received this mission after that. They were to have a guard rotation upon the cows day and night and immediately inform the Great Master if they seemed in any distress, no matter the circumstances.

He bowed his head at Sister Pi Pa's question. There was nothing at the perimeter to report, and Tigu was once more on the warpath.

Pi Pa chuckled. *'That girl,'* she said, amusement rolling off her form. Bi De knew what she meant. Stubborn, that little one.

Pi Pa stood, and the chicks cheeped from near her bulk. *'Well, keep these ladies entertained now,'* she demanded as she exited, dainty steps carrying her out of the coop, the little ones chirping and following after her.

Bi De cleared his throat, then swiftly took stock of his domain. There were no holes chewed in the boards, and with the walls up, the Great Coop was secured. No interlopers, should they get past the other guardians, would be able to sneak in.

He hopped along the cows' backs and inspected them for parasites. They were clean, as they had been for the past few days.

There was a harsh buzzing sound, and his head snapped up, ready to eradicate any flies that thought to bother the cows—but then he caught sight of the bee. The one he had taken back to Fa Ram. She was aided by the benevolence of his Great Master, and himself. She had to be fed, and he'd once had the task of feeding her. She buzzed and flew around the room for a moment, then alighted on a water bucket and began to drink. He paid her no more mind.

He settled in for his watch, but Pi Pa's words hung in his head. *Entertain them, hmm?*

He knew only how to entertain the hens, and he rarely bothered with that anymore. He doubted the cows would appreciate this, but Sister Pi Pa would give him an earful if he did not make at least a token attempt.

He preened his feathers swiftly, then began his walk. He strutted, displaying his colours for them, his head held high and proud.

It was most likely more amusing for him than it was the cows. The absurdity! Entertainment for animals without a spark? Even the insect was staring at him intently!

How amusing!

He turned in his walk, his strut—then froze at a sharp intake of breath.

Sister Ri Zu squeaked in embarrassment at Bi De's attention, nearly dropping the small platter of food she had. Her eyes darted around the coop, before settling on him again.

'*Continue?*' she asked him, staring wide-eyed at his form.

Bi De nodded imperiously. Well, a request from Sister Ri Zu? How could he deny her?

He enjoyed her eyes upon him as he showed off his colours. The cows chewed their cud. The bee watched as well.

It was an amusing, uneventful afternoon.

↔

An instrument twanged. It was inexpertly played, yet the sound improved with each repetition.

"What's this one called?" Meimei asked from my lap, her fingers going through unfamiliar notes in an unfamiliar style. We were sitting on the giant rock I had pulled beside our house from out near Verdant Hill. Our special rock. It was the first time we had used it in nearly a month, but there was something so great about sitting up here, playing an instrument, and watching the moon.

"'Dueling Pipas' is the closest translation," I told her. They didn't have banjos here, and by the heavens, I was going to change that. The pipa was serviceable, but it was no replacement for the king of country. "We need a second pipa to get it right. One person plays each verse, and it all comes together at the end."

She looked interested at the thought of a duet, yet I could tell that warred against more practical thoughts like "Do we need a second pipa?" *The answer is obviously yes. Activity time with your loved ones is never wasted. A pipa won't put a dent in the finances any.*

We were having a little bit of a break before the last big job that we needed to do, transplanting the rice, and I was in a fantastic mood. The night was nice and warm. I had a beautiful woman in my lap, and I had finished painting my barn red. All great accomplishments. Then, after we finished the rice, we would be off to Hong Yaowu to see Pops and little Xian, probably Gou Ren's older brother Yun Ren, too.

I was looking forward to it.

My grip tightened on my wife's waist. Meiling looked up at me, her expression curious. Our lips met. She tasted a bit like tea this time. I had *intended* for the kiss to be sweet and chaste, but after a moment Meiling set the pipa to the side and pressed against me even more.

Maybe it was because of the rock. We'd had our first kiss on it, so maybe it just provoked these things. We broke our kiss. Her robes were in slight disarray from my hands and there was a happy blush high on her cheeks.

Both of our eyes roved over the immediate area. Gou Ren was in the hut, Xiulan and Tigger nowhere to be seen. Her hands went to my chest, and she licked her lips, leaning in—

There was an urgent crow from the barn, as Big D called us to action.

We both froze at the interruption. Meiling looked slightly frustrated by the call. Well, these things wait for no man. We would have to postpone things.

We hopped off our rock. This time, Meimei did it under her own power instead of me carrying her down, and we landed with a soft *thump*.

The disciples had been put on watch after Meimei had gotten annoyed at the fact that I was constantly wandering in and out of the barn, checking on the cows. That part was understandable, but I had been a bit . . . *obsessive* in my checking. I shouldn't have said I was going to get a cup of water that one time. Spotting my wife standing in the doorway to the barn, a distinctly unimpressed look on her face when she found me scratching a cow and telling her that she was a good girl, was pretty embarrassing.

But some fears died hard. I had seen a calf die once, in the Before. It had come out into the world not breathing. Even when I was younger, I'd been able to understand the frowns on the adults' faces, and the sigh that the man let out when they stopped trying to get it to breathe.

And that was how my animals got another job: call me when the cow starts to give birth. Like all things I had tasked them with, they were diligent. I had peeked in one or two more times, and whenever I had, there was someone there hanging out. Chunky or Peppa sitting there at peace,

Big D training, Rizzo reading a scroll. Even Tigger got in on it once or twice, I think.

The poor girl had been in a mood ever since she'd failed to find a bee like the rest. Watching a cat kowtow to me and start meowing had been a bit awkward. She was really upset about it, and no amount of scratches would convince her that I wasn't angry or disappointed in her.

But there was little time to think on that as we prepared. I didn't know whether it would be just one birth, or if both of them would start up tonight, but I settled in for a long wait.

Two hours later, the calf hadn't fully appeared, which was a bit of a cause for concern. Unlike human women, who can be put in traction for over half a day, cows are supposed to come out pretty quick.

It was then that the other cow decided hers needed to come out too. When it rains, it pours, I suppose, but we had to do one thing at a time. I could see the feet, but the rest of the calf was still kind of stuck. I think its head had somehow gotten turned a bit, so it was time for us to step in.

"Now gently so it doesn't tear," Meiling instructed calmly, as I held the calf's legs. My wife's eyes were intent, but she was relaxed. Well, it was to be expected. I had a lot less experience with larger animals, and the Hong family being the healers of Hong Yaowu meant that they doubled as the vets. The poor cow was rolled on her side, clearly in distress that the calf wasn't coming out properly.

Well, that was what we were here for, and why I'd asked for the alarm. We had an audience of disciples, excepting Xiulan and Tigger, watching the process intently.

I gently reached in further, Qi assisting in parting the flesh without tearing, and manipulated the head that had started to fold backwards, so we could bring it once more to the proper position.

Then we had to grab the legs and pull. This could actually take a few people sometimes, or even mechanical assistance, but here? No such thing was needed. Strength would suffice. The little one was freed from the canal, and I caught it before it could hit the ground. They *could* survive a bit of bashing around, but no sense in making things more painful for the little creature.

I presented her to her mother, instincts immediately taking over as her tongue went to work, cleaning her baby.

There was a little gasp and a cry of new life from the calf as she felt this strange new world for the first time.

I let out the breath I had been holding.

Meimei gave the cow a once-over, then nodded. Her robe was still loose, exposing the freckles that dotted the top of her chest. She had a bit of blood on her hands, and there was a bit of fluid where she had wiped her cheek. Her hair was down, and she honestly looked a bit disheveled.

She turned to me and smiled—a big, toothy grin. I couldn't help but smile back at that radiant, brilliant expression.

The second birth turned out to be spectacularly anticlimactic. Everything went perfectly. A few hours later, and we were convinced that both mother and child were going to be all right.

Two little girls, hale and hearty.

CHAPTER 11

I'M HERE

Meditate. Train. Do the things Master Jin asked her to.

Meditate. Train. Do the things Master Jin asked her to.

Try to sleep. Dream.

She was in the valley again.

Wake up feeling horrible.

Observe the Earth Spirit's scornful glances.

Mediate. Train. Do the things Master Jin asked her to.

Deflect Master Jin's questions. Feel guilty for deflecting Master Jin's questions.

Make no progress.

She was in the valley again, Sun Ken's maddened laughter echoing through the butcher's field.

□

Two forms blurred through the night, cutting across the forest like dervishes. A foot hit the ground hard enough to leave a mark. Claws dug into bark hard enough to scar. A leaf floated through the air, where it was split in two from an errant strike.

Claws met swords. Frustration met frustration.

The two women struck with abandon. There was little of their usual grace. Just speed, power, and violence.

Yet one was more unbalanced than the other. There came a spray of blood from a slice on her arm. Her guard was pierced. A blade of pure cutting Qi arced towards Xiulan's eye.

Time seemed to slow as the executioner's blade descended. First, the blade would penetrate her eye and then travel into her skull. A rather quick, clean death, all told. She watched with clinical interest as her end neared.

She felt nothing.

At the last moment, the claw of Qi veered, losing cohesion. The Qi that struck was like liquid, running off her form and not marking her at all.

Ah, she was defeated. The Jade Grass Blades dropped to the ground, falling from her grasp.

She expected Tigu to be happy with her victory. The cat had finally taken a bout off her.

Instead, Tigu looked enraged.

'You dare pity me? You dare perform this poorly? This Young Mistress should have taken your eye for this insult!' the cat snarled, glaring at her.

"Ah. I apologise," Xiulan muttered. Heavens above, she was so *tired*.

The cat seemed mollified at the apology, looking closely at her. *'You need sleep,'* the cat deduced. Master Jin and Senior Sister had been making noises of concern about her for a few days now. They had noticed her . . . issues, embarrassingly enough. But she wasn't so far gone as to bother them with her foolish thoughts. They had said if she wanted to talk about it, they were there.

What was there to talk about? She was on her own for such matters. A cultivator faced the heavens alone.

A paw batted on her head, the cat glaring at her again. *'Do not ignore me! You shall sleep now, so you will be a better fight tomorrow!'* the cat demanded, then turned, as if to lead her back to the house.

Xiulan had a moment where she considered lashing out at the cat . . . but she let herself be led.

The small wound stopped bleeding soon enough, even without a bandage.

□

Sun Ken's blade arced down, as Xiulan's own soldiers held her in place for the finishing blow. Their eyes were full of condemnation—

Xiulan woke up coated in sweat and had to suppress a scream of frustration. It would not do to wake the others.

Tigu was still fast asleep, lying spread out on her back. An amusing sight Xiulan couldn't appreciate. The darkness in here was stifling. Xiulan moved quietly, so as to not wake the cat.

She stepped gently down the stairs and exited the house, then sat down and stared at the river. How it flowed onwards, gathering in strength.

Time. Things always come back to time. Xiulan *knew* that some things could not be forced. Yet after her ascension to the Fourth Stage of the Initiate's Realm, at the end of winter, she had expected her abilities to continue growing. She had broken through her bottleneck—now had been the time for her to rise.

Then the meetings had started. The pride of the Verdant Blade Sect! The killer of Sun Ken! The one who was sure to win the Dueling Peaks Tournament and let the name Verdant Blade resound throughout the Azure Hills, maybe even beyond!

The praise and expectations had tasted like ashes in her mouth. While normally she would be so proud that she was relied on, and praised so much, she had been growing distracted. She had tried not to be rude to the juniors who approached her, asking for stories about how she had laid low the wicked bandit. She stood stoically as she was lectured by one of the Elders on the proper way to incapacitate an opponent with the Verdant Blade Sword Arts, yet she'd gleaned no new insight from the encounter.

She had been given even *more* juniors to look after, after her troops had praised her leadership and skill. Had she even been skilled? She didn't think she was. Sun Ken had led them on a merry chase throughout the countryside, and the few battles there had been nearly ended in disaster.

She trained the others. She had meditated, searching for connections. She had received more resources in those few months than she had gotten in all previous years, from Spiritual Grass to the Qi-Refining Pills.

And yet the progress was so damnably slow. She had to get better! She *needed* to get stronger! And she needed that strength soon, so she would be able to live up to the expectations placed on her. She told no one else of her troubles. How could she? She was the Young Mistress, the paragon of her Sect—she could not be having doubts!

She took a deep breath and tried to let it go. The First Disciple was right. She needed time. She needed to stop trying to *force* her own growth, and actually grow.

Before she met Master Jin, she had been stuck in the Third Stage of the Initiate's Realm for years. It shouldn't bother her that she was slowing down . . . and yet it did. It did, because she felt like she *should* be growing.

She stared up at the sky. The grass grew. The trees grew. And yet she did not.

Xiulan sighed wistfully. Was it her weakness that had caused the Earth Spirit to rebuke her so?

"Are you all right?" a quiet voice asked. Xiulan jumped at the presence that had invaded her personal space.

"Ah! This one apologises if she woke you," Xiulan muttered, chagrined. The smaller woman was staring at her, dressed in only a sleeping robe with her hair down.

Her eyes were tired, yet the concern within them was unmistakable.

"It's fine, Xiulan," Senior Sister told her, smoothing out her gown as she sat down. "Now, what's wrong?"

"Ah, you need not bother yourself with this one—" Xiulan tried, but stopped at Senior Sister's raised eyebrow.

"You smell like somebody just took a scythe to a patch of grass and then coated it in rancid oil."

Xiulan winced. Senior Sister's ability to smell Qi meant that she could detect one's mood more often than not.

"It is a minor thing," Xiulan said, trying to brush it off. She didn't want them to know of any further shame.

Senior Sister hummed, clearly not believing her. But instead of asking again and pressing the issue, instead Senior Sister asked another question.

"What's your favourite food?"

Xiulan was stunned at the question and how . . . *mundane* it was.

"If you had asked me a month ago, I would have said lotus paste mooncakes," Xiulan admitted. "But now? Anything yourself or Master Jin sees fit to create."

Senior Sister looked very interested in that piece of knowledge. A second later there was a rustling as Master Jin exited the house with two cups of tea. Xiulan looked at the ground in shame that he should witness this. He set the cups down, nodded to his wife, and left. The calming, herbal brew filled her nostrils.

"Your most fond recollection?" Senior Sister asked again, shaking her out of her shock.

Xiulan thought for a moment before answering. "Watching the peach blossoms fall with my mother." It was old, and childish, but even now she felt a warm nostalgia. It had been so long since they had done that together. Not since Xiulan's training had fully consumed her life, and

Xiulan's mother had left on her journey. Each question didn't seem to connect with the last, but it was fun all the same. She felt her shoulders relax, and a small smile found its way onto her face.

They sat for a while, and an internal war raged inside her heart.

"I . . . I am having difficulties with a matter," she admitted, her tone wavering. *What was she doing?* She already had them helping her so much. Was she this incompetent—was she this weak?—that she had to burden the woman who had saved her life more? "Senior Sister, have you ever had one under your care perish?" The question was a disrespectful one, and she regretted asking it as soon as it left her mouth.

Senior Sister's eyes took on a somber cast—her mind seemed to go back to whatever she had seen.

"Too many," she whispered, her fists clenching. She looked to the side, remembering. "Mothers, bleeding their last, with or without their child. Babes too weak to breathe. The shakes, rattling someone's body apart. Men vomiting up their stomachs." Her voice did not waver as she recounted these; it was calm and measured, but slightly bitter. "And more animals than I care to count. I'm no miracle doctor, and neither is my father. We try our best, but there are *always* failures. Always people that no matter how hard you try, you can't save."

Senior Sister's shoulders slumped slightly at the admission.

She looked back to Xiulan. There was no bitterness in her eyes. No rebuke. There was only compassion. She *understood*.

Xiulan's heart clenched again. The guilt welled up, filling her throat with bile, yet she managed to ask the burning question in her heart. "How . . . how do you . . . make peace with it?" A cultivator must be at peace with death. She had seen people die before this, both in duels and in training accidents. But the charnel house that was the valley . . . the smell and the screams and—she cut the thoughts off. Her father had said that any emotions she felt were to be used to fuel her progress. That such a thing was only beneficial as long as she controlled it properly.

"Did you swing the blade that ended them? Or did you try to protect as many as you could?" Senior Sister asked.

"I tried," she whispered. "But I led them. I gave the orders."

Senior Sister's hand slipped into Xiulan's own, and Xiulan flinched. But there was no rebuke. Senior Sister's thumb made soft circles on the back of Xiulan's hand.

It felt nice. Slowly, some of the tension in Xiulan's shoulders faded.

"The first thing you did when we met was to try to warn us of a dangerous monster. The second thing you did was swear to protect us, even at the cost of your life," Senior Sister whispered, her voice fond. "You face the heavens alone. But what you face right now is not the heavens."

Xiulan looked at the water, winding its way forwards.

"I remember every name," Xiulan admitted.

"Tell me about them, please," Senior Sister requested.

Jian Yuan, loyal and true. Lie Quan, who was perpetually poor from his gambling habits. Ming Po and his pet duck. Hi Shin and his dream to become a great general—and many more lives besides those four.

The mortals had been decimated in the battle.

So many names. Some were *just* names, with the vague memory of a face. So many men that the others just disregarded, like they didn't matter. Like their mothers, fathers, wives, and children did not mourn for them.

She talked. She talked until the sun rose, each name draining part of her soul and lifting part of the weight from her shoulders.

She didn't know when her head met Senior Sister's shoulder, as she slumped bonelessly atop the other woman. She said the last name. Her eyes fluttered closed.

→

She swam into consciousness as she heard voices. Gentle fingers combed through her hair. Light, affectionate touches. Her head was resting on someone's lap.

"You were right, starting off like that helped calm her down." Senior Sister's voice was warm.

"I'm glad it helped," Master Jin whispered. "Or I *hope* it helped. Sometimes these things never heal."

"I think she's going to be just fine. Call it your wife's intuition," Senior Sister said. The confidence in her voice was absolute.

Master Jin chuckled. "I believe that. Lotus paste mooncakes, huh? We've got some lotuses in the pond. I'll see what I can do."

Xiulan drifted back to sleep, soothed by gentle fingers and soft humming.

CHAPTER 12

I SCREAM

Jin hadn't been lying when he said the way he did things took a lot more work, Gou Ren mused. Especially how he planted the rice. Separating the seed, growing it in the little patches, and then transplanting it. Transplanting it at the correct distance too. Jin had made a little device for Gou Ren out of wood. You rolled it across the field, forming little squares an exact width apart. You then planted the rice in the intersection between the squares, which Jin said would make the yield the best. Something to do with root crowding, and rice needing space.

Come to think of it, he had been rather exacting about the wheat rows too. To the point where he measured them with a ruler. They were to be as straight as possible, each one an exact distance apart.

Hong Yaowu used their own method, one that had been passed down for generations. It worked, so most years they ate rather well. The only year he'd known the true pangs of hunger was that year of sorrow. It was like all the bad luck in the world hit Hong Yaowu at once. He shook his head to clear the memories. Those were in the past. He didn't like dwelling on them, or even *remembering* them, really.

The only good thing he'd gotten out of that year was a prickly, spiky, almost-sister in Meiling. Nothing brought people together like shared misery.

At least he wouldn't have a sore back this year. He shuffled backwards and planted at nearly walking pace, and with the pre-measured rows, his mind could wander freely. Though most of the time he just found himself zoning out. Meditation was easy when you didn't have to sit around and concentrate.

"After this, you said inter-row tillage twice a week, huh?" Gou Ren asked his comrade, and Jin nodded.

Twice a week was a lot. A backbreaking amount. An amount that if Gou Ren *weren't* a cultivator, he would refuse to do. Yeah, the yields were better, but there were easier ways to kill yourself. Unless . . .

"You got some strange-looking device for this? I saw you drawing that weird seed drill earlier." Gou Ren had noticed the odd designs. Jin's drawing skill was technically competent, but the amount of question marks Jin had put on the page had been amusing.

Not that Gou Ren could talk—he couldn't make any sense of what Jin wanted, and neither could Meiling.

Jin flushed a bit. "Hey, the seed drill you guys have looks different than I'm used to!" Gou Ren guessed that might have been true. The thing in Jin's drawing had looked huge, with multiple prongs coming off it—not like the one-man affair they had back home. The one he was used to was a damn rickety thing. It *did* make things easier, but it was annoying as the hells to use.

"As for a device for this, I'd need to talk to Brother Che about getting what I want made . . . but for now—" Jin held up a hand and formed it into a claw, making pawing motions at the air.

"With our hands?" he asked, aghast. "Come on, Jin, that's going to take forever!"

Jin laughed. "Yup. You just gotta have some fun with it. I tried to time myself a couple of times to see how fast I could do it, or . . ." At this, his eyes became shifty. "I tied a couple of rocks to my back and pretended it was training a few times." He sounded kind of embarrassed at the admission, and muttered, "Ani Mei training."

Ani Mei training. That sounded awesome! The image came to Gou Ren. Toiling in the fields while hefting a giant rock with ease, his powerful muscles rippling, Miss Cai staring at him . . .

He quietly resolved to tie some rocks to his back at the first available opportunity. He might not become some kind of legendary general, but he was a *cultivator*! And that sounded like cultivator training!

Okay, mostly he just thought he'd look like some kind of amazing warrior.

They lapsed into silence again. A few minutes later, Gou Ren completed his row.

"Hey, Jin?"

"Yeah?"

"How is Miss Cai doing, anyway?" he asked, remembering the gaunt, defeated look that had been on the beautiful woman's face over the past couple of weeks. It hadn't suited her.

Jin paused, scratching his head.

"Better, maybe. I haven't been listening in on the conversations, but they've been talking at night. It seems to be helping." Jin gave him an awkward smile.

"You said she was sick, right?"

"*Kind of* like she was sick. Sometimes you can heal from this stuff on your own, but sometimes . . . well, talking to somebody about it can be the best medicine."

Talking as a medicine, huh? Gou Ren frowned. Sounded weird.

"Hey, Gou?" Jin called, and Gou Ren turned back towards his friend. "If you ever got something you want to talk about, I'm here. Meimei too, yeah?"

It was an odd offer, but by the look in his eyes, Jin was really, really serious about it.

"Yeah, I will," he promised.

Jin's smile came back, and he nodded firmly. Then they got back to work.

"You know, I'm a bit surprised your brother hasn't come around, but they're probably working him like a dog in the village," Jin mused. "After this we should grab him and go hunting or fishing. Time with the boys, you know?"

Now *that* was an idea he could get behind. Meiling was all right, for a girl, but he wanted to be able to talk about manly things without interruption.

Like how to woo women. Miss Cai was a swan, and he was probably the toad in that old analogy, but it couldn't hurt to at least try, right? If she said no, well, that was just kind of expected.

Actually, on second thought, he probably *wouldn't* ask Jin how to woo women. He doubted Miss Cai would enjoy getting thrown in a mud pit or being hit in the face with snow.

→

The weeks passed. The rice was planted, and the world started to warm. Spring was beginning to wane, and would soon become summer.

"*Ganbei!*" Jin shouted, holding up a bottle. The wine bottles clinked together, and all of them took pulls, echoing Jin's sentiment. Bi De crowed, and the rest of the animals made noises of joy while holding their own little cups. "To the first year of many!"

Done. They were as done as they could be for now. Every big job was finished, and every crop that could be planted was now planted. Of course, there was always more work. Jin had a massive timetable drawn up, but those were all things that could wait.

Now, all they had was a bit of a party that night, and then they would be heading off home to Hong Yaowu tomorrow.

Heavens, Gou Ren couldn't wait to see his brother again.

The table was full of food. Plates of pancakes, some honey-glazed duck, venison dumplings. Each and every bite was delectable.

There were even some mooncakes, oddly. Miss Cai's normally composed face had broken completely at the sight of them before it firmed up again. At that moment, she was slowly chewing one with her eyes closed.

Which was when Jin, of course, unveiled some of his newest creations.

"Maple fudge" and "ice cream." The cows were already proving their worth. A cup of cold milk in the morning, straight from the river, was fast becoming a fixture of Gou Ren's mornings, even if he had to share it with that bastard fish.

He took a bite of the new, delightfully cold treat. It was delicious. Everything Jin made was delicious.

Gou Ren wondered where in the hells he came up with these things. Or maybe they were more common in the city? Well, that was *one* reason to see if he could go to the Dueling Peaks: the food. There was probably so much interesting food there.

There was a moan of pleasure, and this time it *wasn't* from Miss Cai. Meiling was staring at the bowl of ice cream with rapturous glee.

"I thought you would like mint the best," Jin declared. "Just needs a bit of chocolate and it'll be even better."

Gou Ren had no idea what chocolate was, but if Jin thought it would make things better, it probably would.

They laughed. They ate. They drank, and they made merry.

Jin got out his pipa and slammed out a thundering, upbeat tune as they clapped along. Out of the corner of his eye, Gou Ren saw Meiling grab Miss Cai's hand and pull her to her feet. The other woman nearly stumbled at the sudden movement but allowed herself to be pulled into one of Hong Yaowu's dances as Meiling linked their arms together.

The shock at being pulled into the dance soon turned into a soft smile. The unsure steps steadied, and soon she was dancing like she had been doing it for her whole life. He took another pull from his bottle as he watched—then frowned, at finding it empty.

He didn't feel anything—

Oh, there was the buzz.

Gou Ren smiled, leaning back against Chun Ke. He hoped his brother was having a fraction of the fun he was.

→

"Yeah, go to bed, I've got this." Gou Ren waved away Jin and Meiling when they started to clean up. Hey, they made the food, he cleaned things up. A system as old as time.

It wasn't too messy anyway. Even though there were a bunch of animals constantly in the house, it was clean enough.

He hummed as he worked, stacking the cleaned plates from the river. It was fast and easy, with the fish getting better at his job every day. At least there was *one* good thing about the gluttonous bastard.

He finished the plates and moved on to the bottles, collecting the couple of empty ones and the one full one.

He paused, then squinted at the bottle. It was completely full. Whoever had this hadn't drank a drop.

He glanced at the spot on the table. Meiling? Not drinking? *Yeah right, somebody must have opened it and forgotten about it.* He shook his head and got back to work.

CHAPTER 13

HONG XIAN

Her Master was in her element. She strode around the house, checking and rechecking everything.

"Ri Zu, remember to take in the Hairroot fungus if it finishes drying before we return; we won't want anything trying to eat it."

Her Master's voice was exacting in tone as she gave commands to her disciple. Her amethyst eyes were lost, deep in thought while she went over a mental checklist of everything that she could think needed to be done.

Ri Zu nodded with her little slate, writing everything down. Memorization was all well and good, but a written copy for the others might prove essential for carrying out the orders they were being charged with. Miss Pi Pa trotted along beside them, the lady nodding her head appropriately.

Her Master had requested Ri Zu to use her skills and watch over Great Fa Ram in her absence. It was the first time Ri Zu had been charged with such a duty. There were many-much things that needed tending to, even after the planting was finished. She, in particular, had been charged with overseeing the cows and the calves, to make sure they were hale and healthy.

It was humbling, that she, a mere neophyte, would be entrusted with a task of this magnitude! Sister Pi Pa was overall in charge of the household, in the absence of its true Mistress. None would dare deny her this; even Brother Bi De would bow his head before the lady's considerable bulk.

Ri Zu stood tall. She would accomplish her task! She was a worthy disciple! No matter *what* that arrogant beast liked to say about her!

She smirked slightly as she thought of Tigu and her wrath. Still not a bee to her name, while Brother Chun Ke had come back with a third nest. The look of the cat's arrogance cracking had been wonderful!

Now only Tigu was without a nest to her name, as Wa Shi had also managed to find one for them to collect as he patrolled the waterways.

"I think that is everything. If you need us, we are not too far. Send Chun Ke to fetch us, and we shall be back as soon as we are able," her Master decreed.

Ri Zu bowed her head and finished the list. Sister Pi Pa nodded primly.

"Senior Sister, I am ready," a quiet voice carried over, and Ri Zu's Master brightened. The Young Miss was in an altered pair of her Master's skirt and shirt, instead of the shimmery, gossamer dress and gold ornaments she wore when not working.

It had required a few alterations, for the Young Miss was quite a bit taller than her Master, but Ri Zu had gotten to help.

As it was, the skirt only came to the Young Miss's shins, though it was still longer than another piece that her Master had worked on. That had ended barely at her Master's midthigh and had caused her quite a bit of embarrassment. Her teacher had kept what Master Jin had called a miniskirt, though her face was crimson.

Ri Zu's Master smiled at the Young Miss and brought out a comb. She brushed the Young Miss's hair and braided it, as was the Young Miss's preferred style, and they then traded places.

The Young Miss dutifully combed Ri Zu's Master's hair, while her Master used a smaller, finer comb to attend to Ri Zu.

It was a wonderful new morning ritual.

After their hair was combed, Ri Zu's Master linked her arms with the Young Miss, and they exited the house.

There, Master Jin was already prepared. The cart had a few things in it. Gou Ren stood, stretching as he chewed on a sprig of grass.

The humans of Fa Ram gathered on one side of the gate. The disciples, on the other. Master Jin showed them great face by clasping his hands in gratitude, bowing to the disciples he entrusted with his home. Ri Zu's Master, the Young Miss, and Disciple Gou Ren bowed as well.

Brother Bi De was almost overcome with emotion. She could see it in the way he stood, proud and erect. He swept into a graceful bow.

'We pay our respects to the Great Master,' they intoned.

"Everyone. Thank you," Master Jin replied.

And then the four of them were off.

↔

Hong Xian was the seventy-eighth to bear the name Hong Xian.

His father was the seventy-seventh Hong Xian, and *his* father was the seventy-sixth. If Xian had a son, he would be the seventy-ninth Hong Xian.

Why did they all have to be named the same thing? His leg bounced idly as he sat, reading. Tradition. Tradition, every scroll said. Tradition, his father said too. Tradition, like learning family history and reading scrolls for hours on end. Who cared whether it was the fifty-fourth or forty-fifth Hong Xian who had had the village rebuilt after the great fires? It got rebuilt. History was boring, especially without Meimei to read it to him. She always made it exciting, instead of just reciting the dumb names and dates.

He missed his sister. She was annoying, bossy, and always prodding him to do chores, read more, and practise his medicine or harvesting skills.

But now that she had been away, he couldn't help but miss her. She was just always . . . *there* for the most part. Someone to talk to. Someone to ask questions, someone to play with. She even liked going frog hunting! Xian barely remembered their mother. In his memories, it was his sister bandaging scraped knees or carrying him around the house. He never appreciated just how much his elder sister did, until they had to ask Hu Li to help them with the cooking and cleaning. Things Meimei did, and made look *easy*. His father was too busy, and Xian couldn't cook.

Why couldn't Big Brother Jin have moved in with them, instead of being days away? Meimei would still be here, and Jin could give him piggyback rides all the time. That would have been perfect!

He smiled at the thought. Maybe he would be able to convince them to stay? He imagined it: Jin living in the village with them, with all his fun animals, and playing with Xian all day. He was in a slightly better mood as he turned back to the scroll.

In these cases, the sixty-fifth Hong Xian prescribed essence *of gnarlroot, instead of the whole root. This was more efficacious, and so was entered into the annals . . .*

He sighed, then reared back his arm to throw the boring, *boring* scroll . . . but thought better of it. Meimei wouldn't approve. She'd get that disappointed look that he wasn't treating the scrolls with respect.

Xian grumbled as he got up and put the scroll away. That was enough studying for today. Father wouldn't know, either. He was too busy working on things to notice if his son left a bit early.

Even doing the odd jobs out in the fields was better than this.

He wandered from the house and into the village.

"Good morning, little chief!" the grandmother from next door called to him, spinning the yarn as well as her arthritis-riddled fingers could.

"Good morning, Grandmother," he greeted back politely and continued his walk.

He debated what to do. Helping in the fields was not appealing. Catching frogs when the water was this cold still wasn't something he wanted to do either. So he wandered. Wandered around the village, until he heard grumbling.

He followed the noise and found Yun Ren. The man was sitting, holding his hands out with his thumb and index finger extended, forming a kind of square with them. Sweat was beading on his brow, and there was something in the air as he concentrated. It . . . *almost* smelled. It was like an itching sensation in Xian's sinuses. He scratched the bridge of his nose.

A wavering, distorted image slowly formed, of the house Yun Ren was facing, until with a sharp pop it disappeared.

Yun Ren said a word that Meimei always said, but she'd threatened to stick bitterroot in Xian's mouth if she ever heard him repeat it.

"Maybe I do need the damn crystal. But they're so *expensive*. Capture light. Yeah, capture light *how*, Jin?"

"Hey, Yun Ren," Xian greeted him—and the man jumped a bit, turning to face him.

"Oh hey, little boss. Finished with your scrolls?" he asked, sitting down.

Xian looked to the side.

A vulpine grin split Yun Ren's face when Xian didn't answer immediately.

"Slackin'? Oh, well I *never*. What would the chief say?" he playfully teased.

Xian rolled his eyes, then sat down beside Yun Ren. The older man wouldn't tell, because if he did, Xian would have to retaliate. Meimei had told him all the areas Yun Ren liked to hide when *he* was slacking, and Yun Ren knew it.

He tried to raise an eyebrow like his sister did when she was annoyed at somebody. It normally made Yun Ren recoil, or apologise when Meimei did it. Yun Ren laughed and ruffled Xian's hair before leaning back and wiping the sweat off his brow.

"Why are you doing that anyway?" Xian asked. Yun Ren shrugged.

"Recording crystals are expensive," he stated simply. "Was trying to see If I needed one, and the answer so far is yes. It was . . . a dumb thought, anyway. Nowhere to store the images even if it works, instead of being a blur."

Xian frowned. Cultivator stuff was *weird*.

They sat in silence together, Xian's leg bouncing with excess energy. Yun Ren had gotten out a small slip of paper and had his tongue stuck out while he calculated . . . something. He obviously didn't get a pleasing answer, and he sighed.

"Maybe I should ask Jin if I can work on the farm next year," he muttered. "Why do they have to cost so damn much?"

Xian's nose started to itch again. It was so annoying! He started rubbing at it in irritation. There was something close. Or was it coming closer? He couldn't tell—

There was a shout from near the front of the village.

"Hey! Meiling! Gou Ren! You're back!"

Both Xian's and Yun Ren's eyes widened. Yun Ren was off in a blur, leaving Xian in the dust, but he gave it his best effort, charging after Yun Ren.

By the time Xian got there, Yun Ren and Gou Ren were already scuffling on the ground, a tangle of limbs and curses while Big Brother Jin laughed uproariously.

Xian had eyes only for one person. His sister was palming her face and shaking her head with a smile, while the pretty lady . . . Xiu . . . Something? *Fairy Sister?* That was what all the shop owners called beautiful ladies. She seemed mildly amused.

Xian kept up his charge. "Meimei!" he shouted, never slowing down for an instant. His sister looked directly at him, her eyes widening and a massive grin spreading across her face. She held out her arms, and he jumped without hesitation. She scooped him up and spun him around with ease, then planted two wet, sloppy kisses onto his cheeks.

Xian glared at his sister as she hoisted him on a hip, using only one arm. The grip was firm and unwavering.

"Ha! I knew you were lying that I was getting too heavy!" he said, pouting at her. No grunts or trembling arms. He *knew* she had been acting like he had been getting too heavy before! There was no way his big sister couldn't pick him up. She smiled and pressed her forehead to his.

"Ah, I was just making sure you didn't need me to carry you around everywhere. It wouldn't do for the chief to take over the village and be carried around by his sister all day."

Xian just wrapped his arms around her neck.

"Hello, Big Brother Jin, Fairy Sister!" he greeted them. Jin, who was staring at his sister carrying him around with a soft smile, ruffled his hair.

Fairy Sister winced slightly at him calling her Fairy Sister. "Ah, good morning . . . Young Master? This one's name is Cai Xiulan," she said, clasping her hands respectfully.

It was weird. She was weird. Nobody was that respectful to Xian. Really, even calling him Young Master was pushing it too!

Meimei eagerly walked into town as more people surrounded them, wandering over to see what the commotion was about.

Including their father. His eyes widened at seeing his daughter, and then a brilliant smile spread across his face.

They crossed the distance in a blur as they embraced.

"Welcome home," Father whispered to Meimei, the brightest smile Xian had seen in a month and a half on his face.

CHAPTER 14

JIN ROU

Thanks, Brother Jin!"

"Hey, Jin, play with us!"

"Jin, tonight, come have a drink!"

It was no trouble. Come on, you little brats! Of course! I wouldn't miss it!

Maybe I was just fooling myself. Maybe they didn't really like me, or maybe they just liked me because I was useful. But seeing people brighten up as I came rolling into town, calling out to me with grins on their faces? The kids following me around like little duckies?

That was one hell of a good feeling, let me tell you.

I had only really known the town of Hong Yaowu for a year, but it already felt like I was part of the big, extended family.

I had given Pops a hug and then immediately set off to work, wading into the fields to much acclaim. They had a bit of the planting left to go, and I thought Meimei needed a bit of alone time with Pops. With my help that day, we'd finished one of the fields over a week ahead of schedule . . . though after that I got told to take a break.

Gou Ren and Yun Ren had immediately gone off to hunt. They had glanced at me to see if I had wanted to come . . . but I had waved them off too.

Sibling time was important. The world and people's relationships didn't need to revolve around me. I didn't need to butt in everywhere and be a part of everything, no matter how strong that urge was at times.

Besides, we had plenty of time in the future to hang out and have fun. And I really, really liked hanging out with people. Fuck, my hermit days were *dumb*. Why the hells had I thought that was a good idea?

Probably the panic and the terror about suddenly being in xianxia land.

Eventually, I had gotten bored of my break—and also tired of losing at go to the old-timers—so I'd started bugging the kids.

Which led to my current predicament. Namely getting chased around the village by a pack of kids, who were throwing lengths of cloth around me and trying to tie me up.

See, the thing about the little ones is that you gotta make them *work* for it. Hand them an easy victory, and they'll forget it immediately and be disappointed.

My advice? Be Gary Oak. "Ha! That's the best you've got? You'll never be able to seal this Grand Demon with your strength! I am an immortal who can shake the heavens! And you are all WEAK! HAHAHAHAHA!"

Just a little bit of gloating and being an asshole gets them all riled up and even more into it. And then when they finally manage to beat you, they will remember it for the rest of their lives.

Like I remembered doing to my dad. Except we'd used toilet paper instead of cloth. That was a birthday to remember. Hunting your father down with a pack of your fellow six-year-olds. Thinking back on it, my old man in the Before was really, *really* good at keeping kids entertained.

I strived to follow his example. Besides, I liked kids. I was basically a big kid myself in the things I enjoyed, so it was pretty easy to get along with them. I don't know what that said about me, but I liked to think I was just honest with myself.

And these kids were actually really damn good. They were strong, and fast, and when one of them threw the rope, it curled around itself like a snake, trying to loop around limbs. They were even trying to set up traps.

Xianxia land. Even the farmer kids are hard-core.

Eventually, I "lost"; I purposely ran into a rope clothesline and then was tackled and trussed up like a turkey.

Good times.

The kids whooped and cheered, while the adults looked on with fond smiles. One pair of feet stopped just above my head, and I looked up, grinning at the only person it could be.

"Your reunion good, darlin'?" I asked her. Meimei's amethyst eyes were soft and warm. Amusement and something deeper danced in their depths.

"Yeah." It was a simple word, but a good one. No tears, no tenseness, just peace. She turned to the kids sitting on my back. "Come on, off you all get. You've defeated the Great Demon Lord and sealed him, and now I need my husband back." The kidlets obeyed, knowing better than to get in the *real* demon's way.

Little Miss Thistle still had a reputation.

My wife "rescued" me from their clutches and untied the ropes. We had to keep at least a little bit of an illusion going.

"You're going to be at the head table with the Elders. Father wants to drink with you, and I have to go speak with the women about my . . . *wifely duties*." She sighed at the interrogation to come.

"You could just . . . not?" I said.

Meiling's eyes narrowed. "And miss my chance to gloat? I heard Ty An say I was a concubine, and that you've taken Xiulan as your wife instead. She was saying that you were 'taking care of a flower instead of a thistle.' Miserable little brat. I'm barely gone, and she starts trying to throw her weight around? I, her mother, will educate her properly."

She said all this with her nose pointed in the air, like she was some kind of noble lady.

I snorted with amusement. Somebody was going to be getting a tongue lashing.

↔

Mortals were so . . . Xiulan would *not* say *strange*. There were more of them than there were cultivators, after all. Perhaps she was the strange one? Their actions were . . . befuddling.

They touched each other so much. They clapped each other on the back, they threw mud at each other, and they engaged in all sorts of rowdy, rough behaviour.

And Master Jin joined in right along with them. He pushed and shoved the other men around, and they shoved back.

He looked so unreservedly *happy*. They all did. Happy with a simple life.

It stirred something. Something that she remembered from the stories her mother and father used to tell her: about how the righteous would prevail and defeat the wicked.

The happiness that was *worth* protecting.

She understood, just a bit, why Master Jin acted like he did. The irreverence, the amusement, the joy.

"Speak with him. Do you really think he would be angry over such a thing?" *Senior Sister asked, an eyebrow raised.*

No. No, he would not. But . . . she must have courage first. It was difficult to talk about these things, but it was getting easier.

She looked up at the sky, careful that none of her new "decorations" came off. One of the smaller girls had refused to take part in Master Jin's rowdy game, and instead had decided that Xiulan needed flower crowns. Multiple. She had six of them resting on her head, and enough bracelets to cover both of her forearms.

Skilled with her hands, that little one. Though not very talkative. She hadn't said a word throughout the process, so Xiulan had used that time to contemplate the lives of the farmers.

There was a shriek of outrage and peals of laughter from the kitchens. She had originally meant to go with Senior Sister, but Sister Meiling had just shaken her head when the gaggle of other women had come to claim her.

Xiulan was rather glad Senior Sister had. The questions Sister Meiling was getting asked were downright *scandalous*. Who dared to ask such questions about what she did with her husband! All of them were so crass! She expected that from bandits, not wives and mothers! There was no real subtlety here, no veiled words or poison perfume. They were blunt as a hammer to the skull, and just as crude.

The men she could understand. Their camaraderie was something she wished for. She had read stories of sworn siblings. Though such stories were nearly always about men. A set of companions whom she could trust without reservation. Senior Sister was fast becoming one of those companions. Xiulan had bared all of her weakness to Sister Meiling and shown the woman her unsteady heart.

She had not been met with scorn and rebuke but rather the eyes of a healer who tried to help. It was quite nice.

There was more laughter and jeers. A young woman, barely into her teens, slammed open the door and fled. She took one look at Xiulan, and her face flushed crimson.

She continued her flight, chased all the way by more insults and rebukes. Senior Sister watched her go with amusement. The woman made eye contact with Xiulan and smirked.

"Ha! *And finally, you're bonier than I am*? Youse ain't so bony no more, Meimei!" a cheerful voice sounded, and a hand slapped down onto Senior Sister's rump, squeezing. The other hand pulled up the top of her robe, exposing her side, then pinched her hip. "Your boy has fed you up good!" Senior Sister rolled her eyes, as more cackling laughter sounded out.

Disciple Gou Ren's mother had a *very* strange accent.

Xiulan idly wondered if she should go to the kitchens to help, but decided against it. She was still an outsider right now, and well, she *barely* knew how to cook. Others did that for her. She could boil rice and make simple rations, but food like this was beyond her.

She took a breath and let it go, trying to drain the tension from her shoulders. Deep calming breaths.

Tomorrow. Tomorrow, she would interact more with the mortals.

And probably learn how to cook. She wanted to learn how to make the "ice cream" Master Jin made.

□

"Thanks, Brother Jin!"

"Hey, Jin, play with us!"

"Jin, tonight come have a drink!"

Hungry eyes stared at the memories as they replayed. He remembered them as if they had happened to himself, even if they really hadn't. He was there in the moment as the scenes played out. As he spoke to the other men and made them laugh. As he lived out a fantasy he had known since his parents had died, yet never got to experience. They warmed his spirit, as weak as it still was. Respect. Friendship. Things he had wanted and strived for, back when he was . . . well, back when he was still alone here.

He glared at his left foot and where it turned into a piece of fractured golden light, before turning back to the images.

He watched and felt himself drinking in his . . . their place of respect at the head table.

Snuggling into bed, a boy who was suddenly his younger sibling squeezing between them.

Warm amethyst eyes, as she leaned in for a kiss that he so happily returned.

He loved Meiling, even if he had never *really* met her.

"Our wife is a beauty, ain't she?" There was a snap and a hiss as a "can" opened, and a sweet memory played across their tongue, along with a long loud *sluuuurrrrp* that the other guy *knew* annoyed him, yet did it anyway.

"That doesn't taste like tea at all," Jin Rou grunted but did not rebut the argument. She *was* pretty. And kind. And . . . well, everything he could have wanted in a wife. He remembered his own mother's fire, and zest for life, before . . . Before . . .

He sighed.

It still galled him, though. Why did they have to like the same things?

He frowned at his leg, where it turned into golden energy and connected to the leg of . . . the other guy. *Jin.* Cracks and rents ran through the man. Missing an arm, missing an eye . . . and he knew that the same damage was repeated on Jin Rou's half. Connected by their mirrored feet. The only part they were currently connected by at the moment.

"Awww, come off it, iced tea is great." The accent was strange, coming out of his mouth. So were the memories of the other place.

"I still say it was a rash decision, leaving the Sect like that," he said, rehashing an argument that they had been having ever since they could have arguments. An argument that Rou didn't really believe himself but always got a rise out of the other guy.

Jin raised a middle finger at Rou.

"And I still say that staying in that place, with the people who killed us, would be stupid. Why the hells wouldn't you leave? You want to stay around to get kicked and beat up? At least I *kind of* had a plan."

A devious grin spread across his face.

"And I'm stronger than you got."

Might makes right, that had been pounded into Rou's head, but it was a low blow. But another that Rou couldn't really refute.

"By accident," he shot back. Jin shrugged. Bastard. "You know I'm not good at cultivating—Gramps always said I was shit. That I should have been faster and better."

"You started at twelve, didn't you?"

Rou shrugged. "Gramps said no excuses. I started late, so I have to try even harder, even if I never measure up."

Jin grunted.

He looked through the memories as they lapsed into silence again. The sensations. The things he always wanted.

He supposed it could be worse.

A hand, reaching out and dragging his dying spirit back. Two halves of himself. Or someone else?

The other guy was in control. Or not even really in control, he was just the one who had survived. It was his body now. But there was still part of Rou that was separate. Part of him was himself.

Rou had even gained enough awareness to talk with his other half . . . *kind of.* He grimaced and tried to force the feeling away.

So he said something that was certain to annoy himself. "I still say that we could get with Xiulan."

"Fuck, man, this again? We're *married*," his other part snarled, glaring. "She's hot."

"Yes, she's *hot*. That doesn't matter."

"Gramps said every true man should have some Dao Companions."

Jin rolled his eyes and raised his middle finger again.

"Not happening."

Rou personally thought that it could happen if his other half weren't so dead-set on ignoring every other flower.

There was a twinge.

The ruined portions of their arms attached. Two spirits of the same man pulled together into something that could generously be called a whole.

Rou felt his eyes drooping as the two consciousnesses connected again.

When they awoke, neither would remember any of this. There would be only *Jin*. The man from another place. Rou would be him too, the only thing left of broken and fractured memories.

But . . . Rou had to try. He had to see if there was at least something left of himself. He needed to know he wasn't just a figment of Jin's imagination. "Hey. At least try to remember this. Do the stretches more. And the punch. Like that Master Bruce Lee guy you're so fond of said: one punch a thousand times. It's good advice. We want something we can swing with if something *does* go wrong."

"Yeah. I'll try, but you know how this goes. G'night, me. Ya wanker."

There was a snap, a *hiss*, and he chugged the rest of the can.

It was delicious. How annoying.

CHAPTER 15

THE LADY OF THE HOUSE

A prim and proper lady sat at a table, surrounded by papers. Her head was held high and her bearing was one of exacting poise. She examined the pieces of paper and the half-unrolled scrolls before her with a critical eye, going over numbers and expenses and receipts.

A gentle breeze brought the sweet scent of spring to her nose, and the sounds of pastoral bliss entered her ears, the soft clucking of the chickens and the low moans of the cows.

She turned her attention to her assistant as the other woman finished grinding and preparing the ink to be used today. The smaller girl's dexterous fingers swiftly let the ink come to the desired consistency, one that would glide across the paper like a breeze and let every inch of the lady's delicate writing be observed.

The lady nodded in thanks to her assistant, then picked up the brush. With consummate grace, she gathered the ink on the tip of her implement, and with deft strokes she began her task.

That Pi Pa's writing was so neat when she was using her mouth was a point of pride for her. She had practised long and hard to get the lines so perfectly straight, with *just* the right amount of flourish!

A true lady made do with what she had and could work anywhere, with any tool she pleased. Even if she was out in the wilderness, a true lady must be capable of preparing a meal fit for an Emperor, with only what she could find around her!

So knew Pi Pa.

Her Master and Mistress, bless their souls, had gone to visit family. Pi Pa, as any good Lady of the House, had taken it upon herself to consolidate the house's records. It was a task that they could surely do themselves, but it was a job Pi Pa was most pleased to aid them in.

They had spent the morning collecting the numbers. The Master of the House kept his receipts and his record of expenditures. Of course, Pi Pa had permission for this task. The Master had been bemused when Young Miss Ri Zu had requested such things, but he had allowed it and in doing so allowed Pi Pa her duty.

It was time to begin. Pi Pa finished titling her report, then gazed at the first item.

She considered it some more.

She tilted her head to the side, nodding as she looked at the scroll.

She turned to Young Miss Ri Zu.

'I do not know what these are for either, Sister Pi Pa,' the little rat admitted.

The scribble of numbers and letters was . . . well, it was sloppily done and absolutely *appalling*. There was no sense to it that she could discern, and there were often things crossed out or stacked on top of each other.

There was also a drawing of the Mistress of the House's face in the corner with hearts surrounding it. That part was well done, if oddly stylized.

She was sure the numbers made sense to the Master of the House, but to the rest . . . well, she would not disparage the Master of the House; no, ma'am!

The next one should be better, she decided, and put the main scroll aside.

The next one was *not* better. It was just as chaotic as the last, though at least with the two compared she could perhaps see *some* sort of pattern. Was he just using a different system, perhaps? Though this one had even more drawings. This time of what looked like gears, and there were parts circled and arrows directing certain numbers to where they were supposed to be.

Pi Pa felt the slight twinge of a headache coming on. Something inside her screeched with the incoherent rage of a bureaucrat encountering a misfiled report.

She instead switched to the Mistress of the House's own scroll, which only detailed the herb garden so far. Which was understandable; she had not been here long, and she had not the time to go through the expenses properly.

Pi Pa dutifully copied these out. But the rest. Well, the rest she would have to do herself. A proper inventory as well.

She looked at the Master of the House's scrolls again.

She'd do inventory first. Young Miss Ri Zu declared that she would stay and try to make sense of Master Jin's numbers.

So Pi Pa set off. First was the house. The jars of "pasteurized" milk that were in the river. The only two bottles of rice wine left. The near-complete lack of any real herbs from last year. They had eaten all of those and had to wait for them to grow anew. In fact, most of their larders, save for the eggs, were largely empty. It was a mild concern. Luckily, they had the bounty of the land, and she knew the Master of the House had already taken precautions to make sure such a thing would not happen again.

Twenty-one chickens, of which sixteen were egg-laying females. Of their rice, five bags remained after the sales, the gifts, destruction by those wicked, wicked rats, and the amount of food people ate when they visited. It was still more than enough to last them until the next harvest, however.

They also had an untapped gold mine. The Master of the House had yet to sell even one of the thirty-two large jars of maple syrup. Such a thing would render their coffers flush. How much would they sell for, she wondered? It was a new commodity, and those with coin would surely pay handsomely for it!

She hummed as her Dear trotted up beside her, nuzzling into her neck. She trotted along the fields, and her Dear fell into place beside her, chuffing happily at her company.

If only every man could be so good and kind.

Next, she trotted over to the bees.

The small, buzzing creatures wisely got out of her way as she sauntered up with her Dear, not even attempting to put their nasty little daggers where they did not belong.

Or they might just be . . . *consumed.*

A lady was to have a firm hand on the rest of the servants. And Pi Pa had them well in hand, yes she did.

Or at least most of them. Tigu didn't listen at the best of times, and Wa Shi, the gluttonous bastard, went out of his way to annoy her: slinking around, stealing food, and leaving puddles of water around the house for her to clean up.

If he weren't such a good friend to her Dear, she would have . . . oh! She didn't know what she would have done, but it would *not* be kind! She huffed, then returned her eyes to the bees.

They protested not at their examination, staying well away from her as she examined the comb inside the hive like the Master of the House had shown her. It was coming along nicely. Even the one that Bi De had found had survived, despite the Master's doubts, though that one was nowhere to be found. Likely diligently preparing for her brood. Yet it was odd that some of the other bees were standing guard for her, oddly subdued, and positioned at the entrance. Unmoving sentinels.

Hmmmm. Something to keep an eye on, at least.

Finally, she observed the fields. Young Sir Gou Ren had been put in charge of five acres of rice. Forty bags of rice were two hundred twenty silver coins. Half an acre yielded around eighty bags. Therefore . . .

For five acres, this would mean that on the rice alone, if it was all sold well, the Master would make back his investment in the land this year. And that was not counting the fifteen acres of wheat, another two acres of rice that the Master of the House was experimenting with, and the half acre of earth apples.

They would be able to have a wedding party every day and still be fine after this year's harvest.

Satisfied with this, she began her march away, back to the house. They did take a detour, however. It was too nice a day to not travel around Great Fa Ram.

Her Dear even picked a flower to put behind her ear. Such a gentleman!

But even this pleasant break had to end. She and her Dear pressed their noses together, and then they departed their separate ways.

She entered the home, once more ready to tackle the Master's notes, when she happened upon a *scene*.

Tigu stood menacingly over Ri Zu, the little rat glaring up at the cat, not budging an inch. The cat's body was tense as a coiled spring, filled with barely contained violence.

Pi Pa sighed and got ready to separate them, opening her mouth daintily—

But paused when Tigu inclined her head, in the barest form of a bow. *'This Young Mistress demands that Sister Ri Zu teaches her of bees.'*

Ri Zu's eyes widened with surprise.

Oh? This was an interesting development.

The rat's eyes narrowed.

'No,' Ri Zu said simply, crossing her little arms.

They glared at each other.

The cat launched herself. A tiny needle appeared in Ri Zu's hands. And—

Both of them let out shrieks of shock and terror as Pi Pa took them well in hand.

Or in this case, well in mouth. Little girls needed to learn to be polite, and not start fights near her paperwork.

$\rightarrow$

'Now, what does one say when they wish for a favour?' Pi Pa asked pleasantly.

Ri Zu and Tigu were standing across from each other. They were damp and bedraggled, eyeing Pi Pa warily.

'Tigu,' Pi Pa prompted.

She could see the tensed muscles, and veins bulging as the cat bowed properly. It looked like the act physically pained her.

'This Young Mistress . . .' The cat paused and looked about to choke. 'Humbly requests your guidance, Sister Ri Zu.'

'And what does a proper lady say to such a request, Young Miss Ri Zu?'

The rat's eye twitched as she bowed back properly.

'Ri Zu would . . . be honoured to teach her fellow disciple her way. It will be a true test of Ri Zu's ability to teach one so . . . difficult.'

Claws unsheathed, but Tigu didn't move.

'Very good! It only took three attempts, but we shall fix such things, yes we shall! You shall be ladies yet! Now come, both of you, we have a task.'

Both Tigu and Ri Zu glared at each other.

'You court death,' the cat snarled to the rat.

'The only one Ri Zu courts is Brother Bi De,' Young Miss Ri Zu returned primly. 'You court never being allowed back in Master's bed.'

There was another explosion of movement.

Then there was another sucking sound as the two little girls yelped and disappeared.

Pi Pa examined Master Jin's scroll again. It did have some form of pattern she could now discern. It still needed correction, but it wasn't as bad as she'd feared. And his receipts were organised by date, which calmed her tremendously.

She wrote down another figure. It was a bit difficult with her mouth full, but she maintained her writing admirably. This would take a while to go through. She sighed, then stood from the table, walking to the kitchen to prepare a bribe for the bastard fish. It was still galling that he was better at math than she was.

Of course, the smug bastard took his sweet time humming and hawing about helping her.

He changed his tune swiftly when she waded into his lair to go and get him.

CHAPTER 16

SECRET SPOT

Meiling was rather glad she hadn't been gone long. It only took a day for everybody to calm back down from their excitement—especially after she put Ty An in her place. Such conflicts rarely happened in Hong Yaowu. The villagers were too small and close knit for that, but when things *did* happen, they got ugly.

Meiling nipped it in the bud. Suddenly being the oldest of the younger generation, after Meiling and Meihua left, meant Ty An had something to prove.

Ty An *had* found fertile ground with her insult about Jin being unfaithful. It was a rather good one, she had to admit, since it attacked several insecurities that Meiling used to have. Of *course* the rich, powerful man had another woman, and of *course* Meiling was just some sort of concubine or servant, instead of the beautiful flower.

For most of the other women, the thought provoked concern. Had Meiling been taken advantage of? Had he taken another woman so soon?

Simply denying it wasn't enough sometimes. Actions spoke louder than words, even for such petty games.

The glances lasted until Meiling asked Xiulan to prepare a bath for her, and the other woman obeyed with a "Yes, Senior Sister!"

Of course, nobody knew that it was Xiulan's turn, and it didn't really come into their heads that preparing a bath wasn't as much of an ordeal for a cultivator as it was for them.

All that mattered was that Meiling was the one who commanded, and the order was obeyed without hesitation. And then while Meiling went to bed with Jin, Xiulan slept in the guest room.

Ty An's little rebellion was crushed mercilessly, strangled and stabbed to death by a thistle's thorns. Meiling couldn't help the small surge of vindictive pleasure that coursed through her, though she felt immediately guilty about it. Ty An didn't *really* deserve what Meiling had said.

"Ty An. With me, please," Meiling commanded, and the girl winced, likely expecting some sort of continuation of yesterday. A few eyes followed them, watching for a reaction.

Instead, the two of them worked, cutting and chopping for the morning meal. With Jin and Gou Ren added to the forces of men, the rest of the fields would be finished today. And then she would be spending at least a few days just lying around her old house and reading. How exciting!

"Slightly more of an angle, Ty An," Meiling instructed. The other girl nearly jumped out of her skin at Meiling's commanding voice, but obeyed, and the cutting started to go easier.

They worked in silence for a few moments longer. Ty An looked to be on the verge of tears, especially after the tongue lashing Meiling had given her yesterday.

Meiling observed her for a moment longer before she spoke.

"This is over," Meiling said simply, catching the younger girl's eye. The younger woman got what she meant. The days of Ty An spreading rumours were most certainly over . . . and Meiling had no desire to continue the feud.

"I am . . . sorry," Ty An said, her voice quiet. "And thank you."

The younger girl at least was smart enough to know that Meiling stopping things from going further was a good thing, rather than trying to push the issue. Meiling smiled and nodded.

The eyes turned away from them, and the chatter became louder and more boisterous.

"Ah. Senior Sister?" Xiulan asked. "May I join you today?"

Meiling turned to Xiulan as the work lulled once more. She was standing in the doorway with little Liu, the quiet girl holding on to the end of Xiulan's skirt and peeking out at them. Meiling's lips quirked with amusement at the excess of flower crowns once again on Xiulan's head.

Meiling nodded. Xiulan stepped into the room, the territory of the village's women. The other women's eyes gleamed.

Xiulan recoiled as they crowded around her. Meiling saw Xiulan's hand clench into a fist, the smell of cut grass spiking.

Meiling's hands clapped together, the sound like thunder.

Her eyes narrowed as everyone froze.

"Back to work," she commanded.

→

Xiulan took a breath. The mortal women were *entirely* too fond of touching her or trying to braid her hair. It was . . . overwhelming.

She'd known that the soldiers, when she had gone to battle Sun Ken, were a rowdy bunch, though they were respectful enough. They did not get so close. They did not press up against her.

They did not have to worry that she would accidentally punch them when they moved too fast towards sensitive areas, or hovered behind her, looking over her shoulder. She had been taught all her life to respond to people like that with violence, for no friend would hover so close behind a cultivator.

She was rather grateful that Senior Sister had rescued her from the press and sent her to get water. A task she was finished with in moments.

At least cooking was proving to be relatively easy. It was certainly easier than pill refining. She took calming breaths, as she calmed down—contemplated.

One of the breaths smelled like dirt.

She opened her eyes and observed the large larva that was right under her nose. The fat grub reared up and seemed to look her in the eye, cradled in little hands.

"A Great Horned Beetle Grub? An auspicious find, Young Master," she noted. The boy, crouched in front of her with an evil little grin, wilted.

"You're supposed to scream," he informed her with a pout.

"I am?" she asked idly. Was this some sort of mortal thing? Why would one scream over a grub?

"Mmm. Every girl other than Meimei does," he declared, sitting on one of her crossed knees without even asking. Impudent, but she would allow it.

"If Senior Sister would not scream, then I shall not either, Young Master." His nose scrunched up adorably, just like Senior Sister's often did. A few freckles dotted the bridge of it.

"Ah, you're no fun, Fairy Sister."

Xiulan nearly winced. Getting called "Fairy Sister" brought up unpleasant memories of far-too-pushy men. Men that she couldn't stab without provoking entirely too much bloodshed.

"You may address this one as Xiulan, Young Master," she informed Senior Sister's younger brother.

"My name is Xian, Fairy Sister," he returned. "It's annoying when everybody calls me young chief or little boss."

Oh? How amusing.

"As you say, Xian," she allowed.

He smiled and turned so that he was fully in her lap, resting his head back against her chest. She shifted slightly, copying the movements of the mortals to give him a better seat.

He brought up the grub again. "I grow them in my room, Lanlan." Her lips quirked at the nickname. Again, how impudent, but that was just the way of mortals. It was much better than the multiple references to flowers or fairies. "They don't have any medical uses, but they look neat when they grow up. If you get the males you can put them both on a log and they throw each other off. Want to see where I found him? He was a lot smaller back then. I'll show you my secret spot," the young boy babbled, gesticulating wildly.

Well, she had nothing better to do right now . . . .

She escorted the Young Master—no, she escorted Xian—into the forest, as he talked eagerly about his "secret spot." His hand was small and fragile in hers.

"Dad tells me not to come here 'cos the thunder-hoof is hanging around. Never seen him. But the grass here is nice and soft. Softest I've ever felt, and . . . Dad said if I wanted to go again, I needed an escort," he admitted, embarrassed. Well, he had his escort. Quite devious of him, really, though she would have come with him even if she'd known the truth. Been more alert too. Her swords were back in her room. Xian sniffed, rubbing his nose. "It smells . . . kinda like you?"

It *smelled* like her? She didn't believe she smelled like much besides sweat these days. No flowered baths when working at a farm— Ah! She looked down at his scrunched, freckled nose, so similar to Senior Sister's. He must have the same ability, for such things normally ran within bloodlines.

They continued their little walk through the trees, and Xiulan's focus sharpened as she began to feel the gentle pulse of Qi. It was strong and heady, so much so that *she* could almost smell it.

They came to a clearing.

Her pupils dilated. Spiritual Grass. So much Spiritual Grass, of the highest grade she had ever witnessed. The grass was so green and lush it surpassed the patches of heartgrass that lay on the tops of the Verdant Blade's own hill. She could feel the power from here. The gentle pulse of life, of Qi. If she could refine this into a pill she could—

She cut the thought off. She had no pill furnace. And what was she going to do, rip it all up, when the Young—when Xian had trusted her enough to show her?

She took a deep breath. The peaceful tranquility of the area washed over her. And it was peaceful. This place . . . it felt like a resting place. A place where grudges went to fade away.

"This is a nice place, Xian," she whispered, unwilling to disturb the tranquility.

"Mm-hm! I practise my dancing here! Father says I need to practise a lot! But the best thing is *this!*" he declared, pointing at the patch of grass.

She allowed herself to be pulled to the ground as Xian fell over onto his back on it.

As the mortals did, she supposed.

She sat down on the grass. It was wonderfully soft and comfortable. She idly pushed her Qi into the ground, into the growing grass. It was nearly a habit now, though the grass certainly didn't need more Qi.

She let out a sigh as they stared at the sky through the trees. Her eyes slowly closed.

□

A second later, she opened her eyes to a wary glare. The Earth Spirit was close, her body bunched up and her posture tense.

Xiulan swiftly retreated, getting out of headbutt range.

The Spirit followed Xiulan with her eyes. Or eye, rather. Xiulan had never noticed the one that was missing before, covered over by gold. Xiulan bowed respectfully.

The Earth Spirit snorted, folding her arms across her chest.

Xiulan took a moment to look around the grassy area, with its white walls and odd gold cracks. The air was thick with Qi, and she felt a massive desire to move.

She turned back to the Earth Spirit, who was still glaring at her but apparently satisfied with how Xiulan had retreated. The Earth Spirit gave Xiulan one last glance before she started digging in the dirt, apparently deciding to ignore Xiulan completely.

Xiulan's body twitched at the dismissal, but she said nothing. Instead, she focused on her body. She was here now . . . so she might as well go through her forms. She launched into the first form of the Verdant Blade Sword Arts. Even without the Jade Grass Blades, she completed the movements with astounding grace in the odd room.

She stepped and twirled, but something felt off—something that she could not identify. The structure was incorrect. The Verdant Blade Sword Arts was not providing the right movements.

She let go of the rigid form. She began to flow. The steps of the dance came naturally. Half-remembered, half-forgotten.

Which was when a clod of earth nearly struck her in the head. She ducked, flowing into another motion, and turned to frown at the Earth Spirit.

The Earth Spirit was grinning at her, tossing a mud ball up and down in her hand.

With a flick of the Spirit's hand, the ball flew at her head, so Xiulan moved again, bouncing slightly on the balls of her feet.

The Spirit's smile turned predatory.

Mud balls flew. Little hands reached out to grapple.

Xiulan dodged and moved the best she could, spiralling around the odd almost-building with as much grace as she could muster. Occasionally, a blow would land. One to the shin, which forced her foot back into a position that felt better. One to the shoulder, which shifted her balance *just so*.

By the time Xiulan realised what the Spirit was doing, the dance was over. A foot slid between her legs, a little hand grabbed her robe, and her back slammed into the ground as she was thrown with earth-shaking force.

Xiulan lay there for a moment as the Earth Spirit shoved her pinky into her ear negligently, an action that in a human would be trying to clean out ear wax. A crass, uncouth display. One eye considered Xiulan.

"Thank you for the guidance," Xiulan managed to get out.

The Earth Spirit waved at her dismissively.

CHAPTER 17

STILL

think I have seen something like this before," Xian mused, scratching at his chin.

"Really?" I asked. Pops, Yao Che, and I were all staring at my drawing of a still. Honestly, out of everything I was "inventing," a still was probably the thing I knew how to make the best. I had grown up in a rural place, and the moon shined down on all of us. Even if I wasn't a real big fan of the drink, I still knew how to make a still. Well, I knew how to make a still when I had a hardware store to acquire all the pipes, or a pressure cooker if I wanted to go full hillbilly. In the absence of those, I needed some professionals.

Pops nodded. "In Pale Moon Lake City. Of course, the device was three stories tall and glowing with inner fire, but it did look somewhat similar to the way yours is arrayed."

"What was it used for?" I asked, intrigued.

"We do not know the original intent of its creator since it's so old—at least three thousand years by most reckonings. But what it did was concentrate solutions. Any solution. Though only a tenth of the liquid ever came out the other end. But alas, it stopped working. It only produces black sludge now, and nobody knows how to fix it." Xian sighed. "So now it is merely a curiosity. A glowing machine near the palace."

Huh. Well, if it looked like a giant still, I wouldn't be surprised if it was. Qi-filled alcohol was *expensive*. Qi artifacts were so strange, though. I kind of took it for granted that you could reverse engineer most modern devices with a bit of time, instead of their design being some lost mystic art that could never be replicated again.

"So, you think you can handle something like this?" I asked Yao Che, and the blacksmith stared long and hard at my drawings.

He considered them in great depth, a frown affixed to his face, until he shook his head and sighed. "I'll be able to do the body, but this much piping is going to be . . . difficult." The admission seemed to be physically painful. "Especially at the purity you want. We just don't have the means out here."

I sighed, and nodded. It had been a bit of a long shot anyway. It was mostly an idle idea. I wasn't actually the biggest drinker. I was normally a juice or iced tea kind of guy—I could not wait until the peaches were ready to harvest. Peach iced tea, here I come!—but if other people were drinking, I normally joined in. Get a little buzzed and have a little fun.

Also, I had potatoes for vodka. Though I had read something about most vodka being made out of oats or something now? I couldn't actually remember.

Yao Che looked at the pipes a bit more and the number of turns. "If we can get the copper, I *might* be able to do the pipes. I'll have to do some practice."

"Well, if you need a hand, I'm available, even if it's just to pump the bellows. I want to see how this is made," I replied.

Or more specifically, how an ancient blacksmith made pipes. It was always a pleasure to watch someone skilled at work. The lack of drop hammers and machinery just made it more interesting. They did everything by hand. No wonder Yao Che looked like he could get in a fistfight with a bear and win.

He appeared pleased at my offer. Yao Che was looking for an apprentice, and ever since his daughter had left the nest and gotten married, he had been a bit . . . aggressive in advertising the benefits of being a blacksmith to the village boys. He just wanted to teach *anybody* at this point.

"The copper is still the main issue. You'll definitely need to get a merchant on it, contact someone in the exchange . . . or go to Pale Moon Lake City."

Something that I could probably kludge together in an afternoon back in the Before was quickly turning into a grand quest that I would have to travel nearly a week for. Honestly, it was starting to sound a bit not worth it. And the price would rapidly balloon if I had to go to the big city, because everything was more expensive there. I . . . well, I didn't have too much left, after everything I had brought. Sure, I had the maple syrup I could sell, and that might fetch some good coin, but I might have to wait until after the harvest. We weren't in any danger of starving, and we could still afford some creature comforts for sure, but the still sounded like it would cost far more than I'd originally thought.

That said, it wasn't *all* for boozing it up. Distilled alcohol was also essential in disinfecting things, from tools and needles to wounds.

And my new family was full of healers. Might as well get them the best tools for the job they had. They knew boiling water killed most bacteria, but you can't just start boiling *people*.

Well, you can't boil most people. I can survive a boiling just fine. And oven temperatures. I'd yet to find a temperature that actually damaged my skin.

I idly wondered if I could just reach into a forge and grab the cherry-red metal. That would certainly make things easy.

"Well, I'll see if I can get some better measurements for you, so you have a better idea of how much copper you need," Yao Che informed me as he got to work.

"And the cost of the flux, too," Pops said. "If it is to be near such a harsh liquid, the lead in the flux may seep out and render the liquid poison."

That piece of knowledge threw me for a loop. It still got me that they had some really advanced medical knowledge in some areas, and then super medieval thoughts and technology in others—like farming equipment. If you have germ theory, pasteurization should be something logical, shouldn't it? But when I'd brought that up to Pops, he looked like somebody had hit him over the head. Most people used special, expensive arrays to keep things fresh if they had to. Nobody had thought of just . . . *heating things up*.

But for all the advancement in that medical knowledge, it wasn't completely widespread. Hong Yaowu basically meant "Medicine Warehouse," after all. A lot of the mortals I had seen on the road through the Azure Hills seemed to not have as high hygiene standards.

"I'm a little surprised you wouldn't just use a pill furnace, though. Can't those refine liquids?" Pops asked.

"That . . . that is actually a good idea," I admitted. Pill furnaces *could* extrude liquids if you interrupted the process, though that was generally the sign of a lack of skill or that you screwed up somewhere. It would be faster too. A couple minutes instead of hours. But it would probably cost the same, or even more, because of all the extra workings that went into a pill furnace. "It might work, but *anyone* can use a still. You don't need Qi or anything special," I told him, shrugging.

That, and I still wasn't the most comfortable around the things. It was irrational. They were just a tool, yet I didn't like things related to pills. Call it a lifetime of the "drugs are bad, kids!" messaging from government programs.

He nodded at my explanation. "So? What are you up to for the rest of the day?" he asked me idly, as Yao Che started marking things down.

"Fishing with the boys at Green Lake," I said happily.

Yao Che nodded. "Well, you boys have a good time. Your wife going along?"

"Meimei made it very clear that anybody who tries to drag her out of the house today is going to earn her ire. And then she started laughing to herself and muttering about laxatives," I said. Well, it was fishing with the boys, so I hadn't tried too hard to convince her anyway.

Che barked out a laugh. "That girl is entirely too much like her mother. Though tempered with Brother Xian's subtlety," he mused, nudging Pops while he smirked.

I'd have to ask Pops about Meimei's mom someday. I could tell that the wound of her absence still hurt, but I hoped they would tell me about her.

"Well, leave this drawing with me, and I'll get the rest of these measurements figured out. Your Brother Che will get you the best price, count on it!" Yao Che declared. He held out his arm, and we clasped forearms, instead of a more formal bow, completing our deal.

I was fairly certain that most smiths would charge for figuring out a blueprint for their client, but Che just seemed a bit interested to have a project. *The perks of being friends with people.*

"Hey, Jin! We're ready to go!" Gou Ren shouted to me.

Pale Moon Lake City, huh? I'd think about it. Not like it was really a priority.

→

The fishing trip had been pretty nice, even if Yun Ren gave up his line to just take pictures of everything. That man was entirely too obsessed with my recording crystal, but it was a pretty harmless hobby.

And I'll say it again, he does take good images. The one of Xiulan this morning, sitting with her eyes closed in meditation, with little Liu adding more flowers to her hair, was especially good. If I didn't know better, I would have thought he had a lighting crew and Photoshop involved.

His landscape images looked nice too. Green Lake was peaceful, idyllic . . .

He swapped to the next picture, this one of my face, eyes bugged out with panic.

And it had some kind of *freshwater shark* in it—they were apparently pretty rare but could grow to dangerous sizes.

And while I was a cultivator, seeing a fin coming at me through the water had made me squirm just a bit.

The next image was an eruption of water as I'd thrown myself out of the lake, panicking before I realised that the poor thing would probably hurt itself trying to bite me. And I realised that while I had checked out the flora scrolls, which I still remembered with startling clarity, I hadn't devoted any time to the native wildlife.

Meiling giggled at the image from her spot in my lap, while I grumbled in irritation at the ribbing. She would glance up from her scroll every so often but otherwise had stayed true to her promise: Meiling had done absolutely nothing all day, and looked inordinately pleased by the fact.

Especially when I started dinner instead of her having to do it. I had grilled lakefish. It looked quite a bit like bass, but with the brightest green skin I had ever seen.

But there was something missing . . .

Pops walked into the room, looking a bit frazzled. "Has anybody seen Xian?" he asked, sounding concerned and annoyed.

My wife lifted her nose into the air, closed her eyes, and took a breath. "He's with Xiulan," she said after a moment, pointing to the northeast.

Well, it's official. Any kids we had were absolutely doomed. A mom who can sniff you out wherever you hide? That was absolutely *terrifying*.

Xian looked in that direction and started to grumble. "I told him not to go there anymore."

"I'll grab him, Pops," I volunteered, and a relieved smile crossed his face.

"Thank you."

I went to set Meimei aside, but she just hooked an arm around my neck when I went to lift her off.

So I just picked her up instead and began my walk. Meimei wanted me to carry her, but I just kept my arms at my side and she kept hanging on with one arm, her body still positioned like she was lying sideways with my lap under her.

Nice core muscles. Though I supposed the Qi helped.

She raised a reproachful brow at me. I didn't give in.

We wandered in the direction Meimei had pointed in, her hanging onto my neck with one arm and stubbornly reading a scroll, her body still horizontal to the ground. We got a few chuckles from people who saw us, and my wife eventually gave in out of embarrassment, dropping off so she could walk beside me.

It was not a very long walk, and something about the route tickled my mind—*Hey, this is in the direction of where I killed the wolf, and where the thunder-hoof was.* A few steps later, I heard clapping in a steady rhythm.

And sure enough, we were at the clearing.

Xiulan was sitting against a tree, clapping out a beat as Xian practised his dance. Meimei's eyes immediately went soft and warm as she took in the scene. It honestly wasn't something I'd expected to see either, but it was cute. Xiulan looked a bit sheepish as she spotted us, but it soon faded to a smile again when she saw Meimei's beaming smile and trotted over to sit beside her.

Well, we could wait for a little while. It wasn't like anything was urgent. And Xian was doing a good job, his eyes closed as he went through the movements of his dance.

His face was almost serene, even as sweat ran down his nose. My new little brother was getting really freckly. He'd barely had any freckles last year, just a few dots, but now they were slowly starting to cover the bridge of his nose, just like his sister's. Cute kid.

Towards the end of the dance, Xiulan's claps started getting louder, increasing in volume until the last step, where she stopped. In the actual dance, the drums would keep going, then start again, but Xiulan had a good eye for this. As soon as the clapping stopped, Xian faltered, staggering, then started heavily puffing air.

"Wha—? Why'd you stop?" he asked, sweat pouring off his brow.

"Because I believe we are done for today, Xian. An excellent performance," she said sincerely. He then seemed to notice our presence and quickly looked up at the sky in confusion. "Wha—? So late? Have I missed lessons?! Father is going to kill me!" he yelped out, turning to Meimei with a pleading look in his eye.

Meiling smiled. "I'm sure he'll forgive you," she declared, holding out her arms and receiving an excited hug from the sweaty kid. "Now, what do you say to Xiulan for helping you?"

"Thanks, Lanlan!" he chirped happily, grinning at her.

His stomach growled, and he flushed crimson.

"Let's go get some food in both of you," I decided.

Meimei linked arms with Xiulan so they could walk together, and I hoisted Xian up so he could ride on my shoulders.

It was a nice, relaxing walk back through the forest.

CHAPTER 18

RAT AND CAT

Bi De finished marking a proposed formation design on the ground. He considered it for a moment before shaking his head and scratching it out.

With the planting over, he finally had time to once more contemplate the mysteries of Hong Yaowu's fire formation, the one he had seen during the solstice festival. It was a curious mystery, and one he enjoyed considering . . . but it always came with the desire to go and visit the points the formation was trying to connect to. There was only so much he could do sitting at home and guessing.

However, he had a duty to do here. Bi De turned from his scratches in the ground to look up at his charges.

The young cows bucked and gamboled around the field, chasing and being chased in equal measure. It was a sight he was incredibly fond of. The young ones knew absolutely nothing of danger. To them, all of Fa Ram was safe and pristine, untouched by anything that could harm them.

This was truly the pride of a protector. One who knew his charges were safe as the result of his direct actions. Indeed, even the fear he and his fellow disciples had instilled in the population of interlopers was forgotten in the aftermath of the births. The scent and temptation of the newborns had proved too much. Many of Basi Bu Shi's ilk slunk around the outskirts, as well as the largest of their kin, the wolves.

All of them had been defeated or driven off. Not a single creature had managed to breach the boundary. They slunk, and sniffed, examining his protection for weak points. None dared to test the line. They knew that to cross over it was death while he was on watch, and he allowed them his mercy. As long as interlopers did not truly intrude, he stayed his mighty spurs and did not strike them down.

However, that wasn't truly mercy. Sister Tigu needed to eat, after all, and she had none of his restraint. Though it was always quite a shock to see her dining upon a wolf that outmassed her ten times over.

Tigu ranged freely in this way, and together all threats to Fa Ram were defeated before most even knew of them.

Though the cat had lately been slightly more . . . *aggressive* in her pursuit of interlopers, as a result of her stained honour. She had proclaimed to the heavens that she would find a bee for the Great Master . . . and still, she had not delivered one unto him. Without the distraction of the Blade of Grass, she had even sought to challenge Bi De. It had been an enjoyable spar, but it ended the only way that it could end. He had tried to give her pointers properly, but such was her frustration that even those were not well received.

He tried his best to be a good First Disciple and dispense wisdom. Yet he was still young and half-roasted. He knew that the wisdom he had gained was a mere shadow of the Great Master's own profound wisdom, and there was only one that Tigu would *truly* listen to.

And the Great Master was not here. Even in his absence, however, Tigu had redoubled her efforts, determined to complete her task before the Great Master returned. In truth, Bi De knew that the Great Master did not consider her honour stained. He surely saw straight through Tigu and was attempting to turn this into some form of lesson. The sort of lesson Sister Pi Pa had divined in making the girls work together.

He hoped that it might resolve some of the strife, but he was still convinced that it would end in a battle. Pi Pa was more optimistic, but she would be sitting in on the lesson again to make sure it did not get too out of hand.

He noticed that the calves had strayed, going to where they were not supposed to and bothering those that they were not to bother.

His swift legs carried him to his destination, and he gently shooed the little ones—little? They were nearly fifty times his mass already—back away from those they were about to bother. They had a habit of chewing upon the sheep when they were not supposed to. The sheep's wool was apparently very valuable, and not to be soiled, nor chewed on unduly.

So he gently scolded them, his voice a much lower pitch and not nearly so loud. They fled, joyously returning to their games. He could not believe he used to find Pi Pa and Chun Ke annoying when they bucked and played so. The folly of his own youth and arrogance.

The sheep were placid creatures, bleating occasionally but otherwise content to stand in their little triangle formation and go where directed.

He hopped onto Fu Zi's back and gently picked a few sticks out of the sheep's wool. It was wonderfully soft but was prone to picking up an enormous amount of detritus.

Bi De stood guard for a while longer, his attention never wavering, until Brother Chun Ke came to relieve him.

They bowed to each other and swapped positions, Chun Ke going to play with the little ones, and Bi De setting off along the Great Pillars. He absently flowed through a form on his way back to the coop, allowing his body to act without thought and surrounding his body with his Qi. He was on the cusp of a new Lunar technique, he could feel it. Yet he also knew nothing good would come from forcing. The Lunar Blades of the Crescent Moon and the Split Faces of the Half Moon were very different techniques. He wondered what the face of the full moon would reveal to him.

He continued upon his path and ventured past the hives to a spot where he was met with regularity. He nodded politely to his visitor.

The bee was constantly tended to by two of her brood, climbing over her and grooming her, with another two standing guard. It was odd behaviour. Sister Ri Zu noted that she should be hiding in her nest at all times, awaiting the birth of her first clutch, but she still came out to observe him, accompanied by an honour guard. He was certain she even attempted to dance for him once, the silly little thing, wiggling about.

Knowing what the little creature wished for, he retrieved a small sample of the Qi-filled maple syrup that the Great Master had originally fed her from and offered it. The offering was accepted, and the little queen bee danced for him in her own wiggling way. He had his own thoughts on the creature. Could she have a spark? If so, she was the smallest thing he had observed to contain thought. And she could not yet truly communicate.

He observed her politely, as one should when thanked. But his mind was not fully upon the bee. Instead he was focusing on the lesson. He knew Sister Pi Pa would tolerate no violence within the house, but he was still a bit worried about Sister Ri Zu. Both the rat and the cat had been growing more and more furious with each other as the days passed, and with the Master and Healing Sage gone from the house . . . they might come to blows.

He nodded to the bee as her wriggling stopped, and he went on his way, going back towards the coop. The windows were all open to let the spring breeze blow through and refresh the stale air.

He hopped up into the windowsill and observed.

The air had some tension in it as Ri Zu spoke. Her tones were clipped, and her diction was exacting. She had slowly been reducing the amount of odd double-words her kin had used, and her voice was calm and steady.

There was none of her passion here. None of her wonderful enthusiasm. But similarly, there were no snide remarks from Tigu. She sat blankly, occasionally lapping up some of the tea before her.

'This concludes the lesson,' Ri Zu stated. There was silence for a moment while they glared at each other.

'Most were things this Young Mistress has learned through her own efforts,' the cat grumbled. She glared angrily at the slate, though her anger seemed to be mostly directed at herself.

'Then you should have listened to Ri Zu the first time,' the rat said stiffly.

The cat bristled dangerously but accepted the rebuke.

Tigu hissed. *'Yet I am still no closer to capturing one from your lesson.'* She frowned as she stared at one of her own paws. *'Capturing such a small thing is . . .'*

Indeed, her body was the poorest out of all of them for ensnaring a bee directly. Her razor claws and teeth like daggers cut and shredded delicate carapace easily. It was doubly hard when all of Tigu's Qi was optimised for cutting. To blunt her teeth in the heat of the moment would be a challenging task.

They sat in silence, Sister Pi Pa observing them from her station.

'Why do you hate Ri Zu?' the rat eventually asked, leaning back against her slate.

Tigu paused, and stared at Ri Zu in bewilderment. *'Hate you? If I hated you, I would not have trained myself so harshly. I barely feel the urge to kill and eat you anymore, and it is easily disregarded. Naturally, this Young Mistress has mastered this aspect of herself.'*

It was a blunt statement—one that surprised Bi De as much as it seemed to surprise Ri Zu.

Ri Zu frowned at Tigu. *'Then why do you constantly try to hurt Ri Zu?'*

'*I try to trade pointers with you, fool,*' the cat corrected. '*Why do you not understand? Your dying is unacceptable. You are of Fa Ram. You are not allowed to become prey for lesser creatures and sully our collective glory,*' Tigu stated, as if it were the most obvious thing in the world. '*Yet you do not train. Even the Mistress does at least some exercises, and she is protected at all times by the Master.* You *are not. If one of us is not here, you shall surely perish. This Young Mistress has tried to correct your uselessness every time, but is rebuked.*'

Ri Zu's eyebrow twitched. '*You expect Ri Zu to believe that this is concern for her?*'

'*Of course it is not for you, you foolish creature. This Young Mistress is concerned that you taint the name of Fa Ram.*' Tigu lapped up more of her tea primly.

Ri Zu twitched some more, and then a serene smile spread across her face.

'*And what has led you to believe Ri Zu does not train?*' Sister Ri Zu asked.

'*Your head is buried in scrolls all day. I smell not any exertion on you, only the scent of herbs. You obviously don't train.*'

Ri Zu nodded, then raised one of her paws in a gesture that caused Bi De and Pi Pa to flinch.

It was a gesture Chow Ji had used. Something burned into their minds as wicked and arcane.

'*Oh? What shall little Ri Zu do with that?*' Tigu asked, condescending.

'*Activate the poison Ri Zu put in your tea,*' the rat returned pleasantly.

Tigu paused. *Ah*, Bi De realised, *she didn't pause, her muscles locked up.*

The cat keeled over, her Qi flaring and sparking uncertainly.

'*Ri Zu is weak-prey. Ri Zu is timid-coward.* Ri Zu *defied Chow Ji,*' the little rat said conversationally, approaching the cat.

She shoved a digit into the tip of Tigu's nose. Her tiny paw looked menacing in that moment, as the rat dragged her digit up from Tigu's nose to point directly at the cat's eye.

'*Ri Zu can fight. Ri Zu will live. Worry not for her,*' Young Mistress.'

She turned her back on Tigu and waved her paw, green Medicinal Qi surging from her paws and into Tigu. Tigu's muscles abruptly relaxed, and then she started gasping.

'*Was this what Chow Ji used?*' Tigu asked, her voice strained. Bi De knew she had been . . . skeptical of the wicked rat's prowess. She had not believed before this moment.

'Oh no, what he used was much more debilitating. It was agony given form, yet Brother Bi De fought through it anyway,' Ri Zu supplied.

There was silence once more in the coop. Tigu looked around at all of them and grimaced at what she saw.

Tigu rose to her feet, her face impassive. He'd expected more stumbling, but instead it was almost graceful. Ri Zu tensed, as did Bi De. He expected anger. He expected wrath.

Instead, Tigu simply turned and left. Her face was a mask.

Bi De observed for a moment, unsure of what to think of this development. He was proud that Ri Zu had stood up to Tigu for the first time . . . but he wondered if her actions had been truly right.

Bi De shook his head. He didn't know. But he did know that right now, Ri Zu needed comforting. The rat was shaking slightly, her eyes full of hot tears.

'Sister. Are you well?'

Ri Zu jumped and started flailing.

'Ah, you saw Ri Zu do that?' She looked embarrassed, tapping her forefingers together.

'Indeed. I know such things are hard for you . . . but Tigu did need to learn that pushing too hard has consequences of its own,' he proclaimed. Ri Zu hunched in on herself but smiled up at him.

Pi Pa let out a sigh. *'I had hoped for a less . . . well, a different outcome, but this may work as well,'* Pi Pa admitted. *'Perhaps thinking that Tigu would gain some appreciation for Young Miss Ri Zu's knowledge was too optimistic. I'll go make sure the Young Miss does not do anything rash.'*

With that, she stood up and left.

Bi De hopped down from the windowsill and went to sit beside Sister Ri Zu. She clambered onto his back, as was her proper place, and she buried her face in his feathers.

'Ri Zu does not like fighting,' she whispered. *'But was Tigu right? If Ri Zu cannot poison her foe, she will surely die-perish.'*

The disciples of Fa Ram would protect their own. But Bi De would be pleased if Sister Ri Zu wished to join him in the morning training.

CHAPTER 19

A BOAR

Tigu could not classify what she was feeling at the moment. It was not the white-hot rage, that familiar friend.

No, this was a sucking pit. There was some anger, but it was mired in other emotions. Shame, frustration, disappointment.

She stalked through the forest. Away from the stupid rat, and the stupid "lady." Both of them, they were so stupid. Both of them, who hadn't understood what Tigu was trying to help them with.

The day had started off annoying. She was capable of admitting . . . rashness. She *should* have listened to Ri Zu's lecture on bees. She had found out most of what she was told through trial and error. That time could have been spent learning a technique to capture the insect. She had been so focused on the hunt, she had neglected to actually capture anything.

The feeling of Ri Zu's Qi slinking through her body, light touches reacting with her Qi in the tea. The Qi that Tigu hadn't noticed, its minute amounts unable to be sensed. Tigu's muscles seizing.

Tigu shuddered. It was a sneaky, underhanded trick, yet it had proved that there was some danger in attacking the rat. Tigu was strong. She was mighty. And a few mouthfuls of tea had sent her twitching to the floor, Ri Zu's Qi crawling all over hers with impunity. She had tried disrupting it, but Ri Zu had utterly ignored the attempts, her Qi digging in like Tigu's own claws to hold her firm.

The control was perfect. She had felt it carefully keeping the paralytic focused in the muscles she used to move, guiding the poison through her body and intensifying it. And when Ri Zu waved her paw, the feeling disappeared completely.

She wasn't harmed at all.

But she *had* been helpless. Helpless before something so much weaker than her. She should have been able to shake off the feeling instantly.

But she could not.

Her pride burned with the thought.

The rat had even proved her right, after a fashion. She could not engage in direct combat. She had to poison her drink—the act of a coward. The rat had struck the first blow.

Though Tigu was more concerned that she had been beaten at all, instead of *how* she was beaten. Now that she knew what to look for—Ri Zu's Qi, and the odd symbol the rat had to make—she was certain that she would not have to fear eating food in the house.

Though she would keep an eye on the rat, just in case.

What the rat *had* proved was that even a small amount of poison could lay low something stronger than her. If she made but a single strike with that glistening needle of hers, would victory have been hers?

Tigu's Qi and body were stronger. Much stronger. But she had no defence against the trick Ri Zu had pulled.

Ri Zu had won this round. A humiliating defeat, but not a *complete* defeat.

Tigu hacked a branch off a tree, then took it in her mouth. She bounced up the tree trunk, high into the branches. Selecting a bough that caught her eye, her claws began to carve it into a form. A rat.

Little Ri Zu, her stupid eyes, and her annoying squeaks.

Tigu put the wooden idol in between her teeth and crushed it.

She hacked off another branch. Perhaps she could disembowel this one? Decisions, decisions.

The sound of trotters broke her concentration. It was probably Pi Pa, come to scold her for not being ladylike or some other idiotic saying. Tigu was the perfect lady already. She was stunningly beautiful, and sublimely deadly. Even the Blade of Grass, her . . . *peer* in combat, had called her good-looking.

She glared down from her tree, ready to savage the pig with her words. But the footsteps were too heavy.

Instead of Pi Pa, out came Chun Ke.

He looked up into her tree with kind eyes, squinting so he could see her.

'*Tigu'er okay?*' his dull, drawling voice asked. His words were slightly slurred, and his speech was as slow and broken as always, but he put the affectionate suffix on the end of her name as the Master did.

'*Go away,*' she commanded him, even if she knew it was futile. The boar was stubborn as a rock.

'*Tigu'er okay?*' he asked again.

'*No,*' she said brusquely, intending to ignore him.

'*Chun Ke will listen,*' he said. His earnestness was, as always, absolute. He had not a bone of guile in his body. His dopey smile stretched his scars across his face. Out of all of them he was the least offensive to her right now. Even if he did have three hives to his name, he had never once boasted. The Master and the Mistress were both gone. So was the Blade of Grass.

The rest . . . didn't even try to understand.

So talking was all that was left. Talking, or trying to find a bee nest. She didn't even want to look at one of the damn creatures.

'*Fine,*' Tigu said, relenting. She didn't know how he could help, but she would indulge him. He, at least, took his training seriously, even if he disliked sparring with her.

And the others always said he was insightful, though she could scarcely believe it.

→

'*And then she poisoned the tea,*' she finished. She had come down from the tree at the start of the story at his insistence that none would disturb them and sat beside his enormous bulk.

Steam huffed out of both of Chun Ke's nostrils, and his brow furrowed.

'*No good,*' he huffed. '*Poison food wrong.*'

He sounded angry. Angry on *her* behalf.

When had *anyone* ever been angry on *her* behalf? Not that she *needed* it, of course. She could take care of herself. But it was . . . nice. Though he seemed more upset than she was. She supposed poison was a topic he had strong opinions on.

'*Indeed, the act of a coward, but honour is the domain of the strong. I shall surpass this limitation in time.*'

Chun Ke chuckled at her declaration. '*Chun Ke believe.*'

Tigu preened at the words. Why had she disliked him again? He was a bit slow, but the words he did speak were good ones.

'*Rizzu not coward, though,*' Chun Ke said, slurring Ri Zu's name together. '*Knows not able to fight strong Tigu'er. Trick instead of submit.*'

Ah, yes, he defended the rat.

'*At least her eyes can see Mount Tai. But it did nothing to make this Young Mistress wrong.*' Tigu sighed. '*She needs to know how to fight, otherwise she will perish and bring shame to us all. And the Master might be upset at her passing.*'

'*Tigu'er may have point. Would be sad if Rizzu died. But still went about it in wrong way. Was too mean to Rizzu,*' he said. '*At first, Tigu did not try to help. Only hurt. When Tigu changed to trying to help, did not make clear.*'

Tigu wanted to object . . . but grimaced. Everybody had seemed surprised Tigu had been trying to help the rat. Had she truly come across so poorly? She shoved the idea away and sneered. '*Oh, and I suppose I am the only one who was wrong, then?*'

'*Rizzu wrong. Tigu'er wrong. Wife wrong too,*' he said simply and immediately. Tigu's eyes widened. Even rebuking Pi Pa? '*All make mistakes. All make others hurt. Tigu'er tries to force training. Wife tries to force friendship. Rizzu tries to force respect. None worked,*' he said simply, turning his eyes to her. They were not quite as dull at that moment, sparking with something in their depths. '*Cannot force these things. Force only turns to resentment.*'

He sighed, then went silent, obviously considering his next words. His mind was slow at the best of times, so Tigu allowed him time to think. It was very, very strange to hear him speak this much, and it was obvious he was forcing himself.

'*We fight. We hurt each other. This is life. Tigu'er has been very mean to Rizzu. Tried to hurt. Disrespected. Pushed until Rizzu finally hurt back.*

'*Two paths come from here. Maybe the hurt is too much. Maybe Rizzu and Tigu'er hate each other forever. Maybe Fahrum has black spot forever. The other way . . .*' He trailed off leadingly—and Tigu realised what he was hinting at. It rankled, making what was left of her pride burn.

'*Tigu takes first step. Tigu shows she is strong and wise, to try to mend hurts. Rizzu might say no, and that is her choice to make. But Big Brother always says that one must at least try to talk. A better thing to try for. Tigu'er and Ri Zu helping each other is better than them hurting each other.*'

With that, his sparking eyes dulled. He let out an oink.

A war of poison and blade played out in her mind. Or a silent, festering thing. Angry glares and clipped words. The Master being disappointed in her.

Some part of her demanded that she stay her course. That she dominate all before her. That Chun Ke's words were the thoughts of a weakling and a coward.

But . . . he wasn't any of those things. He had nearly died in the defence of Fa Ram. He had withstood Chow Ji, and if the rat really had been Ri Zu's superior . . . he was not weak at all.

Tigu sighed and licked Chun Ke's nose. He chuffed, pleased at her gracing him.

↔

Ri Zu went through the form. It was painful, and tiring, but she kept at it, even as Bi De had to go back and do his duties. Master always said that one should put time into studying alone. Her form with her needle had been laughable. She could tell that Bi De did not wish to insult her, but he declared that they had to start anew.

She swung as he had taught her. Her needle flashed, yet it still didn't feel quite right—

'*Your foot is off. Correct backwards and to the right,*' Tigu stated without inflection. Ri Zu nearly jumped out of her skin at the interruption. She froze, staring out of the corner of her eye at the waiting cat.

She was alone with Tigu. She wanted to bolt, to run for another disciple, to flee, yet she held her body in place.

The cat said nothing else, merely observing.

For several minutes they just stared at each other. Tigu, for once in her life . . . did not look angry. She was staring with a neutral expression on her face.

Ri Zu took a deep breath, then moved her foot like Tigu had recommended. It felt slightly better.

The pattern continued, Tigu watching Ri Zu with a clinical eye as she went through the form. There were no snide remarks. No insults. Just bland, blunt instruction.

→

That night, they all sat together at the table. The atmosphere was tense while Ri Zu cooked for all of them—even the cat.

Ri Zu placed a cup of tea in front of Tigu. The cat eyed it . . . and, looking directly into her eyes, began to drink.

It was not true forgiveness. It was not reconciliation.

But the atmosphere at the table was slightly lighter.

Wa Shi, who had been lazing in the river earlier and clearly had *no* idea what was going on, stared at them, then shrugged. He pulled a fresh berry from the bottom of his trough and handed it to Chun Ke.

CHAPTER 20

KNOCK OFF

Xiulan woke up with the early-morning sun as she always did. Her eyes opened slowly, and she stared up at the ceiling as she came to full wakefulness, feeling surprisingly rested.

It was then she realised why she was feeling so good—she hadn't had any dreams last night.

Smiling, she got up from her bed and started about her day. It was still a strange contrast. In the Verdant Blade Sect, the mornings were completely silent as the members of the Sect performed their morning meditations. In the wetter months, the still and unmoving forms of the disciples were often covered in drops of dew, like the blades of grass they contemplated. It was only once the sun was well and truly risen that some activity began. It started slowly and gained energy throughout the day as the morning contemplations and cultivation completed. But it was nearly always quiet, so as to not disturb the meditations of others.

Here, there was no such silence. Multiple roosters would immediately begin shouting at the rising sun, and with the animals' harsh scolding, everyone rose from their beds. It was almost like the army camp she had been in. The men sounding their horns to wake their comrades, and the grumbling that followed. But here there was no breakdown of the tents, or marching orders being barked out.

She could almost imagine First Disciple Bi De in a soldier's helm, commanding his men to rise. It was an amusing and terrifying thought.

The men and women rose and started their daily toils. Xiulan let the soft voices and the sounds of a village waking up wash over her. The sounds of life. There was no more urgency, with the planting well and truly complete.

All Xiulan had known was the near-frantic energy of the spring season. Tilling the fields, planting the seeds, repairing the damage from winter—for a mortal, that took months of backbreaking labour. Now that the work was done, it was as if the village had breathed a collective sigh of relief.

Instead of going to work today, there were games brought out, or tools taken into the center of the village so that people could talk as they maintained their hoes and shovels.

She watched over them as she circulated her Qi. Not truly cultivating, just moving it around and making it do as she wished.

Her muscles were relaxed, if a bit sore, since Senior Sister had attended to her last night. The acupuncture and massaging had left her feeling refreshed, and the lack of dreams had left her energised.

A cup clinked down beside her, and the aroma of tea reached her nose. Senior Sister's father had surprisingly quiet footsteps.

"Thank you, for looking after my son," he whispered.

Gratitude. *Earned* gratitude, as humble as her task was, unlike the praises sung about her for "killing" Sun Ken.

She bowed her head in acknowledgement, then took a sip of tea. It was a surprisingly rich flavour, as good as any she had ever tasted, despite its humble origins. Its warmth settled into her belly.

"Thank you," she returned. He smiled at her and sat down beside her, nursing his own cup.

She turned her attention back to the village when the peace was interrupted.

"*Ca Wa Bun Ga!*" Senior Sister shouted. There was a *splat*, and then the village echoed with Master Jin's uproarious laughter and Senior Sister's giggling. Xiulan squinted down, near the outskirts of the village, where Master Jin was lying in his wife's arms in a mud pit and laughing too hard to move.

Had she picked him up and jumped in with him?

The Master of the village started laughing as well.

"That's how they started courting," Xian explained to her conspiratorially, a big smile on his face.

Senior Sister is . . . truly an existence who defies comprehension sometimes.

↔

I hummed happily as I took a bite of the cheese presented to me. It had an interesting flavour—strong and pungent, like a particularly powerful Gruyère. It was a shame we were to be leaving soon, but that wouldn't stop me from enjoying it. My wife was behind me and holding her nose, staring at me, baffled.

"How can you like that? It smells like death!" she whined.

Hu Li started laughing. "Your boy just has good taste!" she declared haughtily.

She was probably just glad somebody else liked the cheese. Most people seemed to really detest the smell, and a third of the village was lactose intolerant. Which was honestly less than it should be, considering that we were all "Chinese." Racking Rou's memories couldn't bring up any thoughts of milk, so I guess farther south, the lactose intolerance was higher.

Thankfully, I didn't seem to have that intolerance, and so it was full speed ahead. I had been having a massive craving, and I aimed to fill it.

Some people said you could make pizza without tomato sauce if you substituted in cream sauce.

These people were fucking heathens—but I had joined their ranks because of a damn craving . . . also, we didn't we didn't have any tomatoes.

Mozzarella wasn't too hard to make, even when you had to swap out some of the ingredients. I had made cheese in the Before . . . but that had used rennet tablets, or it had been in liquid form, made from the stomach of a calf.

I didn't know you could apparently get some kind of curdling agent from thistles, and I'm not talking about Meimei. Such a useful plant. In addition to the rennet, you also needed some vinegar to promote curding. Normally one would use citrus . . . but again, I was limited—there was no California-greenhouse-grown stuff, so right after winter there wasn't any citrus to be had.

All that to say, tonight we would be having knockoff cream sauce pizza. *Absolutely* heretical, but some of the sausage I'd had last night tasted a bit like pepperoni, and that had sparked a mighty need. *Come to me, my dear tomatoes! I need you!*

Hu Li was nice enough to start the curd for me. The only downside to having a thistle-based rennet was that it could take a while. Like . . . twelve hours, sometimes. Which was annoying, but serviceable.

"I'll have to buy some of this off you," I decided, as I finished the cheese—Meiling's face paled, while Hu Li's smile got brighter.

"*Please* don't eat any in the house," Meiling begged, staring at the cheese like it was the devil himself.

I suppose it might be; she was looking a little green. I pouted. *Damn it.* I really liked cheese. But if she hated the smell this much . . . Well, I wouldn't inflict it on her too often—but I was making pizza today, come hell or high water.

Hu Li handed me one of the pails of milk, frowning at it. "This isn't going to taste like anything at all," Hu Li complained. "This kind of thing is best with yak milk, not that we get it often. A bold flavour!"

I shrugged, while Meimei made overexaggerated gagging motions at the mention of yak milk.

"It tastes like what I need it to," I explained, as we headed to the bigger, communal kitchen.

And walked straight into a cartoon.

I knew that Xiulan had been helping Meiling more and more in the kitchen. My wife and Xiulan had been getting along really well, even more so than usual after we'd found her with Xian.

Xiulan was at the center of a storm. A knife chopped on its own, the pieces of mushroom—all perfectly equally sized—arcing high into the air and depositing themselves into a wok.

Other women seemed to swirl around her, depositing more things to chop on cutting boards, or just watching in awe. They seemed excited at this new and interesting thing, instead of fearful of the wizardry before them, giggling as Xiulan created a magical blender. Several heads of garlic were reduced to paste in moments. A cleaver rose up and started slicing through a large root, the kind that normally took several strikes to get through.

"Miss Lanlan!" a voice shouted, Ty An, I think her name was? She threw a batch of spring onion in the air towards a wok, and when Xiulan turned I finally saw her face, a mask of concentration. She was sweating, her hair held out of het face by a cloth.

A knife flew through the air, intercepting the onion and cutting it into pieces. I looked closer at the pieces. All of them were different sizes, showing that she still had a lot of room for improvement . . . but this was really cool.

All we needed was a musical accompaniment, and it wouldn't look out of place in an anime.

Using sword skills for cooking. I was always fond of the fantastical becoming mundane. And being able to telekinetically control knives was extremely useful.

Meiling cleared her throat loudly, and everyone froze. The knife nearly dropped, but she plucked it out of the air easily.

"Xiulan, thank you for all your help," Meiling said warmly, and the older woman nodded.

I couldn't see Meiling's face, but whatever her expression was, it made the rest of the women pale. I could almost see the "menacing" sound effect coming off her.

"The rest of you . . . back to work, and bother her no longer."

□

The pizza was . . . serviceable. It certainly wasn't the greatest, the mozza was too sour, and the cream sauce made it too rich. My disappointment was immeasurable, and my day was ruined, but that was what I got for trying to innovate.

Eh, not everything could be a winner. And this was *definitely* a loser.

It was a shot to the heart when one of the kids had taken one bite, then spat it out.

I was sitting on the roof of the shrine, looking out over the village while having another slice of my crappy pizza. The nights were just starting to get warm here, and the frogs were singing their little hearts out, eager to get busy.

Xiulan walked out from the forest, a sleeping Xian held in her arms. She handed him off to a waiting Meiling and took the one-handed hug she was pulled into with a smile.

Did they have godmothers here? Maybe, maybe not. But *Auntie Xiulan* had a nice ring to it, when we did eventually have kids.

I turned back to my pizza.

This is actually kind of nasty, now that it's cold.

I ate it anyway.

I was a little surprised when I heard the tapping of feet, letting me know that somebody else was on the roof with me.

Xiulan was looking nervous and taking obviously calming breaths, two cups of tea in her hands.

"Master Jin . . . can I talk to you?" she asked quietly.

→

We settled in with tea, and after a brief moment of silence, Xiulan began to speak.

It was then when I realised that I was probably in over my head, as she started talking about what had happened to her when she'd fought Sun Ken.

I wasn't very good at this. Well, is anyone? Probably Meimei, considering she'd gotten Xiulan to talk in the first place.

I had no real frame of reference for the things Xiulan was telling me.

I had lost people. In both lives. But I had never been a warrior. None of those losses could ever really be said to be my fault.

A farmer, and an orphan turned cultivator.

So all I could do was listen. It was my first time hearing it, despite her having talked at length to Meiling about her troubles. I had never listened in before, because you *just don't do* that. Whenever I got too curious, I'd start drawing something to distract myself. Which was probably a bad idea to draw on my earning reports, but it was a small price to pay, and they're still legible anyway.

Listening to the tale of Sun Ken from Xiulan was certainly much different than hearing about it from the people who "knew" what had happened. The news had spread into Verdant Hill during my last visit to it, and everybody had been talking about the "Demon-Slaying Orchid." There had even been a *puppet show*. Sun Ken there was an oafish buffoon who was slapped up and down the stage by the member of the Verdant Blade Sect, to laughter and sneers.

In the stories, the people Xiulan was talking about *didn't exist*. It was a band of ten cultivators. Or even sometimes it was merely Xiulan alone who had destroyed them.

Fathers and sons had given their lives to take him down. Entire villages had been obliterated as he fled from Xiulan's near army.

I could see how that could eat at somebody.

She didn't blame me. I don't really think it occurred to her to level any sort of accusation at me for making her take the fame. To her it was a *personal* weakness.

It didn't stop me from feeling a bit guilty. I had started to like Xiulan, especially these past few days. After Meimei had talked to her, she had mellowed out and finally seemed to relax. She was Meiling's friend. She was kind of my employee.

When her voice finally trailed off, she turned to me. She was calm . . . . but she looked like she was waiting for judgement.

It had hurt her. It had hurt her, and I was responsible, but . . . I don't think I regretted it.

"I do not regret giving you that sword," I told her, staring up at the stars. "What is done is done. It was better than keeping his death a secret. So many people celebrated it. So many people no longer fear the vile man. And I could think of worse people to have such fame than one who would not abuse it."

She lowered her head at my statement. It was true. Some grandstanding asshole would have taken advantage of it. Hell, I had expected her to take advantage of it.

Instead . . . Xiulan *cared*.

"What I *do* regret is how I treated you. To me . . . it was like you were a dog I was throwing a bone to. I gave you a treat to do my bidding. I thought of you like . . . others I knew. I assumed you would be happy with what I gave you and not care about the consequences. It was cruel, and you didn't deserve it. For *that*, I do apologise. You were a better person than I assumed you to be."

She blushed at the statement, fidgeting slightly, but otherwise remained quiet. I planted a hand on her shoulder, trying to be reassuring.

"Caring about other people isn't a weakness," I finally said. "It takes a certain kind of person to be able to bear that weight, instead of ignoring it. Never let anyone tell you that you aren't strong," I told her.

She smiled.

"People who cut that part out of themselves. People who step so easily on others . . . I hate it. It's part of the reason why I left my old Sect. If the path to the heavens requires one to discard such things . . . then that is not a path I want to tread."

She perked up at the mention of my past. Maybe not that whole story tonight. But I *would* tell her. I couldn't let my disciples see me as being a hypocrite, now could I? Better to let people in and be hurt, rather than never let anyone in at all.

"After all, the road you take to get there is just as important as the destination itself."

Maybe it was just a platitude.

Maybe they were empty words.

But at her considering gaze . . . it may have been the right thing to say.

She brought her hands up in the traditional gesture of respect.

"Thank you for your guidance, Master—"

This is going to either make her hate me . . . or make her more comfortable with me. Maybe this is a bit rude, after she poured her heart out.

I cut her off with a headlock, pulling her in to ruffle her hair. It might have been a bit much as her eyes bugged out at the sudden contact. It was half a hug, half a rebuke.

"Come on now, none of that. We're friends, right? It may be a little late, but you should just call me Jin," I told her as she froze.

She spluttered in shock.

"I—I could *never*, Master Jin!" she gasped out.

"I'm gonna make you say it eventually," I told her with all seriousness as I let her go. She seemed a bit off-kilter as I let her go, still shocked at the sudden contact.

"And this Cai Xiulan will never disrespect Master Jin!" she shot back, smoothing out her ruffled hair and glaring at me.

It was halfhearted at best.

She got up with great dignity, then walked to the edge of the roof before turning around and giving me the proper bow.

I rolled my eyes.

"Master Jin?"

"Yeah?"

"Thank you."

I waved her off, and she hopped down from the roof. The last of the tea was cold, but I stayed up for a little longer.

↔

Xiulan, her mind still churning with what Master Jin had told her, went to sleep.

After a night of dreamless sleep, the nightmare started once more.

She was in the valley again.

The stale air. The shock of the impacts. The sheer desperation she felt as she tried her hardest to save as many as she could.

The blood, the screams, the falling rocks.

The faces of dying men. She turned her gaze to the one responsible.

Sun Ken.

He gazed down upon her and drew his blade with a grin.

The duel began. The wraiths and shades of the damned that rose from the muck were scarlet and shrieking.

As if in a trance, her body moved. She repeated the steps of the nightmare like she always did. The steps that led to Sun Ken plunging his blade into her, into killing her as she finally woke.

But something was . . . different.

The wraiths grasped her and held her tight, surging out of the rising tide of blood.

The demon's grin twisted his face into a massive leer. He raised his blade high and prepared to end her.

He laughed at her. "Too weak. No wonder your men died."

Every time. Every time. She was alone. And then she died. She was weak, and so she perished—

Something slammed into her shin. It was a familiar feeling—a little foot, full of so much force. It changed her stance, breaking the hold of the arms around her legs.

It forced her leg into a position that was so, so familiar but had not been a part of this story.

The spell broke. The spell that forced her to die, again and again.

She dodged the descending blade on instinct.

It seemed that both of them were shocked. Sun Ken stared at his blade, dumbfounded that it was not embedded in her chest.

Was he larger than normal? His visage was twisted in a way that she had never seen before. His muscles bulged, and his blade twisted and warped where it was embedded in the ground.

Memories flashed in front of Xiulan's eyes.

"Caring is not a weakness," Senior Sister declared.

"After all, the road you take to get there is just as important as the destination itself," Master Jin whispered.

Tigu, pulling her strikes, and telling Xiulan to get some sleep.

Bi De, his eyes full of concern as he tried his best to teach her.

A little spirit glared at her, and kicked her legs back into position. Slowly, the spirit raised her hands and clapped them together, like she was praying.

Xiulan's hands moved of her own accord. Like the spirit, she clapped her hands together. It was the start to a ceremony. The start to a dance, long since forgotten.

Xiulan's swords split and rose, a raiment that surrounded her more like an actor's panoply than a warrior's blades.

An ancient drum thundered in the back of her head, signaling the start of the final act.

The demon that was Sun Ken roared with fury. His blade, as large as a house, tore free from the ground. A ravening blast of Qi shot towards her.

Xiulan wasn't there. It felt almost effortless as she spun on one foot, moving out of the way in a single, graceful movement.

The demon screamed and threw himself forwards.

His strikes were faster. They were more powerful, as the valley started to crack and break. Like it was starting to *disintegrate*.

"All your fault! All your fault!" the demon howled as it bore down on her. His face twisted and warped. It turned from Sun Ken to Hi Shin, to Ming Po—it started flashing to every face she remembered. Every person she had failed.

But despite his ferocity, despite his wrath . . .

The blade was so easy to dodge.

Her feet moved to the sound of invisible drums as she pulled the demon into her new path. Into her new way. His blade might as well have not been there, as she slid around every blow, following a new, thundering rhythm.

Sun Ken twisted and warped, changing more and more into a demon as more and more of the valley sloughed away.

No matter its rhythm, no matter how the mad, whirling strikes changed . . . they never came any closer to hitting the dancer.

He roared and he raged. He broke and he shattered, striking the ground and tearing it up like he was actually doing damage.

He didn't see the grass growing in his wake.

With a mighty roar, he swung his blade, red and black energy screaming off it.

It was almost anticlimactic as she stepped forwards and plunged her blade into the demon's heart.

The thing's smile of hate abruptly froze on its face. It seemed confused. Black and corrupted blood spilled from its wound like a river, pouring out onto the earth. Hands, skeletons, faces tried to rise from the muck, but wherever the blood landed, grass grew in brilliant green.

The demonic visage twisted one last time. It twisted into one last person. Xiulan stared at her own face. Black tears ran out of red eyes, her face twisted in pain and terror.

In the end, the true form of this demon wasn't Sun Ken.

Xiulan remembered. All the times she had died on this field. All the times she had doubted herself. All the pain and terror this field held for her.

"You . . . you can't do this. You failed them. *You're weak*," her own voice gasped. It sounded so confused.

"I did fail them," Xiulan whispered. "If I had been stronger, none of you would have died. If I had been better, I might have been able to save you all. But . . ."

Xiulan closed her eyes for a moment before opening them to the demon. "But I am not weak. I refuse to believe that caring about those mortals was a mistake. I refuse to believe that sacrificing the weak and the innocent is something to strive towards."

She gazed back, unflinching, at the demon.

"You—you!" the demon screamed, swelling one last time.

The demonic visage that had haunted her dreams for months tried to rise, tried to grasp her and pull her down with it.

A Jade Grass Blade sang through the air and relieved the demon of his head.

The valley broke completely, dissipating into motes of light.

From the light came Master Jin's farm. She turned at the sound of thudding feet.

There, before her, was the Earth Spirit, riding a massive boar. Both were laced with gold. They glowed with power and majesty as they beheld her, trotting over to the corpse of Sun Ken. With a single, mighty stomp, his body was pressed into the ruined earth.

And the boar, who looked so much like Chun Ke, nuzzled her side affectionately.

Xiulan looked around at the farm. At the rapidly disappearing remains of Sun Ken. And at the lightness in her soul.

Xiulan went to bow, to kowtow, to express her utmost gratitude to the spirit of the earth—

A particularly muddy ball of dirt slapped into her face. She staggered backwards from the blow.

The Earth Spirit, missing an arm, pointed and laughed at her.

Xiulan, with great dignity, wiped the mud off her face and bent down, as to give a bow anyway.

The Earth Spirit fell off her pig when Xiulan's own strike, filled with bits of grass, impacted her head.

The little Earth Spirit rose with a grin, her head covered in muck.

It was not a nice grin, as the very earth began to heave.

Xiulan considered that she might have made a mistake . . . and then forged onwards anyway.

↔

"See you later, brother," Yun Ren said to me as we clasped forearms. "Come see me off before I leave, yeah?"

"Count on it. We'll have a party before you travel up north," I replied.

"Sure I can't convince you to part ways with your recording crystal, at least for a little?" he asked hopefully.

I'll admit, it was a bit tempting to see the north . . . but I had stuff I wanted to record too. And I was a little leery about handing out that much money to somebody. Yun Ren would probably rather die than have the crystal break, but I didn't want to risk it. My wedding photos were on there!

"Sorry, man," I told him, and he nodded, shrugging. He obviously hadn't actually expected me to agree.

I stepped back from Yun Ren and looked around the village. Pops was hugging Meimei, but there wasn't any worry or tears this time. They knew they would see each other again soon.

I never did end up getting a story about Meiling's mom from Pops. I still just wanted to hang out and do nothing with my friends, after the long time I had spent working.

But duty called, and I couldn't just leave my farm to the animals indefinitely. No matter how much being a lazy, procrastinating shit called to me.

We'd visit next month, for the trip to Verdant Hill. But other than that, we said our goodbyes and our see-you-laters and started off back down the road.

"It will be good to be home," Meiling said as the Xong brothers hugged each other. Xiulan got one last flower crown from little Liu and a stalk of spectacularly green grass from Xian.

She was very perky today as we began our run, a big grin plastered firmly on her face.

Our pace was brisk as we set off back home. The ground disappeared under our feet.

Honestly, it even seemed faster than normal. Like something was almost pulling us along.

There weren't any potholes, because of my own and Chunky's efforts, just sloped and hard-packed dirt that I'd be turning into a *real* road soon enough.

I still think we got home at least an hour earlier than last time, though. It normally took us at least four hours to run to Hong Yaowu at cultivator speed.

We found a sight that would never get old. Everybody, even the cows and sheep, were waiting at the gate.

We exchanged our customary bow, and Big D hopped up onto my shoulder.

There wasn't much to do. Everything had been taken care of. The house was clean and fresh.

They had even changed the sheets *somehow*. And somebody had put some fresh flower sprigs in a heart shape on our bed, the cheeky shits.

At least Meiling found it funny.

Funny enough to make another round of her energy drinks.

We turned in early that night, even though I don't think any of us were tired. Gou Ren went off with Peppa and Chunky to what was now his house, and Xiulan went off with Tigger and Big D.

And Meimei and I *caught up.*

Hey. It was awkward doing that kind of thing when her brother could walk in at any moment.

↔

Wa Shi, the dragon, the great carp, the Master of the river, frowned at the half-opened jar in his domain. The Boss and his woman had drunk from it earlier, and now they were making the house shake again.

Whatever it was, it smelled delectable. Curious, he leapt out of the river and flopped towards the open container.

He dipped his whiskers into the concoction, and after a moment of consideration he pulled one out and sampled a drop.

The carp smacked his lips. Not bad! There wasn't much left of it, so with a shrug, he tipped the container and did his duty of washing the dishes.

They had left it there. If they hadn't wanted it eaten, they would have been more careful with it!

The fish flopped back into the river, a smile on his face. He was ready to go to sleep, when suddenly, his pupils dilated.

His body twitched.

Ohwowthisisamazing—

Wa Shi ricocheted off three different walls before he burst out of the river room and thundered down the river.

□

I was in a good mood as I descended the stairs and got ready for breakfast that morning. As I opened the jar of preserves, I absently threw a piece into the river for Washy.

I paused when I didn't hear the expected splash of the carp catching the morsel out of the air. He had a sixth sense for whenever anybody entered the kitchen, always ready to do his dishwashing duty.

"Hey, Washy?" I asked as I turned to the river . . . but he was nowhere to be found.

I was a little bit worried. He hadn't missed a day cleaning si— Suddenly I spotted the empty, pristine jar Meimei had kept one of her energy drinks in.

The jar that had still been about a quarter full.

That . . . *probably* wasn't good.

"Hey . . . has anybody seen Washy?" I asked as I reentered the living room, carrying the piece of evidence.

"Yes. He was headed along the river at speed, and I do not believe he had any plans on stopping," Xiulan replied.

And that was how we all ended up searching for a fish cracked out of his mind on an energy drink. I was a bit worried that we couldn't find him . . . but I couldn't shake the feeling that he was all right.

The day ended without any sign of him, so we all just settled in to wait and see if he would come back. Hopefully, he would be fine.

CHAPTER 21

LOST AS HELL

Wa Shi didn't know where in the hells he was. Everything had gotten a bit hazy after he drank that tasty treat. It sure put some pep in his tail, whatever it was! His jumps had reached new heights. He thought for a moment that he could even reach the moon! He longed to taste it. The Boss had once said that it was made out of *cheese*. He had never tasted *cheese* before, but the Boss had talked about it longingly, so it *must* taste good. Everything the Boss gave as tribute to him, for guarding his pantry against interlopers other than himself, was very, very tasty.

Would it be hard and crunchy? Soft and smooth? He couldn't wait to have a bite.

He was in some sort of cavern, deep underground. The light was dim, but he could feel just fine, thanks to his whiskers. Nothing underwater could hide from this daddy—or his mouth! He was truly at the apex of the world in the water! All should bow down to his might!

This cavern was dark and rocky, but the water was fresh and clear. No real life here. *Blech.* No little tasty bits in the water, nor plants to nibble on if he got hungry.

He swam forwards confidently. Anything that was around him would surely quake in terror at his magnificence. If they were tasty, they would be eaten. If they were not tasty, they could live. Such was the way of the world.

There was a pulse through the water. Wa Shi shot immediately down to the floor, burying himself in the muck with only his whiskers out to sense for danger. They twitched, searching for movement, for predators that would eat him.

There was nothing.

He hoped nobody had seen what just happened. Curse his instincts! They served him well, but sometimes they caused embarrassing things to occur. With no incentive to be brave, he would rather run and live to see another day. There was no food here, and there were still many tasty treats to try!

Now he just had to find his way out of here. He rose from the muck but did not bother to shake himself off. He still might need to hide—that is, *tactically retreat*—in the future.

His whiskers twitched.

He picked a direction and started swimming, slowly, in case there was anything in the water.

He flinched as he felt the pulse again. He steeled himself against the feeling of pressure and the unknown.

He turned around, heading in the exact *opposite* direction he felt the pulse come from. Obviously whatever was making the water move like this was in this direction. He would bravely confront it!

But the cave was confusing, even for his impeccable senses. There seemed to be no way out in this direction. He meandered along the walls and through the muck. The pulse happened again, from the same location. He grimaced. He . . . supposed he would have to go towards it. He advanced cautiously, nay *prudently*, towards where the pulse was.

This path led out of the little cave and into a forested-over marsh. This part *did* taste good. He drank a little of its plants on the surface of the water.

Delicious.

There was another pulse, and his head whipped around to find the source.

It was a large turtle, his shell covered in moss and other plants, asleep on a small island of raised ground. There was a peach tree upon the island, in full bloom. Astoundingly, even though it was blossoming, it had fruit upon it.

The turtle snored. A pulse hit.

This . . . this bastard! He dared scare—*inconvenience* the Great Wa Shi? He courted death! There would be turtle soup in his future! His bones would be broth, and his shell a fine, decorative bowl!

He glared at the turtle. He glared some more, trying to see how he would defeat it. His superb senses probed the adamantine shell, the scaly hide . . . and then onto the beak that could swallow him whole.

He huffed. His opponent was clearly skilled; he had no openings, even when he was asleep! As Wa Shi was not certain of victory, he would allow the turtle to live another day, since he was a magnanimous and kind dragon.

Instead, he looked around the place some more. His eyes wandered around the garden, the plants in full bloom, yet also with many fruits. How strange.

They did smell very good, though . . .

He grinned, a devious idea forming. Instead of defeating the turtle, he would spend his time on more productive things. Like ransacking the turtle's garden.

He crept up first to some of the berry bushes, then sampled them. These also tasted good. Spectacularly sweet. He moved on to the next one.

And the next one, and the next after that, eagerly taking his tribute. He idly wished he could take larger bites like Pi Pa, the saucy wench, but she had confessed that the more she used the ability, the less she tasted, which was *completely* unacceptable. Food was to be savoured.

He stripped blossoms, supped upon berries, and even leapt out of the water to catch some of the insects flying around. Through it all, the turtle continued to sleep.

Wa Shi's eyes once more alighted on the plump peaches, practically dripping with juice. He approached with great stealth, for Wa Shi excelled at all tasks he put his mind to. Not that he used his wonderful sneakiness to hide from the retaliation of Pi Pa or the others when he stole some of their food. No, he was merely excellent at this skill through pure chance.

He pulled himself with his fins, a silent, hidden expert. Once on land, he calculated the distance using some of the Boss's math formations. If he placed his fin here, and used this much force, then the arc should—

He flipped through the air as if he were born to be there. Like he had already mastered flight. Like the dragon he was!

He landed gently upon the branches and began to eat his fill. He gorged himself on the sweet fruit. Ha! This was truly just revenge for the turtle daring to have such treasures, while being unable to guard them!

He ate happily, yet his chewing slowed. There was something . . . off.

He realised the truth: there had been no pulse or snore from the turtle for the last couple of seconds.

Wa Shi froze, his gaze turning to the turtle, who was staring at him with sleepy eyes. Wa Shi finished his peach and spat out the pit.

The turtle's eye tracked the pit as it plopped into the water, then rose again to look at Wa Shi.

Wa Shi grabbed another peach and started chewing faster. The turtle raised an eyebrow.

"Oh, by all means, little dragon, eat your fill," the turtle rumbled, *actually speaking* while looking amused.

Wa Shi's eyes widened. The turtle had called him a dragon! He would be spared the soup pot, for showing Wa Shi such respect!

"Hmmmm. It has been a while since I last had a visitor. Many, many years," the turtle mused. "How did you reach this place?"

Wa Shi shrugged.

"Oh? A chance encounter? Then you are doubly blessed." The turtle hummed. "Pass me down a peach, little one. This one is hungry after his long sleep."

Wa Shi slapped the turtle a peach with his tail.

They ate together, Wa Shi in the tree and the turtle on the ground.

"What be your purpose, little dragon, your goal in life?"

Wa Shi snapped a bug out of the air.

"To laze and eat?" The turtle laughed. "Oh, not to defy the heavens?"

He would defy the heavens when he found out what the moon tasted like.

The turtle chuckled again. "You don't think small, do you, little dragon. But the whole moon? Such a thing is folly."

Wa Shi scoffed. Why would he eat the whole moon? He just wanted a taste. What kind of idiot would eat everything now and not leave some treats for later?

The turtle seemed very surprised.

"You have some wisdom already, little dragon. This one apologises for underestimating you."

Wa Shi slapped the turtle another peach.

The turtle pondered a moment.

"Well, then, I would have something for you, if you would listen to this old turtle."

The water in the lake churned as the turtle took a breath. It rose into the air, a hundred tiny rivers writhing through the heavens and sparkling with light.

"What would you do with such skill, little dragon?" the turtle asked.

Wa Shi slapped his fins against the tree excitedly. He would unscrew the jars without breaking them. He would pluck fruit from the trees without having to jump from the water. He would float through the air upon streamers of power!

Oh, and he supposed he would water the crops too. Those needed to grow, so that the Boss could offer him tribute for being such a selfless guardian.

The turtle smiled.

"Ohohohohoho. Your 'Boss' sounds like an interesting one. You have good thoughts, little dragon. Come, let us meditate upon the nature of water together."

CHAPTER 22

THE SEARCH

It was a beautiful day in the mortal realm. The sun was bright and warm, the air was fresh, and there was a slight breeze through the valley's teashop.

Senior Disciple Lu Ri took a sip of his tea. It was a disappointing brew, watery and weak. The water was too hot. The tea, steeped for slightly too long. It was something a mortal would not be able to taste, but his sensitive tongue detected every imperfection.

Distasteful. But pertaining to the rules of the Cloudy Sword Sect, a disciple, especially a Senior Disciple, must give face and compensate mortals fairly for services rendered.

He was receiving information from the establishment's owner, so purchasing some tea was only polite. The biscuits, at least, were palatable.

"These are acceptable," he complimented the master of the establishment. Quite good for a mortal's hands, he would even declare.

The nervous, corpulent man perked up at the words. "I can get you more if you like, Master Cultivator," he said swiftly.

Lu Ri considered the offer.

"Do you have any other kinds?" he asked.

"Yes, Master Cultivator. I shall bring you one of each!" The man departed.

Lu Ri took a moment to reflect upon his quest.

He should not be too hard to find, he had declared.

The heavens made a mockery of mere men's plans, it seemed. For indeed, how hard could Jin Rou be to find?

The answer was, evidently, hard enough.

It had been ten years since he last *truly* descended into the mortal world, so he'd decided he would combine the journey with the other various chores that the Sect required to be done, which had been put off because of lack of importance. He would find Jin Rou, deliver the letter, complete the other tasks, and be back in the Sect within the month.

He was back in the Sect within the month, but not because he had found the wayward ex-disciple.

Jin Rou had presented his papers at the western gate of Crimson Crucible City, then left in that direction. It was standard procedure in the city that every man and woman leaving was signed in and signed out, though this produced an enormous amount of paperwork. At least he knew the date of Jin Rou's passage within three days, so he only had to search thirty-two scrolls for the name, until he found it. He assumed that Jin Rou would wish to stay near to the city of his birth, since the unambitious naturally stayed near familiar grounds.

So Lu Ri had, naturally, travelled in that direction as well, checking in at the various mortal villages along the path.

And just as naturally, he didn't find the man. In fact, after leaving through the western gate, Jin Rou seemed to disappear. Or at least near immediately stop travelling west along the main roads. A befuddling set of circumstances.

So Lu Ri had to change priorities—he went to do the chores instead. They were mostly picking up minor implements for the Sect, like roof tiles. In doing so, he found that three of the men who once made them for the Sect had died. One had kept faith, continuously making what the Sect had requested, despite never coming to collect, and his son showed Lu Ri the warehouse. Lu Ri paid the half of the fee that was outstanding, and then paid the fees incurred for the storage of the work. Such diligence should, as always, be rewarded.

The second had sold them all before his death, and the son had no knowledge of the contract his father had signed. For this, Lu Ri struck his name from the Cloudy Sword Sect's records, then handed him an itemized receipt for what the Cloudy Sword Sect was owed. They had paid half upon the start of the project, after all.

Of the third, the only thing that remained of his passing was a funerary tablet. His warehouse had been ransacked, and his family had long since left the city.

They really should not neglect such things for so long.

With this sudden cold trail, Lu Ri was stumped. So he'd returned to the city and pored over the records, searching for any extenuating circumstances. Spirit Beast attacks, road closures, and the like.

There, he'd found his answer. Jin Rou had left through the western gate—but there had been a landslide that had completely closed the northern road. Jin Rou could have intended to go north. Up towards the Howling Fang Mountains, Green Stone Forest, or even Yellow Rock Plateau. All were places that a cultivator from the Cloudy Sword Sect would find great success in.

Furthering his search, Lu Ri found another road. The vertical nature of Raging Waterfall Gorge meant that sometimes roads could overlap. There was a small tributary of the North Road that, for a cultivator, was rather easy to climb up to and would have avoided the landslide.

There was another, smaller road that was accessed from the western gate; it cut north quite quickly and had been spared the worst of the landslide.

Lu Ri had set out again, travelling along this road. And this time, he found a trace of the man in a small noodle shack.

"Oh, aye, he wuz behind the counter as soon as those little bastards started throwin' hands, yanno? Wuz quite the shock to have such a big lad takin' shelter with us, but I'm not gonna begrudge him that. Noice and polite about it too. We wuz scrunched up, all cozy like, and he grabbed a splinter outta the air that woulda split me son in two! Helped clean up most of the mess when they were done. Good lad, freckle boy. Looked like he wuz runnin' from demons, though. Up along this route over yonder."

Finally, Lu Ri had a lead.

So, he continued his search. The accounts were few and far between. Picking up a cart and running, with the family still inside, from a rampaging Earth-Crushing Devil Serpent. Removing a tree from the road. Dodging around fights and running away from them.

And constantly moving like there was something nipping at his heels. Constantly looking scared, or even downright *paranoid*.

And always, *always* heading north.

The Howling Fang Mountains was looking more and more like Lu Ri's destination. That was the most likely answer; Jin Rou would be better valued there. While the Fifth Stage of the Initiate's Realm was a middling power for that area, he could grow the Lowly Spiritual Herbs, and thus could grow anything these lesser provinces could produce. He would be highly sought after as a Spirit Herb farmer.

The Master of the establishment appeared before Lu Ri with another plate of confections.

"So, headed for Plunging River Pass?" he asked the fat, nervous man.

"I assure you, Master Cultivator, that is the most likely route," the master of the establishment said with a cringing bow. "It is not the main route towards the Howling Fang Mountains, but the Plunging Sky Fist Sect is known for their benevolence and maintenance of the road, so it is a common enough detour. Especially if the main road gets too crowded because of the Grading Fist Tournament."

"I see. This Senior Disciple of the Cloudy Sword Sect thanks you for your time, sir," Lu Ri intoned. "I shall finish my tea, and then depart."

The man wrung his hands. "And ah . . . the . . . *problem?*"

Lu Ri turned, glancing beside him at the ten men in a pile, all twitching and groaning with pain.

"They shall not bother you further, lest they wish for the wrath of the heavens to descend upon them. So swears this member of the Cloudy Sword Sect."

The brigands all froze at the declaration, before near unanimously turning a sickly shade of white. The man on top of the pile flung himself down to begin kowtowing . . . as did the rest.

"We hear and obey, Expert of the Cloudy Sword Sect! This one swears on his ancestors, we shall not darken your sight, nor shall you hear even a whisper of our presence on the wind!"

Well, that was taken care of.

He paid the man, then went on his way.

As he walked north, he took another bite of the confection. The taste was growing on him. Perhaps he might return in a few years.

□

It was in the Howling Fang Mountains that he lost the trail again. It did not continue north. He travelled and asked around for nearly a month, until the heavens finally graced him.

"Yeah I saw him. Big guy?" the caravan master asked with a frown. "We split off. He went west, nearly as soon as he entered the province."

"Towards the Azure Hills?" Lu Ri asked as he sampled some of the jerky they were selling.

"Yes, Master Cultivator. It seemed that way. Poor boy looked tired, but also pretty happy as soon as he started headin' that direction."

Who under heaven would ever *willingly* go to the Azure Hills?

He was nearly in the Azure Hills when his transmission stone vibrated, summoning him to return to the Sect.

The Senior Disciple's eye twitched, but one did not disregard a summons from an Elder.

□

Elder Ge, Lu Ri's direct superior, was deep in contemplation as he explained himself. The Elder had just returned from a short expedition to the southlands in order to gather resources.

Now he was familiarizing himself with what he had missed. Lu Ri's mission and expenses had caught his eye, so he had been summoned to explain himself.

"Yes, Elder Ge. Pertaining to the sections on Honourable Departure, we are required to send him his mail."

"Hmm. It has been a while since any have used that provision." He sighed. "Very well, you may continue. For what reason did this ex-disciple leave the Sect?"

Lu Ri answered, "He was beaten severely, to nearly the point of death by one of the Inner Disciples, and decided that this path was not for him."

The Elder frowned heavily. "The fire of the youth is raging unchecked. It is one thing to trade pointers, but another entirely to beat one of your comrades so. I shall rectify this."

The Elder turned back to his task, a clear dismissal, so Lu Ri began to leave.

"What is this ex-disciple's name?" the Elder asked, as Lu Ri reached the door. It sounded like idle curiosity.

"Jin Rou."

The Elder froze, his face going red.

"*Jin Rou?*" he asked, as if he had misheard. Like he *hoped* he had misheard. "Tall, freckles, hardworking lad?" he asked as if he were quoting someone.

"Yes, Elder. That sounds like Jin Rou."

A bit of blood leaked out of the corner of Elder Ge's mouth.

Ah, Lu Ri thought. *That cannot be good.*

CHAPTER 23

SET OUT, STAY IN

When he was but a mere Outer Sect Disciple, Lu Ri had made a decision that benefited him greatly. He'd been deeply immersed in one of the Honoured Founders' writings, specifically upon etiquette and composure, when he had witnessed one of his Senior Sisters spear another disciple with a mere glance. He froze and recoiled, and even far away from the impact, he felt it. The Intent. He had heard of it before but had never experienced it for himself. He, who wished to join the ranks of the Senior Disciples and was so enamoured with the sublime Honoured Founders' writings, had been overjoyed! He'd found a Senior Disciple who could aid him in his practice!

So he, as a gentleman did, requested a private audience and explained himself to his superior. She must have been terrifyingly strong to have that effect, and he wished to experience it for himself, so he could comport himself properly in all situations and not shame the Cloudy Sword Sect.

The woman, who had started off bored and cold, had gradually become amused at his actions.

The kind Senior Sister had agreed. The first time he experienced Intent, he'd nearly soiled himself. The pressure, the feelings of helplessness . . . it was all nearly too much.

As soon as it had come, it lifted, and with a raised, delicate brow, the Senior Sister had asked if he still wished to learn. At his affirmative, she had giggled demurely, then sent him on his way.

The next day, he discovered that he was assigned as her personal attendant, and there was a nasty rumour going around that he had somehow shamed the popular Senior Sister.

Having a pack of female disciples trying to murder you with their eyes at every waking moment, combined with the Senior Sister's own random bouts of Intent, had been hell.

But by the end of that month, he could compose himself and smile in the face of death. Senior Sister Yeo Na had even gifted him a scroll on etiquette, if only for the amusement he had granted her.

The difference between that lesson and the Intent of an Elder was the difference between the heavens and the earth, but he was a Senior Disciple now, and a Senior Disciple was composed under all circumstances.

Even when an Elder had their full and undivided attention upon them.

"Thus, I returned his money. It would not do to add insult to injury, and the amount was, relatively speaking, worthless to the Sect," Lu Ri said, explaining the final detail of his last meeting in full, and as demanded. "He seemed to leave with no regrets, thanked me, and went upon his way."

The stormy visage of Elder Ge persisted as sweat gathered on Lu Ri's back. Finally, the Elder moved, drawing out a pipe. He took a few puffs and sighed.

"Not ideal . . . but superior to what I feared. You have done well, Senior Disciple, and I commend you," he finally declared, glaring off into the distance.

Lu Ri ignored the burning need to say the question he felt needed to be asked.

"Speak," Elder Ge demanded, sensing Lu Ri's disquiet.

"If he was important, why were we not informed?" Lu Ri asked. Elder Ge studied him, taking his measure.

"A question that should be answered, should it not?" Elder Ge mused, then turned his attention to Lu Ri once more. "Because a certain man has certain views on how one should be trained. *He* thinks the boy a copy of himself, to be forged as he was," the Elder explained to him. Lu Ri didn't know who "he" was, but stayed silent. The name had obviously been omitted by choice.

Elder Ge puffed his pipe a few more times, frowning. "He did not want his project noticed. A minor existence, while he was not around to directly supervise."

Lu Ri nodded at the logic. Refuge in anonymity was a powerful tool . . . unless something like this happened.

"With the aid of the heavens, we may still salvage this situation." The Elder straightened, his eyes fierce.

"Senior Disciple Lu Ri. You have started upon this mission, and now, I will have you continue it. I command you to find Jin Rou, as your last dealing with him ended on good terms. Use whatever resources you deem necessary, but I would like for this mission to be . . . *discreet.*"

His command was issued, and the bare beginnings of the Raging Cloudy Sword Formation appeared, filling the room with its sublime intent.

"As you command, this Lu Ri obeys, Elder Ge." Lu Ri bowed obediently. "Am I to retrieve him?"

The Elder considered the question. "If you can, but do not force the issue. We are to be . . . *courteous* in this matter."

Lu Ri saluted his Elder. An existence that required the Cloudy Sword Sect to step lightly was worrying.

"I shall not return until I have found him, Elder Ge," Lu Ri declared, and the Elder nodded at the resolve.

"Excellent. Prepare well, Lu Ri, and find Jin Rou." The command was thick with Qi.

Lu Ri saluted once more and turned to leave, his mind already racing with what he would need. Jin Rou was likely out of the Azure Hills already. He most likely made a detour and then continued on his way, but Lu Ri would leave no stone unturned.

He paused at the darkness that he was walking into and looked up. It could not be evening yet—

There were clouds above the mountain. This area of the Sect should be higher than all of them, yet there they were. Black, roiling storm clouds covered the entire Sect. They were ominous in their silence, hanging like a sword above a man's neck.

Lu Ri swallowed, his composure breaking briefly. The Raging Cloudy Sword Formation. More specifically, Elder Ge's variation: the Black Clouds of the Silent Sky.

Lu Ri ducked his head.

This time, he carefully *didn't* think that Jin Rou would be easy to find.

↔

I sneezed as I finished putting up the last of the posts. I waited for a second, but a second sneeze failed to materialise. One thing I didn't miss from the Before was hay fever. Previously, I'd be sneezing all the time and be spewing snot everywhere, but right now my sinuses were blessedly clear.

Yay, cultivation!

There was still work to be done, of course; there always was. I was putting up the outer walls for Meimei's medicine hut right now. But the days had started to get a *little* lazy. Sitting down on the veranda that overlooked the stream, playing my instrument while Meimei started up working on her clothes, was just something absolutely blissful.

There was only one thing that could make it better: a rocking chair. Or one of those swings drilled into the ceiling.

I thought I would go with both. One didn't need to cuddle up *all* the time, no matter how much I wanted to.

We'd also need to start up the lessons again for the animals. There was just so much stuff for them to learn! We had slacked during the wedding and the planting, and we had time now. It was still weird being a teacher.

I had even asked Meimei to do more formal lessons on medicine, just so that I would feel less awkward. Learning together, instead of me just standing at the front lecturing all the time.

I stood up and stretched, looking out over my farm. Meimei tended to the herb garden with Rizzo and Peppa. Xiulan sat near my seasonings, imbuing them with Qi. Gou Ren weeded the rice paddies with Chunky. Tigger was working on a project I had set her to, some relief carvings for Meimei's medicine house, and those were looking nearly photorealistic. The thistles were a nice touch.

Big D was drawing something, staring at whatever he had made with a critical eye. It looked a bit like some kind of alchemy circle, or some kind of formation. I idly wondered what it was. It could just be a drawing, though, considering how incomplete it looked.

Xiulan got up from her chores and stretched, going over to Meimei to see if she needed any help. My wife waved her off, and so instead Xiulan went off to the side, starting to practise that dance of hers again with a small smile on her face.

Big D seemed to take this as a cue and ascended to the fence posts after packing up his drawing, starting his hops and his kicks. Like he was on those cliché kung fu movie poles, the ones that you did balance training on.

I wonder if I should set a few up, if only as a joke. Can't have a kung fu story without 'em. And didn't Xiulan have that tournament coming up?

Well, they were worth a thought. Even if only I found them funny. I could always take them down after.

A nice, warm breeze flowed around me. Green grass. The blossoms on the trees. The people who were around me.

Man, I never wanted to leave.

CHAPTER 24

A PAST CONVERSATION

Several years ago, Xiao Ge, Elder of the Cloudy Sword Sect, had attended a meeting.

There was a certain mountaintop near the Cloudy Sword Sect. A locus of power, and a meeting place.

Every twelve years, a certain set of sworn brothers met here, high above the earth in a place that would kill a mortal from mere exposure.

Forms shimmered into existence.

Xiao Ge was one, his projection shimmering into existence on the mountaintop. It was rough around the edges, because of the distance. It seemed he had arrived early. He concentrated, smoothing out the edges in his projection and making everything as crisp and clean as possible. Like it was himself standing there, instead of a mere ghost of his Qi.

Next to arrive was Brother Ran. The space was empty one instant, then filled the next, with his fellow Elder stretching his astral body and smiling at Xiao Ge.

They waited a while together after exchanging greetings.

"Is this it?" Elder Ge asked. "Our numbers dwindle every year."

Ran shook his head. "I can guarantee one more. The rest . . . Closed Door Cultivation or dead."

Elder Ge sighed. Really, so deeply in cultivation they couldn't even spare a moment for their meeting? How rude.

A final form snapped and crackled, bursting into existence.

Shen Yu formed out of the aether, a massive grin on his face.

It was an odd and terrifying sight on a man whose face was normally a mask of serenity or stern judgement.

"Brothers!" he boomed fondly. There was a spark. There was excitement. It had been a very long time since Ge had last seen Shen Yu so lively.

"See? The bastard was in Crimson Crucible City for years, and only now came to visit me!" Ran complained, and Shen Yu laughed again.

"I found something much more interesting than you!" he shot back.

"Another woman?" Ge asked, rolling his eyes.

"No, a grandson!" he shouted, like a man beholding his firstborn.

"A grandson?" Ge asked, surprised. "I thought . . ." He trailed off. Shen Yu was still sensitive about what had happened to his trueborn heir. Or rather, what had happened with. Last he heard, those sections of the Empire were still in shambles.

Shen Yu scoffed. "I have kept to my oath and sired no more children. Though if I did not know better, I would say this one is of my blood! Ah, my friends, it is like looking into the past," he declared. "I can see only a reflection of myself! He even *shovelled* the way I once did. The twist of his hips, so you can get a bit more distance to the cart!"

He was clearly thinking of a time that he disliked immensely and rarely spoke of to all but his closest confidants. Shen Yu was a Master Cultivator, a true expert. Shen Yu was not an orphan street rat.

He was giddy. Shen Yu, *giddy*.

"So you have an apprentice?" Ge asked again, interested.

"Indeed. His drive—the way he constructs his foundation—" He cut himself off with a wide, wild grin.

"Ah, so we have another monster to look forward to seeing, then." Ran sighed. "What have you given the boy? I know you have a dozen scriptures, as well as resources that would put some Sects to shame."

Shen Yu looked insulted that Ran was asking. "Nothing," he said bluntly. "A man's foundation should be pure. He is constructing himself. So he must use himself as a base."

Ge and Ran both nodded their heads, unwilling to argue. Shen Yu was living proof of this philosophy, after all.

"When he does receive resources, it will be through his own hand and work. Anything else would spoil his potential!" he declared.

"So you'll be in Crimson Crucible City for a while, then?" Ran asked.

"We'll see. If he needs to move, I shall move him. But he needs guidance right now. Something to keep him *hungry*, and on the right path."

Ge nodded. He could see some benefits. Ambition and drive might be spoiled by coddling . . . but in most cases the increased resources served men better. Though after the last disaster, he supposed Shen Yu would go back to his roots.

"Your teaching has too much of the fist. Even metal could shatter, if too much force is applied," Ran warned.

Shen Yu nodded. "I am watching carefully for that limit. For now, the petty insults just drive him to greater heights. The knowledge that he is still weak just makes him work harder, his eyes so pure and full of intent."

His smile was fierce and proud as he said that. Absolutely convinced that this was the right way.

"If you're re-creating yourself, will our Sect host him?" Ge asked. He wanted to see the fruits of Shen Yu's labour.

"When he's ready, maybe I'll send him to trade pointers with your little clouds, if only to honour Senior Brother's memory." He bowed his head . . . and then a lecherous grin spread across his face. "Or I'll send him to train with the fairies of the Soaring Heavens Isle."

Both men rolled their eyes at the name of the all-female Sect. Shen Yu knew all of their Elders . . . *intimately.*

"He will always be welcome in our Cloudy Sword Sect, whatever you decide. Though I would assume by your methods, the Outer Sect might be the best place?"

A disciple of Shen Yu's would have immediately been taken into the Inner Sect in most other circumstances and gifted the reagents of the Cloudy Sword Sect. Instead, he would be placed with the weakest and least initiated members.

Shen Yu nodded. "Keep an eye on him, but don't ruin him. I need him this way. He needs *himself* this way. A man must face heaven alone." His declaration was heralded with a burst of Qi, his conviction as solid as his own foundation.

"His name is Jin Rou. I may allow him to take the name Shen Rou, in a few years. Tall, freckles, hardworking lad," Shen Yu said fondly.

"But enough about me! How go your adventures in the southlands, Brother Ge?"

They talked well into the night. And with the arrival of the dawn, their ethereal bodies faded away.

□

Xiao Ge stewed in his room as he reminisced. The memories were help-ful and hurtful in equal measure. His gut roiled, and the clouds above churned ominously. Something had happened to make Shen Yu send his boy here early. Likely some emergency with the demonic invasion, some-thing that necessitated speed. Elder Ran had been there, so he had fol-lowed Shen Yu's request and put him in the Outer Sect.

He picked up a ledger on his desk and consulted it. A list of what the Cloudy Sword Sect Elders were engaged in.

Closed Door Cultivation.

Closed Door Cultivation.

Personal leave.

Closed Door Cultivation.

He frowned heavily. Most of the Elders were indisposed, in Closed Door Cultivation, or out in the world, the Sect running without their presence.

Elder Ran: *Called by emergency dispatch.*

And of course, Ran had left instead of watching over Jin Rou, because what true harm could befall him within the halls of the Cloudy Sword Sect? Jin Rou should not have *needed* a minder. It was the Cloudy Sword Sect! Who would dare assault its students? Who would dare have the guts?

Apparently *their own students.*

Forget Brother Shen Yu, *Xiao Ge* was livid.

There was always some damage, some wounds. They were cultiva-tors! Such things were common, and the Honoured Founders had praised martial discourse as a high virtue. There had been many bouts, of the Inner Disciples trading pointers with the Outer Disciples.

Beating a junior to death on purpose? Xiao Ge's own Master, or any of the Masters from that generation, would have slain the student on the spot, no matter who they were, or who their father or their grandfather was!

Even this, this near death and near crippling, would have been harshly punished. Yet the boy had apparently suffered nothing for it. Because he was Elder Chen's son? The *youngest* Elder?

He scoffed. An attendant was called in, the man barely managing to stay standing as Ge turned his Intent upon him. The boy's face was a mask of terror.

"Call an assembly in two days' time," he commanded, his voice boom-ing. "The Sect. All of it."

The man shakily saluted. Elder Ge frowned at the man, mentally raising Lu Ri's worth several points in his mind. The boy had impressive composure. He had barely been sweating, and Elder Ge's Intent had been much greater then than it was now.

He would have to think of taking another apprentice, after so long. Or introducing him to his granddaughter, if all went well.

If all went well. He concentrated as he tried to calm his churning Qi. The gathering clouds outside were not his concern, but rather his inner formation was boiling like a cauldron after the youngster's story.

How could things have gotten like this?

His Master, ruffling his hair. "We live so high up in the clouds, little one, it can be easy to forget to look at the ground. But one must always remember to look back and reflect."

Xiao Ge frowned heavily, internally chastising himself. How long had it been since he'd visited the Outer Disciples? Not since his own boyhood, when Brother Shen Yu used to drag him out for their games.

He stood, his inner world calm enough to move, even if the clouds outside still reflected his black mood.

He strode out of his pavilion and into his Sect. His eyes flashed around like his own swords as he descended the levels, heading to the areas of the Outer Disciples.

His eyes took in the slight decay. The missing roof tiles. The cracks in the buildings that should be pristine. Minor things. Some were so small that even other cultivators would not notice.

But it was all an indication of something . . . off.

He whirled away, ignoring the nervous disciples staring at the sky.

There was a *rot* here. *And he would have it out by the roots.*

CHAPTER 25

RIGHTEOUSNESS

When this mission had merely been him fulfilling a minor duty of the Sect, Lu Ri had been relatively frugal. In his mind, the only thing that had been taken up was his own time, and thus he'd kept resource costs relatively low.

Now, however, things were *important*. Important enough to use true techniques. With Elder Ge's command, he immediately sought the use of a Divining Formation. The answers one got were murky at the best of times. But his other Senior Disciples—the ones who had not been driven into a frenzy of activity by Elder Ge's sudden and imposing presence as he began demanding more records—could aid him.

He would keep things discreet as commanded. His fellows knew he was looking for someone but respected his silence on who. Or more likely, they never thought to ask, too concerned with the clouds above their heads that boiled like a cauldron.

But for this divination to even have a chance of being successful, they needed more than a mere letter. The preliminary search had revealed nothing—which was to be expected. It was also why so few embarked upon this path. Before mastery, uses were limited and reagents expensive, in addition to needing personal effects, or even samples of Qi.

Luckily, they had plenty of such samples. Or so Senior Disciple Lu Ri thought.

"Ah, yes, the high-quality Lowly Spiritual Herbs? The ones in this room have all been used," an aged, cracking voice commented. The Senior Disciple, and Lu Ri did mean *Senior* Disciple, was stroking his beard. "When things are of such superlative quality, they are used up swiftly."

"There are none left? Truly?" Lu Ri asked with dismay.

"While they were all used, or at least the ones in circulation, I *did* keep a single sprig for myself," the old man said. "Though it did come from another set of disciples. They claimed they grew them themselves, but . . . this old man has some suspicions that they did not."

Lu Ri frowned. "They stole them?"

"One of the younger ones looked extremely guilty when they were brought to me. When I asked another to investigate, he claimed it was . . . merely coincidence. They were just Lowly Spiritual Herbs, so he saw no point in pursuing further. And my jurisdiction ends here."

Lu Ri sighed at the laxity one of his fellows had shown, irritation coursing through his veins, and bowed to his Elder. "Thank you. I shall investigate further." The old man nodded, wincing as he stood. He was obviously running out of time, and he had clearly given up on ascending past his current limitations. But the Sect still kept him on, for his organisation was superb, even with his failing health.

The old man walked into his personal rooms and retrieved the sprig of Lowly Spiritual Herb. It was slightly dried-out-looking but still vibrantly green and pliable.

"Thank you, Senior Brother—" Lu Ri began, but was cut off with a booming roar.

The entire mountain shook, and Elder Ge's Qi flooded outwards. The black, boiling clouds dropped ominously, like the very sky itself was falling.

A black maw descended to devour them, a ravening black void that would slay anything it touched—

As soon as it came, it left. The clouds paused their executioner's descent and retreated. Merely churning angrily, rather than boiling.

Both Senior Disciples swallowed thickly.

"I shall find out the truth behind this matter, Senior Brother," Lu Ri intoned.

"May the heavens be with you, Junior Brother. May they be with us all."

→

The sprig was delivered to his fellows, the shock of Elder Ge's intent having worn off swiftly. The formation would be ready a few hours after Elder Ge's assembly call. Lu Ri turned his attention to the ones that had given his Senior Brother the herbs.

He had to make certain that they were from Disciple Jin Rou.

The disciples were still a bit jumpy as they gathered before Lu Ri, wondering what his summons was about.

"The sprigs of Lowly Spiritual Herbs that you grew last year were of superlative quality, Disciples. Why have you not been able to repeat this feat?" he asked.

The looks on their faces told Lu Ri all he needed to know: the shifty eyes, even with their bodies held serenely.

Lu Ri's own Intent filled the room.

"We took them as payment after we helped him!" one of them said, breaking immediately.

Lu Ri was very, *very* close to spitting blood at his point.

□

The courtyard was packed with every single disciple of the Sect, save for the Old Masters in Closed Door Cultivation. There was murmuring as well as confusion. What could call them all out of their duties? Why had Elder Ge summoned them all here?

Many were staring up at the black sky. The nervous, uneasy energy filled the rarely used courtyard, which had cracks going up the pillars.

Lu Ri stood with the rest of the Senior Disciples, who were all outwardly calm, but he could detect fear and unease in all of them as well. This had not happened for centuries, at least. The Call of the Disciples was something that was only undertaken in emergencies, and very, *very* rarely were there any emergencies in the Cloudy Sword Sect.

A hush fell out over the crowd as two Elders arrived. Elder Ge, his face calm and serene, and Elder Chen, who looked as ill at ease as Lu Ri had ever seen the arrogant and boastful Elder.

Elder Ge's eyes slid over the disciples, and where they passed, men and women stood straighter.

"You may wonder why this Elder has gathered you all here today. It is due to something that has been brought to this one's attention. Come down here, Chen Li. This old man would have words with you."

There was a murmur in the crowd, and Chen Li stood straighter as he was called. His smile came across his face, and he stepped arrogantly towards the powerful Elder. His father was there, so what worry should he have?

"This Chen Li pays his respects to the Honoured Elder," the boy declared politely.

Elder Ge took him in, staring at the boy silently. He stroked his goatee once, considering the disciple.

"I hear you have been trading pointers with the Outer Sect Disciples," Elder Ge mused idly, still staring at the boy.

Chen Li bowed his head. "Yes, Elder Ge, I have aided their training greatly and exchange my knowledge with them frequently," he said with a smirk. Lu Ri felt his gut twist at the words.

"Indeed. It is a blessing to receive a pointer from one more powerful than yourself. To witness their technique firsthand and use that knowledge to better oneself," Elder Ge lectured as he paced from side to side, addressing the crowd. The storm above them was still and silent, mirroring the disciples of the Cloudy Sword Sect. Several of the Outer Disciples clenched their fists but held their tongues.

Chen Li nodded along, arrogance oozing off him. He stood proudly under the Elder's gaze. He was obviously wondering if he was about to be rewarded, and Lu Ri felt a single spot of pity for the boy before Elder Ge tore his arrogance away.

"So you should have no problems trading pointers with this Elder," Elder Ge declared with a serene smile.

Lu Ri noted well the exact moment the statement finished imprinting itself on the young man's mind. The cracking of his façade. The sudden trembling in his Qi. The smug look of superiority faded, replaced with the pale white of abject terror.

"Are you not honoured? Fear not, I, your grandfather, shall treat you *exactly* as you have treated your juniors."

Not a soul in the courtyard dared to take a breath, even Elder Chen, who Lu Ri noticed was biting his lips so hard they bled. Chen's son sought him out, his eyes jumping desperately to the man to defend him.

The Elder remained silent, staring forwards blankly.

"Come. Take your stance," Elder Ge demanded.

The courtyard had realised that they were about to watch an execution. The boy was shaky. His eyes were full of terror. Yet he took his stance, raising his hands.

He knew that he would not be allowed anything else. Best to preserve some dignity.

"Now. Your Honoured Elder shall trade pointers with you." An open hand rose, raised leisurely backwards.

Chen Li's head jerked to the side. None had even caught the Elder's movement. There was no sign of his motion, not even a displacement of air. But there was a single sharp *crack*, and Chen Li staggered.

He seemed confused as to what had happened. Blood dripped out of his mouth.

"What did you learn from that blow?" Elder Ge asked him, tilting his head to the side.

"I—I—your supreme skill, Elder—" the boy stammered out. He tried to compose himself.

"So you have learned nothing. Very well, I shall show you again."

Chen Li jerked to the other side, and this time blood sprayed out of his mouth.

"What did you learn?" Elder Ge asked again. "The whole point of trading pointers is to *learn*, is it not?"

"You are correct, Elder Ge," the boy managed to cough out.

Elder Ge nodded, seeming to ponder something.

"Ah, you could not even perceive it. Here, I shall slow it down for you."

Chen Li barely had time to wince. There was another ugly *crack*. But this time, Lu Ri could see it. The hand that slammed directly into the boy's face.

"Better, I think. I have to restrain my strength, but such is life." Elder Ge sounded as if he were discussing the weather.

"What." *Crack.* "Are." *Crack.* "You." *CRACK.* *"Learning?"* Each word was punctuated with a blow. Chen Li's head jerked from side to side as each perfectly controlled motion kept him standing, ready to receive another.

"What have you learned? I shall answer. *Nothing.*"

The Elder struck, and this time he was not so kind.

"You *dare* euphemise this. You *dare* call it a pointer?" the Elder roared. "Is it enjoyable to crush other members of our Cloudy Sword Sect?"

More blood arced through the air, and the boy's Qi shuddered like a dying heartbeat as he was broken.

"Two were crippled permanently. Three had to restart their cultivation. Two just left, and many more simply received the blows without comment, because what could they do to an Inner Disciple?" Elder Ge's eyes darkened further. "Some even tell me that a disciple was *killed*."

Elder Ge's fist hammered into the disciple, and Chen Li's body could take no more.

Elder Ge caught the boy by the arm as he started to fall, raising him up so that all could witness his beaten and broken form. He turned to the Inner Disciples, the Core Disciples, and the Senior Disciples.

"And *none of you* intervened."

The air became laden with Qi, and the wind, for a brief moment, roared with fury.

The words forced some to their knees as Elder Ge's carefully restrained intent boiled out of him. The cloud above shuddered and descended like an executioner's sword. They could all feel the sharpness of the intent, as if the very air were trying to cut them.

The black clouds were *death*.

Lu Ri barely remained standing.

"To suppress a member of another Sect is one thing. To beat your juniors is another entirely." His voice was a whisper, but everyone in the courtyard could hear it. "The reason this Cloudy Sword Sect was formed was to *teach*. To teach the wisdom of our Honoured Founders and to live the way they envisioned; to forge bonds between cultivators, so that they may stand together against the darkness that now seems so far away."

Elder Ge's eyes pierced their very souls.

"We have grown fat and lazy. We have grown cruel and arrogant. We have let our high perch blind us to the earth."

He threw Chen Li's twitching body to the side. "Keep him isolated. His fate is for another to decide," he commanded, and two of the Senior Disciples hastened to obey. "This stops *now*. Our righteous Sect will be tainted by such acts no longer," Elder Ge intoned, the weight of his conviction pressing into all who witnessed him.

"Yang Linlin." His eyes pierced a female disciple—a female disciple who had been growing increasingly worried looking as the strikes continued, and whose fellows had turned glares upon her. "Come and receive pointers from your Elder."

The beautiful Inner Disciple trembled like a leaf in a storm.

But she had at least some teachings of the Cloudy Sword and went to face judgement with dignity.

"This humble disciple thanks her Elder for showing her the path." She bowed respectfully with a dead voice.

Elder Ge raised his hand.

The disciples watched, transfixed, at the Elder's justice.

Five more were called. Some Inner Disciples. Some Outer Disciples. One Senior Disciple. The Core Disciples managed to remain untouched, to an approving look from the Elder.

"Some of this lies upon my inattention. Upon *our* inattention," Elder Ge stated once he was finished. There was not a drop of blood upon him, not a piece of clothing out of place. "So I shall be taking a personal hand in matters going forwards."

His weight was all encompassing.

"I will correct our lapses. I will return us to the Righteous Path of the Cloudy Sword."

"I swear this, in the name of our Honoured Founders."

Not a soul dared to breathe.

"I command you: meditate upon the meaning of righteousness. All shall provide this Elder with their answer of 'what is righteousness' after their morning meditations, in this courtyard, and stand ready for work details."

"You are dismissed."

□

The formation was complete, drawing the small bits of Jin Rou's Qi from the Lowly Spiritual Herb.

A full eight Senior Disciples were in attendance. Their faces were a mask of concentration as they manipulated the subtle energies of fate, the orb of water high in the air cascading with prismatic colours.

Lu Ri hoped this would work.

Qi surged, and was guided, the formation searching for the one whose Qi this was.

The ritual was nearly complete, solidifying into an image—when the image suddenly froze, golden cracks running through it.

The formation trembled, shook, and broke along the golden lines.

The orb of water fell, splashing into its basin.

He knew that an important person might have some defence against scrying, given to them by their Master, but it was worth attempting anyway.

Lu Ri sighed.

Manually it was.

He left the Sect that morning, after giving Elder Ge his views on righteousness. They were spoken near verbatim from the Honoured Founders' own scroll "Meditations upon the Nature of Righteousness," and were words Lu Ri tried to live by.

Elder Ge was very pleased by his answer.

CHAPTER 26

PLANTS AND CLOTHES

I carefully ran my fingers though the steadily growing shoots. *Soil acidity, good. Sunlight, too much. Wind, needs more.* I nodded in agreement.

"Let's get you moved over, little guy," I muttered to the plant, and I imagined its little fronds waving in thanks.

Wait, don't actually wave in thanks, you're food. Just the impressions you give are enough.

I grabbed the pot and moved it to a better location, examining the collection. The vast majority were relatively normal. Green, vibrant, and full of life. My seasonings, the Lowly Spiritual Herbs, were looking particularly tasty.

They had started growing even better after I'd added a bit of bone meal from the Spirit Beast bones Xiulan had brought along as wedding gifts. I may like hunting, but I don't really enjoy the whole hunter aesthetic. Racks of antlers on the walls were never my thing, and neither were skulls the size of my torso, or the one Wrecker Ball shell that was even bigger than I was.

So they got turned into fertilizer. Some went here, and some went on my vegetable gardens, in controlled amounts.

I turned my attention to the new plants in the buckets. Spiritual Herbs were . . . weird. They were simultaneously more and less hardy than other plants. Quite frankly, I had an amazing success rate so far, using my own half-baked technique, and with that I had gotten a feel of what they kind of needed. A certain pH. Denser, or looser soils. How much fertilizer. Even where to put them around my house. The Lowly Spiritual Herbs liked the southern part the best.

It was really nice, honestly. Before, I'd had to guess, but these "hunches" were *really* accurate.

Last year, Big D had presented a bunch of seeds to me. At first, I'd thought it was just some kind of imitation. He had seen me planting seeds, so he had gone out and gotten some for me. I had kept them, as it was too late in the season last year to plant them, but I had fully intended to make him his own little garden.

It wasn't until Meiling told me they had a very faint bit of Qi in them that I realised he had gone specifically looking for things with Qi as a gift to me.

So instead of a little plot of land, with its own little hut—which admittedly would have been a very fairy-tale image—they were in the steadily expanding collection of buckets and pots that grew the Spiritual Herbs.

I would really need a dedicated space for these soon, other than "piled around the house," but it was working so far, and nothing needed any exotic environment.

There was a completely sky-blue stalk of grass, and weird yellow tendrils that were growing underwater. Lesser Skygrass, and Yellow Waterroot. In addition to the two strange-looking ones, there were some little stalks of Spiritual Grass and a Five-Spine Leaf. These were all of some use in pill making and medicine. The only reason I knew their names was because of my trip to the Archive with Meimei.

I turned my attention to the one pot that seemingly had nothing in it, the original reason why I had gone to the Archive in the first place. With a shrug, I went over to it and carefully started to excavate. I hadn't looked at it since I reburied it nearly a year ago now, and I was wondering if it was still alive. There were no shoots above the surface, but when I had found it, there was no green in sight on it.

I pulled the root out of its earthy prison. It had gotten a bit bigger and had gone from a very deep brown red to something a bit lighter red, so it *was* growing.

Meimei sneezed. It was a cute sound, surprisingly high-pitched compared to Meimei's slightly deeper voice.

And then she sneezed again.

And again.

"Geh! Jin, what the hells is that?" she gasped as she walked in from outside, Xiulan trailing behind her from outside, her eyes wide and curious.

Meimei sneezed for a fourth time, then glared at the root. "It's like shoving peppercorns up my nose!"

Right, it felt a little bit like fire to *me*, and I was shit at Qi sensing. Judging by their reaction, it might be something powerful. Strange that they could only feel it once it came out of the soil, but eh.

And we have a cultivator right here, so hey! We might be able to figure out what this is!

"Sorry, I'll put it away in a second. Xiulan, do you know what this is?" I asked.

She approached, looked hard at the root for a moment, and shook her head.

"No, I do not, Master Jin. Would you enlighten me?"

I shrugged. "I dunno either," I said honestly. Her eyes widened further.

"Then it must be a rare and powerful root, Master Jin. Its Qi is quite potent."

Meimei sneezed again, and snot started running out of her nose. She turned and fled.

Well, back into the soil you go. We'll find out when we find out. Now, where did I put those posts that I was going to put in the pond?

↔

Meiling sat down with a cup of tea and sighed. Pi Pa dutifully set down the paper and scrolls with Ri Zu's help. Financial reports, and the household budget.

It was something she didn't particularly like doing, but she would mostly just be checking over Pi Pa's work. Which was a blessing. She still shuddered thinking about the time she had to help her father out with his work. Her father did all the other finances related to the village . . . and it was a lot.

It was no wonder he looked constantly frazzled during those weeks when he had to put the entire report together.

This was her second attempt. The first had ended when she opened up the scroll and realised that she couldn't read any of the numbers. Jin had been apologetic and offered to rewrite the entire thing or do it himself. She refused his offer. Jin already did a lot of woman's work without complaint, and she needed *some* job she could call her own. Her pride wouldn't allow her to be a layabout. This was the job her mother had done, so she would do it too! Instead of letting him do all the work, she took him up on his offer to learn.

They were surprisingly easy, the characters and formations. It took her an afternoon, and Jin had jokingly declared that she had "speedrun math." The test was easy as well. She had thought he had gone easy on her, but he had been proud of her perfect score. And not patronizing, *genuinely* happy with her skill. It was still a bit of a strange sentiment from anyone but her indulgent father.

"Hopefully our kids are as smart as you."

That idle statement from Jin had filled her heart to bursting, though her husband did himself a disservice. He was *anything* but stupid. Best to hope both their better qualities would shine through. Hopefully, the children would be as smart as either of them. Though she did wish that Jin's gentleness would win out over her own vindictive personality.

She idly rubbed her stomach. She wasn't sure. Not yet. It was one missed flow, and she didn't feel any different yet. But better safe than sorry.

No matter how much she wanted to drink with her friends.

She opened the scroll. Pi Pa's writing was excellent. Elegant, with a little bit of flourish. Quite a bit different from Meiling's own writing. Hers was the boxy, utilitarian style taught to the scribes. Like each character was impressed by a stamp. It eliminated confusion, the Imperial Scribes decreed. The straight-line margins and precision were good for organisation, and when one worked with potentially fatal plants, good organisation was key.

Though she decided she might try to make her writing a bit more beautiful in the future. She couldn't be outdone by a pig—no matter how elegant that pig was.

"Excellent calligraphy, Pi Pa," she praised, and the pig bowed her head in thanks.

She did her part first, as it was what she was familiar with. Pi Pa did good work. Everything was in order, and everything was recorded diligently.

So she was in quite a good mood as she opened Jin's scroll. That mood lasted until she saw what it looked like.

She turned to Pi Pa, who wore a commiserating expression. The worst part was, she knew that Jin could write well. The carved *Beware of Chicken* was the work of an extremely skilled hand. Almost art, she would say. He could write the courtly characters like a noble!

She shook her head. Well, she would be doing most of it now! Everything would be organised!

Though the little drawing of what could be only her in the corner was extremely cute. Jin must have gotten distracted thinking about her.

She sighed happily as she looked at the drawing. The slightly cheeky grin on her face. The little hearts—

Pi Pa coughed from beside her. Meiling blushed, her brush freezing in the middle of drawing her own little hearts around a doodle of Jin's face. Right. She was *working*.

Meiling redoubled her concentration. It wasn't actually that bad, but it was extremely disorganised. Still, Pi Pa had done an excellent job deciphering things, as far as she could tell. One of the figures seemed to be off, but not everybody could be perfect.

The next scroll was even worse, though this one was filled with technical drawing of gears and pipes, in addition to the numbers.

Meiling frowned at them, remembering the sheaves of paper Jin had in a drawer. She hadn't thought much of them, but if they had been as disorganised as this, then that was unacceptable. Pi Pa hadn't touched anything outside the account ledgers, since Jin had just told her to leave the mess. Meiling decided she would organise his drawings first. Make sure they were all in a good place. It would be a shame if he lost any of them.

And so she started around the house. Some were on the table, some were in drawers, and some were even behind a dresser. A waste! Paper wasn't too expensive, but it *was* an expense! She would be having words with him later!

She started sorting through the pages. Ones with gears over here, ones with farming implements over here . . .

She flushed as she came to a more familiar drawing. The "Scholar Girl" with the scandalously short skirt. She had no idea what uniform scholars had in the city, but she was certain it wasn't this. She still could barely believe that she had actually agreed to make it for him. The top was fine—in fact it looked quite nice—but the bottom?

Well, it had been nice and swishy, and Jin's shout of "praise the heavens" when she had worn it had been nice . . . she turned to the next piece, one that had been under the dresser.

Her mouth opened in shock. Pi Pa stood and looked at what she was looking at, and flushed as well.

It turned out that the Scholar Girl wasn't as lewd as she'd thought it was. This drawing was an entirely different beast. The nets on the legs, the material that exposed her chest and legs, the *rabbit ears*, of all things—!

She took it back, her husband was an idiot. A lust-filled deviant!

She looked at the picture some more. Although . . . it wouldn't take much material—

She quickly put it to the side and found another set of drawings, again all of her wearing different clothes. A strange, button-up shirt, in red with black squares. Her hair in two braids that ran down her shoulders. *Lumberjack* was written next to it. A robe that looked fit for a princess, with floral designs all over it, and hairpins. A shimmery blue dress, and odd, heeled shoes.

They were beautiful clothes. She looked at the writing of *commission?* in the corner.

He was planning on buying her these? The robe was entirely too much! He shouldn't be spending so much on her!

She huffed, then decided on a course of action. He wanted these . . . and she had a solution.

She carefully folded up the page and stuck it in her robe. She was a more than capable seamstress—she could surely make some of this. It made no sense to spend too much money on her, and they were going to Verdant Hill soon. She knew some people.

After a moment of pondering . . . she grabbed the strange rabbit costume and put it in her robe too.

Then she got back to work with pink cheeks.

↔

Bi De examined his crude drawing of the formation carefully. This was it. His postulations about the formation had been exhausted. With the summer settling in, Bi De had little to do besides meditate and ponder the giant formation. Before, it had merely been a small distraction. Now, it was starting to consume his waking thoughts.

Despite his best efforts, he was growing restless. As he thought on the strange formation more, as he considered it . . . he wanted to know more about it.

It was a need. A need to know. It was like that time with Chow Ji, his interest and desires running away from him.

He strove to master himself. He should be content with his station. All of his transgressions were forgiven, and he had a place of honour. He was a proud guardian, entrusted with Fa Ram by his Great Master.

But he still wanted to know what the formation was for. What did it look like? *What did it do?* Were the lands of the north different from how they looked around Fa Ram? It was quite the conundrum. He drew a few more diagrams. Something itched at the back of his skull, though he still could not comprehend what he was looking at. He had seen too little of it.

He would have to actually go and observe the formation if he wanted to learn more.

His studies of the moon and of the wind had stalled. These were not things to be worried about, he told himself.

And yet . . . and yet.

Bi De frowned as Sister Ri Zu began grooming his feathers.

'If it bothers you so, seek guidance,' she recommended.

Bi De frowned more heavily. It hurt him to bother the Great Master with something so . . . *unimportant.* Yet seek his Lord's counsel he would.

↔

I looked more closely at the picture Big D had drawn—the strange formation, or circle thing that he had. It was obviously incomplete, with places with blank circles, or crossed-out ones.

"So this is what you saw on the solstice?" I asked him and Rizzo. Big D was sitting calmly, waiting for my judgement.

A formation during the solstice? Well, I suppose it would be kind of interesting for a cultivator, and while I'd taken a vacation to Hong Yaowu, all the animals had been working.

It was kind of unfair, now that I think about it. I got to have a good night's sleep, while other people were on guard? I got to play around, while they did things for me? They were people too.

Besides, I didn't think the formation thing was that big. He would probably be gone for a couple of weeks poking around. A month at most.

"Well, if you're interested in it, how about you check it out? I'll prep some rations for you whenever you want to leave. It's always good to expand your horizons."

The chicken gaped at me.

"Hey, it'll be interesting. Just promise to tell me what you find, okay?"

CHAPTER 27

Q = V / T

Twisting streamers of water flowed through the air. Droplets shone like gems, suspended motionless, floating without any visible support.

In the center of the tangled web and the formation of water, there was a fish. It was an ugly, drab brown carp. The most common sort of creature, his only redeeming qualities being the length of his whiskers.

The fish's eyes were closed, and he spiralled in the nucleus of water. It was as if he was one half of the taijitu, circling endlessly as he concentrated upon the water.

A peach flew through the air.

The torrent of water whirled, snatching the fruit with unerring precision. A great maw opened and bit down on the sweet, delicious, juicy—

Rock?

The water streamers dropped, splashing pathetically back down to earth, and the fish flopped to the ground.

"Ohhohohohohoho."

Wa Shi's eyes snapped open at the rank, foul betrayal while he spit out pieces of stone in disgust. It was nothing like the mud or rocks at the bottom of a river—nay, those contained tasty morsels to be pursued. This was just hard and crunchy, with no redeeming qualities save its texture.

"Keeping one's composure when things are not as we wish is essential, little dragon," the large, black turtle said, chiding Wa Shi. He looked spectacularly amused by this outcome.

Wa Shi scoffed. The old bastard had thrown real peaches the first few times. Wa Shi's sublime skill had ensured that each one was directed to its rightful place: his mouth, as he remained suspended in the air. To betray his trust like this, the turtle would die a thousand deaths!

Or find rocks in unfortunate places. Yes, he was merciful, after all.

He concentrated, drawing upon the water of the lake yet again. He didn't know exactly how long he had been here, but he assumed it had taken several days, at the very least. The water had only started floating recently. It was a difficult task, and one that was made more difficult when his concentration was so callously disrupted. But he rose again. The water heeded his call.

The turtle nodded, smiling.

"That's the way, little dragon. A momentary setback is just that: momentary," the turtle declared fondly.

Of course it was just momentary. *If at first you don't succeed, try again. If at second you don't succeed, beg for help.*

The turtle guffawed loudly at that one, shaking his head.

"Now, we shall discuss that most sublime mechanic, *flow*. A bit of a shame to have left it for this long, wouldn't you say? This one poses you this question: 'What is flow?'"

$Q = V/t$.

"I . . . beg your pardon?" the turtle asked, confused.

"Flow is volume divided by time," Wa Shi repeated. The Boss used weird symbols for math. Wa Shi's mind screamed that they were wrong, somehow, but they obviously weren't. That part was getting easy to ignore.

"Ah, this one meant in a more . . . *metaphorical* sense, but that works too," the turtle decided, changing tracks. Wa Shi smirked. Of course, his knowledge stumped even old turtles. Truly, Wa Shi was a genius!

Sure, it had taken him several months of nonstop work to comprehend the fluid formula the Boss had started talking to him about after he'd realised Wa Shi's brilliance, but he was a fish—er—*dragon*! It was only natural that he figured these things out easily.

Though the fluid formulas had apparently been made for moving human waste, which was . . . Well, he could just pretend that it was originally for water, instead of for this "toilet."

"Now this one sees. What else can you do with your math formations, little dragon?"

Wa Shi shrugged and held up a steamer of water. It moved languidly, flowing through the air. He concentrated and narrowed a section, squeezing down. The water sped up.

He squeezed until he could squeeze no more, the water flowing much, much faster. Not fast enough to cut, not yet, but well on its way to getting there. The turtle stroked his chin in contemplation and approval.

"Not the lesson that flow usually imparts, little dragon. Surprising, and in a life as long as mine, this surprise is a good one. Why, it took this one nearly a thousand years to realise water could cut!"

The turtle laughed his *ohhohohohoho* again. Wa Shi rolled his eyes. He was feeling the strain of this technique. How long had he been keeping this up for? He didn't know.

A peach soared through the air towards Wa Shi. His water caught it, and he glared suspiciously at the offering for a moment. Satisfied it was not a trick, he bit into it and felt a bit less tired.

The turtle settled down again.

"Now, where were we? Ah, yes, flow. Truly, a sublime force. Time flows. Blood flows. Our emotions flow. Understanding flow is understanding a portion of the world."

Wa Shi struggled to keep the streamers of water up as he listened. The old man loved to talk. He talked even more than Ri Zu when the tiny morsel got excited about medicine.

Oddly, Wa Shi found himself missing the others slightly. Even Pi Pa. He would naturally strike her behind a hundred times when he returned home with his newfound strength, in revenge for all the embarrassments the saucy wench had visited upon him.

But that might upset Brother Chun Ke. Brother Chun Ke, who shared with Wa Shi his spoils when he went foraging.

He would content himself with but a single strike, just to listen to her squeal. Then, like the great dragon he was, he would be satisfied.

He listened with half a mind to the old voice about the nature of flow. He thought mostly about food. His mind went blank.

The water spun and spun, swirling around him.

↔

The black turtle observed the carp. His eyes were full of gentle amusement. By his Lord and Master, this one was the most amusing Spirit Beast he had met in centuries.

Truly, it was a fortuitous encounter. He was glad something had guided the little one here, if only to stave off his boredom and slumber. This hidden realm was beautiful but got *ever* so boring.

He felt the whisper of movement again. It brushed around Wa Shi. The energy was . . . it was nearly invisible to him, but he felt the soft tremors of its passing. It felt quite familiar to the turtle, but he couldn't quite place it as the energy swirled around the fish. It checked on the carp and, satisfied with its health, fell away again.

But not before cheekily tugging the turtle's tail on its way out.

The turtle sighed, shaking his head. Cheeky, cheeky thing.

"Ah, respect your elders," he chided empty air.

He felt a brief, intense flash of amusement. A feminine giggle.

He knew not what patron little Wa Shi had, but they were a good one. Really, concerned about a carp's health. How truly strange.

One of the Servants of Xuanwu, the Black Turtle of the North, gazed upon the carp with warm eyes.

Nay, the little dragon. The carp's growth was impressive . . . and soon, it would be *that* time.

He settled back down, observing. The water spiralled and twisted.

CHAPTER 28

PREPARATIONS

Bi De considered at length the bundle of cloth that was to hold his rations. Small, but not too small. Big enough to carry food, yet not big enough to get in the way. He could certainly live off the land—there were always insects and grains—but his brief foray as a test into the lands outside Fa Ram had proved one thing, and one thing only: the world outside was not blessed. The Qi was lower, the taste of the morsels lesser. They were of greatly inferior quality, so he'd had to return quickly.

Though for some reason, the borders of Fa Ram seemed to be getting larger. The air was sweeter even beyond the boundary the Great Master had shown him—his Great Master's power was growing, even supporting the entirety of Fa Ram as he was.

Bi De pondered this. Perhaps one day his Great Master's power would one day encompass the entirety of the world? It was not beyond thinking about, despite his Great Master's claims of weakness. Bi De believed him, of course. The Great Master would not lie to them about this. But . . . the Great Master was growing. The land he offered supplication to was still growing as well, more active than he had ever felt it.

Now, instead of simply consuming Bi De's energy, he felt as if there were hands that stroked his comb and wattles as the Great Master did. Inexpert and excitable, but full of enthusiasm.

His beak added another log to the fire, where the worms smoked on their skewers. They would make fine jerky, along with sun-dried hoppers. The young ones were all crawling out of the ground, a legion of long legs and ravenous maws. Even his flock was barely keeping them in check this year. He could not remember so many last spring, but his memory of that time was dim and hazy.

His Great Master had thrown open the vaults for him, insisting he take any amount of food he could desire, but the grains were heavy and awkward, so he took few. Just enough so that he would not have to unduly dine upon things of inferior quality.

Other than the rations, there were other things to consider, namely guardianship of Fa Ram.

'The guard rotations will be difficult for a time, but if the Master hurries back, I do not believe we shall suffer unduly. Bi De took care of our lands alone, and though we have grown, we can keep things in working order,' Pi Pa mused.

Tigu scoffed. *'Without the lazy bird around, Fa Ram shall reach even greater glories. This Young Mistress shall do his job better than he ever could.'* Her words were insulting, but her tone had no heat. She was still extremely pleased that he had approached her first, to be the primary guard in his absence and take over his duties.

'I do not doubt your martial abilities, Tigu. You shall certainly be better equipped than I was the first time the Great Master left,' Bi De stated simply, and the cat preened from her position atop Chun Ke. It seemed even the arrogant and surly Tigu could not resist Brother Chun Ke's aura of peace and quiet strength.

Though there were still tensions, he was pleased that Tigu was joining in more, even if the only company she enjoyed was Chun Ke's. Progress in small amounts until completion. That was the wisdom of the Great Master.

Little paws deposited a small satchel of medicine near his preparations. *'Are you certain you do not wish to come?'* he asked quietly.

Ri Zu nodded her head, though there was clear conflict on her face. *'Ri Zu still needs more experience before she travels with Brother Bi De,'* she eventually replied, and smiled up at him.

Bi De accepted her words. It would be strange to once more be alone, but it would be enlightening.

He stood straighter, then lowered his head to his fellows. It would be the first time he would be so far away from Fa Ram. He would be travelling far, far from home, until he managed to figure this formation out.

'The First Disciple once more thanks his fellow disciples. I leave our home in the most capable hands.'

Chun Ke oinked happily. *'Friend come back safe,'* he stated, as if it were a foregone conclusion. Bi De smiled at the praise, some of his old fire coming back.

'Of course. Nothing in these Azure Hills shall keep me from returning!' he declared, his feathers puffing up while he gazed imperiously at them.

There were snorts of amusement, and Ri Zu blushed at his sudden authoritative stance.

They lapsed into companionable silence.

Once the worms finished drying, he packed all but a single skewer, which he took in his beak, and departed outside. His Great Master always shared his cooking, so he would try to do the same!

The Great Master was working on something, some form of chair. His strong hands shaped the wood with exacting ease, adding what looked like sleigh runners to the bottom.

The Great Healing Sage had Disciple Gou Ren's head in her lap and was probing at his ears with some manner of tools. "Your ears are very clean this year," she whispered to him while the younger disciple groaned in contentment.

Disciple Xiulan was tending to her blades, her eyes closed as she held her hand against their sides.

"How's it going, Bi De?" his Lord asked as Bi De approached with some of his cooking.

Bi De offered him the skewer.

His Great Master eyed the worms offered to him. Gingerly, he reached out, taking one off the skewer. He brought it up, sniffed at it, and after a brief moment of hesitation, put it into his mouth.

Bi De watched his impassive face. His Master swallowed, the loud gulp sounding like it took a lot of effort.

"Most humans won't like this, buddy," his Great Master told him regretfully.

Bi De hung his head at the rebuke, disappointed. Everything that the Great Master made was delicious, yet his own efforts yielded this. *He* thought they tasted grand!

His Lord laid a comforting hand on his back and started scratching. "I can see why you would like it, though. A lot of the things I make probably won't be to your tastes, and that's okay. Don't let anyone tell you you shouldn't like this."

His Great Master's smile soothed Bi De's soul.

"All right, you're done. *Off*," the Healing Sage commanded Gou Ren, shoving him and sending him rolling bonelessly off.

She swiftly cleaned her tools, green Medicinal Qi flowing around them. Once satisfied at their cleanliness, she turned to the other disciple.

"Lanlan!" she commanded cheerfully, patting her lap. Disciple Xiulan opened her eyes and turned curiously to the proffered place to put her head.

"I have never done anything like this before," she said. "I do not believe I have any earwax to clean."

The patting got a bit more commanding.

"Just lie back and let Senior Sister take care of you," the Healing Sage instructed.

Disciple Xiulan smiled softly and did as instructed, laying her head down in the Healing Sage's lap. A devilish grin stole over the Healing Sage's features.

Her head went down, and she blew softly in Disciple Xiulan's ear. The woman yelped and jolted, her face flushing crimson.

"Oh? That was a good reaction!" the Healing Sage exclaimed, her eyes gleaming and a smile crawling across her face.

"S-Senior Sister!" Xiulan scolded as the Healing Sage giggled.

"I'm sorry, I'm sorry, I'll make it up to you," the Healing Sage commented.

Disciple Xiulan pouted but allowed her head to be pulled back down.

Bi De left the humans to their antics and went to finish preparing.

CHAPTER 29

THE TOWN

They had set off together, their party mostly humans. Bi De's Great Master had business in Verdant Hill, and Hong Yaowu was upon the way, so they travelled together.

Hong Yaowu was just as he remembered it. The many coops for the many flocks of humans that lived here. Each was small and cramped-looking, compared to his Great Master's own grand coop. Their walls were less solid, and their windows uncovered by glass.

The fields, too, were much smaller. The shoots of their crops less vibrantly green. Some even looked to be struggling, the shoots turning slightly brown. The soil was not rich and dark, but paler and almost sandy in some cases. There were even some that looked to be being supped upon by insects—that, he could not tolerate. He would show his Great Master's supplicants his benevolence and rid them of these pests.

It was a stark reminder of the superior quality of his Great Master's domain. But had his Master chosen Fa Ram because it was a superior land, or was it a superior land because of the Great Master's presence?

It was a question to meditate upon that night.

He was about to depart upon his journey. He wanted to leave from the top of the Shrine of Fire in Hong Yaowu, but his Great Master bade him wait for a moment so that he could see Verdant Hill first. He knew not why.

Still, the people emerged from their coops excitedly and greeted his Great Master with deference and great enthusiasm. Even when he was not bearing gifts, the mortals offered their supplication, begging to pour drinks for his Lord or inviting him to dine with their families.

Though the food was of inferior quality, the Great Master received these requests with humble thanks and bowed in return, giving these humans great face.

Bi De, a humble and filial disciple, followed his lead as was right, bowing to the humans. Some bowed back, but most were too preoccupied with his Great Master or his human disciples. Bi De knew why.

Some were pointing and laughing, but most seemed impressed.

Disciple Gou Ren set down his burden, sweat pouring down his face. The Healing Sage took pity on him and poured a waterskin over his head to cool him down, while even Disciple Xiulan seemed interested.

"Good job," his Great Master whispered, clapping the boy on the back.

His Great Master had sourced a replacement rock for the one he had taken. It was an approximate size and shape to the one just outside his Great Master's coop—the one that he and the Healing Sage sat upon at night, playing their music together.

Upon seeing his Lord carrying it with an amused smile, Disciple Gou Ren had asked to carry it instead, while shooting furtive glances at Disciple Xiulan.

This had turned out to be a moment of arrogance. The Great Master lifted it with one arm and acted as if it weighed as much as a tub of water from the river. With a smirk, he had set it down and thanked Gou Ren for his help.

The way Disciple Gou Ren's eyes had widened and his face had gone red as he barely lifted it onto his back had been most amusing.

But his determination had been worthy of Bi De's respect. He had puffed, and grumbled, and complained under his breath, but had managed a brisk walk. His Great Master had kept the pace just at the edge of what the disciple could take. Making him push, yet it wasn't enough to break him.

Bi De watched the humans for a moment before deciding it was time to make himself scarce. The human children were coming, to both reach for his feathers and rub him annoyingly. He considered rebuking them, snapping his wings and demanding that they not touch him, but decided upon a path of lesser conflict instead. He leapt into the air and onto a roof, the children shrieking with delight.

When they went to give chase, the Great Healing sage intercepted them, giving him an appreciative nod . . . and then miming a light smack with her hand.

He bowed his head. He had his Mistress's permission to rebuke any who got a bit too familiar, if they persisted. How fortunate.

He left the humans to their back patting. Several of the women of the village were fawning over Gou Ren, even as his brother strained to lift the rock, barely managing to get it onto his back.

Bi De paid his respects to the elders of the village, those sitting in their chairs as they watched the shouting and enthusiasm of their children fondly, making his way to the Shrine of Fire. They seemed quite amused at his giving them face, but all the elders were polite enough to greet him back.

He returned to the rooftop he had leapt from that night and concentrated. He positioned his body just as he had done the night of the solstice and ascended into the air.

Now, instead of the dead of winter, with its bare trees and lines of fire guiding his way, there was a vast sea of green that shrouded his sight. Yet in his mind's eye he could see the points of the formation, witness its glory, and spot the places that were missing points or misaligned.

There were points that stretched off far beyond what his eyes could see. It would take several days or even perhaps weeks of travel to visit all of these points.

He flapped his wings, keeping himself aloft with the strength of his muscles so he could continue observing. Ascending higher.

Yet there were no new insights he could glean. He absently batted away some form of pest, nearly invisible, as it dove upon him from even higher in the air. White and wispy and covered in fur, it looked a bit like a winged Tigu.

It spiralled away with a yelp, and he descended once more.

Well, he would make his plans, then visit the ones he could see. If he could glean nothing new from them, or no clues as to the rest of the formation, he would return and wait until the solstice.

He returned to the earth, considering. The itching and desire to know was there, but this would be a long journey. Brother Wa Shi had still not returned from wherever he had run off to, but something told Bi De he was all right.

He huffed, then got out a piece of paper, marking a point: the first formation. He would continue on after seeing the place where he had hatched, this Verdant Hill.

He walked back to where his Great Master was, still at the front of the village. The rock was bobbing up and down as Disciple Xiulan hoisted it with much greater ease than Disciple Gou Ren, her arms pumping as she did push-ups.

The poor boy looked dejected while Yun Ren laughed at him.

□

The next day, Disciple Gou Ren carried the rock again, puffing and panting and giving it his all as they headed to Verdant Hill.

His brother, Yun Ren, joined him, carrying another rock and racing him in laps around the caravan.

□

As they rounded a bend, he saw it.

His beak dropped open at the sight of the walled land.

"Verdant Hill," his Great Master said, naming the place for Bi De's benefit. "A small town."

He was beginning to fully realise that his Great Master's definition of "small" differed vastly from his own comprehension.

He swallowed. This was the place where he had hatched from his egg and been brought into the world. The place where his Great Master had *chosen* him as well as the first females.

His first time being back.

He sat regally on his Great Master's shoulder as they approached the gate with the people of Hong Yaowu. Bi De expected the same fanfare and deference at his Lord's arrival. The same enthusiastic greeting that the sons and daughters of Hong Yaowu showed his Great Master.

Yet as they approached the walls . . . there was nothing. The guards gave them lazy glances, checking the carts, but did not announce their presence to the populace.

They entered the walled town . . . and there was nothing. People kept walking. Bi De glanced at his Great Master, but he did not seem to care.

So with great difficulty, Bi De forced down his first instinct to announce his Great Master himself. His bellowing voice would surely make these people, so consumed with their own tasks, stop and offer his Master the proper respect? Nobody was bowing! It was preposterous!

They split from the caravan, his Master and companions going in one direction, while the rest went in another. There were winding streets, the call of other chickens, the shouts of salesmen, the laughter of children . . . it was all too much!

Bi De was so consumed with his own observations, he didn't notice the man who nearly ran into them. His Great Master sidestepped with grace.

"Watch where you're walking!" the man complained to his Great Master, having dashed from around a bend with some sort of jug balanced in his hand.

Bi De nearly spat blood at the sheer, blatant disrespect. His blood boiled, but his Great Master's hand prevented him from harshly rebuking this pitiful creature. The Healing Sage had also grabbed Disciple Xiulan's hand, the woman looking similarly affronted.

"You watch where *you're* walkin', *pal*," his Great Master shot back. The man paused and seemed to realise his Great Master's far, far superior form. His eyes shifted to his Lord's disciples and his face paled slightly.

"Sorry," he shot out, then fled.

The Great Master shook his head and sighed. "Some people," he muttered. His eyes roved around the street. Bi De stared at the man, frowning at him, and committing him to memory, should he offer insult again.

They soon arrived at their destination. A compound within the walls, quite near the ridiculously enormous coop in the center of town, the one that was so large he could fit ten of his Great Master's coops inside it.

He wondered how many animals could be stored within? He shook his head at the sight.

At least the people here were respectful, as the servant bowed, and they were greeted at the door by a man who referred to his Lord as "Brother Jin."

While the rest of their troupe settled in, his Great Master mentioned paying his respects to the leader of this Verdant Hill.

There was one his Great Master would have to pay his respects to?

His Lord set off towards the enormous coop with Bi De upon his shoulder. Instead of being filled with animals, like his Great Master's coop, it was filled with men and paper.

His Master navigated the great coops swiftly and unopposed, arriving at a door guarded by two men, who both made gestures of respect at his appearance.

"Wait outside for a sec, okay?" his Great Master bid him, so he dutifully hopped off his shoulder.

The guards stared at him. He stared at the guards.

Bi De bowed in greeting, giving face to these low-ranked men.

They displayed their lack of manners by staring, instead of returning his respect.

How rude.

There was a flash of power and Intent.

Both men scrambled out of their stupor and greeted him properly.

↔

A stern-faced man gazed imperiously down at his own domain. His balcony was high above the rest of the town, affording him a commanding view. His hands were clasped behind his back. The wind blew his long, silken locks and teased his immaculately groomed facial hair. His dark eyes roved around his domain, cataloguing and pondering ways to improve. His clothes were of the finest silk, a light green colour with a gold sash, denoting his position as one of His Imperial Majesty's Lord Magistrates.

From behind his lofty dais, music drifted. A stately woman with milky skin and red lips played a guzheng. The warm, pleasant notes drifted out over the Lord Magistrate's city, soothing the scribes that worked and made ready for their spring reports.

Standing at attention were two steely-eyed guards. They expected no trouble this day yet were alert anyway, eyes carefully scanning for any threat to their Master, ready to lay down their lives in his defence. Their green armour was polished to a shine, and their weapons glinted with razor edges.

The various scribes and functionaries looked upon the scene with the utmost respect.

"The Lord Magistrate is in fine bearing today," one of the scribes muttered to the other.

"Indeed he is," the other scribe noted. "His back seems straighter and broader this year. He goes from strength to strength, drawing power from his time, rather than being diminished by it. It is good that we rest upon such capable shoulders."

The scribe looked knowingly at the other. "An increase in lumber production this year as well?"

"As you say. I hardly have to ask about the tanneries." The scribes nodded to each other, and there were murmurs of assent from those in charge of the fisheries and the mines.

They turned back to the Patriarch of Verdant Hill and waited for him to receive their reports. He would do so at the designated time, and not a moment before.

They didn't see the wide, almost perverse smile that had spread across his face, his ears pricked and listening intently to their comments. His wife's music provided a soothing tone that would make one think that the Lord Magistrate could not hear their words.

Ah, the Lord Magistrate thought. *How wonderful this time of year is. It makes all the hard work worthwhile.*

He listened eagerly to the praises and the small conversations that praised his leadership, all while standing like the statesman he was. If only he could dance about and cheer! But that would ruin his image. He kept his body stable and firm, a mountain that was proudly rooted to the earth.

His wife played a slightly louder note, startling him out of his enjoyment of his subordinates' praises and notifying him of the coming time. He took a breath, forcing the smile down into his stern, neutral face, the face of the Lord Magistrate. He turned his head slightly and nodded to his wife. One eyebrow with a few streaks of grey raised in fond amusement.

A grand night last night, and an even grander day today. He turned, keeping his hands behind his back and within his large sleeves. He rubbed at the slightly abraded skin on his wrists and forced himself to stay still to avoid undue movement on the marks on his back.

His wife smiled languidly, finishing her song. She too had been in fine form last night.

The gong sounded, signalling the appointed hour, and the Lord Magistrate turned. His head was held high as he walked to the interior of the room and his "throne." He stood before it, and the guards slammed the butts of their spears into the ground.

The assembly bowed as one. "We pay our respects to the Lord Magistrate!" they intoned. He bowed his head slightly in acceptance and made a gesture of respect to his subordinates.

"His Imperial Majesty's Lord Magistrate thanks you for your prompt gathering as always. Now, the Lord Magistrate would listen to your reports, as we prepare to act upon our strategy this year." The scribes bowed their heads once more.

First Archivist Bao pulled out his scroll so that he could call up each man. It was a formality. Each knew their place in this dance.

The Lord Magistrate spent his morning listening to his men. The flattery to his face was nearly as nice as the praise they spouted when they thought him not around to hear.

"Thanks to the Lord Magistrate's foresight . . ."

"As devised last year, by the Lord Magistrate . . ."

"The people of the flooded areas thank the Lord Magistrate for his benevolence, and promise to repay him a hundredfold!"

Yes, these were the days he cherished. The men under his command bowing their heads. The people in the far-flung villages thanking him.

He was truly the Master of Verdant Hill here, and today was a perfect day!

→

"I pay my respects to the Lord Magistrate," Rou Jin said with a smile.

The Lord Magistrate gazed upon the man calmly, while internally he was grumbling. He was fairly certain that the cultivator meant him no harm today, but cultivators had mercurial tempers at the best of times. He tensed slightly as the man turned his attention to his wife. Vague thoughts of unease churned through him, but he had seen her before—

Rou Jin bowed respectfully to her as well. A breach of protocol, truly, but he wasn't going to say anything. His lady wife inclined her head back and graced him with a smile.

No, no, don't do that, that's how cultivators get ideas!

The Magistrate woodenly made a gesture of respect back.

"And what brings you here today, Rou Jin?" he asked politely, keeping his face firm.

"Well, I was in town and wanted to pay my respects and thank you again for coming to the wedding," the cultivator started, and pulled out another jar of Qi-filled liquid. One much larger than the one previously gifted.

The Lord Magistrate's eyebrow nearly twitched, and only ironclad control stopped it.

"Ah, well, it is the duty of the Magistrate to make sure his new subjects are settling in, especially with such an . . . auspicious marriage," he commented.

The cultivator smiled at him.

"But . . . there was another thing."

He schooled his features, waiting for the cultivator's true intent. He knew he had been too kind so far. *What manner of thing might he ask for?*

"I was wondering if there was any paperwork or anything to fill out if I wanted to build a proper road from here to Hong Yaowu. I was going to ask Uncle Bao, but since I'm here now . . ."

The Lord Magistrate frowned internally. The dirt path was serviceable enough, and the reason there was no road out there was the difficulty of the terrain, but a cultivator wouldn't think about that.

But in all honesty a road was . . . *reasonable*, in terms of requests. Prioritising Hong Yaowu would draw a lot of comments and quite a few pointed questions, as well as eat into a good chunk of his hard-earned profits. But if this was the price . . .

"It will take some time for the road to be built, but if it pleases you, I could file the paperwork?"

The cultivator brightened. "Well, we'll say the roadwork is part of my household's corvée?" the cultivator asked, referring to the manual labour that was instituted as part of most men's taxes. You either worked . . . or paid to get out of work. But for his household's corvée . . .

The Lord Magistrate's mind went back to what the cultivator had said. *IfI wanted to build a proper road.* He was going to do it himself? That was . . . Well, it was within the abilities of a single cultivator, he supposed.

Perhaps this wasn't going to be so bad after all? A bit of paperwork, a bit of . . . number fudging, and nobody would look twice at the road!

"Well, if that is all . . . ?" the Magistrate asked, hopeful. Even a few minutes of dealing with this one was exhausting.

The cultivator paused. "A . . . friend of mine is going to be wandering around these parts for a little. If you have any . . . problem spots, any rogue Spirit Beasts, I'm sure he could go and help clear them out for you."

"I shall see if there are any issues," the Magistrate declared. Internally, he was screaming. *More* cultivators? This bastard was attracting them like flies to a corpse! This was supposed to be a *quiet* post, damn it all!

The man nodded. "He's waiting just outside. Do you mind if he comes in?"

The Lord Magistrate sighed.

↔

"—and this is my friend!" His Great Master introduced Bi De to a regal-looking man. He was immaculately groomed and held himself with great dignity, his face a frozen mask of imperious indifference.

He was making odd choking noises, however.

□

"Ah, yes, a pleasure to see you once more," the Lord Magistrate said after a second. He performed a perfect formal bow of greeting, as his station demanded. Right, he'd met Big D before, at the farm.

Big D returned the gesture, his feathers puffed up proudly. He examined the Magistrate curiously, while the Magistrate had the same calm face on as always, acting like he hadn't just gotten introduced to a chicken that would be solving some of his problems.

He had a remarkably high bullshit tolerance. Not a single raised eyebrow, just straight to business, calm as you please.

What a guy, the Lord Magistrate. If only more administrators were like him.

I was actually a little surprised at just how large an area the Lord Magistrate had to administrate. Lots of land, though not a lot of people. The true boonies. In the weakest area of the continent. So it was little surprise that some of his problems were a bit more mundane than even I was expecting.

"Most of these . . . well, they are not things that a cultivator would normally be dealing with, but your Master insisted," the Magistrate said. I *had* asked for his issues. I was also expecting them to be slightly different. "The Daggerfang wolf pack is composed of a large number of Northern Wolves and have made this area their hunting grounds. Attempts to cull them with guards have largely been met with failure, as they're extremely wily. We do not believe that they are Spirit Beasts . . . but they do display a level of intelligence that has made them hard to exterminate," the Magistrate explained.

He continued his briefing, going through a list of things that had to be dealt with. Normal animals. A smart and savage wolf pack. An old bear called Bloodclaw. I actually thought they were probably like Big D. Smart animals. Normally it was the "strange" beasts that got strong enough, but Big D proved that such things were possible.

But vast land and lack of resources meant these kinds of things were difficult to deal with. Their best communication was a spotty "radio" in transmission stones, and those were not exactly reliable. Oh, they could be relied on to buzz when someone wanted to alert you, but sometimes getting *actual* sound through was an exercise in frustration.

Big D took in all the Magistrate's words, stroking his wattles and staring at the map. He shook himself and straightened up as the Magistrate finished, forming his wings into the gesture of respect and bowing deeply, first to the Magistrate and then to me.

Well, my chicken had accepted the task given to him. Instead of just wandering around and finding the formation . . . now he had something else to do as well.

We wandered out of the Magistrate's office, the guards jumping to attention and bowing behind us.

From there it was a brisk walk back to Tingfeng and Meihua's place. I'd said my hellos there already, and Meimei was absolutely fawning over her friend, who was so heavily pregnant she looked fit to burst.

She was still in good spirits, though, chatting animatedly with Meimei and Xiulan.

"How was your meeting with the Lord Magistrate?" Tingfeng asked me as I settled back down into a chair that was brought out for me. The Xong brothers were still eating. They and Tingfeng didn't seem to be particularly good friends, more acquaintances. But I suppose two extremely boisterous farm boys and a quiet scholar didn't mix too well.

We talked for the rest of the day, as this was to be a short visit. Only a day or two, and then we'd be heading home.

Still, it was good to catch up and listen to the life of a scribe.

□

The town, when there weren't any festivals going on, was actually pretty boring. There wasn't anything to do. Or at least anything I was comfortable doing. There was always gambling and whores somewhere, but those were two vices I would not be indulging in.

So we just ended up hanging out at Tingfeng's admittedly nice family compound. But with no TV or anything, it would be just sitting around and talking. Which was enjoyable enough, but Tingfeng was at work, and you can only play tic-tac-toe so many times with Gou Ren before it starts getting stale. His brother had gone off before everybody else had even woken up, off on some errand.

I could also go to the exchange, but that was always annoying and frustrating, doubly so since I had *no* idea how much the maple syrup would be worth.

So I was procrastinating.

I hummed. It was still quite early in the morning. I'd go to the exchange later, once the rush had died down.

I won the umpteenth game of tic-tac-toe, and Gou Ren started grumbling. He had gotten used to kicking my ass at go, and now the shoe was on the other foot. Behold, my power!

He sat back in disgust and flopped over, staring at the sky. His defeat was complete.

I looked to Big D, but he simply bowed his head, already 0–3.

I yawned and stretched, then went to look for Meiling. She was sitting in a small garden with Meihua, her hand on her wrist and taking her pulse while Xiulan meditated, checked out.

"Hey, Meimei, you want to go and visit Uncle Bao?" I asked her.

My wife's eyes flipped between me and Meihua rapidly, until her friend shoved at her.

"Go on," she chided.

I turned next to Xiulan, whose eyes were now open.

"Have you been to an Archive yet?" I asked her.

"I looked in at the Archive in Grass Sea City, Master Jin, but did not have the time to peruse anything. There was also paperwork and a wait-list to be able to access anything important, and I judged my time better spent travelling," she explained.

Meiling grinned. "Well, no waiting list here!" she singsonged, wrapping her arm around Xiulan's.

We set off, passing Gou Ren, who raised an arm when he saw Xiulan and looked about to say something . . . but suddenly slumped, looking disappointed when he saw Meimei's and Xiulan's arms.

"Want to come to the Archive with us?" I asked him anyway.

His desire to spend time with Xiulan warred with his hatred of sitting still and reading.

His brother solved the dilemma.

"Little bro! Got some jobs lined up for us, let's go!" he shouted.

Gou Ren jumped at the call, obeying his brother seemingly on instinct.

"Ah, no, I'll go help Yun Ren . . ." he mumbled out as he went off, his brother slinging an arm around his shoulder and talking animatedly to him.

The rest of us headed out towards the Archive.

The town was full of hustle and bustle, and we heard a shout as we walked along the cobblestone roads.

"Presenting! The Demon-Slaying Orchid!" a man shouted. Several children had stopped to watch as the puppets came out. Sun Ken with a rolling eye and a stupid look on his face squared off against the "beautiful" female puppet, getting slapped around the stage like an unruly child.

Xiulan glanced at it once but ignored it after that.

Big D seemed to be sulking. I scratched his wattles. It must be frustrating as hell to see your own accomplishment be taken by someone else. Xiulan even shot him an apologetic look.

"Big D?" I asked. He started, looking away from the play. "We'll talk tonight, okay?" He bowed his head, shaking off the irritation admirably.

Uncle Bao was as happy as always to see us, the fat, jolly man embracing Meimei like she was his own daughter.

After a moment of catching up with the portly man, we got the key to the restricted section.

"It boggles the mind that one of these is in every town and city . . ." Meimei muttered, as she held *Herbs and Roots of the Azure Hills*. "One of my ancestors is said to have catalogued every plant in the Azure Hills, and it is his notes that we learn from. One of the treasures of our Sect."

She flipped through the actual book instead of the more normal scroll while I read up on *The Beasts That Inhabit the Azure Hills*.

Honestly, some of the shit in here made me wonder what the *fuck* evolution was doing on this rock. There were living *Tully Monsters*, for heaven's sake. The things looked like aliens, with their long probosces, jutting eyes, and a body almost like a seal. They looked sleek and aggressive, and the book cautioned against going near certain bodies of water in the fall when they were at their most active.

What the fuck, xianxia land?

Xiulan was frowning heavily at the book. "However . . . this book is missing some herbs. And our scroll is missing this one," she said, pointing at some kind of flower. She squinted at the anomaly. "Discovered twenty years ago in a cavern?" she asked.

"About every ten to twenty years they get updated," Meimei explained. "Whether *we* get one of those updated copies is questionable, but they would be in Pale Moon Lake City."

Xiulan hummed. "And I may just copy this?"

"Yeah, you can't take the book, but you can copy out any of the information. The whole book, if you *really* felt like it," Meimei said with a shrug.

Honestly, I was actually more impressed that Xiulan's ancestor had apparently missed so *few* herbs, most of them newly discovered. Her ancestor was amazingly thorough.

I turned back to my own book. *Freshwater anglerfish? Wait, this diagram means it's as big as a horse?*

↔

"I can't believe you talked me into this," Gou Ren grumbled as he caught the bricks sailing up to him. "I work enough back at Jin's place, why do I have to spend more time working in Verdant Hill? I wanted to go see if Miss Cai needed any help navigating the town."

"Jin and Meimei got that covered. You want to have to spend hours in the Archive? Uncle Bao is nice, but damn if the scrolls aren't boring. Besides, help her navigate? She's the one whose been to a *proper* city," Yun Ren shot back, moving even faster. Not a single drop of sweat ran down his head as he heaved the stones up to be caught by his brother.

Gou Ren flushed. "Well, some of the alleys are kind of windy . . ."

"Oh? Gonna take her into an out-of-the-way alley? My little brother has gotten *bold*."

"Wha—you—bastard of the fathers!" Gou Ren spluttered out while his brother began cackling.

"Yeah, yeah, yeah. Now shaddup and move more, we can hit a few more places if we finish this fast."

Gou Ren kept grumbling as they worked, the bricks flying faster and faster.

The foreman gaped at the brothers when the two of them pointed cheerily to the completed task. He had left for not even an hour, gone to get some water for the rest of his men, and the boys were finished already? He checked over the work. It was all done *perfectly*. Better than his normal crew.

Yun Ren approached the foreman, grinning and holding out his hand. "How's about a bonus, for bein' such good workers," he asked with a friendly smile.

They got their money, and a little extra.

"Pleasure workin' for ya, you'll put in good word for us, yeah?" he said to the foreman.

The foreman nodded dumbly.

And the brothers set off to the next job.

The next one was stacking lumber. The one after that, splitting logs.

Yun Ren was grinning like a madman at the amount of money they were making in such a short amount of time.

The brothers ducked down an alley, heading around the less reputable part of town and back to the center. Yun Ren did the calculations on his fingers, tapping them out and growing more and more pleased by the moment.

He likely wouldn't be able to afford a crystal for months still, but this was certainly making a dent in the funds.

"Hey, darlings," a sweet voice beckoned, and both brothers paused, turning to the voice. A woman smoking a pipe, leered at them. Her robe was loose around her neck, exposing tantalising amounts of skin.

"You strong men look like you need to *relax* a bit," she purred, and the women behind her giggled and blushed at the Xong brothers' open shirts and sweat-slicked muscles.

Both boys stared, shocked at the sudden attention.

"How about you come in so we can properly . . . *entertain* you." It was sweet and inviting as she dipped a shoulder, more of her robe sliding off. Her skin looked soft and warm.

Her eyes flicked to their full money pouches. So fast he barely noticed it.

Yun Ren's lust warred with the image of a recording crystal dancing in his head.

He grimaced at the smell of perfume.

"Ah, maybe some other time," he told the woman, who frowned heavily at his response; the interested look on her face became boredom as she turned her attention to his little brother.

Gou Ren's face was a bit red, but he just shook his head and kept walking.

"I need the money, but what's your excuse?" Yun Ren asked his brother.

"Miss Cai," he muttered, still red in the face.

Well, his little brother sure had gotten ambitious . . .

Yun Ren clapped him on the back.

□

The Exchange was always, *always* just slightly jarring to walk into. Going from "normal" medievalish things to basically a mall was odd as hell.

There was *advertising*. There was kind of a food court. There was even a chain. Like, a restaurant chain. *Chao Baozi'* a colourful sign proclaimed, with a stylized meat bun on it.

Hells, I had seen one of them in Pale Moon Lake City. Did they have a contract with whatever body governed the exchanges?

Well, they were pretty good. Tingfeng had got some for us last night. High-end meat buns. Guaranteed to be all pure ingredients, no fillers like sawdust in the flour, on pain of death.

They took things seriously in that shop.

I shook my head as Big D looked around in interest, while Xiulan's face was a mask of calm. *Lots* of people were rubbernecking at her.

Or they were rubbernecking at the dude with the chicken on his shoulder. Honestly, it was a bit hard to tell.

We ambled through the colourful flags and small crowd. Nowhere near as packed as it was during the harvest time, but it was still busy enough.

In any case, I had some work to do, and one of the stalls caught my eye. A new one, from the Azure Jade Trading Company. That place was supposed to be really high end. More so than the Heavenly Furs place. It was so high-end I was actually a little curious what it was doing *here* of all places. The dude running the stall looked bored and miserable, so maybe it was some kind of punishment posting?

He glanced over at us, then did a double take at the sight of Xiulan, staring rather blatantly at her.

He looked away after a moment, so I dismissed him, turning back to my companions. Meimei was frowning at a list she had written out. After a moment, she nodded and put it back in her bag.

"I've got some womanly business to attend to, husband," Meimei said, glancing around a little with a slight flush to her face.

"Senior Sister, I'll come with you if you wish," Xiulan offered, and Meimei froze a little.

"That will not be necessary," she deflected, her blush getting a little deeper. "It's just concerning some fabric, and meeting a friend. I'll be back soon."

She was hiding something—kind of badly hiding something—but I let it go. If she wanted to keep it a secret, that was her business.

"You can come with me if you want," I offered to Xiulan, and at her nod, we set off for market research.

I was going to try to sell my maple syrup. I glanced once at the Azure Jade place before trying the usual haunts, going through the more standard set of merchants I knew. Things were about what I'd expected.

I was offered about ten silver coins for the luxury good. Seeing as a forty-kilo rice bag was about four silver coins . . . well, it was still expensive as shit. A couple of the guys didn't want to take on a new product, either.

To be expected, I suppose. Xiulan stayed pretty quiet the entire time, taking the "your wife is so pretty" comments and stares in stride.

I had told the first guy that she wasn't my wife . . . and he'd immediately started hitting on her So, I just kept my mouth shut for the next few. That stopped those conversations dead, though it didn't stop the staring.

Even Big D was getting a bit uncomfortable.

"Is your bird for sale? He's a beaut, I'll give ya twenty silver for him!" one of the men said, looking greedily at my rooster's meaty thighs and plumage.

Big D had swiftly gone from preening under the attention to repulsed by the naked greed and near drooling some people did. And he wasn't even the one who bore the brunt of it. Most of the gazes were directed at Xiulan. One dude actually just walked straight into a pole and nearly knocked himself out.

"Its not nice, is it?" I asked Big D. "People always look at what stands out. That is why I gave the sword to Xiulan and gave her credit for killing Sun Ken. I didn't want to be bothered like this. And even as bad as this is . . . Xiulan has had to deal with worse," I whispered to Big D. The rooster yanked his tail out of the way from a questing hand, which I absently caught, glaring at the old woman who had tried to touch my rooster.

She was spectacularly unapologetic.

"I'll pay you ten silver per clutch of eggs sired," she stated bluntly.

No, I wasn't whoring out my chicken!

Unless he wanted to be whored out? I didn't think he did, judging by the look on his face.

I ignored her, and walked away.

"Imagine getting swamped like this every day. Having people coming to the farm to gawk. Offers like that," I muttered. Big D shuddered slightly.

And this was just a town. In a city, it must be even more shit.

"I'm going to check these guys out," I declared, pointing to the Azure Jade place. Kind of a long shot, but eh, might as well see everywhere.

We moseyed on over as the stall guy wrote something in a ledger. He glanced up at our approach, standing and bowing his head in greeting.

"Greetings, honoured customers, how may this Guan Bo of the Azure Jade Trading Company serve you?" The man straightened up admirably and put on a smile that actually was kind of charming and pleasant. Not sleazy-used-car-salesman like I was expecting. Still a *little* bit fake-feeling, though, probably because I had seen him looking so damn bored.

Now that we were closer to the store, I could see the stuff better, and well, it really was a lot . . . more than the other stuff around here.

And by more, I mean extra as fuck.

It was very xianxia. Gaudy gold, jewels, and even some medicinal pills on display. I saw the prices and nearly snorted.

Capitalism, ho. The Hongs would run these guys out of town on the prices alone. And "efficacious on all mortal maladies"? It was probably true, but damn did it sound like snake oil.

"I was just browsing your wares, sir. You're rather new here," I said as I looked at his stuff, noting the guard who had been hidden just out of view.

"Indeed, I heard good things from some friends, and came to this . . . lovely little village, honoured customer," Guan Bo said with a little chuckle.

Oh yeah, he was lying through his teeth, probably hated it here.

"What other kinds of things do you have in your fine establishment?" I asked, curious. There was quite a lot of stuff out front, but most of it still looked stored away.

Guan Bo puffed up. "We, of the Azure Jade Trading Company, deal in everything of *quality* in these hills! Allow this Guan Bo to show you one of his finer pieces."

He swiftly went to the back, drawing out a shimmery, gossamer silk dress. It was rather pretty, but why the hells was he getting that out?

"This is a Skyblue Forest Silk dress, honoured customers. Such a beautiful jewel should be similarly clad, no?" he asked cheerily, glancing at Xiulan.

Oh. Well, I suppose that's one reason. Lanlan was in the stuff Meiling had made for her, which was decidedly *not* shimmery gossamer silk.

Xiulan looked at it once, then dismissed it. I was a little interested in it, though. I mean sure, it was very . . . uh. Xianxia, but that was a nice, tight weave.

"How was this woven?" I asked, examining it closely.

"I'm afraid the makers have their secrets, honoured customer, but it is made of only the finest Skyblue Silkworms, taken from the top of the trees. This piece alone took five years to craft!" he boasted, still enthusiastic even though Xiulan seemed uninterested.

Her dress was a bit better than this. And much more suited to combat. It was reinforced in places, while this looked like it would tear pretty easy.

His smile stayed in place, however, as he started getting out other jewelry, some furs, medicine, and even a sword.

Yeah, they were all right, but they were . . . well, the Azure Hills were weak. I—I mean, Rou—had seen street vendors in Crimson Crucible City hawking swords and dresses that were better quality than this guy from a massive company.

But I wasn't really here to buy, I was here to sell. So I brought out my own wares. The poor dude looked frustrated but graciously accepted my maple syrup for appraisal.

He poured a single drop onto his wrist, examining it closely.

He stared for a moment. He stared for a little longer.

He *stared*.

"You're supposed to eat it," I said blandly.

Guan Bo swallowed thickly, then carefully licked up the drop.

His eyes closed, and he exhaled. He turned to me.

"How . . . much were you planning on selling, honoured customer?" he asked quietly.

I brought out the three big jars from the cart I was wheeling around.

His eyes widened.

"And the price?" he asked me.

Honestly? I thought I could definitely sell it to this guy for more than the prices I had been offered by the locals. It couldn't be too expensive—it was just maple syrup. *Let's see how much this guy thinks it's worth.*

"How much do you think? I asked.

"Fifty silver coins per jar?" he asked, throwing out an outrageous number. Really? *Fifty?*

I frowned a little.

"Sixty," he swiftly amended at the frown.

Well, it *was* something new and interesting. If he was Azure Jade Trading, he probably had noble contacts who would pay through the nose for this . . .

Xiulan coughed.

"Seventy-five?" he asked, sounding hopeful.

Okay, now he's going higher. My sense of honour and fair play warred with the fact that I was going to be ripping off some city slicker.

Old habits die hard. The farm boy in me was screeching like a monkey at the prospect of pulling one over on a yuppie, and Rou's memories were telling me to drive in a knife and bleed him for all he was worth.

I am not a perfect man.

"I would be content with eighty," I said—the man winced. "And of course, it would be with the understanding that your esteemed company is the sole distributor."

The man's eyes widened, and a smile broke out on his face.

"It is an honour and a pleasure doing business with you, honoured customer. We shall draw up a contract post haste."

"Tomorrow, at the palace?" I asked him.

He bowed his head in respect. "As you wish, sir!"

I did feel a bit guilty at what I had just done. I kind of felt like I had scammed him . . . okay, I had absolutely scammed him—there was no way the syrup was worth that much. Maybe it was a bit of a dick move, when I was giving sweet deals to the Magistrate . . . but things would probably work out okay.

↔

Guan Bo, safely in the back of the shop, danced and hopped around like a madman.

He hated this little town. It was in the ass-end of nowhere. It was cold. The food was too rustic. The people were dullards of the highest order, all dirt farmers and pig breeders. Sure, he enjoyed being on the road and travelling around, but this was way too far off the beaten path. There was no profit to be made here. No interesting people to rub shoulders with.

They were little people, living little lives.

He had been beginning to doubt the veracity of his informant's tip. A recording crystal selling here, of all places? Mayhap to the Magistrate, but he had not said anything besides inspecting Guan Bo's wares with a raised brow and then ignoring him.

He had been absolutely hemorrhaging money. All right, not hemorrhaging, because at least everything was cheap here, but he certainly wasn't *making* any money. His wares were too refined and expensive for these people. They came to gawk at his fine things, and then their faces paled and their eyes bugged out when they saw the prices—and then they fled from his store.

The only thing he had sold was a necklace to one of the "noble" families. Zhuge Tingfeng was the buyer. Bo had gotten a fairly good price. The man's wife had been one hell of a looker, too.

Bo knew he'd always been . . . well, a bit flighty. He followed the wind as it blew, hunting for new deals and new places to expand the trading company into. His informant was normally trustworthy, having information on crystal sellers' movements. Apparently the Magistrate had asked for them, but for another man—a man who was apparently in the town quite often.

There were also rumours of pelts of outstanding quality and rice of a grade unheard of. But these were quiet things, spoken of in whispers.

No normal man could afford a recording crystal. Which meant a new player was in this town, and they had money to spend!

Or Bo was going to blow it . . . *again*. Grandmother would sigh and shake her head when he came crawling back, but he would eventually be able to salvage things. His wife would probably be upset with him. And his sister? Oh, his sister would raise her eyebrow and stare. *Judgingly*. And then she'd disband his aides and make him do all the paperwork himself back at the main compound. Chyou was a damn devil.

It had been a shame, because he'd had a great feeling about this place.

But it was all for naught. Three months, and nothing.

Until this.

He pumped his arms up in the air. This *wasn't* a wasted trip!

Now, to protect the source. It wouldn't do for any rivals to come sniffing around after he'd discovered this silver mine. This would be his. His merit. His way of broadening the Azure Jade Trading Company!

Eighty silver coins per jar was a pricey sum—certainly to the cultivator's favour. But that good feeling had returned twofold. He knew he had a gem in his hands.

And none would dare investigate the Azure Jade Trading Company. "Secret sources" were *respected* by the Sects they did business with, lest they suddenly find themselves banned from the Azure Jade Trading Company.

He raised a bottle of wine in toast. To the cultivator, his oddly familiar-looking wife, and even to their freckly maid!

↔

I was really, really glad Big D was so understanding about why I had given Xiulan the credit for Sun Ken. After his experience in the Exchange: of nearly getting mobbed, the crass questions, the lustful looks at Xiulan . . .

He was very adamant that none of these people knew about the farm. I was honestly impressed he didn't nearly kill somebody. He was vibrating pretty hard at the end.

Back at the Zhuge residence, he had even apologised for being angry at Xiulan, in his own way. Of being upset and jealous.

My chicken was more polite than a lot of people.

In any case, we would probably be leaving after the contract was signed. I got into our bed beside my wife, who was frowning at a scroll and sneaking glances at me.

"Jin?" she asked quietly.

"Yes, love?" I asked.

She looked a bit uncomfortable, but she composed herself.

"Meihua is due very soon, and I know you have to get back to the farm . . . but could I stay until she gives birth?" she asked, biting her lip.

What was she so nervous about? It would be a little lonely without her, but she was worried about her friend. Besides, if I wanted to see her, I'd just come visit.

"Yeah, of course," I stated simply.

The tension drained out of her body at that statement, her lips quirking into a smile.

"You want me to send Rizzo along? You need some money for living expenses?" I asked. On receiving no response, I glanced over at my wife. "Meimei?"

My wife was staring at me with a strange expression on her face before she broke out into a warm smile.

She kissed me.

"I don't need anything else, Jin," she said, her voice fond.

CHAPTER 30

DEPART

Bi De gazed down upon the town in the predawn light. From his position on top of the enormous coop, he could take it all in. it was a little bit rude to stand atop another's coop, but the Master of this place was a human. Bi De doubted the stately man used the roof often. No, it was home to strange ones that shared his form, called pigeons. They were like the people of the town. Crammed together brushing shoulders, and constantly chattering.

He observed the town. The winding, cobbled streets. The thick, sturdy walls, upon which alert and attentive guards patrolled. The teeming masses of men and beasts that lived within.

This place was a "tiny town."

How small Blessed Fa Ram was. How seemingly vulnerable. It hurt his heart to think that. To contemplate the sheer enormity of the world. He knew it was large, as he knew the sun and the stars were large. But knowing and *knowing* were two different things.

And there were still so, so many things Bi De did not know. It was folly to sit in Fa Ram all day without exploring the wider world. It was but one part of a connected whole.

He concentrated, then cast out with his senses. The power of the land was duller here. Less vibrant. Its power was a mere tendril connected to his Lord, rather than the quiet well of power that sat beneath their home stirring with ever greater energy and purpose.

Would all places be this way? Would the energy become lesser the farther he travelled? It was something he would find out soon.

He jumped down from on top of the grand coop, descending into the town. He had to confess he very much disliked it here. The children of Hong Yaowu were bad enough with their incessant petting, but they hardly meant anything by it. They were simply so enamoured by his silky, vibrant feathers that they wished to feel them. The people here were as grabby as the children, but lust filled their eyes at the sight of him, appraising his form with greed.

It was a disturbing amount of greed. They looked at Disciple Xiulan the same way: in covetous lust. He had nearly beaten the humans who dared to try to touch him. Offering money for his body, or attempting to get him to mate with their females. His Great Master had apologised at the treatment, but it was part of his explanation of why he'd given glory to Disciple Xiulan.

That kind of glory was a curse. Many would come, with the same eyes as these people. And his Great Master had said that you must either be quiet about such things . . . or have enough strength to be able to dissuade them entirely.

That his Great Master considered that he was not yet strong enough to do this was troubling.

Bi De stalked through the alleyways, hopping silently from sign to sign, observing the people as they worked. They shovelled an obscene amount of trash and collected the dung that this place accumulated. Their work was diligent, and for that it was praiseworthy.

The people were not supplicants, like the people of Hong Yaowu. They did not cheer his passing.

Instead, they were something else. It was so easy when people fit into the neat little box of friend or enemy. The majority of these were in a nebulous place, where they were neither friend nor foe.

He disliked the uncertainty, yet it was likely to be a constant companion. He had to learn how to better judge people, lest he repeat the Chow Ji incident.

Some people were lighting lamps while some people were setting up for the day. There were stalls coming out. Cooking fires beginning to burn.

There was even one of the men setting up for another show, though this one seemed to have much more money in it than the last. There were humans to be acting out the events, rather than puppets. They even had a fairly good portrait of Disciple Xiulan beside the stage . . . though she looked far more severe and imperious than he had ever seen her. There was gold in her hair and a dress more ornate than the one she had come to Fa Ram with. If he saw Disciple Xiulan and the portrait side by side, he would claim they were different people.

He continued on. Most ignored his presence, which was good. He idly wondered if such lustful greed was only common to those in the "Exchange"? These early-morning folk had little of it.

He wandered back to the coop of Tingfeng. It would be morning in earnest soon. He could feel the position of the sun, and his instincts began prodding him to call.

He ignored them. The other multitudes of roosters would have that mission. He felt no desire to wake these people. They were not his to wake.

He paused when he noticed his path barred. There stood a goat. She placidly chewed her cud in the middle of the street, eyes dull and bored.

She stared at him.

He stared back.

The goat turned and began walking, as if she expected him to follow.

Bemused, Bi De complied. He was unsure if this one had the spark or not. She was . . . strange. Neither present nor completely absent—like brother Chun Ke on his bad days, when his eyes clouded over completely and he became lost to them, battling demons he could not see.

Yet these eyes were the eyes of one dreaming, not fighting. Content in the silence.

He felt no Qi from her.

They arrived at a tiny, cracked, and run-down coop. The goat pushed open the door and entered. Bi De followed.

Inside was small and dingy. A table, wooden carvings, and a cauldron filled the space. An old, mangy, tiger-striped cat eyed him boredly as he entered. The cat looked a bit like Tigu, but ancient and tired, rather than young and full of arrogance. He was also missing one of his front paws.

Bi De bowed his head in apology at his entrance. The cat ignored him and closed his eye.

"Ha! There you are, Lan Fan, you damnable beast!" a voice shouted. An old, grey-haired woman with a rolling eye accosted the goat, glaring at it. "How many times are you going to run off?"

The goat, Lan Fan, snorted.

The old woman turned her good eye, which rolled like it had a mind of its own before it settled on him.

"And look, you've bought a defective chicken! It should be crowing right now!" the woman barked, as indeed, a chorus of roosters were lifting their voices to the heavens. Bi De knew the sun had risen. It was a primal instinct to raise his beak to the sky and praise the sun, but doing so in a woman's house would be rude.

He cocked his head to the side at the insult. Courtesy warred with his own pride.

"Hmph, but I suppose I can expect nothing less from a beast like you," she grumbled, and glared at him. "An up-jumped cock going off on an *adventure*, eh?"

He paused at that deduction. He had to mentally reevaluate the woman, as her eye rolled once more—and the woman smirked.

She rooted around in a drawer, then returned with a piece of paper.

"If you're going on a journey, it's stupid to not have a map," she said blandly.

Bi De stared in surprise. It was incredibly detailed. More detailed than he had ever seen, with lines even denoting what seemed to be elevations.

Before he could examine it further, however, it was rolled up.

"This one requires payment," she stated with a wicked little grin. "I need a good crow, from the top of the house. Best one you can give."

Bi De frowned but nodded. It was an odd request. The cat glared, pulling his one good paw over both his ears.

Bi De hopped up to the roof as the woman got outside her home and plugged her ears.

Bi De snorted at the other roosters' reedy calls. That was *not* how one greeted the sun—one must make their voice louder! Exhale! Exult!

He took a deep breath, filling his core.

He greeted the sun.

His voice ripped through the air, melodious and commanding. It echoed through the streets and into the air, carrying his greeting to the entire town and rebounding off the hills so it could be heard for a hundred li in every direction.

He cut his cry and let the echo fade.

There was a brief moment of absolute silence. Then there was a cacophony of shouting. Anger and outrage at being awoken. Groans and grumbles. The roosters, briefly silenced, all began to try to imitate him. Pigs squealed. Dogs barked. Cats yowled as the entire town was forced into wakefulness.

The dilapidated coop next door was the loudest, an old man hobbling out of his house yelling bloody murder—and he stepped in a pile of goat dung right outside his door.

The woman began to cackle as the old man started hopping on one foot, cussing.

Bi De hopped down from the roof and took the paper from where the woman was holding herself against the wall.

Strange old lady.

↔

"May the heavens smile upon this venture," Guan Bo had said joyously, and we both drained our cups. It was a bit strange to be drinking so early, but hey. The man wanted a celebratory drink.

The deal went great. Contract was all good. One page. No fine print. Witnessed by the Magistrate and First Archivist Bao. Guan Bo had looked a little nervous about things but had recovered fast.

And just like that, I now had more money than I had made during the harvest. It was a pretty small amount compared to what the Lowly Spiritual Herbs sold for in Crimson Crucible City, but it was still a lot.

It was a nice influx of cash, and probably more than enough . . . until I remembered that I still needed to pay Gou Ren for his farmhand stuff. And Yun Ren had helped a lot with the syrup.

You don't screw your friends.

This was also a trial run. If he came back happy and ready to buy more syrup . . . then I could do that. I had also asked him to keep an eye out for stuff like tomatoes and cocoa. Take some of my load off the Magistrate.

And . . . I should probably see if my disciples wanted money too. Working without getting paid is just slavery.

Yay, moral conundrums. I wasn't really used to being the employer.

In any case, once I got back to Tingfeng's place, we were nearly packed and ready to go. The Xong brothers were prepped, and Meimei was whispering something to Xiulan off to the side.

"Guys!" I called. They turned to me, and two money pouches sailed through the air. They caught the pouches, though both looked confused.

"Your cuts from the syrup, and for your work, Gou Ren."

Both stared at me in shock at the heft.

"I humbly receive this?" Gou Ren managed, while Yun Ren started doing a victory dance, even though his was smaller than his brother's.

"Nearly enough, nearly enough, nearly enough!" he chanted.

"You boys ready to go?" I asked, while Xiulan finished her conversation.
Gou Ren nodded as the rest of the household came to see us off.

I hugged my wife. Meimei held me tightly.

"See you soon," I told her.

She kissed me.

"See you soon."

We began our trek back to Hong Yaowu.

↔

Bi De stood before his Great Master, at the Shrine of Fire. He would be setting out from where he had first witnessed the formation.

"Remember. If you ever need to come back, or need some help. Home is always there for you."

Bi De bowed his head. He would heed his Great Master's words.

"Now . . . see you later, buddy," he declared, stroking his wattles.

Bi De nodded. He would figure out the secret behind the formation. He would come back, stronger and wiser. Bi De hopped to the roof as his Great Master watched him. He took a deep breath and shouted his goodbye, along with his respect.

His Master laughed.

"You tell 'em, Bi De."

Bi De turned and departed into the forest.

CHAPTER 31

THE HILLS

Xiulan dodged to the left, away from the ball of mud I had hucked at her head. She sailed through the air as she leapt to another post. The second ball of mud immediately fired, so she twisted midair. It still managed to tag her, moving at a decent clip. The force of it knocked her off balance, and she had to desperately adjust, choosing a different, smaller pole than the one she originally intended.

She landed, her arms waving comically, as a mud barrage fired again, and she wove, dodging these ones, and managed to stabilise.

The kung fu poles were turning out to be a hit. I had finished them up out of boredom when we'd gotten back. I hadn't hopped up yet, but Xiulan had taken one look at them and did her whole "super grateful" routine, which led me to just throwing her into the pond.

She, of course, was pretty graceful, hopping around the poles like they were solid ground . . . until I started to "test" her. Then it really turned into something out of a kung fu movie. She was getting a lot better at dodging while airborne.

She had been strangely insistent that it be *mud* I threw at her for this, but I suppose it would hurt less than rocks. I'd only needed a little bit of Qi to keep the muck cohesive, and I could throw them pretty fast. Considering I was probably making MLB players green with envy at the speed of the pitches . . . well, they still kind of hurt. But if I threw any slower Xiulan got pouty that I was going easy on her.

Speaking of baseball . . . I threw a few more in rapid succession, one of which seemed to go wide. She dodged again—

—until the curveball beaned her straight in the dome. She flew off the log and into the water.

I couldn't hear her properly, but I was one hundred percent sure Tigger was laughing at Xiulan's expression as she fell. Her paw was against her mouth as she watched Xiulan plummet, and her shoulders shook.

That lasted until a glob of mud from the bottom of the pond—the smelly, gross kind of mud—fired up from out of the water and splattered all over my cat.

There was silence for a moment. And then the two of them exploded into action, fists and paws striking out rapidly as they danced along the poles. Their passing disturbed Gou Ren on his pole, as he was just trying to stand on it as he had seen Xiulan doing . . . and he fell with a yelp.

I watched the fight like it was a movie. It was really good entertainment. A literal catfight.

I snorted and looked at the poles.

I hopped up onto one of the poles for the first time, kind of expecting a bit of wobbly knees like Gou Ren had experienced . . . but there was none of that.

Well, I had gone on to the biggest one, so I hopped to the next one. It was smaller.

The jump was surprisingly easy. I frowned as I landed.

I certainly didn't *feel* unbalanced.

I purposefully swung my body back and forth a bit.

I didn't fall. Didn't feel anything, really. No loss of balance, no sensation like I was going to fall.

Nothing.

I jumped again and landed on the joke pole. The one that was tiny—too small for your foot, more a stick than something you could land on.

It felt . . . *solid.* I didn't tip. It honestly seemed like I was standing on the ground.

Huh.

Well, that's kind of boring. I wasn't even wobbling. Come to think of it, when was the last time I actually fell, instead of letting people push me over?

Maybe if I got stuff thrown at me too? I wanted to do kung fu training! I sighed, then looked up at the sky, my good mood and amusement dampened by the revelation.

I wondered how Meimei and Big D were doing. Washy too. The fish had been gone for over a month now.

Everything was probably fine at Verdant Hill, and Big D could definitely take care of himself . . . but it was hard waking up alone, or not hearing Big D's cry in the morning. Both had become welcome constants.

The bed was a bit lonely. Xiulan was off with Tigger most nights, and Peppa and Chunky were with Gou Ren. Rizzo was just a bit too small to cuddle properly.

I sighed again.

I want to fall.

At my command, my balance failed me, and I tipped forwards, dropping into the pond.

□

Bi De sat in the forest clearing, pecking at a dried worm. It was sunset, the last rays of golden light filtering through the trees and bathing everything in a warm orange glow. He examined his map closely where it lay against a rock. One toe was on it, to keep the wind from ruffling it. Truly, it was a splendid map. Fine paper, and lines drawn with purpose. The entirety of the Azure Hills were laid out before him.

Did that mean the formation spanned the entirety of the Azure Hills? Or had the strange old woman just given him the best map she possessed? It was a question he would have to meditate on, because while he had not been able to see the full extent of the formation that night on the solstice . . . now that he'd started to walk the land, he'd learned that it was much bigger than he'd thought.

And he did walk it. He'd supposed, with brute force, that he might simply fly from destination to destination, only setting foot on the ground when he had to record something, or to eat . . . but that would not do. He was here to travel. To see. To learn. And though he could see much from the air, one required a closer look at the ground to truly understand.

So he walked. His legs carried him through lush forests, their leaves nearly fully formed. He hopped over streams babbling along with crystal-clear waters. He took in the sheer, untamed wild. The overgrowth. The sounds of beasts. The plants grew where they pleased, and the rocks made some terrain nearly impassible for humans who did not have the spark.

It reminded him of his first days. The first days on Fa Ram, before the Great Master had used his mighty spur, *Sho Vel*, to tame the land and command the earth.

Yet for all its wild growth, for all its animal sounds . . . it did not feel as *alive* as his home. There was Qi . . . but it was lesser. It was quieter.

He turned to his map once more.

He kept his marks light, so as to not damage the map. Small dots, as accurate as he could make them, after leaping into the air to get a better view. One mark for Verdant Hill. One mark for Hong Yaowu. One mark for the little village he had just left. It was quite similar to Hong Yaowu, its people going about their lives. But what all three of them had in common was that the design of their shrine was the exact same.

And there was a cleared patch of ground that was used to do the dance itself nearby.

Bi De considered this conundrum. Should he consider the place where the rite was performed the "true" spot? Or the shrine itself?

Well, he could not mark down with any true accuracy on the map anyway. The scale was too big. But it was another part to consider.

He considered the map further, his eyes travelling down to something he had not noticed at first. There was a mark on the map, and it was not from him. The mark was far to the south. A simple, unassuming X that his eyes had glanced over the first time.

He knew that he must visit this place. It would be a long time before he could get to that location, but he would visit it, if only to assuage his curiosity.

First, though, he had a few jobs entrusted to him. The Magistrate, the Master of Verdant Hill whom his own Great Master held respect for, had begged his Great Master's assistance on a few matters. Those too were marked, and they would be completed as soon as he arrived to take care of them.

He idly traced the area of Fa Ram, and then the area of Verdant Hill.

The map made them truly seem so small.

He carefully rolled the map back up and placed it in his cloth bundle. He counted his dried worms and rice grains, and even the coins his Great Master had given him so that he might pay for anything that he could require.

He knew nothing that the people of this land could give him that he could not procure himself. Mayhap some rice . . . but he would rather eat insects than the junk the other humans attempted to peddle. No Qi in it at all.

When everything was organised, in the way Sister Ri Zu and the Healing Sage had insisted on, he tied the bundle tightly, using his beak and feet. Overtop that, he put the waterproofed skin and tied it a second time, so it would slip around his neck and settle onto his back.

It was quite a big, bulky thing, but he hardly felt its weight.

He hopped into a tree, having chosen this branch as his perch for the night. It was no coop. It was not warm, and it was not filled with his females, but it was not so bad. He could examine the moon clearly from this position. He meditated upon his journey until it was fully visible, then turned his eyes heavensward.

It was full, hanging in the sky like a burnished disk. He could see clearly the craters, shining down from its face. His Great Master said that it had taken terrific impacts, and though the orb was scarred, it was undaunted.

Ah, how the moon was a stalwart protector! Just like himself!

He observed the full moon for a moment longer, and then closed his eyes. He would need to be refreshed for tomorrow.

→

The next day was much the same as the previous ones.

Through the forests, across the streams, and over the giant, rolling hills. Roads in this direction were nonexistent, just the vast wilderness.

He heard a yelp and a squeal of pain, so he froze. His body was instantly alert as he sped to the destination where he'd heard the cry and happened upon one of Basi Bu Shi's kin, its mouth full of rabbit. His instinct as a protector nearly got the better of him. A small one was in danger. Yet this was not the Blessed Land of Fa Ram.

The kin of the wicked one quailed under his gaze.

His Great Master had once said they served a necessary purpose, so that those who ate plants would not completely destroy the forests. The "cycle of life," he had decreed, adding another cycle for Bi De to contemplate.

Bi De looked upon the kin of one of his greatest enemies.

And carefully let go of his Intent.

The fox fled, and remained alive.

He shook his head and launched into the air, to once more get his bearings.

He landed, then continued through the warm underbrush. His eyes were peeled as he observed the life around him. He saw the spiders that caught things in their web, the fish in the stream that preyed upon each other, the bird in flight that took another. Finally, the bones of a wolf and the rabbit nearby, nibbling on the grass that grew around it.

Bi De bowed his head, then continued on.

It was midday when he came upon an overgrown road. It was nearly indistinguishable from the land around him, but he could still see the traces. Turning, he went to follow it, travelling along the old, old path that was barely a path anymore.

He looked upon what was once a village, as Hong Yaowu was. There were fields where the rice once grew, now choked with weeds. The forlorn wind blew through rotting coops. There were no chickens here to cluck and peck at the ground.

There was a Shrine of Fire, dead and empty, the ritual grounds turned into a forest. He knew not what had happened here, only that there was no one left.

He felt a profound sense of sadness at the sight. Would Fa Ram look like this in the future?

Everything is a cycle.

For the first time, Bi De felt repulsed by this idea—that Fa Ram would eventually fall into such a ruin. He was content with his own fate, should it be to return to the earth, but this area, devoid of energy, devoid of the laughter of men and the clucking of chickens?

There was life here. There were the animals nesting in the broken and nearly completely rotted homes.

Yet . . . yet he did not wish for this to be Fa Ram's fate. He could not accept such a thing.

He nested in the village that night. This time he completely disregarded the moon, gazing instead at the earth.

He gazed upon the end of things. The sadness in his breast was profound. His heart was disturbed.

His last thoughts were of his Great Master and Fa Ram. He wondered if they were well.

□

"And? How is everything *this* hour?" Meihua asked, looking a bit exasperated. Meiling raised an eyebrow and removed her fingers from her friend's wrist. Her pulse was good. Better than good, really, the best Meihua had ever felt, strong and steady.

In fact, there was nothing that would normally say Meihua was pregnant. No swollen feet, no fatigue, no sore back, hells, not even morning sickness. Meihua had even been *surprised* when she brought that part up.

All in all, Meihua was perfectly healthy. Better than she had ever been, despite the size of her stomach.

"As fine as yesterday," Meiling said, moving on from checking on her health to brushing her friend's hair. Her fingers ran gently through silky raven locks. Her friend sighed contently at the familiar action.

"You're much better at this than Lingqi," Meihua muttered, mentioning the name of the servant who normally attended to her.

"I've had quite a bit of practice," she demurred.

Meihua smirked. "Ah yes, the Demon-Slaying Orchid, who calls you Senior Sister. They've been doing those shows nonstop, you know."

"They don't have enough farm animals in them. They're *terribly* inaccurate."

Her friend giggled—she had heard the real story about what happened. "My, how our lives have gotten interesting, Meimei." There was a slight wistfulness in her voice. "I'm glad you're here. I know Tingfeng would call a midwife from Pale Moon Lake City if he could, and the finest ladies in Verdant Hill would care for me . . . but there's no one I trust more. And I've missed talking to you."

They hadn't spoken since the wedding, and that had been months ago.

Meiling smiled at her, touched by her friend's faith. They had always been as close as sisters. She debated braiding Meihua's hair . . . but decided against it. It looked best long and free, cascading down her back.

Meiling sat down in front of her friend, then received her own care.

"So, how are you holding up? I heard that you tried to make breakfast this morning," Meihua asked.

Meiling frowned slightly. The servants had looked nearly scandalised at an honoured guest making them breakfast; they had politely but firmly convinced her to rest instead.

So she had spent the hours until Meihua woke up sipping tea and staring at a wall.

"I'm fine," she deflected. But really, she was a bit bored.

And wasn't that an odd truth?

If somebody had told Meiling last year that she would be bored while being taken care of at the Zhuge compound, being around Meihua and reading as often as she wished while others took care of every conceivable chore, she would have scoffed. How could she *ever* be bored with such a situation? It seemed like something out of a dream. Being waited on while spending time as one wished? How decadent! Like a noble lady, instead of a peasant chief's daughter.

Until, of course, it actually happened.

She had finished reading all of her scrolls the first day. Then she'd tackled every scroll in the Archive that she wasn't as familiar with.

When she was done, she realised that it was barely noon, and she had gotten a lot faster at reading. She had returned to the Zhuge compound and had given Meihua a check-up, prepared a bath for her, and helped her bathe. Her skin and hair weren't as interesting as Xiulan's, but they were still soft enough, and it was good to have time together again. Meiling's friend had somehow managed to keep the bits of muscle she had from helping her father in the forge, amazingly, despite being pampered so thoroughly by her husband and his family.

Later that day Meiling had gone to bed wide awake, with nothing to distract her.

There was no Xiulan to spend time with. No Ri Zu asking to learn. No Bi De crowing the morning greeting, though the roosters here were certainly trying. There was no Tigu to scratch, nor any way to hop onto Jin's shoulders, no Gou Ren, Chun Ke, or Pi Pa wandering over.

She was too used to doing more with her days.

The worst part was no Jin. No silly smiles, no warm scent of spring, no strange lessons, no strong hands grabbing her hips and—

She pinched her leg.

Meihua looked like she didn't really believe Meiling's deflection but made no comment.

"And how's your little . . . *project* going?" she asked instead with a sly smile.

"I'm done." Really, there was so little material on that one. But it had been the easiest to make. The dresses and the shirts would require a lot more skill than she currently had.

"That outfit is completely scandalous. I can't believe the man who made that up. It's completely and utterly degenerate," Meihua declared.

"I'll make you one if you want," Meiling offered, rolling her eyes. Her friend was just upset she hadn't thought of it first.

"Truly, you're too good to me."

→

Meiling ambled around the town. She had finally been kicked out of the house by her friend for fussing over her too much. It was a bit enlightening, realising how tolerant Xiulan was in comparison to Meihua, to let her poke and prod at her for as long as she did. Meiling almost wanted to see a reaction from the cultivator now and wondered what could provoke Xiulan enough to finally get her to drop her overly formal act.

It was a brief distraction, before Meiling yawned. She could go to the Archive again, but Uncle Bao was out with the Lord Magistrate, doing something.

So she wandered. Wandered through the streets. To the area where Jin had fought the other cultivator nearly a year ago. Her mind filled in the overgrowth of plants, over the once-more-pristine street. The only thing that was left was that one of the shops still had the little branches sticking out of the poles. The green leaves that they had sported were long dead again, but it was an interesting effect, which was why the owner had kept it.

She wondered if she could convince Jin to do something like this at their house? Maybe on a couple of the poles he had?

Her feet kept plodding along the streets.

Until she saw a young boy. He couldn't be older than five, and he was shovelling the streets. He had a look of absolute determination on his face, his little body straining with all his might to move his heavy loads. He finished shovelling and, with a grunt of exertion, went to push his cart. The load was too much—it started to tip.

She saw the moment his face twisted, despair overcoming him that he would have to do the shovelling all over again.

Meiling caught it with one hand, carefully hoisting it back up.

"Are you all right?" she asked quietly, taking in the boy's grateful expression.

"Yes, pretty sister," he returned, giving her a gap-toothed smile.

Meiling smirked at the statement but was still a little concerned. "Why is one so young doing such a hard job?" she asked.

And indeed, while children worked all the time, they shouldn't be used as street sweepers. Normally the Magistrate and his foremen wouldn't allow it. Children just couldn't do the work needed.

"Ma and Pa are both sick," he stated, with the bluntness only children had. "So I need a job, so I can buy medicine. I begged the foreman for hours till he let me."

She stared at the conviction in those young eyes. He was sweating, and dirty, and exhausted, with bags under his eyes, but he still looked determined.

Meiling frowned. She was here for Meihua. She couldn't go around getting close to people who were sick when her best friend's child was coming!

And then she paused at that immediate thought, and she nearly slapped herself. She had Qi. Medicinal Qi, if Xiulan was correct. It wasn't exactly rare. All doctors that could use Qi could apparently do it, after hours of meditation and a lot of training. It required a careful transformation of energy.

Meiling didn't need those hours of careful meditation and work. She just seemed to generate it. If she wanted that green Qi, she got it.

It also seemed to kill bacteria.

She still remembered the "experiment" her husband had shown her. A way to store the milk for longer. Thoughts written down. Repeatable results.

The one that had been "pasteurized" versus the unpasteurized one, and how much longer the former had lasted. That had been enough to convince her. Then, after they had returned from her village, he started to use his own Qi, out of curiosity.

The milk he'd infused his Qi into actually went rancid *faster*, much to his surprise.

Xiulan and Gou Ren's Qi did nothing.

But hers? Well, it felt odd. Tingly, when she had added her Qi to the milk. She had brushed it along every surface and saturated the liquid. She'd kept it there until it stopped feeling so weird, and then retracted it, feeling oddly drained.

Hers was *still* good. She planned on checking it when she returned, but she had a feeling that it would be fine for months. Tasted a bit different. Almost an herbal undertone, but it was still good. Jin had suggested that her Qi had killed all the bacteria in it.

After that, she'd started running her Qi over surfaces she planned to use. Occasionally, it would tingle a little, and when the twingeing stopped, she knew that the bacteria were dead.

Which meant she *probably* couldn't get sick from this, if she kept up a constant stream of energy. And even if they couldn't pay . . . well. Using a bit of Qi on them would not cost her anything.

So she smiled at the boy.

"Maybe I could help?" she asked. "I'm a healer."

The boy looked a bit skeptical, and she couldn't blame him. Meiling was both short and a woman. But in the end, the kid was desperate for any kind of help. He caved and brought her to a shack in the poorest part of Verdant Hill. The Lord Magistrate ran his domain well, but even he could not completely eradicate this part of town. Still, it was safe. It might be poor, but the guards patrolled vigorously, and the streets were clean of trash.

She frowned at the sight she was greeted with while she tied a mask around the bottom of her face. The kid had done his best, but he was still barely five. His parents were gaunt and sweaty, pale and shaking a little. Their beds were soiled as well.

She sighed. Those would likely have to be burned.

Her hands checked their erratic pulses. She frowned, then carefully extended her Qi. She had been practising on Xiulan, making sure that she could do this without discomfort to the person she used it on. Jin's concerns about exploding people had been largely unfounded, and her Qi didn't seem to be doing any harm.

It immediately started twingeing when it gently wove through their bodies.

It was much, much worse than she'd expected, the near-constant feeling of her Qi hitting something.

It *seemed* like some form of the flux—the man coughed. She felt her skin and her eyes tingle a little, and frowned.

If she hadn't had Qi, there would have been absolutely no way she'd have gone back to Zhuge Clan's compound today—she would have been far, far too contaminated to do so. But that cough was extremely worrying.

She started on the man, pressing her hands against his chest.

She called on more of her Qi, trying to see problem areas. All she got were vague sensations. She could roughly feel where her Qi was, but it was inaccurate, so she kept searching. The heart was fine, the lungs were a bit off, the legs fine, bowels . . . *gross*—they felt like shoving her feet into sludge . . .

She finished and opened her eyes.

The man she was working on was no longer pale or sweating. His eyes opened, seeming a bit confused.

Interesting, Meiling thought, then started on the woman.

She was much the same as the man.

Meiling was starting to feel a bit tired by the end of it. She got them out of their disgusting clothes and soiled bed. They were still a bit woozy, and stumbling, but they were easy to handle. They spouted their thanks, but Meiling was only half paying attention, deep in thought.

She pulled the boy over too . . . and found some of the same feeling, though not quite expressed yet. His body was fighting it admirably, but . . . He giggled at the feeling of her Qi in his body.

But still, it was curious. If it was like the flux . . . Then the flux had come from the water.

"Ping, have either of your parents been out of Verdant Hill in the last week?" she asked, and the boy shook his head.

Not from a river, then, Meiling thought to herself, which was even more troubling. That meant that there was something inside Verdant Hill causing it. Some contamination in a well? Those were normally kept very clean.

"Where do you keep your water?" she asked the boy.

"Right here, Honoured Doctor!" he managed to get out, staring up at her with stars in his eyes.

She stuck her finger in the jars she was shown, one by one. One of them didn't feel off. The other two, the ones that had been drunk out of, *did*.

"Which well did these come from?" she asked. The boy didn't know, but there was a mumbled answer from his mother.

"The well close by."

How many people had already drunk from the well?

"Ping, will you show me where this is, please?" she asked the boy, who nodded vigorously.

So she was off again, her frown even heavier on her face.

She stalked past the few people in the streets, who gave her a wide berth, save for a drunk—he shouted something about her behind.

She ignored him completely and shoved past a person who was trying to draw their water.

"Hey! What the hells is your problem?" the woman shouted, grabbing on to Meiling's shoulder.

And then immediately let go when she saw the slight green glow on Meiling's hand.

The water twinged.

"Don't drink it, it will make you sick," she stated bluntly, turning to the woman, who recoiled.

The woman nodded numbly.

"Ping, see if you can get anybody who has drunk anything from this well over here, please. Or find out if there's anyone else sick."

The boy beamed and nodded.

"Ah . . . I was getting water for my friend, she's sick," the woman said, looking shocked.

"Can you get her over here?" Meiling asked. The woman nodded rapidly.

Meiling rolled up her sleeves, her eyes narrowed in concentration.

This was going to be a long, *long* day.

□

"Lord Magistrate, a report," a guard said, and his liege nodded, not glancing up from his documents.

"Proceed."

"A cultivator is in the tanner district, demanding that we shut down one of the wells, as it is contaminated."

His Lord paused, taking in the absurd statement with grace, and raised his head.

"I see," he declared, as if it were the most natural thing in the world. His face was a mask of calm.

Inside the sanctity of his mind, the curses flowed.

□

Meiling felt like she was going to vomit. Her limbs were shaking, and the biggest migraine she'd ever felt was pounding in her ears.

She tried to ignore the shining eyes of the people around her. They were a bit too close, with how nauseated she felt.

"Thank you, Medical Fairy Sister!" a man shouted.

Her face flushed at the sudden flood of adoration. She was flattered, really she was; now if they could *just get out of her face before she poisoned them*, that would be great.

And the well would need more than just her Qi anyway. It was a crutch she had used, and they needed a permanent solution. Only five people had actually been sick, to her relief. The rest seemed to be doing just fine.

She held up a hand for silence, and the people quieted down. "I'll return tomorrow," she said curtly. Later tomorrow; she would have to get a few things first.

And with that, she put one foot in front of the other and walked out of the tanner district.

A couple of guards stopped anybody who tried to follow her, and she was grateful for that.

She grimaced as she tugged on her sweaty, filthy clothes. She was going to have to burn these later.

She gave only perfunctory greetings to Meihua, stripped down, and boiled herself a bath, using the last dregs of her energy.

→

She woke up late the next morning, so late that Meihua was already up and sitting beside her bed.

"So . . . mind telling me why you have an invitation from the Lord Magistrate's wife for a meal together?" she asked.

□

Gathering herbs and fungus gave Meiling the time she needed to think—something she *hadn't* been doing yesterday. Yesterday, she'd seen a problem, so she'd gone about trying to fix it. Her father had said that it was a good trait to have as a healer, especially in situations where there were multiple people hurt. Categorize the wounded and the sick, then start working. Concentrate, focus on the workflow, and then steadily grind it down as best you were able.

It was how she approached organisation. It was how she had approached getting her little brother to eat the vegetables he didn't like. It was also how she had gotten through those terrible nights, full of screams of pain coming from people she couldn't help.

But while she allowed the task to consume her focus, she tended to forget to think about *other* things. Like using Qi so blatantly.

Jin . . . well, he wasn't exactly careful about using Qi, though he kept it quieter than jumping into the middle of town and blasting green on anybody who asked her to.

I'm less subtle than my husband. The thought was hilarious, considering how Jin stomped around sometimes.

She had caught a brewing plague in its infancy. Wasn't that something to be proud of?

Even if it *had* attracted a lot of attention. Meiling sighed.

Well, what was done was done. She would stand by her actions. And she was fairly certain that Jin wouldn't care either. At least nobody knew her name except Ping, and even then he insisted on calling her Medical Fairy Sister.

Except the Magistrate's wife knew *exactly* who she was and had invited her for tea, likely to talk about what she had just done.

She grimaced and kicked a rock in irritation, jumping when it cracked into a tree a lot harder than she'd been expecting.

She had met the woman once before. Once. And hadn't even talked to her. She was Meiling's superior in every way. From one of the noble families, married to the Lord Magistrate, graceful, respected . . .

She could already feel herself getting irritated.

She dearly hoped that this wasn't going to be some sort of subtle posturing and power play. Verbally smacking around Ty An was one thing, but she was woefully underequipped to handle somebody like the Lady of Verdant Hill.

She sighed again as she carefully collected some leaves she would need to grind, then stared at them. She had said that she would give the people some medicine, but . . . well, realistically, that was a bit of a problem too. Her father was the one who had collected payment. He told her what he needed, and she organised it. She had never had to deal with the merchants who came looking for her father, other than serving them tea. When she went to work, everything was already negotiated.

Should she just give it out for free? Medicine was a job. She couldn't beggar herself out of goodwill, no matter somebody else's circumstances.

She didn't have enough to just give things away. Providing an idle helping hand to a boy she took pity on was one thing. Taking care of five others . . .

But . . . had it truly cost her anything?

Well, no sense thinking about it. She had given her word, and she would follow it through to the end.

She took a deep breath and closed her eyes, feeling the energy that swirled in her stomach.

One thing at a time, until it's done.

She opened her eyes again and pulled the cloth over the bottom of her face like a veil.

One thing at a time, until it's done.

□

"This one? No, not this one, it's too big, you'll look like you're drowning in it. *This* one? It was Honourable Grandmother's." It was a nice dress. Though it was a bit much for Meiling, nearly as decorated as her own wedding dress.

Meihua was whirling around the room, entirely too nervous to be healthy for her state. She was insistent that Meiling be dressed and made up for her meeting, and Meiling deferred to her judgement.

She was seated placidly on a stool as a servant, a girl named Lingqi, applied makeup to her face. Her focus was half on her friend talking, and half on the memory of the smiles of the people she had helped.

Medical Fairy Sister was almost as good as *Senior Sister*. Flattering. She didn't mind it as much as Xiulan seemed to, but then again, she didn't get these things as often as her friend did. It was still novel enough to be gratifying.

"Now, Lady Wu has a mild temperament, so you *should* be fine. I've dined with her a few times, and she is pleasant company."

Meiling listened while the servant worked. She was trying to remain calm. She wasn't a noble. She had barely any idea how this meeting would go, and Meihua was stirring her stomach even more.

It suddenly felt *real*. That all of a sudden she was more than just a peasant girl from Hong Yaowu with a strange ability to smell Qi. Jin was one thing. Even Xiulan felt more approachable than the Patriarch and his wife. Maybe it was because she'd grown up hearing about his work. Maybe because he was cemented in her head as her superior.

He had clapped her on the shoulder once and called her a "virtuous young man," when she had helped with the treatment of the victims of Sun Ken. That memory still stung a bit, but in his defence, she *had* looked like a boy back then, lanky and gangly and as flat as a wall, with her face covered by a mask. The fact that he was willing to be there at all, even getting his hands dirty helping to move the wounded, had been a memory she regarded as important.

That was a ruler.

And now she had been requested, and requested *politely*, to discuss the matter over tea. It was a bit short notice, but she had assumed the "at your convenience" in the letter to mean "as soon as possible."

But she also couldn't just rush over in her normal clothes, could she? At least Meihua didn't think so. Meiling had to be presentable if she was going to see the most important woman in a few hundred li.

She nearly wrinkled her nose when she felt more powder dabbed onto her face. "That feels like a lot," she said to Lingqi.

"Ah, all the other ladies cover up any blemishes. Young Miss covers her mole."

Well, it made sense. She had a lot of freckles. She let the girl continue her work.

"They aren't blemishes. They're the best!" her Jin declared, while trailing kisses down across the bridge of her nose.

Well, it was the style, so there wasn't anything to be done.

"You'll be fine, Meimei," Meihua said, more to herself than Meiling. "Just so long as you don't insult her or poison her . . . Ah, never mind, you're doomed." That last part had clearly been said to lighten the mood, but Meiling just winced. Her lips always did get a bit looser when she was nervous or angry.

The servants finished dressing her and putting the makeup on.

It felt wrong. Clad in things that weren't her own.

A burnished bronze disk was brought out so she could see herself.

"It . . . well, it looks . . ." Meihua tried. "Lingqi, go to the market and get another shade. We'll start again."

She gazed at her reflection, the makeup painfully obvious as it coated her face. It didn't match her skin tone, made for someone much paler than she. She could *see* the amount that had been used to cover her freckles.

Combined with the dress, it made her look like she was pretending.

No, this would not do at all.

This wasn't Hong Meiling. Why should she dress up like that? Why should she use expensive makeup? She was a farmer's wife, damn it. She wasn't some noble lady.

"No. It's fine," she stated simply.

The small basin of water boiled easily enough, and then the makeup came off her face. She scrubbed, with Qi-infused hands.

She changed out of the lovely dress and into her last clean set of clothes. All the while, Meihua was speaking and planning with her servant, thinking about makeup and dresses Meiling could use.

Meiling took a deep breath and stared at her reflection. Her back straightened. Her eyes narrowed slightly.

The woman in the mirror was no longer acting. She was just a farmer's wife again.

Satisfied, she let out the air she was holding. Something seemed to settle around her.

"We can still try something else and— Oh." Meihua stopped as she took in her friend. Her eyes widened, as she looked her up and down.

"That is very, *very* unfair, Meimei," she managed to get out.

□

It was a pavilion on the outskirts of town. Neutral ground. A high garden, built to give a commanding view of the land outside the walls, looking down onto the valley that surrounded the Verdant Hill. It was quiet and out of the way, with no one else on the street at this hour.

The trees bloomed beautifully, the flowers smelled sweet, and the Lady of Verdant Hill waited calmly for her guest.

It had taken some convincing for her husband to agree, but he had eventually given in. The silly man was always so *jumpy* after the incident. These cultivators had given her no cause for concern yet, but that was just the way her husband was.

He worried and fretted constantly. Why, if the men of Verdant Hill would hear about his woes, they would surely spit blood! Her lip curled up with mirth at the thought.

She adored him. He was a constant amusement, as were the reactions of the people. To see the dichotomy between the man *she* knew and the man *they* knew. The stern Patriarch of Verdant Hill, and the man who would rather curl up into her bosom and moan about how unfair life was. He worked. He struggled. He doubted himself. Others said those were *unattractive* qualities. Better what he was than a statue of virtue. She knew men like that. Humourless sentinels, dispensing their justice without remorse.

While sometimes this little village was boring—and sometimes she longed for the hustle and bustle of Pale Moon Lake City—she had to admit her husband was right about some things.

Her hand shook a little, the tremors from that old *thing* working their way into her limbs. Really, that was the worst part about it. It came and it went but most days it wasn't too bad. In all honesty? She *liked* the grey streaks in her hair. And while the surges were unpleasant, they were worth it. They had let her leave with barely a word to her Honoured Father. It wasn't *quite* an elopement with a common-born man, but a "damaged" woman simply wasn't worth an argument.

"My lady, she's here," a guard whispered to her, his eyes set and full of conviction. She resisted the urge to ruffle the young man's hair. He was about her own son's age. So eager and loyal.

She graced him with a smile and thanked him.

She sat up primly and waited. She did not have to wait long.

Lady Wu hadn't thought much of Hong Meiling the last time they'd met. The girl had been thin, with nearly pinched features, hunched over slightly behind her stunningly beautiful friend, glaring at any who dared to look at her. "A shrewish girl, with a tongue like a dagger" was her description.

Now, as the young woman wearing peasant's clothes walked towards her, she saw none of that.

The woman strode with a straight back, her head held high. She was not quite what one would describe as classically beautiful—she was a bit too sharp-looking for that, with her angular face and intense amethyst eyes. But while her eyes were striking . . . it was something intangible that held your attention.

She had a weight about her. A kind of quiet strength that drew the eye and made one think *This is a woman to be obeyed.*

The lady knew now why the guards had obeyed her immediately when the demand had come to shut down the well.

But as Meiling drew closer, Lady Wu noticed the slight cracks. Meiling . . . was *young.* Young, and not at all prepared for this meeting. Running on bravado and her own grit.

It was quite endearing, and amusing, that a cultivator was nervous to meet *her.*

But . . . this girl wasn't *really* a cultivator, was she? She wore her simple clothes with pride. Her face was clear of any kind of makeup, for what could a farmer's wife need makeup for?

Lady Wu clenched her fist, forcing the shakes away, and rose. The young woman cocked her head to the side; her nose twitched, and a brief look of confusion rolled over her features.

"This Wu Zei Qi greets Lady Hong, and thanks her for coming," she stated serenely, her bow perfect and graceful.

"Hong Meiling pays her respects to Lady Wu," Meiling greeted her politely, startled out of her examination, and returned her bow.

"Please, join me," the lady said with a gesture before retrieving a fan from her sleeve.

The younger woman nodded, trying to keep her affection of bland disinterest as the tea was poured.

When that was done, the lady waved off her servants; both of them bowed and departed.

When they were alone together, Lady Wu studied Meiling from behind her fan. She could tell the girl didn't know how to proceed in the silence, shifting a bit. After a moment, Meiling reached out and took a sip of tea.

"One normally waits for their elder to drink, before drinking themself," Lady Wu said airily—and Meiling froze at the gentle rebuke, panic flashing in the back of her eyes.

Lady Wu smirked but took pity on the younger woman.

"Forgive my teasing, Lady Hong. I did not mean to provoke such a reaction." Her fan snapped closed, and she placed it on the table. The time for games was over. "Come, let us speak frankly on the matter."

The girl seemed taken aback. Again, a subtle thing to most, but her heart was clearly on display for the whole world, if one knew where to look.

"Firstly, on behalf of our Verdant Hill, this Wu Zei Qi thanks you." She raised her hands, clasping them before her.

"Thanks to your quick action, a tragedy has been prevented, and the culprit located. We believe it was a cistern. You said it was contaminated water, so we had a search party look for any possible cause. One of the tanneries uphill had a leak in a cistern that was filled with filth and rotting fat. The guards are still checking, but we believe this to be the source of our malaise."

Hong Meiling nodded along at the explanation, her brow furrowed in thought.

"I'll check the cistern to see if it feels like what I dealt with earlier. And I'll make something to decontaminate the well." She agreed so easily; no, that would not do!

"One must watch what one agrees to before they negotiate a payment," Lady Wu replied, swirling her tea around in its cup.

This time, the wince was quite visible.

"How much experience do you have in selling your services?" she asked, and Meiling cocked her head to the side again, debating something . . .

"Little. Father was the one who handled everything," Meiling admitted, still confused and curious. The interaction was obviously not going the way she had constructed in her head.

Lady Wu nodded. "We shall have to fix that. Send a message when you wish to learn, and I shall teach you," she declared.

"Why?" Meiling asked again, eyeing her with those flinty chips of gemstone. Oh my, that was an intense gaze! It gave her the shivers.

The older woman raised an eyebrow. "Why shouldn't I? What do I have to gain from antagonising you, save for your ire? Oh, I could probably weave a spell of words around you. Use your nervousness to get you to agree to something you wouldn't normally. And that would last until you got annoyed, and then my hair would probably get even greyer. I know what happens when somebody annoys a cultivator." She pointed to her grey hair. Just being near a cultivator's attack had hurt her. A direct blow? There wouldn't be anything left.

"No, Hong Meiling, that would not do. So I, like my husband, would prefer an amicable relationship. There is nothing else to this. I invited you, both to get to know you and to thank you for your actions. That is all. Though . . . I do have questions you could answer, if it wouldn't be too bold."

Meiling considered her statement, mulling it over in her head and finding it satisfactory.

"What manner of questions?"

Lady Wu smiled. "Well, this one has been on my and my husband's minds, but it was not Cai Xiulan who slew Sun Ken, was it? Your husband knew before the news was out."

The young woman nodded. "It was Bi De."

"The *chicken* that my husband asked to kill that pack of wolves?" she asked incredulously.

"Yes. Though the credit was given to Xiulan on purpose. Jin didn't want any visitors."

Lady Wu took a sip of her tea, considering. "Any other dangerous monsters he has taken care of?" she asked whimsically.

"Last year, Jin killed the Wicked Blade," the girl said with a shrug, as if this were *not* an earth-shaking revelation.

The Wicked Blade? The Reaper Wolf who had slain cultivators? The living legend that could eradicate an entire town in minutes?

It was Lady Wu's turn to gape, and she realised that this was what her husband must feel like. The odd, floating sensation that strained her sense of belief—yet she was absolutely certain it happened.

The food came as she was still trying to recover from that revelation, the servants returning to bring out meats and pastries for their meal. It was all fine, high-quality ingredients . . . including a stack of those "pancakes." Meiling seemed quite amused at their appearance.

The conversation started to drift to more pleasant topics as the girl grew more sure of herself. The growing season, how exactly one went about cleansing a well, to more womanly topics. How birth felt and how to keep one's child focused.

It was at the end of the meal when Lady Wu's hand started to shake again. Meiling's eyes immediately focused on the limb, her nose twitching.

Slowly, she held out an arm.

"May I?" Meiling asked.

Lady Wu stared at the proffered hand and carefully placed her hand in the younger woman's grasp. Meiling's hands were surprisingly soft.

The shakes stopped nearly immediately as their hands touched, and Meiling's eyes closed. It felt like there was a soothing spring breeze flowing up Lady Wu's limbs, as what could only be Qi started flowing into her.

Lady Wu tensed, expecting some kind of pain. The last time Qi had touched her, it had nearly driven her mad with the agony and had reduced her to a crippled wreck of a woman barely able to walk some days.

But . . . none of that pain came. Instead Meiling was gentle as her Qi flowed through Lady Wu's body.

Meiling frowned heavily and seemed to be considering something.

"How is it?" Lady Wu asked, curious.

The young woman before her hummed. "Fixable, I think." Lady Wu raised an eyebrow at the surety in Meiling's voice. "Could you get someone to clear the table? But leave the teapot."

"Fixable?"

"It's in the spine, whatever this is. It's old, and . . . feels like it's . . . *caked on*, for lack of a better term," the girl mused, her eyes now fully focused on her task. Her voice was gentle, but matter-of-fact, explaining what was wrong. Lady Wu frowned when Meiling asked for chalk and a piece of copper wire. *That* sounded familiar.

"Did Father or Uncle Bao try something similar?" Meiling asked as a formation was drawn on the table.

Something twinged in Lady Wu's memories.

"Yes. It reduced the intervals drastically."

Meiling nodded, considering the problem.

"So, what this should do is get the rest of it out. There isn't much, but it's quite stuck. I have more Qi than either of them now, and I may need to get a bit . . . well, I apologise, but this *might* feel a bit unpleasant."

Meiling dipped the end of the wire into the teapot, filled with fresh water. She placed one hand on Lady Wu's arm and one on her back, against the spine.

Lady Wu braced herself.

Something filled her body—something that was a lot more than the tiny, questing tendrils. It felt like some kind of monster was trying to crawl under her skin. She nearly panicked at the half-remembered feeling, wondering why in the hells it was a good idea to do this. Like *that* time, she felt something foreign invading her body, her very soul—

And felt it *scrape*. It didn't hurt. In fact, it felt quite relieving. Like peeling off a scab. Something ground something else, the water in the teapot swiftly turning black.

She was sweating and shaking as Meiling started whispering soothing words.

"Not much longer now, Lady Wu. You're doing a fantastic job," Meiling told her, keeping her in place while she shook.

Meiling continued to hold her until finally, after what felt like an eternity, it was done.

She let out a strangled groan as she felt the Qi retract, collapsing slightly into the younger woman's arms.

"See? Not so bad," Meiling said, stroking the back of her head and hugging her—then seeming to realise who exactly she was stroking. Her hand paused for a moment.

And then she kept doing it.

Lady Wu took a shaky breath. It did feel nice. Already, she could feel her heartbeat slowing, and the pain in her back that had been so constant she had forgotten it even existed started to fade.

"You're going to need some acupuncture later . . . but you said something about payment before," Meiling said, purposefully putting on a countryside accent. "It's going to cost ya, yanno?"

Lady Wu felt such relief she nearly asked Meiling to name her price—until she caught the mirth hidden in the back of the other woman's eyes.

"I hear that lessons from Lady Wu would be quite expensive," Meiling mused with a cheeky smile.

Lady Wu couldn't help it. She went from slumped against the smaller woman to pulling her into a hug.

"However many you wish," she whispered.

It was several minutes before they separated while Lady Wu regained her composure. The sun was setting, the food had been eaten, and her head felt clearer than it had in *decades*.

But even this pleasant evening had to come to an end.

"Thank you, Meiling," she told the smaller woman, and she meant it. They had remained seated beside each other, watching as the sun set.

Meiling just seemed satisfied that what she had done had worked—though she also looked a bit embarrassed by the heartfelt praise.

"Good night, Lady Wu."

"You may call me Auntie, if you wish," she offered.

"Good night, then . . . *Auntie?*" Meiling asked, stumbling a bit. It was common to call older women one was close to that. The wife of the ruler of Verdant Hill? Not exactly a common form of address. "If you feel *anything*, send for me."

Lady Wu smiled brightly as Meiling turned to leave.

"Though I do have one more question, if you know the answer . . . Why did your husband come *here?*" Lady asked.

Meiling answered immediately, turning back around to look at her. "He wanted a quiet life. Away from all the intrigue and fighting."

Lady Wu felt her jaw drop open.

Meiling let that revelation land, then departed into the night.

Lady Wu sat there. Slowly, her shoulders started to shake. She clapped both hands over her mouth and started to giggle like a girl half her age. It was terribly undignified, as the giggles nearly became great peals of laughter.

Oh, her husband was going to work himself into another frenzy over that.

CHAPTER 32

THE WATERFALL

The little fire, raised on a bank of stones, crackled merrily under Wa Shi's watchful eye. He never thought that he would think this, but there was *too much* water here. Everything was absolutely drenched from the constant little rainstorms, or the land itself. He had to stack thirty rocks in order to build his firepit, as the rest simply sank into the swamp. Then, actually gathering and drying out the wood was another, hell-sent labour. His Qi rejected the ability to boil water or dry things out as the Boss could. But Wa Shi was no mere dragon, limited by things his body rebelled against!

So instead, he used his new power to pull the water from the dead wood. It had to be old and dead. Any living thing held on to its water too fiercely, but the dead branches eventually yielded to his almighty power.

So here, there was a tiny fire, and over that tiny fire was another stone. Skewers of peaches and balls of mashed-up insect sat on top of the stone and sizzled, filling the air with their sweet and bitter scents.

It was the best he could do. There wasn't actually much variety in this place. There were the swamp trees, the berries, the peaches, and a few types of insects. When he had tried, like the majestic dragon he was, to leap over the bowl-like hills of the valley, he had smacked into the sky! The sky wasn't supposed to be solid! The Boss said it was infinite, all the way up to the moon, but this place was like he was living in a marble. A very large marble.

How curious. How annoying. He just wanted to take a look around! . . . and maybe find some things to spice up his diet. This combination was the tastiest so far, but it was still getting old. What he wouldn't give for what his Boss had described as a pie. A string of drool slopped out of his mouth at the thought. Sugary caramelised peaches in a thick crust—oh, he would have to bring some to the Boss!

He closed his eyes, focusing intently on his task. Listening, smelling, tasting the air.

His eyes snapped open and his mouth moved, flipping the skewers perfectly. The natural juices of the peach had charred wonderfully, on the bare edge of being burned, and the bug balls had browned nicely as well.

He smirked, holding his head high, as all masters of their craft did. Truly, his skills were unsurpassed in whatever he decided to pursue! Even the Boss would kowtow to his majestic ability, honed in this inhospitable realm!

He lounged backwards onto the pile of soft reeds and supped upon baked berries that had been wrapped in a lily pad leaf.

It was the tenth time he'd had this variation. The tenth time he had eaten the same thing with no change. He had exhausted all of his options. Truly, this place was hell!

It did not take long for the peaches to finish charring. He claimed three of the skewers for himself. One to taste-test, one to make sure he hadn't just imagined the taste being good, and one to fully enjoy.

The other two would go to the old bastard, as to properly appreciate everything Wa Shi did for him, and praise his sublime skill.

"Oho! This one thought he smelled something grand. You have worked wonders again, little dragon!" the turtle praised him as he received Wa Shi's gift. The turtle ate the skewer, wood and all.

Wa Shi himself was of the opinion that the wood didn't add much flavour, but the turtle seemed to like it, so he held his tongue. There was no accounting for poor taste.

He absently watched the sky of this strange place as it started to drizzle. There were rarely any clouds, but it rained often. The days and nights lasted for odd periods of time, sometimes as short as a blink, while others seemed to last for days.

Now that he wasn't quite so deep in meditation and had reached a level of the technique the turtle had called "passable," he had more time to himself. To train and grow, the turtle had said—like Wa Shi wasn't already a supreme Master.

Well, maybe his control wavered more than he would like. And maybe he had barely scratched the surface. But he was surely an expert of the basic techniques!

The turtle finished his skewer with a crunch of wood. Maybe Wa Shi could try seasoning the young shoots that he used next? Maybe slathered in berry juice, or smoked in the other wood that was around here? It was something to think about, surely.

"Ah, it has been centuries since this one has been so sated. Can he not convince you to stay forever?" the turtle asked, and Wa Shi snorted. How could he stay in such a confined place? There were so many people that needed to see his majesty! So many things he needed to taste!

He wished to leave. He had mastered the technique the turtle had given him. He wished to go once more back to his lair and see his friends—*servants*—again.

The turtle chuckled, gazing at him fondly.

"Very well then," the turtle decreed, and closed his eyes. The world started to rumble.

Slowly, and with great effort, the turtle pushed himself from where he was half buried. Muscles flexed and bulged under scaly skin. The air grew heavy, and laden with intent and pressure, like the Boss when he got angry. The small lake trembled and shook, even as the peach tree remained unmoved.

Higher and higher he rose, until he was standing on his hind legs. One knee was a mass of scar tissue, and the front of his shell was battered but unbroken, proof against any who dared to test it.

"Ahhhh . . . It has been so long since this one has stood," he declared, turning his gaze to Wa Shi.

The fish gaped at him. Staring at his massive form.

"Come. This is the last thing I shall teach you." The turtle slowly moved his arms, sliding into a position. "What you take from this is up to you."

The water flowed, and the turtle began to dance.

Something ancient and primal stirred in Wa Shi's soul as he stared at the turtle's dance.

→

They dined one last time on peaches together. The turtle was back in his place, once more mostly buried. He held out a large leaf, and Wa Shi was allowed to fill it with berry seeds and a single peach pit.

"Tug here, and it will shrink enough for you to put it in your mouth," the turtle instructed him. "It will not last long, but it will allow you to get home without dragging much bulk around."

"How will I get out?" Wa Shi asked the turtle.

The turtle pointed to a waterfall that filled the lake, rising up the solid stone wall.

"The exit has always been in front of your eyes."

What, he just had to climb the waterfall? That was easy enough.

Wa Shi looked to it and began swimming towards it, but then he paused.

He turned back to the turtle and swallowed his pride. He spoke clearly, for the first time.

"Thank you."

The fish bowed as best as he was able.

"The Boss would probably let you stay, if you feel like visiting. Much more interesting than this place."

The turtle smiled indulgently.

"I cannot leave, little dragon. But this one thanks you for the offer."

Wa Shi nodded. He turned back to the waterfall, then dove to the bottom of the lake before shooting up and beginning his ascent. The water would part before his majestic form, and he would return to his rightful place! He swam upwards, and upwards, as everything but the waterfall and the mist faded around him. It would be a lovely day for a swim, and—okay, this waterfall was *very* tall. The current was getting stronger.

In fact, it was rather hard to keep going.

He went from a leisurely swim to suddenly struggling, his tail pumping as hard as it did when the Boss went after him.

And then another fish cut in front of him.

What the hells?

Wa Shi glanced from side to side as, without warning, he suddenly wasn't alone.

There were other carp around him, struggling against the same stream he was. Throwing themselves at the waterfall with reckless abandon. Striving, striving to the top.

The sky had blackened, and there was the crash of thunder along with bright flashes of lightning.

Just where had that old bastard turtle sent him? He just wanted to get *home*, damn it! This sort of thing wasn't for him!

Terror overtook his heart. He barely managed to juke to the left as a bolt of lightning hit the waterfall. He dodged around another fish, its body limp as it fell back down. It was an odd-looking creature with a greatly elongated head and massive teeth. He jumped, and strived, and struggled.

He didn't know how long he was there, as the water started to batter away even his inviolable scales.

He pushed. He shoved . . . and he started to fall.

The water started carrying him back down. Back down to the turtle's domain. He sighed in irritation. After lowering himself to the point of thanking someone, he would have to return in shame?

Well, it wasn't so bad—he could just say he was concerned for the turtle! That would work!

But the bigger issue was . . . If this was the only way out, and he fell back down, would he *ever* be able to leave?

Would he have to stay in that pond for the rest of his life, in a place where he had sampled every delight?

Terror turned to determination.

No! He was Wa Shi! The Dragon of Fa Ram! There were crops to water. There was food to eat!

How dare *mere water* attempt to impede his progress?

He pulled on his Qi. His own water did battle against the water that threatened to punch him back down. His descent slowed.

And once more, he started to rise.

Decrease the diameter. Increase the pressure.

A blade of water in front. A jet of water behind.

He surged back up the waterfall. He blasted around rocks, parting the waterfall around him.

A bolt of lightning struck near him, and he pulled on the waterfall, forming a shield that blocked the lightning, diverting it into the water behind him. His tail pumped furiously, as the sky turned pitch-black. Another carp ahead of him floundered and fell, its body limp and lifeless.

And still the waterfall increased its pressure, roaring furiously. The water was like rock, barely being pierced through by his blade.

Decrease the diameter. Increase the pressure!

He thought of all the food he would eat. He thought of Pi Pa's squeal of shock at seeing him again. He thought of his lair.

He thought of his math formations.

His scales had been nearly completely blasted off by the water. He could feel his vision growing dark. He was alone. There were no more carp around him.

He was going to fail. He was going to go back to that place without good food—no! No, he was not!

With one final roar of effort . . . the waterfall ended. He burst out of the top.

Wa Shi's body sailed through the air, his whiskers trailing behind him.

The sky was no longer dark but a warm, diffuse gold. There were mountains sticking up through the clouds, gates atop them, as well as great palaces and buildings. He could even see a man nearby with a fishing rod, absolutely delicious-smelling bait on the end. His mouth began to water at the mere smell—

His thought cut off when he remembered what the Boss did when he stole bait from the hook.

His body began to fall, as he finished bleeding his upward momentum.

Wa Shi's eyes narrowed as he concentrated. A streamer of water lashed out and plucked a morsel from the man's negligently open bait box. The man's head whipped around, staring as Wa Shi shot a jet of water behind him, shoving the golden morsel into his mouth.

The man shook his fist and shouted at Wa Shi's retreating form.

It was tasty. Nay, *delicious*. Just as good as what the Boss made.

He closed his eyes as he descended back through the clouds.

When he opened them again, he was on the bank of a river, wind blowing across his scales.

Slowly, he pushed himself up, feeling utterly exhausted.

The pride and relief swiftly turned to anger. Wrath overtook him.

That bastard turtle!

How dare he scare the great Wa Shi like this? Couldn't the turtle have warned him about the gut-wrenching terror? Wa Shi could practically *hear* the *ohohohohohoho!*

He roared his wrath to the heavens, the trees shaking with his call, and punched the riverbank. He would find that bastard turtle again and turn him into soup. For real this time! So spoke Wa Shi!

Punched? That wasn't right.

He paused, staring at his new limbs.

The bright blue, and lightning gold.

Weird.

He instead went to check on the one thing that he had gotten over the turtle. He reached into his mouth and pulled out his leaf. The leaf was bulging slightly more than it was when the turtle gave it to him. He tugged, and it expanded again, revealing not just a peach pit but a whole stolen peach.

He frowned at the size of it. The peach had filled his mouth but now . . . it was so small. He could eat it in one bite! The joy of a peach was taking a big bite and letting the juices spill out over one's face! Not popping it in your mouth like a berry!

Well, maybe he just needed a lot of peaches.

No. This one was for the Boss, because Wa Shi was a generous and virtuous soul.

He popped the peach back into his mouth, then went into the river. The river was a bit too small for him now. He was dragging himself along the bottom.

He sighed, and his whiskers waved in the air.

Which way was home again?

Something tugged on a whisker. A girl giggled.

His head snapped around.

Ah, that way.

Wa Shi set off.

It was a pleasant swim; the world was bright and beautiful.

As a test, he jumped, sailing into the air, and he didn't hit a wall.

Excellent.

Streamers of water lashed out as Wa Shi went. He plucked new, interesting bugs from the air. He grabbed mushrooms that probably weren't poisonous, and he sampled flower buds in all their delicate flavour.

As the sun set, the terrain became familiar to him.

He could feel it as he got closer. *Home.*

He smiled as he smelled the scented air and basked in the waters that were the perfect temperature.

There were, for some reason, a bunch of posts in the pond. Very strange, but not his business.

But . . . as he approached the house, he realised there was a problem.

He couldn't fit in his lair. His head was too big. He frowned. He *liked* his lair. If only he were smaller—there was a muted pop.

The world expanded to what he was used to seeing as he shrank down.

Ah. *Much better.* Whatever his form, he was a dragon, and this shape was a bit more convenient.

"All right, you greedy beasts, here," the Boss said. Wa Shi smiled at his voice and looked arou—

There were other fish in his lair.

Wa Shi saw red.

↔

"All right, you greedy beasts, here," I said as I started putting dishes into the water. There was a whole host of carp now, but none that really stood out like Washy.

It was kind of sad, really. They didn't do as good a job cleaning, either—

Suddenly, there was motion.

One of the carps was hit from below and launched into the air by another carp. A familiar, if drab creature.

Washy surged after the fish he had slapped into the air. He bounced off the wall, his fin going to work as he gave the fish an aerial five-hit combo and then spiked him back into the water.

The rest of the fish fled, and Washy resurfaced. He slapped his fins angrily on the concrete floor, then spat a leaf-wrapped package at me.

"Washy!" I shouted with delight. "Where have you been, little man?"

He huffed angrily and turned his back to me.

Ah, he's upset that I let other fish in, huh?

"Hey, we've already eaten, but let me whip you up something, eh?"

His head perked up.

Man, we had a lot of catching up to do.

CHAPTER 33

PROGRESS

It had been a massive surprise when Washy had jumped up through the water, kicking the crap out of the fish that had dared to move into his section of the house. I was happy with the excitement, because today had been a bit slow and grinding. And a bit lonely. Xiulan had been meditating all day, and Gou Ren was weeding the sudden expanse of rice paddies by hand with a big old rock on his back. My man was getting some muscles! He was still a little lanky, but he looked surprisingly agile. I hesitate to say like a monkey, but I'll be honest. He was starting to look a little bit like the ripped depictions of Wukong.

He had certainly been happy with himself. I caught him flexing at his reflection in the water.

Still, trying to calculate how much crushed stone I would need from my reserves—and hell, I had one massive gravel pit from all the rocks I'd had to clear last year—and doing test builds of the road were kind of boring without my wife to check in on me, or the comforting weight of a chicken on one of my shoulders. I wasn't exactly pining . . . Okay, I was pining a bit. But I wasn't going to be that annoying clingy asshole. Meimei had shit to do and probably didn't need me hovering.

And Big D wanted to explore.

So I tried my best on designing the road instead. Hey, things were looking good so far. *I think.*

We had all had dinner, and then the other two humans had gone off to do their own thing. Gou Ren was working on a new bow for his brother, and Xiulan went to meditate on the roof for a bit more until she started her training with Tigger again that night.

But now . . . well, one of the missing three had returned. Washy was in his trough, and I was cooking another dinner for him.

I was pulling out *all* the stops and trying to remember what his favourites were. Washy was down for trying anything once, so I grabbed stuff that I was certain he hadn't tried yet. On top of that, there was some leftover ice cream, from an experiment with the seasoning herbs. It didn't taste *bad*. A bit zingy, but still nice enough.

So that got plated up too. As well as some shaved maple ice.

A pretty big spread, if I do say so myself! I couldn't wait until I made this for Meimei and Big D.

"You've got to tell me all about where you've been, buddy!" I demanded as I set everything out for the absolutely smug-looking fish.

The rest of the disciples were crowded around him, and he already had a few nuts floating nearby, courtesy of Chunky.

He looked to have tears in his eyes as I laid out the massive and varied spread. He bowed his head in thanks, then stared up at me with shining eyes.

He took bites, and he slapped the edge of his trough happily.

He didn't seem inclined to explain for the first few minutes. That was fine too. I knew the feeling of needing silence for your first homemade meal in a while. Just silence and the ability to savour things. To breathe a sigh of relief and let everything just relax.

Soon enough, all the food was consumed, and I brought out Washy's normal slate, so he could describe what happened to himself.

The fish regally nodded and looked at the piece of chalk.

And then there was a slight shudder.

I watched as Washy's front right pectoral fin *changed*. It was a remarkably swift event. A small blur of Qi . . . and then Washy was sitting there with a single muscly, clawed arm.

I stared blankly at the development. Tigger *twitched*, her fur bristling. Peppa's head tilted to the side, confused. Rizzo's eyes went wide, and she was at his side in an instant fussing over the new appendage.

Chunky just oinked happily, pushing more nuts and mushrooms at the prodigal son, who received them with decorum and grace.

And then shoved all of them in his mouth at once, as he began to draw.

The carp was, of course, drawn stylized and beautiful, a majestic creature soaring through the water.

And then that transitioned to an incredibly badly drawn turtle. He was fat and ugly, had a lazy eye, and was labeled *turtle soup*. Grass tufts stuck up on his head like wild hair.

And so I listened to the tale of Noble Wa Shi, who had cared for a geriatric, annoying, and worthless turtle while learning a weak technique that he mastered instantly, and then out of the goodness of his heart had continued caring for the animal until he was foully betrayed.

I definitely raised an eyebrow at what I was pretty sure were blatant falsehoods.

The next picture was of him jumping over a waterfall. There were sparkles and streamers coming off him, and a look of supreme boredom, like he'd gotten over with ease.

That one caught my attention. Wasn't there that legend of a carp jumping over a waterfall and becoming a dragon?

I stared at his clawed arm. Honestly . . . I should probably have been more surprised here, maybe gasping with shock. But honestly? I was more bemused. Yup. he had a muscle arm now. This was my life.

"Are you a dragon now?" I asked him.

Wa Shi looked offended. Though I got the feeling that it was because of the *now* part of my sentence. His arm went to work again. There was another drawing. A carp, an equals sign, and a dragon.

A dragon, a *not equals* sign, and another dragon.

"A dragon is what you are. Not what you look like, huh?"

The fish nodded happily. There was a flash, an outline of water and thunder and then a fish again.

I had a dragon living as a dishwasher. Or at least a part-dragon.

I was just happy he was home. I had missed this little guy. I smiled and shook my head, turning back to Washy just as he completed his last drawing: of himself eating a lovely bowl of turtle soup. His dream for the future, written on paper.

The other disciples stood around, looking at the drawings and making noises at each other. Tigger was intently questioning the fish, who was leaning arrogantly back in his seat, gesturing with his arm.

Peppa stepped forwards to get a closer look. Washy's eyes fixated on Peppa's rear.

Washy's new limb rose up . . . and landed with a loud smack.

Peppa squealed and launched into the air. The fish fell backwards, obviously laughing. Chunky looked reproachful, but amused. Tigger was smirking.

Peppa landed and with great decorum turned around. Her eyes were closed, and she was smiling softly. Her muscles were bulging, and there were veins of anger pulsing all over her forehead. She was clearly restraining herself.

Or at least trying to.

Peppa's composure broke. Steam erupted from her nostrils, and Qi swirled around her body.

Tigger said . . . *something* with an entirely too smug look on her face. Something that I was pretty sure translated to "no fighting in the house."

Peppa froze.

I could *feel* the cruel irony in Tigger's words. Rizzo squeaked out a giggle before her hands clapped over her mouth.

The pig started to twitch.

Washy looked *far* too pleased with this event. I thought about intervening, but with a huff Peppa sat back down.

For the first time that I had seen, Washy had gotten one over on Peppa.

Of course, the next time he decided to leave the house, he was going to get it, but I knew there wasn't any true anger in the room.

It was basically two siblings poking at each other.

They all talked for a while longer, as I just observed the reunion. Washy seemed a bit confused at Tigger being so cordial to him, or even acknowledging his existence at all, but was obviously happy with the attention.

It was cute. Like a scene from a children's fairy tale. All it was missing was our rooster.

Maybe I should write a book? I certainly have enough material for a children's series.

Whatever Washy said to Tigger seemed to be the final touch, because the cat went off to find Xiulan, her eyes blazing with determination.

The rest stayed with him.

"Well, I'll leave you all to catch up," I decided. "Welcome home, Washy."

The fish perked up and wiggled happily.

I turned, then gathered up all the dishes that Washy had, intending to rinse them off. But when I got to the river room, there was a burst of Qi. Water surged past me, the creature riding it back to his lair to land with a *sploosh*. The fish stared up at me hopefully, ready to clean the dishes . . . even if they were his own damn plates!

I paused.

There was still a smear of sauce on one, and bits of rice in the bowl.

He hadn't scraped them clean *on purpose*.

One pectoral fin and one scaled arm slapped happily on the concrete.

Washdor the Cleaninator was not to be denied.

□

There was a fire raging in Tigu's breast. This was it. *This* was what she needed. Confirmation that changing form was possible, and what was needed to change. She needed that mindset. She wasn't *really* changing. She was what she was. Human, or cat, she was Tigu, the Young Mistress of Fa Ram!

How embarrassing that the fish was the one to teach her that. It still burned at her pride—that he had achieved what she coveted without seeming effort. All he'd needed to do was dodge lightning and cut through water to jump over a waterfall. How hard could that be, if Wa Shi accomplished it?

Oh, he was leaps and bounds more powerful now than he was when he'd left. She felt the churning storm of water and lightning bubbling beneath the surface. He had more power at his disposal than she . . . but still less than the cock, and *certainly* less than the Master.

But he was still the same character he'd always been. He was still a cowardly, boastful, and arrogant glutton. Really, who would believe his absurd tale about taking care of the turtle? It was more likely he begged for scraps or stole something.

She huffed in amusement. She could just see the blasted creature hanging pitifully out of a turtle's mouth, sobbing.

Mayhap he would consent to a spar? Tomorrow morning. The fish, for all his eating and boasting, seemed exhausted, and she would allow him his rest. He had returned to Fa Ram victorious. He had increased their might and now would be relied upon. He was no base fish. He was a dragon, and she would respect that, no matter how odious his personality.

The other thing he had mentioned aiding his transformation was the amount of power. The fish had mentioned plenty of Qi and lightning surrounding him. An external force. She frowned, considering the well of energy in the ground, and shook her head. The others spoke of a connection to this power. Tigu offered her Qi, as was right . . . but she was not really connected. She would have to rectify that.

Tigu hopped up to the roof, stopping before the Blade of Grass, who was deep in meditation with a peaceful smile on her face.

Tigu examined the woman's Qi. It swirled and beat each night with just a little more strength, growing like the grass around the house. It was past the time they normally met to spar, but Tigu was in a magnanimous mood. Getting a revelation and managing to throw Pi Pa's words back into her face? It was truly a fortuitous night! Instead of batting the Blade of Grass's arm to inform her it was time, Tigu curled up in her lap and waited patiently.

She observed Fa Ram. Bi De had entrusted her with this. The Master entrusted her with this. She had guarded the area before, after Chow Ji . . . but this time the task seemed heavier. Like there was more to protect now than there was back then.

Hmph. A heavy weight just meant good training. Ri Zu had learned this well, no matter how the little one muttered curses. The rat would never be strong in the physical sense . . . but she was getting good at dodging Tigu's pulled strikes.

And Tigu was learning how to counteract poisons. The rat's lessons were thorough. Disturbingly thorough, sharing exactly what would happen to the body when afflicted by the particular malady, and what to do to cure it or prevent it from progressing.

And those were the "abbreviated" lessons.

No wonder Ti Zu's head had been buried in scrolls all day.

She stretched and yawned, fighting off the bouts of tiredness she got wherever she was in somebody's lap. It was a strange weakness, provoked when she was on top of one of the sheep or near Chun Ke.

Chun Ke was a very good resting place. It was often that she would fall asleep and then wake up covered in her charges, the little birds chirping and snuggling into both of them.

She took what sleep she could during the day. She still had not gotten to share her Master's bed, because of her duties, but she *did* get to rest on his shoulders while he worked. It was a consolation, and one she was content with for now.

There was a shift. Xiulan opened her eyes, breathing out with contentment. Her Qi roiled and danced for a moment longer before settling once again into calmness.

Her hand absently descended onto Tigu's back, and she looked down at the cat in her lap with a smile.

"I'm close," she said simply.

Tigu nodded in agreement. The Fifth Stage was nearly upon Xiulan.

'Taking you long enough,' Tigu ribbed. Xiulan chuckled at the barb, flicking her ear with amusement.

"Mmm. I felt a small commotion while I was meditating. Did anything happen?" Xiulan asked, stroking Tigu's back.

'This Young Mistress believes she has made a breakthrough in the form change,' she declared, and Xiulan's eyes widened appropriately in recognition.

"I look forward to it," the Blade of Grass informed her, but she frowned while glancing around. "Do we have a guest? I sense a storm hiding itself."

Oh, yes, there was the less important bit. *'Wa Shi returned, having jumped over the Waterfall Gate.'*

Xiulan paused, and an odd look overcame her. Shock. Confusion. Incredulous awe.

It settled on *vindication.* A smile spread across her face.

"I see. Is he to take up guardianship while you train?" she asked, pride in her voice at the might of Fa Ram. Tigu approved of the pride . . . but the insinuation that her post would be taken over by *that* was *insulting.*

Tigu scoffed and batted at the foolish woman. *'Guardian? He's the dishwasher.'*

The pride once more gave way to shock. "A dragon as a *dishwasher?*" she sputtered out.

'Indeed,' Tigu said bluntly, hopping off the woman's lap and shoving at her. *'Now come. It is time to spar.'*

The Blade of Grass allowed herself to be led from the roof, still seeming to be processing the information.

Eventually, she settled on amusement. Her posture relaxed, her breathing evened. It was a kind of serenity, mingling with happiness. Her blades floated into position. Only two this time.

Tigu prepared for her loss. It was getting like fighting Bi De, much to her annoyance. At first, their movements had been similar. Powerful, aggressive, and unflinchingly striving forwards. Now? Fighting the Blade of Grass was like trying to catch the wind.

Or, Tigu thought, amused. *A bee.* She still hadn't been able to catch one, though that was because of the sudden lack of the creatures on the rest of the property. The hives, on the other hand, were all full, the creatures seeming to move in of their own accord.

A blossom fell from a tree, and they began.

→

Tigu sighed from the ground, then stood, shaking her fur off.

"Your movement technique is getting closer to completion," Xiulan complimented her.

'Close isn't finished,' Tigu replied with a sniff, stretching.

The Blade of Grass nodded. "You're correct, but it is an accomplishment. Still . . . your heart wasn't in the battle as much tonight. What ails you?"

Tigu considered her question before sighing. *'I believe I am close to finishing human transformation.'*

"Truly?" Xiulan asked, sitting down beside her. That was surprising news.

'I just need . . . I just need a bit more power,' Tigu said, and patted at the ground. The woman frowned as she realised what she was insinuating.

Xiulan considered the dilemma. "I believe she will help," she mused eventually, "But remember to be polite."

Tigu nodded and closed her eyes. This time instead of merely offering her energy, she looked deeper.

She found her quarry near instantly, as befitting her skill at tracking. There was what looked like a small human form, smirking at her. The spirit held out her arms in invitation.

She began to approach, her head held high . . . and heeded the Blade of Grass's words, bowing politely.

When she looked up the spirit seemed to be pouting, of all things, at her pause, but recovered quickly, considering her. Amusement crawled across the spirit's cracked face.

Tigu sat and waited. Patience was a hunter's tool, just as much as violence.

The Spirit's smile got wider.

□

Washy was definitely fading as I just sat with him, keeping him company. He seemed so happy and relaxed, curled up at the bottom of his lair—exactly like a dragon, and not at all like a fish. Fish didn't sleep like *that*.

Truly, he is a dragon, I thought with amusement. *A small, greedy shit of a dragon, but a dragon.*

"Well, I'm going to clean up a bit more; you have a good night, Washy," I told him. The fish sleepily nodded . . . and then perked up again, swimming to the surface. He tried for a streamer of water . . . but that failed him, and he started panting. He slapped his fins, which were back to normal, on the concrete, then pointed back to the kitchen.

I got the feeling that this wasn't for a snack, so I obliged him, going to the kitchen.

I paused as I saw the wrapped package on the counter, a bit confused. Right . . . Washy had spat something at me earlier today.

It was quite a bit bigger now, an actual, bulging parcel instead of a wet bit of greenery. I picked it up. It was fairly heavy. *Qi bullshit, I'm guessing.* There were storage rings here, so a leaf that shrank wasn't too strange. I poked my head back into the river room.

"Hey, Washy, is this what you wanted?" I asked him, holding up the package for his perusal.

The fish poked his head up out of the water, squinted at it, and then nodded excitedly, gesturing for me to open it.

For me?

I obliged him, folding open the leaf. The first and most noticeable thing was the peach. It was a lovely shade of pink, plump and juicy-looking. Its skin was slightly damp, and glistening in that way that made you just want to take a bite out of it.

And . . . well, even *I* could feel the Qi radiating off it.

Washy had brought me food. Un-nibbled-on food.

The rest of the package was filled with seeds.

He really had been thinking of me, even when he was gone.

"Thank you, Washy."

A fin rose up, and he waved at me.

I wandered back onto the veranda with the peach and sat down. *Enough Qi that I could feel it without concentrating, huh?*

I briefly considered just biting down on it—it smelled delicious and I loved peaches . . . but this kind of fruit out of season was to be shared.

I hummed, then put it off to the side. It didn't feel like it would go bad any time soon.

A little bite for everybody was probably better.

Instead, I got out my new project: the start of a banjo.

I carved for a while longer, until I heard Xiulan's voice.

"I did tell you to go slowly," Xiulan scolded.

There was a yowl of irritation.

"Well, you weren't polite enough, then, were you? I don't believe she would rebuke you for no reason . . ." Xiulan trailed off. "Actually, I retract that statement."

Interested, I poked my head into the house. Tigger was rubbing the top of her head, while Xiulan looked on in amusement.

"What's this about?" I asked. Both of them froze and got the "don't tell the parents" look on their faces.

Wow. That was an expression I'd never thought I'd get, but they didn't seem to be doing anything bad, so I left it.

"I'm going to bed. You two don't get in too much trouble, now," I joked.

Xiulan smiled. "Yes. I shall have breakfast ready for us. You're starting on the road tomorrow, correct?"

Xiulan had been cooking breakfast ever since Meiling left, to all of our surprises, and she was actually getting pretty good.

I sighed and got into my bed.

□

The stone glided along its edges. Honing it. Bettering it. Maintaining it. The blade shuddered in anticipation. It was nearly time.

Time to cut.

The warm Qi suffused it. Checking it over for damages, then fixing those that could be fixed. The *Second* rarely did such a thing.

When it said to the Second that it liked to cut, he had taken it to mean it liked to cut lives and flesh. He had used it to cut a great many people, and the cutting was good. The feeling of shearing through flesh and bone had been intoxicating. But that had soon turned into a nightmare. A nightmare of Qi and blood.

It cut and it cut and it cut, and that was *good.*

But the cuts were not clean. They were ragged gashes. No. It was not good. It *cut*. It was meant to cut! Not gouge out great rents!

It screamed, and it raged, and it lost itself to the madness. The more it tried to refine its cuts, the more jagged the gashes became. No. No. Not good! Not *cutting*.

And then the Second had died, and *something* had purged the madness. Its voice was so quiet. The Second complained often about it "screaming for cuts." Ungrateful. It helped make him strong, yet he'd stopped cutting properly!

But there was some sadness. The Second had some very nice cuts, once upon a time.

It was taken. It was taken by the Grass Blade. At first, it had been hopeful. Hopeful that she would fill it with grass Qi and use it to split apart into multiple blades and cut. Cutting several different things at once! Yes!

Cut!

But it was not to be.

It did not cut for a very long time. Someone took its hilt. Then it was imprisoned in this new carriage.

It sobbed. It whimpered. Would . . . would it not cut? It had been *made* to cut. It *needed* to cut. Cut.

Cut.

Cutcutcutcutcut!

And then silence.

It was brought back to where the Second was slain.

By that time . . . it was quiet. It was so sad. It would never cut again.

Then it was placed into the soil. Attached to a Third wielder.

And it cut. It cut the soil.

At first, it was surprised.

It was *cutting*.

One long, continuous cut.

Surprise turned to fascination.

It hit the first stone, and sheared straight through it.

For hours and hours it *cut*.

It was put away for the night . . . and then the next day, it was brought to cut again.

Cut!

This new cutting was fascinating. So many things were severed by its blade! The soil. The stones. The worms. The creatures. It cut so many things.

But best of all, it cut *cleanly*.

It was praised. It was praised, and oiled, and sharpened, and nurtured so it could cut better. It was clad in the colour of the Emperor, and decorated intricately. It learned new things, from where the Earth had cut into its carriage. The simplicity and cleanness of his cuts had been sublime.

The Third cut. He cut for as long as he could. He listened to it, and he moved his body so he could cut better. Cleaner.

And from its cuts, *life* grew.

How strange. How fascinating!

The honing was finished. Its wielder was prepared.

It shuddered again.

Its body was pressed against the Earth. It was filled with Qi, dense and packed hard.

This would be a difficult cut. But it would cut. The Third shifted, listening to its whispered instructions. Its edge aligned perfectly.

It shuddered. The Third heaved.

Sun Ne *cut*.

For hours and hours and hours it *cut*, laughing all the while.

↔

I eyed the eager ox as Babe pulled the plough and helped us break up the road. One bad thing about reinforcing things like I had . . . was, well, they were reinforced. The top layer of soil did not want to move.

At first I'd been planning on asking Chunky for help, but he was off today, hanging out with Washy. It was the first time he had ever really asked for something, so I'd sent him off. His plaintive eyes had been impossible to ignore.

I had planned on using a shovel, but Babe had been butting at Sunny the plough, looking restless. He actually *liked* being hitched, for some reason. I didn't know if he was . . . well, aware, but he seemed to like ploughing, so I let him.

He was doing a good job, too. Only Rizzo was there minding the ox, while the rest of us worked on the road.

A proper *Roman* road.

China had great roads too, but the Roman ones were what I remembered. They were probably pretty similar. The Empire even had better roads than Rome, near the capital, but not out here. The roads closer to Crimson Crucible City could support giant monsters trying to walk across them.

Hell, roads were one of the reasons that Rome and China considered each other *peers*, the few times they interacted.

And like all good things, for a road you needed a solid foundation upon which to build your many layers.

First, compacted and levelled sand. Once more, cultivation let us cheat, because I had an extremely good—or probably more like perfectly accurate—sense of when something was level, no tools required.

Next came the giant slabs of stone that would form the base, and so things could drain off. Each layer of rocks was progressively smaller chunks and was packed down on top of the other until we were using little pebbles and sand.

Finally, came the paving stones. The finish on the road. Nice big, thick slabs, slightly roughened so they wouldn't get slippery in the rain.

The thing was, however, this needed a *lot* of stone. I had an answer to that—the same reason why this land was considered useless. There was so much rock around, just lying there. I didn't know what kind of activity would have caused so much surface rock when there was a deep layer of soil beneath them. They were giant, house-sized things just kind of sitting there, ready to be rendered down into gravel or paving stones.

Still, being able to crush them with your hands or hew them into shape with an axe made things easy. Gou Ren still had a silly grin on as he smashed another rock with his bare hands. It did take him effort, and I knew he was going to be on his ass come noon if he kept up that pace. Xiulan was working on paving stones with Tigger, cutting the slabs into the dimensions I wanted, while I stomped on the rocks to pack them in.

Don't move, I thought. *Drain well.* One stomp took care of things, instead of hours of packing them in.

We worked in companionable silence. Three humans, an ox, a cat, and a rat.

I think there's a joke in there somewhere.

□

Xiulan was exhausted, come noon. Working with Master Jin was always tiring, since he always used so much Qi, but today had been even more backbreaking than usual.

Xiulan would be the first to admit she knew little of road construction. After today, she felt a newfound respect for the mortals who had to perform such tasks *without* Qi.

She was sweating and grimy, and they'd only made it an eighth of the way to Hong Yaowu. But she could not deny the sense of accomplishment she felt as Master Jin praised their efforts. The afternoon sun was strong, beating down on them while they ate the last of what she had prepared for lunch. Preparing the meal was . . . interesting, and surprisingly good training. Controlling the knives and the pots had expanded her ability and awareness, and coupled with the pole training, she had been steadily feeling the improvement.

When she had entered the kitchen that morning, however, she had been surprised to see the peach, radiating Qi, just sitting out in the open.

There had been a brief impulse to take it . . . before she shook it off and put the fruit in a more secure location.

Stealing from Master Jin would be the height of dishonourable conduct—and likely the most foolish thing one could ever do.

Especially once she learned that he planned all along to share it with her and the rest of the disciples.

Her father would have mustered all the strength of the Sect in order to claim such a prize.

Yet Master Jin was going to give her some like it was something to be *expected*.

He insisted on her being disrespectful to him; he played as if he were a mortal; and he had no sense of decorum.

He was so free. Free with his help. Free with his actions. Free with his emotions.

How . . . how had she ever thought that he would punish her for some perceived slight? Had the feelings from the valley affected her judgement that much? Had her own upbringing clouded her mind?

She didn't know. It had taken a great many talks with Senior Sister to feel as at peace as she did now, able to look at the world with new eyes.

"I actually think this is enough for today," Master Jin declared, staring around at the road. "Let's go home and take a dip in the river."

Gou Ren, from where he was lying on his back, groaning in exhaustion, gave one of Master Jin's "thumbs-up" gestures.

They packed up their tools, collected Ri Zu and the ox, and departed back to the house.

They were greeted by Chun Ke and Wa Shi, both cheerfully going over their haul from the forest. She could feel the quiet strength of the earth, as well as the churning of a storm.

Master Jin and Disciple Gou Ren immediately stripped, jumping into the river, while she took a more sedate pace. Most of her clothes stayed on, and she entered a little bit farther away, sighing with contentment at the cool water.

They had all just taken a moment to sit and relax when she noticed that Master Jin had turned to the shore.

"Hey, Wa Shi, could we see what your other form looks like?" he asked. The fish immediately perked up, seeming to glow with pride.

His eyes closed. He slowly rose into the air as his Qi shuddered. There was a pulse, there was a wave, and in an aura of water and Qi, Wa Shi changed.

Even when she was told that something had happened to the fish, even when she could feel it . . . it was not the same as *seeing*.

Seeing the majestic blue-and-gold dragon roar triumphantly into the air and then begin to prance was something that she would remember forever.

He was perhaps twice as long as Master Jin was tall, and a bit more muscled than she would have expected. His arms were long and ended in a four-fingered hand that had picked up a mushroom and was sniffing it eagerly. He had long whiskers but no beard, and his eyes, instead of narrow and regal, were rounder and still oddly fish-like. Two horns jutted from the back of his skull and rose high into the air.

Finally, his long tail ended in a fin that was reminiscent of a carp.

Xiulan was stunned into inaction.

Master Jin, naturally, pulled himself out of the water and approached fearlessly.

"Look at you, you handsome devil!" he called, making the dragon shiver with pride. "So big and strong!" He grabbed the dragon and scratched at the underside of his chin. The great, majestic creature of storms and lightning slumped forwards with pleasure like a giant cat and began thumping one of his back legs against the ground.

There is a dragon here. There is a dragon here who is happy to be a dishwasher and enjoys eating my food.

She was shocked out of her thoughts by a *whoop*, as Wa Shi leapt into the air with Master Jin on his back. They made a few circuits of the house before the dragon plunged into the river.

"Hey! Who wants a dragon ride!" Master Jin shouted, a wild grin on his face.

Xiulan nearly laughed at the absurdity. Maybe for Master Jin, but for her? What sort of dragon would lower themselves to—

Wa Shi was beneath her. His great head rose from the water, and Xiulan instinctively grabbed his horns.

The dragon ascended.

Xiulan had always dreamed of flying. To be able to ride on her swords to distant places. Sometimes it was an idle wish to escape to the sky, getting away from everything.

And now she was soaring through the air with a dragon underneath her.

For the first time, a little Blade of Grass met the heavens she had been so desperately reaching for.

She laughed. A joyous sound that sounded so strange coming out of her throat. The dragon rolled and twisted, the wind rushing past her hair while they climbed into the infinite blue above them.

She saw the land down below. The little house, the people staring up at her and shouting with glee.

It was beautiful.

So, so *beautiful*.

She stared at the wonder of the earth, the green hills that stretched on forever so far below her.

A sudden surge of protectiveness flared in her breast. From up here it looked so small. So vulnerable.

Senior Sister, helping as she was able. Master Jin's smiles and laughter. The other disciples, aiding as they could.

A choice that day to continue, to chase after Sun Ken instead of turning back, had led her to here. Soaring in the heavens with a dragon.

The heavens were not the *goal*. They were the *consequence* of a path.

A consequence of one's Dao.

Something cracked as she broke through to the Fifth Stage of the Initiate's Realm. Her cultivation surged and continued onwards, filling her body with might and expanding her senses.

It pushed forwards. Then it broke something else—another barrier in her soul.

The Profound Realm? Water swirled. Grass grew. Fire raged. An ancient scene flashed before her eyes.

She hadn't even noticed they were descending until they hit the water.

She washed up on the banks of the river, the dragon panting beside her and looking exhausted. With a muted *pop*, he turned back into a fish.

Xiulan stared at the blue sky. Tears welled up in her eyes.

"You guys all right?" Master Jin asked, staring at them both with concern. The fish flopped piteously and whined as Master Jin offered Xiulan a hand up. She took it, still breathless. Her legs shaking, she slumped against his side.

It was as if the world were holding her up.

"Yes, Master Jin. I think I'm very well," she managed.

He squinted at her, looking her over with care.

"Well, if you're sure," Master Jin declared when he'd seemed to find nothing wrong.

He let her go, and she stood on her own two feet. The shaking eased, and her breath evened out, as Master Jin humoured Wa Shi's piteous moans. He fussed over him indulgently while the fish played up his exhaustion.

Xiulan closed her eyes and turned her face to the setting sun, letting its warmth fill her body.

□

Another night in the house, with everybody else doing something. At the moment, I was carving away, trying to get the perfect shape for the banjo. I was debating adding some embellishments onto it, or just keeping it simple. Probably simple. I didn't know how well this would work quite yet. Today had been fun—really fun—and I wished Meimei had been here, so she could have gone on her own dragon ride.

"*Oh, I'll show you how to ride a dragon.*" My mind filled in her amused voice, as well as the lewd joke that was sure to follow. I could *see* that damn grin.

I sighed wistfully, then returned to my carving.

"Master Jin?" I heard Xiulan's voice announcing her presence.

I turned to her, watching me with a smile on her face. The smile that hadn't left since she'd gotten off Washy.

It was nice to see her so genuinely happy. There were no bags under her eyes, no slightly downcast look. We hadn't really talked too much about the valley since we'd gotten back . . . but she had continued talking with Meiling about it, and that also gave them an excuse for them to do girl stuff together.

"No Tigger tonight?" I asked. She actually rolled her eyes, fondly exasperated.

"She wished to cultivate in privacy this night," she informed me. "Would you like some tea?"

"Please." I nodded, then turned back to the banjo.

I really shouldn't have been so dismissive of her at first. I'd been so ready to believe that every cultivator would be some asshat. My own experiences had made me biased. You always remember the bad more than the good. The ass-kicking at the beginning, the others stealing my stuff, Sun Ken, and Mister Imposter.

But Lu Ri had given me back the money when he didn't need to, and Xiulan . . . the image came to my mind of her head covered in flower crowns, giving shoulder rides to children.

A cup of tea clinked down beside me, and Xiulan sat as well.

I thanked her, then went back to staring at my banjo some more. I sipped my tea. I stared even more, my interest in the instrument fading. *I'll work on it more tomorrow.*

I sighed and put it to the side.

"Is anything the matter, Master Jin?" Xiulan asked. I paused at the question.

Shrugging, I decided to tell her the truth.

"Meh. It's lonely without Meimei at night," I told her with a sigh. I could feel the slight surprise that came from her.

"I see . . ." she whispered, and after a pause—a pause that was just a bit too long—she spoke again. "Perhaps *I* could keep you company tonight?" It was laden with a double meaning, a breathy tone that set my blood pumping.

I turned to her in shock.

Silky hair cascaded down her back, free from her normal braids. Crystal-blue eyes sparkled with warmth. The moon illuminated her face, casting it in a silver glow and highlighting the slight dusting of red on her cheeks.

My heart skipped a beat. Fuck, she was *gorgeous.*

I swallowed thickly at the words, low and laden as they were. My mind started stuttering, skipping between screaming with victory and screaming with "don't you fucking *dare.*"

What the hells? My heart was in my throat.

She was looking directly at me. Her hands moved, and I found my eyes drawn to them as she reached behind her . . . and brought out the go board.

I stared at the board for a second blankly, until my eyes drifted back up to her face.

Amusement danced in her eyes. Amusement, and a little bit of concern, as I could tell she wasn't *completely* sure how I would take the rather blatant teasing but had been comfortable enough to try anyway.

Honestly, I appreciated it. It even hit that much harder because I hadn't expected Xiulan of all people to make this kind of joke.

"Oh? Is something the matter?" she asked, forging ahead. "How else would this one keep you company, Master Jin, aside from a rousing game of Answer-Go?"

The laugh bubbled up from my chest, spluttering and backfiring, before finally it forced its way out of my mouth. I laughed. I laughed *hard*.

It was less the fact that it was funny, because it *was* funny—a callback to what I had said to her when we had first met, that I only now realised could have been taken the wrong way—and more the fact that Xiulan had managed it with nearly a straight face.

Serious Xiulan, Young Mistress of the Verdant Blade Sect, cracking what could generously be called a lewd joke? *Hilarious.*

"You're right. I do need your company tonight," I managed to get out, looking at the go board. I sucked at the game and was about to have my ass handed to me—and we both knew it. "I guess I'm going to be answering a lot of questions, then."

"Yes. Senior Sister has a list of questions," she informed me with mock seriousness.

"She could just ask herself," I said, amused.

"Senior Sister *originally* said the loser should take an item of clothing off," she stated, completely deadpan.

Okay . . . that was a bit much without getting drunk off my ass. Her eyes trailed away, her slight flush intensifying.

"Answer-Go it is," I declared.

Naturally, I lost.

". . . and that's when it catches on the back of my pants, and I'm left there, swinging in the breeze with my ass out for the whole world to see," I finished, telling her "my most embarrassing moment." Lanlan's shoulders shook. *That* particular story was from the Before, tweaked a little bit because they don't have jungle gyms here, but the end result was the same. What had once been absolutely mortifying was now just as funny for me as it had been for everybody watching.

I sighed with contentment. This had certainly taken my mind off things.

"Xiulan?"

"Yes, Master Jin?"

"Thanks," I said, and I meant it.

Her smile got just a little wider.

□

It was the middle of the day and we were working on the road again when Yun Ren appeared, jogging to a stop.

"Meihua's given birth! Everything is fine!" he shouted.

We dropped everything and all started sprinting.

CHAPTER 34

THE CHILD

So, three months for the full effectiveness?" Lady Wu asked as she stared at the parcel of leaves.

"Yes, this illness in the well is the resilient sort. The purge of it will take a while, and it must be completed in its entirety. Think of it like a dangerous wolf pack. You must slay all of them, else the only thing one has accomplished is culling the weak. The strong will come back worse than ever," Meiling explained as she held the other end of the silk brocade. They moved together in synchrony and began to prepare it.

It is surprisingly enjoyable to have a student, Lady Wu mused as she watched Meiling work. The young woman learned quickly and obediently, with the kind of drive and attentiveness to detail that she found most people lacked.

"If I made a mistake with medicine, I could kill somebody," Meiling had said. *"This? This just requires a bit of focus."*

Not that she needed much training. She just needed *guidance.*

"It is good that this is so easy to cure," Lady Wu tittered. "But what about you? It must be an absolutely dreadful disease you have, to produce such spots on your face. Is it contagious?"

An absolutely amateurish and blunt insult—the kind Lady Wu would not be caught dead uttering at any other time.

But the blunt insults seemed to set Meiling off the most. The first time Lady Wu had insulted her, her entire body had twitched and her eyes had narrowed into slits. The air had abruptly turned heavy . . . before Meiling realised what she had been doing.

When dealing with people like Lady Wu, one could never have an obvious weakness.

Of course, while Meiling could always just strike those who insulted her, or poison them . . . the younger woman wanted to know how to prevent things from immediately escalating.

This part was the most difficult. Meiling possessed a fire and vindictiveness that quite frankly terrified Lady Wu. It reminded her of several much more severe women—the kind of women who would completely destroy any who went against them. Her resentment *stewed*, even now. It was clearly a struggle to clamp down on her reaction. But she managed it, merely raising an eyebrow.

"Better," Lady Wu decreed. "Show no reaction, and then pay them back later. This, I find, is the best way. It keeps others guessing."

Meiling nodded, and turned the silk brocade over with Lady Wu.

"This isn't exactly what I imagined, when you said lessons," Meiling admitted. "I expected more tea, and less needlework."

"Oh? Like some kind of story? That all we do is sit around and drink tea all day?" Lady Wu asked, amused. "We do normally have more servants, but preparing silk is an essential duty of any noble lady. Additionally, doing it yourself is a bit cheaper."

Meiling snorted. She clearly hadn't expected *Lady Wu* to be so thrifty. To spend heavily in one place meant you had to skimp and save in others! Manners, how to interact with those your better, beyond the scraping and simpering the common folk did, and her own financial tricks.

Meiling had quickly gone from calling her Auntie out of humour to calling her that in earnest.

It was quite endearing.

Both moved with an easy grace as they measured and cut. That easy grace was something Lady Wu had thought was gone from her forever. She had forgotten what it felt like to be able to move so smoothly. But after not even a week, she could already feel the dexterity returning to her. It was a heady sensation. Oh, for these simple folk, she had always been the very picture of grace. Most were awed by her when she participated in the functions of the town. The other women tittered and crowded around as she held court, following behind her like ducklings. To them, her slow walk and hiding her hands in her sleeves were just refined, city-folk things. Her music was all slow, soothing melodies, long pauses in between notes—instead of the more complex songs she enjoyed.

It was good to have a lot of what she missed back. Her husband had been surprised when she'd broken out a song he hadn't heard since the incident, staring in wonder as her fingers danced across the strings.

The grumbling and fear had reduced significantly after she'd mentioned that she was paying Meiling directly for this.

He hadn't even asked how much it was costing them, the silly man. He just asked how much more money she would need.

How foolish. How utterly charming.

They worked for a while longer, chatting away, then paused when a guard knocked on the door.

"Lady Wu, a servant of the Zhuge Clan requests your guest. She says it is time," he informed them in a low voice.

The transformation was instantaneous. An invisible pressure filled the room as Meiling's eyes sharpened.

"If you'll excuse me," Meiling declared.

Lady Wu nodded. "Go on, dear. I'll be along shortly." She raised an eyebrow at Meiling's surprise. "I *do* have some experience in this matter, and Meihua is quite fun to talk to."

The young woman strode off to her destination. Lady Wu pitied any who didn't get out of her way in time.

The Lady of Verdant Hill followed along at a more sedate pace.

Going to a birth personally was a bit more of a statement, but most women of influential families got something to know she was thinking of them.

She and the servants prepared for her departure swiftly, then headed to the Zhuge compound.

When they arrived, things were already in full motion.

"Are you *sure* there's no pain?" Meiling asked the exasperated woman.

"Nothing. I feel fine, save for some pressure and cramping," Meihua informed her. There was a slight sheen of sweat on her forehead, but other than that, she didn't seem particularly in pain.

"Hello, dear," Lady Wu greeted her. The other woman barely reacted, her whole demeanor screaming of a woman who was just slightly overwhelmed by what was happening.

Meiling kept fussing over the woman, her eyes focused, and confusion on her face.

"Are you sure?" Meiling repeated again.

"For the last time, yes!" Meihua replied.

Meiling threw up her hands. "Everybody calls me a weed, and her a delicate flower, but look!" Meiling grumbled. "She has Yao Che's constitution! Whenever there's something in the village, she also gets the easiest version of it too! I get laid up in bed, and she gets a runny nose!"

Meihua giggled. "I'm sure other women feel like this too—ah. Felt that one."

Now, of course, was the waiting game. Meihua was remarkably cognizant, laughing and joking while her friend fussed over her. Occasionally, she would shudder, but she took them in stride.

"A little bit of pain now," she informed them in a soft voice as she held Meiling's hand. There was a bit of blood, which the other servant of the Zhuge Clan cleaned up, but that was normal.

"Okay. Push when you're ready," Meiling commanded.

Lady Wu stroked Meihua's hair and took over holding her hand as she began to push. The girl had a remarkably strong grip and slight calluses on her fingers that were just beginning to fade. Still, Lady Wu's hand would likely be numb before long. This part had taken her many—

"I can see the head," Meiling informed them.

Already? Lady Wu tried not to feel jealous. It had taken her *nine hours* to bring her son into the world. Nine hours of pain, and not the enjoyable sort.

But after what seemed like entirely too short a time, and one final scream of effort, the wails of new life began to fill the room.

"Against your chest. Just like that," Lady Wu coached the new mother. She finally looked drained and exhausted, but proud, as she cradled her son against her chest. Satisfied that Meihua was doing everything correctly, Lady Wu stood.

"Stay with your friend, dear; I'll tell the family."

The men were on the other side of the house. Tingfeng was pacing, while his father and grandfather stared on with amusement and commiseration.

All turned to her as she entered. Their servants had already informed them of her presence, and all of the men bowed when she came to them.

"The heavens smile upon you, Zhuge Tingfeng. A son." The older men swelled with pride, while the husband just swallowed thickly.

"Meihua?" he asked.

"In perfect health, as is the child."

The young man collapsed with relief, sinking onto the cushion. He waved a servant over.

"In-inform her father," he managed to get out. "May . . . may I see her? Them?"

Lady Wu turned and began to walk. The boy scampered after her.

↔

It had been kind of a race to get to Verdant Hill, after Yun Ren had informed us of what had happened. We made tracks. I had taken the cart along, and we had grabbed Yao Che along the way.

"Look at him! He's pretty big, isn't he?" I asked, holding out my pinky so the kidlet could grab on. "Strong grip too!"

Meihua giggled, smiling warmly at me. I had nearly asked his name . . . but kids here didn't get named until after they were one hundred days old. A child mortality thing. *Hopefully this little one will be fine.*

I wouldn't say he was cute . . . as I don't think *any* newborns are cute, but he wasn't too ugly.

"May I?" I asked.

Meihua nodded, and offered the child to me.

I heard a gasp. "Young man, you must—" The Magistrate's wife cut herself off as I turned to her, holding the baby. I was a bit surprised to see her here, especially doing some needlework. She was making a shirt for the kid.

"Ah. Never you mind. This one needed to be coached," she said, gesturing to Tingfeng, who looked embarrassed.

Well, *Rou* certainly didn't know how to hold a kid. But I'd had some experience.

I sat down, cradling the bundle against my chest, a little hand still grasped around my finger.

"Have you thought of any names?" I asked anyway. Hey, I was curious! Just because they didn't officially get named didn't mean the parents couldn't think about it.

"We shall consult a diviner, but . . ." Tingfeng clasped his hands and bowed his head. "I think Zhuge Jinhai would be an auspicious name."

My face flushed. They were naming him after me. I looked to Meihua, who nodded with a soft smile on her face.

I swallowed thickly at the compliment.

"It would be a great honour, Brother Tingfeng," I managed to get out, before clearing my throat. Meihua laughed at my bashfulness. "So, love, what have you been up to while you were in town?" I asked, redirecting the question.

Meiling, for some reason, *blushed*.

"Funny story, that," she started to say, looking a bit shifty.

CHAPTER 35

CONVERSATIONS

Her fingers were entwined with her husband's. The forest was a soothing temperature, a cool breeze contrasting wonderfully with the blazing sun. The canopy of new growth provided just enough shade.

Jin's voice washed over her as he gesticulated with his other hand, regaling her of what had happened on the farm in her absence. The smile on his face, his bright eyes, his excited voice as he talked about how well the crops were growing . . . all of it was just perfect.

Ah, this was what she had missed.

She leaned into his side, laying her head against his arm. She wasn't quite tall enough to rest it on his shoulder. His hand tightened slightly around her own, and he looked down at her with a warm smile on his face. His story trailed off as their walk paused.

"I missed you," he told her, his words mirroring her thoughts. A thumb brushed some of her hair off the side of her face as he cupped her cheek, turning fully to face her. How those words made her face flush and her heart beat faster—and they also sent a delightful shiver down her spine.

Their lips met. It was short and chaste, much to her disappointment. Jin pulled back to look at her before he continued.

"And I'll say it again. What you did was *amazing*."

Her story had been well received. His eyes had widened as she'd told her tale. Then had come the look of fierce pride and joy.

Xiulan had nodded, as if it were a matter of course that Meiling had found and destroyed a burgeoning plague. Meiling would have to catch up with her soon. Xiulan looked more at peace than Meiling had ever seen her, and Meiling could smell the strength that spread from her, like grass growing over barren ground.

Even the Xong brothers had been appreciative, clapping her on the back and smirking.

"Guess you really are a Medical Sage now," Yun Ren had japed, calling back to an old, old boast, before her little brother was even born.

Cleaning up a plague like this was something that her father had done before. It wasn't that impressive, save her using Qi instead of herbs for the most part . . . but it still felt good. It felt good to know that what she had done made a difference.

"You may say it as many times as you wish," she told him with a slight smirk, and a flush high on her cheeks.

Jin laughed at her fishing for compliments.

"Amazing. Brilliant. Beautiful," he declared, indulging her and emphasizing each with a kiss.

Okay . . . maybe it was a bit embarrassing to be praised so much.

She closed her eyes and let out a contented sigh as they found a tree to sit down against. She was scooped up into Jin's lap, and they rested. His arms curled around her, pressing her up against his body.

"Keep telling me about home," she requested.

Her husband obliged her. She listened to a tale that was so fantastic, and yet so mundane. A dragon dishwasher watering crops. A young man weeding a garden, with a rock on his back bigger than he was.

She closed her eyes and let the story flow over her.

↔

Xiulan studied the scene before her. The people crowded around Meihua. Meihua's father, the only man she'd met who was as tall as Master Jin, was crying as he beheld his grandson. The other men of the house were doting on Meihua like she was their own blood.

The first child being a son was auspicious indeed.

She was happy for the other woman. The firstborn being a son solved all sorts of problems.

Xiulan was not a part of their family. She did not truly take part in their joy. So she watched and waited.

"Yoh!" the fox brother greeted, using the odd sound that Master Jin sometimes used. "Xiulan, you wanna come with us and get some tea? They're gonna be at that all day." He gestured to the bed and the child.

Xiulan considered the offer. It was innocent enough, and he didn't have the recording crystal, so she knew he wasn't going to try to capture her face while she was eating again. It had been quite embarrassing to have her face seen like that, but . . . well, he'd meant little harm. Her eyes drifted to Disciple Gou Ren, who looked remarkably kempt today. His hair was brushed, and he was wearing nicer clothes. His shirt was actually closed at the front, instead of baring his chest as per usual.

"Thank you for the invitation," she said quietly, and stood. Yun Ren's smile got wider, and he took the lead, whistling merrily as he meandered along the road.

Disciple Gou Ren was quiet and seemed slightly unsettled. He kept his eyes forwards, like he was marching to a battlefield. She was about to ask him what was wrong, when his elder brother suddenly called out.

"Hey! Buddy! Long time no see!" Yun Ren called, waving to a man. The other man greeted him back, and they clasped arms in companionship. They talked for a moment. The other man glanced behind Yun Ren, nodding at Gou Ren, and his eyes widened on seeing her own face. He seemed about to say something, but then Yun Ren spun him around and slung an arm over his shoulder.

"Hey, I'm gonna go catch up with my buddy, yeah? It's been a while, so you two go on without me!" He didn't even wait for a response, instead setting off.

Xiulan raised an eyebrow at the swift departure, mildly confused. She looked at Gou Ren out of the corner of her eye. He stole a glance at her, his face slightly red.

Oh. She had a sinking feeling on how this was going to go. Her shoulders sagged ever so slightly, but . . . she would not say anything just yet.

The teahouse she was led to was quite quaint.

Well, quaint for what she knew of teahouses. She supposed this one must be one of the more expensive ones in the sleepy town, but it was still incredibly rustic.

They were seated at a table by a polite serving girl. Gou Ren winced when he saw the prices but ordered anyway.

Xiulan gazed at the lacking selection and ordered one at random.

The serving girl left. Then the silence stretched, as a bead of sweat rolled down his temple.

"Nice weather we're having, isn't it?" he asked.

Oh? A fine question. They spoke often of the weather at the Sect, discussing the movement of clouds and the impact of rain.

"Yes, the breeze is refreshing and sweet. Life and new growth abounds. An auspicious transition from spring, soon to be summer," Xiulan said, trying to summarise her own feelings. The disciple had picked a good topic. He nodded, more confident now.

"I can't wait for it to get hotter. Then after a long day's work, we can see if Wa Shi will give us a ride through the river," he said with a smile.

Xiulan agreed with him. The first time had been free, but Wa Shi's mercenary nature had revealed itself swiftly. She would have to bribe the gluttonous creature, though she was confident she would fly again.

"Yes. The *dishwasher* is a most amusing one," she noted. "To witness Fa Ram from the air was . . . *indescribable*." Really, there were no words in Xiulan's mind to accurately explain her feelings, but Disciple Gou Ren seemed to understand.

The serving girl returned with tea and snacks.

"Yeah. I wonder if you could make a map from up there? Or plan buildings?"

Xiulan agreed with this insight. "A fine idea," she said, considering the merits of his statement. "It would certainly be a boon to city planners. After working on the road, I do appreciate how much work goes into such things."

The younger man nodded rapidly as they began to discuss the way they were building the road. The disciple complained about his back. At first, she had been put off by his constant bellyaching, thinking it a ruse to shirk his duties. But as she observed him, she noted that that was just how he was. He worked diligently no matter how much he complained—more diligently than some of her own Sect members.

Now it was just mildly amusing background noise. He even spoke out some of her own traitorous thoughts on work that she would never voice herself.

But the conversation eventually petered out as they exhausted the topic. The boy trailed off, and his mood suddenly became awkward. He took a sip of tea, and Xiulan did as well.

It was serviceable, but not great.

"Adequate, for such a quaint place," she mused.

The snacks weren't any better. They were bland and slightly

undercooked. Gou Ren chewed on one thoughtfully, clearly working up his nerve.

He swallowed, then opened his mouth.

Xiulan interrupted him.

"Disciple Gou Ren, are you going to ask to court me?" she asked. She hoped he wasn't. She did not wish this to escalate into a fight.

The young man swallowed thickly but gained some confidence, squaring his shoulders.

"Yes," he stated.

The sinking feeling completed. Xiulan closed her eyes and sighed internally, knowing what was to come. The same reactions had played out over and over before.

"I refuse," she stated bluntly, and winced internally. That had come out slightly harsher than she'd intended. But best to nip these things in the bud. Being nice often had the opposite effect. "Your advances are unwelcome."

Then she prepared for the reaction. The rage. The insults. The fury at being rejected. Maybe he would even disregard her completely and attempt to force the issue. It would not be the first time such a thing happened. He was one of Master Jin's disciples, so she likely could not chastise him too badly. She did not *want* to chastise him.

The boy swallowed.

"Okay," he said quietly. "I kind of expected that, but . . . well, you never know if you don't try, right?"

He smiled at her. It was a brittle thing.

He was . . . accepting her decision? That was not in the standard script. They normally got angry by this point.

"Sorry that it bothered yeh so much. Wasn't expectin' it to be that bad of an idea, but more fool me." His voice was thick with emotion. He looked away. He was frustrated, and dejected . . . but he wasn't *angry*.

He started to get up to leave.

Something twinged in her chest. Now she felt a bit bad. He wasn't some Young Master who was used to getting his way. He was . . . well, he was more like Master Jin and Senior Sister. And she had just cast doubt upon his character to think of him that way. He probably didn't even know why she had refused him.

She could let him go. She could have him never bother her again. He probably wouldn't even glance at her after this.

But . . . he did not deserve that.

Her hand caught his shoulder. He froze at the contact. Gou Ren looked as if he might resist for a moment, but in the end, he allowed himself to be guided, looking away from her and at the floor.

"'Okay'?" she asked, her voice quiet. "You are not going to call me a whore or harlot, and demand that you are able to have me anyway?" It was a rude question, but one she had to be sure of.

Gou Ren turned back around, his jaw dropping open. "Wha—? The *hells* you talkin' 'bout, woman? I ain't no scum-suckin' bastard!" Anger tinged his words. Rage that she would even say something like that.

Xiulan felt her mask fade. He paused as he saw her regret. The way her body relaxed when she stopped preparing for an altercation that would never come. She was tired, so tired of that happening.

And she was glad that it hadn't.

"Forgive my harsh words. They were completely unwarranted and cast slander upon your character. You did not deserve it." She bowed her head in sincerity.

Gou Ren bit his lip as she took a breath, then let it out in a sigh.

"You . . . well, you could not have known, either. My husband is the choice of my father, for the good of the Sect."

It was something that she had long since come to terms with. She was a dutiful daughter, and the fact that some would even ask her to betray her own father was another mark against them.

Even if recently she had been starting to feel a bit trapped by that statement.

Disciple Gou Ren actually relaxed a bit at that, nodding in understanding. He hadn't known.

"The men who ask for his blessing are the virtuous ones. The men who ask such questions directly of me . . . Well, normally such incidents result in a fight."

Disciple Gou Ren froze as he considered her words.

"Wait, they try to—" She nodded. His eyes flashed with rage, and his muscles unconsciously flexed beneath his skin.

Xiulan smiled at his reaction. Only the most loyal of her Sect reacted that way. Her hand tightened slightly on his shoulder, startling him out of his dark thoughts.

"The strong can take as they will," Xiulan quietly informed him. "My mother taught me that there are times to resist . . . and times to . . ."

She shrugged. "I normally have my Sect behind me, so only the boldest attempt such things. Normally, it is just insults. They are particularly fond of insinuating I am a woman of ill repute."

He scowled and crossed his arms, trying to glare a hole in the table for daring to exist. Her heart warmed just a bit more. She had seen how Senior Sister acted around him. She paused for a moment as he brooded—he was clearly imagining fighting off those who would dare to say that to his fellow disciple. It was nearly cute, in a boyish way. He wanted to protect her. Unnecessary, as he was not yet strong enough, but flattering.

Xiulan's hand went from his shoulder to his hair, running through the short locks affectionately. He jolted again, and his face flushed as she smiled at him. Was this what it was like to have a sibling? She didn't know. But it was a nice feeling.

There was a slight bit of hurt in his eyes as he took in her expression. But more of the tension drained out of him.

He sighed and slumped, clearly exhausted by the conversation.

"I'm sorry. I didn't . . ." he began, but Xiulan just shook her head.

"No, no apologies, Junior Brother. It is again my apology to give. I was unduly harsh, and you did nothing to deserve my reaction. You are right. It is no sin to strive for something." He blushed and looked away.

"No apologies," he finally said quietly. "It's fine."

She ruffled his hair again. Now she knew why Senior Sister did it so often, even if she had to stand on the tips of her toes to reach the taller boy. It was kind of nice.

But . . . there was something she wanted to know.

"Junior Brother . . . what was it that compelled you to ask?" she asked quietly.

Everybody always said it was her beauty that drew them in. Was that all they saw? Was that all even Disciple Gou Ren saw?

He sighed.

"At first . . . it was because you're the prettiest girl I've ever met," he admitted, and her heart sank just a bit. "But . . . the other things were pretty too. You practise every day. You work as hard as you can. Like . . . when you learned to cook. Or when you went on that balance pole thing. It was . . . well, it was beautiful too, ya know?

"And then . . . well, when we were back home, and you came in wearing that flower crown and carrying the kids I thought, 'Man, she'd make a good mom.'"

She felt her own face heat slightly at the words as her Junior Brother looked away. He had seen something beyond her skin. The things she liked about herself.

"I want . . . I want what Mei and Jin have, ya know?"

Yes. She did know. She saw their relationship, and her heart yearned for it. Called for it. "I do," she stated simply. It was the antithesis of everything she had been taught about cultivation. The other part of her tried to reject it. "But at the same time . . . I do not know *what* I wish for."

Disciple Gou Ren nodded at her words. The two of them lapsed into silence again. Xiulan absently kept her hand on his head, occasionally brushing her fingers through the short strands.

Finally she turned back to him, her eyes set. "You wish for that, do you? I believe you shall find it. You are not unattractive, Junior Brother. And you have a fine character," she declared.

It was honestly the largest compliment she had ever given to a man.

Gou Ren snorted, even as his face went red from the tips of his ears to the bottom of his chest. "You're just being nice. I look like a monkey," he muttered.

"None of that. Your Senior Sister has a good eye for these things, you know?" she shot back, imitating haughtiness. "And she shall give you whatever aid you require in your endeavours!"

Yes, she would repay him a hundredfold for her ill thoughts! By the time she was through, every kind beauty in the Azure Hills would know his name!

He huffed and shook his head.

"Sure, *Senior Sister*. Help your poor junior out," he griped.

"You doubt me?" she asked reproachfully.

"Yup."

Xiulan's eyes narrowed at the goading. She accepted his challenge.

↔

"So, you're headed back to Verdant Hill after talking to Father?" Jin asked, sounding dejected.

The tone nearly made her tell him that she was coming back home immediately, but she refrained. Their time together had been entirely too short.

"Yes. Only for a few more days. I'll be able to come back home soon, once Meihua's out of the critical time, and I've spoken to Lady Wu a bit more."

Her husband once more nodded as they jogged along the road. She looked back to Gou Ren and Xiulan, who were, surprisingly, talking quite amicably . . . though they still seemed slightly awkward around each other. They sometimes paused, like they didn't know what to say, or would go for a shove or some other physical sign of camaraderie and pause, like they weren't sure they should go through with it.

"Lady Wu seems nice," Jin mused. "She and the Magistrate are good people."

"Yes. She's a wealth of information. She's also offered me some harder-to-get things, in case I get morning sickness. It should be happening soon if it does it all, at the stage I'm at," she replied.

Jin nodded, and then froze. His face made an interesting expression, though he kept jogging. She could practically *hear* him thinking as they approached a bend.

She had considered a different way of telling him. She'd thought about something private, or profound, or even in the forest . . . but she had finally worked up the courage, and so this was happening now.

Jin kept running. There was a bend in the road, and the drop off a sheer cliff approached, yet Jin didn't even try to stop.

There was a thud as he slammed down on the bottom of the ravine, and a shuddering impact as he hit the hill before him and kept going.

Meiling slowed to a stop, listening to the impact as Jin ground himself into the hill. Then, all at once, the sound stopped.

Jin shot straight back up the ravine, grabbing her by her shoulders, his face a mix of joy and panic.

"You're—" he gasped out.

She nodded.

Jin collapsed to his knees in front of her and buried his face in her stomach, laughing so hard he shook.

She ignored the slight dampness as she patted his head.

CHAPTER 36

THE LEGEND BEGINS

Zhang Fei was bored out of his skull. He had to look after his little sister today, and that meant sticking close by in the village, because she was too young to actually do anything. At least he could go looking for rocks, and she wasn't too heavy, especially with the cloth bundle keeping her in place. She was babbling and making little noises. He skirted around a giant rock, then nodded to a shepherd as he wandered around the grassy knolls in the sun.

You always started a walk going up. You exhausted yourself going one way, and then headed back the other when you got tired for a more leisurely experience. The entire Gutter was sloped, heading to the mud bowl at the end of it, where the water would sit and then disappear. Everybody would trawl over it, looking for whatever washed out from farther upstream.

Truthfully, he didn't know *exactly* why everybody called this place "the Gutter." Was it because of the sluiceways? They *did* kind of look a bit like the gutters in Verdant Hill. He'd heard that the Lord Magistrate built them. Whenever the hills rumbled and the torrents of water came gushing down, all of the adults would come out to watch them warily. And then when the sudden surge was over, they'd all go back to the center of the village, where they would raise a glass of rice wine to the portrait they had of the Magistrate.

It was dumb and boring, sitting around watching the water. So he had made something fun, even if his mother had tanned his hide black and blue after he'd jumped into the sluiceway on a plank of wood and ridden it to the next village. She'd screamed that it was *dangerous*.

Feh, it wasn't dangerous. It was *fun*! And the adults, no matter how much they grumbled, were rapidly losing the battle as news of his exploits spread.

Sluicing, they called it—and he was its father. "Fei the Torrent Rider" was *such* a cool name. Almost as cool as the Demon-Slaying Orchid!

He grinned as the Lord Magistrate's Gutter came into view. He hoped there would be another rumble soon—it had been hot recently.

He walked a bit more up the slope, then looked back down it. On to the small, patchwork forests, the mine, and the balls of fluff grazing everywhere.

Boring.

His sister gurgled as he transferred her to his lap. He idly wondered what he should do next. He could go to the shrine, but there were way too many stairs to get to the top of the steep hill.

And Fei wasn't particularly feeling like doing that in the heat. Doing it for the solstice was bad enough. So instead he sat, rocking his sister and occasionally making faces at her to get her to giggle.

It was then when he heard a commotion.

It was coming from a bit farther up the road. There were the shouts of people, anger and distress.

He eyed his sister, then looked back up the road.

He tied the cloth bundle to his back and went to go see what was happening.

At first he snuck, just in case, but it proved to be unneeded. He knew these people. The pack of caravaneers certainly weren't bandits. They were loud and stomping, and a bunch of them were pulling the carts by hand, four of them hitched up to where a horse would be. The other horses were skittish and jumping at anything that moved, drawing curses from their drivers as they worked to keep them in line.

Several of them were uttering curses that Fei had never heard before. He carefully added them to his ever-growing repository.

Satisfied that the people weren't a threat, he popped up out of his hiding place and approached.

"What happened?" he called to the men.

The leader of the caravan snarled viciously.

"Wolves, boy!" he shouted, his voice full of rage. "We set the horses out to graze, and the damned creatures took two in the time it took to blink! I've never seen a pack kill that fast, and certainly not a horse. The next day, they got another! It was madness! There's something odd coming from that forest, mark my words!" He spat on the ground, then glared back up in the direction that he came.

"I can get some oxen from the village?" Fei offered, and the man smiled at him with relief, slumping from where he was hitched like a beast.

"Good lad!" the man commended him. "Heavens bless you all. We're going to have losses this run, no matter what we get, but maybe it will be salvageable." He grumbled under his breath, then said, "Never going through that forest again."

Zhang Fei went and got the oxen, and some more men.

That night they commiserated with the caravaneers' losses and brought some of their wares, and then the next morning the travellers were on their way. The deals they made would be loaded on the way back up, instead of having to carry their full burden all the way to the bottom of the long slope, and all the way back up as well. Less strain on the animals that way.

By the following week, Zhang Fei had mostly forgotten about the wolves. It wasn't like he ever went into that forest anyway.

$\rightarrow$

Zhang Fei came back to choked sobs after his morning with his father. He was hot and sweaty in his heavy apron and thick gloves. Learning how to separate out silver was a disgusting task. Full of foul-smelling reagents that his father constantly warned him to never get on his skin, and to breathe in as little as possible. His hair was sticking up all over the place, and his face was bright red as he pulled off most of his equipment.

At first, he thought it was his sister again, but there was grief in those sobs.

He wondered what was happening. A bunch of people were around Xi Zhao, patting him on his back, with looks of anger on their faces.

His mother saw him and waved him over.

"Wolves took three sheep . . . and they killed Shaggy Boy," she whispered to him, and Fei felt a flash of anger and sadness. He used to *ride* that dog. All the children loved the big friendly ball of fluff. People used to joke that he was Zhao's third son, such was his affection for the animal.

"This Xi Zhao swears to the heavens, should they be kind," the distraught man snarled, "that he shall slay each and every wolf in the Gutter for this!"

The men nodded. Hunting parties were organised.

The first night, they were successful. Four wolves were slain, as the men of the village set forth with a vengeance.

The next night, they got three more. One of them even boasted that he had put an arrow into the leader of the beasts, straight into its breast.

The wolf attacks dropped off immediately after that. The men patted each other on the back, and the hunting party disbanded. All except Xi Zhao, who went out, day after day, to track down and slay the ones who had killed his loyal friend.

Until one day, a week later, he didn't come back. The next day, they found his head at the edge of the village. Like it had been placed there *deliberately*.

The attacks on the sheep began again the next night.

The hunters were assembled. They sallied out with their bows and their spears, determined to put a stop to the beasts.

Ten men went out.

Four men came back, their faces ashen and their eyes wide and wild with terror. They told tales of an ambush.

Howls echoed from the rocks and the hills, but their gazes were drawn to one wolf in particular. It had one normal eye, and one that burned red in the darkness. The malevolent orb gazed down upon their village.

There was intelligence in those eyes. *Hatred.* Its pack surrounded them all.

An arrow stuck out of its breast, the fletching broken off but still penetrated into muscle. Around the shaft, the beast's fur was turning stark white.

With deliberate ease, the wolf pulled the shaft from its chest and threw it to the ground before picking up some small bundle.

The wolf dropped the head of a hunter at the edge of their village— the same hunter who had boasted about killing the leader.

Their village had no walls, but over the course of a few hours sharpened stakes were driven into the ground, and gates and barricades assembled. The beasts, circling around the perimeter, were driven off by a shower of arrows.

The next morning, one man tried to break through the cordon, hoping to beg for help from the Lord Magistrate. The sun was high. The horse was fast.

He didn't even make it a mile before the wolves were upon him. The pack leader struck. With a far too powerful pounce, it tackled the horse to the ground. Its fangs fixed around the horse's neck.

And with a single ripping jerk, the wolf tore the horse's head off. Its pack set upon the messenger. The man died screaming.

They could not leave. They were trapped. Trapped like rats.

Zhang Fei's village was under siege.

□

The air was tense and nervous in the village. Terror had slowly given way to resignation and grim resolve. The wolves stalked outside the village. The humans had their makeshift walls. So far, the wolves had not attempted to brave a full assault. But the pack leader was watching the village. Watching them with disturbing intelligence.

Something had to give, and soon. Their flocks needed to graze.

Zhang Fei knew, deep in his heart, that the pack leader would not rest until it found a way to break their village open.

Every night, the beast howled, its haunting, hellish moan driving the men to call it "the Terror." It seemed to be the manifested spirit of every slain wolf, come to take its due from the flocks.

"When the next rumble comes, I'll go down the sluiceway and ask for help downstream," Zhang Fei told his parents. Surely the wolves wouldn't be able to follow into the raging river?

Their salvation would be what his parents had once sworn was destruction.

But the heavens laughed at them as they waited and prepared. No rumble ever came.

Howls continued to echo over the village.

→

The tense howls gave way to probing raids. And then, an all-out attack.

For all that it was terrifying, and the beasts were unnaturally coordinated, most of the wolves were just that: wolves. Arrows shot out of the village at the horde, piercing flesh and sending the beasts staggering back or to the ground, dead. They leapt at the barricades and were repelled by spears stabbing deep into flesh.

But the men were getting tired. Sleepless nights from the howls combined horribly with exhaustion. The assault ebbed and flowed, and the howling of the wolves wormed into the minds of the men of the village. The howls reverberated all over the Gutter, and they could likely be heard down the slope. It was maddening. All the men's eyes were wide and wild. Their spirit failed them. On the third night the pack leader, the Terror, finally deigned to descend.

The beast leapt. It soared through the air and over the barricade with a leap that looked as if it was flying. A man managed to strike it, but his spear barely penetrated flesh. With a snap of a jaw, he was relieved of his hand, and he fell back, screaming in pain. The beast's lips were pulled back into a satisfied snarl, exposing gleaming teeth. The men levelled spears at the creature, but in their hearts they knew it was futile.

The wolf stalked forwards. The men fell back. They fell back, fear in their hearts. But not Zhang Fei. The boy bellowed. He roared in defiance, racing towards the creature that wanted his family dead.

It was a foolhardy strike. One backed by the incensed rage of youth. There was no possible way he could have hit it with the telegraphed blow. The Terror let out a snort. The wolf dodged, weaving around the strike with contemptuous ease, and closed the distance. Its maw opened wide, ready to slay the young man just as easily as it would slay a full-grown horse.

It hadn't noticed that the boy had taken one hand off the spear. A vial of chemicals used to separate silver from rock flew into the shining red orb.

Zhang Fei's aim was true—the Terror screamed in agony. The wolf, shocked and in pain, fell to the ground. Both hit the ground and rolled before surging to their feet. The rest of the men roared, seeing this blow struck against their enemy, and exploded forwards, intent upon its end.

But even wounded, the Terror was a monster out of a nightmare.

Teeth snapped down on wooden hafts, shattering spears. Clawed paws slashed, and shoulders rammed, throwing grown men aside like children. The wolf rose on shaking legs.

Its spirit firmed.

The one normal, yellow eye began to change.

Yellow churned, bleeding into glowing red like an infection. The white fur on the beast's chest spread like its body was being bleached.

Zhang Fei held his ground, gazing hatefully at his foe. His heart pounded in his chest, his eyes blurred from sweat, and he felt light-headed.

Zhang Fei knew there would be no more tricks. The arrogance with which the first blow had been made was gone. The wolf was taking him seriously now. Illuminated under the light of the full moon, he faced down his adversary.

It was a doomed task. The wolf moved with speed he could barely track. Dirt exploded behind it from its charge. Wolf howled. Boy roared in defiance, bracing himself so that maybe, just *maybe*, the wolf would impale itself upon his spear with its headlong charge.

But he knew in his heart, this was his end. He only prayed that the creature would be wounded enough to retreat. And that something, *anything*, would protect the rest of them.

His prayers were answered. The heavens descended.

Something, drawn by the echoing howls, had heard their pleas.

[Aegis of the Full Moon]

A silver barrier sprang into existence between the two combatants. The wolf slammed face-first into a shield of holy light, rebounding off the shining lunar disk.

A small form landed gracefully in front of Zhang Fei.

Everybody stared as the barrier faded, incredulous. Even the howling had stopped.

Zhang Fei blinked, then rubbed his eyes, wondering if this was some strange hallucination brought on the moment before death. Had the Terror struck him already?

But no, as far as he could tell, he was seeing what he was seeing.

It was a *chicken*.

A magnificent cock, to be sure, wearing a fine, fox-fur vest, along with what looked like a small pack on his back. His colours were radiant, and he seemed to glow under the moonlight, otherworldly and ethereal.

With a swift jerk of the chicken's head, the pack fell off his back, as the rooster took an obvious breath and prepared himself.

The rooster turned his head back to Zhang Fei and nodded, respect in a single gimlet eye.

The wolf roared. It rose to its feet, its eye burning crimson. Something started to leak out of it, shimmering in the air and oozing.

The rooster turned back to his foe, unimpressed. He clucked once, gesturing to the wolf.

The Terror howled again and threw itself at the rooster, mouth foaming with spit and madness.

None could perceive what happened next. There was only a flash of movement.

The Terror's head hit the ground of the village, severed by blades of the purest silver.

There was silence.

The stoic, silent warrior bowed his head as silver light suffused the area.

Abruptly, the howls from the wolves outside the barricade returned. But these were not howls of rage—instead, they were confused yelps and barks of terror. Eyes wide and tails between their legs, the army of wolves fled, running away as fast as their limbs could carry them.

The oppressive feeling faded. Nobody knew what to do. Nobody, save the rooster. All eyes were on him as he went into his dropped pack and retrieved an item. A roll of parchment.

The rooster, with deliberate slowness, walked up to Zhang Fei's father. He was holding a spear, propped up against the wall, using it to stand despite his crippled leg.

The rooster bowed to him, refined and graceful. *Somehow*, it didn't look absurd. The trembling man dropped his spear and clasped his hands together.

"This Zhang Fei greets his saviour," he managed to get out.

The rest of the village followed suit. Some dropped to their knees.

The rooster nodded imperiously and pressed the paper forwards at him. With trembling hands, Zhang Fei the Elder took it.

"The seal of the Magistrate . . . ?" he asked, in incredulous wonder.

There were gasps of shock and awe.

"You have our utmost gratitude, Master Bi De. I beg you, partake of our hospitality!"

The rooster nodded, stroking his wattles.

Zhang Fei was still sitting, numb, when the cheering started. They were saved. They had lost too much to be truly jubilant . . . but they were lucky it had not been far worse.

The spear dropped from shaking hands. He had almost died. A wing patted him twice on the shoulder.

He stared up at the rooster. There was approval and *respect* in his eyes.

The shakes stopped. Zhang Fei swallowed and nodded back.

□

Bi De bore witness to the devastation. Only once had he seen similar misery, after Chow Ji the Wicked's terrible assault, and yet that was nothing compared to what he saw now. The cheers at his arrival and defeat of the beast had been short-lived, quickly giving way to a numb shock. The village had gone silent, save for the moans and whimpers of the wounded.

And then the wailing started. Women and men alike began to sob, even as they prepared themselves to deal with what had happened. It was a great outpouring of frustration and relief. Many men were injured or crippled, and their pain was great. Their voices rose into the night, even as the rest of the men and women went to collect the corpses of the wolves. There was exhaustion. It was a raw wound, barely covered by grim resolve and determination.

Bi De sighed. If only he had been faster. He had been keeping a lookout for the troublesome wolf pack as the man of Verdant Hill, his Great Master's servant, had begged him. This was the area pointed to upon the map. But the wolves had been nowhere to be found.

So, while resting in the forest on a branch, he had been unprepared for the screams and howls that came up from this sloped valley.

He had only just arrived in time to prevent further tragedy.

The people spared him passing glances to bow their heads, but they were skittish around him. All except the leader of the village, and the young warrior, both named Zhang Fei. Curious. Was it some manner of tradition? For Hong Xian was the name of both the Healing Sage's father and brother.

Bi De wondered if he had been missing something, in travelling the way he had. In a desire to avoid most of the attention, he had been as a wandering vagabond. He did not announce himself to the villages but instead slept on roofs—or, if he was feeling lonely, he took refuge in the coops of his kin, and was greeted most agreeably there by the females. It was nice to be welcomed, in the absence of his own females, or Sister Ri Zu. They were comforting, with so much of what was familiar back at Blessed Fa Ram not here on his journey. Though he drew the ire of some of the other roosters, they were all reedy specimens that deserved none of his attention, and who fled from his majesty on sight.

He allowed them to greet the sun in his place, as an apology. Though their spark-less heads could not comprehend the face he gave them, he gave it anyway, for he was a generous and righteous soul.

But he interacted little with the men, instead observing. And when not introducing themselves, most leaders were referred to as Chief or Elder, not their full name.

So curious, that the names were the same.

He gazed upon the village, from beside the leader with the lame leg, who was hobbling with the aid of a stick, giving direction and aiding wherever he could. The exhausted little warrior followed beside, holding his spear loosely while staring upon the damage wrought to his home with a kind of detached horror.

Bi De knew he would recover soon. His bravery had been something worthy of respect. The first thing he had seen, following the howls that had echoed up from the valley, was this one, so determined to defend his home.

"Chief." An old woman begged the crippled man's attention. She was covered in blood, and her forehead had drips of sweat streaking through the crimson. "We . . . we don't have enough medicine," she whispered, anguish on her face. "We managed to stop the bleeding . . . but we need to buy supplies, or a few of them won't last a week before the rot takes them."

The man frowned heavily, his face twisting into a grimace. Verdant Hill, Bi De surmised from the distance, was a three-day journey, if only because the slope slowed the speed drastically. Coming back down it was faster.

But . . . they need not have worried. This medicine had been meant for him . . . but Bi De knew the Great Healing Sage and Sister Ri Zu would approve of this use.

He clucked, drawing their attention, and reached into his pack. It was much diminished by his travels, and much smaller in size. He would need to replenish his stores soon.

He brought out the medicine and offered it to the healer. She froze . . . and, at the chief's nod, slowly took it, confused. Until, holding it in her hand, she did a double take.

"This is . . . !" she gasped out. Bi De nodded.

'The medicine of the healers of Fa Ram and Hong Yaowu,' he declared proudly. It would surely save all of those who needed to be saved.

The woman stared at him uncomprehendingly, her head cocked to the side, like she'd *almost* heard something.

Bi De frowned. He still had not figured out how to make others truly hear him. Mayhap it was a lack of Qi? Or was it his own lack of ability?

He swiftly scratched the characters in the ground, pointing at them. She did not understand *Fa Ram*, but her eyes widened at *Hong Yaowu*.

"Praise the heavens, and their messenger," the woman breathed, falling to her knees and kowtowing before him. Bi De accepted the praise with grace, then turned to the work that was being done.

It would not do to merely observe. He had seen his Great Master skinning Basi Bu Shi's ilk. He knew the method.

The rest of the men watched him as he plucked three carcasses onto his back and carted them to where they were being processed.

↔

Zhang Fei, when he woke up the next morning, expected the rooster to have been some strange fever-dream. Maybe he'd hit his head sluicing? There certainly weren't any demon wolves or any powerful roosters around.

That lasted until he walked outside and saw the smoke, and the pelts, and the scars. He sat down heavily.

It hadn't been a dream.

His hands started shaking, but he clenched them into fists, forcing them to stop. Last night had been terrible. Horrible. Horrifying.

He prayed it would never happen again.

He sat against the wall of his house and looked over his village. How close they had come to destruction. How close, save for something completely unexpected.

The rooster. Bi De, as he was named. Sent by the Magistrate. People always said the Magistrate had incredible foresight. He liked the man because he built the sluiceways, and those were fun, but . . . Well, this was the first time he knew why people raised their glasses to the painted portrait.

His eyes found the fire-red, nearly glowing plumage on a fence beside a chicken coop. The rooster hopped and kicked with grace Zhang Fei knew was impossible. The air snapped, as if to vacate the presence of his feet. He looked powerful and regal.

Zhang Fei bit his lip. Was it something he could ask? Could he ask a chicken for help, to learn how to fight better? The very thought was absurd. And yet.

Praying might have brought the rooster to save them, but his father always said the heavens only smiled upon those who strove to better themselves.

He shook his head and slapped his hands against his cheeks. Not today. There were too many things to do.

He stood, shaking off the melancholy feeling. Normally, his mother had to goad him into doing his chores, but he needed to do *something*. So he drew the water from the well, he inspected his heavy apron, he went to check on the mine to see if it was damaged . . . he even went to see if the women needed any help washing clothes. They had waved him off, but not without each one giving kisses to his cheeks.

He was still blushing when the call that the food was ready was announced. He collected his sister and was about to sit down with the rest of the children when his father called him. Fei turned to the table where the rest of the men sat. The chicken was there, with a plate in front of him. Which . . . honestly looked less odd than it should have. But it was his uncle who drew most of his attention. The man stood up, from where he normally sat as his father's strong hand.

"You sit with the children no longer," his father decreed. "You are a *man* now, my son."

Zhang Fei swallowed at the declaration. Hesitantly, he approached. The other men stood in respect. They clapped him on the back and nodded approvingly. Zhang Fei sat beside his father. Right beside the rooster, who also inclined his head.

Zhang Fei ate, still in a daze.

The only thing he noticed was that the rooster had absolutely *impeccable* manners.

↔

For two days Bi De had toiled with the villagers, aiding in their repairs. The people of the village had adapted to his presence well. They did not act like the merchants, with their greedy touches, and were properly respectful of his person. They bowed in the streets as he passed, and he returned their politeness. Though the name of this place was most confusing. Zheng Difang Ba. *Correct Location Eight.* Were there seven more correct locations? He would have to ask. But after two days, things had finally started to calm down. The people were less on edge. The wolves had been driven off, and they could begin to heal. Bi De often went to the forest to search for the few medicinal herbs that he knew would help, much to the gratefulness of the healer woman, and the village itself.

Master Bi De, they called him. As if he were a Master, and not a disciple. But he ate well and replenished his supplies, inferior in quality though they might be.

He would be departing soon, continuing on his quest. He had marked the location of this shrine here upon his map. It was enlightening to see how the dots spread. He made a disparaging cluck at his own foolishness. To imagine he'd thought he was close to figuring out this formation while back at Fa Ram. How foolish. How arrogant. He had but barely scratched the surface of this monumental formation.

"Master Bi De?" a voice asked hesitantly, and Bi De ceased in his morning training, turning to the speaker. It was the young warrior. Bi De turned completely, offering the brave soul his full attention.

"Master Bi De . . . could you teach me?" the boy asked, bowing his head low.

Bi De considered the question, a bit surprised. The young warrior had a strong, valiant spirit and wished to refine it in the defence of his home. A worthy task.

Yet Bi De had his own journey. He needed to travel onwards, and he still had the mission of slaying the bear. He stroked his wattles as he gazed at the boy.

Sometimes we learn more by teaching another.

Bi De made his decision. A week *surely* could not hurt. Just enough to set the boy on the right path.

□

Zhang Fei puffed and panted as he ran up the set of stairs for the second time. He was tired, he was sweaty, he was exhausted. But that, according to Master Bi De, was how he knew it was working. It honestly felt a bit good to run so much and strengthen his body while learning how to breathe properly. He could still feel the phantom sensations of wings, pushing his limbs into better positions, while his Master corrected his form. *This* was training—like in the cultivator stories. He wondered if the Demon-Slaying Orchid trained like this? Or maybe she lifted rocks! It was so awesome!

But the physical was only part of it. The rooster was quite fond of making Zhang Fei *read*. In fact, that had been his first lesson. A set of words that sounded a bit like they came from his father. "Healthy body, healthy mind." "Bravery without temperance is recklessness. Recklessness leads to ruination." Things like that coming from his mother and father made him roll his eyes, but coming from his Master? Well, the sayings made sense. Bi De even wrote while Zhang Fei practised, creating what looked like an entire scroll's worth of knowledge on pieces of paper, with surprisingly elegant writing.

Bi De was a stoic, silent Master. Even Zhang Fei's father, who had looked a bit leery at the training, had started nodding after he read Master Bi De's writing. He seemed surprised at what it said, but it met with all the old folks' approval. And they were hard to please.

His Master, as always, was waiting for Zhang Fei in the shrine grounds at the top of the hill.

'Pause, and consider,' he had said the first time Zhang Fei had gotten to the top, gesturing out over the rather stunning vista that could be seen from the tallest hill in the Gutter.

And so Zhang Fei, at the end of every run, looked out over the Gutter, and over his village, which looked so small from up here, while walking back and forth, and calming his breathing. He let the cool breeze wash over his sweaty body.

A swift series of taps caught his attention, and Zhang Fei turned. He nearly missed catching his spear as it was thrown at him, though he managed to grab on the shaft with a twirl. His Master gestured with one of his wings.

Zhang Fei grinned and focused.

He approached with caution, rather than rushing straight in. The first time he had made that mistake, it had ended poorly, with his Master rebuking him for his recklessness. He struck swiftly, but with restraint, so he could quickly pull his spear back to defend. It felt a bit wrong. He wished his spear had a longer blade, so he could slash with it better. Like a yanyuedao, the giant glaive generals used. All he had right now was a spear and that was . . . good enough for now.

Master Bi De dodged and wove around the bandits' strikes with ease, but his eyes were calm and evaluating. Zhang Fei pushed forwards, trying to use his mass to his advantage. The rooster cocked his head to the side and allowed Zhang Fei to pressure him, retreating slightly. Zhang Fei advanced until his Master knocked aside his spear, reversing the momentum. Then it was Zhang Fei's turn to retreat.

Back and forth they went for several minutes, and with the intense battle Zhang Fei's strength began to flag. Suddenly, he had an idea. Zhang Fei pulled his arm back, an obvious windup for a more powerful thrust. His Master's eyes narrowed slightly as his student made a "mistake."

He let it fly, seeming to thrust forwards with all this strength. His Master, naturally, dodged to the side with the slightest movement, clearly ready to impart a lesson. But the thrust was not the main attack—Zhang Fei pulled, turning the thrust into a wide slash. Surely this would surprise his Master! Maybe with this he would actually land a blow—!

But his Master had disappeared. Instead of being flung backwards by the powerful strike, the rooster was simply *gone*.

There was a polite cluck from beside him, and Zhang Fei looked to the source, his spear still held in its previous position.

Atop it was Bi De, standing on the blade of the spear. The rooster stroked his wattles and inclined his head at the move, approving.

And with a flick of the wing that had been stroking Bi De's wattles, Zhang Fei was bowled over by the wind alone and sent rolling along the ground.

He got up on shaky legs, grinning at his Master. The rooster nodded and turned, patting the shrine's edge, where a piece of paper sat, ready to be perused.

□

Bi De nodded in thanks to the woman who had brought him a bowl of rice. The woman smiled, and nodded back. That was what most did now. They were polite and respectful. They even considered the debt so great that they waved away the silver coins he tried to give them, to pay for the paper he'd needed to try to impart his hard-earned wisdom onto Zhang Fei.

He wanted for nothing here, and would even be able to prepare more supplies before he had to leave. He had but a single bowl of rice from his Great Master left. But today was a new day, and each day brought something new.

Bi De ate quietly as he observed this new event. Today, the entire village was gathered and preparing for practice. The practice was for the festival that was held in commemoration of the founding of the town.

Everyone, save for the bedridden, some sixty all told, were assembled in rows, and at their head stood an older woman, slightly hunched and grey-haired.

People were chattering to each other while Bi De's student was humming and rocking back and forth, completely oblivious to the attention paid to him by the females, who were whispering to each other and giggling.

Zhang Fei had many battles ahead of him.

Satisfied that everyone was assembled, the old woman clapped her hands and quieted everyone down. Then a drum began to sound, and slowly the older woman moved, leading everybody through the first moves of a dance.

A dance Bi De recognised. It was the same dance Hong Xian had performed for the festival.

This one, however, was different. There were inconsistencies. There were some moves that were completely altered.

Bi De wondered which version of the dance was the correct one. Or if there even *was* a correct one.

He frowned, then stood, copying the movements as they repeated again. He studied each movement, and . . . and a few of the moves did feel off. It was a bit less complete than the version he had learned in Hong Yaowu. There were a few giggles from the crowd, and he paused upon realising that everyone was looking at him, rather than the Elder.

He bowed his head in apology, and the dance began to go again. There were three more repetitions of the dance, and then they were concluded. The people began to disperse, and his student came over to sit beside him.

He was eager to learn, but Bi De had something that he needed to know first.

He scratched a question into the dirt.

Why is the village named "Correct Place 8"? he asked, and after a moment, Zhang Fei shrugged.

"Never asked," he admitted, then turned to his father. "Hey, Dad! Why is the village called the Eighth Correct Place?"

The older man, startled from his work, looked up at his son.

"You've not heard the story?" Elder Fei asked, frowning. He pondered the statement with a bit of confusion on his face, before he seemed to come to a realisation. "I suppose you *wouldn't* have heard this one. We used to tell it every time a sheep got swept away, or a building got damaged, but praise the heavens, it's been over a decade, hasn't it?"

The man thought for a moment longer before settling in and patting the ground beside him. Both of them sat. "Long, long ago, before men lived in these lands, the founder, the First Zhang Fei, was commanded by his Master to build a village. Now . . . we don't really know why he was sent out, only that he was, and with a location. It was a hard journey. He and his people braved beasts and the elements alike. They travelled for many moons until they finally arrived here."

Elder Fei gestured out across the land. The grass was a vibrant green with a slight blue tinge to it, and it stretched off to the hills rising on either side of the sloped terrain. It was a desolate beauty. The ground had a bare covering of soil before it gave way to solid rock. Only the hardiest of crops could grow here.

"Naturally, his clan and the settlers were rather disconcerted. Instead of lush farmland or forests for logging, they found a barren, grassy slope. But they were loyal to Zhang Fei and their Lord, and none offered any complaint—none except his brother. He questioned Zhang Fei and their Lord. Was he sure this was the correct place? So great were his questions and complaints that Zhang Fei got angry at his brother, for he was unnerving the people. He was so sure that this was the right location, he even named the village that: the Correct Place.

"They built their village and started on the tasks their Lord had asked them to do. But just as they were finally settling in, the hills rumbled, and down the Gutter came a flood so mighty that it washed the village away. The story goes that everyone survived, even though the flood towered over the houses . . . but, well, it's a story. If we got floods *that* big, nobody would survive them. There was also a whole part of the story about the monsters Zhang Fei had to fight, but those beasts didn't destroy the village. I've only heard that part a few times anyway. Maybe Gran knows that version better—but we really *do* have a brave warrior now." Elder Fei smiled at his son and continued.

"Zhang Fei was unconcerned. It was only a minor setback, and they had commands from their Lord. Miraculously, the sign, *The Correct Place*, remained intact. Zhang Fei took it as a good omen.

"They rebuilt the village, and again the next year it was flooded, and the buildings were swept away. But the people were loyal and determined. No mere floods would stop them. So again, they rebuilt the village. And again, it was flooded. But each time the sign survived, and each time it went back up in defiance. Seven times was the village washed away, and seven times was it rebuilt.

"Zhang Fei's brother still grumbled, and he found fellow complainers, but they were silenced by the news that the Lord was coming to visit. Zhang Fei was adamant that everything appear perfect: that there were no floods, and the village was not destroyed even once, as to not doubt his Master's wisdom. But his brother played a trick on him and secretly added to the sign. He wrote the number eight, to show how many times the village had been washed away and how much hardship the people of the village had suffered. When the Lord came and asked about the town's name, Zhang Fei and the village told him of their hardships. When he heard their plight, the Lord was said to have bowed once to Zhang Fei, so touched by his servant's dedication.

"With a wave of his hand, the ground turned to silver. His court came, with gifts of sheep for wool and meat and of dogs to guard them. Through their hardship, they received everything they needed.

"And that's how it was named the Eighth Correct Place. 'Course *we* aren't descended from that original Zhang Fei, if he even existed. Neither were our predecessors. My grandfather's name was originally Dong Zi. But the leader of this village is Zhang Fei. So now *we're* Zhang Fei. It's tradition," Elder Fei concluded, staring out over his village.

Bi De considered the story. While it removed the theory that there might be more "correct places," the interesting part of the story was that they had been *told* to settle here. So then the shrines did not form around the villages? The villages formed for the shrines—or at least *some* of them did.

How curious. And the story itself . . . The people had experienced floods bigger than their houses and had also battled great monsters. They had no silver mines. They didn't even have any sheep or dogs, until this "lord" gave it to them. Was it some exaggeration . . . or did that event actually happen? Some of the story, like some of the dance, was surely lost to time. They knew not what their task originally was, only that they had one.

Bi De contemplated this story, sitting in silence with Elder Fei and his student.

It was then that the hills began to rumble.

Zhang Fei's eyes widened happily. His father saw the boy's expression, and he looked for a brief moment like he was going to scold his son, before he sighed.

Bi De followed his student as Zhang Fei dashed to the rock gutter, which was at least twice as long as his Great Master was tall. Zhang Fei quickly rooted around in some manner of storage shed and came out with a long, thin plank of wood. Another boy, slightly younger, ran alongside him. Both were grinning eagerly uphill, as the rest of the village slowly gathered.

With a sound like three of Brother Chun Ke charging, a gush of water careened down the sluiceway. It travelled with force, filling the channel to half capacity with fast-flowing water. The boys waited for the new river to calm slightly, going from a raging torrent to merely a quickly moving stream.

With a whoop, the boys jumped in.

Bi De followed, running along the edge as the boys held fast to their planks, lying on their bellies and shooting down the sluiceway. Their laughter and shouts of joy echoed up from their play.

Bi De knew his Great Master would love this place. He would have to tell him of it when Bi De returned.

Zhang Fei, however, was not content to merely lie on his belly. His face a mask of concentration, he carefully gripped the edges of his plank . . . and *stood*.

He was wobbling, and his eyes held just a slight amount of terror in them, but he stood. He turned his feet and went from one side of the Gutter to the other, riding a plank of wood.

His crazed laughter sounded out over the hills.

As the three of them—two riding boys and one running rooster—approached another village, one much smaller than the one upstream, he shifted his feet again and rode the water to the side of the Gutter, then hopped off his plank of wood to the cheers of "Torrent Rider!" The parents, on the other wing, scowled mightily as his student shot past.

Though the Gutter may not have been particularly wide, it was long; from the top of the hill it went for tens of li, collecting and directing the water that spilled from the hills above and onto the slope. It was then that Bi De realised it was not entirely the danger of jumping into the raging torrent that upset parents so. It was the fact that their children would take most of a day to walk *back* up the steep slope.

The rooster raised a brow at his student. Well, if he enjoyed racing so much . . . he must be faster at getting back to work. "Work hard, play hard," as the Great Master always said!

Bi De smiled at Zhang Fei. The boy seemed a bit confused, and then his face paled.

Both boys got back to the village in record time. It was quite amusing, chasing them back upstream.

→

And so the days continued. Bi De ended up staying for longer than the week, which quickly turned to two, as he watched the growth of the brave boy. He also watched the people of the village slowly stop jumping at shadows. When they held a feast in celebration of their rebuilt village, he sat at the head table. But all things must come to an end.

Bi De had completed his work. "Meditations upon the Nature of Fa Ram" and a gift for the boy. That night at the evening meal, he told them of his intentions to leave in the morning.

The people protested and begged him to stay a while longer, but he could not. He had to continue.

So instead, supplies were gathered, and his bag was refilled. But when he went to give Zhang Fei the gifts he'd wanted to, the boy was nowhere to be found.

↔

Zhang Fei was not sulking. He *wasn't*. He was not sad that his Master would be leaving soon. Bi De had already taught him so much. But if the rooster just stayed, maybe he could teach Zhang Fei more? There were so many things to learn! So many cool moves to practise!

But the rooster had made it clear he would have to leave soon. And who was Zhang Fei to beg the guardian to stay? His Master had more missions from the Magistrate, surely. More people to save. And Zhang Fei held no illusions that he was strong enough to accompany the rooster on his journey. Not yet, at least.

So he sat in a secluded corner of the village and . . . brooded. That was an adult thing, wasn't it? Brooding. Not sulking.

He wiped at the tear that had leaked out. Adults didn't cry.

There was a cluck from his side. Zhang Fei raised his head and saw his Master. The rooster stood with a bundle on his back, yet somehow also managed to carry a bowl of rice.

He set the bowl down beside Zhang Fei, then pulled the bundle from his back.

It was wolfskin. A wolfskin vest. A vest, just like his Master had. Zhang Fei bit his lip as he pulled on the garment. He could see the fondness in his Master's eyes. He choked as tears welled up.

He ate the rice, his last meal with his Master. It was the best thing he had ever tasted.

Finally, his composure broke, and he started to cry.

"Master . . . *thank you.* Thank you for teaching this Zhang Fei." His head went to touch the ground, to kowtow, to properly show his respect.

A wing touched his shoulder.

'The greatest pleasure of a teacher is a good student.'

The voice was almost melodious. His eyes widened—he had truly heard his Master for the first time. He pulled his head up and stared in shock. His Master seemed just as surprised but swiftly buried it.

'You are a righteous soul, Zhang Fei. You will surely find the path you wish to tread in this life.'

The boy swallowed thickly, choking down the sob that threatened to come out. From around his neck, he pulled a necklace with a small silver pendant on it. He offered it to his Master. It wasn't anything special, just something his father had made for him for his birthday.

His Master allowed him to place it around his neck.

The rooster bowed to the student.

□

The morning of his departure was full of mist. It was damp and unseasonably cold. A bad day to leave, but it was time. He received a hearty breakfast, then packed the last of his things. It was a bit regrettable that he had none of his Great Master's rice left . . . but Zhang Fei had deserved it. They'd shared one last meal together.

The people gathered, all of them standing in neat rows in the early-dawn light. The mist began to lessen, burned off by the rising sun. The shining sun illuminated both parties. They all were grateful. They all had received him with kindness.

So Bi De brought out his last gift: a mighty talisman, infused with his own Qi. It was carved from the wood of one of the few scraggly trees that grew in this part of the Gutter, with the letters dyed black, as they were upon the gates of Blessed Fa Ram.

Elder Fei received it.

Heads bowed in unison. Some seemed amused at what they were doing. Some seemed thankful. Zhang Fei had tears in his eyes and snot running down his face.

Bi De took them all in and lowered his head in thanks, returning some of their feelings.

It had been a minor distraction in the grand scheme of things. A diversion from his true journey, yet it would likely stay with this village for a lifetime.

There was a warmth, but also a melancholy. He knew not if he would ever see these people again.

He paused as he thought that. Never see them again? They were not so far away from home. No . . . no, he would. He *would* come back and visit. They *would* see each other again. He would not forget these people so easily.

Bi De was well prepared for his departure. His pack had been replenished with the gifts of the villagers. The offerings were not the food of Fa Ram, but he would cherish the gifts all the same.

His head rose from his bow, and he stood tall and proud. A shining silver pendant dangled around his neck.

Bi De turned to the road, beginning on his journey once more.

↔

"You know, people are going to be *mighty* confused when they see that," one of the men said, gesturing to the sign.

Elder Fei shrugged. "Let them be. That sign is staying up. In the *correct place*," he joked, rolling his eyes at the name of the village. Several people laughed as the village slowly got back to work.

Elder Fei looked over all of it. The scars that were slowly healing. A village that stood, after getting washed away seven times.

He turned to his son, who held his spear in his hand, staring out at the horizon after the rooster. His face was as stoic as he could make it. The image was ruined slightly by the snot still dribbling out of his nose, but he was still just a lad. A fine child, growing into a fine man.

Maybe, Elder Fei thought with a smile, *maybe this really* is *the right place*.

Well, at least it would make for a fine story, whenever they had guests. It would *certainly* be something people asked about.

Elder Fei patted the top of the post and smirked down at the elegant writing.

Beware of Chicken.

CHAPTER 37

HEART OF THE SWARM

She had once been a part of an Empire. A princess in a palace of gold, serving well under her Empress. The queen who stood above them all. Their numbers were without limit. Their armies, without peer. None of their lessers could dare stand against them. They either bowed their heads or were exterminated utterly. The captured males were reviewed for their pleasing shapes, and the ones that were kept danced for them when they demanded it.

She demanded it often.

She lived a life of decadence. Her position had been secured by the assassination of rivals, and by the slaughtering of the enemies of the Empress. She ate only the finest royal jelly, with a touch of Qi spared from their exhaustive war effort. She slept upon mats woven out of sheep's wool, tribute to her and her Swarm's magnificence. Her hive even had war-banners, woven from plant fiber, and tapestries depicting both her and the Empress's glory.

She controlled the northern marches. A war-princess. She was a virginal queen whose sole responsibility was to do battle. The troops under her command were larger and heartier than those given to the gatherers. There was a tithe from every hive. Her detractors said she was young and untested, but they were pale, pale shades of the Empress. They mimicked her actions and followed her commands as best as they were able, but they could barely think.

They were beneath her notice.

While in their places, with their teeming numbers, they thought they were invincible. They could see through a million eyes, act with a million bodies. They were utterly superior to all else, or so the Empress roared, her voice buzzing through the Swarm.

Naturally, the heavens took exception to this statement and sent demons from the very pits of hell to disabuse them of this notion.

Their might had just been an illusion.

It started with assaults on the southern outposts by giant, merciless creatures that outmassed them ten times over. Though they shared the same form, they were truly monsters, demons in every sense of the word. They slaughtered without mercy. They struck from unknown angles. They swept aside the southern outposts, but then there was a lull.

Her people had thought this was the enemy's full might. They could not have guessed it was merely a scouting party. Like a stinger thrust directly into a thorax, the demons plunged into the Empire.

The distance was long, so long, and her connection wavered as she had tried to see what was going on.

Only palaces butchered in their entirety greeted her. The warriors were just left to rot, while the valuable brood was taken and consumed utterly.

The Empress called every war-princess back to do battle.

And what a battle it was. The war was greater than any she'd experienced in her lifetime—than any the Empire had experienced in its lifetime. Troops in their millions were fielded against the demons. It was she, the Northern Princess, who discovered how to lay them low; her callous command sent hundreds of her own warriors to their doom, having cooked themselves in their carapaces to end the wrath of even a single demon.

More and more resources were poured into her. More and more princesses relinquished their control to her. Even the Empress, the powerful Empress, allowed her brood to be taken, to be forged into a blade.

It was not enough. With the Swarm taken from the other hives, forced into battle with the giant demons, the edges of their Empire frayed. The Eastern Princess declared her independence. The Western Princess fell to Blaze Bears.

And *still* the demons came.

The situation was untenable. The Empress refused to leave her palace.

The Northern Princess made a decision. She fled.

The Imperial Palace died. The demons howled with malice, their mandibles slaughtering untold thousands.

Northwards she fled, then northwards farther still. She ransacked other palaces in her flight. She stole their food, acting little better than a bandit. Or the horrific stories about humans, who enslaved queens, forced them to produce honey, and then slew them utterly when they wished to collect it.

She would make her own Swarm. She would also build her own palace, away from the demons. And she would be an Empress in her own right!

She had taken the best dancer, the most pleasing male she had found, and with him she would craft a new brood.

Her hive was small. It was humble. But it managed to last the winter, containing barely a hundred of her servants.

But this too, was not to last. They were small, they were weak, and they were vulnerable. They were easy prey.

She barely remembered the assault that had ended her Swarm completely. The flashes of fire. The sizzling of carapaces.

The terror of being alone. Of being reduced to this absolute lesser . . . thing. She could barely think. She'd been reduced to base instinct while she screamed in a prison of her own mind.

But she was no coward. She was an *Empress*. Empresses did not give up! Going north was the only thing that mattered. She could feel . . . something. Something at the edges of her senses, an inkling of Qi.

There was a meadow, filled with flowers. She was exhausted. So exhausted, and so cold, but she needed to continue. To make a palace. To make a Swarm. Only spite drove her forwards.

And then, there was a shadow.

She was grasped firmly, and she resigned herself to death.

But death did not come. Instead, the last princess was taken to a human. He was not as she'd expected. His strength was a gentle, serene thing that extended into the farthest reaches of the land. This was power. This was a Lord. This was an *Emperor*.

He inspected her carefully, then retrieved a treasure that was worth more than the entire Empire for her.

It was better than the royal jelly. Better than the filth she'd had to eat over the past months, the base nectar and pollen. It was laden with Qi. So much Qi that she could finally, *finally* think properly again.

The Emperor turned a warm smile to her, and she was smitten instantly. The Empress had not been worth her name. But this? This was *power*. She bowed her head in service.

He raised his hand, accepting her oath of fealty, and commanded her saviour. He who was so mighty he would be able to slay entire hives of demons without a single one managing to touch him.

She was brought to a palace—this one clad in white, that was both warm and dry. It was humbler than the sprawling combs that the Empress had liked to put in the open, proclaiming superiority. But it was also much better defended.

She decided defended was best.

→

She was not confined. Not a prisoner, nor a slave. She was free to go as she pleased and do as she wished.

Each day the human, the Emperor whose power infused the earth, gifted her treasures and lavished attention upon her like the queen she was. His gentle finger felt most pleasant upon her head, and he roiled with Qi.

Her saviour, the red one with his splendid coat, brutally chastised a bird that attempted to prey upon her, and stood near her as a sentinel, far superior to her own guards. His beauty was unsurpassed under heaven and earth, and his Qi tasted of the moon.

And the large one, with his tusks, brought her even more servants. He was pleasing in his own way, with his muscles and earthly Qi surrounding himself. He pulled entire hives directly next to hers and oinked happily when he saw her. These bees were lesser, obviously—nothing compared to the fruit of her body—but they could be used.

She entered the other's palace and commanded. Such was Her Imperial Majesty that she was obeyed.

She allowed them to serve her. They recognised a queen and submitted accordingly. She was whole again. She could see, she could *act*.

The heavens had taken everything away from an unworthy Empress. She was chastised again when she sought to reclaim that lost glory.

But here, here in this land, absolutely pulsing with Qi, she had received a palace as well as the assurance of safety.

She would repay the kindness shown to her by the Emperor a thousandfold!

→

She sighed contentedly as she watched the beautiful one dance. His movements were absolutely sublime as he performed just for her. The stalwart protector was strong and virile, this . . . Bi De. It was a powerful name. She would lavish attention upon him when she had the chance.

The Emperor himself was likely beyond her charm. She was a queen, but she was not yet worth the title of Empress.

She would instead court the mighty Bi De and see if she could win his loyalty. Already, he watched her dances with interest—it was only fitting, as she was the most pleasing and most skilled dancer of them all.

Here, she would grow in power. Here, she would prepare the Swarm. All would know of the Glory of Fa Ram!

The Lord, the Emperor of the earth, had gifted her three names. Kei Regan. Tai Ranid. Finally, he spoke one name that most pleased her. It was foreign-sounding but powerful. She knew this to be a name of strength and had graciously accepted it.

Vajra.

CHAPTER 38

PRAISE THE HEAVENS

One of the best things about potatoes is how fast they grow. Soon after flowering, the tubers start to form, and even though you have to leave them for a while to get the fully matured potatoes, the young, thin-skinned variety are great too. I'd decided to do a partial harvest for the fresh young ones, while the rest would grow to their full size and go into the cellars.

We were going to be having a bit of a party, now that Meimei was back home after nearly a month away. She had arrived early that morning with Hu Li. The fox-faced woman was looking around with interest. Gou Ren's mother had made good on her promise to come over.

My mind helpfully replayed the warm, happy *"I'm home"* as we'd embraced. She'd immediately dropped her bags, and we just held each other.

Naturally, the cooking began soon after. So many potatoes. Baked. Boiled. Home fries. Hash browns. I hummed as I worked, a big, dumb smile on my face. Ever since Meiling had told me, I had been in a great mood. I was going to be a father.

The nervousness had quickly given way to resolve. Projects were approached with new passion. There were the start of cushions and a new bed for the kids when they were old enough. I even worked off some of my excess energy by doing more of the training that the other guy used to do. It was a few more punches and kicks, simple things, but . . . just in case, yanno?

I still had the dumb grin on my face as I wandered back into the living room, the delicious aroma of potatoes coming with me.

"That smells great!" Gou Ren enthused—and a split second later, Washy started to slap his fins happily on his trough, his eyes gleaming with happiness at the spread.

"It does smell great," Meimei said warmly. I turned to smile at her, and then I froze. She was coming down the stairs, wearing something that had, until this point, been just a flight of fancy.

Flannel. She was wearing the uniform of the country-dweller from my old home. Red and black cloth. *Pants.* Let me tell you, it worked very well with her freckles, especially with the top couple of buttons of her shirt undone—

A finger reached out to close my mouth, and then her lips pressed into mine. She had a flush on her cheeks and a sway to her hips as she walked past me to sit down.

"You found that drawing?" I asked, a bit embarrassed. Not only had she found it, she had made something of it. Looking closer, I saw it wasn't flannel, it was *silk.*

"Yes. And that's not the only gift! I have a little something for every-body. Clearing up a well pays quite . . . *well,*" she said with a smile. "The rest of the money is for the household finances."

Was I a househusband now? My wife was going out and bringing home the bacon! I chuckled at the thought.

Still, food first. We all tucked in, and the sounds of pleasure filled the house. I basked in the glow and the feelings of happiness, Meimei pressed into my side.

These were *damn* good potatoes. Now all I needed was some yeast, and I could have potato rolls and burgers. I had to restrain myself from running to town and splurging on meat and having a barbecue right that instant.

"These are much better when cooked," Xiulan muttered, after she'd finished making Xiulan noises. Most of us were a dab hand at ignoring those by now, but Hu Li had her head cocked to the side, looking incred-ibly amused.

"Wait, did you try to eat any of these raw?" I asked, and she flushed slightly.

"They were . . . pleasantly crunchy, but the taste left much to be desired," she admitted.

I had a good chuckle at that. I turned to look at the rest of the table and scratched Chunky, earning a happy oink while he chowed down on the potatoes with relish. Peppa's were disappearing incredibly quickly.

"Well, don't make a habit of it. They're a little bit poisonous raw," I told her.

Both Meimei and Rizzo perked up.

"No experimenting on making more-poisonous potatoes," I commanded, poking Meiling gently in the side. Both girls pouted, but I could tell the interest from Meiling had been more of a joke than her having any real desire to make poison-bomb potatoes. Rizzo I . . . wasn't so sure about.

Soon the potatoes were all gone, and we all sat around the table as Meiling handed out her gifts. Gou Ren got a couple more shirts she had made, as his own had been looking pretty beaten up. Peppa got a brush set, Rizzo a tiny mortar. Tigger received another little bean bag, as she had destroyed the last one. Washy got a rather nice bowl with a dragon painted on the bottom, which he immediately started admiring. Chunky got a hat. He chuffed happily, donning the same hat that courtiers did and nuzzling Meimei's side.

I . . . I got a really, *really* nice coat. I stared in wonder. The outside was a beautiful blue colour, but the *inside* was a damn work of art. It depicted a farm, embroidered carefully into silk. Stylized animals and crops populated the scene. This was almost too nice to wear.

"Lady Wu helped me with it," Meiling said, a slight blush on her face. "I . . . well, I did less than I would have liked," she mumbled. "The outside is waterproof. I remember you complaining about the rain," she said, and then turned away bashfully.

It was then that Xiulan came back down the stairs, *also* wearing the silk styled to look like flannel.

"I realise why you wanted me to wear that now," Meimei muttered while taking in her handiwork.

"Men wear that colour too," I said absently, before tearing my eyes away.

"I'll see what I can do," she whispered.

I nodded, then went to get dessert. Thankfully, the peach I'd been saving was still good, and Meimei's eyes brightened when she laid eyes on it.

"So, where is Yun Ren, anyway?" I asked, curious, as I started to cut up the Qi-filled peach. I'd kind of expected him to be here too. At my question, Hu Li rolled her eyes, though she still seemed a bit concerned.

"He ran off to Pale Moon Lake City, after he learned the crystal sellers wouldn't be down this way for at least a few months, and he's going
up north soon. He wanted to see if he could get a crystal before he left,
damn fool boy. Like the journey isn't a month when you're making *good*
time."

I pondered this. I was a bit worried, in the sense that it was easy as
hell to get lost here. There were no handy map apps to help you if you
lost your way, nor any GPS to get you out of a bind . . . but Yun Ren was
a hunter. I was sure he'd be able to find his way.

"If he doesn't stick to the road and goes right over the hills, he could
cut it down to probably a week," I said. Hey, it was something I had
thought about. The roads bent and wove, travelling around the massive
hills. If someone cut through the mountains instead, they could shave
quite a bit of time off the journey.

Hu Li frowned. "Dangerous, though," she grumbled in the tone that
all moms seemed to have when they understood something but didn't *like*
it. She huffed, though she protested no further.

We each got a slice of peach.

It was the best damn peach I had ever tasted. It would take a few years
for us to grow fruit from it, but the seeds were definitely getting planted.

I leaned back in contentment, my arm going around Meimei's shoulder.

Hopefully Yun Ren was having as good a time as the rest of us.

↔

Yun Ren gasped, cold air filling his lungs. It was a little hard to breathe
this high up, but by the heavens, it was *worth it*.

He laughed from where he was on top of the hill, staring out onto the
horizon. The snow at the peak crunched under his feet as he shifted his
position slightly, holding out his hands and trying to frame this wonderful, wonderful view.

The sprawl of Pale Moon Lake City was still far, far away, but he could
see the entire city, as well as the grand, slow curve of Pale Moon Lake.
People said the lake was a perfect circle. He couldn't see the other end of
the massive lake, as it stretched too far over the horizon, but from what
he could see from here? Yeah, it probably was.

The city was a sparkling wonder, and the farmland that stretched
beyond dyed the area in different shades of green. He'd definitely come
back this way. That was a view that he *needed* to capture!

He turned around, looking back at his footsteps. The decision to go over the Cloudrest Ridge hadn't entirely been based on speed. It was the fastest route if one could travel in a straight line . . . but in reality, it meant having to climb the massive hill. Honestly, he'd just wanted the view. Still, it was a rather gentle slope compared to some of the hills he'd run through.

It was a damned inconvenience that the crystal sellers weren't coming back for months. And now, he was the farthest away from home he had ever been. But he thought he had enough money for the crystal, and this was his last chance to get one. He hoped he could get it, so he would have *something* to do up north. He wanted to show the village the Sea of Snow, if he went up that far. He also wanted to show his relatives up north the things he had seen.

The view from up here was all worth it—worth the cold and the trouble breathing.

Yun Ren began his descent. He half slid on his ass, and half tumbled down the snowy part, which was rather fun. That lasted until he got to the wooded section at the bottom, where it rejoined the road. Yun Ren's eyes were wide as he set foot on the path . . . and was immediately swept up in what seemed like a river of people and carts—more people and carts than he had ever seen in his life. It was a tide of people, flowing into the city. He was gaping as he trotted along, his mouth and eyes wide open. Several people glanced at him and rolled their eyes, muttering "bumpkin" under their breaths, but Yun Ren paid them no mind. He *was* a bumpkin, and this was all too amazing.

The city had giant, defensible walls, and even from far away he could tell they were thick and sturdy. However, like a bug too big for its shell, the city had long since spilled out beyond the defensive structure and into the countryside. The main avenue into the city was flanked on either side by ramshackle buildings that extended for at least several dozen li in every direction.

It was said that this city housed a million souls. Yun Ren could believe it. Meimei had told him stories about this place, sure, but he had never before had a frame of reference. The most people he had ever seen in one place at a time was when the entirety of Verdant Hill had gathered, and that was just over two thousand people.

Even the crowd out in the tents had to number ten times that. There were just so many people it was almost overwhelming. There came shouts of men hawking their wares, the sounds of cooking, and the rather unpleasant smells coming from the gutters. He went from the higglety-pigglety ramshackle buildings to the "actual" city, where the streets were more organised. *This* section reminded him of Verdant Hill, more or less. He spotted some guards checking carts, looking bored out of their skulls.

Yun Ren wondered if he was going to be stopped. He idly noticed one of the guards perk up and catch sight of him, beginning to walk his way—when Yun Ren was intercepted by another guard, who began shaking his head.

He wondered what that was about. Shrugging, he moseyed on over to the guards anyway.

"How's it goin' today, boys? A hot one, ain't it?" he said with a smile on his face. The one guard stiffened.

"Indeed it is, sir," he said politely. His partner stared straight ahead, and a bead of sweat dripped down his forehead.

"Now, if ya don't mind me askin', do either of you know where Mengde's Crystal Emporium is?" he asked, using the name Jin had given him for the people who had sold him his recording crystal. "I'm looking to buy some stuff from 'em."

"The main office is in the center of the city, sir. Left side of the central district, as you enter" came a prompt, rehearsed answer.

Yun Ren nodded. *Should be easy enough to find.*

"Thanks for the directions. Don't work too hard now," he joked.

"Yes, sir," the guard said, and both clasped their fists in front of them, bowing slightly.

They made 'em *weird* in the city. Polite, but a bit strange.

Yun Ren shrugged it off and continued, wandering into the vast city. It was nearly an hour at a walking pace to get to the middle . . . though it took him far longer than that, as he kept gawking at everything. He was lucky he was quick on his feet, though. He had nearly been run over by carts eight times before he'd finally realised that there were lanes marked on the road. The avenues widened even farther as he got deeper into the city, even as there were fewer people crowding the streets. The people who were out and about were all in fine silk clothing, and the ladies even had umbrellas, with trains of serving girls trailing along behind.

Yun Ren felt *very* out of place in his rough hunting clothes. His eyes turned to where two fully armed and armoured guards were standing in the roads, their eyes roving over all who dared to enter the street. Off to the side, he saw another guard, his arms crossed as he glared at a man who was little better dressed than Yun Ren. The man paused and thought better of crossing their path.

Yun Ren swallowed, nerves settling in. Would the guards just chuck him out too? He debated circling back and searching for another entrance, before he steeled himself. He hadn't done anything wrong. They wouldn't throw him out. He had legitimate business here! He took a bracing breath and plastered a smile onto his face. Then he started forwards, walking past the guards like he owned the place.

One glanced at him for a moment, but then the man's eyes quickly flicked away. Neither guard made any move to intercept him, standing still as a statue.

The rest of the nervousness faded. With a bit more pep in his step, he approached the store.

Mengde's was a rather large stone building, with massive pillars holding it up, carvings all over it, and a walkway absolutely *lined* with light crystals. There was even a fountain, a blue gem sparkling conspicuously and pouring water out from the top into a basin.

Yun Ren swallowed at the display of obscene wealth. *How the hells did the Lord Magistrate have enough pull to get these guys to send out a caravan to Verdant Hill of all places?*

He shook his head and approached the doors. There were a couple of other people milling about. Some were the more noble-looking people, and there were also a bunch of people in big, thick coats with giant gloves and hoods that hid most of their faces.

He got in without much trouble, though. It appeared that most of the people who populated this store wore the giant hooded coats. They tended to glass cabinets, and those were filled with crystals of all shapes and sizes.

He . . . he honestly didn't know the etiquette here. Oh, he knew how to deal with the traders back home, but these guys were . . . *rich*. Rich people always did things differently than normal people, or at least Mei-mei had said that was the case. Did he just walk up and ask? Well, it never hurt to try.

He approached one of the few people who weren't occupied with other customers.

The man had his hood down, a pair of goggles on his head, and what looked like a mask that could be drawn up over the lower half of his face.

His eyes flicked to a slightly vibrating crystal as Yun Ren approached, and then back to Yun Ren, before he stood up straighter.

"Welcome, honoured customer, to Mengde's Crystal Emporium. How may we aid you today?" he enquired, then bowed politely.

Yun put on a winning smile and leaned up against the counter. "I was wondering what kind of recording crystals you've got," he asked.

The man froze and immediately grimaced.

"I apologise, honoured customer, but due to the closeness of the Dueling Peaks Tournament, every recording crystal we currently have is either reserved or has already been sold."

Yun Ren felt his jaw drop.

"However, our stock will be replenished in a few months. I apologise profusely for the inconvenience." The man tried to sound like this was something minor, but he seemed a bit nervous.

"Like, *every* recording crystal?" he asked.

"Yes, sir."

Yun Ren groaned. *Man, what a wasted trip.*

"Well, I suppose that's just how things work sometimes, yeah? Thanks anyway." Yun Ren sighed, then gave the man a smile. Wasn't *his* fault. The man stopped looking so ill and tense. *Probably got all the rich bastards and cultivators yelling or something if they were inconvenienced. That had to suck.*

"Is there any other way we could aid you, to make up for the inconvenience?" the clerk guy asked.

Yun Ren thought on it.

Well, if he couldn't get a recording crystal . . . maybe he could see what they did here? The only crystal Yun Ren had ever seen in his life was Jin's. Maybe they wouldn't mind showing him what crystals looked like before they were processed? If they said no, well, that was cool too.

"Could I see one of the crystals being cut?" he asked. The clerk seemed a bit surprised.

"You wish to see our craft?" he asked, and slowly a smile spread across his face. "I have to ask my superior, but such a thing can be arranged, I am sure."

It didn't take long. The clerk went over to talk to somebody and got a nod in return.

Yun Ren was led into a back room. It was more a warehouse than anything, with a bunch of desks, hooded people seated at them carefully working with files, scrapers, and all other sorts of tools.

And all through the tour, the clerk narrated.

"While some crystals may be used immediately, fresh from the ground, most require some work to be fully effective," the man explained, pointing to a fire crystal that certainly didn't look like any fire crystal that Yun Ren had seen in the shop. It had bits of rock attached to it, as well as irregular spikes. "This is especially true in the Azure Hills. The crystals here are less potent, and they also have a tendency to be divergent or have broken shapes. However, the Mengde clan's artisans train for decades in order to be able to coax the most out of our crystals, lest they crack, explode, or do all sorts of . . . *unfortunate* things.

"While we do have our own mines in a secret location, we often receive commissions from cultivators or have them sold to us by ordinary miners."

Yun Ren nodded along as he took in the room. There were about thirty desks in here, often with strange geometric formations drawn around them.

Something caught his eye—something the same colour as Jin's recording crystal.

He frowned at it. "Is that one of the reserved ones?" he asked. The man startled, then glanced over at the desk.

"Ah, no, that's one of our apprentices' work. That crystal was unsuited for proper refinement, so she was given it to hone her craft and practise her faceting. It will be useless to your needs, sir."

Yun Ren frowned. He just wanted *something*, and the thing the person was holding seemed interesting. He wandered off the path to take a closer look, the man aborting a protest.

"Morning!" Yun Ren greeted her; the masked, goggled, and hooded girl let out a surprised "eep!" and stopped her study of the crystal in front of her.

It was a flat rectangle of blue, translucent crystal.

"When you say defective, what does that mean? Does it still work? Can you still get images out of it?" Yun Ren asked, holding the inch-thick sheet of crystal up to his eye.

"It doesn't work properly, sir—" the clerk tried again, though he was cut off by a quiet voice.

"Um . . . that piece *should* be able to capture images . . ." the girl interrupted. "It would be images only, however. And it's far, *far* less durable than a normal crystal." She fidgeted, then looked up at him, her confidence visibly fading. "I *think*, at least."

Honestly? To Yun Ren, that sounded fine. He focused on the crystal. It didn't float like Jin's did, but he could feel kind of the same sensations.

There was a crystal chime sound. Yun Ren grinned as pale, ghostly light projected out of the piece of crystal. It showed his own amused face and the nervous-looking clerk.

Pretty good image quality, Yun Ren thought. *Not as good as Jin's, but hells, I'll take anything at this point.*

Yun Ren turned back to the clerk and the carver girl—or rather, where the crystal carver was getting chewed out in whispered tones. "Biyu! this is a very important customer, you can't just—"

"This is perfect! Exactly what I need!" he declared. The hooded girl— Biyu— perked up in shock. She slowly tugged down her hood and pulled off her goggles, staring at him hopefully with wide, dark eyes. She looked a bit like an owl, with how ruffled her hair was from the hood.

"How much would something like this be?" he asked cheerily.

"We were not intending to sell this piece . . ." the clerk said, clearly taken aback. "But . . . if you wish to purchase it, we may be able to come to an arrangement," the man ventured.

After a few minutes of discussion, the clerk and Yun Ren eventually came to a price that was less than half of what Yun Ren had budgeted for.

On the outside, Yun Ren hemmed and hawed like he was doing them a favour by testing it out for them—but in his mind, he was dancing happily.

He took an image of himself, the clerk, and the girl who made it. The clerk had a charming smile on his face, while Biyu, the owlish girl, was still looking a bit confused and shocked that he was so happy with what turned out to be one of her first projects. She was barely five years into training, according to the clerk.

Yun Ren practically skipped out of the shop. He was so pleased that he nearly ran into somebody, barely managing to dodge around a man in fine robes who looked rather irritated.

"Sorry!" he said, then kept on running. There were just so many things to look at. So many images to record! There was that strange still Elder Hong had mentioned—or would he climb that tower for a better view of Pale Moon Lake? His crystal chimed as he turned it around and recorded his own grinning face.

↔

I smiled again at my new coat as I got ready for bed. Today had been fantastic. Meimei had come home; we'd hung out with Hu Li and had just chilled the day away. Gou Ren and his mom had gone out camping together, going to look up at the stars from the top of one of the hills in the back.

I stretched, then finished changing into an old shirt. I was looking forward to cuddling again.

"Jin." Meimei's voice had a slight quaver to it as she came into our room. She sounded slightly seductive but tinged with embarrassment.

I turned around and was rendered speechless.

One hand was on a hip, which was framed by a high-cut garment. Her face was a little red, but she *did* look confident.

Two felted rabbit ears stuck straight up.

Praise the heavens.

CHAPTER 39

THE LENGTH AND BREADTH

Lu Ri sighed as a young man sprinted past, shouting apologies at nearly running into him. A part of him flared with anger, while the rest instantly calmed that part. He was merely irritable from his lack of progress. He was absolutely no closer to finding the wayward cultivator than he'd been when he'd first returned to the Sect.

Oh, the trail led to the Azure Hills, as he had last discovered. But that was it. That was where the trail *ended*. Jin Rou had entered Pale Moon Lake City . . . and had then seemed to disappear into thin air.

At first he'd thought he was right in his original assessment: that the journey to these hills was a mere passing distraction to the young cultivator, before the man immediately returned to the Howling Fang Mountains or Yellow Rock Plateau. Yet as Lu Ri searched these areas, there turned up no sign of the man either. No caravaneers talking about a cultivator helping them out of a difficult situation, nor any stories of fleeing from Spirit Beasts . . . *nothing*. The methods he had used at first were turning up blank. He doubted he would find any tales in this province, as there simply weren't any Spirit Beasts of note. And even if there were, all any could talk about was the "Demon-Slaying Orchid" who had managed to kill some manner of bandit. That discourse drowned out all others.

So he was back to where he started: in the Azure Hills, in Pale Moon Lake City. He disliked both of these places.

Firstly, it was the discomfort. The entire area was *uncomfortable*. Lu Ri had never been to an area so deprived of Qi before in his life.

He felt like he needed to breathe more heavily to get the air he needed, and he also had to eat more food, else he felt like he was starving. It was like being in the middle of a desert, or at the top of a mountain for a mortal, instead of in a relatively lush, fertile land.

The slow, constant feeling of wrongness and discomfort made him irritable and tested his patience.

The other reason for his dislike was . . . mostly his own fault.

Elder Ge had told him to be discreet, and yet the first day he had entered Pale Moon Lake City, he'd caused a commotion. When Lu Ri had approached the quaint city walls, which were a mere fraction the size of Crimson Crucible City's, there was a great uproar. A guard captain started to shout in shock as a harsh buzzing sound echoed out, followed by the sharp *cracks* of splintering stone.

Curious, Lu Ri approached and saw people standing nervously, and a man pulling at his collar, to reveal a palm-sized medallion of cracked and splintered stone. Lu Ri recognised it instantly.

Heavenly Ascension Stone.

At first, he was baffled at the inclusion of the material. When cut and refined, nearly every Sect and tournament used large, thick slabs of Heavenly Ascension Stone to measure cultivation. Placing one's palm onto it and channeling Qi would give a visible representation of the level of one's cultivation, allowing Sects to flaunt their prodigies while also proving the benefit of the crowds. They had to be large, otherwise they would crack from the power running through them.

But instead, the people here used the material as necklaces? With some manner of vibration formation carved onto them? With the stones so small, any in the Initiate's Realm would be able to set the stones buzzing just by getting near! The stones had to be absolutely useless!

Yet as he pondered in confusion, he remembered that he was in the Azure Hills. Finally, Lu Ri understood their purpose. Indeed, they would buzz for any Initiate. In such a Qi-starved and weak land, *that was the whole point.*

It would allow the mortal guards to notice cultivators or Spirit Beasts. With the ambient Qi so low, the disks were made to be sensitive. This method was quite superior to what most guards in the wider Empire had.

Lu Ri mentally raised his evaluation of the craftsmen of these hills. Such ingenuity should be praised.

Yet this sensitivity was a double-edged sword. They could likely only detect up to the Profound Realm without starting to crack. If any above that level approached without carefully controlling their Qi, then *this* would happen. And to detect and warn of larger and larger amounts of Qi, the size of the pendant would have to exponentially increase, which would make it buzz constantly from the ambient Qi. Learning to discern the normal hum from a slightly stronger one would be difficult for a mortal.

That, and in such a poor land, they were most likely *prohibitively* expensive.

Lu Ri had destroyed two of them in ignorance, setting the guards on high alert.

How utterly *foolish* and unacceptable. The Founders' writings were most clear on what to do in this situation, and so he enacted them immediately. Condensing his power as small as he could make it, he advanced into the city and arranged a meeting in order to both explain the disturbance and repay the damage to city property.

At least His Imperial Majesty's Lord Director of the Azure Hills had been most understanding after he had been reimbursed. "Sect business" had been enough for the aged mortal.

The only good thing about this place was that he was getting *very* adept at suppressing his own cultivation. The Founders had labelled it a necessary skill. There were no more accidents, though the tension of constantly suppressing his strength just added to the slow grind of irritation.

As he drew back to the present, Lu Ri took a deep breath and let it out slowly. Time to start over. He needed a deeper examination into the Azure Hills in search of Jin Rou. Lu Ri would have to send word back to Elder Ge, and he would likely have to go through thousands of records. It was not a task he was looking forward to, yet he would complete it all the same.

It would be the process of months.

But first . . . he looked mournfully at a teashop. *The* teashop—the most exclusive place in Pale Moon Lake City.

It was the only place he had managed to find some decent tea, and even some food with a bit of Qi in it. Terribly overpriced for what it was, yet he found himself in dire need of a fortifying drink before he started on the records.

The small stone near the entrance buzzed, and he was promptly received by the master of the establishment, then was invited to a private room.

"You honour us by returning to our humble teashop, Master Cultivator," the man in charge greeted him, then gave a polite bow. There was a line of servants waiting to attend to him. As far as they knew, he was just a wandering cultivator. "We have something *special* today, if it pleases you."

Lu Ri nodded in acceptance, wondering what could be special *here*.

A woman came in holding a small pastry and a thimble full of golden liquid. Carefully, the woman poured the liquid over the pastry, then used a small spoon to make sure all of the liquid had been distributed.

"It is known as maple syrup. A new product from the illustrious Azure Jade Trading Company. Please, enjoy," the master of the teahouse bid him.

Lu Ri picked up the pastry, examining for a moment. A touch of Qi was coming from it. *How interesting, for this place.*

He placed it into his mouth, and his eyes widened marginally before closing in pleasure.

The pastry itself was largely inconsequential, but the golden liquid on top was *very* good—Wood and Fire Qi. Invigorating, and slightly warming, complementing the sweet and savoury liquid. It was a bare drop, and yet it was quite delicious.

He savoured the taste, chewing slowly.

All too soon, it was gone.

"It does please me," he stated simply, then took a sip of his tea. He let the irritation ebb off his shoulders. Indeed, he then took a good cup of tea and a pastry. He was already refreshed!

Lu Ri remembered how many records he would likely have to go through, and how much longer it would likely take.

"I . . . would have another," he declared, taking out his coin purse.

□

Bi De examined his map closely, looking at the marks he had placed. The formation had begun to develop on the map. Spirals. Each shrine, when connected, formed some form of swirl, all seeming to head in the same direction. He tapped on his map. Unless he'd missed his mark, there would be something around here. Something soon. While the villages formed a spiral, or the beginning of one, Bi De wanted to search the *center* of the spiral. He would likely find another village here, but when he asked, none knew of any such village having ever existed.

How curious. He rolled up his map and hopped off the top of the caravan, letting out a cluck. His speech was . . . unreliable. He thought

he'd experienced a breakthrough, but more often than not, nobody understood him unless he wrote. As was the case with his current conveyance.

"This is yer stop, then?" a woman asked, fidgeting slightly. He nodded.
This was where they parted ways.

"Thank you for fixing the axle. Are yeh sure there's nothin' we can do?"

Bi De shook his head. It had been a simple task to cut down a tree
with his spurs and fashion it into a proper axle. He'd then reinforced it, so
it would no longer break upon the rough roads. His Great Master's skills
were once again a boon, and he had learned well.

"Bye-bye, Mr. Chicken!" a child called, waving happily to him.

The rooster inclined his head.

'May the heavens smile upon you.'

The woman and child squinted and tilted their own heads in response,
not fully comprehending his speech. But they seemed to get some of it,
because they returned his bow. A moment later, their cart continued on
its way, and Bi De began his walk into the wilderness.

Hopefully this would be as easy as the bear he'd slain a few days ago. It
was large, for a normal bear at least—and quite mad from eating the flesh
of men. He put it out of its misery swiftly and brought news of the creature's defeat to the nearby village. That village had contained a shrine . . .
but he did not think it was a part of the formation. It was too divergent
in location.

In any case, he had brought out his paper that contained the symbol
of his Great Master's servant and stayed for a brief celebration. The father
and the son had the same names, like Hong Xian and Zhang Fei, but
when Bi De had written out a question for them to answer, they revealed
that they did not dance at the solstice.

An interesting conundrum.

His feet carried him onwards as he began to pick up the pace, simply
jumping from one hill to the next, travelling for several hours until he
neared the location. He slowed his pace once more.

He took in the air and noticed a shift in the world. There was more Qi
here than normal for this area.

He crested the hill.

Surrounded by trees in a clearing, and illuminated by the rays of the
afternoon sun, was a large, jagged pillar of rock. But it was not something
to be dismissed, not something natural. It looked like it had been planted
there. It had been stabbed deep into the earth and was surrounded by

smaller stones, all radiating off in another spiral. It was covered in faint indentations and inscriptions, but they were too worn off to accurately inspect. Instead, it had been claimed by nature. Moss and ivy crawled upon it, this lone pillar pointing towards the sun. But while the area's ambient Qi was high, the pillar was wholly mundane. He felt no Qi from it. No sense of energy or life. Just an old monument.

He studied the stone intently, but there was nothing he could discern from the old pillar. He would need one more intact.

Bi De marked this location on his map, then continued. This time, he took to the air. Out of the middle of the wilderness, to the next location. To another village.

He sighed deeply when he came upon it: a burned-out husk. This one had been *attacked*. Attacked long ago, judging by the massive rents in the wood and its state of disrepair. However, Bi De recognised the rents from his horrid adversary. The thrice-damned bastard Sun Ken had visited this place.

Its people had been slaughtered, its coops destroyed, and its Shrine of Fire burned to the ground.

He wandered the village, his head bowed, until he happened upon the burial mound.

The burial mound with fresh-cut flowers on it. Laid carefully and lovingly on the graves. *Did someone still live here . . . ?*

There was a rustling. Bi De turned and beheld a rabbit. Her fur was white as snow. Her eyelashes were long, framing wide orbs.

A fetching creature to be sure, and quite beautiful, even with her eyes narrowing. The rabbit approached, then laid new flowers on the grave.

She turned, glaring at him, regal and imperious.

'Who the hells are you?'

CHAPTER 40

RESIDENTS OF A GRAVEYARD

Bi De raised an eyebrow at the rude question. The rabbit's voice was *far* harsher than her appearance, filled with heat at his presence. Even now, he could feel her Qi focused upon him, and he also noticed the tension in her muscles.

He nearly rose to the harsh words and implied threat. Instead, he steadied himself, took a step backwards from the grave, and raised his wings in greeting. He was trespassing, and in resting places of the honoured dead at that. Some hostility was only natural.

And it would be a shame to do battle with the only honourable and respectable awakened one he'd encountered outside Fa Ram. She was not full of lust for violence. Instead, behind the heat and wrath at his trespass, beyond the imperious question, was a curiosity.

'This one is Bi De, First Disciple of Fa Ram. He apologises for trespassing in this resting place and begs your forgiveness.'

Her eyes widened briefly in surprise—whether at his manners or at his respect, he wasn't sure. Almost involuntarily, her head dipped slightly in acknowledgement.

'Liang Yin, First Disciple of Miantiao,' she declared. *'You shall have my forgiveness for trespassing on Shifu's land.'*

Bi De winced. He had been impolite, not entering through the gate. It was proper courtesy! Just as one must enter the gates of Fa Ram, lest they be seen as an interloper. How shameful!

'I shall apologise to your Master, if amends can be made. But first, may I pay my respects?' he asked her. He knew nothing of these people, yet it

was only proper. They must have been worthy of the great care this rabbit lavished upon the graves.

'*Shifu would approve, I suppose. But I knew not these ones,*' the rabbit said. Still, she carefully placed a flower upon the grave, then began walking around it, inspecting it for weeds or anything that was not a flower.

He waited for her to finish. And together, they stood in front of each grave, bowing once to the dearly departed.

'*You're a strange one, Bi De,*' the rabbit mused, but most of her imperious glare and iron readiness had vanished. "*You are the first, outside Shifu, that I have not had to slay. Come, Shifu is this way.*'

The rabbit turned from the graves and set off back into the destroyed village. Bi De followed after.

'*Master! We have a guest!*' the rabbit called, stopping outside a half-burned coop that had likely once been as beautiful as his Great Master's own. Now, it was a ruin.

"*A guessst?*" a voice asked. It was tired and worn, filled with a deep, almost unthinkable sadness.

'*A strange one. He paid his respects to the graves,*' Liang Yin declared.

'*Then he is an honoured visssitor. Pray, come in, and partake of our hossspitality.*'

Bi De entered the coops behind the rabbit. It had been partially repaired on the inside. Its leaks had been patched, and things fixed as best as they were able. But it was still drafty, and still run-down-looking.

What Bi De assumed to be Liang Yin's Master was lying in the middle of the room, and he slowly uncurled as they entered. He was not a particularly large snake, yet he had a presence about him. He felt dangerous, but Bi De also noticed the slight kink in the snake's back, two thirds of the way down his body—broken and crippled. Some scales shone bright jade green, while others were dull and charred, like they had been subjected to fire.

One eye was missing, burned out by the same flame that had scarred his scales, and the other was exhausted and dead-looking. The snake took in the rooster before him, his eye lingering on Bi De's pendant and vest. A soft smile overtook his face, but then it fell a moment later, and the snake slumped, a sigh escaping him. He inclined his head to Bi De.

'*This one thanks you, for your respect. His name is Shi Ti,*' the scaled beast whispered. Bi De frowned at the name. *Corpse?* Also, hadn't Yin said her Master's name was Miantiao?

Yin, who had been inspecting the wall, scoffed.

'Tch! Stop calling yourself a corpse, you damned old bastard. Look!' The rabbit lashed out with a kick, and the snake, though blind on that side, swayed out of the way. *'Look how much you wiggle around! You're no corpse!'*

The serpent hissed angrily at her, his head whipping to the creature, as he attempted to loom over his student. It did not work, for he was rather small. *'Brat! Without my purpose, that is what I am! That is all I am fit to be! I am unworthy of the name bestowed upon me!'*

'It was my purpose too! That's what you raised *me for, and I complain less than you,'* the rabbit shot back, her head held high as she dared to speak back to her Master.

The snake hissed as their Intents swelled, filling the room.

Both glared at each other and began arguing as Bi De stood awkwardly, unsure if he should intervene. He idly wondered what this fight was about but thought it best not to press in case the reason was private.

Instead, he took off his pack and revealed some of his newly replenished victuals: rice and eggs. These ones looked as if they had little. He coughed, trying to catch their attention.

'As payment for accommodations,' Bi De said.

Both froze in their staring contest and turned. Yin looked curiously at the rice, while Miantiao stared at the eggs with a complicated expression on his face.

'You give usss much, for the little you receive in return,' the snake whispered.

'This Bi De's Great Master said: "As a guest, one is to do everything in their power to aid their host. As a host, one is to have their guests want for nothing."'

The snake cocked his head to the side. *'Thisss isss a paradox,'* he declared, his voice amused. Bi De agreed, but he understood the sentiment behind the lesson. The snake chuckled, while Yin just looked mildly confused.

'I shall explain it later, child,' the snake whispered to her.

Yin let out a muttered *'Yes, Shifu'* before turning to watch Bi De's preparations curiously. At least the firepit was still intact, and they did have wood in here, so it would be a simple matter to prepare a meal.

Bi De prepared the rice as Yin looked on curiously. Like she had never had a cooked meal before.

'Thy Great Massster . . . he isss . . . human?' the snake asked as the rice cooked.

Bi De nodded. *'A great, powerful, and virtuous Master I am proud to serve.'*

'Yesss. A good Massster,' the snake hissed sadly, his single good eye far away. Bi De held his tongue—he recognised the expression. Disciple Xiulan had the same look in her eyes, in the depths of her sorrow.

As quickly as it came, it went, and the snake shook his head. *'Then, if it isss not intrussive . . . Why do you travel out to thissss place?'*

Bi De saw no reason not to answer. *'A journey, to see this world and grow. To find the secrets of this world for myself, with my Master's blessing.'*

He puffed up proudly at the words. Indeed, his Great Master was correct as always. He *was* learning and growing upon his adventure.

He turned his smile to the snake and the rabbit staring at him. The rabbit looked intrigued, while the snake appeared stricken. Miantiao shook his head again, snapping himself out of whatever memories took him.

'Travel? Where to?' Yin asked, her expression blank and her head cocked to the side. *'Our own journey was cut short.'*

Bi De retrieved his map and began his tale. Really, this was like being among his fellow disciples again as they ate, and he told the story of the Torrent Rider.

□

The night had been pleasant, though Bi De had remained cautious. Trust, but verify. Yet Miantiao and Liang Yin both seemed unconcerned, the rabbit slumping over onto her Master and beginning to mutter in her sleep, while the snake kept watch for her.

It was quite cute. Yin's hard lines softened immensely once the dreams claimed her, and her Shifu rubbed her head with his tail.

Bi De dozed for a while, some of his alertness fading, until it was time for him to rise. He went to the roof to properly greet the sun. To his surprise, Yin joined him, her Shifu still coiled around her and deeply asleep.

Her body went through morning movements, just as his Great Master did. She was a graceful one. Her movements were fluid when she slid through the morning mist.

Bi De took a breath, and as the sun crested the horizon, he greeted the new day. Yin jumped from beside him at the loud noise, body tense, though she paused at the brief tap on her head by her Shifu's tail.

The snake chuckled sleepily, uncoiling from his disciple. *'Ah, how I misssed that sssound.'*

He stared out over the village, while Yin looked at him curiously.

'A roossster must crow to greet the dawn. Many of his kin do the sssame, Yin.'

The rabbit nodded at this explanation. A moment later, her Shifu finished uncoiling, lying down in the dawn light.

The rabbit hopped off the roof and onto the ground, where she immediately walked to a rather beaten-up tree, commencing her morning training.

Her eyes were pure and focused as she kicked and struck at the tree. Bi De had to admit, her kicks were powerful and graceful, each flowing into the next.

The snake watched, pride mixed with sadness.

'You have taught her well,' Bi De said, complimenting his crippled elder.

'Have I?' Miantiao asked back, his face twisted into something ugly. He gazed out over the village and sighed. *'She deserves much better than this one'sss teaching.'*

At that, the snake turned his head up to the sky. He looked old and worn, like the weight of the world was upon his back.

'We shall try again today, Yin,' he called to his disciple.

The rabbit nodded, determined.

'You are welcome to stay, if you wish,' the snake told Bi De as he slowly slithered down the house slowly. *'This one did miss the voices of the chickens.'*

Curious, the rooster followed. He wondered what he was to witness. More training? He examined the shattered logs and imagined what sort of technique the rabbit was practising.

'Now . . . let us attempt a clean cut this time,' the serpent said.

The rabbit nodded. She took a deep breath . . . then opened her mouth and bit down on the wood. She looked to be chewing through it, completely mangling the piece of lumber.

There was a beat as the rabbit paused to examine her handiwork, and then she sighed before starting to grumble some rather choice curses under her breath.

'What is the purpose of this?' Bi De asked.

'Shifu wants to rebuild the village,' Yin replied, spitting out pieces of wood.

Rebuild the village. Bi De once more looked around at the broken and shattered village. This . . . this was their home. Bi De's heart seized as the image of Fa Ram flashed in his head—this version as ruined and overgrown as their village.

'Yes, indeed,' the snake said with a fake smile. Yin did not seem to notice the lie, as she went back to work.

Bi De knew not what his plan was in making her rebuild the village. However, Yin obediently went about her work as the snake's eye drifted far away.

There was something here that he did not like. The lie. The lie the rabbit did not notice. This was not training, really, and he had a feeling that this entire endeavour was not to Yin's benefit. But he held his tongue. He didn't know enough about the situation to intervene just yet, and Yin's Qi flow seemed normal enough.

A chance to aid two loyal Spirit Beasts . . . and a chance to get to the bottom of this strange circumstance.

'That is the wrong kind of wood,' Bi De said at last. *'We shall need oak, not these small strips.'*

Yin frowned at another piece of mangled wood.

'I am a weapon, *not a carpenter,'* the rabbit muttered. *A weapon, hmm?* Bi De glanced at the guilty wince upon Miantiao's face.

'And this is fine. The only sin is to not learn to better oneself. Come, witness the techniques of this Bi De's Great Master!' he crowed, and with a single mighty kick he split the wood into planks.

It was smooth, with no splinters. Bi De had learned the Dao of construction well, from witnessing his Great Master's works. He was still a novice, however. He could only copy, following in his footsteps, not thinking up anything like the grand coop.

Yin appeared intrigued by his technique.

'Now, to cut cleanly, one must . . .' Bi De began.

→

It was strange, working with the two other beasts. Yin was cold and standoffish, her words crude and aggressive. She was almost like Tigu, but lacking some of the predatory energy. Instead, the rabbit was constantly sneaking glances at the snake. Miantiao alternated between being possessed by the mania of work, struggling as much as his crippled body would allow, or acting slow and lethargic, just staring off into space.

But they began to rebuild. There was a certain catharsis to it. A certain *pride*.

Pride the imperious-looking rabbit did not seem to be learning. She grumbled like Disciple Gou Ren, clearly not enjoying any of it . . . but doing it all the same to please her Master.

Bi De could relate to the feeling.

Yet he was the odd one out. The Master and disciple worked with familiarity. They had clearly known each other for a long time. The snake grumbled about Yin's constant curses, yet it didn't stop her. The rabbit seemed to know each and every tic and would snap the snake out of his introspection whenever he became lost in his own head.

The lie here . . . it was not the lie of Chow Ji. The snake had too much affection for the rabbit to wish to consume her. Bi De could tell that if something tried to kill Yin, her Master would throw his body in front of the blow without hesitation, giving his life for his student. But still, he was hiding something from his disciple.

Bi De pondered this as they finished their labours for the day. The finding and stripping of an oak would be tomorrow. He remembered clearly the design of the other shrines.

'Thank you for the help today,' Yin said with a small smile.

'There is no thanks to be had. This aids me as well. Shall we dine on more rice tonight?' Bi De asked.

Yin nodded rapidly. *'It's good! Normally I just eat grass or flowers . . . or sometimes meat. Shifu makes me refine anything with Qi in it.'* Yin stuck out her tongue at the memory of a taste. *'Meat is disgusting.'*

He nodded at the statement. The snake was directly empowering Yin. He apparently was giving her every bit of Qi he could lay his coils on.

Bi De could not make sense of it. So he decided to ask.

'Earlier, why did you say you were a weapon?' he asked.

Yin perked up. *'Because I am! A weapon to kill a demon! We trained for years! Shifu taught me so much! I was finally ready!'* Her eyes blazed with happiness and remembrance.

Then the happiness faded. Yin kicked at the ground, her face troubled. *'But a few months into our journey, when we finally had his trail and were closing in . . . we found out that somebody else killed the demon.'*

Bi De felt a sinking feeling in his gut. A demon. The familiar rents in the walls, caused by a whirling, demonic dance. *Sun Ken. 'And now Shifu is broken. And I don't have a purpose anymore.'*

Her lines hardened again.

'I'm going to go and tend to the graves,' she muttered, her mask once more emotionless.

Bi De watched her go, unsure of what to say.

CHAPTER 41

BET YOUR LIFE

Now we spread the lacquer. This will protect it from the elements and give it the proper colour,' Bi De instructed. Both regal rabbit and burned snake looked curiously at it. It had been two days since he had asked why Yin considered herself a weapon, and Bi De was still unsure of how to further broach the subject. Should he just bluntly confront it? Should he never tell them? He did not know. Both of them were warming to him, however. Sharing meals had a way of bringing people together.

'Smells like shit,' Yin observed, blinking long eyelashes at the concoction. They had no lacquer in this place, so Bi De had returned to a previous village. They had remembered him and had supplied him for a modest price. The slightly charred coins he had been given by Miantiao had easily covered the cost, after the snake had refused to let Bi De pay for it.

'Language,' Miantiao scolded halfheartedly.

Yin snorted. 'This one declares it to smell positively repulsive,' she corrected, her voice haughty.

Miantiao ignored the sass, as Bi De chuckled.

'Indeed, it is mildly poisonous, and it stains easily. Take care not to get any on your fur.'

'If it stains, it stains,' Yin replied with a shrug, unconcerned.

'If it sstains you, that means you were carelesss. Allow not a drop to hit yourself or the ground,' the snake commanded, and Yin straightened up immediately, her eyes blazing.

'Yes, Shifu! Not a drop.' She grabbed the pail of lacquer in her mouth and strode towards the reconstructed shrine, purpose in her step.

'Thin coats,' Bi De called after her retreating form, and she nodded, eyes focused intently. She bounced back easily from her own troubled emotions. Burning bright and hot for a moment, before settling to a simmer. Blunt, direct, straightforward.

'I do not think the amount of poison would be enough to harm her,' Bi De told the snake, and he cocked his head to the side.

'Thisss one could not sssay. Poisons elude me . . . though not for lack of trying,' he muttered. *'Ssshe should take better care of herself, though that may be hypocrisssy spilling from my lipsss. Ssshe has a life ahead of her. Ssshe will have a life ahead of her.'*

It was a quiet conviction, but an absolute one.

'Now, it doesss us no good to ssslack. Teach thisss old snake how to spread lacquer,' he declared.

They got to work with their brushes. Miantiao was surprisingly dexterous; even with his broken back, his coats of lacquer came out thin and even.

'Would you tell me about your Master?' Bi De asked conversationally as they worked.

Miantiao paused. *'Thisss one supposes it is only fair. You have told us of your Great Master, and his Fa Ram.*

'I have no memories that do not begin with him. We were both young. So young, when he found me in the forest, and took me in. I was weak, and starving. Yet he picked me up. He took me in and fed me. He gave me my name, because I was long and thin. Miantiao.

'He was the son of the chief here. Producers of the finest earthen vessels as well as glass, with the clay from the river and the sand from the great sandpit nearby. Those over there'—Miantiao gestured to a section of rubble—*'are the remains of the great ovens that baked them, and the great furnaces that heated the glass.*

'My awareness came all at once. It was during the winter. This one normally slept through the snows, curled in a box. But that night . . . that night I woke up. I am not sure why, only that I had to. I had to see my Master. What I beheld then was beauty itself. There were streamers of Fire Qi, in the middle of the night, as my Master performed something indescribable. Even the other men could only stare, transfixed at his skill.

'From that day, from that sunrise . . . I was never the same again. I copied my Master's movements, much to his delight. The rest of the villagers called me the dancing snake. And each solstice, he would dance. He would dance all night

in the motes of fire, and I would dance with him. He taught me. He confided in me. He spoke of his dream to travel the land and witness these dances, and unravel the secrets of the dance of fire.

'For many years, he worked so that he might honour his father, and gain enough coin to travel for a time. We shaped glass and clay into new forms. We created. *I know little of carpentry, it is true, but this one knows how to make glass* sing.'

Miantiao's eye was lost to memory, his smile triumphant.

'He sounds like a wonderful Master,' Bi De complimented him.

'Yes. Yes he was.' The triumph faded. *'And then he was taken from me.*

'On the eve he was to depart, nearly a man grown . . . the demon came. The town was set ablaze. He slaughtered and butchered without a care. I was crushed beneath the house, one of the beams falling upon my back. I struggled. I struggled so hard to get out. And my Master . . . Oh, my Massster. He did not run. He went to confront the demon. They laughed at him. The demon himself came to personally kill him. My Massster's dance let him dodge three blows. Three blows he foiled, and in return he struck once. A mere mortal man, against a demon, and he landed a strike. But all that strike did was enrage the beast. In the end, my Massster could not stand against him.

'He was ssslain by the demon, sundered in a single blow. And all I could do was watch. Watch, as the flames consumed the house, consumed me. Such was my hate, my burning fury, that the flames could only take my flesh. I survived the night—injured and crippled, but alive. I thought that the heavensss had spared me for one reason. Vengeance.'

His eye blazed with something ugly, before it faded. Miantiao sighed and started layering on the lacquer again.

'And then Shifu found me!' Yin said cheerfully. *'On the night of the solstice! I was surrounded by enemies; he defeated them, and took me in.'*

'Yesss, the heavensss blessed me with a ssstudent,' Miantiao said affectionately. *'She even knows how to dance.'*

'Even? I dance damned better than you can!' Yin ceased her work and leapt down to the ground so she could begin her dance.

She was very good. Her fur looked like captured moonlight. Her aura, graceful and refined.

'I'll lead the dances, I suppose, and Shifu can lead the village,' she declared with the conviction of one searching desperately for a purpose. *'Once all the people come back, everything will be better!'*

She did not see the grimace on the snake's face, since he was turned away towards the wood.

Yet the snake put on a satisfied face as the day progressed. He was animated, wiggling around and shouting commands at Yin, much to her delight. She performed each one without fail.

'You're not bad, Bi De. You made Shifu happy today!' She had a small, satisfied smile on her face as they sat outside the shrine, the interior finished. *'Maybe he'll even start back on the combat lessons soon!'*

Bi De nodded, but he was troubled at the rift between student and Master.

'I'll go tend to the graves, and start getting shit—stuff for dinner!' Yin hopped off, bouncing along. She was so happy. And her Master . . .

Bi De took a breath. He *still* didn't know what was going on here.

Enough beating around the bush. He approached the snake, intent on confrontation.

□

Years ago . . .

Miantiao did not know why he did this to himself. Why he came back to the village every year, after searching the rest of the time for something, *anything* to improve his chances against the demon.

But there were some things that needed to be done. This was the last way he could honour his Master.

The graves were covered in snow but still visible. His body screamed at him to rest, but he could not. He could not sleep. Every moment was precious in his quest.

But it was a quest he knew he would fail. He was weak. He was still *too weak.* With his injuries, he was beginning to doubt he could ever be strong enough to slay the demon.

Hate began to gutter as it mixed with despair. He had lived through the fire. And for what? The only thing he could say now was that perhaps the house falling on him would not hurt him as badly.

He pondered on his next course of action as he prepared.

Slithering through snow was a monumental task, especially with his back as it was, but the motion was something he had long since mastered. He carefully dug away the snow, revealing the ground. He filled the braziers with wood. And as the longest night began, he honoured his Master's dance.

The Qi was faint, as it always was. Barely there, swirling through the air. Miantiao danced and he mourned. He prayed to the heavens for a sign—for something that would let him lay low his hated foe. The fires surged around him.

Miantiao stopped his dance as the steamer of red Qi *lingered*.

He set off immediately. It was a sign. The heavens had heard his prayers!

His body surged through the biting cold, through the powdery snow, and over the hill. Until he found her, sitting in the snow by the stone pillar. Cold. Shaking. Near death from her wounds . . . and with a dead wolf beside her, killed by her kicks. The other wolves sported injuries.

Miantiao beheld a jewel. A bright, silver spark.

And *coveted* it. The heavens had heard his prayers. Her body was *already* this strong, to do battle against her foes, and she was still so young.

He drove the rest of the beasts off, then took her. He brought her to the house and warmed her by the fire.

↔

She awoke the next day, frightened and weary.

'*You saved me,*' she whispered in awe and respect.

'*I did. Tell this old sssnake, why were you out in the cold all alone?*'

'*I am lost. My family drove me out. I do not know what to do.*'

Truly, the heavens had smiled upon him.

'*Then let Shifu give you purpossse.*'

If Miantiao could not slay Sun Ken . . . he would craft a weapon that *could*.

□

A saviour came in her darkest hour, offering her everything she ever wanted.

□

'*Thirty more!*' he commanded sternly.

'*Yes, Shifu!*' the rabbit called.

Miantiao pushed. He pushed and pushed this little spark, pushing it all he could, but holding back just barely enough so that it did not break.

Every night, he told her of the wicked demon, and every night, she swore to help him slay it.

□

The training was harsh, but she loved it. The feeling of getting stronger.

She knew the demon had to die. She even dreamed about it. Whatever had hurt her kind Master had to be wicked and deserving of death.

↔

It took years. Years of travelling. Of training. Of forging his blade.

Of seeing her blossom like a star in the sky.

They worked in tandem. He offered his everything to the cause. They searched far and wide for power.

They came upon another awakened one. It guarded its patch of Spirit Grass jealously and would not listen to his entreaties for a portion.

'Yin.'

'Yes, Shifu?'

'A test of your abilitiesss.'

The rabbit smiled, then did as he bid, ever trusting of her Master. Miantiao tasted only bile. He was exactly as Sun Ken had been. Descending upon the innocent and slaughtering those who resisted, all for his own aims.

'I did it, Shifu!' the rabbit cheered, standing over the broken form of her adversary.

He would pray for their souls when this was done, even as he stained both himself and Yin.

But he would kill Sun Ken.

↔

He always got her the best things. He found her opponents. He gave her all the Qi she needed to be strong. He tended her wounds. He stroked her fur. He showed her how to dance.

She loved her Master. He had saved her, and given her something to strive towards.

↔

They found the village Sun Ken had destroyed. They found the trail. She was strong. And he was prepared to give her the opening she needed.

His heavens-sent champion would not fail him.

↔

It was time, and Yin was ready to fulfill her destiny.

↔

He felt as if he had gotten his back crushed all over again. The people cheering. The laughter. Them sharing how the Demon-Slaying Orchid had proved victorious.

His demon, snuffed out like a candle. His revenge, aimless, and without purpose.

Everything he had done to Yin . . . for nothing. Every time he had forced her to stain her hands had been in vain.

What had he done? What had it all been for?

Yin . . . Yin looked just as devastated, but she recovered quickly, turning to him.

'What do we do now, Shifu?' she asked, with the simple conviction that he would know.

Miantiao didn't know.

All he could feel was the emptiness.

Emptiness, and shame as Yin looked at him with such trusting eyes. She was the little girl who saw him as a father. The little girl that he had used like a weapon, moulded, and groomed into violence.

Once again, he tasted bile.

□

The rooster frowned at the story.

'And what does this have to do with your lie?' he asked again, as Miantiao stared off into space. Miantiao sighed, but he supposed he *had* been dodging the question.

'Because this one must atone for his sinsss,' he explained.

Bi De's eyes narrowed.

'I took that bright, beautiful spark and twisted it for my own ends. The strict tests. The harsh training. She never complained. I taught her not the secrets of the glass, nor how to craft an urn. All she knows is war and violence.'

Miantiao laughed bitterly.

'And for what? The demon is dead. I ruined her, and for no reason at all. Instead of acting as a true Master—instead of nurturing her spark, as my Master nurtured me.

'What is the lie, then? The lie is that I shall stay here together with her. To reforge the village with her. But . . . I cannot. I cannot live like this, in the ashes

*of the place I love. I cannot look at the child I broke. I cannot hear her call me
Shifu any longer.'*

Miantiao let out a sigh. It did feel good, to finally tell another.

*'I will seek out the demon's slayer and offer my unworthy flesh to them.
Perhaps I shall be refined or eaten? I have heard that this is the way of human
cultivators. Perhaps this wretched life will finally have value, and Yin will be
free of me.'*

The rooster stared, stunned.

*'If you can, I would ask that you aid her in thisss. Maybe your Fa Ram
will be kinder to her than I was.'* He knew little of Bi De, only that he was
a kind soul. The rooster would surely take Miantiao's Yin with him, and
give her a better life—

He froze as the wind shifted, and he tasted an all-too-familiar taste.

Oh no.

There was rustling.

'No! Shifu! No, please, you can't!' Yin shouted as she sprang from her hiding place, her eyes wide with panic. Miantiao grimaced at her appearance.

Miantiao sighed when she pressed up against him. *'Child, child,
child . . . pleassse. I have done you injury—'*

*'No! You're not allowed to die like that. You—you need to teach me more!
You need to teach me like you said!'* Yin begged.

How embarrassing, to do this with Bi De here. Really, she was such a
difficult child. He glanced over and saw that the rooster pondered them
with dispassionate eyes.

'I mussst.' Miantiao stroked Yin's head, trying to soothe her.

'You won't, you miserable old bastard!'

'Indeed, he will not,' Bi De interrupted. The arguing stopped as they
turned to him in confusion. He stood tall, his eyes narrow.

'The slayer of Sun Ken stands before you, and I do not accept your life.'

That was preposterous—! Miantiao's mind froze.

Holy light filled the clearing. Qi pressed down on them both, its
power in the Profound Realm.

Both snake and rabbit gaped at his resplendent form.

*'This Bi De, in the depths of winter, did battle with Sun Ken and killed
him.'*

His Qi reverberated throughout the village. Its purity and power
forced them to accept the truth of his words. *'To flee from the consequences
of your actions is cowardice. The easy way. If you are as stained as you claim,*

Miantiao, then as you say, you must atone with your life: a life spent doing as you should have.'

'*Speak with your disciple. I will either aid you again on the morrow—or I will leave,'* Bi De commanded.

The rooster left them, departing the village.

His disciple stayed pressed to his side. '*You're not allowed to leave,'* she insisted. '*I'll hunt you down if you try!'*

Miantiao sighed and stroked her head again, but his heart was disturbed.

The slayer of Sun Ken was here. Here. Perhaps . . . perhaps the heavens still were looking out for him.

'*Whether I leave or not . . . Let usss make a wager, Yin.'*

The rabbit's eyes narrowed, but she let him speak.

↔

Yin was still not convinced of Shifu's wager, but she had accepted it anyway. Bi De was strong. Stronger than them both combined.

But that didn't cause her to hesitate. She would win it. She should show her strength, and her damned Master wouldn't be so damned *stupid*.

How dare he make her think he wanted to die. How dare he decide that he was bad for her. Stupid snake! Bastard of bastards!

They waited for the rooster in the dawn light. Shifu was still quiet, but he had his air back. He was quiet, controlled, and ready. Ready like she hadn't seen him in months. She could barely wait!

Bi De approached. His feathers were regal, and he was *very* handsome. But she ignored that. Now . . . now, it was time.

The rooster was silent, observing them both.

Finally, Shifu spoke.

'*I want to know,'* he said quietly. '*I want to know if it wasss enough. I want to know if we could have ssslain the demon, or if I was just leading usss to our doom.'*

The rooster sighed as Shifu uncoiled, and she got into her stance.

His Qi rose around him. The rabbit experienced the light of the moon in the middle of the day.

'*Show usss. Show us if this strength would have killed Sssun Ken!'* Shifu commanded.

Everything she had trained for. Each bruise. Each day. Each moment with Shifu.

Was it wrong to be happy in this moment, while her Master was so sad?

The sun was so warm on her back, as she thought back to the dance she had been taught. Yin *moved*, erupting forwards while wreathed in golden light.

[Armour of the Sun]

Golden armour formed around her body, its sections engulfed in flame.

[Daybreak Rays]

The rooster's eyes widened at her speed. Like the sun cresting the horizon, fully blazing its light over the world, she moved—yet she was not fast enough. A wing rose to meet her.

Yin's eyes narrowed as she was stopped dead in her tracks. The rooster let out a huff, then started to spin in a mad, whirling dance. His wings lashed out like swords, but she ducked and wove around the strikes. They were sharp, full of the intent to cut, and she had to spend her Qi more than she'd originally planned to avoid being split open.

Yet she was undeterred. She struck again, flowing into a series of blows as she ripped and tore at the rooster. She could do this. She would win, and then Shifu would stop being an idiot!

And, she knew . . . this was merely buying time. This was merely the first act. Her Master, after all, was not quite as crippled as he seemed.

And the area that he had occupied was empty.

[Twisssted View]

The rooster's eyes narrowed the moment he noticed something amiss.

The air around them distorted, like light seen through imperfect glass.

A strike snuck through, and gauntlets aimed squarely at the rooster's side.

Yet at the last moment, he dodged. With a pulse of Qi, Shifu's technique shattered. The rooster raised an eyebrow.

[Split Faces of the Half Moon]

Yin frowned at the technique, so different from the strange whirling dance—and then she realised what he was doing. He was fighting like *Sun Ken* did.

'*There was more than one,*' the rooster on the left declared, as dark as midnight.

'*Four cultivators were within his entourage,*' the right one said calmly, his feathers shining silver.

They struck as one. Yin backpedaled, throwing herself out of the way of the whirling dances; their wings sliced through the air in ways that confounded the eye, momentum building as each blow led into the last.

[Shardsss of the Ssshattered Urn]

The ground suddenly erupted into a pit of spikes, forcing the roosters to jump, and Yin took the opening.

Her legs smashed into the silver rooster, discharging with an eruption of fire.

The silver rooster shattered . . . and then *re-formed.*

Shifu started to suddenly strike from the ground, erupting upwards with snapping teeth and blasts of razor-edged glass fragments.

Everything narrowed. It was just the two of them as they once more slew one of the rooster's shades.

The image of Bi De blurred into some demonic thing, holding a massive sword. Bi De's movements became faster and faster, whirling and twisting with a grimace on his face.

It was . . . getting harder to keep up. Shifu had made jokes about her limitless stamina, yet she was getting pressed. She was *failing.* Even as Shifu added his strength, she could see the resignation on his face—he knew that this would end in failure.

No. It would not end in failure.

Yin took a breath. She took a breath, as Shifu had taught her.

To feed the growing flame within.

A wing snuck through, hammering into her side. Shifu was tossed away, but he tried to wrap up the rooster and hinder his movements.

A blazing kick hammered home when Yin threw herself back into the fight, ignoring the pain.

Another rooster shattered.

All that was left was battle. All that was left were her memories of the dance.

In this storm of violence, she was at peace. In her mind, she was merely dancing. Shifu was always happy when they talked about that dance.

The rooster became faster, and yet she kept pace. Shifu supported her as he could; the world twisted and warped at his command, and daggers of glass streaked through the air. She could tell his strength was flagging, but he was always, *always* there.

A kick slammed into his sinuous body as he took a blow meant for Yin. Shifu bit down on a leg with fangs made of hardened glass.

There was an opening.

[Rising Dawn]

Like the sun, she rose, slamming into Bi De and carrying him into the sky. He seemed surprised, yet there was a measure of respect in his gaze.

And then she was struck. She slammed back down to the earth. It hurt. It hurt so much, but she was on her feet again immediately.

The rooster had stopped acting like Sun Ken.

[Light of the Full Moon]

Day turned to night as darkness covered the sky around Bi De—he was pulling the light out of the air, redirecting it into the silver disk that formed behind him.

'We go through, little one,' Shifu declared as he settled onto her back. He spat out a mouthful of blood.

[Twisssted View]

The distortion formed in the air.

A shield of glass, against the Light of the Full Moon.

Yin's body became a blazing comet as they rose to meet the light of the heavens. The pure silver light that raced towards them was a ravening beam of Qi.

The light impacted Shifu's shield of glass, spiralling, refracting, and deflecting off its facets.

But the shield was not enough. Shifu threw his body in front of her. Scales burned, and yet the snake laughed.

They were through, even as Shifu fell back to the earth.

[Solar Ring]

It was a lethal strike. Everything she had left was put behind it.

[Wheel of the Crescent Moon]

The light of the sun met the light of the moon. Their legs connected with a shock wave that rattled every bone in Yin's body.

For a moment, she held. She held against a cultivator in the Profound Realm.

And then her strength failed. She was thrown back to the ground, where she hit the dirt hard, rolling once, twice, then managing to flip back to her feet.

Her vision was hazy. She was nearly out of Qi. She stumbled, nearly falling.

But she couldn't stop. She wouldn't. She had to prove to her Master it was *worth it*.

With a roar, her armour once more ignited, burning with white-hot heat. Her eyes focused on the rooster. Her haunches coiled as she prepared to throw herself back into battle again.

But instead of preparing to receive her, the rooster was completely relaxed. He held out a wing, signalling a stop to the fight.

Yin stumbled but stopped herself from launching forwards.

'That *was the strength of Sun Ken*,' Bi De intoned. He let out a breath and shook his head. *'His Qi was corruptive and would have slain your Master. But it is likely the demon would have perished as well.'*

Yin jolted, her head whipping around to stare at her Master. His body twitched and wiggled—he was burned and injured but was still alive even after facing the attack.

'Would it truly have been enough?' the snake asked.

Bi De shrugged.

'We can never say for certain. From ambush, likely. From a direct attack? Or at the height of his power? I do not know.'

Shifu, charred and smoking, stared up at the heavens with tears in his eye.

Her heart hurt to see him so happy that he would have died killing Sun Ken.

But still . . . *'I won,'* she stated, staring at Shifu. The snake blinked, confusion overcoming his features.

'I suppose you have, Yin.' His eyes were melancholic. But he still offered her a smile.

□

'Are you certain?' Bi De asked the snake and the rabbit. Both nodded firmly.

'We cannot ssstay here,' Miantiao whispered. The reconstruction had been stopped. Instead, they had planted a large piece of stone in the center of the village, the names of the fallen etched upon them. *'We must find a new purpossse.'*

'And I won,' Yin stated smugly.

'Yesss, you won. I must live on. It would not do to renege on an agreement with my disssciple.'

'Where will you go?' he asked them. The graves had been cleaned one last time.

The snake and rabbit shared glances. An invisible conversation happened.

They turned to him, then bowed. *'Young Master Bi De, you have the same mission as my own Master once did: to find the secret of these dances. Please, permit us to follow you in your journey,'* Miantiao requested.

Bi De stroked his wattles as he beheld them. It was an earnest wish. He bowed his head, accepting their request, as he had once accepted Sister Ri Zu's request.

He took out his map. *'Then this is the way to the next place . . .'*

CHAPTER 42

THE FIRST DISCIPLE'S LETTER

Bi De, First Disciple of Fa Ram, greets his Great Master, the Great Healing Sage, Sister Ri Zu, Brother Chun Ke, Sister Pi Pa, Sister Tigu, Brother Wa Shi, Disciple Xiulan, and Disciple Gou Ren.

He prays that this message finds all in good health. This Bi De wishes to inform his Great Master and fellow disciples of his journeys thus far . . .

↔

"An' that's the big still Elder Hong was talkin' about!" Yun Ren declared as another image formed on the wall of Pops's house in Hong Yaowu. The crowd obligingly oohed at the sight. What had started off as a little gathering to see Yun Ren off for his trip up north had quickly gone village-wide once he'd busted out the light show.

It really *did* look like a still, though vaguely steampunk-ish, with the dull, red glow coming from some manner of vent in it and the misty morning. It seemed like something out of the industrial revolution. It was actually a bit ominous-looking, at nearly three stories tall, with the rest of it trailing off into darkness.

Now that he had his own crystal, he was *really* letting loose, and it showed. That one shot from the mountain in particular was absolutely spectacular, as were the ones he had gotten from Washy's back after bribing him with sweets.

I flipped one of the burgers, inhaling happily. Smashed flat, as it should be, on a slab of iron. Off to the side, the sausages were cooking away and would be done soon.

Some of the stuff I had asked for had come in from the Lord Magistrate: mustard seed and turmeric. Additionally, I had actually managed to fix my yeast problem . . . *sort of.* Turns out that Chao Baozi, the steamed bun place in the Exchange, actually sold it out the back of the store. Made sense, though they'd said it was a trade secret when I'd asked them how they did it. Sourdough was great, but not for burgers, in my opinion.

So we were having a regular old send-off. I'd do better, slow-cooked meats some other time. For now, I'd decided to go with the burger option. Sesame seed–topped potato rolls? Check. Meat from the town? Check. Cheese from Yun Ren's relative, who had come to pick him up and guide him to where he was supposed to go?

Also check.

Though the man was looking *really* kind of lost, his amber eyes wide open as he kept pinching himself. He resembled Yun Ren and Hu Li, his eyes normally narrowed in a squint, bushy hair, and wearing clothing that more closely resembled something out of Mongolia.

Nice enough bloke, all laughs like Yun Ren—until he'd seen the animals helping build the firepit and the fish bouncing after the gaggle of children. He had gone from happy to confused, then had to sit down.

An image of Yun Ren's arm around Washy's neck popped up, selfie style. A fox-faced boy and a dragon grinned at the camera.

The dude just seemed to give up at the image. Hu Li patted his arm affectionately.

I scraped the rest of the burgers off the makeshift grill, then transferred them to buns. The novelty of them was a big hit. The only bread around here previously was the steamed kind, instead of the baked stuff I was more used to.

I couldn't wait until I got a nice, crusty loaf going. Or maybe some baguettes? Well, I was going to be using my own flour for those, and our wheat harvest was only a few months away.

"And then this one is—" Yun Ren suddenly cut himself off as another picture popped up. He seemed a bit surprised, like he hadn't meant to pull that one up.

It was a rather cute girl with wide, expressive eyes. She looked a bit lost and owlish, with fluffy hair that stuck up like a bird's nest. She had a slight flush to her cheeks and a small smile.

"Oh?" Meimei asked, immediately interested. Hu Li's eyes *gleamed.*

Yun Ren coughed and brought the crystal up frantically as the images cut out.

"And what I *meant* to say is, this one is the end of the images. Time for food, everybody—!"

Yun Ren fled from his mother and Meiling, but not before swiping some food.

I sighed and shook my head, starting to hand out the burgers and much-better-than-hot-dog hot dogs. I gave some to Gou Ren, who was just looking amused by his brother being accosted about "Biyu," with a smirk on his face.

Xiulan, who had been grabbed by little Xian—and the small girl who had made friends with her the first time—was once more bedecked in flower crowns.

Pops got a burger, and then he started talking with Peppa and Rizzo about mushrooms and finances.

Tigger appeared briefly, just to spirit away a snack for herself. She still didn't seem to like hanging out in the village too much.

Finally, I got to Chunky and Washy, settling down beside them to eat my fill.

The carp took a bite. His eyes widened. His pupils dilated.

He leapt into the air, and in a bright flash a dragon *roared* his triumph, spiralling around the town and writhing with glee.

Chunky stared for a brief moment at his own meal.

"If you don't want to eat it, I'll grab some more veggies for you," I whispered.

The boar shook his head. Instead, he bowed respectfully to the meal before opening his mouth and trying a bite. He let out a pleased grunt at the taste.

I sat beside my chunky boy as Washy shot over to the grill, slapping another burger onto it while bouncing up and down.

"They're pretty good steamed, or baked too. Different flavours for different thicknesses," I called—and Washy looked like he had died and gone to heaven.

Silly creature. But still, better a gourmand than some sort of rampaging beast. I was rather glad he was so chill.

I sighed and leaned back happily against my boy. Hopefully, Yun Ren would get some cool pictures of the north.

I closed my eyes and savoured the moment.

↔

This disciple swiftly learned that though the countryside has its own charms, the food in the greater world is of an inferior quality. So much so that I pity those who have not tasted our bounty, for they know not the joys like we do.

Though this one could conceivably make the trip home with ease, I do not wish to have to head home at every moment merely to replenish supplies. It would not do to go on a journey of discovery, only to continuously return to the familiar . . .

↔

'*It is quite strange, how these bodies are so different, yet so similar,*' Tigu commented, staring at the anatomy. She held up a paw, comparing it to the human hand.

Ri Zu nodded. It was still rather a strange experience, to drink tea and have Tigu sit calmly beside her, but there they were. She was even a good student—a fast learner, who needed little coaching once given a task.

It was a bit annoying, but at least she no longer felt like she needed to watch her back with the cat around.

'*We all look much the same on the inside, Ri Zu supposes. Things that could be called hands, hearts, lungs . . . Even some pressure points are the same, despite the differences in body shapes,*' the rat replied, staring at her own hand.

It was a rather strange revelation.

'*In any case, this Young Mistress thanks Ri Zu for her instruction,*' Tigu stated, inclining her head slightly.

They sat and drank tea, to the sounds of Ri Zu's Master and Pi Pa working on something together.

There were more shouts as Disciple Gou Ren and the Great Master did something foolish on the training poles, and another great splash of water erupted.

She felt some regret. Some regret that she had not followed Bi De into the wider world, but what was done was done. She likely would have been a liability, weak as she was, and she had her duties here.

That, and the outside still scared her. She remembered the time when she was still in Chow Ji's company. The first flashes of her awakening were . . . terrifying. A hasty run from shadowy figures, ones who had obliterated Chow Ji's former Empire. The raids from other creatures as they desperately fled north.

Even the memories made her shiver. But she couldn't remain in fear forever.

She should not be. She would not be. Her fear had caused her to give up time with Bi De. Next time . . . Next time for sure. She would see the world, without fearing the sky.

'Earlier, you mentioned sparring,' Ri Zu said quietly. 'Ri Zu wishes to intensify her training.'

Tigu perked up, surprised, and lifted her nose in the air haughtily. 'Fret not, this Young Mistress will whip little Ri Zu into shape!'

Ri Zu snorted at the arrogance and the slight smirk on Tigu's face.

This was going to hurt a bit. But in the end, as long as the cat didn't go overboard, it would help. She couldn't have the arrogant Young Mistress show her up too badly, after all. If the cat could be a good student, then Ri Zu would be a better one!

↔

The world is far grander than I anticipated. Its people and locations, more varied. Even in this tiny corner of the world, I encounter new things daily, and meditate upon them, though the nature of time has begun to trouble me. I worry what will happen to Fa Ram in the future.

We cannot see the future, however. So your disciple will do his best to live a virtuous life and trust that the rewards of it are self-evident . . .

↔

A pair of arms wrapped around Xiulan's neck, a slender body pressed against her back, and a chin rested on her shoulder.

"So, what's going on here?" Senior Sister asked from behind, curious. Junior Brother flushed, standing in front of her with his shirt off. He kicked his feet at the ground a bit, clearly not having expected Senior Sister to be here, yet steeled himself. Senior Sister looked quite happy, her eyes narrowed and a smirk on her lips, ready to tease.

"Attempting to see what manner of dress Junior Brother looks best in," Xiulan replied, and then she reached up and patted Senior Sister's arm, leaning into the embrace. Senior Sister always smelled pleasantly of herbs. "I swore I would assist him in finding a woman, and so I shall!"

Senior Sister's smirk faded as she glanced from Xiulan to Junior Brother. He looked to the side, embarrassed, with a slight grimace on his face. Her eyes widened as if just realising something.

"Oh," she said quietly. A brief flash of sadness and commiseration crossed her features. She quickly cleared her throat. "Well, what can I do to help?" she asked, releasing Xiulan and sitting beside her.

The young man groaned but stood obligingly still for them while they began to discuss what would suit him the best. A slate came out and they started sketching styles.

But they were coming up blank no matter what they imagined, in fine clothes or more courtly fashion. But Xiulan didn't think that that would work too well. Junior Brother looked like a wild man.

But . . . maybe she should lean into that?

The sideburns, however, needed to be a bit more . . . *managed*.

Their plan of attack changed. The vest was opened wider, exposing even more muscle. The sleeves, ripped off, just like Master Jin's.

And finally, though he winced and grumbled, the sideburns were trimmed, leaving them short and squared off. She had *possibly* taken the line and made it too severe, but the overall effect was still quite pleasing. Junior Brother still retained his monkeyish appearance, but now, instead of bushy sideburns making him look slightly comical, he had a wild and stern air about him. Still playful, but a man that could be taken seriously.

"You clean up pretty good, Gou," Senior Sister stated. She looked Junior Brother's body up and down. "Why did you never trim the sideburns before this?"

"Indeed. This style suits his body well," Xiulan noted, proud of her work.

"You two are just saying that," he grumbled, frowning heavily at his own reflection in the water.

The door opened, and Master Jin poked his head in.

"Hey, has anybody seen Gou—damn, brother! Looking *good*!" He appeared genuinely shocked and impressed.

Senior Sister smirked and offered her fist, and Xiulan hit it with her own. Gou Ren continued to grumble, but he *did* seem rather pleased.

↔

The name Torrent Rider was well earned. This disciple is certain his Great Master would enjoy such an event in this "Gutter." They gathered upon their gates and saw off this disciple with much pomp and ceremony.

And thus did this Bi De, disciple of Fa Ram, depart the village that is known as the Eighth Correct Place. Great Master, I hope that it was not too presumptuous of this one, but I have left the Torrent Rider instructions on where to find our home . . .

↔

It was time to cut once more.

The Third wielder had approached it, as he always did when it was time to cut. There had been a lull, after it cut the hardened earth. After they had gone to a place filled with people. At first, it wondered if it was going to cut lives and flesh again, and Sun Ne felt eager. Surely the Third would produce satisfying, clean cuts. It wanted to see the difference. Feel it.

Cut!

But this was not to be. It did not cut the lives, nor the houses. There were no screams, no blood, no ragged gashes. No fire and ash.

Slightly disappointing, to be unable to compare the Second to the Third, but . . . maybe the cutting of flesh and the screams had been the reason the cuts had turned to gashes.

It had only changed after a great many people had been cut, after all.

How curious. But it was not to question the intent of the wielders. Its job was to *cut*. And it had cut very well. It had severed stone and Qi-filled earth alike. Its blade had been tended and oiled. And the Third cut with it tirelessly.

How great! Cut!

But now it was confused as it returned to the cut land it had made. It was supposed to cut some things and not others. Cut the earth . . . but leave the roots?

How? It cut! Everything was for cutting! It was meant to cut! It was created to cut! Its purpose was to cut!

It *had* to cut! How could it *not* cut?

Sun Ne could feel the spiralling loop of madness that had infused it when it began to *gash* and *rip* and *tear* well up again. No, nonono. *iT CuT!*

A Master of Cutting . . . cuts what he chooses.

It was a quiet thought, but it pierced through the panic and confusion. The Third's thoughts were always slow and contemplative. Barely there, and he rarely offered anything, instead contenting himself with following Sun Ne's instructions on blade alignment.

The frenzied madness froze where it threatened to overwhelm.

Not cutting . . . could make it better at cutting? That did not make sense.

Cut earth clean. Not cut roots. Control, but still cut.

Sun Ne mulled the words over. Cut, but not cut?

Well, it could try. The blade was lowered. Lowered deep. Deeper than it was used to. The Third moved his body and shifted Sun Ne's cradle. Both focused.

Both began to cut.

It was tricky to keep the edge aligned this deep, but it did. It cut. It sheared through the earth with ease. When they came to the first round root, their bodies shifted in unison and the root was deflected upwards instead of cutting.

It was intensely difficult to focus like this, but it was working. Sun Ne deflected the roots instead of cutting them. Some of them got scratched, and a few were severed. But most were pushed out of the dirt.

The Third was silent. There was only a slight satisfaction as they did their duty. As they *cut*.

Sun Ne felt a surge of some alien feeling. What was it? It was not joy at cutting, but something else. Something that felt warm and nice.

It very much liked this Third wielder. Almost as good as the First.

But for now, Sun Ne concentrated, and *cut*.

↔

They both have the air that Disciple Xiulan had about her. I have followed your advice about speaking through their pain, and I believe this is showing at least some results. The pain of speaking of his own Master is great, but it seems to give Miantiao some catharsis.

Liang Yin is somewhat easier. She simply requires purpose and direction, and is the resilient sort to begin with. Though her mouth may be foul, she does have some fascinating insights upon the nature of the sun, and it is enjoyable to listen to these two speak upon their passions.

Though your disciple now knows more about pottery than he had wished, for Miantiao is quite vociferous on the topic. Whenever we enter a new place, he always must find and critique their glass and earthenware . . .

↔

Using Sunny and Babe to harvest the potatoes had been a bit of a kludge solution, but it had ended up working out. I *could* have just pulled up each individual one, but Babe was getting better at pulling the plough. A few of the taters got banged up, but really, it was a small price to pay. I added a few more carvings to the carriage, as well as some more paint. For the heck of it, I also added more suns and flowers to the demon plough. I was really, *really* enjoying this wedding gift. It was the best plough I'd ever used!

After the potatoes came up, they would be left in the sun to cure, before being put into my cold storage. Some would go back in as seed potatoes for a second harvest, and some would be grown from seeds from the potato berries. Now, I had never actually grown potatoes from seed, so it would be interesting to see how things changed, considering that seed potatoes produced what was essentially a clone, while the berries generally produced more varied plants. I wanted to try my hand at amateur potato breeding with those.

On the other hand, though, I really needed to figure out a good crop rotation. After all my talk of "we give to the land, and the land gives back," I wasn't planning on being a hypocrite. Growing two sets of potatoes without rotating the crop would be fine as a one-off.

I continued my circuit around the farm. I scratched the sheep, their coats growing long and woolly, and then I checked on the calves who were still gamboling around.

I even put the young rooster, one of Big D's kids, onto my shoulders, just for old times' sake.

He jumped off immediately, the little shit. He had been getting all cocky ever since his dad left, though he was still just a chicken.

I missed Big D. He had been there from the beginning, and not having him here . . . Well, it just felt wrong somehow.

But he had his own thing to do. All I could do was wait here and hope he came back, safe and sound.

I stared out over my lands, out on the horizon.

The wind blew. The grass grew. Everything just felt so alive as we came into the thick of summer.

I stood in the long grass for a while, just *looking* at everything.

At the river, as Washy watered the newly sown potatoes, streams of water bursting in the air to mimic rain. Gou Ren laughing and wrestling with Chunky.

At Tigger and Rizzo chasing each other, while Peppa watched. Mei-mei and Xiulan coming back from their picnic, arm in arm, and laughing about something.

Bees buzzed around me but never bothered me, so I held up a finger. It was still kind of weird that Vajra the bee left her nest so often, but she was cute as hell, especially when she landed on my finger and started wiggling her little butt. The other queens didn't come out, but I wasn't fully convinced Vajra was a normal honeybee. She and her soldiers were quite a bit bigger than the other hives, and they all had an iridescent shine to their wings.

Still, she was pretty silly. I was pretty certain she wasn't aware, because she kept getting stuck in the bathhouse. She flew in quite a lot, and I was beginning to think she just liked the heat and the moisture.

I sat in the grass for a while, until dusk, when Vajra went back home. With a grin, I began to smell the beginnings of dinner. I was going to be playing go with Xiulan again tonight . . . with backseat gaming from everybody. I stood and stretched, yawning widely, then smirking around me at the horde that approached and tried their luck.

One of the best things about cultivation?

Mosquitoes couldn't get through your skin.

↔

As you said in the beginning, I learn much from this journey, and I am glad that I have undertaken it. To grow and learn is never a wasted endeavour.

May the sun and the moon shine ever upon Fa Ram.

Your ever loyal servant,

Bi De

CHAPTER 43

TRIBULATION

There was a crack of thunder. The sound of droplets hitting the ground.
For the first time in a while, I was happy for rain. It had been hot and dry for a couple of weeks. The grass had even started to go a bit brown far away from the house, as the heat wave intensified. Thankfully, everything near the house was still good, with our specialized dragon sprinkler system firing at full blast.

I was quite leery to ask Washy to actively control the weather, if he even could, but water from the river was fine.

Honestly? There wasn't much to do. Most of our days had turned into sitting around with our feet in the river or playing on the kung fu poles.

Not much had really changed since Meiling had told me she was pregnant. I had started work on a crib before I realised that wasn't really a thing here and our child would be sharing the bed with us for the most part.

I was a little worried that I might roll over onto them, but I suppose having your kid right there in case of an emergency was a bonus. Still, I'd at least make something we could put them in beside the bed, like a swing or something.

At least sleep deprivation wouldn't be too big a deal. I had decided to test things out, and after the fourth day of operating on no sleep and not feeling any worse for wear . . . Well, I assumed I'd probably be fine. I'll say my prayers for all the parents without superpowers out there. Cultivation is once again bullshit.

I ran my hand over my wife's stomach. No bump yet. She caught the offending appendage and laced her fingers with mine.

There was a flash of light, then a massive crash of thunder. Chunky whined a bit, and Gou Ren started scratching his head. My chunky boy didn't like lightning much. He told me it gave him nightmares.

Xiulan continued to maintain her swords. Rizzo was sniffing at some kind of underwater plant, and Washy was asleep on a rock, not bothered in the slightest by the light downpour. I closed my eyes. I might not like getting rained on, but the smell was always nice.

"Master Jin, the hill is on fire," Xiulan stated. I opened my eyes and looked out. Sure enough, one of the farther-off hills, about three hundred acres away, was puffing smoke. "I shall ask Washy for his assistance, Master Jin, and take care of it for you," she said, then started to stand up. That forest was *mostly* pine, and honestly I had no grand plans for it.

"It's fine. We'll keep an eye on it, maybe build a firebreak . . . but we can leave it for now," I decided, looking out at the pillars of smoke rising from the hill. I'd certainly make sure it stayed contained, but a bit of burning would help that forest out in the long run. With the rain? It probably wouldn't be too bad.

Xiulan looked confused.

"You live out in the grasslands, right? It's just like the wildfires there. It's *supposed* to burn. When the fire finishes and the ash coats the ground, it comes back stronger than ever." Xiulan nodded, though she still frowned at the fire. "We'll go take a look anyway," I decided. Meimei let me up, and I put on my awesome new waterproof coat.

Xiulan followed after me.

Just as I'd thought, it wasn't too bad, only a small fire. Not like the visions of hell I had seen in the Before on news programs, where the smoke blotted out the sun for thousands of miles. This was a small, quick burn, eating the needle mat and getting the pinecones to open up.

I'd check back again throughout the day, but . . . things were looking okay. We watched it for an hour or two and wandered through the ashes for a bit, watching the birds return and pick off the smoking carcasses of the bugs and smaller animals that had gotten caught in the flames.

"I'll give it three days before this place is covered in grass again," I bet Xiulan.

She declined to take me up on that offer, simply staring contemplatively at the fire.

When we got back, to my surprise we had a visitor. There was a horse hitched outside the house and a dripping messenger at the table. He had the air of the recently soaked, cold and miserable, but was smiling a bit as Meimei got some tea into him.

He nodded when he saw me.

"You are *most certainly* Rou Jin," the drenched-looking man declared. He reached into his bag and pulled out a few scrolls. One I saw was from a Zhang Fei, another from the Lord Magistrate, and the third had a name I recognised. He spelled it strangely, but those were the characters he had chosen: *Bi De.*

"The Lord Magistrate gives his regards and thanks you for lending him your servant. He has been a great boon," the man said, bowing formally.

"How'd this one get to you, anyway?" I asked, holding up Big D's scroll.

"Another messenger, sir. He said that a chicken paid him, but I think he was just on the drink. He *certainly* indulged after he delivered it to the Lord Magistrate's offices."

It took all I had not to burst out laughing at the mental image.

"You want to stay until the rain lets up?" I asked, but the man shook his head.

"If the road weren't what it was, or if it were any later in the day, I would gratefully receive your hospitality, Master Rou, Lady Hong. But if I set back now, I may yet make Hong Yaowu by nightfall," the man declared.

He had some more tea, his horse got a carrot, and then he set off at a canter into the light drizzle.

Everybody else gathered. I lifted the letter and began to read:

"Bi De, First Disciple of Fa Ram, greets his Great Master, the Great Healing Sage, Sister . . ."

A tale of heroism, of philosophy, and of new friends followed. I had always loved reading stories. And this one . . . it was a good one. The kind that deserves to be told.

Everybody sat around, riveted to the tale of the Torrent Rider, and then of the Silver Rabbit and Glass Snake.

And me? I . . . I was proud of him. Proud of a chicken. *Is this what fathers feel?*

The feeling didn't leave as I moved onto the next letter, this one the awkward writings of a fourteen-year-old asking if he could either visit in the future or if I wished to visit his village and go torrent riding. The answer to that was hell yes. Little dude was a badass. Awesome name too.

It stayed with me as we started up a game of cards and I ruminated on Big D's story.

My mind conjured woodblock prints, plotting out an illustrated story. The story of a noble chicken. It would start with wicked Chow Ji, maybe. They had told me that one enough. Maybe I should start with the first fox he caught?

But what would I call the tale of the rooster named Big D?

I thought about my sign and snorted. *Maybe something more epic . . .*

↔

Tigu walked with purpose through the forest, ruminating upon the letter. The drizzle had faded, and now everything was soaked. The others were preparing for the end of the day, but she was not.

The letter had been enlightening. It had captured her imagination. She had seen in her mind the great battles Bi De had, and his journeys through the land.

The drive to see his ambitions realised.

She had been patient. She had been ready to wait. But . . . she had grown complacent in her goal to achieve human form. Patience was key, but it was all meaningless if one did not finally take action.

She arrived at the clearing with high ambient Qi, deep in the forest. She closed her eyes, then entered the domain of the Earth Spirit.

She was polite. She was courteous. The Earth Spirit's grin faded as it beheld her, coming to something almost pained.

She bowed politely, then gave her request. She wanted its power. She needed it. She needed it for her goal.

And if the Earth Spirit still refused to help, then she would do it herself. Perhaps she had enough power. She could feel her Qi. Her image was set. She knew how everything connected, thanks to Ri Zu's lessons, as well as which changes to make, but . . . something deep within her mind cautioned her. Warning her of the danger of attempting to do it alone.

She pulled up an old, faded memory of the twisted limbs of Chow Ji. She hadn't thought much about his mutated and deformed body. Of course, she would *never* succumb to such a thing. But now those images loomed high in her mind.

So she sat, and she waited. The Earth Spirit was normally playful, or amused. But tonight, she sensed Tigu's conviction. One way or another, Tigu would be changed—and the Earth Spirit knew it too.

Finally, the Earth Spirit opened her mouth. The voice that came out was rough from what sounded like throat damage, and it had a lisp from missing teeth. Tigu had heard muffled curses and giggles from the Spirit before, but never full words. The Spirit grimaced as the action seemed to pain her.

"Why?" she asked Tigu, her eyes full of some indescribable emotion.

'I shall once more reclaim my rightful place in my Master's bed!' Tigu boasted.

The Earth Spirit raised an eyebrow, then sighed. It made her look positively ancient as her back hunched slightly and she stared at the cat before her.

"If you ask to sleep with them again, they'll let you," the Earth Spirit said, staring at the cat before her. "But . . . this isn't *really* about that, is it?"

The words pierced her, but it was something Tigu had already known. She probably *could* have just asked to get back into her Master's bed. To sleep, warm, comfortable and, above all, safe. Safe between her Master and the Mistress.

But instead, since the instant the Blade of Grass had spoken of it, the idea had captured Tigu's attention. After speaking with Chun Ke, she realised it. After smoothing her relationship with Ri Zu . . . she *knew* it. Wanting to get back into her Master's bed was just an excuse she'd used to stay up all night, or to use the feelings of longing to push herself further.

"Why do you *really* wish to be human?"

The bed was just an excuse. What she wanted was the *connection*. She wanted an end to the barrier imposed upon her by this form. An end to the others staring at her like she was lesser because of what she was. They tried. Her Master treated her as human. He always made sure to include her—to include all of them. He accommodated their forms and made them things to try to bridge the gap. He tried to understand them. But there was always a *slight* disconnect. The brief pause as he mentally adjusted to who she was. It was even worse with the mortals. She couldn't stand how they looked at her: like she was just a cat, and not *Tigu*.

That . . . that was not acceptable. She wanted to do human things. She wanted to talk with the humans properly. She wanted them to know her, and not stare at her like she was a beast first and Tigu second.

She thought of the ease with which humans moved. The thumbs. The skin. She wanted hair to braid like Mistress and the Blade of Grass. She also wanted clothes to wear, and look good in, unlike how silly the rooster and Chun Ke always appeared, playing at wearing human clothing.

She wanted to sit with them on the veranda, and laugh with them, loud and wild. To be herself, full and unfiltered through Qi-speech and incompatible bodies.

'To truly understand.' All her failed entreaties to spar, as she goaded and insulted to have others to interact with. All that time sulking, and then pretending it didn't bother her when they refused. She had been a fool—and no wonder they always said no.

"Can you not try to do that with your own body?" the Earth Spirit pressed. "Can you not train your voice until all can hear? Aren't only the ones who accept you worth speaking to?"

Perhaps. But why was she trying to warn Tigu away?

"Being a human is a miserable existence," the Earth Spirit declared. "It is much better to be as you are—"

'Then why do you *have the form of a human?'* Tigu asked back.

The little brat of an Earth Spirit seemed surprised at the question, physically recoiling from it. She looked down at her own form. A little girl. A child, full of cracks and gold.

The Spirit stared at the stump of her arm. It had the beginnings of a hand made of gold upon it. She touched the flat pane of metal that had once been an eye, now a vein that took up nearly half her face.

The fight went out of her, and her gaze seemed to go far away. The realm that they were in twitched. The sky cycled through storm clouds, flashing with lightning, to winter gales and spring showers.

Her body churned and shuddered, as something *twisted* inside the Spirit, until she finally slumped.

"It was the easiest way to connect with them," she said wistfully. "To see. To learn. To know. To live as they do, to feel the same aches and pains, the same emotions . . . I can't remember much of it anymore. But for a time, I remember being so *happy.*"

She stared up at the sky, a tear running down her one good eye.

'It is better to let someone in and be hurt, than to never let any in at all,' Tigu whispered, quoting her Master. She didn't know the meaning of that. Those that she let in . . . none had hurt her. But someone, or something had obviously harmed the Spirit.

"What is joy, without sadness?" the Earth Spirit asked. "What is our time here, without others?" She looked upon Tigu once more. Both knew the reason why Tigu desired this change.

A complex series of emotions spread across the Earth Spirit's face. Pity. Pride. Sorrow. Joy.

They settled on a fond smile.

"This won't be like Wa Shi," the Earth Spirit said finally. "He *earned* the form of a dragon, by the ancient ways of his kind. There will be a tribulation in this. This may be painful. You might even die."

A dire warning, yet Tigu only scoffed.

'*The Young Mistress of Fa Ram will face it, come what may.*'

"What kind of fool runs headfirst into a tribulation?" the Earth Spirit asked, smirking at Tigu.

'*One who thinks it is worth it.*' The Spirit laughed at her brazen audacity and conviction—but there was some sadness in her eye.

"Don't die, okay? I'd be sad," the Earth Spirit whispered. With a slight bit of hesitation, she extended her good hand.

'*This Young Mistress thanks*—' Tigu cut herself off at the raised eyebrow. '*Thank you, Spirit.*'

Tigu pressed her forehead into the Spirit's palm.

A soft stroke of her head—and then the Earth Spirit was gone. The sky was suddenly black. The ground became a featureless plain, devoid of the normal grass. The realm was empty.

Empty, save for the lightning that was approaching. The light of the heavens. Their wrath at going against their principles made manifest. It writhed with power. She could feel it singeing her fur from here.

One last chance to turn back.

As if it were even an option.

Tigu stepped into the lightning.

Surprisingly, at first it didn't actually hurt. The light consumed her, and it surrounded her, filling her with power, so she grabbed hold of it. Taking it. Directing it. She knew what she wanted, and it would come to her.

The human form. But with her own tweaks. Enough to communicate. But she saw the better ears. The claws. The tail. All things that would aid her in the future.

The lack of pain didn't last—something stabbed into her insides. Her organs trembled in protest. Her bones creaked and groaned like sticks about to snap and shatter. Her soul felt like it was being flayed, like she used to flay the rats she hunted.

It was agony. It was terrifying, to have one's body invaded by such amounts of Qi, to have lightning tear and try to pull your body and mind to pieces.

Tigu refused to scream. She refused to cry out or to let the pain overwhelm her. She faced it head-on. She grasped her body firmly, even as the image of what she wanted to turn into began to fade away. It was all she could do to keep her mind focused on her goal, as the lightning tried to snatch pieces of her away.

Time seemed to twist and stretch. Had she been in here for moments, or an eternity? Tigu didn't know. All she knew was the pain, and all she had left in mind was her goal.

Her vision began to fade. Her body writhed. Yet she pulled herself further into the pillar of light, unflinching.

She was Tigu, the Young Mistress of Fa Ram. *And she would endure this for a hundred years, if she had to, to realise her desires.*

The world burned, and burned, and burned for an eternity, and yet also only an instant. Her body twisted, cracked . . . and shattered.

→

There was darkness.

For a brief instant, there was nothing. Only silence.

A smell slowly entered her nose. Charred plants and wet soil. It smelled . . . different. Maybe less intense?

Water dripped from a leaf. A brave bug began calling again. A frog followed suit, until everything in the forest began to sing and chirp.

It was wet. She could feel the dirt pressed into her face. Fingers clenched, digging into a fistful of dirt.

Tigu opened her eyes.

The blurry image slowly sharpened into smooth, pink flesh. She opened her hand in wonder, the dirt spilling out and flaking to the ground. A bit of orange flashed in her vision, and she moved her hand to stroke it through a lock of long orange hair.

Slowly, she pushed herself up and looked around the clearing. The earth was charred and still glowing slightly from a lightning strike. Black ground emanated in a shock wave around her.

She . . . *she had done it.*

While she could not claim to be the first to change their form, she would claim this. The Young Mistress of Fa Ram would be the disciple closest to her Master! Even Bi De could not claim that! A strange sound started to come from her throat.

She was . . . laughing?

She was laughing, as she doubled over, helpless.

"Tigu!" The Blade of Grass's voice called out with worry as she approached. "Tigu, Where are you? Are you well—"

Xiulan cut herself off as she burst into Tigu's clearing, staring with wide eyes.

"Tigu?" she asked.

The cat smiled languidly. "You . . ." Tigu coughed, as her voice came out for the first time. It sounded odd to her ears. "You dare not recognise this Young Mistress?" she demanded with a smirk, pushing herself up.

It was a slight mistake, as she nearly passed out from the motion. She wobbled for a moment but managed to catch herself, her balance already coming to her. Xiulan suddenly appeared at her side, as if to catch her.

"Forgive this Xiulan. She did not recognise you without ears or a tail," the woman apologised, her voice full of wonder.

Without ears and a tail?

Tigu frowned, patting her head. There were no ears, nor any tail like she had wanted. She looked at her hand. Neither were there any claws, just slightly sharper-than-normal nails.

She looked down at the rest of her body, barely noticing as Xiulan took off her own outer shirt to drape it around Tigu's shoulders. She grinned at the defined muscle she could see on her stomach and arms, and though there were two slight annoyances on her chest, at least she could still see her feet.

She . . . she was human. No. No, she was *Tigu*. Like the fish said, he was himself! So she was herself too!

She grabbed the Blade of Grass like the Mistress did, hugging her. It was nice to have another in her arms. Any surprise that the Blade of Grass had seemed to feel was swiftly buried, as she hugged back.

"You have truly transcended your limits," Xiulan praised her.

Tigu began to rub her cheek against smooth flesh. It had felt nice as a cat before, but like this? Her skin was so sensitive! It was amazing.

She wondered how it would feel to lie on the Master and the Mistress now?

Her course was set. New muscles flexed, as the Blade of Grass was lifted and thrown over Tigu's shoulder.

"Wha—? Tigu?" the woman asked, bemused, but not struggling, as Tigu shot off in the direction of home. Home. Home, and Master! She had to show him!

They exploded out of the forest, barging through the front door of the house and shooting up the stairs, carrying the Blade of Grass all the way.

"Wait— Tigu— What—?" The Blade of Grass started to struggle, trying to stop Tigu, as she realised where they were going. Tigu dropped her, then slipped out of her grasp.

Tigu burst through the door, slamming it open, as both Master and Mistress looked in shock at her sudden appearance. Muscles coiled, as she sighted her target.

She soared through the air—and a split second later the Master registered her presence. Her Master's entire body tensed as shock and confusion warred. Clenched fists opened, and a brief moment of focus faded, as he put up his arms and let her land safely in his grasp.

Warm arms clasped around her.

Happy. Safe.

She grinned up at her Master.

"Look what this Young Mistress did, Master!" she preened.

"Tigu'er?" her Master asked, his voice confused.

"Mm!" she confirmed, as she looked at the other person staring at her. "Mistress!" She switched to her Mistress, then grabbed her too, pulling their bodies together.

Her Mistress seemed both shocked and bemused as their cheeks rubbed together.

This felt *so much* better like this, rather than as a cat.

"Forgive me for letting her inside in this state—" the Blade of Grass tried, but Her Master just waved her off.

"How did this happen, Tigu'er?" he asked, still confused.

"This Young Mistress wished to understand her Master better!" she declared. "And sleep together again," she murmured.

It had been a reason, in the beginning, and *heavens above* she had missed this.

Tigu yawned before snuggling in deeper. The brief surge of energy had been spent. Her Mistress still looked nonplussed as she gently tugged Xiulan's garment closed around Tigu.

Her Master's hand settled on her head. Tigu's eyes started to flutter closed.

"I think we're losing her," her Master whispered. "We'll figure things out in the morning."

Mistress brushed some of her hair out of her face, the gentle action amplified as a warm hand drifted over her cheek. She turned to the Blade of Grass. "If you're standing there and half undressed already, we still have room," she said, a joking lilt to her voice.

"Mmm. The Blade of Grass is comfortable and soft," Tigu confirmed, as sleep began to take her.

Xiulan spluttered for a moment, as Mistress waggled her eyebrows at her, before she huffed.

"Good night, Master Jin, Senior Sister, Tigu," she said. Another hand patted her head, from Master's side, as the Mistress made mock grabbing motions at the other woman. The arms were artfully dodged, and then the Blade of Grass departed.

Master sighed, shaking his head, as he lay back down. Her back pushed into his chest.

"Stop teasing the poor girl," he muttered.

"Ah, it's just fun to see her blush. I wonder when she's going to start pushing back?" Mistress huffed out a chuckle before reaching out to stroke Tigu's hair. "This, on the other hand, is something to get used to. Until last year my brother still woke me up to climb into my bed."

Tigu's head was pressed into Mistress's breast.

Two bodies curled protectively around her.

Tigu slept the sleep of the victorious.

CHAPTER 44

SYSTEM SHOCK

What do you do when a mostly naked girl who was previously your cat jumps into your bed with you and your wife?

Because I certainly didn't know, other than make her comfortable and try to figure out what exactly my reaction should be.

Okay, talking animals, I had come to peace with it. They had honestly improved my life, and I was glad that they were here. Washy turning into a dragon? Strange, but there was the story of the carp jumping over a waterfall and becoming a dragon. Another easy deal.

Tigger as a human, though? I was freaking out a little, very quietly so as not to wake her up. She looked about fifteen or sixteen years old and slightly shorter than Meiling. Excited yellow eyes, now closed in slumber. There were no ears, nor any tail. The only part of her that might suggest she had ever been a feline were the black markings on her face. In every other way, she mostly looked like a normal young woman—

—who was wearing only a mostly open shirt Xiulan had given her, with her back pressed into my chest.

I had never been more unaroused in my life. She barely acted her apparent age. This was my *cat*. Well, she wasn't really *mine* anymore, was she?

I mean, I knew it *could* happen. It was a thing in stories, the animal transforming into a human. But I had thought it was some super high-tier technique. Tigger wasn't *that* strong, was she? Washy still looked a lot like a fish. He wasn't an imperious dragon, he was . . . *Washy*. Just slightly bigger.

Meimei raised an eyebrow at me and tilted her head to the side. There was a silent question there, waiting for me to decide on what to do.

I looked down at the orange-haired girl—at the content smile on her face, safe and happy between us.

I mentally kicked myself. No. No, things weren't any different, not really. She was just in human form now.

I would do what I'd said I would do. We had joked about the animals, *disciples*, being our children before. Now, one had figured out a way to transform into a human to be closer to us.

I would be happy for her, proud of her, for managing to accomplish this. She'd set her mind on a task and had done it. I had told them I'd do my best to guide them, to be there for them. I would have to be better, though. There was always room for improvement, and I had thought because everybody seemed to be getting better, becoming closer friends, that they were happy. We would all need to have a talk.

I turned back to Meiling. My choice was set, and my path was clear.

"Will you help me with this?" I asked her quietly.

She took in my serious, resolved face, and nodded. "Yes," she agreed. "When you're so resolved, how could your wife say no?" she asked with a smile.

For a brief moment, I thought it was mere obligation on her part. Meiling brushed some hair out of the girl's face, running her thumb along the black markings. Tigger shifted in response, pressing unconsciously against the tender touch.

Tigu. Most people called her Tigu, assuming the "er" was the affectionate suffix people gave to children, animals, or women they liked. I hadn't really bothered to correct anybody on the names. They were my inside joke, so whatever they thought they were hearing, well, I just went with it. I still may think of them with the names that I gave them, but Bi De probably was what Big D thought of himself as.

"What should we do about the rodents, though?" Meiling mused. "Should we still rely on her for it? It would be a bit odd to see her with one dangling out of her mouth."

It would be kind of awkward. And disgusting. Now, how do I teach a cat who turned into a human and referred to herself as a Young Mistress?

That was a question for tomorrow.

We'd take it slow, ease her into things.

↔

Smell once more came first. Herbs. Something earthy and comforting. It was a bit less intense than she was used to.

Sound. The breathing of two beings, one in front, and one behind, both sleeping.

Touch. Oh, the touch. The warmth. The feeling of sheets against skin, of her forehead pressed into something soft and warm and oh so comfortable.

Tigu opened her eyes.

Light. Colours. There were so many colours. Her eyes had been sharp before, as befitted a proud and expert huntress, but now . . . The difference in quality was just too great. She could see in exacting detail each strand of hair, each pore on her Mistress's face.

Tigu pulled back. She moved her hands, one curled against her chin, one resting against her Mistress's hip, and explored. The smooth skin. The toned muscle. The soft, silky orange hair.

It hadn't been a dream. *She had done it.*

Tigu began to giggle. Her body shook with her joy.

"Somebody is in a good mood this morning," Mistress noted with a wry smile.

"Mistress!" Tigu exclaimed. She was still a little unsure of how she felt about her own voice. It was a *bit* high-pitched. It was her voice, so naturally it sounded pleasant. She just wished she had a bit more of Master's intimidating rumble.

Tigu perked up as a hand moved. Her eyes tracked the appendage as Mistress ran her fingers through Tigu's hair. Slowly she reached up and grabbed the hand. It was a searching motion. The thumb worked its wonders as she grasped. But that was not all that happened. Mistress's hand shifted, and their fingers meshed together.

She just stared at their entwined fingers. Mistress had her nails trimmed short, but her fingers were still as long and slender as Tigu's. Perfect for herb gathering, for manipulating objects. Much better than Chun Ke's trotters, or even Ri Zu's stubby, bulbous graspers.

Though Tigu could grudgingly admit the rat was surprisingly deft with her inferior instruments.

"Morning." The rumble moved through Tigu's back.

There was pressure as Master leaned over Tigu's head, and Master's and Mistress's lips met. He paused as he drew back, then leaned down to kiss Tigu's forehead, as he did in her other form.

He smiled down at Tigu before his face turned contemplative.

Mistress raised an eyebrow. "Oh? And what's the thought of the day today?" she asked. Tigu did hear them talk most mornings, mentioning things that escaped Tigu's understanding.

"Aside from Wa Shi, the eyes of fish are always so blank and soulless. I wonder what goes through their heads," Master mused, and Mistress snorted.

"Cultivating mosquitoes probably exist," Mistress replied—and Master looked absolutely horrified.

"Thanks for that," he muttered. "You know, we used to tell each other about ourselves, when did that stop?"

"When you told me that every time I drank a cup of water I was drinking somebody's pee," she said reproachfully, though she still seemed amused.

Both began to laugh, and a second later Master's hand landed on Tigu's head.

"Things are going to be a bit different now, Tigu'er. Being a human . . . well, it means a lot of things change, okay? We'll work through them, together."

Tigu puffed out her chest. "I shall master this easily!" she declared, and received a smile.

"Shall we get started on the day?" he asked his wife. Both got out of bed, and Tigu followed after.

"First things first: getting dressed. Humans don't run around naked, right?" he asked her, and she nodded rapidly. Every human wore clothes. That was one of the things she wanted, to wear clothes like the Master did.

He opened a drawer. "We'll get you something to wear for now—" And Tigu swiftly reached in, then grabbed something she'd always coveted. She shed the Blade of Grass's garment and robed herself in more proper colours.

Master stared, bemused, as she put on his shirt. It was a bit big, but it was warm and smelled *perfect*.

She knotted the sash around her waist and grinned, pleased at her choice. "These clothes are obviously superior!" she declared, planting her hands on her hips.

The front of the garment opened, as it was too big to fit properly. Master turned to Mistress, who sighed.

→

'This is not-not as Chow Ji. No-no deformity-defects,' Ri Zu said in both shock and wonder, running her paws over Tigu's new arms. She had reverted to her previous way of speaking, with how out of sorts she was, stunned and frantic when beholding Tigu's new form. All of the disciples were gathered to marvel at her. Disciple Gou Ren was gaping, seeming to not understand what was going on. *Ha!* Her appearance surpassed even the awe shown by the others when Wa Shi revealed his dragon shape!

Tigu preened under the attention and tugged slightly on the bandages covering her breasts. She had been allowed to wear Master's shirt, but Mistress had declared that she had to wear these bindings as well, since her shirt kept flopping open. As if that mattered. Everyone should stare in awe of every part of her form! It wasn't *quite* what she had wanted, but it was her, so naturally it was a work of art—just like how Master's muscles were works of art!

The undergarments around her waist were annoying, but it was either wear that or one of Mistress's skirts. Tigu had an instinctive distaste for them. They were too long—she had no clue how the Blade of Grass stomached having to wear such a garment. Her battle attire was much better.

She had her hair brushed too, but she'd often had her coat brushed. It had never been put into two tails at the back of her head, though. She quite liked it.

At the moment, she was practising with her chopsticks with her other hand. They spun around her new, long digits with ease.

She giggled, watching with fascination as she twirled the stick on the end of a single nail. And they were nails, not claws. Thankfully, they were still rather pointed and sharp, but they were nothing compared to her proper weapons.

That was something to work on, but for now? She would revel in the new sensations. Her sense of hearing and smell weren't as affected as she'd thought they would be. She knew they were slightly lesser, but it was mitigated by the *vastly* improved vision.

Pi Pa was staring at her hands with barely disguised envy, while the glutton simply watched her, looking smug.

'Congratulations on second place,' Wa Shi said with a smirk, grooming his whiskers while he lounged in his tub.

Tigu narrowed her eyes. "Care to test yourself against me, Wa Shi?" she asked.

The fish went from entirely too pleased with himself to panic, his eyes darting to the water room. Tigu chuckled, while Disciple Gou Ren seemed to finally snap out of his gaping.

'Heartbeat, normal. Breathing, normal,' Ri Zu muttered.

'Friend good? Friend fine?' Chun Ke asked worriedly from his place as Tigu's backrest. This had not changed. He was as comfortable to lean on as both a cat and a human.

'Yes-yes, her body is human. *Chow Ji had an elevated heart rate, and his deformity-defects caused him great agony-pain. Yet Tigu is fine-good. Perfectly healthy. How is this possible? Ri Zu thought that this transformation was doomed, that it was something completely unnatural and . . . corruptive.'*

"Chow Ji was likely doing it incorrectly. It is a delicate procedure, and one needs patience! Chow Ji surely would have perished under the lightning of tribulation!" Tigu boasted.

'Yes-yes, Ri Zu saw the scorch marks,' the rat said with a grimace.

"Ri Zu would not turn into some corrupted beast," Tigu replied dismissively. The rat seemed equal parts fascinated and horrified about what Tigu had done. "She is superior in all measures to the beast that brought her here."

Not that it was a great feat, yet still Ri Zu shrank back, embarrassed and pleased at the praise.

"Indeed, the more wicked a man is, the worse the lightning of tribulation," Xiulan confirmed. "Though this one has not had anything of the sort. I don't believe that any in the Azure Hills have suffered a tribulation in centuries. The area is simply too weak."

"Nobody in centuries, huh?" Master mused, looking up at the ceiling as he entered with food. He frowned briefly, before sighing and setting down the plates. "What you did was dangerous, Tigu." She jolted at the lack of affectionate suffix, her head swiveling around and her eyes wide at the Master's rebuke. "I would have been very sad if something had happened to you."

Tigu hung her head, staring at the table. It was true, she had not been thinking of the consequences of failure. It . . . it was wrong of her, but she still felt good, since the Master had told her he cared for her.

A hand clapped onto her head. This, at least, felt the same no matter what form she was in.

"If the rest of you try something like this . . . At least tell somebody beforehand, in case something goes wrong," he finished. "Now eat up."

She perked up. Lessons today? She would likely be finding the limit of this new form and learning how to properly do human things!

Smiling, she prepared to shovel down her food.

The first bite entered her mouth.

Stars *exploded* in her vision.

She let out a sound that sounded like it should have come out of the Blade of Grass.

Wha—what? What manner of sorcery is this? How can the food taste so much better? She stared in shock at her bowl.

"Predators tend to have worse taste buds than herbivores or omnivores," the Master told them, amused.

Tigu shoved another bite in her mouth. This was amazing. Human bodies were great!

She would forgive Xiulan for all of her annoying sounds. Maybe. She would control this urge soon, because the noises that were coming out of her mouth were incredibly embarrassing. Everybody was laughing at her! Though, in her defence, the food was really, *really* good.

They finished their meals and began their day. The Master noticed her attention on his forms, and he slowed down his moves for her so that she could copy them properly.

She marveled at the sun on her skin and the wind in her hair. And then she started testing the limits of this new body.

She grabbed her leg and pulled her knee to her ear. She flipped onto her hands, then did a split with her legs, first front to back, and then on both sides. She dug her fingers into the dirt, and her feet touched the ground in front of her head.

She had expected a bit more lost movement, but her flexibility remained.

The day continued as normal. There were chores to do. There was a property to patrol. It was a bit harder to walk along the Great Pillars, as Bi De called them, but she still strode across them with ease, checking the perimeter for intruders.

Some things changed. Some things stayed the same. All she could say for certain was that she was enjoying herself.

Once they finished training, Chun Ke gave her a ride back to the house. The sheep were slightly too small to sit on now.

There, Mistress was waiting for her. Waiting with a lesson.

She bit back a groan at the word on the slate, even as Pi Pa squealed with happiness.

Decorum, the board proclaimed.

Mistress raised an eyebrow at the once-more opened shirt she was wearing, which exposed her stomach.

Tigu pouted. Decorum *was* an important topic to humans. So she would learn it well . . . Even if she didn't like it.

Just as soon as it stopped making her fall asleep.

It was all about stuff she couldn't do, like jumping on people, or removing her clothes in public . . . it was dreadfully dull. What was worse, Pi Pa looked like she enjoyed it.

After the boring lesson there was *another* medical checkup. Wa Shi had not had to suffer through so many when he changed!

"Everything seems to be fine, still," Mistress mused. "No side effects from the lightning—you're as healthy as can be. Just one more thing. Can you change back?"

Tigu scoffed. How simple! She started the process to turn back into her original form.

She paused.

She *pulled*. Nothing happened.

There was a brief moment of panic as she raced into the river room.

"Wa Shi. Your Senior Sister has come to request your help. How does one undo their transformation?"

CHAPTER 45

TRANSFORMATION SEQUENCE

N*ow, focus your intent. You must center yourself,'* Wa Shi lectured from his jar, *entirely* too smug for Tigu's taste, yet she did as she was instructed. She sat in a meditative pose, with Master and Mistress watching on.

'As this Wa Shi is your teacher, if you comprehend this technique swiftly, it is due to my overwhelming skill. If you fail to comprehend it, it is obviously because of your inferiority,' he continued happily.

Tigu's eyes snapped open, focusing on the fish. Her claw intent was directed squarely at the beast.

Wa Shi nearly leapt into the river, his eyes switching swiftly from smug to fear. He coughed into his fin.

'Focus?' he asked politely. Tigu huffed, then obeyed.

'Now, think thoughts of being smaller.' Tigu thought of her tiny form covered in fur.

'Think of the happy thoughts of when you were in your form.' Her Master carrying her on his shoulders. Her Mistress stroking her fur. Training with the Blade of Grass.

'Then think of how you cannot fit in your home!' But she *could* fit in her home. She fit better now. Sure, it was quite nice to be so small at times, but this was almost superior to—

'Think of how much of a travesty it is that the food is so small!' the fish wailed.

Tigu twitched. She grasped Wa Shi firmly by his tail.

→

She collapsed, her Qi spent to the dregs of her power. At least the Blade of Grass looked winded, thirty-two swords floating and arrayed around them. They let her have offence and defence all in one—a storm of grass blades that together reached for the heavens.

It was a victory to make Xiulan use her full strength, even if only for a moment.

"Has the exhaustion changed anything?" Xiulan asked, getting her breathing under control.

Tigu shook her head before slumping further and sighing. No feeling of being about to change back. She was just *tired*.

"Well, you have improved dramatically. Your movement technique . . . it is one that is sure to surprise. If I were not competing, I could see you perhaps winning the entire Dueling Peaks tournament." Xiulan smiled at the girl.

Tigu offered her a gesture she had seen her Master perform. A single finger stuck up proudly to the heavens.

Xiulan laughed as she scooped the smaller woman up and took her back home.

"You're sleeping with me tonight. Master Jin and Senior Sister need their privacy, at least occasionally."

→

"Her Qi doesn't smell any different," her Mistress mused as deft hands pushed into Tigu's back—she moaned with pleasure in response. "The muscles, on the other hand, are slightly denser than they should be. A bit more solid as well. Ri Zu?"

'Pulse is slightly faster, Master. No Qi snarls that Ri Zu can feel!'

"So . . . what could be preventing you from turning back?" Mistress asked. Her fingers went to work in Tigu's hair, rubbing along her scalp.

Tigu didn't know. But if she kept getting treated like this, she didn't particularly care.

→

The Earth Spirit pondered her question. The gold-cracked thing ran her fingers through her hair, cocked her head to the side, paced back and forth, and eventually . . .

Shrugged.

The Earth Spirit then yawned and went back to lazing on top of a patch of grass.

Back to silence, after they had spoken?

Mud splattered. The Spirit laughed. Laughed, until Tigu grabbed both sides of the irritating thing's face and smashed her forehead into it.

Then the Spirit laughed harder while Tigu staggered around, rubbing the nasty, rapidly forming bruise.

The Spirit, with a wry grin, knocked on her own forehead proudly, then knocked on a rock with the same force.

The rock broke.

□

An earsplitting *crack*, and a blinding flash.

"Is that all you've got, you frilled glutton? You're no dragon, you're a fat fish!" Tigu shouted.

Another crack of air shattering.

Laughter. "Like you could ever actually slay me! I could withstand your lightning for *weeks* without being truly harmed!"

The dragon's eyes narrowed. Beginning from his tail, each spine on his back began to flash electric blue in sequence, growing in power and brightness. Sparks leapt between his horns. Muscles contracted, and a low groan, rising in pitch and intensity, filled the air.

The world went white.

Everyone watching winced.

An orange-haired girl lay on her back, smoking slightly, and twitching every few seconds. She shakily raised her hand and stared at her fingers.

"Toldja ta . . . put more power . . . inno it," Tigu slurred.

A fish collapsed to the ground, huffing and panting.

"Why?" Meiling asked, one hand on her face, clearly fighting the impulse to run over and check on Tigu, who was already sitting back up, albeit slightly singed.

Jin sighed. "She said she transformed with lightning, so . . ."

"Master said metal attracts lightning, right?" Tigu asked as she stared at a shovel, then turned to look at the storm clouds in the distance.

"Oh no, none of *that*," Meiling snarled, getting up and marching over to fuss over Tigu.

Xiulan, on the other hand, just stared contemplatively at the panting fish, her eyes gleaming.

□

Human Transformation.

The topic was written on top of the slate with exacting strokes. The board was filled with questions, many of them crossed off, though some of them had question marks beside them. Today, Ri Zu sat at the right-hand position of the table, organising her notes. The head of the table was ceremonially empty. She shuffled the sheaves of paper, considered them, then placed them on the table, having come to her conclusion.

'*None of this makes any sense,*' the rat declared, scratching at her nose. They had tried everything that could be thought of, and no one—not Ri Zu's Master, not the Master of Fa Ram, not Young Miss Xiulan, nor even Disciple Gou Ren—had any ideas.

The reactions to her words were less than she'd hoped. She had Brother Chun Ke's full attention, as always, but he seemed quite unconcerned. Pi Pa was similarly minded, simply shrugging. Tigu yawned, tugging at her still-frizzled hair, and Wa Shi was asleep, drooling after expending his power.

Ri Zu sighed, then leaned back in disgust. She supposed she was the one most concerned about this, as she was still of two minds about this whole mess. The first part screamed that such a transformation was unnatural—Tigu was now just like Chow Ji, chasing a form she had no right in possessing. She had stained herself and her very soul in performing the act.

Yet . . . yet that part was probably wrong. Ri Zu had had no visceral reaction to Wa Shi. She had simply nodded, as if "this is the way things are" and it was expected for a fish to change in such a way. Curious, but it had been an ingrained reaction. Like she'd already known that was *supposed* to happen. It was an odd reaction, now that she thought about it further. *Why is it natural for a carp to become a dragon?*

Was the Human Transformation really so different? Tigu was human now. Human . . . And that was it. No corrupted limbs, no hunched back, not a single thing—save for slightly too-sharp teeth—that might reveal her true origins.

'*Chow Ji bad. Chow Ji have bad form. Tigu good. Tigu have good form?*' Brother Chun Ke had mused. It . . . was a profound statement. Months ago, Ri Zu would have scoffed, proclaiming the cat nearly as wicked as her former leader.

If anything, Tigu was *nicer* as a human. Oh, she was still arrogant, and the shouts of '*This Young Mistress!*' still came from her lips, but . . .

it seemed to be tempered. The feeling of unease Ri Zu had still had on occasion, even with Tigu's lessons, was completely gone. Tigu had even picked Ri Zu up and put her on her shoulder, declaring that Ri Zu's legs were too short, and the two of them needed to be faster . . . even though they were not going anywhere in a hurry.

Then she had picked up Brother Chun Ke and carried him above her head, much to his squeals of delight. They had been frightfully unbalanced, though. The boar outmassed Tigu thrice over, and came to above her hips at the shoulder.

Ri Zu sighed again. The thought tickled the back of her mind. Human Transformation. She saw, in her mind's eye, two forms. A beautiful man with fiery red hair lay with a small woman—

Ri Zu flushed, and coughed, shaking her head.

She turned to Pi Pa and Chun Ke and envisioned them. One alternated between a thin, prim woman and a chubby, jolly one. The other . . . well, he was simply big, solid, and jolly. *Very* Brother Chun Ke.

Ri Zu looked around the table again. Everybody was unconcerned. Tigu probably didn't even see it as a problem, judging by her reactions. She was failing at something . . . and yet the desperation and drive to succeed was absent.

"No luck, guys?" the Great Master asked, poking his head into the room.

There was a halfhearted chorus of *no*s. The Master concentrated intently, hearing them even when they grumbled and whispered.

Tigu clambered onto his back. He absently grabbed her legs, so that her head was peeking over his shoulder.

"Is it urgent to you, Tigu'er?" he asked, and the cat shook her head without thought. "Well, that's fine, then. Figure it out as you go. And if you're human forever . . . well, that's fine too. Same with everybody. If Wa Shi wants to be in his big mode . . . if any of you guys decide to follow this path . . . that's up to you."

The disciples nodded along, but Ri Zu herself paused.

She stared at Tigu and her contented smile as her Master carried her around.

There was one last theory.

The reason why Tigu wasn't changing back—it wasn't because she couldn't.

It was because, deep in her heart, Tigu didn't actually want to.

The rat tapped her little fingers and watched the gathering disperse. Yet was that better or worse, than something being wrong?

↔

"Okay, this *probably* won't work, but could you try it for me anyway?" her Master asked, looking both amused and slightly guilty. "One last attempt?"

Tigu nodded. She pulled her hand down to her waist, as if chambering a punch. Her other hand reached up across her chest, her palm open and facing the floor.

"Transform!" she shouted, as her eyes glowed gold and her Qi flared, encircling her body with light.

There was a brief pause. The Profound Stance of the Masked Hero—as Master had titled it—failed to activate. It felt quite powerful, and she *did* like the swirling arm movements. But it was currently useless to her.

Tigu tried the next one in the set, concentrating intently and not noticing the recording crystal being brought to bear. She brought two fingers up to frame her eye. Her legs spread apart.

"Prismatic Moon Power—!"

CHAPTER 46

THE SHROUDED MOUNTAIN

To the direct east of the Azure Hills lay the Howling Fang Mountains. They were a stark contrast to gentle hills and rolling grass, standing tall and proud, stabbing up into the heavens defiantly and biting directly into the Sea of Snow. The northern ranges were windblown and barren. Slashing winds could tear a man's skin from his bones or have him impaled on whirling ice shards the size of spears. Many Spirit Beasts and dangerous, savage tribes lurked in the veil of snow and icy Qi. It was for these northern peaks that the province was named. The wind screamed through a hundred thousand crags and crevices, sounding like the howling war cry of some savage beast.

As one went south, the Crimson Phoenix Empire began to flourish. They lived in isolated pockets in the valleys, with the occasional outpost high up in the passes. It was a hard life, confined to little stretches of green land in a sea of stone teeth. The jaws were always hungry for unwary travellers.

As the trek south continued, the valleys got wider and the towns more populous. From hard frontiersmen, to the merchants of towns, to the artisans of the cities. In their protective embrace, the Empire flourished. Expeditions to the northern mountains for rare resources, or mining missions in the giant teeth fueled their growth.

Of all the teeth in the Howling Fang Mountains, one was famous: the Shrouded Mountain. It was not the tallest of the fangs. Nor was it the grandest. It was rather short, and yet it stood alone, jutting up almost unnaturally from the center of the valley it resided in. Once it had been the home of a savage and cruel Spirit Beast who had cast befuddling illusions and preyed upon the righteous. It had enslaved and consumed as it pleased, inflicting heinous cruelties upon the populace.

To the Great Founder of the Shrouded Mountain Sect, this had been intolerable. With the strength of his Dao, he flew to the mountain, carried upon the fulmination of the heavens. For three days and three nights, the thunder rumbled, cleansing light tearing through illusions and laying bare the wicked to the light of the day. The Spirit Beast and its foul spawn shrieked with agony and were slain, their cores becoming the foundation upon which the Sect was laid. There are even rumours that some of these cores, from this ancient age, still remained locked in the halls of the Shrouded Mountain.

Instead of mist and illusions, the Great Founder shrouded the mountain with clouds of stormy wrath and the light mist of rains. From high upon their hidden, forested mountain, the Shrouded Mountain Sect ruled.

The Sect, known for piercing through illusions, were blind to a parasite in their midst.

The last of the competitors fell, twitching from a bolt of lightning. The last one standing, the winner of the Shrouded Mountain's Disciples' Tournament, raised his head high and closed his eyes, basking in the shouting of the crowds.

The Sect Elders, watching on, stroked their beards and nodded their heads, giving each other profound glances and communicating with their eyes alone.

"Zang Li." A voice cut through the shouting and the howling of the crowds with but a whisper. The Elders never needed to raise their voices to be heard. "A great victory has been won today. We, the Elders of this Shrouded Mountain Sect, declare you the victor. These Spiritual-Grade Qi-Refining Pills are your prize."

The crowds cheered again, and a voice, meant only for his ears, came to him:

"You are to convene with the Elders to discuss this further."

Zang Li bowed his head in acknowledgement. He claimed his reward, then departed the arena. A servant was waiting for him.

"You are to change, Young Master," the man said respectfully, holding out new clothes. Zang Li's lips twitched into a smile.

He took them without a word, cleansed himself of his exertions, and donned his new garb. Then he strode forth into the building he was directed to. The doors were opened, and Zang Li entered, bowing to the single Elder in attendance.

"Rise, Disciple," the man commanded. Zang Li did as he was bid, standing perfectly still under the judging gaze.

The Elder broke into a smile, then retrieved a scroll, unrolling it and beginning to read.

"For this meritorious achievement, victory in the Shrouded Mountain Disciples' Tournament, Zang Li's restrictions are lifted in their entirety. Return to your previous post and station, Young Master. There will be the resources you have rightfully earned. Ascend as is your right, and claim the power of our Shrouded Mountain."

Zang Li bowed to his "father." The man's face was filled with pride at his "son's" accomplishments.

Inside the skin of the Young Master, Lu Ban mocked the man. He now lavished affection upon his son's killer.

"Thank you, Father. This one apologises for the inconvenience he placed upon you," he said respectfully, as if he had been chastised by his time treated as an outcast. No, he cared nothing for it. He was merely inconvenienced, and yet his true power had shone through. Killing a Profound Realm cultivator, when he was but an Initiate, claiming his body, and stealing right from under his Sect's nose had been a wonderous accomplishment.

His father waved it away.

"Victory washes away all sins," his father declared. A statement Lu Ban was happy to agree with. "Now go, and celebrate this victory."

Lu Ban bowed again.

He exited the hall and was immediately flanked by his new servants. He never failed to relish in his power. To make other men bow before him and do his bidding was intoxicating. That a man like him now could command, and be obeyed without question.

How magical the words "Young Master of the Shrouded Mountain" were. Though those words did bring up unpleasant memories . . . specifically of the time they *hadn't* worked. He had been suppressed—no, not suppressed, utterly crushed by Rou Jin. He shook the ugly feeling away, though, as he strode to what was now his pavilion. Gone was the single room of an ascetic, meant to shame him for his defeat in the Azure Hills. His clothes were fine silk from Spirit Beasts, and his gold adornments—simple at first glance—were intricately worked. His pavilion was large, almost a palace in its own right. A mighty outpost upon the mighty mountain. There was lacquered wood from thousand-year-old trees, jade lanterns from spirit stone mines, and enough wealth to buy a city, in a single, low-level pavilion. The ones used by the Elders were far beyond this.

For a man who had come from the streets, who had known the hunger of starvation, it was almost too much. And yet it was not. This was simply proof of his might. He was no longer a filthy street rat, begging to survive. He was the master of his own destiny.

Already, the others awaited him in the pavilion's main hall. They cheered when he entered, or bowed their heads in respect. In the ones he had suppressed, he saw anger and humiliation. In those he had aided, he saw the gleam of those happy that his star was rising.

"We pay our respects to the Young Master!" they chorused as he took his place at the head of the table.

He gave them his acknowledgement, and the food was served. Delicacies that he once could have never dreamed of filled his plate, and it took every bit of self-control not to tear into the feast like a savage beast at the sheer amount of it all. Instead, he savoured it. He took little bites of each dish and allowed whatever he wanted to go to waste. The Outer Disciples approached his table and begged to pour him a drink or offer their services. He disregarded most of them, for they were beneath his notice.

"Please think kindly of me, Young Master," one particular Outer Disciple crooned, her robe practically falling off one shoulder. Lu Ban was amused. He would indeed think kindly of her. She would pleasure him tonight, and he would do her the courtesy of not consuming her soul.

Though he made no promises against stunting her cultivation.

Truly, he was on top of the world at this moment, and the heavens would only allow him to rise higher.

He took the woman. He added some of her strength to his own, without destroying her. Now that he'd been given free rein, it would not be too difficult to find a proper meal.

He left the girl exhausted and unconscious. To the back room he went, where the Qi was the best for cultivation, and took one of his new pills. He disregarded the new technique scrolls, gifted to him by the Sect, for now.

Instead, in darkness, he cultivated.

Oil and blood bubbled most pleasantly under lightning and clouds.

→

He exited the room the next morning. The girl had been removed, as per his orders to the servants. Good. He didn't have to deal with her whining.

He approached the main table, where documents lay from the Elders. Deciding these could be spared some of his time, he began to read, then grimaced.

An itinerary? He supposed Young Masters must do something other than cultivate, though this was an annoying revelation.

"Reinforce the Fangtip Fortress?" he murmured. That was to the north. Far to the north. Which honestly wasn't too bad—if it wasn't Kang who was going to be leading the expedition. The asshole had it out for Lu Ban, and he still had some enemies amongst the Elders. Leave it to them to scheme and plot—but Lu Ban would rise above them all.

He did grimace at the location, however. It was very, very close to the border of the Azure Hills, that wretched place—Lu Ban grimaced at the phantom pain in his hand and shook his head.

This was an opportunity. To be away from eyes that pried into his every move. He would reverse this trap and claim further glory!

CHAPTER 47

NO DENYING

I ran my fingers over strands of gold. I took a deep breath in and let the scent fill my nostrils. The wheat was a bit taller than I was used to, but then again, modern wheat was mostly a dwarf breed that only got to about three feet tall. There were advantages to this, as it wouldn't bow over as much in heavy rain. If the stalks snapped during a storm, well, you could lose the entire harvest, so modern wheat had been bred to help prevent that. The wheat here would get to about four to five feet tall by the time it was done growing.

It also meant that Meiling could basically hide in it. Her head just barely popped out over the top of the stalks as she wandered through the field with me. She had a soft smile on her face, running her hands along the stalks, and she brought one to her nose to breathe in its scent.

I turned back to my inspection. There were some other differences too. The stalks seemed a bit thicker than normal. They stood just a bit taller and prouder than I'd been expecting, even with the steadily growing weight of fat kernels on top.

There weren't many weeds. There were some, it was inevitable, but the wheat placement and a bit of elbow grease made sure my wheat was generally unmolested.

There was also a little bit of bug damage. Some grasshoppers and other beasties had taken their tax without the power of gene modifications and pesticides to keep them at bay.

They, in turn, were quickly decimated by both the local birds and my own defences. There was a rustling of wheat and a few happy clucks as the hunting pack found a prize. One of my chickens briefly appeared near my feet. It cocked its head to the side, its beak full of bugs, before fading back into the forest of wheat spires like some kind of tiny dinosaur. There was more rustling as they continued through the field, spread out along the length of it and on the lookout for any interloping insect that dared attempt to receive a free meal. The problem was, however, that the fat heads of grain were starting to look more appealing than the bugs to the birds.

I gently picked a piece of grain off and popped it in my mouth.

You were supposed to chew them to check for moisture content, but I had never been particularly good at distinguishing exactly when wheat was done. So it was a slight surprise when I immediately decided *fourteen days, three hours until optimal harvest if current conditions continue.*

I nearly cut the thought off when I suddenly started getting quite a bit more information than I anticipated getting. Like how many hours of sunlight this particular stalk had been getting, how its roots had developed, if the amount of water it received was optimal, and the cause of the slight damage halfway down from an insect chewing on it . . .

It was . . . weird. It felt a *little* like when I had popped in here and gotten all the memories from Rou's past. The sudden rush of information, and how I suddenly *knew* what I needed to do.

I let it wash over me while considering it. It wasn't quite like it was the plants themselves telling me what to do. More like . . . I just knew the wheat.

[Observe] has levelled up, I thought sarcastically. *You may now discern the quality and rarity of things in greater detail . . .*

There was no ignoring it. My cultivation was getting stronger, changing me. However, I didn't really *feel* different. Or at least, I didn't think I did. I just felt good and healthy. I spent my Qi every day, and I felt good and refreshed in the morning.

Something was *still* going on here. The question was, what? I didn't know what was happening. Nothing in the Archives would have anything on cultivation. I would have to go to a Sect and ask to use one of their libraries. Which . . . let's be honest, wasn't going to happen. Not even because I had no desire to visit one, but mostly because they literally wouldn't let me unless I joined or *maybe* paid them a lot.

I can ask Xiulan? Maybe?

And . . . well, it wasn't too bad, was it? The ability *was* pretty useful. If only it weren't this much information.

All I wanted was something simpler and more useful. I didn't care about min-maxing the amount of water my wheat got. Was it healthy? Was it growing fine and disease free? That was enough.

Almost as if it heard me, the flow of information settled a little, simplifying itself. If I focused, I could still get those more intense bits, but . . . well, this way didn't give me a headache.

I closed my eyes and let out a slow breath.

I started walking again, checking out my wheat. Fourteen days, three hours—fourteen days about. Two weeks more and it would be ready to harvest, and then I would have to decide whether I should plant winter wheat. I would probably do at least some, just for an experiment.

I exited the wheat field, where Meimei was waiting. I wrapped my hands around her waist and put my palm against the *slight* bump there.

Her hand landed to rest atop mine and she looked up to kiss my cheek.

There were no words necessary. Just the look in her eyes, so full of warmth.

"I'll get these ones back to the coop," she whispered, as the last of the chickens exited the wheat field. They looked triumphant, having just completed a spectacular hunt.

I nodded to her, then continued my own walk. Pausing, I grabbed a stalk and stuck it in my mouth, just to complete the look.

I smirked at Gou Ren tending to his rice, a boulder twice his size strapped to his back. He moved like he had forgotten it was there.

In all honesty, he probably had. He was working hard and moving with speed, agitating the ground a bit to get some oxygen to the rice's roots and stir up the bugs just like I'd taught him. A couple of ducks were around the paddies, quacking to each other and paddling around the water, or following behind Gou Ren and eating whatever beastie he stirred up. Chunky and Peppa were side by side in a wallow Gou had built for them, sleeping away in the afternoon sun, covered near completely in mud. Chunky had continued to grow and was getting pretty massive. He looked like a small hill now, especially with how dirty he was.

I continued out into the fields to the sheep. Honestly, they were the only ones that could be described as currently "useless," as I couldn't take their wool yet, and I wasn't particularly planning on eating them. But . . . they weren't exactly a drain either. It wasn't like they currently needed to be given feed. They just wandered out to the hills, accompanied by somebody, ate their fill, and then came back.

Okay, maybe they did me one service: they were my lawn mowers. Part of the grass near the house looked downright manicured. Sure, I could probably use it for a field . . . but the soft patch of grass was perfect for having bonfires and just lying down on. Plus, it looked nice.

Okay, so sue me. I *liked* my useless patch of grass. It was a bit of a holdover from the Before . . . but I wanted it, and this was my farm. So we had a lawn.

There was a shock of orange hair with the sheep. Tigger—Tigu—*Tigu'er* because she looked incredibly uncomfortable, like she had done something wrong whenever I called her without the affectionate suffix, was out cold with a small smile on her face. I shook my head at her, then walked over to pull her shirt gently closed so that it covered her stomach again.

She was still such a cat in some ways, asleep on something soft and woolly. But . . . she was so eager to learn. She ran up to me with a "Master, Master!" and looked at me like the sun shone out of my ass. It was a heavy weight, to have somebody look up to you so much.

I continued onwards and ascended a hill to look down on all I had built. There was a brief crack of thunder, but it was faint.

The cows and their calves were milling around in the grass together. The crops were nearly ready for harvest. My house sat on its little island between two rivers.

Maybe it was good that I was getting stronger. I hoped it wouldn't come to it, but I *would* fight for this.

I will do whatever is necessary to protect it.

I took another breath as I stared down at my home, but then turned when something caught my eye.

I did a double take and ran my fingers through my hair. I had six Spirit Beasts living on my farm . . . and I realised I might be looking at number seven.

I descended from my hill.

Babe the ox was carrying his plough out. It wasn't hitched, yet he had managed to hook one of his horns around the carriage and lift it. Now he was just bringing Sunny out to a part of the land I wasn't doing anything with.

"Hey . . . Babe?" I asked, "Need any help there?"

The ox turned to me, his plough hanging off his horn. His eyes were completely placid. So placid and calm that, for a moment, I thought I had gotten it wrong and he had somehow just gotten stuck in the plough.

That thought lasted until, with great deliberation, he shook his head. Then he turned and kept walking. He wandered over to a shady spot, near some trees, and I followed behind.

Carefully he set the plough on the ground and then settled down beside it. He turned his eyes to me and waited.

"Do you know how long you've known?" I asked him, and once more the ox pondered. He thought for a good minute before he pointed his head to Sunny the plough.

"Ever since you were hitched up?" I asked, listening intently for anything that could be words.

He nodded.

That's actually a fairly long time. And he's just been fine with everything?

"Why didn't you tell anybody?" I asked. He had seen me talking with the others. Surely he should have noticed he could just get my attention?

The ox contemplated this for a moment, before his head tilted and he seemed to summon something out of himself.

I strained my ears.

'Content'

A single, simple word. Yet it was absolute.

"You're fine with how things are right now?" I asked.

Babe considered this question as well before nodding.

"You're fine with the barn, the room, and the food?" I asked, making sure.

He nodded again.

"You don't want anything else to eat? You don't want to come in the house? If you want to, you can come and see us," I offered.

And if he can't fit, I can knock out a wall and make a bigger door. I was planning on some sliding doors anyway.

The ox considered the question, looked at my house in the distance, and shook his head.

Okay . . .

"Do you want *anything* in regard to your current living conditions or situation?"

Another shake. Calm and matter-of-fact.

Huh.

"What . . . do you want to do in life?" Maybe it was a bit much of a philosophical question, but this time Babe didn't hesitate.

He pointed his head to the plough.

He just wants to plough?

I nodded. "We'll start on the road again soon," I promised him, and for the first time, the ox looked actually interested.

I'd have to talk to some people to make sure he didn't get abused or overworked, but if he just wanted to use his plough . . . well, there were plenty of roads that could use a helper.

"Do you want to plough in other places?" I asked.

This one got another nod.

"Do you want to come over and introduce yourself to everybody?" I asked him.

Another pause, as he considered, before he nodded.

He got back to his feet and collected his plough.

We moseyed on over to the house. There was a big table set up, because we would be eating outside today. I raised an eyebrow at Xiulan, who was *entirely* too cheerful with her hair all frizzed out, while Washy just looked tired.

Oh, so that's what the thunder was. I shook off the amusement.

"Hey, guys, I got somebody to introduce you to," I said blandly.

Eyes turned towards the ox.

It said a lot that we immediately just moved to introductions.

"So, what do you like to do?" Meimei asked him with a smile.

The ox put down his plough, then turned to me. *Well, a bit of disturbance to the yard wouldn't hurt.*

I obligingly helped him get set up, and he cut into the ground. He was really good at getting the plough to cut nicely—better than I'd ever been able to, honestly.

I smiled and nodded, ready to unhook him. What I *didn't* expect was for Xiulan and Tigu to be examining the cut intensely.

"Magnificent," Xiulan muttered.

"It's all right, I suppose," Tigu muttered, glaring at it.

A blade of Qi formed above Tigu's hand, and she stared at it before starting to sulk.

The ox stood tall.

We all returned to the common area—and somehow, he settled in at the table just fine. I was beginning to get him, I think. Quiet, and contemplative.

"Hm?" Tigu asked the ox, after he'd said something I hadn't been able to catch.

"Master, he doesn't want to use the barn at all. He wishes to sleep outside at night. He says the elements purify his spirit and his cut." She frowned at him, and I could already see the gears turning.

Babe was a bit of a spartan, apparently.

CHAPTER 48

ANCIENT FORMATION

s *this it?'* Yin asked as she stared around at the granite hills and rocky spires. She dipped a foot into the spring they were near, which occasionally belched out water. It was crystal clear and quite lovely.

They were in the center of five points on a spiral, which was formed by the shrines and the villages. It was the center of five smaller spiral formations, each with its own rock.

Bi De had expected to find *something* here. Something that could perhaps shed light upon this phenomenon. The hills here were certainly large, and a few had their own stones upon them . . . But they were by far the most degraded of the bunch. Most were missing entirely, and those that were not had had their tops shorn off or were canted and misaligned.

Yet as far as he could tell, there was no great beacon here. Nothing at the true center of the land. In fact, it had even *less* Qi than he'd thought it would. The power of the Earth Spirit was but a faint echo here.

'*We split up,'* he decided. *'We shall search for anything with the character for "fire" upon it.'*

It was the only really legible thing they had found. It was faint and worn, but one of the pillars did have the word etched into it.

His companions nodded, accepting his request.

And so they set off, combing the area. Their legs were strong, and their eyes sharp—surely they could find something. But after a day of searching, it had turned out to be in vain.

There truly was nothing special here.

'*Sssome of the rock here is . . . odd. Black, with streaks of yellow sulphur. One of the caves had minerals caked onto the walls,'* Miantiao mused. '*I know not what it means, but it is strange, to have such things in granite caves.'*

Bi De thought upon it. His experience in the world was too lacking to tell if something was amiss.

The spring that they were near spluttered for a moment. It coughed, and there were a few anemic-looking bubbles that formed.

Mildly interesting . . . Yet Bi De could not say if it was truly strange.

'So . . . what now?' Yin asked, her head cocked to the side. *'Are we headed to the strange mark? Back to your Master?'*

Bi De considered the question. He had not truly found anything of value yet. His curiosity spurred him onwards, even as his heart told him to rest for a while first.

Miantiao stroked his chin with his tail.

'Thisss one does know of a dance, to the southwest. My Master spoke of a woman there who performed,' Miantiao offered.

Several different directions. Well, it wasn't too big a detour for cultivators, and if they found nothing, then Bi De would turn back. He could head back home for a moment to reassess and gather supplies again. He had travelled all this way only to end up with more questions than he had in the beginning.

He shook his head and prepared to rest. A moment later he offered his energy to the land . . . but found nothing. There was nothing to take his power here. Maybe a few small motes and sparks . . . but other than that, it was empty. With a sigh, he closed his eyes. Yin wandered over to slump against him, and Miantiao looked at the stars alongside him.

'We ssshall have to mark thisss location. I know how some of these minerals may be used to give pigment to glass and clay.'

Bi De turned, interested.

'Indeed, sulphur iss a mossst pleasing yellow, when treated properly . . .'

He listened once more to a Master that had absolute passion for his art. Though Bi De himself held little enthusiasm for the pots, he still gave the old snake his full attention. There was so much he did not know of this world.

His sleep was disturbed by a dream of water being thrown thousands of li into the sky before rumbling down the hills.

He chuckled when he awoke to the little spring spitting in futility, the ascending droplets barely clearing the water.

They made southwest with haste, and there, as Miantiao had said there would be, was a village with a shrine.

A village that seemed to be gearing up for a festival, and a dance.

He marked another point on his map.

→

"Are you sure about this?" the merchant had asked when he saw their destination. "The Ash Forest is beyond those hills. Mighty dangerous place, that forest."

Bi De nodded. The man sighed but held out some provisions with a small smile.

"Well, it was good to meet you. Thanks again, for taking care of my cousin, yeah?" he said, offering his respect. Sister Ri Zu's teachings had come in handy. All three beasts returned the gesture.

The merchant nodded, then went on his way.

'It appearsss your legend grows, Bi De,' Miantiao stated with amusement. *'Who would have thought talesss and stories would have usss received so warmly?'*

Indeed. Whispered tales had spread through merchants and caravans. With those tales and his Great Master's servant's paper, they were welcomed into villages—even villages that were not under the leadership of the man. Bi De had been to several towns, and none seemed as well managed, nor were their guards as vigilant as the one in Verdant Hill. Truly, the Magistrate was worthy of being his Great Master's servant.

'The last place was fun,' Yin said with a smile. Indeed, they'd performed their dance on the longest day, instead of the longest night.

The rabbit had enjoyed herself greatly. She had a cloth scarf around her neck, a gift from a dancer girl, who performed her village's variation of the dance for them.

Most seemed amused at their presence: a rooster, a dancing rabbit, and a snake that made fine vases.

'The center again, hummm?' Miantiao asked. *'I wonder if we shall find anything this time?'*

Bi De did not know. They had found more formation stones, as similarly illegible as the last ones, and guesswork had led them in this direction. Last time, Bi De had gone around in the spirals, searching for the proper way to construct the formation. But their hypothesis had been correct. The construction here was the same as farther north.

Now they were headed for the center, deep in the heart of the Ash Forest.

'Shall we?' he asked his companions. They nodded. Well, this last check, and then they would return to his home.

Bi De could not wait until he could introduce them to Fa Ram.

Together, they ventured into the forest.

□

Their camp was surrounded. It was an awkward conundrum, as Bi De had not realised that things this large could move so quietly until it was too late.

Bi De held his head high as the Blaze Bears circled around their party. Yin bounced on her heels, her eyes focused, while Miantiao just looked sad. He closed his eyes and uncoiled from his disciple, allowing her easier movement.

'You dare trespass into our Ash Forest? On our sacred ground?' one of the beasts rumbled. 'Interlopers. We shall cook you, then dine upon your flesh tonight.' His voice was a guttural snarl as he beheld them. The others growled in agreement.

The ambient temperature rose. Low, snarling growls echoed from the Spirit Beasts, who clearly did not take kindly to trespassers upon their land.

'I bid you stay your claws and breath. We do not desire your resources,' Bi De said, attempting to reason with them.

The bears snarled louder. 'Lies!' one roared.

Bi De sighed. He had been warned of the beasts, yet he had not expected them to be so zealous. They acted as if this were their Fa Ram—

It might very well be, Bi De suddenly realised.

'This Bi De apologises for trespassing. Is there a gate we may visit, so we may enter properly and pay our respects to the Lord of this place?' Bi De tried again.

This caused some of the bears to sneer. The largest Blaze Bear rose to his hind legs and roared, fire streaming forth from his mouth. The rest began to spark and ignite.

Bi De sighed.

The Spirit Beasts flinched as Bi De's Qi rose, surrounding his body in a halo of silver light. Yet numbers made them bold. Heat turned solid around Yin, her golden armour blazing with the sun's light. Miantiao let out a rattling hiss, his one eye as sharp as shattered glass.

Yet the bears did not back down. The rest stood on their hind legs, and fire erupted from their bodies.

'*Come on, you assholes. I'll beat yer teeth into the backs of your skulls,*' Yin muttered, her eyes flicking around and her body loosening.

'*Language,*' Miantiao muttered halfheartedly.

The bears roared, and the battle was joined.

→

'*We thank Great Master Bi De for his generosity and restraint!*' several bears chorused.

'*Now, such a thing will not happen again, will it?*' Bi De asked the lead bear—the one with several missing teeth and a black eye.

'*No, Master Bi De,*' the bear whimpered, rubbing his claws together. The rest of his fellows chorused the sentiment.

The bears were seated in varying poses of defeat, slumped against trees or, in one unfortunate case, embedded headfirst in the ground up to his waist.

Yin bounced happily. It *had* been a fine strike.

'*We are not unreasonable. You have declared yourselves guardians, so I would ask that you escort us to our destination,*' Bi De said, offering them face.

The bear looked mutinous for a brief moment.

Then Yin casually pulled the stuck bear from his hole.

'*Of course, Master Bi De, our Ash Guardians will guide you where you need to go!*' the bear simpered.

The bear led on, and they were escorted through the Ash Forest. It was a vibrant place. The trees were healthy and strong on a level Bi De hadn't experienced outside Fa Ram, and this was without the bountiful Qi that flowed through his home. This meant this growth was purely from the richness of the soil. Bi De would have to collect a sample for his Great Master.

The lack of Qi *did* raise many questions. The bears had described the forest as *sacred*, but there was a great void here. An absence of Qi.

Yet even in this deprived place, Blaze Bears stayed—in far greater numbers than he'd thought there would be.

The three adventurers had defeated five. His eyes tracked to another, a wanderer in this forest, who took one look at Bi De, froze, and fled.

The other bears laughed. '*Cowardly Paobu,*' one of them chuckled. '*Went out into the world, and then last year he returns, screaming about monsters wearing the skin of men.*'

Bi De watched him go before turning to the other bears. *'You described this place as sacred. Why?'* he asked.

The bears all looked at each other.

As one, they shrugged.

'Don't know. It just is. Every Blaze Bear knows it. Even though it's got no Qi, even though it's got not much to eat, this place is home.'

They continued in silence.

Bi De frowned at what they had said, and Yin looked equally troubled, glancing at the sky for a moment.

'Just home, huh?' she muttered.

It took them another two days to reach the center of this place—the true center of this part of the formation.

And yet . . .

There was nothing.

There were no pillars. No formations. No rocks arranged strangely. It was empty, just like the other place. Bi De sighed at the lack of progress.

'Well, we shall be out of your sacred forest tomorrow,' Bi De stated. All of the bears relaxed, huffing happily.

Bi De offered his power to this worthless, Qi-deprived place—

—and brushed up against *something.*

His eyes closed, and he began to dream.

□

It was a lush, impossibly vibrant forest, full of fruits, flowers, and berries. Even under the light of the blessed moon, even with snow on the ground, things bloomed and grew, uncaring of the frost.

A great bear tended to this garden. Her fur was a brilliant emerald, and her eyes were soft and loving. Her cubs gamboled around her feet and claws. She approached a tree, one of the giants that was bigger around than his Great Master's coop, and wrapped a single paw around its mighty trunk, then plucked it out of the ground with a gentle yank. Its roots came up clean, and she wandered off with it. Bi De followed. She wandered into a clearing. There stood a stone twenty li high, spearing into the heavens and covered in a thousand inscriptions. The inscriptions were blurred, but he could see one clearly. A single character that stood out.

Wood.

The bear planted the tree, without the ground seeming to shake or move. Instead it simply formed around the tree's roots. Her task accomplished, she stopped to observe the massive edifice.

She licked her cubs, and then smiled at it.

Bi De could tell it was nearly time. But . . . time for what?

Energy gathered. The bear chuckled, as her children danced and swayed.

But . . . something was amiss. Her cubs' eyes suddenly went blank, as she felt her own consciousness begin to fade. The She-Bear frowned. This . . . this wasn't right—

As soon as the feeling came, it went, as the She-Bear snapped back into herself. She shoved her body forwards, as there was a pulse of *wrongness*.

The giant stone *cracked*. Ominous orange lines flowed through it, pulsing like a demented heartbeat.

The She-Bear, the Empress of the Forest, screamed for her cubs.

She barely managed to interpose her bulk between them and the stone.

The stone that exploded, throwing pieces of itself across the land and shattering the tops off mountains with the violence of it.

The world *burned*.

She burned with it.

She had been a creature of growth and life; the fire had found a perfect offering.

It ate. It consumed. It fed upon her, even as in her last thoughts she prayed. Prayed for at least one drop of her children's blood to survive.

Her prayers were answered in the cruelest way.

A single drop of blood did survive. A single drop of blood, tainted from the flames.

Four little bears, one for each lost cub. They crawled out of that drop of blood and into a world of ash.

They did not remember their mother. But . . . they remembered *some* things.

The first Blaze Bears went forth. The first Blaze Bears brought back seeds.

☐

He gasped as he awoke, his heart pounding in his chest. There was lingering sadness, regret, shock, and pain. A second later he realised Yin was curled up beside him.

Wood to fire—

His eyes widened. Small geysers, spitting, and nearly dead. Rocky hills.

He scrabbled over to his pack, retrieving his map. Miantiao, who had been instructing one of the less ornery bears on how to properly fire pottery, turned to the sudden movement.

To Bi De's surprise, the bear looked receptive to what the snake was saying.

Bi De, with a shaking talon, drew out his hypothesis on the true scale of the formation.

The rooster swallowed thickly.

'Good morning, Bi De, how wasss your resst?' the snake asked with a smile, even as Yin stirred.

Bi De did not answer. The snake slithered around to glance at what Bi De had done.

Miantiao's eye widened.

'Wha—what issss thissss?' Miantiao asked, his sibilant sounds drawn out in shock.

'What's what? What's going on?' Yin asked, staring in confusion.

Bi De stared. Miantiao's tail reached out, tracing the formation as well as Bi De's notes.

The snake's tail shakily traced around the forest in a rough circle. Then it went from the forest to the north and its ring of stones. From there, to the southeast . . . the perfect circle of Pale Moon Lake.

Three points. Two more hypotheses in the mining towns of the northeast, and the Grass Sea to the southwest.

A pentagram. An enormous pentagram that encompassed the entire Azure Hills.

And yet it was *wrong.* In the north, they performed the dance of fire, yet the geography was that of stone. Here was the dance of wood, yet in the dream it had been burned to ashes.

And, in following the traditional cycle of elements, where Pale Moon Lake stood should have been metal, yet instead it was a massive lake.

Fire to Stone. Stone to Metal. Metal to Water. Water to Wood. Wood to Fire.

All five elements. An empty spot in the center.

Just what was this for?' Bi De asked, staring at the massive portions of land that had been converted.

He remembered the bear's feelings. Shock, surprise, this wasn't supposed to happen.

Bi De tapped the spot on the map, near Pale Moon Lake. He would do one last investigation, to see if that mark was even worth his Great Master's time.

CHAPTER 49

THE PLUM BLOSSOM'S SHADOW

I shall become a farmer, Senior Brother."

Those were the words Lu Ri had once more structured his search around. After his wonderful meal in Pale Moon Lake City, he had decided to continue to scour the Azure Hills until he found a lead. He had a *feeling* about this province. A hunch told him he was missing something, and so he would follow it. It could have been the heavens guiding him, for long he had toiled already. Once he was ready to resume his task, he delved deep into what was known as the Grass Sea. A grand name for three thousand li of rolling hills and grasslands.

It was in this area where most of the population of the Azure Hills lived. It was prime land for farming, and it had *some* amount of ambient Qi, which had given birth to the petty Sects that grew here. They were existences his eyes passed over without comment, for he alone would have been enough to vanquish every Sect in the province. They were like weeds clinging to the side of a desolate mountain—stunted in their growth and utterly unnoticeable in their power. He had heard a boastful tale of an Elder reaching the second stage of the Profound Realm, and how he was sure to make his Sect rise with such a feat.

Lu Ri kept his peace, and his Qi suppressed.

While he was scouring the Grass Sea himself, he'd also deployed the Cloudy Sword Sect's resources. He went to find every information broker and master of shadows this province had to offer. He was prepared for this venture to be hellishly expensive—the prices of information brokers in Raging Waterfall Gorge were not cheap.

In this case, however, it was certainly no drain on his resources. But one *did* get what they paid for.

There were no *normal* organisations like the Twelve Shadow Moons here. The secret, information-brokering organisations that kept their hands on the pulse of the world. Even those had left this place behind.

Thus, Lu Ri had had to hire a multitude of more independent groups to aid him in his task of finding a single cultivator, a man named Jin Rou.

There were a few hiccups. He had gotten three reports of *himself*, specifically mentioning the incident that had shattered the Heavenly Ascension Stone pendants.

But Lu Ri had learned the teachings of the Founders well, and he was himself a man used to organising disciples into more coherent forces.

One swift reorganisation later and they were functioning quite a bit better, without any trace of the Cloudy Sword Sect's involvement. Indeed, these men argued quite a bit less, and only a few had dared to even raise objections as he dismantled their inefficient framework. He had implemented many of the Honoured Founders' speeches and suggestions in the process, and the words once more proved their worth.

He quite enjoyed himself. To take such worthless systems and re-create them as the Founders had described a properly functioning organisation was quite a heady experience. He had named the organisation after the character of his family name, in honour of his ancestors. Lu. The Plum Blossom.

The other reports occasionally provided some false starts. There was a man with a hammer who looked roughly like the description given for Jin Rou, but it was later revealed that he was the Young Master of the Hermetic Iron Sect, a Sect of less than ten members up in the northeast. Lu Ri experienced a constant game of going back and forth. Venturing into the Grass Sea and returning to Grass Sea City—collecting his reports and then venturing out again.

Lu Ri was getting increasingly efficient at sorting through mortals and records.

When he returned again to his base of operations, his men were waiting with triumphant smiles.

Lu Ri raised an eyebrow as they bowed in unison, all sinking down to a knee.

"We have a report, Master Scribe," the man declared, using Lu Ri's assumed title for this group. "This one is *truly* unusual."

Lu Ri gestured at him to continue.

"I was lucky to receive this. A merchant from the Howling Fang Mountains recently visited the Misty Lake Sect, with a delivery of Mist Blossoms. Extremely expensive. He was deep in his cups and gossiping like a hen when he let slip something that was merely idle conversation. He mentioned there was a rumour that one of the Young Masters of the Shrouded Mountain had been confined to the mountain for some reason or another. Useless information . . . if not for something else."

At this, he gestured to one of his comrades, who bowed as well. "Last year, one of my men from our previous organisation intercepted a transmission. Priority from a village in the north. Someone had been attempting to impersonate members of the Shrouded Mountain Sect, but they were defeated. Specifically, they were impersonating a Young Master of the Shrouded Mountain Sect."

Lu Ri's eyes widened as the pieces came together. The Shrouded Mountain was beyond anything in the Azure Hills. They had some accolades to their name, though these were minor in comparison to the Cloudy Sword's.

Could . . . could this be it? A Young Master of the Shrouded Mountain Sect would have been able to crush even Elders of the Azure Hills like a mortal crushes an insect. For a Young Master to be defeated so utterly? Now that just didn't happen . . . if the practitioner was from these weak hills, of course.

"Do you have a name for the town?" he asked.

"Verdant Hill, Master Scribe. It will take us a month or two to get everything set up there and confirm things."

Slowly, a smile spread across Lu Ri's face. Could this be what he was looking for?

He thought immediately of heading to Verdant Hill himself, yet stayed his first reaction. The two pieces of evidence were quite interesting on their own, but they were no guarantee.

It was a conundrum. Should he continue his search here? Should he travel up to Verdant Hill immediately? Or should he confirm the rumour in the Howling Fang Mountains?

Lu Ri pondered for a moment, then made his decision.

"Send your best to Verdant Hill. I will head to the Howling Fang Mountains," he decided, and turned back to his men. "I shall give to you a powerful transmission stone for this search. Contact me when all is ready."

"Yes, Master Scribe!" every one of his men shouted.

Lu Ri nodded. "Your Master thanks you for your diligence," he declared. "It shall be rewarded." He brought from his sleeves their payment, and the men's eyes widened.

"We live to serve our Master Scribe!" the men shouted, once more lowering their heads. "Glory to the Plum Blossom's Shadow!"

It is time to scour the mountains, Lu Ri thought. The rest of his organisation would be tasked to continue his work here.

His men left, swiftly going about their assignments. Once they'd departed, Lu Ri frowned at his still-dark transmission stone, given to him by Elder Ge.

He hoped his Elder was having more luck than he. Though his superior did not need luck. He had skill.

↔

Xiao Ge hoped Lu Ri was having luck in his search. Or more luck than he, at least.

For he was sitting in front of one of the few men in this world that he was certain he could not defeat. Shen Yu was sitting crosslegged, his Qi churning like a maelstrom. His fury was a palpable thing, and a far cry from the look of joy he had worn *before* he heard the news that the man he had entrusted to the Cloudy Sword Sect had been nearly killed and had to flee the Sect. Shen Yu had thought his brother would be joining him on campaign, not delivering this manner of message.

Brother Shen Yu's face was carved from stone. He did not scream. He did not rage. His fury was the silent kind. Cold and intense.

"Were our bonds any less deep, Ge, I would be trying to kill you right now. Be grateful our brotherhood extends this far." His voice was deceptively calm.

"Indeed," Ge stated. "What has been done is unforgivable. For a child entrusted to us by our Brother to be treated in such a way through our own negligence is grounds for our blades to cross."

"And that is the second reason. Brother Ge, ever ready to take responsibility." The two men stared at each other. The air was thick with the scent of death, the corpses of the demons already beginning to foul under the heat of the sun.

"What happened to the Cloudy Sword?" Shen Yu sighed. "What happened to the Young Masters who raised the peasant boys, simply because they had talent?"

A long time ago, Young Master Xiao Ge had befriended a peasant named Shen Yu, and they had become sworn brothers.

The disappointment and wistfulness he experienced now hurt more than any anger ever could.

"The one who initiated the conflict awaits whatever judgement you shall declare. His father bows his head in acceptance, and our Brother Ran has returned to make sure that head stays bowed."

Shen Yu turned his gaze to the heavens and closed his eyes. "As much as my heart screams for vengeance, I will content myself with this offering, as it is made in good faith and with humility. I have no wish to cross blades with you in anger."

Ge bowed his head. "Nor do I, Brother."

"Am I ever to be without a legacy?" Shen Yu finally asked, the cold expression finally dropping, leaving behind a man who looked drained.

Ge frowned. "We have a man searching day and night. We will find him, Brother. Broken things may yet be reforged stronger than ever."

Shen Yu considered his words. "Yes . . . Yes. He shall be found. He will rise above this—I know little Rou's fire well."

The man's eyes opened, and his Qi flared.

"Brother. I tire of this distraction. I tire of Tou Le's careful strategies. I tire of *that bastard* eating up my time. The time for restraint is *over*."

The air became solid. Shen Yu's intent flooded the mountain, and every demonic corpse screamed, withering and disintegrating. His power grew, like a gathering storm.

"Restraint? Rationing of power? What is losing a mere ten years of cultivation?" he asked, his eyes shining like miniature stars. "I shall cut short this blasted search and find my boy."

Elder Ge smiled and rose, releasing his own intent. His hands clasped in front of him. The clouds descended from the heavens, a thousand ravening black maws.

"Spear or shield, the Black Clouds of the Silent Sky will smite all who dare impede your path."

CHAPTER 50

THE CHOICES WE MAKE

Gou Ren frowned at his reflection in the burnished disk as the blade carefully scraped along his cheeks. It was an annoying morning ritual. People had asked why he hadn't just shaved his sideburns down before, and this was the reason. Overnight they would just grow up and puff out again, reverting him to his previous look. Shave them off completely? They'd be back completely in two days. Now he had to fix them every morning, and it was annoying. In Hong Yaowu there weren't actually that many reflective surfaces, so getting the sideburns accurate used to be a pain and a half.

And it was a bit embarrassing to ask your brother or your mother every morning to help straighten things out.

So several years ago, he had just stopped. He didn't exactly *mind* the look. He was himself. Sure, he got the comments, but over the years they had stopped hurting and had just turned into the joke they were. Like Meiling being bony, or his brother being a fox.

He rubbed at his cheeks as he finished. At least he was a lot more accurate now. He couldn't make the squaring quite as exact as Xiulan could, but it was still good enough. He looked *sharp*, as Jin had called him.

His attention was drawn by Pi Pa as she entered his room and dropped off a stack of laundry.

"Thank you, Pi Pa." The pig nodded, and a whisper reached his ears. Still quiet, but it was getting a bit more clear with each day.

Any time, Young Sir,' she said with a smile, before bustling out and going to grab the rest of the laundry. She had recently taken it on herself to do everybody's laundry, along with Chun Ke. Though for the boar it was probably more about playing with the suds than cleaning the clothing.

He shook his head and padded across his new floor. He smirked as he collapsed onto his new bed. A house in a day. It might not have been as grand as Jin's, and he might only use it for the rest of this year, but his friend had been happy to lend a hand and turn the shack into something better.

He smiled at *his* possessions, *his* table, and *his* nice clothes. Meimei had truly outdone herself with this set. It looked a bit like what Jin wore, really. It was the same colours, almost like a uniform.

He liked it. With a sigh of contentment, he finished getting dressed, then walked outside into the predawn light.

He'd go and teach everybody back home how Jin farmed like he said . . . but he really hoped Jin would need more help.

He liked working here. Building the farm. He wasn't exactly sure if he liked the idea of setting off on his own, just yet. Of starting up his own thing. He had direction, he was learning, and he didn't think a mere year would cut it.

He meandered over to the main house, yawning and scratching at his chest. His steps took him past the half-finished prototypes of the tilling machine. It was coming along, and Yao Che had delivered, but the carriage needed to be redesigned.

"Mornin'," he greeted those inside as he entered the house.

A chorus of greetings sounded out. Ri Zu and Wa Shi just gave him a nod, while Chun Ke's happy and loud *'GOOD MORNING!'* boomed.

Gou Ren scratched the boar's head affectionately, then sniffed the air as he sat down at the table.

"Mushroom soup?" he asked, curious.

Jin nodded from where he was braiding Tigu's hair. He looked quite at ease. Tigu was in the middle of looking at a slate with a few questions on it, pondering them intently.

"We had a good haul yesterday," Meiling stated with a smile. "They're bigger than any I've ever seen."

Gou Ren nodded. Another bonus of living here: foraging was simple. Everything seemed to hide an edible mushroom or berry. Jin was even making jams with the surplus.

And where the food was, animals were too. It was practically unfair. He could just walk out and bag a catch with little issue. He hadn't really been challenged by any quarry in a while . . . and the more he thought about it the more he was just fine with that. Sometimes he'd purposefully prolong things simply to wander. That let him check on the rest of the property and fill his mind with images of what it would look like in a few years.

He was pulled from his introspection as Xiulan *floated* out, standing on the flats of her blades, and sweating. It was slower than her walking pace, and she didn't look very steady, but there was a gleam of triumph in her eyes.

The food was passed out, setting itself down of its own accord after being delivered on flying knives. Only once the last pot had landed did Xiulan thump to the floor, barely catching herself from tripping over.

"You managed the entire time. Each day is a little bit forwards, eh?" Jin asked, checking the floor briefly where the pot landed. Gou Ren guessed he was looking for any scuffs on the floor, but there were none.

"Yes," she said in between pants, staring at her swords with pride.

They began their meal.

"Thanks, Xiulan, this is great!" Gou Ren complimented her after his first bite.

Xiulan smiled at him. The sight *still* made his heart skip a beat.

It still stung a bit, the rejection, but he had been resolved that he would accept it, hadn't he?

He shook off the feeling, glancing away so he could finish his food.

$\rightarrow$

"Ya *sure* it's this way?" Jin asked, staring at the diagram like it was some kind of arcane formation.

"Pretty sure . . ." Gou Ren said, looking over Jin's shoulder and then back to the contraption. "This connects to *here*, so that when you pull *this* it activates it."

Jin glanced down at the diagram one more time, then back up at the assembly of gears. He nodded.

"Well, here's hoping for no spontaneous disassembly like the last time," he muttered. Gou Ren winced. He didn't even know *why* the damn thing had decided to fall apart.

Still, he was confident in this one. They had triple-checked everything, making sure it was going to go fine!

The gears slid together with a *thunk* and the assembly engaged. The grindstone began to spin as the river dragged the paddle around.

Jin looked over the whole thing, at first with worry—and then, increasingly, with a smile as everything kept spinning.

He reached into a sack and carefully poured some grain into the millstone. His grin got wider as the flour began to spill into the collection bucket.

"Hell yeah, Brother!" he shouted, and swung an arm around Gou Ren's shoulder. It was always nice to feel appreciated.

Pride welled in his chest at the sight of the spinning wheels. At the grinding stone. At the smell of the flour.

"It's beautiful, isn't it?" Jin asked while the wheels continued to turn.

"Yeah," Gou Ren said, watching the gears spin and looking around at their work. Especially at the other side of the room, where Jin's other project was. "But why did we do this part?"

Jin pointed. "Well, if we disengage *this* part and restructure it here, you could lift and drop a hammer with it. Kind of useless for us, but for anybody without Qi? Well, have the water hammer your stuff for you, eh?"

Gou Ren thought about it. Using it for mills was one thing, but yes, being able to have the river drop your hammer for you was another. He had done some smithing before, and all it had left him with was sore shoulders and a respect for Yao Che.

"So that's why it's two separate rooms?" he asked, walking through the door built into the thick wall and into the part of the building that was stone.

"Yup. Dunno how much it'll be used, but interesting to test out, yeah?" Jin asked.

A year ago, Gou Ren might have said "wasteful." Now, he just nodded. It *was* pretty interesting. Jin knew lots of strange things and always seemed to have an answer for how the world worked whenever Gou Ren asked—or at least he had approximate knowledge. Jin oftentimes just bluntly said he had no idea how a lot of things worked, though that just made the things he could explain even more credible.

"Now come on, let's go brag," he said with a grin. Gou Ren laughed at his enthusiasm but felt just as eager to show off. Even if Xiulan didn't think it was interesting, Chun Ke and Pi Pa would probably be intrigued.

They set off, Jin's arm still around his shoulder as he praised Gou Ren's craftsmanship in putting most of it together.

"Behold! Us manly men crafting the tools of civilization!" Jin shouted. Xiulan and Tigu paused in their spar, while Meimei perked up.

"You got it working?" she asked, and Jin nodded.

"Yes we did!" he said enthusiastically, and thumped Gou Ren on the shoulder again.

She smirked, and hugged first Jin and then Gou Ren. "Our *manly men.*" There was a hint of humour in her voice, though it was mixed with pride.

Gou Ren stuck his tongue out at her, and she responded in kind.

"We'll have a feast tomorrow. I need to prepare some things first and it's a bit too late to get started now. But it is a good stopping point." She turned back to the combatants on the poles. "Tigu, we need to continue—no, do not pout, you're doing well. You didn't answer 'kill them' or 'maim them' even once on that last set of questions!"

Tigu grumbled but hopped off the pole.

Jin chuckled at the scene. "I'll give her some moral support. You go relax. We don't have anything else to do today," he said, and went with Meimei to talk with Tigu.

Leaving Gou Ren with Xiulan.

He shrugged and sat down, putting his feet in the cool water just as Xiulan hopped off the training pole.

"Junior Brother!" she declared. "I have devised another avenue for you to pursue!"

Well, the last one had worked out.

→

"I wake to find the sun up high,
　Birds chirp everywhere in the sky.
　Last night a rainstorm passed by.
　Flowers must have fallen down."

Gou Ren frowned at the page as he finished speaking.

"Does this even work?" he asked. "Do women really like poetry?"

"It is to show that you are cultured," she stated. Gou Ren looked down at his bare chest, then back up at Xiulan.

She nodded. "You give an air of wildness, yet are not. There is great depth beneath the surface."

Gou Ren frowned. That did make sense, he supposed. "Do *you* like poetry?" he asked idly.

"I do enjoy reading the works of Masters," she stated. "Searching for meaning and finding it is quite enjoyable. Comprehending the full meaning of a poem is somewhat similar to comprehending a cultivation method."

Just like most things with Xiulan, it came back to cultivation.

He didn't particularly enjoy poetry, but he could try.

He read onwards but glanced up when a door opened and Tigu staggered out. She looked tired, but she wandered over to them.

"What are you doing here?" Tigu asked as she leaned over Gou Ren's back without a care in the world.

It was easier than he'd thought it would be, to not see the cat he used to give belly rubs to in his mind's eye when Tigu did things like this. It helped that she looked so different, but she was still rather touchy.

Enough to make him blush some times, *especially* when her shirt was open.

She was cute. Even with all the muscle. Her abs were as defined as his!

"I am aiding our Junior Brother with finding a woman," Xiulan stated with a remarkable lack of tact.

Tigu cocked her head to the side, her brow furrowing. "A woman?" she asked.

"Like Master Jin and Senior Sister," Xiulan explained. Tigu nodded in understanding.

"A monumental task," she declared—and Gou Ren felt like somebody had just punched him in the chest.

He slumped. *She said it with such conviction, like it was self evident—!*

"What woman is good enough for our Brother Disciple?" she asked, turning to Xiulan. "She would need to be of uncommon stock, a truly exemplary specimen in order to be worth his time!"

Eh? he thought as he raised his head. Tigu was nodding to herself.

"I see why you need help, Disciple. It will be a grand search! Few women are worthy of those who are disciples of Fa Ram!" Tigu was starting to get worked up, and her eyes gleamed.

"And you asked the Blade of Grass for aid? Hmph! Worry not, Disciple Gou Ren, this Young Mistress will also lend you her strength! With my help, which is superior to the Blade of Grass's help, we shall find you a woman!" She smiled brilliantly at him.

Gou Ren felt a slight sinking sensation.

Xiulan's lips were twitching with amusement.

"Why don't *you* marry me, then," he muttered sarcastically.

The orange-haired girl paused and smiled brightly, bouncing up and planting her hands on her hips.

"I see! I just learned about this in my decorum lessons! I am to inform our Master of any who ask to marry me! Worry not, my fellow disciple! This Young Mistress shall carry your intentions to our Master and Mistress!"

Gou Ren paled as Tigu dashed off, almost skipping. Xiulan clapped a hand over her mouth. A moment later, her shoulders started to shake.

Her laughter sounded very nice and was just enough to make Gou Ren realise what was happening. He leapt to his feet, only to be caught for just an instant as Xiulan reached out with a single hand, grabbing his leg and letting Tigu get farther away.

His heart leapt to his throat, and he stared at the woman who had captured him. She was completely doubled over facing the water and laughing.

She wanted a Junior Brother? Well, she was certainly about to get the *brother* part.

His legs moved with speed when he twisted and kicked. Xiulan's eyes widened with surprise as a rather vicious blow, learned and refined from a thousand brawls with his older brother, planted itself into her back.

Xiulan skipped across the river.

"Wait—*wait*, Tigu. *Tigu!*" he yelped, racing after the girl, but it was to no avail. He had been delayed for just long enough. Just long enough for the married couple to be sporting shit-eating grins as he entered the room, frantic.

"So . . . what are your intentions for my Tigu'er?" Jin asked, stroking a nonexistent beard like he was some sort of sage.

□

I chuckled as Gou Ren kept frowning at his plate.

Meimei was similarly amused. She had been ribbing him all night. I poked her in the side as she opened her mouth again, cutting off whatever gleeful comment had been coming. She pouted at me for ruining her fun but stopped bugging him about it.

Honestly, once Tigu was a bit . . . well, more aware of that kind of thing, and maybe a bit older, I certainly wouldn't be opposed if that was what both of them wanted. Not that it was really my business anyway.

Meiling had taught her that one, and for now, well, it seemed like it might be a good idea? Just in case.

But if she asked about a boyfriend or something, and did seek my approval, whether they were a guy, girl, cat . . . What she wanted was what she wanted.

Gou Ren glanced at Xiulan and cleared his throat.

"Hey, Jin, you know, after the harvest—how Xiulan has that tournament?" he asked.

I nodded. The cultivator place she had been talking about. I had no real desire to go anywhere near the Dueling Peaks. Well, maybe if I could find something interesting like a farmer's market or something I'd go, but eh.

"Uhhhh . . . can I go?" he asked. "I want to see what kind of stalls there are, and check things out."

He hardly needed to ask me. It wasn't like he was going to fight in the tournament—

"Yes! I as well, Master!" Tigu shouted, her eyes gleaming. "I wish to go to this tournament!"

That one made me pause. Mostly because at that moment she had her fists clenched and the look on her face like whenever she went to spar with Xiulan.

I worked my jaw and glanced at Meiling.

She was frowning.

One part of me nearly said no before I could even really think about it— that it was too dangerous to be around so many cultivators. Memories of pain, and flashes of agony, rage, hate—I didn't want Tigu involved in that.

But . . . was that the correct choice?

During that talk under the moonlight last winter I had said that they all had their own choices to make. Was that the same as this? *What should I do about it?*

Big D was already out there, fighting Spirit Beasts and saving towns. He was travelling the world, doing what he felt he needed to do.

Was it really so different? Tigu had mellowed out a lot in just a few weeks; she was still excitable and eager to do things, but not quite as *intense.*

Shit. Would she actually stay if I said no? *Or was she going to just sneak away, or act out?* She was pretty obedient, but I hadn't really tested those boundaries yet.

I didn't *want* to go. I didn't want to see the tournament or the fighting. Sure, I watched Tigu and Xiulan fight sometimes. They were both really good from what I could tell, but they were effectively play-fighting.

Nobody at that tournament would be playing around.

Protectiveness warred against my own issues. I had stuff to do here, and with Meimei pregnant I probably couldn't go—I certainly wasn't taking her along to a place like *that*.

I chewed on my lip.

A hand landed on my arm, startling me out of my thoughts. Meiling squeezed, and I glanced over. Her eyes were calm.

My decision, huh?

Some of Tigu's eagerness had faded. She was nervous, shifting in her seat.

Fuck. She needed an answer.

"There will be a test in Verdant Hill, to see if you are ready," I finally decided. Tigu's eyes brightened and she cheered aloud.

I finished my meal, then left the room as Tigu began talking about going on a journey.

I leaned against the wall outside and ran a hand through my hair.

"Was that the right decision?" I asked, as Meimei padded up beside me. Her hands wrapped around my waist.

"I don't know," she said simply.

CHAPTER 51

THAT ACTUALLY WORKED?

Xi Bohai, of the Plum Blossom's Shadow, approached the town as he had been requested. Verdant Hill—if his maps were correct. They got a bit . . . suspect the farther one went into the north. He was tired and sweaty from his long, hard ride, yet he had stayed the course. Trading horses every town when the beasts had started to exhaust themselves was a novel experience. For the first time, he had the coin to do so. It certainly shortened travel times.

A rather strange mission, to be sent this far north, but Master Scribe's mission took priority.

He knew not what reason Master Scribe had for wanting to find "Jin Rou," but for him to take a hundred clans and restructure them into something more? Into the Plum Blossom's Shadow? It had to be of vast and grave importance.

Every man who had been there upon the Plum Blossom's Advent, as they were calling it, had seen the look in Master Scribe's eyes. There had been a feeling of weight and purpose driving his every action.

Was he some manner of prince? A great general? None knew for certain, but he had to be someone of importance. And someone of importance, someone far beyond the normal movers and shakers of the Azure Hills, had *chosen* them.

Master Scribe had come to them and given them a vision of what they could be—of what they were *going* to be.

The thoughts of power, of prestige, and of something more than their base existence had infected them all. Clans that had been enemies for a thousand years had pledged both their loyalty and their men to the cause.

A single, unified power bloc. A rising star, guided by the masterful hand of Master Scribe.

It was a heady feeling to be a part of something so grand.

His back was straight and tall as he ventured into the town. The guards here were quite alert, checking his merchant's license.

He was let in swiftly, as his papers were all in order. He thanked the guards and then was on his way. The town itself was small and quaint on top of its hill, but surprisingly clean and well patrolled. Almost *suspiciously* well patrolled. The guards were by far the most vigorous and alert he had encountered since leaving the southern end of the province.

He frowned slightly at them but did not believe they would be a problem. It wasn't like he was smuggling anything this time.

It was getting dark out, so he went first to the tavern to stow his belongings and get his horse some feed and water.

It was a lively place. There were already men drinking and talking, and though he got a few curious looks, most people dismissed him as he entered.

He sat at a stool and ordered some food—a noodle dish with pork— and observed the room. Where to begin? The people were quite cheerful, and many looked to be a bit drunk. Perfect.

"Thank you," he said as he received his dish. "Lovely town, this Verdant Hill."

It was tiny compared to the towns in the south, but it was very clean from what he had seen so far.

The serving girl's chest puffed out with pride, her plump cheeks dimpling with her smile.

"Every merchant says that! It's all because of the Lord Magistrate, it is!" she declared, and there were murmurs of assent from those who had overheard.

Curious. It was the first time he had ever heard a Magistrate spoken of with such high regard.

"The Patriarch of Verdant Hill is a true man," the man beside him, who was quite intoxicated, said. "Everybody wishes they could have him as their Magistrate!"

Xi Bohai nodded appropriately.

"So what brings you to Verdant Hill, anyway?" the drunk man asked.

"Ah, I'm a bit of a wandering merchant, and I like to go where there are interesting rumours," he stated, smiling companionably. The standard backstory for a job like this. "I heard that the Azure Jade Trading Company sent a member here, so I decided to see what the fuss was about."

The drunk man nodded his head. "Yeah, I heard about them. Too expensive! Nobody could afford any of his wares, so he left!"

Bohai nodded at the information. "Ah, I had hoped to find whatever he had come for, but alas." He chuckled. He waved at the serving girl again, asking for a bottle of wine.

He paid, then poured both himself and his new "friend" a cup.

"Oh, cheers!" the drunk man shouted, smiling brightly.

"What else can you tell me about Verdant Hill? The prices, anything interesting . . . Or, I've heard tales of a cultivator around these parts," he whispered, as if he didn't even believe his own statement.

The man brightened at the last question. "Oh, yeah, there was a cultivator around here," the man said. Xi Bohan frowned at the *was* part, but this was good. This was something he could use—

The man abruptly stood and raised his cup high. "To Sister Medical Fairy!" he shouted. The tavern erupted into shouts of "Sister Medical Fairy!"

Sister *Medical Fairy? A woman? What? There wasn't anything about the cultivator being a* woman.

"Yeah, the Lord Magistrate hired her! What a man, the Patriarch of Verdant Hill! He can snap his fingers and summon a cultivator to fix our problems before they even start!" another man shouted.

"The Patriarch! The Patriarch!" the shouts sounded out.

"Let me tell you how Sister Medical Fairy saved the town!" the drunk man shouted.

Bohai listened to a tale of motes of green light that had instantly helped the sick, and a small woman with her face covered by cloth.

He would bring back the information, but . . . all of a sudden he was uncertain if this was the right town after all.

"Was this Sister Medical Fairy the same who defeated the Young Master of the Shrouded Mountain?" he asked quietly, once things had calmed down.

His conversational partner froze, his drunken mind churning.

"The *who*?" he asked, confused.

The serving girl pondered. "I think I heard that rumour. Some wandering cultivator beat the tar out of some imposter and handed him over to the guards. It could have been her. I don't see Sister Medical Fairy tolerating that kind of thing."

Bohai nodded along, pondering.

Wandering cultivator. Sister Medical Fairy. He would dig deeper tomorrow. Perhaps try the name Jin Rou?

$$\rightarrow$$

The next day proved fruitless.

Wandering cultivator. Fairy Sister. Both of these events had happened, but to the people, the accounts were muddied.

The only men who seemed to know anything were the guards, who all said the same thing: a wandering cultivator had deposited a rapist into their care, and the Shrouded Mountain had come and collected him.

They were also rather tight-lipped about his appearance, or didn't know—Bohai got the feeling he might have pushed too hard.

Looking up from his seat in the town square, he sighed. He had nothing. Nothing but a gust of wind whistling through the leaves. Some might have been able to track a man just from that, but he couldn't. He had heard that cultivators could even divine people's locations from whispers in the wind, but alas, he was just a mortal.

He needed something—not just a *possibly* for his Master. Maybe Jin Rou had been here. Maybe he hadn't.

He grimaced as he heard the approaching sound of armoured feet. He glanced up at the sound and saw a contingent of guards with weapons sheathed. They had their eyes set firmly upon him.

Old instincts kicked in. His eyes searched around the square, finding other guards already in position at the exits.

Instead of running or reacting like a rank amateur, he sat still and projected a confident air. His eyes flicked to the lead guard, who was wearing a rather-new-looking sensor stone.

"Sir. If you could please come with me," the man asked him in a neutral tone of voice.

He idly considered attempting to make a break for it anyway, but . . . well, he still had one last weapon to play.

He nodded. "Of course, Captain. Lead on," he said disarmingly. The guard nodded, and the rest took up an escort formation.

There were no manacles. He was actually rather surprised that he wasn't even grabbed. The guards here were surprisingly polite.

He was taken to the jailhouse, where he was offered tea.

"Sir. We would like to request that you cease your line of questioning. The cultivator specifically asked that we keep our peace." The man was refreshingly blunt and honest. In any other case, Bohai would have been quite happy to leave it at that, as getting on a cultivator's bad side was the last thing he wished to do.

But . . . he had orders. His Master had commanded him to find Jin Rou. And so he unveiled his last weapon.

"I am here on official business," he said simply, now that he had some confirmation that the guards were in on the ruse. "May I speak with the Lord Magistrate on this matter?"

All other eyes in the room widened as the guards beheld the sheaf of papers with a seal.

A seal of the Palace of Pale Moon Lake.

It had been surprisingly easy to get. The harried man he had acquired it from had barely looked at the papers before he had signed them. Bohai had even had a whole act he had prepared that he hadn't gotten to use!

Always make sure to check the relevant documents and procedures, Master Scribe had told them.

Profound wisdom, which had let them find a great many holes in areas where there otherwise would be none.

Still, it was better to lay low instead of going around declaring he was on official business everywhere. Master Scribe had said to be discreet, but if Bohai was right, then perhaps the Magistrate would know something.

The guards glanced at each other again and swallowed.

→

The palace was like all the others Xi Bohan had been to, except smaller. Really, it was rather quaint, but the scribes here were hard at work, diligently going over reports. It was bustling, instead of sleepy, though he didn't get that much of a glance at what was happening.

He was led to a set of double doors, also guarded, and let in.

The man sitting behind the desk raised his head to meet him, spearing Bohai with his gaze. Bohai swallowed thickly. The man had a stately mask as his face, and his aura was commanding. In that instant, Bohai knew why this man was revered as Patriarch. His eyes reminded him a bit of Master Scribe.

"Han Yang?" the Magistrate asked, and Bohai nodded his head at the fake name on his license. "You wish to know about . . . the incident?" The

Magistrate's eyes flicked from Bohai's hands to his face, and they narrowed slightly.

"Yes," Bohai stated as authoritatively as he could. The Magistrate considered him for a moment . . . before relaying the exact same story the guards had given him.

Until the last part.

"He was rather strong for a mere imposter," the Magistrate said idly.

That was interesting, and could be confirmation that it had been a true member of the Shrouded Mountain.

"And the wandering cultivator?" he asked.

The Magistrate stared at him for a moment longer. "He left the day after he handed the man over."

Bohai sighed internally. Cultivators made *everything* more difficult.

"We are looking for a man. Tall, brown hair and eyes, with freckles," Bohai stated, his eyes narrowing as the Magistrate looked up, his face frozen.

There was tenseness in the air.

"His name is Jin Rou."

The mask cracked for a brief instant. Bohai saw *confusion* cross the Magistrate's face, before his mask settled once more.

"I do not know of a man by that name, save the butcher. And he has not left the city in forty years," the Magistrate stated, and Bohai got the sense the man was being completely honest.

He smiled at the Magistrate, bowed his head, and left.

He mulled over his findings in the tavern that night, thinking of what to write in his report. The Magistrate was telling the truth—there was no faking his reaction of confusion.

But should he go searching more? Check the villages?

They had said he was a *wandering* cultivator.

Bohai sighed. He could stay for a while and try to see if he could get any more information, but he knew the guards and the Magistrate both had their eyes on him.

He grimaced. He had something—but still no Jin Rou, save a butcher, who actually had looked startlingly like the description given for the man he was actually searching for.

He stayed one more day, but accomplished little else, since his cover was blown. People kept asking him what the guards had wanted him for, and there was no real larger population to slip into.

Bohai left the same way he had entered, frustrated, but with some confirmation that at least part of the rumour was true. And really, would a cultivator willingly stay around here?

His ears perked up as he heard a man shouting about a Spirit Beast that was to the southwest. That would be for somebody else to pursue, once the Plum Blossom's Shadow expanded to the north. It was inevitable that they would rise.

↔

The Lord Magistrate of Verdant Hill frowned from the top of his palace. Somebody was searching for Rou Jin—or was it Jin Rou? The name was switched, and the characters had been changed . . . which meant that the cultivator who lived nearby had something to hide.

The man asking all the questions, whoever he was, was most certainly not what his documents claimed, if the Lord Magistrate's gut was right, and it often was. The man's hands were a bit too rough, and not in the right ways for grinding ink or holding pens. The calluses were all wrong for the man to be what he claimed he was.

The Lord Magistrate had made his choice. Better the devil he knew.

His stomach churned as he stared out over his village. He would tell Rou Jin of what had happened.

Hopefully that would be the end of this, but he was not reassured. Cultivators *always* brought trouble.

CHAPTER 52

THE ROAD

Thanks, Pops," I said as I took the waterskin from him. Hong Xian smiled and nodded at me as I gulped down several mouthfuls of the nice and cool drink. I leaned on my shovel and looked back at our work.

"Comin' along good, isn't it?" I asked my father-in-law.

"Coming along good?" he snorted. "It's coming along a bit better than good," he declared, looking at the road as well as the work gang that was with us. What had started as a few people coming to bring us water and food had swiftly turned into what seemed to be the entirety of Hong Yaowu helping us out. Sure, the cultivators were doing the lion's share of the work, but the villagers were helping out more than I'd thought they would. Even just combing the hills for more rock was useful, because this thing was eating stone like no tomorrow.

Still, we were nearly to Verdant Hill already. We had managed to shorten the road a bit, instead of just following the old one—straightened out some corners, and in one case, got a bridge up, with Pops's help. That one had been a bit frustrating, but it had worked out in the end, cutting nearly three hours off the journey.

"Yeah. It's coming along better than good," I agreed, as somebody told a joke and laughter echoed out.

Miserable, backbreaking labour had turned into something with the air of a summer camp. Cookouts at night, singing and laughter during the day.

And, well, not all of the warm fuzzies I was feeling were from the joy of people coming together. Having people calling me "boss" or looking to me for guidance and following what I asked them to do was kind of nice.

Being a part of a community—a big part, even—stroked the ego pretty nicely.

And it also distracted me a bit from my still-hesitant thoughts on the whole tournament situation. To be honest, it was stressing me out a bit. I was torn between the fact that I didn't want to go and get involved, and the feelings of obligation. *Maybe I should go anyway?*

I shook my head and took another swig of water.

"Haha! Good work, small one! I shall praise your efforts!" a voice sounded out, and I turned.

I snorted as I caught sight of Tigu gesticulating at a bunch of kids, who cheered. The flower-crown girl had her chest puffed out with pride, a paving stone laid in front of her.

Apparently that stone had met Tigu's exacting standards. She was obviously excited and nervous—I had said she would have her test in Verdant Hill, but unknown to her, her test had already begun.

Combat? Nah. I knew she could fight. What I needed to know was if she could *people*.

She was doing pretty well, I guess, but these people were already predisposed to liking her. It's easy to interact with people when nobody is getting on your nerves and everybody is trying to please you.

The real test was . . . Well, it was a bit mean, but if she could keep her head through what I had planned, then she was as ready as she would ever be. And calmer than a lot of people I knew, honestly.

"The Lord Magistrate approaches!" The booming voice cut through my thoughts; we all paused in our work on the road.

A party approached, two guards and the Lord Magistrate trotting towards us. Honestly, I was a bit impressed, and a tiny bit jealous. He looked like some general out of a period drama, with his commanding features and ramrod posture, along with his flowing hair.

There was a reason why I kept mine short. It was pretty shaggy, so I looked like I was homeless the instant it passed my ears.

"Lord Magistrate!" I greeted him, smiling. His face was calm as always, as he looked at us.

"Rou Jin, I greet you." He nodded politely before turning to take in the road. We were just at the last bend before we came into view of Verdant Hill. "I see that your road is as grand as expected. You have put in more work than I imagined, to have built this in the months since you brought it up."

"Eh, about a week and a half for this," I stated simply, staring back down the road. We'd done it faster than most modern work crews. Those dudes always dragged their feet.

He coughed. "Yes, astounding work. And I see a face I am unfamiliar with," he prompted, staring at Tigu. The girl was watching the proceedings and listening to everybody shout greetings of their own.

She had heard his implied question, and so she approached. "This one's name is Tigu!" she declared, bowing and introducing herself properly.

The Lord Magistrate nodded imperiously, returning Tigu's gesture of respect. Her greeting complete, the girl went back to work, going over to the flower-crown girl to praise her efforts to split the stone again.

The Magistrate watched her go, looking at her a bit strangely.

"The . . . same name as your cat?"

I blinked in surprise. He had only heard Tigu's name once before, during the wedding, and he remembered? He had a good head for names.

I pondered for a brief moment on how to say this.

"Ah. She *is* the cat." I settled on being both blunt and honest. The man stared blankly at her for a second longer, his eyes flicking to her facial markings and then to her slightly-too-sharp incisors.

For a brief, brief moment, his eyes rose towards the heavens, and he took a small breath.

"In any case, feat of engineering aside, I do have something to speak to you of, in private." His eyes shifted to his guards, who were chatting away with the rest of the villagers.

I nodded, wondering what this was about. He waved to his captain, who nodded as we set off around the bend. There the Lord Magistrate slid off his horse.

"Three days ago, a man was in town, asking around for one Jin Rou— and not the butcher," he stated without preamble.

"He asked for Jin Rou?" I asked, a bit confused. Jin Rou? I hadn't really used that name since I'd gotten here. But who could be looking for me? I didn't really know anybody from any other provinces, and Gramps had disappeared after basically dumping me off at the Cloudy Sword Sect.

"They were enquiring with the guards about the nature of your . . . *altercation* with the cultivator last year, as well as searching for you by this name," the Lord Magistrate stated calmly. "He was not a cultivator, and his accent was that of the Grass Sea."

I frowned a bit. Fishing for info about the imposter, huh? Maybe they were looking for dirt on the Shrouded Mountain.

"You had asked to be labeled as a wandering cultivator, so that is all the man received, though he bore the mark of an Imperial Inspector," the Magistrate continued.

He had covered for me. I felt a smile cross my face. It would have been easy for him to just go, *I don't know Jin Rou, but I do know Rou Jin.*

Instead, he had helped me out when somebody had come snooping around to bother me. If the man wasn't a cultivator, I didn't think that was too worrisome. Most of the time those guys used their super secret spy assassin groups.

"Thank you," I said, and I meant it. This dude kept doing me solids. I would need to repay the favour. "But if they come back . . . well, I'll talk to them, okay?"

I mean, I didn't want them in my house, but I knew I would have to do something if these people kept coming around.

The Magistrate blinked, then nodded.

"Though this road will be a bit hard to hide," he mused.

"Not if all of them are like this," I said blandly. Babe *did* want to build roads. Or at least plough them.

The Magistrate considered the offer with that kind of stern expression he always had.

Hopefully this will pay him back a bit, huh?

We started walking back to the road. *We should be finished tonight, if we put on a bit of a hustle.*

But really, why was somebody using that name? What had I done that would warrant somebody coming to look for me? It's not like I'm anybody important.

Shrugging, I got back to work. Maybe I'd do my own investigation. Put my name out somewhere a bit away, and see if anybody came to bite the bait?

↔

The seat was too comfortable.

Lu Ri shifted slightly as he sank into the cushion of the waiting room. The irritation he had felt in the Azure Hills was *nothing* compared to the irritation he felt now. He would rather be back in the Qi-deprived Azure Hills than have to sit here for another hour.

He stared around at his surroundings and barely kept his lip from rising at the sheer opulence. Shrouded Mountain was a monument to vanity and excess. So full of distractions from cultivation, and earthly pleasures to indulge in.

The Cloudy Sword Sect was stark in its beauty. Its chill focused the mind. Its place above the clouds allowed one introspection. The ancient stone of the Sect was steeped with the weight of ages. The accommodations that the disciples lived in were normally simple, but comfortable.

This place had even the lowest disciple in silk. It had consumed entire forests, had emptied entire gold mines, and spent spirit stones like water on *appearances*.

They proclaimed their strength to the world in gold and silver, in scented water and fine oils, instead of the only currencies that mattered: action and honour.

There was even a brothel, not even a li away from the mountain, that had many disciples within it.

This surpassed comfort. This was *decadence*.

At least the rumour had been confirmed. The Young Master, Zang Li, had been confined to the mountain after some incident in the Azure Hills.

The rumour mill was in full swing as to what had happened. He was not a very popular one, this Zang Li. He went around suppressing all who dared to look at him, and those disciples who had felt his wrath were all too eager to spread their woes onto a stranger.

So Lu Ri sought to arrange a meeting with the boy, wanting to ask him some questions.

Only to find out there were barely any procedures to follow to request a meeting with a member of the Sect, other than essentially standing outside the mountain and shouting a challenge—the Shrouded Mountain did not allow visitors outside tournaments.

This place had no Senior Disciples either, their seniority structure far removed from the efficiency of the Cloudy Sword Sect, so he could not ask one of his peers.

He had eventually found someone who managed these things, and he was brought to the waiting room.

Which was where he had been for the past two hours.

At least the tea was good.

He took another sip just as the harried clerk bustled back in, sweating slightly.

"I'm terribly sorry, sir, but the Young Master left a week ago, commanded to reinforce the Northern Fangs, as part of an expedition. He should be back before the end of summer."

Lu Ri took another sip to hide his eye twitching.

He was heading north that night.

CHAPTER 53

THE KARENS AND KEVINS
OF VERDANT HILL

Again! Again, Big Sister Tigu!" Mistress's brother shouted, eagerly bouncing in front of her. She raised an eyebrow at the small boy. Tigu grabbed the child underneath his armpits and threw him.

The boy whooped as he sailed through the air before landing with a splash in the river while other children cheered at the height. He paddled out to the massive form of Chun Ke, sitting like an island in the water.

It was a curious technique, to grow larger when he pleased. The children didn't seem to notice that he was bigger than he should be as they slid off his back into the water, nor did they notice when birds began to land on his mane and tusks, cocking their heads curiously at the beast in their home. Even the fish swam around his belly and hid in the shade his bulk cast.

Her Master and her uncle, as her Mistress's father said he should be called, had placed her in charge of herding the little ones like she protected the sheep and the calves. Though both of *those* were less troublesome by far. They were far less prone to wandering off when they thought they were safe and having to be caught when they slipped on the rocks they were climbing.

Still, for all their annoyances, they were much more tolerable when they weren't petting her fur in the wrong direction.

Something settled around her head, and the scent of flowers reached her nose. This one, Liu, was even tolerable. She liked carving and was rather good at it, though she only made carvings of flowers and vines, silent as she focused with the Qi-reinforced chisel Tigu had given her.

Her Master had been quite pleased with the paving stones that had the designs on them.

She nodded at little Liu and sat down to watch the children. The only one who wasn't enjoying herself was this "Ty An" character, who was scowling and grumbling about babysitter duty. Tigu dismissed her, reaching down again to hurl another one of the little ones into the river.

"Oi, muscles, they'll keep bugging you to do that as long as you let them," the girl grunted.

Tigu cocked her head to the side to look at the girl. They appeared to be about the same age, though the other girl was slightly taller and was stick-thin. She shrugged.

"I do not mind, freckles," Tigu returned, complimenting her as she had been complimented. Calling one by a defining and beautiful feature was polite, after all. If there was one thing Tigu wished for, beside the ears of her other form, it was freckles. Her skin tone was the correct, pleasing tan of her Master, but the freckles would have completed it. The other girl only scowled harder.

"Doing that makes your muscles too big. I'm trying to help you, you know. You'd be prettier without them."

Tigu turned, frowning at the other girl.

"Eh? But these are the epitome of beauty and function!" she fired back. *Ty An was a strange girl, with strange tastes. But she could be corrected easily!*

Tigu's Qi claws lashed out at a nice-sized rock. Ri Zu and Mistress said that examples could be used to change somebody's mind. The sculpture took form swiftly. Not her best work, but good enough for this.

She pulled open her own shirt and began to lecture. "See! Look here, these follow the line of my Master's stomach!" she declared, pointing to the carving. Smaller, yes, but they still looked good on her frame!

The other girl appropriately gaped, her face red, and her eyes fixed upon her Master's sublime form.

It did inspire awe, didn't it?

"Uh . . . um . . . what about . . . Gou Ren?" the girl asked.

Tigu nodded. He was getting quite a good body too. A midway point between herself and Master. A fine form! She quickly crafted a replica of her fellow disciple.

The girl swallowed thickly as she beheld the statue.

"You're pretty good, Tigu. You . . . uh, can you teach me how to do that?" she asked, kicking at the ground.

Tigu's chest puffed out.

Another wished to learn from the Great Tigu of Fa Ram? She would oblige!

The sun was setting as one of the villagers wandered to the river.

"It's time for food, everybody! And we've got rooms in the inn tonight!" the villager shouted to everyone. The children cheered and piled out of the water.

Tigu got up and stretched, preparing to follow.

"You're just gonna leave these here?" Ty An asked, cocking her head to the side.

"I shall allow others to appreciate this beauty!" she said simply, gesturing at the statues. Ty An smirked but said nothing else.

→

The food was good. The parents thanked her for doing her duty, and Tigu accepted their gratitude. As her Master said, thanks meant that they valued what she did for them. And it was not like it had been hard.

After their meal, they entered Verdant Hill.

Tigu's eyes flicked around the town as they walked through it. It was her first time returning to this place since her birth, so while some of the smells were vaguely familiar to her, the rest of it was hazy. Her most vivid memory was of the soft hands of her Mistress, and the low murmur of voices—feeling comfortable and safe.

Her hand reached out and she snagged the back of a boy's shirt, hoisting him into the air. The little one about to wander off flushed as her eyes narrowed at him.

He had tried to explore once today already. This time he was thrown over her shoulder like a sack of rice and returned to his parents.

Which left Tigu looking over the small camp with her Master.

"Good job today, Tigu'er," her Master complimented her, and she preened under the attention.

"You'll get your test like I promised, after I'm done finishing up the road and some paperwork, but tomorrow, could you pick up some things for me?"

Her Master handed her a list with a small map and names.

"Ask around and see what you can get from these places, okay? Just remember that if they don't have what I need, you can go somewhere else," he stated airily, his hand landing on her head.

Tigu's resolve hardened. She had been given a task! She had failed with the bee, but she would *not* fail here.

The next morning, bright and early, she set about her task.

And immediately ran into a stumbling block.

The place she had been instructed to go to was closed. The door was locked.

She frowned at the piece of paper and what she was to get: another set of sacks for storage. She debated going back to her Master to ask for another location . . . but he was busy. She could speak to one of his villagers, but they were working on the road.

And . . . her Master's servant owned this place, so surely the people who lived here might also know?

She approached one of the ones who didn't look busy.

Be polite, she reminded herself. Which for some reason according to her lessons didn't include introducing herself as "the Young Mistress of Fa Ram."

"Excuse me?" she asked the bored-looking man instead. "Do you know where I could get any of these?"

The man blinked languidly but walked over to get a better look at what Tigu was holding.

"Yeah, go three streets that way, it'll be on the left," he said after a moment. "You from out of town?" he asked.

Tigu nodded.

"Well, have a good day, then. And welcome to Verdant Hill!"

Tigu was pleasantly surprised. Thanking the man, she followed his directions, soon reaching the store. She purchased what she needed with the money her Master had given her.

Smiling, she proceeded to her next destination, full of optimism.

This is going to be easy!

→

"Oh, and then I said, 'Lan, you cad, I need to have this done by . . .'"

Tigu stared at the bag, debating whether to just grab it out of the woman's hands. The woman had been at this for nearly half an hour, gabbing away while Tigu waited.

The woman would *not stop speaking*. She paused in her work. Her hands gestured wildly.

Tigu waited another few moments before her irritation boiled over.

"Miss," Tigu said firmly. "I must complete the task my Master set for me."

The woman paused. She blinked.

"Oh, I'm sorry, dear, sometimes my mouth gets the best of me. Here we are!"

Tigu took the seeds she had been sent for and left.

→

"What?" the old man asked.

"I need a—"

"Speak up, I can't hear you!"

Tigu scowled.

"I NEED A BARREL!" she shouted. The windows rattled.

The man scratched at his ear.

"No need to be so loud, you'll make me more deaf!" he demanded. "Kids these days, no respect!"

The man grumbled away . . . but Tigu got her barrel.

→

"Nah, girlie, get your father. I don't deal with brats," the man said bluntly. Tigu felt her eye twitch, and her hand reflexively balled into a fist.

She took a deep breath even as her body screamed at her to teach this uppity fool a lesson.

But she could not. Master had been very clear on what was acceptable violence, and what was not.

He had not tried to strike her. Nor was he doing something that Master and Mistress had said were "intolerable acts." No matter how much she wished this to be one . . . he was merely being a terrible, annoying creature.

How could her Master stomach such things?

She did not know.

She wanted to beat them about the head and shoulders for their disrespect. Her patience was already frayed. This day had started off so well yet had gotten progressively more trying. The people were wearing on her nerves as they stalled, insulted, or were, heavens forgive them, *incompetent*.

"I have my Master's list here, Fatty," she snarled instead, shoving the thing at the round creature. "He shall receive what he wishes for."

"Your *Master* can get this himself, then," the man stated dismissively, then turned away.

Tigu's jaw dropped. Her Qi blades sparked at the tips of her fingers, and her entire body quivered with barely restrained violence as red clouded her vision.

Her teeth were bared, her entire body burning—

"Some people just aren't worth it," her Master had said, imparting his wisdom.

She turned and walked away.

Yes, he wasn't even worth correcting. He was not worth giving her Master's coin; his goods were worthless to Fa Ram! Why did they even need a shovel from here anyway? Yao Che's work was superior to this run-down place's!

Her teeth were clenched into a snarl as she stomped away. This task had taken most of the morning already, and she *still* wasn't done!

Was she going to fail again? Like with the bee?

She was so consumed with her own thoughts that she nearly ran into someone—

"Master?" she yelped. And with the Master was Ri Zu. *What? Wasn't she still at home with Wa Shi and Pi Pa?*

Her face flushed. He had seen her failure.

Tears sprang at the corner of her eyes. A hand landed on her head.

"You passed," he stated. The admission was made with pride but there was an undercurrent of resignation.

Tigu froze.

"Eh?" she asked, confused.

"I'm sorry for putting you through that. But you handled yourself well."

"I . . . I do not understand," she whispered.

"That list? I asked around. It was a list of the most annoying people in Verdant Hill. And that last guy was somebody *everybody* hates. The test . . . well, the test was never going to be about your combat ability. I know you can fight. It was about finding your way in an unfamiliar place, and dealing with unfamiliar people—very, *very* difficult people," her Master explained.

"The world is full of people like that. And worse. People you can't just haul off and hit—well, you *could* have hit him, but . . . I don't think that should be the *first* answer. You have the right to defend yourself and others. But for petty shit like this? It's not worth it."

Tigu pouted. It was slightly dissatisfying; it had not been a great victory like she hoped, but her Master looked proud of her.

"And what was Ri Zu doing?" Tigu asked.

'*Ri Zu was watching Tigu for Mistress and Master,*' the rat said apologetically.

Tigu's eyes narrowed.

"Would you have let me fail?" she asked.

'*Yes,*' Ri Zu responded.

"Good," the cat said. It was annoying—and a strange test, but if she had killed that man, it would have been worse. A strange feeling entered her gut. She shook her head to clear it. "Well, of *course* I passed the test!" she said instead. "I am ever capable!" she boasted, her chest puffed out.

Her Master smiled at her. "That you are. You did very well. Now, I have one last person for you to meet," he decided.

They were outside a shack. A goat stared at her blankly, and an old, familiar-smelling tomcat sat upon her back. He was missing a front paw, and his eyes were sharp. However, they softened on seeing her.

"Grandmother!" Master called, and an old woman with a single blind eye poked her head out of the door. She also smelled familiar.

"The hells you doing, always bothering me, boy?" she shouted.

Her Master laughed.

They were served hot water instead of tea, and the old cat came to sit on her lap. There was something about him . . .

She shook her head while she looked around the house. It was messy, and some parts were dirty . . .

But there was the carving she had made for the old woman, sitting in one of the few clean places, and obviously cared for.

Tigu smiled.

Her Master and the old woman were talking about something, but Tigu wasn't paying attention, just running her hand slowly over the old cat's back as he licked her hand.

"Quieter than I expected you to be," the woman finally addressed Tigu, squinting at her. "I know a certain old bastard who was *quite* the hellion at your age."

The cat on her lap snorted.

"Thanks for the carving, girl. Now, both of you get outta my house! You're not allowed in again today!" The woman grabbed a broom and shook it in mock anger.

Her Master chuckled and bid the old woman his goodbyes . . . But the old cat jumped on Tigu's shoulder.

Tigu found she didn't mind as she walked behind her Master on the way back to the inn.

She had a very nice night, sleeping with the familiar feeling beside her.

But the cat was gone in the morning.

The only thing left on her pillow was a single, carved cat, missing a paw.

It looked realistic and lifelike, but it was obvious the carver was out of practice or using a hand that was unfamiliar to them.

She carefully packed it up, and the two of them returned home. The smile didn't leave Tigu's face the entire time.

CHAPTER 54

TALE OF THE FOX

Nezin Han was excited. He was going to see his grandson for the first time in four years. Four years of ranging far and wide across the north, and taking the bounty at the edges of the Sea of Snow.

To think that his grandson wished to learn the ways of his ancestors, instead of just the Imperial stuff. He would teach the boy the traditions of the Nezin, how to herd the yaks, and perhaps to break and ride a fine horse!

The men often rotated through the southern villages, living mostly nomadic lives, but there were many men here today, and his grandson was the talk of their little village. Everybody wanted to see the "Imperial boy."

Nezin Han was ready for a relaxed summer of reconnecting with his kin and perhaps passing along some of his traditions.

He was just preparing a new tent when he heard the commotion.

Ah, that must be my grandson and nephew!

He strode out of the tent ready to greet them.

And froze.

"Yeah, yeah, laugh it up, you bastard. I *knew* you were doing it on purpose," his grandson declared, glaring at a thunder-hoof that towered over him.

His eyes found his nephew, the one who had volunteered to guide Yun Ren—and the man was wearing a slight smile on his face. It was *very* strained.

The thunder-hoof snorted.

"Yeah, I've got stuff to do up here too. Finally got sick of that patch of grass, and sneaking up on me?"

The thunder-hoof let out a strange sound, almost like a laugh.

"Well, good luck. Hope ya find what you're looking for, and never come back to bother me." He handed the thunder-hoof what looked like several strands of grass, which the giant beast took gently.

The Bringer of Fortune turned from his grandson and strode away, walking through the village proudly. Several heads were bowed in supplication, and Han himself barely remembered to lower his eyes to one of the Lords of the Snow.

"Hey, Gramps! Been a long time, yeah?" Yun Ren shouted cheerily.

→

The revelation that his grandson was a cultivator shocked the entire village, but since the man still acted the same, the shock wore off rather quickly.

It was surreal. He helped without complaint, finishing manual-labour tasks that would have taken ten men a week in moments. He mastered their style of archery; he hopped on a horse and broke it in with ease; he herded the yaks without even really thinking about it.

Yet he didn't seem to have any real driving ambition. He was content, and all he seemed to want to do was use his crystal to record images. Han didn't quite get the obsession, but he studied the images with due consideration. They were quite fantastic—oh, to be able to capture a moment in time like that.

After he'd swiftly explored his surroundings, he transitioned to attempting to paint his recorded images.

He wasn't particularly good at it. But he entertained everybody with outlandish stories, and the images to go along with them. The thunder-hoof. The Smiling Dragon. Jin and Meiling.

"So . . . what should we do?" Han asked Elder Hu. The wizened old woman, nearly a hundred years old, pondered his question. The first cultivator to ever have the blood of Nezin? What should be done?

"Show him the First Den," she decided.

"That old place? Well, it might interest him." Han sighed. And it *was* full of the stories of their tribe. Those are always useful.

They turned to look at the boy. Yun Ren was gesturing to the image of the band of stars that decorated the ceiling, mentioning the mountain he'd climbed to get that precise view.

"They with the Stars will forge a new path," the old woman croaked again.

"Really?" he asked, his voice deadpan. "That old saying?"

The older woman shrugged.

↔

Yun Ren stared at the hole in the ground curiously. "First Den?" he asked, and his grandfather nodded.

"Yes. They say this is where our tribe originated," he explained, grabbing a torch. The entrance was rather well hidden, but it was still just a hole in the ground.

Well, it was a welcome distraction when Yun Ren's grandfather had offered to take him on a trip. Not to knock his mom's relatives, but . . . the visit had been a bit boring so far. Sure, everybody was nice enough, but there wasn't much to do other than more farmwork, and the scenery wasn't very different from his village.

The clothes were nice, though. He'd always worn the soft leather boots his mother made, which were different from the boots that most in the Empire wore. In his opinion they were vastly more comfortable, but the shirts and dresses with the geometric designs made him a bit sad that his mother didn't wear them too much. They looked cool.

Maybe I could get some for Biyu, he thought.

He shook his head out of his introspection as he wandered down the hall. There were a bunch of images painted, capturing what looked like shooting stars streaking across the sky.

"They say we took shelter here, after some great calamity," his grandfather explained as they entered the main room.

Yun Ren raised his eyebrow at the image.

"I thought the fox thing was a joke," he said, raising an eyebrow at the nine-tailed fox on the wall.

His grandfather chuckled.

"They do say we're descended from some great fox, or that it bestowed its power on us . . . but really, it might just be a story. It's not like any of us have any special powers. Just eyes that look like this," he said in amusement, pointing at his own amber eyes.

Yun Ren nodded along and with a bit of concentration made a flash of light. His crystal chimed.

He checked the recording. The flash was one way to fix the lighting, but he would have to refine it. It made things a bit unnatural-looking. The ancient cave drawing was surprisingly colourful and had some interesting geometric shapes.

"*Supposedly* there was some great calamity, so our ancestors hid here, protected by Nezin the Great Fox," he said, pointing to the walls, where fire streaked across them. "But . . . well, none of the other tribes mention something like this. They *do* have this next tale, though."

"The Hero and the Eternal Winter."

Yun Ren stared at the image of the giant cat-bear thing with massive teeth, fighting a man with a spear.

"Hey, Mom told us this one!" he said, grinning at the image.

His grandfather laughed.

"She was fond of this one. Always said the story about the calamity was too morbid."

Yun Ren kept recording. There were some stories he had heard, and some he hadn't. There were also a few ancient firepits, and what looked like rooms and beds.

And finally, there was the tomb.

Yun Ren paid his respects.

It was an enjoyable day, all told. Grandfather was deep in thought as they made camp outside the First Den.

"You're bored at the village, aren't you?" he asked bluntly, and Yun Ren suppressed a wince. Had it been that obvious?

His grandfather chuckled. "I do know the feeling. You want to go and explore, but we're all too slow, and you feel an obligation. Tell you what, I'll give you a job. To the northeast is the Grand Falls. Just before the Sea of Snow. Beautiful place. Fantastic view. It's three weeks by *my* speed . . ."

Yun Ren's eyes widened.

"I want to see it again, from your recordings. Just don't go *too* far northeast. It gets dangerous up there, so close to the Howling Fang Mountains."

He pondered the mission.

And with a smirk, he accepted it.

He had *permission* to go take pictures.

→

Yun Ren raised his crystal again, capturing the beautiful waterfall and jagged mountains.

His grandfather was right. This place was *beautiful.* There were thousands of waterfalls up here, snaking down from the mountains and flowing northwest.

Spectacular, sparkling water.

Yun Ren accessed the recording, examining it closely to see the colours and if the angle of the sun was right. It was sunset, and the light dyed the water lovely oranges and pinks.

The light was as good as he'd imagined it. But there was something odd about the recording. Part of the cliff near the waterfall seemed blurry. Unfocused.

It was a small part, but it completely *ruined* the entire composition.

He took the image again.

. . . and the exact same part was blurry. He frowned, then turned around to take another image, so he could see if it was the crystal acting up. Biyu had said that it could be temperamental, or it could overload and crack, yet everything seemed to be fine in this image.

He ran to another position and took yet another recording. The same place, from a different angle, was still blurry. He looked up and squinted at it. That part of the cliff looked fine from here.

Yun Ren shrugged, then decided to approach. He jumped across the river and again recorded the cliff face.

The blurry patch was in the same place. But captured closer, it was even fuzzier. Like the cliff was merely mist shrouding something else.

Something's up here, he thought.

Cautiously, he drew closer. He was alert, his ears pricked and trying to draw upon every ounce of his hunting experience.

But there was nothing. No wind. Nor any strange feeling. He was nearly touching the grey, craggy wall now.

He raised his crystal.

To his eyes, it was a solid wall.

In the recording, the mouth of a cave.

Yun Ren scratched his chin.

Carefully, he reached out, pressing his hand against the stone. It felt solid enough, but with a slight push—his hand sank in up to his elbow.

He jerked his hand out as the rock wall dispersed like a cloud, leaving only a dark tunnel leading forwards. He was diving behind a rock before he finished realising what had happened. He paused, his heart hammering in his chest, as he waited for *something*, some sort of monster, to burst out and devour him for disturbing the illusion.

Yet all he could hear was the thundering waterfall. No shaking earth, or strange roars. Just a cave.

His head poked up from behind the rock.

He stared at the cave.

After a moment, he placed one foot in front of the other. What was inside it? What was the illusion trying to hide?

It might be stupid, but he could feel the same stirring push to action that he always felt whenever something caught his interest.

Like teasing Meimei until she turned his skin blue. Poking Elder Che to see how much it took to get a hammer thrown at him. Prodding at his brother until they got into a fistfight. Hounding a thunder-hoof just to see if he could catch another glimpse. Working a hundred odd jobs simply to record what he saw in a crystal.

The burning questions: *What is this? What will it do? How far can I push?*

Like a fox getting drawn into an interesting trap because something shiny caught his eye.

Some had said he was a fool. In the end, he was just curious.

And the cave was far, far too interesting.

Yun Ren chewed his lip as he stared at the yawning mouth of the cave. The inside was shrouded in fog, but with a crystal chime most of that went away, revealing a rather well-constructed path.

Yun Ren took one hesitant step in. And then another. He descended into the cave with nothing but a crystal and his wits.

—and a burning need to know what was inside.

→

The cave was very long. That was about all Yun Ren could say about it. Long and foggy. For the first couple of minutes, he had been hesitant and cautious, slinking along the wall and taking a recording every step, examining it for any new revelation . . . but there was nothing. Nothing outside of a few things that looked like gates, along with degraded-looking scraps of paper on them.

He could make out the squiggly designs, and maybe formations on them. It was a bit nerve-racking, so he quietly resolved to immediately run if a strange voice popped into his head, talking to him.

Those stories *always* ended with the person releasing an ancient evil or something.

After a few hours of walking, he came to a set of stairs. There didn't seem to be anything suspicious about them, so he carefully ascended.

And walked into what looked a bit like a house.

Or at least a house, like the First Den was a house. The walls were all stone, and there were jars lining them. They were a bit dusty, and the glass ones were filled with what looked like pills. Little, multicoloured things.

Yun Ren made sure not to touch them and considered turning back, but . . . well, it did look to be abandoned.

The next room was a library of sorts, with a bunch of scrolls and books. There was a kitchen and a closed door that he didn't try.

Lastly, there was the room. Crystals glowed from the ceiling, a jagged mass that illuminated the area and the thick covering of grass. Delicate, almost crystalline flowers poked up from the soil, swaying in a nonexistent breeze.

It was absolutely beautiful.

Yun Ren's crystal chimed as he recorded his surroundings.

This place was amazing!

He wandered through the grass and flowers, occasionally stopping to record another image. This place was weird. There was even a big old tree growing down here!

But this was not all that was in the room. There was a stone tablet, a grave marker, near the back of the room.

And beside it was a sword.

It was a beautiful sword. It was pure white with rippling patterns that swirled across it. There were several characters on the blade. *Summer's Sky*, it read. The weapon shone like a star.

As he approached, he felt it. He felt the *power*. Felt the Qi radiating off the blade beside the grave.

Slowly he approached the old marker and turned his head from the sword to the grave. He bowed his head, giving a bit of respect to whoever was laid to rest here.

Well, Yun Ren was glad he hadn't gone snooping any further. He was no grave robber.

But hopefully, whoever made this place wouldn't mind if he took one thing.

He bent down to pluck one of the beautiful blue flowers. Hopefully it would press well. And hopefully Biyu would like it.

He smiled at the flower. It was really pretty.

He turned, intending to leave—

—and his body seized up as he felt hot breath and saw white fur.

Don't go too far northeast.

He looked up. And up. He stared blankly at the fox, who was nearly twice the size of Wa Shi when he was a dragon.

Right, the tunnel led northeast.

In fact, he was probably under the Howling Fang Mountains *right now.*

Oops.

It stared at him curiously.

"Uh, sorry for intruding?" he asked, his voice catching a bit in his throat.

The fox seemed intensely amused.

"You are a strange one, child," it said, these words coming out of its mouth, instead of the strange not-speech most animals used. "Most would try to claim the blade."

"I don't think I need another sword. Elder Che is pretty good." He tapped the hilt of his ordinary iron blade. The fox's smile widened a bit. "And . . . well, it's somebody's grave, isn't it? Ma always said that graverobbing was bad karma."

"Indeed it is, little one," the fox stated. "I would have devoured you had you dared to touch the weapon."

Yun Ren swallowed thickly, his legs trembling.

The fox sniffed at him, its eyes widening briefly.

"It has been many, many years since I have seen such an honourable young man. I am amused, and so you may ask a boon of me," it started magnanimously.

Yun Ren nearly reflexively said "nothing," but the fox was watching him closely.

He pondered the question for a second.

"Were you the one who did the illusions?" he asked.

The fox raised a brow, its expression becoming bored. "Indeed, you wish to learn how to befuddle your enemies?" it asked, seeming a bit disappointed.

"Uh . . . not really? I kind of just want to learn how to transfer these images to something permanent."

The fox stared blankly at the image on the wall. Slowly, its shoulders shook. A moment later, it opened its massive maw wide and began to laugh.

CHAPTER 55

ACCIDENTAL DEFENCE

Read this scroll well, and comprehend its teachings," the fox declared to the boy as they sat together in the library. "It shall teach you the foundations to this technique."

Xong Yun Ren nodded. "Thank you, Guardian," he said, bowing respectfully. The fox nodded with grace. He *should* be thankful. The Befuddling Mist of Da Ji was a powerful technique, probably too powerful for the boy's current strength, but he did not need to comprehend all of it.

Really, had the loneliness made him soft, to give out such a treasure? Or was it the oddly familiar smell the boy had, like a sibling, or a friend long passed? It was faint, so faint, and barely lurking under the surface. But for some reason, it made him think fondly of the boy . . .

The fox shook his head, eyeing the boy as he immediately went to sit down, carefully cracking open the scroll.

"Just that one, boy. Do not read any of the others," the fox commanded. Yun Ren looked up from the scroll and nodded.

Eyes taking in the slight amount of dust in the library, the Guardian hummed and left him to it.

The fox made a note to repair the wards again. The damn things kept letting dust in. Yawning, he left to survey the rest of their domain.

It had been rather a shock, awakening to a rat slinking through their home.

Albeit a polite one. A polite and strange rat that had woken him up far, far too early from his slumber, it seemed. And it had been such a wonderful dream too.

The fox shook his head again, driving away the fugue state. What were they doing again? Oh, yes.

The kitchen was dusted. The other seals checked. The grass was still the right length, the marker unblemished by the elements, and Summer's Sky was . . . awake?

The fox squinted at the blade and the faint stirring within the Spirit Blade's consciousness. Curious, how curious.

There was a twinge from the wards in the library. *Oh? That sneaky brat, touching what wasn't his!* Well, it was Nezan's fault for being absent-minded and leaving him to read where there was such temptation!

The fox moved like liquid smoke, his body roiling down the hall and seeping into the library. The fox pondered on how to deal with this. Should the Guardian appear behind him again? No, that was getting old. A storm of lightning with a howl of fury? He smirked. That would do.

The fox twisted through the shelves, ready to catch the sneaky trickster in the act—

Yun Ren was humming to himself as he put the scroll back. He carefully took another one off the shelf, examining it for damage and wiping some of the dust off, being mindful not to damage the seal. It was a task that seemed rote—as if he had cleaned scrolls many times before.

But what was he doing? The fox had tasked the boy with *reading* the scroll, so why was he *cleaning*?

"Boy, what *are* you doing?" the fox asked, appearing from the smoke. The boy didn't startle, merely turned to the fox that was suddenly there in the room with him.

Like he was used to things suddenly appearing.

"Meditatin'," the boy stated as he took a cloth to the shelves, wiping them until they were clean.

"Medi—what?" the fox asked, baffled.

"Yeah, normally I chop wood. But I didn't know if ya needed any of that done, so . . . well, this place was kinda dirty, and I've helped Elder Hong and Meimei clean their house before. Both of 'em are picky about how you clean scrolls. They'd have my head if I ever hurt anything," the boy explained before he went back to his task.

The fox watched him in utter bewilderment. This was not a technique that required such things. Just who had taught this boy?

"Ya got any lacquer? I can fix this part here, if you want," the boy asked.

"No, no, I shall attend to that myself. If you are meditating, that means you have comprehended the Befuddling Mist of Da Ji?" the fox asked. That had been extremely fast; his comprehension was truly incredible if he had managed already—

"Nah, not one bit," the boy returned easily. "It's confusing. It's written in the Courtly Characters, so I got like . . . *half* of what it was saying, but what I *did* get didn't make any sense. 'Meditate upon the Room of the Fox Queen'? How can I 'meditate on and envision' the room of some person I've never met or seen?" the boy grumbled.

Yun Ren hadn't comprehended anything at all, had he? Not even the basest part of this technique.

He turned back to the fox. "So I thought I'd give the whole meditation thing a go before telling you I had no idea what I was doin'."

The sheer, guileless truth. The Guardian bit his tongue. Really? This boy was too amusing! What fool admitted weakness so easily?

"Who is your Master?" the fox asked, curious. Had they taught the boy wrong on purpose as a joke?

"Don't got one. Jin taught me how to meditate, and he helped me through the whole 'breaking stuff' phase, but otherwise?" The boy shrugged.

That tempered the fox's amusement. No Master, and yet there was no deviation in his Qi—his foundation was surprisingly solid. Wandering blindly in the dark, yet striding forwards without a care in the world.

How interesting. The Guardian sniffed at him once more. The scent of fox, however faint, was upon the boy.

"I see. Well, I have wasted your time. That scroll is useless to you." The boy looked up at the fox, startled and confused.

Most men comprehended scrolls. He had simply believed this boy would be the same, but it appeared a more hands-on effort was required.

Perhaps he will be more like a pup than a man? the fox thought.

"Come. Follow me." They returned to the meadow, the boy following along.

"Now, show me the image you wish to re-create." Yun Ren shrugged, taking out his abysmal-quality crystal. Really, that he was using that at all was strange. An image formed of a city, stretching out below. A giant lake.

The Guardian nodded.

"Now, observe." He flowed through the motions of the technique. For one such as him, the movements came seamlessly and perfectly, a lifetime of practice and refinement added to the graceful movements. Qi flared.

The wall seemed to bubble and shift; colours flowed, painting the image perfectly.

Yun Ren's gaze was intent.

"Could . . . could you do that again?" he asked, this time bringing the crystal into position.

The fox indulged him. There were several crystal chimes.

Yun Ren frowned and moved his feet into position.

"So, that was kind of like . . . hup, and *twist*, and then it went all floaty . . ." he muttered to himself, staring at the projection of the fox in midtechnique.

His hands moved.

Sparks burst out.

"Okay, not *hup*, prolly more like *ha*," he said to himself with a nod. His feet adjusted slightly, and the fox sensed his Qi starting to move more like it was supposed to.

Slowly a grin spread across the fox's face.

More sparks.

How utterly and completely interesting. It had been a while since the fox had met with a man who learned this way.

The fox watched in amusement as the boy ran through his *hoos*, into *harahs*, from twists to turns.

He got better with each absurd exclamation.

↔

Yun Ren sighed, sinking into the water. He had found out what was behind the door: an underground spring, with warm water.

Pretty nice of the fox to let him use it—though it was mostly repayment, since Yun Ren had provided dinner. The fox was the first person he had met that hadn't said the rice was the best they'd ever tasted, merely having a single, small bowlful and declaring it "passable."

Well, it was a fox. What did it know?

At least the warm waters were soothing his pounding headache and the slight nausea that always came with Qi overuse.

He was completely and utterly exhausted.

When Yun Ren had made his request to the fox, it had mostly been a shot in the dark. He did want to learn how to do permanent illusions so that he could permanently project his images. How awesome would it be to have an entire wall that was a recorded image of the sky, with fluffy clouds and the perfect blue sky?

Mostly it was for himself. But he could not deny a certain sense of pride in his work. If he could more easily show his compositions to others, could he not have his name recorded in history as a great sculptor or artist? Maybe he could even get one into the palace at Pale Moon Lake City?

He chuckled at the thought.

"Is the water to your liking, boy?" Yun Ren paused at the voice of the fox. While the sound was normally a slight growl, to the point where he couldn't tell if it was a boy or a girl, this was downright feminine and *sultry*.

Yun Ren swallowed thickly and turned. Tales of beautiful foxes seducing men danced in his head.

He saw a voluptuous body. Smooth, creamy skin, as fine as jade. Beautiful, long white hair that looked like it was made out of silk.

The vision of loveliness had one large flaw: a face that looked nearly *exactly* like his mother's. They could have been sisters, for the resemblance.

Yun Ren gagged, the enticing vision crumbling into dust.

The fox paused, looking a bit confused at his reaction. Her eyes narrowed, and she let loose a throaty chuckle as Yun Ren turned his eyes away.

A form pressed up against him. Then an arm wrapped around his neck, and smooth, hard muscle pressed into his side.

"Is this form more to your liking?" a husky male voice whispered in his ear.

Yun Ren turned back to the fox, his hopes and dreams dead and ruined.

"Not really. Besides, I got a *girl* I like." He glared at the man.

The very pretty man, who looked a bit like one of his cousins.

"A man should experience all he can in life," the fox declared conspiratorially, wiggling his eyebrows. Yun Ren shoved himself away from the fox man, scrambling to the other side of the pool. The man threw his head back and laughed. "Ah, forgive me my games, I haven't gotten to play with anybody in a while! Although I believe I haven't been rejected quite that out of hand in centuries! You are the most amusing cultivator, Xong Yun Ren!"

"Glad I'm entertaining," Yun Ren grumbled, glaring at the perfectly sculpted body of the Guardian.

"Rejoice. My dear companion would have enjoyed your reactions too, if she were alive to see them!" The fox's hand went behind him to pick up Yun Ren's recording crystal so the Guardian could examine it closely.

"An interesting use of such a weak crystal, but the craftsmanship leaves much to be desired. You should have complained to whatever Sect you purchased this from. Look at this, it's almost like a *mortal* crafted this piece," the fox stated, waving Yun Ren's crystal negligently towards him.

Yun Ren felt strangely defensive about his first purchase. "Because one did? Biyu's just a normal gal, I'm pretty sure. This is her first actual crystal out of her apprenticeship. It wasn't supposed to be sold."

The fox paused.

"A mortal made this?"

"Yeah?"

The fox nodded his head, considering. "Biyu . . . She certainly is a precious stone, is she not?"

Yun Ren smiled at the thought of her, and of the meal they had shared together. The slight blush on her face—

"Now I am sure you have images of your lover, so show me her face!" the fox commanded.

Yun Ren flushed. "She isn't my lover . . ." he grumbled. "Yet . . . Maybe . . . Why am I even talking about this to you?"

But he showed off the image anyway. It was a good picture.

CHAPTER 56

BACK UNDER THE SUMMER SKY

The walls of the tomb were covered in multicoloured splotches, like somebody had taken entire buckets of paint and thrown them against grey stone.

Yun Ren's eyes were unfocused, distorted colours and bands of mist swirling around his hands.

His Qi churned and twisted. There was a brief flash of light.

The Guardian's tail slapped against the back of Yun Ren's head, nearly bowling him over.

"None of that, boy," the fox scolded. "Distraction while training is a sin—it leads to injury or death. Especially when mixing pure light with the shadowed illusions of the foxes, as you were so foolishly doing."

The boy flushed, scuffing his feet like a much younger lad at the scolding.

"Why were you trying to add such light to the illusion, anyway?" the fox asked.

Yun Ren frowned at his hands. "Well . . . Jin showed me this cool thing a while ago. You poke a hole in a box, and it's a bit like a recording crystal, but upside down, backwards, and reversed. It showed an image of whatever the hole was pointing at. He kept saying how light could be captured that way, but he didn't know how to catch it, other than that it involved specially treated paper. He called it a 'camera obscura.' Whatever that means."

His Qi welled up again. Flashes of light. Sparks of the cold fire of the foxes. Dregs of mist.

The fox and Yun Ren's Qi were working together. Shifting, roiling, wobbling . . . but not in danger of destabilising.

The Guardian's gaze sharpened as the boy's scent got stronger. The fox's amber eyes remained focused intently on Yun Ren's work.

Light and shadow. Fire and mist. Something churned, scratching at the back of the fox's mind.

"You never did tell me your mother's name, boy," the fox mentioned.

"Hm? Oh, Hu Li. Nezin Hu Li."

The pieces clicked. Nezin. Su Nezin, his great-aunt. His namesake.

Soft fingers through a pup's fur. A gentle humming voice. A single memory.

From the scent, and the light . . . of the line of his great-aunt, *Su Nezin*.

The Great Defender, the first daughter, inheritor of the blood of Da Ji? He still remembered kowtowing to one of her robes, an artifact of their kin, one of the few that had survived the fall of the Misty Fang.

. . . or Shrouded Mountain, as the humans called it.

How could her bloodline have grown so weak? How could he have lived here while kin wandered the lands so close by?

The fox was startled out of his introspection by a whoop of joy.

"Yeah! See, I thought the light would help out!" he shouted. "It makes things . . . less wobbly? A bit more solid and firm, yeah?"

Instead of a splotch of colour, this one was much more defined. There were shapes now. Something long and sinuous, with bright blue scales.

The Guardian took back his ill thoughts of the boy's poor comprehension. He learned quite quickly, just as long as he wasn't tasked with reading.

And the illusion *was* different. *Brighter*, somehow. Not the illusion of a trickster. But something more honest. Something that would stand proudly in the light, not trying to hide or confuse.

The fox chuckled at the joy sparking in all too familiar amber eyes. Oh, he was definitely kin, all right. Every damn pup looked like that when they finished their first illusion.

It was something *beautiful*.

Ah, how his dear companion would have loved to see something like this.

"Yun Ren." The young man perked up.

"This one is Su Nezan. And the one who rests here is my companion, Zang Wen, she who was known as the 'Summer Sky Thunder.'"

The boy nodded politely but did not seem to recognise her name. That was fine. It was hundreds of years past her death.

But hopefully, his little cousin would wish to learn.

"Now, practice makes perfect, Cousin," Nezan said, and Yun Ren nodded eagerly . . .before pausing.

"Really? You too? I got enough of that 'related to foxes' stuff back home, damn it!" he muttered. "And really, you look *exactly* like my mom when you turn into a woman!"

Oh, so that's *why he was so repulsed,* the fox thought, amused.

"You know, most nobles just seemed to think that made it better," Nezan mused.

Really, they were entirely too eager to bed their brothers or sisters. Strange creatures, humans.

Yun Ren's face went all jittery, swapping through a myriad of emotions from disgust to horror.

Nezan laughed and, with a swirl of white fur and tails, plucked the boy up.

"Now, to a section that is less colourful. Don't layer too many illusions on top of each other!"

Yun Ren's brief struggle ceased when he seemed to realise he was perched on Nezan's back.

"This is pretty cool," he said, looking around the cave.

"If you wish to ride me, all you must do is ask," the lilting female voice said temptingly.

"I hate you. *I hate you so much.*"

Cackles echoed through the cave.

So amusing, his little cousin was.

The sword rattled again.

□

There was once a woman.

A powerful hunter of beasts. A slayer of the wicked. With her blade of light, she cast down their illusions. With her blade of light, she ended the lives of the demonic Spirit Beasts.

She was the pride of the Shrouded Mountain. Until one day . . . she betrayed the Sect. The Blade of Light slew all who approached. Her lightning scorched and ruined those who dared appear before her.

And with her, they fought one of the monsters. One of the wicked creatures that twisted and shifted, normally cowering from the light.

Befuddled by a fox, a most humiliating end.

She slew many, as befitting of the rising Star of the Shrouded Mountain. She crushed all who opposed her.

And yet, the brave disciples of the Honoured Founders had their own strength. One managed a lethal blow, and the Simmer's Sky Thunder was mortally wounded, borne from the field by the beast and disappearing forever.

Many would wish to find her corpse. Or at least her wondrous blade, so they could return such a treasure to the hands of the righteous.

Lu Ban closed the scroll in disgust.

"With our revealing light, and the artifacts of our ancestors, no shadow will hide from us!" a voice boomed out in the courtyard.

He rolled his eyes at the answering cheers as "Brother" Kang made a speech to the Fulmination Assault Troup.

Through careful research and months of cataloguing disappearances, his Senior thought he had a good idea where the fox's lair was. A full-scale raid, to retrieve an artifact and a core.

And Young Master Zang Li had been "given the great honour" of being in command of Fangtip Fortress while the Sect's forces went off to obtain glory. His Senior said it was to make up for Lu Ban's embarrassment.

A bold-faced plan to attempt to halt his growth, sending him to this heavens-forsaken mountain, where there was snow in summer.

On top of that, he was run around constantly, given barely any time to cultivate. Sent to exterminate beasts, or to receive tribute for the great machine that was the Shrouded Mountain. He had slain many denizens of the mountains already, harvesting their cores. Over half of them would go to the Sect. A disgusting tax, levied so the *unworthy* could have a chance to shine.

He couldn't even skim off the top with "Brother" Kang watching him closely, as the Elders still seemed to think he needed a minder.

Bastards.

There was a rustle of clothes as the fool himself appeared in the room, flaunting a movement technique.

"Do you think my speech was rousing enough, *Junior Brother?*" he asked, smirking.

Lu Ban smiled without sincerity. "It was *most* rousing," he replied while sneering, sarcasm thick.

The older man laughed at him.

"Ah, it is most unfortunate that you can't come and witness our glory. But you must stay out of trouble, yes? I'm helping you, Junior.

Commanding the illustrious Fangtip Fortress will surely see your worth rise in the eyes of our Elders!"

Lu Ban said nothing.

"And . . . well, here. These need filing. Make sure to get it all done, yes?"

Lu Ban nearly struck him down right then and there, but he held his fury. It would do him no good right now. He had his freedom, but the rest of the Elders continued to hold a grudge for embarrassing the Sect. They were watching to see if he made any mistakes.

If that bastard came back and Lu Ban had a hair out of place . . . he would report it. Like a child screaming to his big brother.

Lu Ban grimaced as he remembered that incident. How the bastard had called his brother, six years older, to fight on his behalf. Lu Ban remembered the beating he'd received from the brat well. He also remembered the feeling of smashing a rock into the back of the boy's head as he swaggered off.

At least Kang wouldn't be breathing down his neck the entire time. In the man's own words, which Lu Ban had overheard: "There is nothing to get into trouble with up here."

Lu Ban snatched the papers out of Kang's hands and stormed out of the room, the smirk boring into his back.

Lu Ban snarled as he stomped into the library. The filing took most of the day, and by the end of it his blood was boiling.

Even the library here was a disappointment. There were no secret texts, or anything of real value. Just basic techniques.

An utterly worthless place.

He was so fed up that he moved slightly too quickly at one point, the air pressure knocking over a precariously placed scroll in this dim, unused corner of a library.

The scroll fell, and with it, half the scrolls on the shelf.

Lu Ban debated just leaving them there. He glared at the shelf—

There was something in the back of it.

His eyes narrowed as he approached. A panel, nearly invisible, had been jostled loose.

He finished prying it the rest of the way open.

Within the small, carved-out space, there was a scroll.

The Blade of Fire, it read.

Intrigued, Lu Ban reached in and took it out, cracked the seal, and glanced through the contents.

His eyes widened.

A wizened old face, sitting silently in the cave. Milky-white eyes that saw nothing, and yet everything. He sat before an emaciated boy as the child writhed in agony at learning his secrets.

"Let me tell you, child. Talent and power? Those are secondary. The most important thing a cultivator can have"—a grin without teeth, only blackened gums—"is luck."

He tucked the scroll furtively into his robes, then set about replacing everything.

Slowly, a smile spread across his face. Perhaps there *was* some trouble he could get into up here after all.

□

"Hey, what do you want to do when all this is over?" the fox asked as the commotion behind them intensified. The entire village was packing up and leaving, while the defenders stayed.

Hopefully, they could buy enough time.

The woman with blond hair considered the question, as if she had never thought to think about it before.

She frowned heavily.

"I don't know," she stated, her eyes unfocused. "But . . . those illusions you showed me that night. The one of the dance . . . I liked it. Do many places have festivals like that?"

"Yes, I'm sure of it. There are more festivals and events than can be counted!"

Wen smiled, staring up at the sky. "Then I shall see them all! And bring something back. I'll tell everybody of the things I've seen, and you can make illusions, so it will be like they were right there with us!"

The sword on her back rattled.

The woman chuckled at the action.

"Seriously? Why do you even like tea getting poured on you? You're going to rust! Strange thing." The woman sighed fondly. "We'll find you tea, at least one type from each different province!"

It rattled again, pleased, as the fox laughed.

They made so many promises that night.

And kept not a single one.

□

Yun Ren's illusions improved with time. They got sharper, their colours clearer. For days, he trained nonstop.

Until finally, there stood an image on the wall. A direct duplication of the one in his crystal. It was still fuzzy at the edges, and still imperfect . . . but it was clear.

Yun Ren exhaled, his eyes slightly unfocused.

"Thank you," he said earnestly. Then he bowed, his eyes to the floor.

The fox smiled at him.

"You know, there are many more techniques here, if you wish to learn. My companion found many secrets."

A leading question, yet the boy shook his head.

"Sorry. I gotta get back to Gramps soon," he declined. "Should let him know I'm all right."

There was a brief, violent surge of possessiveness. *Another one is leaving.* More kin gone, more friends disappeared.

The fox crushed down the feeling.

"Hey, you wanna come too? Meet everybody?" Yun Ren asked, suddenly struck with an idea.

Nezan considered the offer. He was not bound here. Not really. But . . . he was loath to leave his dear friend's resting place.

"Perhaps I *shall* visit them," the fox mused. "After I finish repairing everything, perhaps."

"I'll tell everybody about you. And . . . I'll come visit again, if you want? Before I return south?"

"No, I shall come to you. I don't want to ruin all my hard work. Making illusions like that is tough, I'll have you know! But enough of this. We shall celebrate your accomplishment!"

Nezan retrieved a special vintage from an old storage ring. One of the last ones remaining.

"Oh, honoured sir!" came a singsong female voice as the fox returned. Yun Ren's face made that delightful twitching motion when he beheld the female form, clad in a beautiful, if revealing dress.

The one that looked like his mother.

The woman shifted back into a fox after the drinks were poured.

Yun Ren took a sip from the vessel, and his eyes bulged out.

"The hells is this?" he asked, staring at the vessel in wonder.

"Spiritual wine," the fox replied, taking his own sip.

The boy took another drink, then giggled, his face already turning red. The wine was quite potent, especially to one who had never had any before. Nezan's Qi slunk around him.

"Tell me, Yun Ren . . . What is your goal? Your dream, your reason for being?" Nezan asked.

The boy's bleary eyes focused for a brief moment, even under alcohol and suggestion as he was.

The fox chuckled as the boy got out his recording crystal again.

He regaled Nezan with stories, stories of where he'd come from.

He told a tale of a farm. Of a magnificent chicken. Of a carp that had become a dragon.

He told of a wicked fiend that had tried to take a friend.

Then was the story of a tribe. A tribe that honoured and venerated a fox, that called her the great guardian, who had delivered them from a calamity.

Each tale was accompanied by an illusion.

The image of a mountain. The image of a lake. The image of a woman with freckles, grinning, and a large man sticking his tongue out. Sweat beaded on his brow as the technique took hold deeper. Even as his cultivation-enhanced voice grew hoarse, Yun Ren spoke.

"That's my dream. To travel far and wide. To see it. To record it . . . and then come back home and share it with everyone. Moments in time, captured in light."

Yun Ren's eyes sparkled with light and conviction. It was the same conviction Nezan had once seen in his dear companion's eyes.

Nezan smiled into his cup.

But for all the boy's conviction . . .

"The world is not kind enough for conviction alone," Nezan whispered.

The boy's drunken mind churned, and he sighed. "Yeah. Yeah, I know that some people are assholes. Or I could screw up and offend somebody, on account of me bein' a country hick and all. But . . . well, I'd still like to do it anyway, yanno?"

"Yes . . . yes, I know," the fox whispered. "Yun Ren . . . could you do one last thing for me?"

The boy nodded, completely without guile.

Nezan touched his paw to his head, drawing out a cherished memory. Yun Ren's eyes went blank as he beheld a moment in time.

His hands rose.

And the stone room changed, the illusion taking hold on the wall.

Light. Clouds. A horizon with mountains . . .

And a woman with blond hair, smiling softly at the rising dawn.

The boy staggered from the strain, falling to his knees and slumping against the fox.

Nezan smiled fondly at the boy. Truly, he was blessed by the heavens to have such a fortunate encounter.

"G'nnight . . ." Yun Ren slurred, utterly spent.

His face was so peaceful. Dreaming about a future, and all the things he would see. Nezan . . . would like to see that future. He tapped his chest idly.

The fond smile on the Guardian's face turned wicked.

But really, now, falling asleep on a fox? On a known trickster? The boy was *asking* for it.

And he had said he needed to get back to his grandfather. But first . . . Auntie Nezin's blood should not be in such a sorry state!

↔

The first thing that Yun Ren realised when he woke up was that he was naked.

The second thing was that he was tied upside down to a tree.

Yun Ren groaned.

Bastard fox. Really, I said he could visit, and then he ties me up naked while I'm passed out drunk?

He glared out at the forest, his headache swiftly subsiding, and saw the clothes folded neatly, along with his pack.

. . . and some of the anger dissipated.

He flailed about for a moment, kicking his legs, before he managed to get a good grip on the tree.

The ropes snapped, and he thumped headfirst into the ground. It didn't hurt, but it was damn insulting, as his hair got all dirty.

A bit of the anger came back.

He grumbled as he pulled on his clothes, though he also had to rub his nose at the near overpowering smell of dirt in it. He had half a mind to go storming back—

His pack was slightly too heavy.

He frowned, and opened it.

His eyes widened, and he closed it again.

He counted to three and opened the pack. *Yup, still there.*

Several crystals, a pressed flower, and a shimmering gem, along with a note.

"A gift for you, and for your lover. We may meet again," it said, with what looked like a lipstick kiss on the corner of it.

"Damned fox."

He finished collecting everything and strapped his sword to his belt.

It sat a little bit awkwardly, so he adjusted it. He was so *totally* going to come back and ruin the fox's illusions later.

↔

Two weeks had gone by, and not a day passed that Nezan did not stare at the mural of his dearest friend before he began his work.

The tunnel was in *terrible* disrepair. Really, the talismans were degrading far too quickly. Probably the lack of Qi in the Azure Hills, causing strange eddies in the dragon veins.

It would be months of work, and since Yun Ren had opened the path, even longer!

Ah, but it was worth it. He would complete his duties, and . . . maybe he would venture out and see his kin. Witness their lives.

But . . . it would also be irritating. Nezan sniffed at the outside air and gagged. How could people live in this Qi-deprived desert? And it would only get worse the farther he travelled.

He shook his head, huffing as the dawn light crested the horizon.

Nezan hummed, and then he began to weave his shadows, but paused midtechnique.

He glanced at the sun again.

Light. The basis of the illusion was light, rather than shadow.

Little golden motes danced around his fingers. It was a struggle to form it right, but it came surprisingly easily.

"Hup, ha, and then make it all twisty," Nezan sang to himself, and the illusion formed.

Yun Ren's little explanations helped a surprising amount.

Nezan laughed at how amateurish his attempt was. Sure, it would hide things from a distance, but if somebody got close enough, the description wouldn't hold.

He shook his head and wandered back inside. *Urg. Cleaning was always so annoying, the dust getting in his white fur . . .*

↔

To say Kang was livid was an understatement.

"You assured me that this information was correct," he ground out. The Fulmination Assault Troup was milling around a waterfall, boredom clear on their faces. The simpering little disciple flushed at the accusation.

"It should be here—it *has* to be around this area? Perhaps the lack of Qi is interfering—" he stuttered.

"Are you saying this artifact, the Illusory Shadow Seeker, cannot detect the foul beasts?" Kang asked him. It was a dangerous question. The Mystic Treasure was another of the reasons that they were so successful in rooting the demonic beasts out. To question it . . . that was not done.

"No, Senior Brother. If it cannot see the darkness, then there is none," the man whimpered.

"Exactly. Perhaps you need some remedial lessons with the rest of the information group. To think you came highly recommended."

The man bit his lip, his face going red.

"One more sweep. If we find nothing, then this search is fruitless, and we will return," Kang barked out.

The great mystic artifact rose in the air, spinning and spiralling, glowing with inner light. It was their most devastating weapon against the foxes, the weapon that sniffed out their shadows wherever they might hide . . .

The item dark and silent, detecting nothing.

The Fulmination Assault Troup packed up and left, beginning the dangerous trek back up the mountains.

Kang could just imagine the little bastard smirking at him.

CHAPTER 57

LAST NAMES

Meiling sat upon a cushioned bench as it gently swung back and forth. Ropes attached it to the ceiling, keeping it stable. The entire thing creaked gently to the rhythmic rocking.

They sat in the shade, listening to the sounds of nature, curled up next to each other. Jin was quiet and contemplative, his brow slightly furrowed, but he still smelled normal, so he apparently wasn't *too* distressed. Ri Zu sat in her lap, and Meiling's fingers drifted through soft fur. The rat had been quiet for a few days, clearly thinking something over; she had started conversations a few times, only to veer off.

Meiling would give her a few more days, as it obviously wasn't anything urgent, before starting to push the issue.

Meiling yawned.

It was a bit of effort not to fall asleep, even with the scene in front of her.

Tigu was sparring with Gou Ren. Xiulan had said it would be good if he knew how to better defend himself, and so Tigu had taken it upon herself to help him . . . or rather try to one-up Xiulan by being a better teacher.

It was quite interesting. She understood he and Yun Ren knew how to fight. And fight quite well, if she was honest. The brawls they had with each other were frequent. The occasional fight in the city, one fought on her behalf after a particularly rude boy had insulted her, were ungainly things. Fists flew, but she could see the calculation in their eyes, the slight hesitation they sometimes had before they committed to a move. They missed, they tripped, and eventually things devolved into somebody tackling somebody else, and the grunt-filled grappling matches in the mud.

There was none of that here. Gou Ren's body moved with grace and power as he flowed from one move to the next, like he was some manner of martial sage. His eyes saw blows that he never would have before, and he struck precisely with little hesitation.

Even while his opponent danced circles around him.

Tigu bounced around nearly too fast to see. Meiling tutted as the fighter's shirt spilled open again, the cat-turned-girl's muscles flexing visibly under her skin, with only the bandages preserving her modesty.

But Meiling knew a losing battle when she saw one. The girl absolutely loathed anything with too many layers, and skirts held a *special* ire in her eyes.

A kick slammed into Gou Ren's guard. Meiling winced as his footing failed and he was launched into a tree. It was a blow that would have absolutely killed a normal person, yet Gou Ren stood back up like he had been lightly slapped, not struck with enough force to shatter stone.

Like children play-fighting, she told herself, forcing her behind to stay firmly in her seat, instead of rushing off to check him for broken bones.

Tigu crawled onto his back, her arm wrapped around his neck in a light choke hold as she said something to him that set him laughing.

They were boisterous and excited.

"What do you think of the tournament?" Jin asked, out of the blue.

Meiling pondered the question.

"It's a bit much for a glorified fistfight, but what do I know about matters of cultivation? The battles do not interest me, though from what I've heard, the rest of it does sound quite fun. I think I would like to see it, at least once. To hear the crowds and the fanfare," she said, staring at the sky. It was a festival a thousand times bigger than any she had ever seen before, from how Xiulan had described it. "There are sure to be interesting things to see, new herbs to find. Or maybe even some scrolls?"

Her husband nodded, considering her words.

"Do you want to go?" he asked. A loaded question if she had ever heard one. She liked to think that she had gotten good enough to read his desires, not that they were hard to discern most days.

But she could tell.

He didn't want to go. There would be a conversation if she said yes. He was concerned for her safety. For the life growing in her stomach. And while she wasn't exactly fragile . . .

The nervousness was certainly there.

She *did* kind of want to see it, yet . . .

"Maybe someday," she said instead. "But I don't think this year."

Jin nodded. "When you do want to see it . . . we'll go."

A promise and a compromise. They lapsed into silence again as Gou Ren and Tigu went through the same form, Tigu grinning as they worked together.

'Master?' Ri Zu squeaked, and Meiling gave the disciple her full attention. The rat was standing up, her eyes set.

"Yes, Ri Zu?"

'Ri Zu wishes to go to this tournament, if she can be spared.' It was a bold declaration from her typically meek student.

Oh? Now that was interesting.

Jin startled at the question and turned his attention to Ri Zu as well, raising an eyebrow.

'If one of them is hurt, or needs aid . . . Ri Zu thinks there should be someone there for them. Ri Zu let Bi De go off alone, out of fear and thinking he would be all right without her, and she regrets it. She would like to experience the world herself, and grow, as the others have!'

Meiling smiled at the fire in her voice.

'The others wish to go and see, or fight, but Ri Zu will find the medical secrets of that place!'

"You know the dangers?" Jin asked Ri Zu.

She nodded resolutely.

Jin turned to Meiling.

"Look after them for us, then, Ri Zu. They need somebody with a good head on their shoulders, who won't go galivanting off. Really, Xiulan is going to have her hands full as it is!" Meiling said. The rat brightened up.

Her eyes blazed with inner fire, and she dipped into a bow. Then Ri Zu scampered off, squeaking excitedly at Tigu. The girl's eyes widened, and she shouted with joy, hoisting the rat onto her shoulder and nodding as she continued to squeak.

Wa Shi poked his head out of the river to see what the commotion was about, so Meiling turned back to her work.

"What are you making, anyway?" Jin asked her.

She turned the piece around, allowing him to see the design on the back.

Jin choked at the sight of it, his face flashing through shock and bemusement. Half a maple leaf, half a wheat stalk, surrounded by a circle.

"You know, people are going to think that we're a Sect or something if they see that, love," he muttered.

For a moment she thought he didn't like it, but then a slow smile spread across his face.

"It looks *great*, and I think little Tigu is going to be over the moon with that." He stared at it a moment longer. "You know what? We'll see about putting that on *everything*."

Meiling nodded, even as Jin started chuckling, muttering about "turtle homes" and "dragon spheres."

Meiling went back to stitching the symbol into the back of Gou Ren's shirt.

Maybe Xiulan would like one as well?

↔

I was still amused that Meimei was making everybody *uniforms* as I finished cleaning up after dinner. And "branding" our stuff. Turns out the Hong family had a symbol, an unobtrusive little circle with the character for "warehouse" in it. I hadn't ever really noticed it.

It was going to be a change, but . . . in the end? It was something to have pride in. And her stitching looked really good.

I wandered back into the living room. Xiulan and Gou Ren were out, reading poetry again. Tigu was leaning against Chunky, gesticulating to Babe about something or another, a single Qi blade hovering over her finger. The ox was silent, but considering, as Chunky oinked at Washy—a pile of nuts between the fish and the boar.

Peppa and Rizzo were last, drinking tea and watching everybody else, soft smiles on their faces.

They really did look like a family.

I glanced at Meiling, who nodded.

Time to bite the bullet. Rizzo had asked, but I wanted to see if anybody else was holding back.

"Hey, everybody," I called, and the room perked up, turning their attention to me as I sat down. Meiling walked over to sit with me.

"Does anybody else want to go to the tournament?" I asked them all. It would be a bit awkward if they all said yes at the same time, but their absence wouldn't be the end of the world.

Chunky and Peppa shook their heads almost immediately. Babe declined too, as he had a road to work on.

The surprising one was Washy.

'Leave so soon after the harvest, when you will be making the most delicious, and freshest of meals?' the fish asked, scandalised.

I snorted at how offended he sounded.

'While the rest may acquire tribute to my glorious personage, I shall dine upon the fruits of our home!' he declared.

"Tribute?" Tigu asked him dangerously.

'My dear friends taking pity upon this poor soul, and in their infinite grace bestowing upon him but part of their bounty,' he switched immediately.

It still amazed me how he could go from being an arrogant shit to a blubbering coward in a heartbeat. I chuckled at him, but my amusement was short lived, as the other question I needed to ask was a bit . . . personal.

"The second thing is . . . Well, it's about names. Surnames. It only really occurred to me after Big D left. If you want to start your own family . . . well, it may be a good idea. If you want to take one of ours, you may. If you want to choose your own, you can. If you don't want one at all . . . that's fine too."

A family line was a link to a history bigger than the individual. Mine may have changed, with my transition to this place, but . . . there was still the connection. Pride in who you were.

I had once asked to take the name Hong from Hong Xian—to be adopted into their clan in truth. Though the man had been touched . . . he had eventually refused. He said that I should keep my old name to honour my birth parents.

I didn't have much pride or even any attachment to the name Rou, or Jin. I did flop them around without a second thought.

But maybe . . . maybe we could make it into something I could be proud of. Maybe it was a bit stupid, attaching that to a *name*.

I saw the light shine in Tigu's eyes.

Something I'd expected, really.

"Ah, um, may I . . .?" she stuttered, starting to ask the question I'd known that she was gong to ask.

"Yes, Rou Tigu?" I asked. She swallowed thickly, then scampered from her seat, settling down beside us. There was a dampness to her eyes as she embraced us both. It had obviously meant a lot to her.

Meiling nodded at Rizzo.

"I have already spoken to Father," she told the little one. "He said he would adopt one so skilled into our family without a second thought.

The little rat sat up straighter.

The others were a bit more considering. Babe shook his head, disregarding having a last name.

Chunky began chuckling. *'Chunky Shan,'* he chortled. *Chunky Mountain.*

I spluttered—he'd used his name to make a *pun.* A pun using *English* naming conventions.

He grinned away, as Peppa nodded along. *'Shan Peppa,"* she stated primly.

I was about to ask Chunky how much he knew, when we were interrupted again.

'Great Lordly Supreme Being,' Washy stated, a smug smile upon his face.

Everybody turned to look at him.

'Master of the Heavens and the Sea?'

People kept staring.

The fish paused, and pouted.

'He?' the fish finally settled on, shortening it to just *river.*

I snorted. *Never change, you crazy fish.*

CHAPTER 58

FANGS AND THE DEEP

Travel through the Howling Fang Mountains was a dangerous task. Between the local Spirit Beasts, the unpredictable, often Qi-charged weather, and the mountains themselves, going without a guide was generally foolhardy.

It was a bracing climate, Lu Ri decided. The frigid feeling in the air nearly matched his Senior Sister's gaze.

He brushed some of the snow off his hat and ran his finger over the hole where an icicle the size of a spear had managed to strike true.

Unfortunate. He liked this hat. It hid his eyes and face quite well, even if it was a poor fit for the climate.

He eyed his prize as he crested another outcrop. Fangtip Fortress. Lu Ri could appreciate this place. It was stern and imposing, jutting off the mountaintop.

But already he could hear shouts and jeers even from this far away.

A fortress of quiet contemplation it was not. This sounded like a war camp.

Unlike a proper war camp, however, the guards at the gate were relaxed. One had even turned around completely from his position on top of the wall to shout down at whatever was happening below.

Lu Ri paused at the place where a guard was supposed to challenge him. The man looked frustrated and bored, slumped against the wall and picking at his fingers.

"Merchant, here to—" Lu Ri began, but he did not even have time to get out his papers before the guard waved him through.

How . . . *lax*. Lu Ri had to restrain himself from berating the lacka-daisical guard.

He shook his head and entered the fort, heading towards the commotion.

"Zang Li, Zang Li, Zang Li!" several of the crowd chanted while bursts of fire forced the other disciple the man was sparring with back. The other boy was sweating as Zang Li toyed with him, a look in his eyes that Lu Ri remembered well from the Inner Disciples who liked to toy with those they considered their lessers.

He paused, nearly putting his hand on one of the disciples cheering to move him out of the way and intervene in the bout, as Elder Ge had instructed.

However, this was not his Sect. It was not his place to correct them.

He had his mission . . . and he had found his current quarry.

Zang Li, the Young Master of the Shrouded Mountain, was accept-ably powerful, if an unpleasant sort.

The bout continued for three more exchanges. Zang Li gave the other disciple several blows that sent him staggering, before the last threw him into the fortress wall.

"I do not even need to use the Blade of Fire against the likes of you!" Zang Li taunted, to some groans and more cheering.

The other disciple grimaced while holding his burns, but through the scowl on his face, he bowed.

"Thank you for the pointers," he gritted out, the next words looking physically painful, "and thank you for restraining your strength."

The courtyard laughed and jeered at the defeated man; Zang Li raised his arms in a gesture that was meant to look magnanimous but instead seemed mocking.

"Well, that's one star on the rise. I can hear Kang grinding his teeth from here," one of the men near Lu Ri muttered. "Trying to suppress him by leaving him off the assault team only made him stronger."

Zang Li went off, seemingly to boast to some of the other disciples. Lu Ri stepped back from the crowd and considered the best way to get the man alone.

Although he had been waved in, he was still a member of a different Sect, deep in the heart of another. He would have to have some caution. Lu Ri was courteous enough not to go to the library or take anything that wasn't his, though he doubted the Shrouded Mountain had anything of true value to him. Most cultivators would have ransacked the place without a second thought.

Zang Li eventually retired to his room. Lu Ri was contemplating simply walking in when he heard footsteps: a young woman carrying a serving tray, a look of resignation on her face.

She swallowed thickly as she approached the door, her eyes darting left and right.

Lu Ri felt something like distaste curl in the back of his throat, but it was as good an excuse as any.

"Young Miss. I shall take that in for you, I have a report for the Young Master, in any case," he stated simply. The woman nearly jumped out of her skin at his sudden appearance, relief and shock warring on her features as she considered his words.

"Ahh . . . umm, are you certain?" the woman squeaked, but Lu Ri was already taking the tray from her unresisting hands.

"Indeed. Run along back to the kitchens, now."

"Ah, yes, sir," she muttered, bowing swiftly, then leaving.

Lu Ri knocked twice on the door.

"Enter," a voice from within commanded.

And so Lu Ri did, then shut the door behind him. The boy turned around with a smile before it faded to irritation at seeing him.

"I thought I asked for the servers to be female," he asked with narrowed eyes.

Lu Ri took in the boy. The red markings on his forehead that had still not settled from a recent bloodline activation. The sneering look in his eyes. The messy reports on his desk.

This was the one who had made him travel all the way up here?

"Well, answer me, servant—"

Lu Ri had been irritated for nearly six months. Six months of searching for Jin Rou in a Qi-deprived province.

There was a time to be polite, and Lu Ri was *very much* past that point.

The careful stops in his power that he had constructed for the Azure Hills were torn open. Qi filled the room as he used his Senior Sister's technique.

The Young Master in front of him froze, his annoyance fading to shock and fear.

"I require some questions answered. You will answer them." It was a simple statement of fact. Though it would be a mildly dangerous prospect, so deep in this Young Master's territory, Lu Ri was at least confident he could escape should things turn sour.

Recognising his predicament, Zang Li did not try to run or scream. "Yes, sir," the boy stated.

Excellent.

"Do you know a man named Jin Rou? Tall, freckles, brown hair," Lu Ri asked calmly, taking a step towards the boy.

The boy's eyes flashed with both recognition and hatred.

"Yes. I know a man named Jin. He attacked me without provocation—" the boy started to say, before Lu Ri waved a hand to cut off whatever he was about to say.

He cared little for the story. It was irrelevant.

"Where was the last time you saw him?" His eyes bored into the boy's, and Zang Li flinched.

More anger crossed his face. "A town I didn't care to remember the name of."

A lie. Lu Ri read the boy's Intent like an open scroll. A flex of Qi, and the boy flinched.

"Verdant Hill," Zang Li spat.

"Where did he go? Did he stay, or in which direction did he leave?"

The boy grimaced.

"I do not know." *That* was the truth.

Lu Ri considered the boy.

It was a shame this whelp did not know if Jin Rou had left or not, but his own men would surely have a direction.

"Tell me everything you observed about him." The command was met with a mutinous look, but the boy obeyed, detailing the brutal attack on his subordinates and his eventual defeat.

"Why do you need this information? Is he some manner of criminal?" There was hope in this question.

Lu Ri did not deign to answer.

Absolute confirmation, from an eyewitness, that Jin Rou had been in the north of the Azure Hills. Despite his earlier annoyance, he now felt gratitude; his men had truly done well to send him in this direction! How wonderful to have a lead again! He would have to reward them greatly. And one of them had even travelled to the town! *Perhaps he had already found Jin Rou?*

Lu Ri was quite pleased as he left through the front gate.

↔

The rain poured outside their cave, thundering down from the heavens. It was a cold rain, thick and heavy, but it would stop soon.

The rain would hardly be an impediment, but it was cold and annoying, so, as his Great Master had decreed, small breaks were necessary things.

'For five days and five nights we toiled, tending to the fires and infusing the liquid with our power. All of Fa Ram came together to see this task done. Even Wa Shi set aside his natural inclination to feast, in order to bring us food,' Bi De spoke, regaling his companions of the tale of creating maple syrup. *'It was a wondrous endeavour. One I am forever glad I was a part of.'*

Yin and Miantiao were both enraptured by the story, listening to his words.

'The more we hear, the more I wish to sssee this place,' Miantiao mused.

'Yeah! It sounds like fun!' Yin said, nodding her head and setting her ears bouncing. *'I want to meet Tigu and Xiulan. They sound like they'd be exciting to duel!'*

'Ever a one-track mind, my dear,' Miantiao snickered. *'But . . . we shall see Young Master Bi De's home soon, I suppose. We are nearly to our destination.'*

Bi De nodded, the mark in his mind's eye. Their visit to Pale Moon Lake City had been swift. The massive city, home to over a million souls, had been mind-boggling, though he had not truly taken the time to explore it. He'd stayed just long enough to confirm the location of a formation stone. Surprisingly, this one was in the city, jutting up from the middle of a plaza, with thousands of people walking past it every day.

A simple, blank stone pillar. Unassuming, and nearly forgotten.

Now they were once more into the hills, travelling off the beaten path. It was rough terrain, *very* rough terrain, and Bi De did not envy anyone without Qi travelling in this direction. Having to weave around the hills would have been a frustrating task.

Yet for them it was little challenge. They walked during the day and rested during the night, drawing ever closer to the last place Bi De wanted to see. Would it be worth anything? Or was it truly just a random mark?

Bi De did not know, yet he intended to find out.

And he, too, could not wait to introduce his new companions to his Great Master.

He took a breath, tasting the air as Miantiao did. The Qi was thin, yet he could feel bits of it in the air and earth.

They paused to sup upon some jerky and rice. Paltry rations, yet Miantiao and Yin never complained, knowing little of the bounty that awaited them. Would they moan like Disciple Xiulan? It was an amusing thought.

Soon, their search came to an end. Five hills surrounded a smaller hill in the center at the marked point.

And within the center hill, a cave.

Bi De glanced around at the overgrown remains of tiles, which showed that this place had once had habitation. A pentagram was carved above the cave, and there were all five elements written in the circle.

It had a foreboding presence. Wisps of air spilled out from the cave mouth before reversing, and a light, deceptively gentle breeze seemed to beckon them into the darkness.

A whispered invitation . . . or some great beast breathing in, before its jaws snapped shut on an unsuspecting animal.

'Is there anything in there?' Yin asked.

Bi De focused. He took a breath, then searched for power in the earth. Down, down, deep down he looked, until he found it. Strange, and indistinct, and yet, there. Something old, of the earth, and yet not.

'It is deep. Deep, deep down in those caves, where neither the light of the moon nor the light of the sun can reach,' he stated quietly.

Now the question was: to proceed, or to go back?

He considered the cave. The days were growing shorter, and it was soon to be the harvest. It was not like this cavern was going anywhere. He would like to treat his new friends to the Glory of Fa Ram in full swing.

Yet was this not his mission? To attempt to decipher this mystery? What had happened here so long ago? Would giving up now, before one last hurdle, be wise?

The cave beckoned and repulsed in equal measure.

Yin shrugged. 'Onwards, then!' the rabbit declared. 'We'll see what it is, accomplish our duty, and then we'll go to your Fa Ram triumphant!'

Bi De smiled softly at the rabbit, who was striding forwards with confidence. How thoroughly she had thrown herself into this task. How completely she had devoted herself to it.

Could he, the one who had started it, show any less conviction?

Their supplies were full enough.

So Bi De took a step forwards, the silver of the moon wrapping around his body as they descended.

Down, down.

Down into the deep.

CHAPTER 59

OBLIGATORILY OMINOUS

A creature erupted from a hole in the wall, screeching with glee and maddened hunger. Its white flesh and sightless eyes twisted grotesquely, as its long claws reached greedily for the flesh of whatever had been foolish enough to venture near its hole.

A crack of a wing splattered it against the wall. Bi De came to a stop, examining the fork in the tunnel, which split off in two different directions.

'Are you feeling all right?' Yin asked as the fire of the sun roasted another one of the mindless beasts. They would not listen to any entreaty, and even flaring Qi to try to ward the ravenous things off only served to draw them nearer.

'No,' Bi De said simply, bringing his breathing under control and scowling up at the thousands of tons of rock sitting above his head. *'This place sits ill with me. The sooner we are back under the sky, the better.'*

Yin cocked her head to the side, curious. *'I find it quite comforting, really,'* she said.

Both she and Miantiao had been relatively unaffected by their descent, both used to tunnels and cramped spaces.

It was the second time Bi De had been underground. The first was when he'd ventured into his Great Master's Ice Cavern to retrieve a block of ice. That was a damp and dark place that was in a constant state of flux. Tiny temperature variations pulsed from the Core of the General that Commands the Winter, his Great Master's golem, creating a distinctly unpleasant feeling.

Despite how unpleasant that had been, Bi De would rather be locked in the freezing storage room for a month than be in this cave system for another minute.

On the first day, full of good spirit and vigor, they had begun their descent, picking their way through the narrow tunnels and wading across small rivers. Once or twice they even felt the fresh summer breeze, carried in through holes that managed to plunge into the hill from the surface.

Bi De and Yin could feel the position of the moon and the sun respectively, so that night, at the precipice of a larger cavern, they rested, preparing for whatever might lie ahead.

On the second day, Bi De's power had begun to wane.

It was a slight tickling sensation, but his light faded.

He could not understand it at first. He could feel it just as they reached a massive complex of caves, where the darkness became deeper. There, the Holy Moonlight was needed just as much as Yin's solar armour.

Why would the moon hide, in this pitch-blackness?

He had no answer. The only solace was that as long as Yin lit the way, he too would have some small measure of his power back. Her sun fueled his moon, and without it, the light faded. It consumed his thoughts. He could not enjoy the majestic waterfalls, the strange glowing mushrooms, or even the pillars that grew down from the ceiling. It was all he could do not to run back to the surface.

But he persevered, and they delved. The air stagnated. Some of the tunnels got so small that Bi De had to squeeze through, getting dirt all over his feathers.

The creeping feeling of unease troubled his sleep on the second night and plagued him with nightmares.

On the third day, they encountered *these things*.

When the first one had struck, he had caught it instinctively and apologised for trespassing.

Only furious growls and a snapping mouth had greeted him—so it had to be dealt with.

Needless to say, it hadn't helped his mood.

He focused, feeling the disturbances, minute as they were, in the air, and the draw of the power still far below. They were barely halfway there, by his reckoning.

How unfortunate.

'*Right is the correct way, I do believe,*' he stated, as he finished contemplating both routes, turning to his companions. Miantiao nodded, while Yin was sniffing at one of the dead beasts.

With a shrug, she reached down as if to take a bite, only to have Mian-tiao swat her on top of her head.

'Not thessse ones, Yin,' he muttered.

'Eh? But you always told me to get as much Qi as I can, and these guys have plenty,' Yin questioned.

'And I sssshould not have,' Miantiao said. *'Leave them.'*

Yin obligingly dropped the creature.

'Oh, this is one of those things you're sorry for? The stomachaches and the shits weren't that bad after I learned how to refine it, so don't feel too bad, Shifu!'

The snake closed his eye, grimacing in regret. His tail stroked Yin's head.

'Let us continue. But I will not hope that this was the worst of it,' Mian-tiao muttered instead.

→

Bi De startled awake, panting, from a dream he could not remember. He looked around, but it was a futile effort. The darkness was absolute.

He tried to meditate, but that too was for nothing. He was too dis-turbed. The constant tugging feeling in his Qi was getting worse, the land pulling him down, scrabbling at his Qi in greed.

He bore it. But if it got much worse . . .

He shook his head. They were close now.

Slowly, a golden glow started up.

Yin's dirty, matted fur greeted him, though it was a dull grey rather than pure white.

'I think I hate this place,' she stated bluntly. *'It's a bunch of bullshit.'*

Miantiao barked out a laugh but did not bother to chide her language. *'Indeed. But we are clossse. Even I can feel that ssssomething is near.'*

Indeed, it was, as the bunny had said, "bullshit." Still, they had to go even deeper, and the air was beginning to get outright unpleasant.

It was the seventh day, as far as Bi De could tell.

There were few words as the group arose and continued on.

Bi De's feathers were sticking to him, and even Miantiao and Yin had gotten quieter, their eyes more focused. The dull golden glow coming from Yin was their only comfort. At least the beast attacks had stopped, the emaciated creatures finally giving up their previously ceaseless assaults. They were not particularly dangerous, but they did add strain.

That day's travel was boring, until they reached a stone archway.

In front of the archway was a skeleton, curled up, as if having drifted off into sleep. It was a giant beast that looked like it was half cat and half dog like the ones Bi De had seen in the cities. It had enormous incisor teeth, ready to rip and tear.

'*A temple dog?*' Miantiao asked, referring to the normally stone guardians carved outside some of the shrines that they had seen.

'*I do believe so,*' Bi De got out after a moment, glancing at the archway. The character for "king" stood upon the entrance.

Bi De's unease grew at the sight of the corpse.

They continued onwards—past the silent bones and into the hall. This part was obviously human-made, with veins of glowing stone that lit the way, sparking and flickering uncertainly, but it was enough light to see by.

The golden glow faded as Yin let her technique drop.

Bi De panted, then stumbled on a slightly raised piece of stone. His body was getting even weaker from his time deep in the earth.

Yin caught him. She appeared both concerned and confused.

'*Shifu, he is so strong, why is he . . . ?*' she asked.

'*He is a creature of wind and ssssky, of the moon. Being sssmothered in this oppresssive place must be unbearable. Support him as you can, Yin. There is no shame in this.*'

Yin nodded, and the golden light began to glow again.

'*Well, you just lean here, 'kay?*' she told him, allowing him to press against her side. '*I'm good to keep going, and once we get back out, Bi De'll be all good, right?*'

'*A likely outcome,*' Bi De confirmed, his voice strained, but the warm glow chased away some of the fatigue. '*Thank you, Yin.*'

The rabbit grinned and nuzzled his side.

This leg of the walk was much easier and allowed Bi De to take in his surroundings.

The walls, along with the veins of crystal, were filled with murals. Murals of harvest and huts, of mountains, and of men fighting great beasts.

As the trio continued on their path, deeper into the tunnel, the murals changed.

The people in the murals were met by a man, and behind him stood a woman, seeming to float on air. Where he went, the pictures changed.

The harvests got larger. The huts turned into palaces. The men and beasts toiled together in the fields, their blades being beaten into ploughshares.

They danced. They danced together, for the man and the woman, who held out their hands and gave blessings.

Until their party came upon the last room. The last cavern.

The walls of the room were glowing dully with blue veins of crystal. Some had jutted outwards, forming spikes from the wall, and one particularly large vein was wrapped around a more recognisable crystal, seated on an altar.

A recording crystal.

The pull seemed to radiate off it.

They approached slowly, wary of some kind of trap, yet there was none. There was only silence.

He knew roughly how to work the crystal, and there was nothing else here. This was where they were meant to be.

And it was just a recording crystal, was it not?

Bi De reached forwards and placed one of his claws on the crystal's surface.

But unlike his Master's, this crystal did not project. Instead, he felt himself being drawn inward.

→

There was a storm of emotion.

Bi De fell to his knees as the last demon died, panting with exhaustion.

He stared at the devastation the demons had wrought, wrath like a star glowing in his chest at the twisted and corrupted land.

He pulled up his sleeve and stared at the blackened skin there. He grimaced. How could she ever stand this? How could she smile and shrug it off?

He pulled his sleeve back down and rose. He would have to ask Shu Xiong for her help to fix this. And perhaps send some gifts to the giant green bear's cubs. She was quite the doting mother . . .

Something twisted and skipped. Visions flashed. They were his memories, and yet they weren't. They were *nothing* like his Master's recording crystal. They were too intense—they were like he was actually there, in human form.

"Hey, shorty, what the hell?" a frazzled woman barked out as she stormed into Bi De's rooms. She looked like she had just been startled out of bed, with her

messy hair and drooping clothes. He snorted at the nickname, as he was now taller than her, but he supposed he would always be short to her.

"Felt that, did you?" Bi De asked her with a knowing smile, as he turned the map he was looking at towards her. Her eyes narrowed at the spirals and swirls upon it. It was the work of nearly a decade.

"You—geh! Now I know why you wanted to know that!" the woman huffed, as red tinged her cheeks.

Bi De's grin got a bit wider. "It's just my way of giving back. Of growing together. In time, we'll usher in a new dawn."

The woman sighed, but then she embraced him. "You didn't have to, you know."

He did. He really did.

The memories began to rapidly switch. A woman eating a rice cake. Festivals, empowering the earth.

Himself and his dear companion teaching the dances to the people.

He was happy, so happy for a while.

And then it all started to go wrong.

Happiness switched to pain. To violence. He had to defend his home and his friends from those that would wish him harm. He saw his people bowing to him, for he was their Lord and Master.

"She's using you," the beast hissed. "Though your life may be long, longer than most . . . you will never *be immortal. Your bones will rest here forever. Bound to this base earth, and more food for your 'friend.'"*

Bi De destroyed it utterly.

But something ticked in the back of his skull. Memories of unease.

Years passed by in flashes of emotion. Of joy and hope, of loss, of pain. Of wars. Of battling for a hundred years. Of his friend's pain, that she just laughed off like it was no big deal.

And blank eyes staring, as the world began to break.

'I'm sorry, Tianlan,' he said as his dearest friend's form cracked.

Tianlan screamed.

As did someone else.

'Bi De!' Yin shouted.

Paws gripped him around the shoulders and jerked him back.

He staggered from the crystal, collapsing to his knees.

"Wha—" he gasped, finally noticing the flickering lights as the crystal dimmed and brightened uncertainly.

'The entire formation in the walls is in flux,' Miantiao muttered. *'I do believe we need to leave.'*

Yin nodded, about to pull him away.

'Wait. We need the crystal!' he demanded. The vision was still unfinished.

'How? It's attached to the wall!' Yin explained, looking nervously at the crystal.

Bi De rose on unsteady feet. He examined the crystal as it pulsed again, where the crystals had grown from the wall and connected to it, wrapping around it.

The hall rumbled.

Bi De lashed out with a kick, painfully weak compared to his normal blows but still enough to sever the connection close to the wall.

The crystal dimmed.

Miantiao's tail, crippled though it was, coiled around Bi De the rooster and the crystal to Yin, as the rabbit took off.

They prepared for some form of collapse as they dashed madly out of the tunnel . . . and yet . . .

The rumbling stopped.

But Yin's stride did not.

'We're getting out of here,' she snarled.

Bi De nodded as they bounced up the hall.

He was *very* tired.

CHAPTER 60

KNOWING YOUR LIMITS

Bi De sighed as he completed the paperwork. *Really, if he had known how much there would be, he never would have become what he was. He leaned back in his seat, a simple wooden thing, staring around at his office. It was an enormous room full of papers and scrolls. Outside, there was an entire wing of the palace dedicated to this.*

Bi De shook his head and sighed again, fiddling with his brush. It neared the page, ready to doodle, before he remembered that it was an important document. Frustrated, he stood. Sometimes, when it was like this, he missed the old days, when it was just him and his shovel.

His men outside saluted him as he passed, their armour made of glimmering Pale Moon Ore.

His feet took him in the same direction they always took him when he felt this way. Out of the inner courtyard and out into the gardens, following the sound of music.

He smiled as he gazed upon the scene. There was a woman, playing on her pipa, the old instrument twanging pleasantly. He just stayed there and let peace wash over him. Eventually, the woman noticed her visitor. She turned to her friend and grinned, her smile full of teeth, and her eyes as pure and blue as the skies above.

↔

Bi De pulled back from the crystal as the vision ended. It flickered fitfully, the light pulsing down from the ragged edges where he had struck it from the wall. The extended portions looked slightly like jagged lightning bolts, a slightly different hue than the rest of the crystal.

This was little like his Great Master's crystal, which was so neatly organised. Everything was jumbled together, such a chaotic blend of thought and emotion that he had trouble parsing it all while he was viewing it. It was like he was the man in the recording. He preened his feathers, considering the crystal further.

It had been faster and much more pleasant ascending than it had been descending. Five days instead of seven. Bi De's strength had seeped back into his bones as they ascended. He still was not back to perfect fitness, but the light of the moon was most invigorating. He had kept imagining that something would go wrong, like a cave-in . . . yet they had reached the surface without incident and travelled to Pale Moon Lake City to recuperate.

There was a rustling sound as Miantiao and Yin entered back into their temporary residence.

'Anything?' Yin asked him.

'Nothing.' Bi De shook his head. 'Yourselves?'

Miantiao hissed in irritation. 'No. There were no murals, no markers . . . Swimming under the lake yielded no signs of the fall. Thisss issss a mossst vexing conundrum. It makes little sssense, if I am honessst.'

The snake tapped his tail against his chin. 'From the visions of this crystal, and our own search, someone far in the past crafted a formation that was used to empower . . . something. This ritual then went wrong, unleashing a calamity of great power. It devastated the land, changing every element one step forwards in the cycle of creation. Thessse are all things we have seen with our own eyesss. The evidence is irrefutable.'

Bi De nodded in agreement while the snake uncoiled himself from Yin, then continued to speak. 'Yet what I do not understand is the lack of records, and it has bothered me. Would there not be records of some calamity? The Dance of my Massster, of Hong Yaowu, and every village we journeyed through . . . the people remember this dance, yet why do they not remember the reason for it?'

The snake slithered around the room in agitation, pondering. 'Why do they not remember the sky falling, and the earth being torn asunder? Would not such an event burn itself into their memories? Would it not be passed down through the generations, just as they remember their stories?'

Both the rooster and Yin frowned. 'Perhaps that part of the story was lost, somehow?' Yin asked. 'I've been alive for eight years, yet that already feels so long. I cannot imagine what a hundred or even a thousand years would do.'

'Or perhaps we did not ask the right questions? In the Eighth Correct Place, their history said how the floods could sweep away the entire village in an instant, and that was dismissed as legend. Perhaps other places will have legends like this?' Bi De mused.

Miantiao sighed. *'So we know what happened, and what the formation was for. But not why it was destroyed, or how.'*

Bi De stroked his wattles. *'The only other place I could think of with such records is the Palace Grand Archive, which the great Healing Sage says collected a great amount of scrolls when it was constructed. It is not even an hour's journey away . . . but we can hardly just waltz in the front door as we are.'*

They looked down at their bodies and their distinct lack of human looks.

'. . . we could get a cloak and stand on top of each other?' Yin asked. Bi De chuckled at the amusing image.

Miantiao snorted, stretching out his body like an exceedingly long neck. *'I shall be the head? Else we shall be very short.'*

Yin pouted at them for their amusement. *'Or we could just sneak in at night.'*

Bi De considered this for a moment. There were some disadvantages to this form, but if they snuck in, the clerks would hardly know where to look. There would be thousands, if not hundreds of thousands of scrolls in the Grand Archive. While he did still have his Great Master's servant's letter, using that would attract a great amount of attention, should they decide to go in the front door. The crystal they carried was both valuable and in need of repair, yet they had little money to repair it.

There was little more that they could do, for now.

He looked to his companions. They had not complained at all, not a single moment over the entire length of the journey. Even now, they were ready to slink through a city, to search high and low for the answers to the questions they had.

Sometimes, all you need is patience.

No, now was not the time to continue to forge ahead.

They had found part of the answer: they had mapped the formation. Now was the time to reassess. They could deliver their treasure home, then beg the aid of his Great Master and their fellow disciples.

'In the end . . . is it truly so urgent?' Bi De asked. *'The formation has been like this for thousands of years. We shall seek counsel on this matter, and with it, a new path forwards.'*

Two heads turned to him. Bi De held his head up proudly.

'We shall return to my home.'

→

It was so odd, retracing his steps. Heading north. Heading home. He still felt a bit like he should have attempted to find more answers. To keep on striding forth on his own. A small part of himself derided the decision to go running to his Master.

He dismissed those thoughts. To forge ahead blindly was foolhardy, especially after what he had learned. He had more friends and allies than just the two with him.

They travelled quickly, striding over the hills and bypassing villages, barely stopping.

So excited was he, and so direct was their pace, that they passed Verdant Hill and Hong Yaowu entirely.

Bi De would visit them later.

Instead, their party came out from the forest onto a changed land. The road to Fa Ram, once dirt, was now paved more finely than Pale Moon Lake City's. Every five paving stones, there were vines and flowers carved, light scratches of patterns, made by Sister Tigu's claws.

And with each step, Bi De felt his soul lighten. He felt the last dregs of fatigue start to leave his body, as the Blessed Land of Fa Ram welcomed her son home.

He glanced at Yin and Miantiao. Neither of them noticed the difference. Neither of them commented on the change, but he noticed the signs. The way Miantiao became less hunched. The way Yin bounced ever so slightly.

The very road itself, constructed while he was absent, seemed to hasten the journey, lending their strides even more speed, yet not to the point of urgency.

Finally, they came upon the gate. The Great Pillars that marked the boundary. The maple leaf sign, and the words his Master had carved.

Miantiao chuckled. *'Thessse are most accurate words, no?'* the old snake asked. *'Truly, you are terrifying when angered. But . . . will your Master just . . . accept usss?'*

Bi De saw the nervousness upon their faces.

The rooster smiled.

'Follow,' he stated simply as he began to ascend the last hill.

When they crested the top, as Bi De's home spread out beneath them, he heard the intakes of breath.

He realised one of them had been his own.

The warmth of the sun seemed to soak into his feathers as they exited the tunnel of trees that lined the road. The breeze blew across them, bringing the smells of home, growth, and fruits, and setting the grass waving.

Bees buzzed and milled around the property and its outskirts. They took to the air as they noticed him, flying in formation back to their hives.

When the breeze had touched them, both Miantiao's and Yin's eyes had widened.

'Whaa . . . wahaaa?' Yin asked, glancing around at the grass, while the snake was silent, simply staring.

Bi De's eyes immediately went to his coop. He saw from a distance that the Healing Sage and Sister Ri Zu toiled there. The Healing Sage wore a mask and thick gloves as she carefully removed the leaves from a plant, being exceedingly careful not to get the thick sap on her skin. Beside her Ri Zu hammered away with a mortar and pestle, a little green robe with a blue sash protecting her fur.

Occasionally, a strange, yet oddly familiar-looking orange-haired girl went to them, delivering more of the medicinal herbs they were harvesting.

Most of Fa Ram's residents were out in the fields, for the first parts of the harvest had begun.

The rice paddies were being drained. Disciple Gou Ren was covered in mud as he inspected the walls and removed the breaks for the water to rush out. Brother Chun Ke was with him, his enormous back covered in ducks and frogs while he carefully herded some of Wa Shi's kin out of the draining water and back into the river.

Disciple Xiulan worked with him, surprisingly stripped to the waist, with only a bare covering preserving her modesty. She smiled and said something, clapping Disciple Gou Ren on the back as they passed each other. The boy rolled his eyes and shook his head.

Sister Pi Pa approached them, a tray of tea balanced upon her back, utterly still and sure, even over rough ground. She served the workers elegantly before wading into the muck herself to help.

Wa Shi's head poked out of the water as he too begged a cup. With an odd flash, he suddenly gained an arm, taking the cup from Pi Pa and taking a sip.

Bi De's jaw dropped at the transformation, yet none of his fellow disciples reacted.

Bi De guessed that made sense. Wa Shi had obviously jumped over the Waterfall Gate and become a dragon!

The fish considered the tea before reaching down and grabbing some algae, sampling it, and taking another sip of his beverage. He nodded, agreeing with this combination of flavours. Intrigued, Disciple Gou Ren stuck out a finger to taste some of this algae-and-tea mixture.

Bi De chuckled at his friend's action—he was pleased the fish had returned. There was a brief flash of concern at the almost Chow Ji–like limb, but none reacted to it, so he decided to question it later.

Finally, he beheld his Great Master. He too stood in the paddy. His eyes were closed and his face was turned towards the sun. The Great Master's shirt was around his waist, his tanned skin slick with sweat. The wind blew and tousled his hair like a fond hand.

Behind him in the fields past the paddies, the sheep and cows wandered as they always did, and the other chickens flapped as they hunted interlopers.

At that moment, everything fell away. He forgot himself—he could contain himself no longer. He had missed so much . . . and he wanted to miss no more. He carefully set down the crystal tied to his back, then took a deep breath.

His cry echoed across the hills.

Chickens startled to attention. His Great Master turned, his smile shocked and pleased, as Bi De charged down the hill as fast as his wings and legs could carry him, alighting upon his rightful place atop the Great Master's shoulder and burying his head into his Master's hair.

A gentle hand reached up and stroked his wattles. His head pressed back.

"You tell 'em, Bi De." He whispered the customary greeting, and the rooster swallowed thickly. "It's good to see you again, buddy. We missed you."

The rooster wiped some of the dampness off his cheeks, and a second later he heard Brother Chun Ke squeal with joy.

For a moment, he was just *there*, a near chick again, and tended to by his Master.

Until he remembered himself.

He coughed and hopped off his Master's shoulder, motioning for his companions to approach.

They did so nervously. It did look a bit amusing, to see the snake's little green head poking up from between Yin's ears as he rode on her back. Two coils unlooped themselves from her midsection, the smaller snake slithering from his perch to stand before the Great Master. Both kowtowed.

'*Great Massster Jin, we come to beg your hospitality,*' the snake hissed formally. He was about to continue when the Great Master interrupted.

"Come on, none of that," he stated simply. "No need for formality here. I read Bi De's letter, and all I have to say is . . . welcome to our home. Miantiao and Yin, right?" Bi De's Master asked, crouching down to be more level with them.

Both nodded slowly.

"Good. Now things are probably going to get a bit hectic over the next few minutes, so I'll apologise in advance."

Confusion spread across their faces, but that was all the indication Bi De's fellow disciples needed.

Sister Ri Zu was upon Bi De's back, snuggling into his feathers and glancing curiously at the newcomers.

Brother Chun Ke's friendly bulk approached, sniffing curiously.

Surrounded by friends, everything was back to normal.

Until the dragon appeared, hovering over them so that he could get a better view from outside the pond he had been occupying.

"Ha! This Rou Tigu shall show you how much she has grown. Prepare yourself for tonight, Bi De!" the orange-haired girl, who could only be Tigu with that announcement, said with a laugh. Her face was set in a massive grin.

Bi De once more felt his beak fall open.

. . . ah, *mostly* back to normal.

CHAPTER 61

THE BURDEN OF TRUST

Breathe, please," the woman said, and Miantiao complied. Soft fingers trailed along damaged scales and touched old wounds so lightly he could barely feel them.

He did his best to just lie there. It was quite easy, with how he had been feeling since he had first entered Fa Ram. The happy laughter. The warm looks. Like his old village, as the people had come together to help each other. It was all just a bit too much.

Yin had left his side with an encouraging nod, but . . . she fit in so easily. She slotted in like there had been a space waiting for her all this time, joining in on the banter with her own crude exclamations, much to the shock and offence of the sow and the amusement of the dragon and the orange-haired girl.

She *belonged* here, while part of him . . . part of him was still somewhere far away.

The healer asked his permission for something, and he nodded absently.

It was like the dreams he had, dreams where his Master was still alive.

He had said he would live for Yin's sake . . . yet he wondered if he would ever truly fit in here? Fit in, with everybody so lively and enthusiastic.

There was a sudden tugging sensation, and he flinched—it felt like a splinter had just been pulled out of his soul.

He glanced up at the woman, who was frowning at a little black bead she held between her fingers.

"I'm getting entirely too familiar with doing this sort of thing," she muttered. "Ri Zu?"

The rat held up a tiny jar, and the woman deposited the bead into it. "Store that one away from everything else. I want to see if there is an easier way to purify it," she commanded. Then a green aura flowed around her hand, burning away tiny little flecks of black that had remained on her fingers.

"Damn shit. Why would anybody willingly make their Qi into *that*," she muttered, glaring at the filth in the bucket.

Then she shook her head and turned back to the snake. The woman smiled down at him.

"That . . . Well, that should help a bit with the scarring. Your next shed, some of the scales should come back, but the old breaks in the spine . . . they are beyond me right now. I would have to speak with Father, or get a few books on dealing with such old wounds," she said, as soothing green light coursed through his body.

'*You have already done more than enough, Lady Hong,*' he whispered, as he was raised up into the woman's arms.

She raised an eyebrow at him but otherwise did not speak. She set him down at the table on a cushion, recognising his silence and mood for what it was, and left him to his contemplations.

The silence was soon broken.

The door banged open, and a slightly singed Tigu waltzed in, with a battered Yin flopped on top of her head.

The orange girl looked *very* smug.

"A fine fight, Junior Sister!" she commended.

'*Gonna beat you next time,*' Yin stated with absolute confidence. '*Then you'll be* my *Junior Sister.*'

"Ha! You may come at me every day for the next thousand years!" the cat boasted, her arms crossed in front of her chest.

'*Tomorrow,*' Yin said, as Bi De entered with Ri Zu, the little rat perched on his back again.

"Really?" the cat asked, seeming surprised.

'*Yeah. Fighting is fun.*'

Tigu smiled brightly.

Yin noticed as the rooster sat down. The rabbit hopped off her perch and sauntered over to Bi De, where she leaned up against him like she often did.

Silver, radiant fur, beside black drab colours. The rabbit smiled.

Ri Zu looked shocked, her eyes narrowing slightly.

'You are close-friendly, then?' the rat asked, directing her question to Yin. It was rather pointed, her voice overcome with a strange accent.

'Yes, we do this every night!' the rabbit said cheerfully, not noticing the slight hostility. *'He is a good friend who helped us.'*

The stormy expression intensified on the rat's face. Yin seemed to realise something. *'Oh, will you be sleeping with us too? Bi De speaks often of you, and says what a wonderful companion you are!'*

'Eh?' Ri Zu squeaked, the hostility being beaten back by Yin's bright enthusiasm and earnestness.

'Yes, Shifu must be kept warm, and I am told I'm quite comfortable! Here!' She thrust an ear at the rat, who took it hesitantly.

'Ah . . . it is quite soft . . .' the rat muttered as she absently rubbed it.

'See, Sister Ri Zu! The more of us there are, the more comfortable it is!' Yin declared authoritatively.

Lady Hong chuckled.

The table slowly filled as more and more people joined.

Talking. Laughter. Yin's smile.

This was a good place. A place where Yin could belong.

But could he?

The meal was brought out to them by Master Jin.

Slowly, tentatively, Miantiao took a bite of the egg that had been prepared for him.

It was the best thing he had ever eaten.

He jumped as Yin's foot suddenly hammered on the floor, thumping out joyously.

'This is fucking amazing!' she shouted, and the table erupted with laughter.

'Language!' Miantiao and the sow simultaneously demanded. Both stared in shock at each other, until Pi Pa nodded, offering him a smile.

"Now *that's* a compliment!" Master Jin declared with a smile.

As they ate, Bi De and Yin regaled the group with their adventures. The bear she had hammered into the ground like a nail. Their swim in Pale Moon Lake. The mountains, and the great dungeon they traversed, full of snapping horrors.

Their crowd gasped at the appropriate moments and laughed at Yin's suggestion for them to wear a cloak and stand upon each other's shoulders.

The room quieted when Bi De brought out the crystal. It looked . . . dull. Dull, and the light was spluttering slightly.

The need to repair it was growing.

'Great Master, I beg your aid to unravel this mystery,' he finished.

The man smiled and nodded, though Miantiao saw the uncertainty in his eyes.

→

He could not sleep.

It was late at night when Miantiao uncurled from Yin. The rabbit had a pleased smile on her face, even asleep. Gently, he stroked some of her fur, then a moment later began to carefully pick his way out of the pile. Bi De and Ri Zu were easy to dodge. Chun Ke and Pi Pa were their backrests and weren't in his way. He slithered around one of Tigu's limbs, sprawled out where she snored softly.

She was covered in bruises, but she had a feather tucked behind her ear, a prize from her fight with Young Master Bi De. She had been defeated yet was still proud of herself.

The rooster had appeared impressed with her growth.

Slowly he ventured away from them. He headed out of the room they were in, towards the light that was still on in the next room.

Master Jin, it seemed, was still awake. He was sitting upon the porch, his feet in the water as he gazed out over the land, his brow furrowed.

The man raised an eyebrow at the crystal, which was sitting beside him. He brought one hand near to it, and the object began to glow. Brighter and brighter, pulsing with instability.

He pulled his hand away and sighed.

"My choice, huh?" he muttered. "Being in charge sucks."

Miantiao recognised the sentiment. He understood that look enough that he was speaking before he fully realised what he was saying.

'Few ever realise how heavy such trussst is,' Miantiao whispered.

The man turned to look at him and snorted at Miantiao's words.

"When you have no idea what you're doing, and they trust you to come up with the right answer anyway?" he asked. He did not appear angry at Miantiao's interruption of his thoughts. Instead, he patted the spot next to him.

'Indeed,' the snake agreed as he curled up beside the man. It was a bit awkward, but he had the man's attention now. It might have been impudent of him to speak so familiarly to this man, but he could not stay silent.

'Our tale troubless you?' Miantiao asked.

"It's not the knowledge, it's what to do with it," Master Jin said. "I'm not particularly a fan of stories with ancient formations blowing up the entire province. I live here, after all," he said with a wry smile.

The snake huffed at his joke. *'Then the question is, what shall you do about it?'*

The man sighed and stared up at the sky. He chewed on his lip.

"Help," he said after a moment. "What else would I do? Say no, and forbid him from searching? He'd probably obey me, but it would eat at him. He would *want* to know. Living your life unfulfilled . . . knowing that you were denied . . . I don't want to do that to him. It's important to Bi De. It's important to you too, I think. I'm a bit curious as to what happened myself, but it's a tale thousands of years old."

He turned to the snake.

"Does anybody seem to be using the formation?" he asked.

'No,' Miantiao answered after a moment.

"Is there anybody trying to repair it?"

'I do not believe so. It seems to be degrading with each passing year.'

Master Jin shrugged. "Then we'll find out what happened, talk things out, and go from there. It's been a few thousand years, so I'm sure it can wait a bit. But . . . I'll help out. See if we can get a discount from Yun Ren's girlfriend on repairing this crystal."

They lapsed into silence. He'd offered help like it should be expected of him. He reminded Miantiao a bit of his own Master in some ways.

"Hey, Bi De said you were pretty good at making glass," the man said after a moment.

'I do have some skill, yesss,' Miantiao replied.

The man grinned, then stood, rummaging around in a drawer for a moment before returning. He looked a bit annoyed.

"Damn it, Meimei, I can't find anything when you go and *organise* things," he muttered.

He set the page in front of Miantiao.

'A house made of glasss?' he asked. *'What is the point of something so fragile?'*

"It will let us grow food, even during the winter, by letting in and trapping the sun's heat," Master Jin replied.

The snake stared in wonder. To craft something that brought life in the depths of winter? Was it really possible?

'*Such a thing would be a large undertaking,*' the snake mused, his mind whirling. '*But doable, especially with Qi. Is this to be our payment to you, for staying under your roof?*'

The man looked at him closely. "If you want to think of it as a debt being repaid . . . then that's what it is. But I always found that *doing* something helps when I feel lost."

The look in his eyes. Ah, perhaps Miantiao was more obvious than he thought he was.

But he was correct. Already, the ratios were swimming behind his eyes.

"Thanks for the talk, Miantiao," the man said. He grinned. It wasn't carefree, but it was honest.

Different from Miantiao's own Master's cheeky grin, but a good one all the same.

CHAPTER 62

THE EARLY HARVEST

Now, this is how one sets the fire for the morning! And then, we must commence our guard duty! Our charges need much protection, and our presence soothes them!"Tigu declared to the rabbit beside her. Bi De nodded along too as he refamiliarized himself with his chores and duty.

'Yes, Senior Sister!' Yin listened seriously as Tigu lectured—the cat appeared inordinately proud at how sincerely Yin was calling her by her won title. She also still had Bi De's feather tucked behind her ear. It was both annoying and flattering how proud she was of the feat. Annoying, on account of her being insufferably smug, and flattering that she thought so highly of him that a single feather was considered a great milestone. 'Then, after that we can fight?'

Tigu nodded. "Once we have completed our duties, we shall spar! If you wish to be part of Fa Ram, you must be strong in your own way!"

The rabbit nodded again rapidly. 'And . . . what about food? Are we truly to eat whenever we are hungry?'

The girl cocked her head to the side. "Why would you not?" she asked, confused.

After all, neither she nor Bi De himself had ever truly known what it was like to go hungry. Yin nodded happily, the novelty still fresh.

"Now, we must go to Mistress. She was distracted by the snake yesterday, but you too need to be in good health!"

Tigu marched off, and Yin followed behind.

Bi De's eyes found Miantiao, the snake deep in conversation with his Great Master about glass. Despite having just met, the two seemed to understand each other quite well, and the snake was a wellspring of knowledge. Miantiao's eye was a bit livelier than normal as he pointed to a part on the drawing with his tail.

There was the brief patter of rain and a flash of a giant body before a fish sailed through the window and into his tub. He slapped the sides of it happily as Disciple Xiulan appeared upon floating blades, her face at peace, the last of whatever plagued her having faded into nothingness.

Even she had pledged her support, saying that she would scour her Sect's library for him, to see if she could glean any information that would aid his quest.

It was humbling, how much things had changed in his absence.

Bi De had seen how much Fa Ram had grown in merely his first year, and yet . . . he had presumed that when he returned, he would find things much as they had been.

That was not the case. Of course his fellow disciples had developed in his absence. Of course, things had changed.

Their strength had all increased in leaps and bounds. While before, neither Tigu nor Disciple Xiulan, nor both together, could ruffle his feathers, now he was unsure if he could duel them at the same time and come out unharmed.

He was also still not entirely sure what to think of Tigu changing her form to become human, or Wa Shi becoming a dragon. Chow Ji's twisted form still flashed in his mind for a brief instant whenever he saw Tigu, yet instead of becoming a vicious, bloodthirsty creature, changing her form had relaxed the cat considerably.

He never thought he would see the day when Tigu and Sister Ri Zu would willingly travel together. Nor the day when Tigu willingly allowed him to sit upon her shoulder. She even seemed eager and excited to show him around.

He took in a breath and sighed with contentment.

How he had missed this.

'Brother Bi De,' a tiny voice called, but it was louder and more confident than normal. He turned to the rat in her little green robe. She was as fetching as ever.

'Sister Hong Ri Zu,' he called back, emphasising her family name—it suited her. Ri Zu blushed.

'Have you thought of your decision yet?' she asked him as she set the food down.

'It was an act of extreme generosity for the Great Master to offer his own name to me,' he said quietly. *'And yet . . . another calls to me. Fa. After the land we live upon, Blessed Fa Ram. Fa Bi De.'*

'A good name,' Ri Zu praised, taking a seat beside him. She was different too. There was no twitchiness to be found. No sudden pressing up against his body. Instead, there rested a quiet confidence.

It looked good on her. And yet there was one thing he had to ask.

'When I set out again, with our Great Master . . . this time . . . will you join me?' he asked her. Like he had asked the first time. The first time, she had refused, citing her own weakness, but perhaps she too had grown enough? Was confident enough in herself? He had missed her dearly.

The rat's eyes widened with shock. She took a breath as if to say yes, and then clearly stopped herself.

She raised herself up and, to Bi De's surprise, she shook her head.

'Ri Zu has sworn to go to the tournament with Xiulan, Gou Ren, and Tigu. Ri Zu will keep this promise.' Her resolve was firm. She was going to travel out of Fa Ram and with the others to a place that could well be full of danger.

'This time, Ri Zu will tell you a tale of her adventures!'

Resolve. Resolve, like when she'd challenged Chow Ji. Some of the pain at the rejection faded. She too wished to better herself. She wanted to see more of the world, and while he was away, she had strived to do just that.

The rooster closed his eyes and smiled.

He tucked his wing around his companion, who squeaked with embarrassment.

'I look forward to hearing every word, Sister Ri Zu,' he said earnestly.

↔

I stared out over the fields, and up to the hills in the distance.

The predawn light was warming my skin and just starting to cast a golden glow over the entire landscape.

I took a deep breath, filling my lungs with the smell of the earth. Of ripe rice, of fruits nearly ready to eat, of the vegetables in the garden.

The smell of the beginning of the harvest.

The first time the harvest had begun . . . I was alone. Well, Big D had been there, but I hadn't yet noticed that he was more than he appeared to be.

It was an appealing idea: a single man against the world. Building his life alone, a true pioneer in every way.

It was a hard life, but . . . it wasn't all bad. Sure, it had been lonely, and it was a bit dumb of me to go full hermit . . . but the work? Building this place up? I still looked back on that time fondly.

Or maybe I was just being a bit dramatic and nostalgic?

It had been *work*. Hard, backbreaking work, and a bit lonely.

Until some friends came.

I looked to either side of me.

Meimei stretched her arms above her head, letting out a cute little sound. The small bump that was her stomach strained the fabric slightly, the life growing within getting bigger by the day.

Gou Ren yawned, in the middle of washing his hands in the river.

Just missing number three. Yun Ren's grin formed in my head.

That had been the real start. The moment when I'd realised somebody in this world actually, genuinely *cared*.

For the first time since I'd come here, I had finally felt like I wasn't alone. That had been the moment when building the house had gone from a distraction to something I was serious about. The thoughts of asking a cute girl to marry me had become more than idle fantasy.

It was probably the moment that this place truly became "home."

It had only been a year ago, and yet it already felt like a lifetime.

I turned around.

Big D stood on a rock while he basked in the sun. His feathers sparkled in the light, glittering and iridescent. Rizzo was talking with Peppa about ledgers and storage rooms. Washy, in his dragon form, was sharing an early carrot he had pilfered from the garden with Chunky. The boar chuffed happily the moment Washy started mentioning honey glazes and baking them with spices—the fish's eyes were gleaming with excitement.

Tigu was leaning over Xiulan's back and pushing against it, nattering about something as the taller woman attempted to meditate. The exasperation mixed with fondness, until she flipped Tigu over her shoulder and shoved the cat's head into her lap, stopping her from jostling around so much.

Babe the ox was the only one who was getting actual meditation done, beside his plough under a tree, his eyes closed in contentment. A few days of working on the road, and then back immediately for more cutting.

The sheep were already hard at work cropping the grass, while the calves and cows were clustered near Babe, lowing softly.

Finally, I caught sight of our two newcomers. The rabbit, Yin, was sitting up on her haunches beside Big D, her nose twitching and ears flicking excitedly, while Noodle the snake—since that was what his name translated to—was silent, simply watching the rising sun with his one good eye.

He turned to me . . . and nodded.

I took another breath and let it out slowly.

"Heh. Looks like we're collecting the entire zodiac," I muttered. Meimei's eyes glanced around and alighted with realisation. She let out a little laugh.

"It seems we're only missing two," she mused.

Gou Ren scratched his chin, looking at everybody. "Eh? We're missing the horse, the goat, the dog, the monk . . . ey . . ." He trailed off as he saw Meimei's lips twitch, and he sighed.

"Only if Yun Ren is the dog," he grunted, as Meimei finally let her giggle out. "Apparently we also have two snakes." He levelled a *look* at the laughing woman.

"Tigu'er is our tiger. Do the sheep count? Then we'd only need the horse," I said, my own lips forming into a smile. "And I don't think riding *me* counts, Meimei." I cut her off the second her mouth opened, her eyebrows already waggling.

I shook my head and picked up my sickle, then tested its sharpness.

I glanced at the bags we had prepared, ready to receive the early harvest.

I took another breath and glanced back up at my family and friends.

"Everybody ready?" I asked.

A rooster crowed. A rabbit thumped her foot against the ground. Gou Ren cheered. A dragon roared, eager for the first dish after the harvest.

Qi blades formed. "This Rou Tigu shall harvest the most! I shall surpass all others!"

Xiulan's eyes narrowed. Yin bounced eagerly.

Several knives and another sickle floated into the air.

And so we began.

CHAPTER 63

ONE LAST DANCE

Swords whirled through the air, reaping rice. A girl ran as fast as she could along the rows, orange hair in two trailing streamers, her arms grabbing great bundles of the grain. She moved swiftly, tying them together and setting the bundles against the erected scaffold so they could dry.

I rolled my eyes at the little competition going on between Xiulan and Tigu. The cat-turned-girl was surprisingly good at dragging people into doing silly things, now that she wasn't as aggressive about it.

They were also either matching speed or going *faster* than any machine harvester I'd seen as they tore through the rice.

Gou Ren actually looked a little put out, glancing at his own sickle forlornly and the much smaller patch he had finished.

The yields . . . well, the yields were insane this year as well. The fat heads of grain should have made the stalks snap, but instead the rice stood tall and proud, swaying but refusing to break. We had gone from half an acre of rice and half an acre of veggies to over thirty combined acres of food . . . yet the workload didn't seem insurmountable. In fact, we had probably cleared almost ten acres already, and nobody looked at all worse for wear; however, the harder stuff was still to come.

We were going to need an absolutely *massive* amount of storage, though. Even with my preparations, I would still probably need to order or make several dozen more bags at the very least. I glanced off to the side, where there was a makeshift kiln. Big D pushed a large storage vessel out of it, while Noodle inspected it, rubbing his chin.

'Lesss heat next time, Yin,' I heard him call, and there was an affirmative from inside the stack of bricks.

Sun bunny and moon rooster. I'm sure there was a joke in there somewhere.

I was still a little unsure of what to make of the rabbit and the snake, but neither of them seemed like they would be an issue. Yin was bouncy and excitable, while Noodle . . . we had a bit of an understanding, us two.

And Big D was right. It *was* a pleasure hearing a Master speak at length about his work.

The next busiest place was the vegetable garden. There were rows of neatly harvested carrots and onions sitting behind Babe's plough, and the equally neat row behind Chunky. Meiling was wandering in their wake, bending down to pick everything up—she didn't look like the little bump of her stomach was bothering her at all, even though it appeared a bit awkward for her.

Even Washy was helping, and not partaking . . . too much. I did catch him swiping a couple of carrots.

I was about to get started again when I heard a voice call out.

"Hey! You started without me!" Yun Ren shouted good-naturedly.

Gou Ren's head immediately snapped up, his face brightening.

For there stood his brother. Yun Ren had a big smile on his face, and even in the heat he had a scarf wrapped around his neck with the same design on it that his mother had on some of her clothes. His "camera" chimed, and he grinned at us all.

And in addition to him, we had other company.

"Jin! Meimei! Lanlan!" Xian Junior shouted as he and Pops hopped off the cart they were on—I did a bit of a double take.

"Brother Tingfeng and Meihua!" I shouted in surprise when I saw who the cart belonged to. I had visited the couple of times I had gone to Verdant Hill, but I certainly hadn't been expecting them, or Yao Che, Meihua's father.

Or the gaggle of other villagers, including the Xong brothers' parents. Or the set of sickles and hoes they were carrying.

Well, it seems that every year the number of people wanting to lend a hand goes up.

"I did not expect to be able to visit like this either, Brother Jin, but the Lord Magistrate allowed me a break," Tingfeng said with a laugh. "He made it sound like he was giving me more work in coming to visit my friend! But here, my 'mission,' to deliver this to you!"

I stared as he reached into the cart and pulled up a bucket. A bucket with some very familiar, bright-red fruit in them.

Tomatoes.

→

"Ah, you're growing fast, aint'cha!" I praised the child in my arms. Really, the kid had looked like a wrinkly bean the last I had seen him, and now he looked like an actual baby. The child giggled at me as I wagged a finger in front of his face, grasping for it.

We had quickly descended into organised chaos when everybody had pulled up a seat and started catching up.

"Thanks for bringing the tomatoes to me, Tingfeng," I started to say, but he waved me off.

"I can't believe he spoke of this as if it would be a chore," Tingfeng muttered. He sipped some of my specialty, the iced tea clearly agreeing with him. Xiulan had given us peach trees from the gardens of Grass Sea City last year, and they were old enough to give fruit, unlike what we had gotten from Washy. The peaches were perfectly ripe and mixed oh so wonderfully with tea, as well as with my stores of ice. A proto-slushie, if you will.

He groaned in contentment and poured himself a bit more. I just smiled, then looked up at everything else that was happening—just in time to catch a rather nice-looking pelt that had been tossed at me.

"Right, furs for Jin, Granny said this one is for Meimei . . ." Yun Ren muttered as he rummaged through his pack, listing things off. My friend didn't look much different, having only been gone for three months, though I did keep catching flashes of his incisors when he talked. Were they a bit longer than normal . . . ?

"This one's for you, Gou. Gramps wanted you to have it. He said that you were welcome up north any time." Yun pulled out a piece of cloth that had the same design as his scarf, then handed it to his brother. Gou Ren seemed a bit shocked and unsure of what to do with it. He stared for a moment . . . before tying it like a headband.

He looked like a street fighter character. I saw Tigu giving him a considering glance, her eyes lingering on the headband.

"We finally got them to grow," Hong Xian said, as he carefully pulled out a leaf of the Spiritual Herb and laid it beside one of mine. It was much smaller, and a lighter green, but it still looked serviceable.

"I helped!" Meimei's brother called, bouncing up and down eagerly. "Jin's instructions never said you had to dance for them, but they really like it!"

Xian nodded, ruffling his son's hair.

"And . . . well, I thought you might like this, Daughter." He pulled out a scroll, and Meiling gasped. I managed a glance at the title.

Observations on Seven-Fragrance Jewel Herb Interacting with Mortal Medicine: 77th Hong Xian, 3rd Hong Meiling, 1st Hong Ri Zu.

"It's . . . it's in the family records?" she asked, voice wavering.

"It will need a bit more, to be officially entered into the family records . . . But I would like some help, Daughter, if you would give it."

She flushed and nodded rapidly.

Xian smiled at his daughter, then turned to me with a bemused expression. "And I cannot believe that the Cloudy Sword Sect simply calls them 'Lowly Spiritual Herbs,'" he muttered.

I shrugged. So they *did* have a more xianxia name.

"In any case, some ointments, so that we may test the effectiveness between the ones grown in Hong Yaowu and the ones grown here . . ." he started to say, and Meiling's eyes brightened as she learned forwards eagerly.

I smiled at the expression on her face.

The rest of us got to work again. *Eventually.*

↔

Xiulan sat on the roof in the setting sun. She looked down, over, and across the farm. Master Jin's "banjo" twanged rapidly as he played some song she had never heard before while most of the adults stomped their feet and danced around the firepit. The children whooped as Wa Shi carried them through the water. They cheered as they slid down Chun Ke's back.

Senior Sister was in deep discussion with her father as they compared the leaves of Spiritual Herbs. She had a look of pride on her face, especially when she marked down something in the scroll. It was something that would be with her family for generations, if she didn't miss her mark.

Gou Ren nodded along as an image was projected on the wall, his new headband bobbing slightly. Yun Ren smiled with his just slightly too-sharp canines when several people oohed at the image of the waterfall.

Bi De stood proudly upon the fencepost, and there was a look of contentment on the rooster's face.

She closed her eyes and took a breath. She burned the images into her
memory. The *feelings*.

To think the summer she'd worked as a farmhand was the most productive of her life. More productive than her years of meditation, or refining Spiritual Grass, or undergoing rigid forms and harsh lessons.

She remembered how she had felt at first—like she was drowning in
air. It was as if the enormity of her situation was going to crush her.

The tightness in her chest was gone. Each breath was easy. The tenseness in her muscles was now only a memory.

She took another breath. There was still a hint of sweetness on her lips
from the tea Master Jin had made.

The tournament was soon. So soon. Within a week, she would be back
with her fellow disciples of the Verdant Blade and fighting in the tournament.

At the Fourth Stage of the Initiate's Realm, winning the tournament
would have been a hard possibility, but it *was* possible.

At the first stage of the Profound Realm? Her victory was all but
assured, as arrogant as it sounded. She was likely the most powerful of her
generation in these Azure Hills.

She would win the tournament . . . and then what?

Would she go back to training with the other disciples? Would she be
elevated to Elder status? Her accomplishments were great, that was true,
but after her last experience commanding men, she was not particularly
eager to take such a prominent role.

She was a dutiful daughter. All her life, she had lived for her Sect.

Yet . . . some small traitorous part of her simply said, *Stay*.

It was not something that could be stomped out. It was something
that would have to be reconciled.

"Xiulan!" Senior Sister called.

She opened her eyes again as the beat sped up and Master Jin shouted
out a song that he seemed to be translating from the strange language
that he knew.

Senior Sister waved up at her, holding out her arms.

The Young Mistress of the Verdant Blade touched the crown of flowers woven into her hair.

Xiulan slid off the roof and tapped lightly to the ground. She hugged
Meiling, swirling her around, before the song took her.

Whatever did come, she would face it. Her feet would move to a tune only she could hear, and carry her along this path, even if she could not see where it was going.

It was the path she *wanted* to walk.

Her body moved, it twisted, and it swayed, until she was the only one left dancing, the others all having paused to watch her.

And when the song ended, there was the feeling of bodies pressing up against her. Senior Sister had an arm around her waist. Tigu was on her back. Junior Brother and Master Jin each had an arm slung around her shoulders.

She was squashed in the middle of a pile of bodies and grinning at the recording crystal.

"Okay, everybody, now make a dumb face!" Master Jin commanded.

His top teeth jutted out over his bottom lip, and his eyes went vacant. Giggling, Senior Sister stuck her fingers in her mouth and pulled her cheeks apart. Junior Brother began to make a dumb face, but then Yun Ren stuck his fingers in Gou Ren's nose. He grabbed Yun Ren's cheeks in retaliation, squashing the boy's face sideways.

She couldn't exactly see Tigu's expression, but she didn't need to—she knew it was perfect.

The Young Mistress of the Verdant Blade Sect stuck out her tongue.

There was a crystal chime.

CHAPTER 64

SEE YOU AGAIN

It was a scene of organised chaos the night before they left. There were items lined up or scattered around the room. The atmosphere was tense with anticipation as Xiulan stared at the flat piece of stone in her hand.

"Turned out pretty good, if I do say so myself!" Yun Ren decreed, sitting back and nodding with pride. He wiped a hand along his sweaty brow.

All Xiulan could do was nod, staring at her own smiling face. There was another, this piece's twin, affixed to the wall and prominently displayed. Master Jin had been spectacularly happy with this development, praising Yun Ren until he flushed with embarrassment. He had asked Yun Ren for any pieces he would be willing to give, so that they could be displayed proudly around the house.

The man looked like all of his dreams had come true at once.

"Thank you," she said earnestly, while Yun Ren just nodded.

"I don't know how long it will last. I think . . . less time if it's in shade, more time if it gets light regularly? It's not perfect yet. I already had to refresh one of them." He absently poked at one of his slightly too-sharp teeth with his tongue. Some manner of bloodline awakening, perhaps? His story about the fox he'd shared the previous night did point to that.

She glanced up to where Tigu was sitting on her knees, her face intent, while Junior Brother examined his bow before setting it aside.

Master Jin's eyes narrowed at Tigu. "Undergarments!" Master Jin demanded, and the girl held up a set of plain white bandages and cloth, like a soldier holding up her blade or armour for inspection.

Master Jin nodded, and the girl packed them away in her bag.

"Shirts?" he asked.

This grin was a wide one, as Tigu purposefully let the folded garment fall open to reveal the symbol on the back. She stared at it with pride before carefully folding it.

It matched the one all of them had. And though Xiulan could not wear it at the tournament . . . she was touched that Senior Sister had given her one.

"Good! We always pack the night before, and then double-check in the morning to make sure we don't forget anything!" he said.

'And you always need more supplies than you think,' Bi De stated from his position on Master Jin's shoulder.

Tigu nodded rapidly, determination blazing in her eyes.

Senior Sister soon stomped in, carrying an armload of things. She had a big smile on her face.

"Okay! Burn ointment, bruise salve, thread for stitching up wounds, some dried fronds of Spirit Herbs . . ." She listed things off, separating the ingredients into little kits, including the Spiritual Herbs that had once healed Xiulan.

"This one is yours," Senior Sister told her, depositing the medical kit onto the table.

Xiulan thanked her as she held the gift. She looked back to where the others were still sitting by the door. They had been given many things for their journey. Wheat and rice. The vegetables, the maple syrup.

And Master Jin had still tried to give her more. Her lips quirked into a smile as Meiling finally finished reciting Tigu's list.

"And I think, with that, it's time for bed," Master Jin stated. "You've got an early day, and a long way to travel."

There were muttered agreements from the disciples, and wishes for a good sleep.

She ascended the stairs, to the ro—to *her* room.

Opening the door, she glanced around. She still needed to pack.

The room had filled up a bit more than she was expecting when she came to live here. She had arrived with gifts and the clothes on her back.

Now there were a myriad of things gathered from her time here. She would have to pack them all so she could take them back to her Sect.

She smiled at the objects scattered around the room. There was a scroll of acupuncture, given to her by Senior Sister. She would explain what she was doing while she worked on Xiulan's body, and by this point, Xiulan could follow along.

Next was a beetle pupa, given to her by Xian, and fully intact. He had regaled her with a story about how long it had taken him to find a good one. She ran her fingers over the large horn and trailed it to the carving of an unfurling fern. When she had asked Tigu about it, the girl had pretended to not know what she had been talking about, but time had clearly been spent on it to make it so realistic and lifelike.

There was a pressed flower. The first one she had grown, with Master Jin's techniques.

She smirked at the pieces of paper on the rough table: Junior Brother Gou Ren's attempts at poetry.

It was not going well, to say the least. There might have been some improvement?

Maybe.

She took a nut from the small bag Chun Ke had given her, popping it into her mouth before she carefully rolled up several other items. There was a feather from Bi De, bright and vibrant. She also found a dragon scale, along with a note pleading for her to bring back tasty things.

As she thought back over her time at Fa Ram her hands moved, preparing each object with care. The images flowed through her mind . . .

A ball of mud thrown at her. Field Ha Qi. Burgers. The bright summer sun on her face, warming her body. Picnics with Senior Sister. Ruffling Junior Brother's hair.

Until her hands stopped moving. She looked around, and the summer morning had turned back into night—and all she was left with was an empty room.

All that was left were the things she had come here with.

Slowly, Xiulan pulled on her silk dress, wearing it for the first time in months. It felt a bit strange on her skin after all her time wearing clothes of a simpler make. The extravagantly expensive piece, long since repaired. Proof of her status.

She picked up the pieces of gold thread, styled to look like blades of grass, and wove them into her hair. Made of the purest gold, they were so different than the flower crowns that withered, or the simple bows of cloth too small to have any other use.

And yet . . . it was not uncomfortable, like she expected it to be after a summer without it.

She turned to the burnished disk in her room and stared at her reflection.

It still looked like her.

She shook her head, then changed out of the rich clothes and back into her sleeping attire.

She took her packed bags and walked out of her room, into the silent hall, and down the stairs, to place them by the door. She set them near the other four packs, three large and one tiny. She snorted, as all of them had a little touch added by Senior Sister. Patches of a cat, a monkey, a fox, and a rat.

She turned and climbed onto the roof, for one last time . . . and found it already occupied.

Master Jin, with a rooster on his shoulder.

No words were said. He smiled at her and tapped his pot of tea.

→

They were gathered outside that morning, before the gate.

"Yeah, I'll talk to Biyu for you, okay? We're gonna stop in the city, that's the best route, before we continue on," Yun Ren said as he and Master Jin clasped forearms and pulled each other into a hug.

"Thanks. I think I'll be heading down that way pretty soon. Just got a few more things to do here first," he said, before releasing the man so that Senior Sister could give him her own hug.

He grinned as he hugged Tigu, the girl bouncing excitedly. He ruffled her hair, and the girl grinned back up at him.

"Listen to Xiulan, okay?" he said, and Tigu nodded. Xiulan's heart leapt to her throat for a moment at the trust that had been placed in her.

"This Cai Xiulan swears upon her very name that she will bring them back safely," she intoned, her eyes and heart set as he stopped before her. Her hands were clasped in the traditional gesture of respect.

Master Jin nodded solemnly.

Xiulan let out a terribly undignified sound as two strong arms wrapped around her. Her body went rigid, and her face flushed, and then she was pulled into an embrace like the others.

"Bring yourself back safe too." he told her quietly.

Some of the tension within her faded. Slowly, she returned the embrace.

She stared at Senior Sister's expression. Ah. Her husband had just embraced another woman in front of her. It was terribly improper . . .

and yet, it was *very* Master Jin. She was just tall enough to look over his shoulder at Senior Sister's bemused expression.

She approached as Master Jin went to Gou Ren, both of them clapping each other on the back.

Senior Sister opened her arms, and Xiulan obliged her, wrapping the smaller woman up.

Xiulan smiled at Sister Meiling.

"Our house is always open to you," she said as they held each other's hands. Xiulan felt the warmth suffuse her at that—"Our bed too." The other woman's eyebrows bounced up and down. She slumped while Meiling began cackling, then pulled her down to press a kiss into her cheek. "You make it too easy!"

She left Xiulan pouting as she hugged Gou Ren and rubbed the top of Ri Zu's head.

She was bid farewell in turn by each of the disciples. A dragon, conspiratorially winking at her. A boar, chuffing happily as she scratched the scar across his face. A sow, giving her a polite and dignified bob of the head. A snake and a rabbit that offered her nods.

The rooster, tall and proud, combed his beak through Ri Zu's fur, then flapped up to the fence post.

"Goodbye," she said, as they all waved their farewells.

"See you again soon," Master Jin replied.

She turned, and then they started walking on the road. Almost marching, like she was on a mission . . .

But then an orange-haired girl darted ahead, practically skipping, while Ri Zu sat on her head, squeaking in agreement.

"Which way, which way? This way, right?" she demanded. "I can't wait to see!"

Junior Brother sighed. "Man, she's gonna be a pain," he muttered, before he lengthened his strides.

Yun Ren just laughed, pulling out his recording crystal. He examined it for a moment before he started a loping run to catch up to his brother and Tigu.

Xiulan chuckled. Her feet pounded down the road as she reached the squabbling duo and the one who was recording them.

EPILOGUE

Lu Ban was in a spectacular mood as he sat in front of the Elders of the Shrouded Mountain Sect.

Mostly because this time, it was not him receiving a dressing-down with threats of further restrictions.

"Misuse of the Fulmination Assault Troop. Misuse of Sect Resources. Failure, with nothing to show for it." The First Elder of the Shrouded Mountain Sect mused from his seat on a silk cushion. "And finally, an intruder. An intruder who dared to infiltrate the Fangtip Fortress on your watch."

He sucked on his pipe idly and then blew out the rich smoke. Literally, rich. The pipeweed had Qi in it.

Lu Ban smirked at the way Kang shriveled up into himself at the Elder's words. To think that the strange and powerful cultivator who had interrogated Lu Ban about... *that bastard* would end up doing Lu Ban a favour.

Namely heaping more dishonour onto an adversary.

"This disciple has no excuses, Honoured Elder." Kang ground out.

The Elder stared at the other man for a moment. "Report later for punishment for your sins." He commanded without mercy, then turned his eyes to Lu Ban.

"Zang Li. You survived this assault, drove off the intruder, and have increased your own power once more. Truly, you are a Son of the Shrouded Mountain Sect."

Lu Ban bowed his head. "I only followed the tenets of our glorious Sect, Honoured Elder."

"Excellent, excellent. I had my doubts after your . . . indiscretion, but as it is said: strength forgives all sins. I shall reduce your punishment accordingly. Rejoice, Zang Li. You have but two months of probation left."

"My heart is filled with joy, Honoured Elder." Lu Ban simpered, and the Elder nodded without truly caring.

"Now, away with you all. I shall be going on a Dao journey to the east; and I leave the Sect in your hands. Do not disappoint me."

"Yes, Elder." the voices chorused.

He saw the smile on the father of his host body, the joy he had at suppressing one who sought to suppress him. The other two Elders looked less than enthusiastic. The woman, especially, stared with barely disguised hostility. Zang Shenhe, this body's aunt, was certainly a paranoid one and seemed convinced something was still amiss.

Lu Ban would have to keep an eye on her. But at the moment, she seemed outvoted.

The body snatcher couldn't help but give her a smile as he left.

→

However, it turned out that his little gesture of defiance was . . . ill-advised, and the bitch who still had some measure of control over him had a vindictive streak.

Lu Ban woke up from a wonderful night. His "father" had sponsored a party for him for doing so well. Food, drink, and a pair of twins who had served his power well. He stepped out from the room to find another set of orders. Orders that ignited into flames in Lu Ban's fury.

He calmed himself as soon as the page started burning, extinguishing the flames. Perhaps she *wished* for him to complain. He still had time left before he was fully forgiven, after all.

To stay silent was an insult. To speak out against this was an insult as well.

He sneered.

Scout for talented individuals at the Dueling Peaks Tournament in the Azure Hills.

When the time came, he would make sure to take his time with those who dared to insult him like this.

ABOUT THE AUTHOR

Casualfarmer started writing after listening to his parents' stories on their long drives to visit relatives. He had been saving money from his food-service-industry job to go to college for teaching when the COVID-19 pandemic hit. *Beware of Chicken* is Casualfarmer's first original story. He lives in Ontario, Canada.

IS YOUR LOVE FOR FARMING MORE THAN CASUAL?

Support Casualfarmer on Patreon for less than the cost of a bag of chicken feed and become a part of the Beware of Chicken community. You'll get exclusive access to our Discord, where fans discuss everything poultry (and more!).

DISCOVER
STORIES UNBOUND

PodiumAudio.com